Musics of Latin America

Musics of Latin America

Robin Moore, General Editor
University of Texas–Austin

Walter Aaron Clark, Contributing Editor
University of California–Riverside

Contributing Authors

John Koegel
California State University–Fullerton

Cristina Magaldi
Towson University

Daniel Party
St. Mary's College

Jonathan Ritter
University of California–Riverside

Deborah Schwartz-Kates
University of Miami

T.M. Scruggs
Independent Scholar

Susan Thomas
University of Georgia

W. W. NORTON & COMPANY
NEW YORK   LONDON

W. W. Norton & Company has been independent since its founding in 1923, when William Warder Norton and Mary D. Herter Norton first published lectures delivered at the People's Institute, the adult education division of New York City's Cooper Union. The Nortons soon expanded their program beyond the Institute, publishing books by celebrated academics from America and abroad. By mid-century, the two major pillars of Norton's publishing program—trade books and college texts—were firmly established. In the 1950s, the Norton family transferred control of the company to its employees, and today—with a staff of four hundred and a comparable number of trade, college, and professional titles published each year—W. W. Norton & Company stands as the largest and oldest publishing house owned wholly by its employees.

First Edition

Editor: Maribeth Payne
Assistant editor: Ariella Foss
Emedia editor: Steve Hoge
Project editor: Justin Hoffman
Copyeditor: Heather Dubnick
Proofreader: Debra Nichols
Director of production, College: Jane Searle
Production manager: Chris Granville
Permissions manager, College: Megan Jackson
Marketing manager: Nicole Albas
Design director: Rubina Yeh
Designer: Lissi Sigillo
Photo editor: Stephanie Romeo
Composition: Preparè, Inc.
Manufacturing: Sheridan Printing

Library of Congress Cataloging-in-Publication Data
Musics of Latin America / Robin Moore, general editor, University of Texas, Austin; Walter Aaron Clark, contributing editor, University of California, Riverside. — First edition.
    p. cm.
  Includes bibliographical references and index.
  ISBN 978-0-393-92965-2   (pbk.)
 1. Music—Latin America—History and criticism.   I. Moore, Robin, 1964-   II. Clark, Walter Aaron.
  ML199.M886 2012
  780.98—dc23

2012004809

W. W. Norton & Company, Inc., 500 Fifth Avenue, New York, NY 10110
www.wwnorton.com

W. W. Norton & Company Ltd., Castle House, 75/76 Wells Street, London W1T 3QT

1 2 3 4 5 6 7 8 9 0

To Gilbert Chase, Gerard Béhague, Robert Stevenson,
and countless others whose work supports the essays in this volume

BRIEF CONTENTS

CONTENTS

1

Introduction | ROBIN MOORE 2

2

Music, Conquest, and Colonialism |
SUSAN THOMAS 24

3

Mexico | JOHN KOEGEL 76

LISTENING GUIDES

Chapter 7 Argentina and the Rioplatense Region

Chapter 8 Peru and the Andes

Chapter 9 Latin American Impact on Contemporary Classical Music

IN DEPTH

PREFACE

The nine contributors to *Musics of Latin America* recognize a pressing need for additional teaching materials in English about the music of Latin America, and we are excited to provide you—students and teachers alike—a comprehensive, up-to-date resource. This volume covers one of the most musically diverse regions in the world and emphasizes music as a means of understanding culture and society. A fundamental component of history and politics, music frequently reflects broader social tensions involving race, class, and gender. Accordingly, musical study is relevant to students across disciplines, from Latin American studies to anthropology, sociology, history, modern languages, international studies, and communications.

Organization and Scope

While much of the text necessarily centers on descriptive information that introduces the general characteristics of regional musical genres, we have framed individual chapters with particular issues in mind. Chapter 1 introduces major themes, such as colonialism, cultural fusion and mestizaje, and urbanization and modernization that have influenced Latin American music. These topics resurface in almost every chapter. We hope that an issue-oriented approach will encourage you to think about overarching processes associated with Latin American cultural forms.

Chapter 2 of *Musics of Latin America* begins with a discussion of colonial-era performance, providing a foundation for understanding the development of regional styles in later years. The next six chapters (Chapters 3–8) are organized geographically; each begins with an overview of a region, examining its history, geography, and demographics, before covering representative traditional idioms, commercial and popular repertoire, and finally classical music. In studying a country or region's music, you will simultaneously gain an understanding of its history and culture.

We account for the most recent developments in Latin American music: wherever possible, each chapter incorporates several examples from the past ten years. Chapters 9 and 10, "Latin American Impact on Contemporary Classical Music" and "Twenty-First Century Latin American and Latino Popular Music," focus exclusively on contemporary music. In addition, Chapter 10 highlights the artistry of immigrant populations and U.S.

citizens of Latin heritage, emphasizing musical styles from the U.S.–Mexico border and the Hispanic Caribbean.

The textbook keeps technical musical language and foreign terminology to a manageable level. Key terms appear in bold upon first usage; they are discussed in the text itself, appear in a list at the end of each chapter, and are defined again in the glossary. An Appendix, "The Elements of Music," introduces general musical terminology and provides a concise overview of music fundamentals with examples of rhythm, melody, harmony, texture, and form drawn from the text's repertoire. Ending with an exploration of the aesthetics of indigenous, Afro-descendant, and European-derived music, the Appendix shows you how these musics differ and provides examples of how to listen to and write about all Latin American music analytically.

Each chapter gives students the tools they need to understand a diversity of musical genres. Musical examples and listening guides illustrate genres' defining characteristics, while Explore and In Depth boxes go beyond the text, drawing students' attention to important resources and examining significant figures and events.

Musical Examples

Throughout the text, selected musical transcriptions enhance the discussion of particular musical styles. Information about the characteristics of many genres, from Colombian gaita to Argentine chacarera, is not easily available in current English-language literature, and in some cases any literature. Therefore, most chapters provide half a dozen transcriptions of rhythmic and melodic patterns associated with a given region. They are notated in Western staff notation for more experienced musicians and, whenever possible, in time unit box system (TUBS) notation for those without formal musical training. An explanation of TUBS notation appears in the introduction.

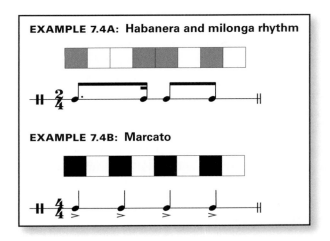

EXAMPLE 7.4A: Habanera and milonga rhythm

EXAMPLE 7.4B: Marcato

Using the Listening Guides

Musics of Latin America presents a wide variety of repertoire and seeks to increase your ability to listen critically to and understand the music you study. Eight to ten detailed listening guides are integrated into each chapter. Links to purchase recordings of each work discussed are available on StudySpace (wwnorton.com/studyspace), Norton's online resource for students. Some listening guides, especially those considering recent repertoire, include only partial lyrics due to the high cost of reprinting material under copyright; students are encouraged to search for the complete lyrics on their own. The listening guides consist of the following elements:

- A list of "What to Listen for"

- Concise head notes specifying the date of composition, composer, lyricist, performers, instrumentation, form, and tempo

- Minute-by-minute commentary with time markers to provide a detailed description of the piece's unique characteristics

- Lyrics in their original language with a parallel translation

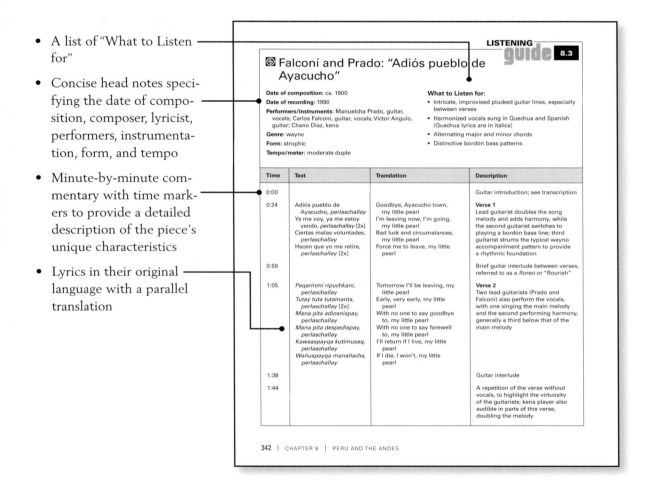

LISTENING guide 8.3

⊚ Falconí and Prado: "Adiós pueblo de Ayacucho"

Date of composition: ca. 1900
Date of recording: 1990
Performers/instruments: Manuelcha Prado, guitar, vocals; Carlos Falconí, guitar, vocals; Victor Angulo, guitar; Chano Diaz, kena
Genre: wayno
Form: strophic
Tempo/meter: moderate duple

What to Listen for:
- Intricate, improvised plucked guitar lines, especially between verses
- Harmonized vocals sung in Quechua and Spanish (Quechua lyrics are in italics)
- Alternating major and minor chords
- Distinctive bordón bass patterns

Time	Text	Translation	Description
0:00			Guitar introduction; see transcription
0:24	Adiós pueblo de Ayacucho, *perlaschallay* Ya me voy, ya me estoy yendo, *perlaschallay* [2x] Ciertas malas voluntades, *perlaschallay* Hacen que yo me retire, *perlaschallay* [2x]	Goodbye, Ayacucho town, my little pearl I'm leaving now, I'm going, my little pearl Bad luck and circumstances, my little pearl Force me to leave, my little pearl	**Verse 1** Lead guitarist doubles the song melody and adds harmony, while the second guitarist switches to playing a bordón bass line; third guitarist strums the typical wayno accompaniment pattern to provide a rhythmic foundation
0:59			Brief guitar interlude between verses, referred to as a *floreo* or "flourish"
1:05	*Paqarinmi ripuchkani, perlaschallay* *Tutay tuta tutamanta, perlaschallay* [2x] *Mana pita adiosnispay, perlaschallay* *Mana pita despedispay, perlaschallay* *Kawsaspayqa kutimusaq, perlaschallay* *Wañuspayqa manañacha, perlaschallay*	Tomorrow I'll be leaving, my little pearl Early, very early, my little pearl With no one to say goodbye to, my little pearl With no one to say farewell to, my little pearl I'll return if I live, my little pearl If I die, I won't, my little pearl	**Verse 2** Two lead guitarists (Prado and Falconi) also perform the vocals, with one singing the main melody and the second performing harmony, generally a third below that of the main melody
1:38			Guitar interlude
1:44			A repetition of the verse without vocals, to highlight the virtuosity of the guitarists; kena player also audible in parts of this verse, doubling the melody

In Depth Boxes

In Depth boxes throughout the text provide nuanced insight into important historical events, instruments, composers, and cultural trends. Among other topics, these boxes examine the construction of a Central American marimba, the music of shamanistic healing rituals, and "testimonial songs" that commemorate the many who died as the result of violence surrounding the Shining Path guerilla movement.

❄ In Depth 2.2

Sor Juana Inés de la Cruz

Sor Juana Inés de la Cruz was born Juana Ramírez de Asbaje in either 1648 or 1651 near Mexico City. Due to her grandfather's extensive library and her strong intellectual drive, she received a thorough education, unusual for a woman of her day. Her grandfather died when she was an adolescent, and she moved to Mexico City where her musical and literary talents endeared her to the viceregal court. Courtly intrigues were not to her liking, however, and at the age of 18 she joined the Convent of San Gerónimo, where she remained for the rest of her life. The convent had a rich musical life. The sisters practiced and studied the musical arts daily and gave performances. In the relative absence of male authority, they had near total autonomy over the musical environment. Additionally, the rather liberal order allowed Sor Juana to continue to her studies and writing, and she is considered by many to have been the most prominent author of New Spain, male or female. Sor Juana's exceptional status as an educated and exceptionally talented woman may have enabled her to produce more controversial writings than most men, as authorities did not initially view women as a possible source of dissent. In her insistence that women should be valued equally with men, she directly clashed with the church. At the same time, she cloaked her feminism within religious expressions of Marian devotion, a practice that

FIGURE 2.8 Sor Juana Inés de la Cruz

may have spared her from the Inquisition. Sor Juana wrote prolifically over a short life span; she died in 1691, in her early forties. While her theological writings have garnered considerable study and critique, her many villancico texts are less well known. Between 1676 and 1692, she published at least 22 sets of villancicos in Mexico City and Puebla. Churches performed the works throughout New Spain, with music provided by a separate composer.

Explore Boxes

Explore boxes suggest opportunities for independent research, directing you to recordings, videos, and other resources. In Chapter 7, for instance, you are referred to videos of payadas de contrapunto (musical dueling) among Argentine guitarists; audiovisual and written sources on Mercedes Sosa, a central figure of the politically engaged nueva cancion (new song) movement; and documentaries on the chamamé.

explore

If you liked the traditional chacarera, you might enjoy modern examples, such as the electronic "Chacarera for Argentina" by Angelini Music or the jazz fusion "Chacarera de la esperanza" (Chacarera of Hope) by the Pablo Ablanedo Octet.

Additional Resources

The end of each chapter includes a list of eight to ten additional resources intended to support individual research. Divided into further reading, listening, and viewing, the lists include the material most useful for students and instructors. A much more comprehensive bibliography, videography, and discography is available on StudySpace. It includes literature that we relied on to write our chapters; other written sources on Latin American music in English, Spanish, and Portuguese; and lists of commercially available recordings and videos.

Acknowledgments

The process of bringing this volume to publication has been long—almost six years—and we are especially pleased to see it completed for that reason. Many individuals have helped shape the content of this volume. We would like to thank the staff at W. W. Norton, specifically Maribeth Payne, Ariella Foss, Justin Hoffman, and Imogen Leigh Howes, who contributed untold hours collecting and organizing data, editing chapters, and providing guidance to each author. Stephanie Romeo and Donna Ranieri provided invaluable help tracking down and securing permissions for visual images, Megan Jackson pursued copyright permissions for printed lyrics, and Debra Nichols was our expert proofreader.

Finally, we are very grateful to the reviewers who evaluated our draft chapters to provide detailed and insightful feedback. Those who have disclosed their names include Gage Averill (University of British Columbia), Alfredo Colman (Baylor University), Drew Edward Davies (Northwestern University), Eric A. Galm (Trinity College), Jonathon Grasse (California State University–Dominguez Hills), Deborah Pacini Hernandez (Tufts University), Carol A. Hess (Michigan State University), Jonathan Kulp (University of Louisiana–Lafayette), Javier León (Indiana University), Alejandro L. Madrid (University of Illinois–Chicago), Peter Manuel (CUNY Graduate Center), Leonora Saavedra (University of California–Riverside), Anthony Seeger (University of California–Los Angeles), Daniel Sheehy (Smithsonian Folkways Recordings), Kay Kaufman Shelemay (Harvard University), Louise K. Stein (University of Michigan), Thomas Turino (University of Illinois–Urbana-Champaign), Grayson Wagstaff (Catholic University of America), and Ketty Wong (University of Kansas).

Robin Moore
University of Texas–Austin
April 2012

Musics of Latin America

1

Introduction

ROBIN MOORE

Performers assemble on stage for a concert by the Nortec Collective from Tijuana, Mexico. Two DJs, Bostich and Fussible, stand in the center with their backs to the audience in front of a large console, glowing rectangular panels in their hands. Flanking them are performers facing forward who play music from distinct traditions of the northern border region; their instruments include the button accordion, bajo sexto (p. 107), tuba, and trumpet. Suddenly the hall comes to life with the throbbing pulse of dance beats. Some consist of sampled Afro-Latin percussion, some are electronically generated, some are reminiscent of U.S. soul from the 1970s, some re-create the sound of a Mexican polka. The rhythms change every few minutes, with one groove eliding almost seamlessly into the next. Live musicians improvise short melodies against the rhythms, making their traditional instruments sound rather avant-garde. At the same time, a video jockey projects images onto a large central screen and manipulates smaller projectors tilted toward the ceiling and side walls. Images projected include scenes of working-class Mexican life, well-known buildings in Tijuana, Mexican cowboys, old U.S. automobiles, as well as kaleidoscopic distortions of faces, instruments, animation, and written slogans, all in scintillating color. The wild mix of traditional and sampled sounds assembled by the Nortec Collective allows the group to explore the border experience, linkages between U.S. and Latin American culture, between the rural and cosmopolitan, and between the developed and developing worlds.

Twenty-five hundred miles to the south in the state Huehuetenango, Guatemala, the rock group Sobrevivencia (Survival) uses music to help

◄ **FIGURE 1.1** Map of Latin America

FIGURE 1.2 Brazilian Rapper MV Bill

preserve traditional indigenous cultures in danger of extinction as they reconcile traditional songs and instruments with international trends. The group's CDs from 2001 and 2002 feature compositions in the native Mam language as well as in Spanish, and accompany indigenous flutes and percussion with the electric guitar. Members use indigenous rock to draw attention to pressing concerns of Mayan descendants—land disputes, poverty, environmental damage, lack of access to education—and to pressure the national government for support.

Another four thousand miles to the southeast in Rio de Janeiro, Brazilian rapper MV Bill (Alex Pereira Barbosa, "Mensageiro da Verdade" or "Messenger of Truth"; Figure 1.2) uses hip-hop sung in Portuguese in a similar way, describing conditions within the infamous slum where he was raised, the Cidade de Deus (City of God). This neighborhood has been immortalized in a powerful film, also called *City of God*. MV Bill not only advocates forcefully for social justice through music, but has organized a network of NGOs (non-governmental organizations) that provide academic support and artistic training to underprivileged youth. His music frequently references drug trafficking and related violence in Rio, as well as police corruption, the need to valorize African heritage, and the importance of education as a means of getting ahead in life. His first single, "Soldado do Morro" (Soldier of the Slum), was banned by the police after they misconstrued it as glorifying violence.

In Bogotá, Colombia, audiences gather in a prominent concert venue to listen to a performance of the experimental classical piece *Creación de la Tierra* (Creation of the Earth) by composer Jacqueline Nova Sondag (1935–1975). Nova won accolades at the First Festival of Latin American Music in Caracas and went on to study at the famed Instituto Torcuato Di Tella in Buenos Aires. She uses as the basis of this composition a recording of an indigenous shaman who recites several chants, including some describing mythic tales about the earth's creation. Nova alters the shaman's voice electronically, separating it into multiple short segments, looping them and playing them backward and forward at various speeds against one another, creating a chorus of unintelligible sounds and rhythms, all derived from the same recording. Only at the end of the work is the shamanic voice heard in its original form. She uses her composition as a way of commenting obliquely on the Latin American experience, the confluence of the modern and the traditional in daily life, and of the contested nature of Latin American identity.

On a stage in Havana's Plaza of the Revolution, a very different sort of Colombian artist faces a crowd of over a million enthusiastic fans at a "Concert for Peace." Juanes (Juan Esteban Aristizábal Vásquez) organized the event in September 2009 in an attempt to improve U.S.-Cuban relations through the use of music, suggesting it was time to "put aside ideological differences" (Figure 1.3). Other performers and groups in attendance include Cubans Silvio Rodríguez and Los Van Van; Puerto Ricans Danny Rivera and Olga Tañón, Juan Fernando Velasco from Ecuador, CuCu Diamante from Venezuela, and the U.S.-based Yerbabuena. Cuban crews transmit free footage of the five-hour event to international television stations Univision and Telemundo, who in turn broadcast the concert throughout the hemisphere. Both the U.S. and Cuban governments provide support, issuing special visas to allow for the travel of performers and technical production teams. Juanes, who lives in southern Florida, receives at least one death threat

FIGURE 1.3 Juanes performing at the Concert for Peace in Havana, Cuba

from Cuban-American activists opposed to his performance in the wake of the event. A small anti-Castro group known as Vigilia Mambisa brings an industrial steamroller and sledge hammers out onto the streets of Miami, publicly crushing his CDs in protest.

These brief descriptions of music making in present-day Latin America underscore its diversity, its vibrancy, and its linkages to an array of pressing concerns for the region and the hemisphere. Many such concerns appear in later chapters of this textbook, and are discussed further. Music is a vital component of Latin American culture and an important means of understanding it. While the study of Latin American society in a broad sense helps us understand and appreciate Latin American music, the music itself provides an opportunity to learn about the broader society as well. In terms of its sound structures and instrumentation, its performances, its associations with particular communities and activities, and its lyrics, music can focus our attention on important aspects of the region, historically and in the present.

The histories of Latin America and the United States are closely intertwined, and in fact part of the same story. The entire Western Hemisphere developed through a common process of European colonization, for instance, and has maintained economic, political, and cultural contact for centuries. All parts of the Americas had native populations whose cultures tended to be misunderstood and ignored by European colonists, if not actively persecuted. Colonists throughout the Americas forcibly brought West Africans to work on plantations or cities as part of the Atlantic slave trade. And of course large parts of what is now the United States actually belonged to Spain or to Mexico up until the mid-nineteenth century.

Latin American immigrants and Latinos (U.S. residents of Latin American ancestry) now constitute the most rapidly expanding part of the U.S. population and suggest that the United States too is becoming "Latinized." As of the year 2000, Latinos became the country's largest minority group, surpassing African Americans; their ranks grew to more than 16 percent of the total population as of 2010. Projections indicate that by 2050 the Latino/Latin American community in the United States will increase to more than one hundred million and constitute 29 percent of the total population. Large sections of southern Florida and the southwest are primarily Spanish-speaking already, a harbinger of further changes to come.

Definitions and Themes

How exactly can we define Latin America as a region and as a musical area? Generally, the term "Latin America" applies to those parts of the Americas in which languages derived from Latin, especially Spanish and Portuguese, are spoken by a majority of residents, as well as to Catholic countries that have traditionally observed Sunday Mass in Latin. Collectively, these countries cover a vast territory spanning two continents, with a total population roughly double that of the United States. Many scholars and critics have questioned the appropriateness of the term "Latin America," given that numerous ethnicities, languages, and immigrants can be found in the region, and that their ties to "Latin" culture or Catholicism are often tenuous, but the term is widely used nevertheless. Latin America can be divided into several smaller areas based on geographic and cultural differences, including North America (comprising Mexico and the U.S. Latino population), Central America (Guatemala, Belize, El Salvador, Honduras, Nicaragua, Costa Rica, Panama), the Spanish-speaking Caribbean and circum-Caribbean (Cuba, Puerto Rico, Dominican Republic, and Caribbean coastal areas of Central America, Colombia, and Venezuela), the Portuguese-speaking Americas (primarily Brazil), the Southern Cone (Argentina, Chile, Paraguay, Uruguay), and the Andean region (Ecuador, Peru, Bolivia, Chile, and parts of Argentina, Colombia, and Venezuela). Most consider French-speaking countries of the Americas (e.g., the francophone Caribbean) part of Latin America as well, and English- or Dutch-speaking Caribbean or circum-Caribbean areas. However, they are not discussed extensively in this volume in order to focus greater attention on Spanish-speaking areas whose music and culture share many attributes with those discussed in other chapters.

Given the diversity of countries and populations comprising Latin America, it is difficult to determine the common denominators that unite them in a cultural or musical sense. Some commonalities exist, however, and each speaks to important factors that have shaped the experience of Latin American people. A few examples are provided.

Colonialism

As mentioned, one experience shared by Latin American nations is a history as colonial possessions of Spain, Portugal, or other European powers. Colonialism refers to the process by which one nation invades a foreign country or region, claiming the territory as their own and placing the local population forcibly under their control. Aggression of this sort has a history dating back to ancient times, but in the case of Latin America the conquest by Iberian powers took place largely between the fifteenth and nineteenth centuries. The impetus for colonialist expansion there derived largely from profits to be made from exploiting the natural resources, and a desire to extend European influence globally. Technological advances in seafaring and in military weapons—especially the use of gunpowder—made possible the control of new territories by relatively small European armies.

Columbus claimed all new territories he encountered as colonial possessions during his first voyages across the Atlantic. After he returned to Europe to tell of the new lands, Spanish and Portuguese rulers made a pact with Pope Alexander VI to divide the Americas between them. The Pope's decree suggested that the goals of the colonizers included "civilizing" any indigenous groups encountered and bringing them the Christian faith, but documents written by early missionaries suggest that this was actually a low priority. Friar Bartolomé de las Casas's *Short History of the Destruction of the Indies*, for instance, asserts that Spanish explorers cared little for native peoples and often treated them with unparalleled cruelty (Figure 1.4). It appears that the first decades of conquest in the hemisphere led directly or indirectly to the deaths of millions.

FIGURE 1.4 *The Conquest of Tenochtitlán*, a sixteenth-century Spanish oil painting depicting the sacking of the Aztec city by Hernán Cortés

As one might expect, Latin American colonies in the Americas tended to adopt the values and cultural orientation of the European powers that governed them. The ruling elite promoted music associated with the Catholic Church and Europe's aristocracy, while soldiers and settlers of more humble origins brought with them instruments and traditional genres from various parts of Spain and Portugal. Though they came into contact with new forms of music, most colonizers (especially elites) ascribed to notions of European superiority and tended to belittle the cultural forms of the non-European peoples whose territories they controlled. Such negative attitudes persisted for some time and began to change significantly only in the early twentieth century. This book represents part of an ongoing process of rectification, an attempt to introduce the reader to all kinds of Latin American music on equal terms.

Musical examples demonstrating the effects of colonialism are found throughout this volume, but perhaps most consistently in Chapter 2. Pieces such as "Hanacpachap cussicuinin" (Listening Guide 2.1) document the way that colonial authorities shaped native practices of listening and ritual worship to conform to Catholic orthodoxy. The countless musicians of racially mixed backgrounds who have composed music in European-derived styles since the conquest testify to the strong influence of Iberian heritage in cultural terms, and to the social prestige and potential for lucrative employment with which it is associated. Examples of indigenous or Afro-descendant composers in the classical idiom range from Juventino Rosas, a musician of Otomí Indian descent active in nineteenth-century Mexico (see Chapter 3) to Tania León, a Afro-Cuban composer active today and discussed in Chapter 9.

Race and Mestizaje

Any overview of Latin America must inevitably address issues of race and cultural hybridity, which are fundamental to the region. Especially in literature from past decades, Latin America is often described as having a "tri-ethnic" heritage. The three facets of heritage in question are indigenous, sub-Saharan African, and European; all three have contributed centrally to Latin American culture and society. Influences from these and other ethnicities have combined in many ways over time, resulting in complex cultural forms that have no single point of origin. Scholars of Latin America use a dizzying array of terms to describe this process of fusion: hybridity, mestizaje, creolization, transculturation, syncretism, and others. **Mestizaje** (or *mestiçagem* in Portuguese), perhaps the most common term, derives from the Latin word for "mixture." It referred initially to racial mixture, and later to hybrid cultural practices as well. Beginning in the early twentieth century, authors such as José Vasconcelos in Mexico and Gilberto Freyre in Brazil began to advocate a conception of the Latin American character in which mestizaje figured as a central component. Over time, their views have been adopted widely, particularly in the construction of nationalist discourses. It is important to recognize that early writings on the subject often celebrated the notion of mestizaje in the abstract, without attention to the brutal and often dehumanizing realities of colonial domination that gave rise to it.

Scholars estimate that more than one hundred million indigenous people may have inhabited the Americas at the time of Columbus's arrival, divided into thousands of distinct linguistic and social groups. The greatest concentrations lived in present-day Mexico, Central America, and the Andes, but substantial numbers lived in virtually all areas. Their populations dwindled dramatically after the conquest as they fell victim to European diseases as well as starvation, armed conflict, overwork (as many were enslaved), and other factors. Despite this, some countries continue to boast large indigenous populations today including Bolivia, Brazil, Guatemala, Mexico, and Peru. Indigenous groups perpetuate their own unique forms of musical expression that run the gamut from traditional to mestizo to cosmopolitan. Examples discussed in the following chapters include instrumental flute and drum repertoire (see "Huistan, Fiesta of San Miguel, 1974. Three Drums and Small Flute," Listening Guide 3.1), songs associated with girls' rites of passage ("Nhuiti ngrere," Listening Guide 6.1), and patron-saint festival music ("Sikuri taquileño," Listening Guide 8.2). No individual's race determines their musical preferences definitively, of course, but only suggests stronger exposure to certain forms of traditional music, and possibly stronger identification with it.

Colonists brought approximately twelve million West Africans to Latin America as slaves, where they and their descendants suffered horribly yet persevered as a group and strongly affected musical traditions in many areas. Most worked initially on plantations that cultivated sugar and other goods for export. More Africans were taken to Brazil than any other single country, approximately 39 percent of the total, and the Caribbean as a region became home to another 40 percent. Chapters devoted to these areas will discuss distinct African-influenced Latin American musical traditions, and the ethnic groups with which they are associated, in greater detail. Colonists took the remaining 21 percent of the West African population to other parts of Central, North, and South America, with only about 5 percent ending up in the United States. Needless to say, the demographics of particular regions with a large Afro-Latin presence have resulted in styles of musical expression distinct from those in areas dominated by European settlers or native groups. Listen to brief segments of "Elegguá, Oggún, Ochosi II," a Yoruba-influenced religious piece (Listening Guide 5.2); "En opuestas regiones," a

Kongo-derived piece (Listening Guide 5.3); "Um a um," a recording of an African musical bow and percussion (Listening Guide 6.5); and "Gaita de las flores," which combines African-derived percussion with indigenous reed flutes (Listening Guide 4.5) in order to compare a few of the diverse sounds of overt Afro-Latin heritage. The authors of this book discuss these and other African-influenced styles, such as Ecuadorian *currulao* music, represented in Figure 1.5 by the well-known group Berejú.

In the same way that indigenous and African-derived traditions in the Americas represent hundreds of distinct ethnic groups with their own instruments, dances, and musical repertoire, European traditions in the Americas demonstrate many specific influences. Traditional music from the Iberian Peninsula itself contains strong influences from North Africa, owing to the many centuries that Arabs ruled the region. Guitar and lute playing, for example—highly influential within Spain and elsewhere—developed from Arab culture and instruments. Spanish cities such as Madrid had populations of sub-Saharan African slaves as well who influenced musical life there long before the conquest of the Americas began. These and other facts underscore how problematic it can be to adopt broad categories such as "European music," "indigenous music," or "African music" without qualification. On a fundamental level, almost all music demonstrates cultural fusion to greater or lesser extents.

European colonization in Latin America, as opposed to the United States, began with relatively small numbers of immigrant families. Instead, soldiers, government administrators, businessmen, adventurers, and the like—the vast majority of them men—settled the colonies. They often developed relationships with black and indigenous women, and thus issues of racial mixture in their children came to the fore quickly. It is no exaggeration to say that

FIGURE 1.5 The *currulao* group Berejú, performing in San Lorenzo, Ecuador, 2000. Instruments featured include the paired *cununo* drums, a hanging *bombo* drum, and the marimba.

colonial Latin American societies obsessed over issues of race for centuries. Prevailing ethnocentric views until recently suggested that non-European people were not as "evolved" as Europeans and that mixture caused potential damage to further generations. Paintings and writings from the eighteenth century demonstrate this perspective, and the multitude of terms generated to distinguish various gradations of racial mixture: in Spanish such terms include **mulato** (half African, half European), mestizo (half indigenous, half European), *castizo* (half mestizo, half European), *morisco* (half mulato, half European), *lobo* (half indigenous, half African), *sambaygo* (half indigenous, half *lobo*), *coyote* (half indigenous, half mestizo), and so on. Some of this vocabulary has survived into the present, and other terms have emerged more recently.

Similarly, a vast array of music has emerged in the Latin American context, some of it very European-sounding, some quite **mestizo** or hybridized, some derived directly from indigenous or West African heritage of various sorts. This range of expression underscores the fact that although Latin America is characterized by racial and cultural mestizaje generally, it is far from homogenous. Distinct class-based and ethnic groups persist that negotiate among many musical influences. They may choose to perpetuate their own unique forms of music in relative isolation. They may forsake traditional genres in favor of modern mass-mediated music, attempt some synthesis of the traditional and modern, or cultivate multiple forms of music making in distinct contexts.

FIGURE 1.6 Eighteenth-century oil painting from the collection *Las castas mexicanas* (*The Mexican Caste System*) depicting four racial types: Spanish (Español), mulato, *salto atrás* (literally, "throw back"), and *lobo*

Mixed-race people themselves figure prominently in the historical development of hybridized musics; as a group, many have been caught between distinct cultural worlds, which must be reconciled or juxtaposed. Latin American music represents a relatively democratic space in this sense, giving voice to expression from the margins of colonial and postcolonial society. Often the wealthy and powerful, who tend to be of European heritage, initially reject music popularized by working-class and mixed-race people, believing it crass or uninteresting. Yet the same music tends to gain popularity among ever-wider segments of the population and eventually emerges as an important form of collective national expression (the same could be said of jazz, rock, and rap in the United States). Despite a certain ongoing ambivalence about native and African-derived culture on the part of elites, populations as a whole have come to realize that mestizo musics serve as an important marker of the Latin American experience.

Urbanization and Modernization

The degree of urbanization of Latin America since the mid-twentieth century is striking and represents a significant trend in every country. In the 1940s and 1950s, most residents still lived in fairly isolated, rural areas; they performed at least some forms of community-based traditional music and maintained a certain cultural distance from others. At present, however, roughly 75 percent of Latin Americans live in cities. Recent rural migrants have tended to settle in shantytowns on city peripheries, or in the tenement houses of poorer urban sectors, bringing once-rural music and dance traditions with them. In these new contexts, rural expression often changes, incorporating new sounds and influences from both the region and from around the world.

In this sense, the twentieth and twenty-first centuries have accelerated trends toward cultural fusion evident since the first years of colonization. The invention of mestizo string instruments such as the charango (Figure 8.7) centuries ago in the Andes can be viewed as part of a similar process involving the reconciliation of European and indigenous influences, as one example. But of course the degree and complexity of hybridity has increased of late. Argentine tango (Figure 7.8) and Dominican bachata (In Depth 5.2) both developed in urban areas, for instance, and both fused countless international and local influences together. Other examples of intercultural exchange include reggae-influenced samba variants from northeast Brazil and experiments fusing salsa and flamenco music in Spain and in the Caribbean.

Many communities thus live with one foot in the practices of the rural past and one in transnational urban contexts. Music itself often embodies such discrepancies and tensions through the incorporation of new forms of instrumentation, rhythm, contexts for performance, the juxtaposition of disparate elements, and so on. A traditional indigenous rattle or shamanic chant may be heard on a recording in tandem with synthesized sounds, much as in the case of Jacqueline Nova's music, discussed earlier; traditional repertoire from a specific region may be sampled, combined with a backbeat, and reinterpreted as dance music throughout the hemisphere and beyond. Néstor García Canclini is one of many authors to study this phenomenon. He notes that performers such as Panamanian Rubén Blades or Argentine Ástor Piazzolla regularly combine a diversity of elements in their compositions including influences from jazz, local traditional music, and international classical repertoire. As a result, it is increasingly difficult to make hard-and-fast distinctions between urban and rural traditions in the region, or to categorize them in other ways.

A trend related to urbanization is that of constant migration or movement in search of work, either within a particular country or outside of it.

FIGURE 1.7 Los Destellos, a well-known Peruvian chicha group from the 1970s

Migrants have contributed to and popularized many of the musical genres discussed in this volume. Examples include música sertaneja (p. 242) and dance rhythms such as baião from northeastern Brazil (p. 239) that now have a strong presence in the large urban centers of the Brazilian central and coastal areas because of internal displacement of rural populations. Various styles of Andean music, like chicha (Figure 1.7; In Depth 8.4), emerged out of a similar synthesis of rural dance music brought by highland immigrants to Lima, along with rhythms from commercial Colombian genres and elements from foreign pop music. More broadly, the intense nostalgia for rural life and imagery found in much traditional music of Mexico, Argentina, and other countries derives in large part from the movement of rural populations to cities in recent years.

International migration and movement are also increasingly common, as are the experiences of life on or across borders and the frequent crossing of cultural boundaries of various kinds. Individuals from Mexico or Central America may travel to and from the United States in search of employment, bringing their music with them and also acquiring a taste for mainstream U.S. artists; South Americans may do the same, or travel to and from European cities. All of this has led to a marked deterritorialization and diversification of heritage. Together with the expansion of the mass media, it has created a situation in which music circulates more widely and rapidly than ever before. Latin American musical forms can no longer be associated exclusively with Latin America, and the music performed by Latin Americans themselves often sounds quite cosmopolitan, heavily influenced by international pop or other repertoire.

Sound-reproduction technology itself has influenced the development of Latin American music in significant ways, beginning at least in the 1920s. The international popularization of genres such as the Latin American bolero at that time (see Chapter 5) owes much to the emergence of commercial radio, for instance, and the sale of 78-rpm records. Many genres such as Mexican mariachi (p. 93) music gained prominence as a national musical form as the result of dissemination through motion pictures, and changed significantly in stylistic terms as part of that process. More recently, LP records, television broadcasts, cassettes, CDs, music videos, Internet broadcasts, and mp3 downloads have all had an impact on musical dissemination and the development of new genres.

In the past, large business interests controlled technologies such as record and CD production and largely determined what sorts of music to record and distribute on them. However, the relatively low costs associated with Internet-streaming audio and inexpensive digital-recording techniques appear to be putting control of music making and dissemination back in the hands of individual performers and communities. CD piracy and the black market economy have also shifted control of recorded music sales away from corporations and toward local communities in many cases.

FIGURE 1.8 Mexican mariachi singer Pedro Infante, who achieved widespread popularity through radio broadcasts and movies of the 1940s and 1950s

Finally, tourism and self-conscious displays of heritage represent an increasingly important factor in the representation of Latin American music, and point to the broader theme of cultural movement just discussed. In our increasingly globalized and interconnected world, performers who once made music only for themselves or their immediate community now primarily entertain visitors from elsewhere. In carefully crafted displays of musical tradition, individuals make decisions about what repertoire to include and exclude, which pieces best represent themselves to others, where to perform, what to wear, whether to charge admission, and so on. All of this fundamentally shapes the musical experience, needless to say, often altering performance radically relative to earlier times.

International organizations, federal governments, regional officials, local communities, and performers themselves all frequently support displays of heritage, each with their own unique interests and motivations for doing so. Performers may simply hope to earn a living from tourists, or to achieve greater recognition for local music that has been marginalized or ignored. State or federal governments may also support music making because of its potential to attract revenue, or as part of politically motivated projects that use music as symbols to unify the population. International organizations often promote local heritage as part of development projects, or to support

FIGURE 1.9 El Güegüense festival, a form of street protest dating from colonial times, as performed in the city of Diriamba, Nicaragua, 2007

endangered traditions. The UNESCO Intangible Cultural Heritage initiative, for instance, has documented many kinds of Latin American music, uploading photos, video, and commentary about them to the web. They have supported Afro-Uruguayan candombe (p. 293) and Afro-Dominican drumming of various sorts; indigenous Aymara festivals from Bolivia, Chile, and Peru; Garifuna music in Belize, Guatemala, and Honduras; El Güegüense street celebrations in Nicaragua (Figure 1.9); indigenous *voladores* rituals in Mexico (Figure 3.2), and many others.

Carnival parades represent perhaps the best-known example of Latin American heritage and draw huge international crowds, whether to Rio de Janeiro, Oruro in Bolivia, or Trinidad and Tobago. Other high-profile events include Inti Raymi, the Festival of the Sun (a reenactment of preconquest Incan rites that takes place in Machu Picchu, Peru), or the Día de los Muertos (Day of the Dead) celebrations on Lake Pátzcuaro in Michoacán, Mexico. Thousands of smaller regional events take place throughout Latin America as well. They include the annual Viña del Mar music festival in Chile, the Cosquín folklore festival in Argentina, boi-bumbá celebrations in various parts of Brazil (Figure 6.4), and so on. Individual hotels frequently organize presentations of local heritage, and musicians themselves may cater to the perceived preferences of tourists, as mentioned. One example of the latter phenomenon is the proliferation of trios and quartets in Havana, Cuba, that formed in the wake of the Wim Wenders film *Buena Vista Social Club*, all of them playing the same half-dozen songs from the sound track again and again.

Many related trends could be mentioned that impact the development of Latin American music and that receive attention in this volume. The marked wealth disparities associated with most Latin American countries, as one example, have their corollary in frequent musical dialogues among various groups, representing the centers and peripheries of their populations. The turbulent political history of the region has been documented in and influenced by a legacy of socially engaged music of various sorts, bringing attention to injustices or inspiring collective action. The machismo associated with much Latin American culture is reflected in the male-dominated nature of music performance and the lyrics of many songs. The region's emphasis on social dance has contributed to its preeminence as an international exporter of dance rhythms, from the earliest centuries of colonization to the present. And the fractured nature of many Latin American populations has led to ongoing debates over the sorts of music that most effectively represent national or regional character.

Goals and Definitions

The authors of this text have multiple goals in mind. They hope to provide you with a feel for the diversity of Latin American music and the history of the development of major genres, as well as a description of their unique musical characteristics and of the local meanings and contexts associated with them. All chapters strive to provide you with an appropriate vocabulary for analyzing Latin American music and expand your ability to speak and write about such repertoire. All chapters identify broad tendencies that have influenced the development of music within the regions they analyze in detail. And all intend to serve as a point of departure for further study by providing additional reading and listening suggestions. The latter are especially important given the many topics touched on only briefly because of space constraints. As a means of encouraging an international perspective on musical scholarship, and in order to recognize the contributions of scholars from Latin America to their own musical histories, the authors have included additional reading suggestions in Spanish, Portuguese, or other languages in addition to English at the end of the volume.

In some cases, a discussion of musical characteristics has necessitated the transcription of short segments of music within the text. Whenever possible, these examples are included in two formats: Western staff notation (for those familiar with it) and an alternate form of notation, such as numeric ciphers or something known as **TUBS (Time Unit Box System)**. It is hoped that the use of multiple notation formats will afford easier access to this information for those unable to read Western music.

The appendix includes background information about common musical terminology and suggestions as to how one might approach the analysis of Latin American music.

TUBS merits brief explanation for those unfamiliar with it. This form of notation was developed by James Koetting and other scholars of West African music in the 1960s and 1970s who were looking for new ways to notate complex rhythms. It involves drawing a series of boxes in horizontal lines, as many as needed to depict rhythms being played against one another in a given musical example. Each box represents the same small unit of time, most typically an eighth note. Markings within particular boxes indicate that a sound is played on an instrument at that moment, while empty boxes represent rests during which no sound is heard. The lines of boxes are understood to represent looped or repeated rhythms in most cases, so students can interpret them by counting through the boxes in sequence, clapping or tapping when indicated by a marked box, and then immediately starting the same counting process over from the beginning of the same line when they reach the end. TUBS notation cannot indicate pitches or harmonies as staff notation does, but it is very effective in analyzing complex rhythms often found in mestizo and African-derived musics, and in understanding the relation of various rhythmic units to one another.

In order to make each chapter consistent, contributors have divided their essays into sections that include a discussion of **traditional music**, **popular music**, and **classical music**. These terms deserve some explanation; though they are useful as a means of classifying music in a general sense, the distinctions between them are often far from precise. They should be viewed not as entirely separate categories, but rather as a means of emphasizing predominant characteristics.

Traditional music (also called "folk music") is typically associated with rural contexts, with specific places or regions, and with groups of people that have cultivated the music for generations. Performers often learn such repertoire by ear from friends and family, rather than through formal study, and may never write it down in notated form. Such music invariably changes over time, but often not as rapidly as in the case of popular or classical music. Community members typically perform it for themselves as a form of entertainment, as part of religious worship, or in similar contexts. They would not tend to stage the music for an audience, but rather integrate it into their own day-to-day activities. Naturally, exceptions can be found for almost all of the characteristics listed; many performers of traditional repertoire do perform in formal contexts for money, for example, and some traditional music is played or listened to far from its place of origin. The urbanization and globalization of music making just described has strained existing conceptions of "the traditional."

Popular music (sometimes called commercial music) is usually associated with urban contexts and dissemination through the mass media. Its audience base tends to be diverse in terms of ethnicity, age, sex, and other factors; often, fans of a particular artist may live in different countries or on different continents. Popular music performers almost always expect payment for their shows and recordings. They frequently make a living from their music, and they may or may not have extensive formal training. They often play on electrified instruments, incorporating influences from U.S. or European genres. Popular music tends to change rapidly in a stylistic sense, following trends and fads of the consumer market.

Problems exist with this definition as well. Some popular musics do not have a terribly diverse audience, for instance, and cater instead to specific minority groups. In the twenty-first century, virtually all forms of music tend to be mass-mediated, whether or not they are commercial. Some popular musicians begin their careers as musicians of traditional repertoire, or as classical musicians, and thus defy easy classification. It is also important to recognize that the phrase "popular music" (*música popular*) within Latin America has connotations different from those in the United States. In Latin America, it might be translated as "music of the people" and can refer to traditional as well as commercial music; often the phrase has political or oppositional connotations. This textbook ascribes to the standard English usage of "popular music" unless otherwise indicated.

Ethnomusicologist Thomas Turino has developed a further critique of terms such as "traditional" and "popular," noting that while they provide some insight into the origin of musical styles, their associations with particular people and places, or their relation to the media in broad strokes, they provide little insight into the nature of music making as a social activity. He suggests alternate categories focused on music making including **participatory performance** (events in which few divisions between performer and audience exist) and **presentational performance** (events in which one group of musicians or dancers provides music for a relatively passive group of spectators). Turino further distinguishes between various types of recorded or electronically generated music including "high fidelity" (recorded songs intended to represent the sound of live performance) and "studio audio art" (the manipulation of sampled or other sounds not intended to reference live performance). Of course, divisions between these "fields" or categories frequently become blurry as well and may overlap substantially. Nevertheless, it is useful to examine genres discussed in the following chapters from the perspective of Turino's model, since many traditional and popular forms of music may be performed simultaneously in community settings and on stages, are manipulated and recorded in studio contexts, and circulate socially in multiple ways.

Classical music of European derivation (also known as "academic music" because of its association with conservatories, or "art music") first developed as the music of the aristocracy, and of the Catholic Church, before spreading to the American colonies. It is a virtuosic tradition, one that typically requires years of study in formal contexts to master. Usually, the music is notated and supported by a substantial body of written theory that describes the appropriate ways to compose and interpret it. Over the past century, classical repertoire in the European tradition has become increasingly experimental as composers search for ever-new and more unconventional ways of organizing sound. Many different types of classical music exist around the world, including genres derived from court traditions in India, Japan, and Indonesia; however, this book uses the term to refer to compositions written by Latin Americans, based primarily on European models.

Classical music may be the least problematic of the three categories discussed here, but it too can be difficult to distinguish from others. For example, musicians of many different backgrounds now boast some classical training or incorporate classical influences into traditional or popular repertoires. Traditional and popular musics can be virtuosic in their own right, making it difficult to differentiate between repertoires in that respect. Classical composers for their part often fuse elements of traditional and popular musics into their compositions as well, further blurring the categories. Classical music is no longer associated with an aristocracy, but is increasingly performed and listened to by audiences of diverse backgrounds, and circulates commercially as a product to be bought and sold.

Musicology and Ethnomusicology

Two related disciplines have contributed to the scholarship in this textbook, providing at least partially distinct focuses and modes of analysis. The first is **musicology**, which in its modern form dates from the late nineteenth century. Musicology, broadly defined, is the scholarly study of music as a physical, aesthetic, and cultural phenomenon. Though its objectives are ample, in practice many musicologists (especially of past decades) have specialized in the analysis of classical repertoire, on the historical development of instruments or genres, or on the careers of particular composers or performers. Alternately, some musicologists have studied performance practice, the appropriate interpretation of primarily classical repertoire from earlier historical periods. Much musicological work takes place in archives with musical scores and written documents from the past. Given Latin America's long colonial history—over approximately five hundred years—and the substantial body of classical repertoire composed there, studies of this nature have much to offer.

The other discipline that has contributed to this textbook is **ethnomu-sicology**, a younger field dating from the 1950s and more influenced by anthropology than history. The "ethno-" in ethnomusicology comes from **ethnography**, the systematic study of human societies through direct observation and interaction. Emphasis within this discipline is on the relationship between musical and social activity, and on the meanings of music for particular groups. It should be noted that greater attention to the contexts for music making—that is, an analytical shift from a focus on musical "products" (instruments, precomposed musical works, recordings) to the processes of music making and on the reception of music by the public—have affected musicology and other disciplines in the humanities. For the most part, ethnomusicologists have tended to study the music of developing countries or immigrant groups, though increasingly they also examine music from the United States or Europe. They may study the classical repertoire of various countries, but more often traditional or popular styles. Their analysis, based on extended stays within the communities they study, usually emphasizes present-day music making rather than genres from the past.

The approach adopted by the authors of this textbook combines insights and approaches from both musicology and ethnomusicology. They incorporate historical analysis, the analysis of musical sound, and an interpretation of the music's meanings and uses in particular settings. They introduce the reader to as many kinds of music as possible and consider it from various perspectives, though special emphasis is placed on genres that are heard in Latin America today or that have strongly influenced present-day music making. The authors give equal weight to indigenous, European-derived, and African-derived musical heritage, mestizo and commercial forms, as well as classical music. They have conceived the book as celebrating all musics and as contributing to a time in which the distinctions between musicology and ethnomusicology will no longer exist.

Latin America itself has a long and distinguished history of musical scholarship and documentation. Formal histories involving music undoubtedly existed among libraries kept by the Aztecs, Mayas, and others, but the Spanish burned these documents, and thus most of the information has been lost. Informal accounts of music making by Europeans date back to the first missionaries who came to the Americas in the fifteenth century, and other accounts appear subsequently in the form of travel diaries, memoirs, and similar texts. Formal musicological studies began in earnest in the early twentieth century, as a rise in nationalist consciousness led to a gradual recognition of the importance of local repertoire. Pioneers such as Carlos Vega in Argentina, Mario de Andrade in Brazil, and Fernando Ortiz in Cuba provided research that has served as the foundation for subsequent publications in Latin America, the United States, and elsewhere. Many prominent researchers from the past hundred years are featured in the lists of additional bibliographic resources in the appendices, should you wish to consult them directly, and some are mentioned in individual chapters.

Musical study within Latin America continues to be influential today. The regional section of the International Association for the Study of Popular Music (IASPM América Latina), to cite one example, has become a vibrant forum for research, hosting annual conferences and lively e-mail debates. Well-established programs for the study of Latin American music in all its many permutations now exist in Rio de Janeiro and other Brazilian cities; in Bogotá, Mexico City, Santiago de Chile; and elsewhere. Musicologists continue to emerge throughout Latin America whose writings have broad international influence. One contemporary example includes Coriún Aharonián from Uruguay, cited in the references at the end of this essay.

One might think of music as resembling language in a certain sense: it consists of both sounds and meanings associated with sounds. Early studies of music among both musicologists and ethnomusicologists tended to prioritize the analysis of sound. Musicologists worked with excerpts from manuscripts or scores, while ethnomusicologists transcribed traditional melodies and analyzed scales, rhythms, and so on. Only since the 1970s have scholars paid more attention to the meanings associated with sound. They realize now that music is part of a broader cultural reality and that it can be studied as music but also "read" as a narrative or story.

The stories told by music revolve around issues of community, cultural negotiation or accommodation, gender relations, political dominance, protest, technological change, and so forth. Every instrument, rhythm, and melody with its unique history provides insights into particular countries, broad demographic trends, as well as the inherited practices of distinct social groups and their active reinterpretation of heritage. From this perspective, an instrument such as the timbales could be analyzed in terms of the rhythms played on it, or might be viewed as telling a story about the "Africanization" of European-style military percussion. This instrument developed out of European timpani drums used by black and mulato Cuban soldiers in the nineteenth century. They began to use their sticks to play on the sides of the drums as well as on the head, as is common in West Africa, to dampen the head with their hand as they played to alter the timbre, and so on. These techniques continue to be employed today.

Similarly, a dance band cumbia by Lucho Bermúdez ("Gaita de las flores," Listening Guide 4.5) could be studied as musical composition or thought of as a text encoded with information about Colombian history. Songs such as this one make implicit reference to the history of Cartagena as a major slave port during the colonial era, to the gradual fusion of indigenous and African musics into a host of traditional genres on the Atlantic coast (commercial cumbia takes inspiration from music fusing indigenous flute playing with African-derived drumming), to the stylization of such repertoire on the part of middle-class composers, and to the strong influence of big-band jazz in Latin America of the 1950s, among other things.

The many stories of Latin American music continue into the future; their sounds and meanings change frequently, responding to the preferences of new generations and to the ever-new situations that confront them. Given this, no textbook can hope to provide an exhaustive overview of Latin American music. Use the following chapters as a frame for thinking about the region and its heritage as you learn more about music you may be familiar with already and discover other sounds that are entirely new.

KEY TERMS

classical music	mulato	presentational performance
ethnography	musicology	traditional music
ethnomusicology	participatory performance	TUBS (Time Unit Box System)
mestizaje		
mestizo	popular music	

FURTHER READING

Aharonián, Coriún. *Conversaciones sobre música, cultura e identidad*. Montevideo, Uruguay: OMBU, 1992.

Béhague, Gerard. "Reflections on the Ideological History of Latin American Ethnomusicology." In *Comparative Musicology and Anthropology of Music. Essays on the History of Ethnomusicology*, edited by Bruno Nettl and Philip Bohlman, 56–68. Chicago: University of Chicago Press, 1991.

Bethell, Leslie. *A Cultural History of Latin America. Literature, Music and the Visual Arts in the Nineteenth and Twentieth Centuries*. New York: Cambridge University Press, 1998.

García Canclini, Néstor. *Hybrid Cultures: Strategies for Entering and Leaving Modernity*. Translated by Christopher L. Chiappari and Silvia L. López. Minneapolis: University of Minnesota Press, 1995.

Green, Duncan. *Faces of Latin America*. London: Latin American Bureau, 1997.

Koetting, James. "Analysis and Notation of West African Drum Ensemble Music." *Selected Reports in Ethnomusicology* 13 (1970): 115–46.

Nettl, Bruno. *The Study of Ethnomusicology: Thirty-one Issues and Concepts*. Urbana: University of Illinois Press, 2005.

Rowe, William, and Vivian Schelling. *Memory and Modernity. Popular Culture in Latin America*. London: Verso, 1991.

Treitler, Leo. L. *Music and the Historical Imagination*. Cambridge, MA: Harvard University Press, 1989.

Turino, Thomas. *Music as Social Life. The Politics of Participation*. Chicago, IL: The University of Chicago Press, 2008.

Los Angeles

San Diego

Viceroyalty of New Spain (est. 1521)

Atlantic Ocean

Havana

Mexico City • • Puebla

Santiago de Cuba

Puerto Rico

Oaxaca •

Santo Domingo

Captaincy General of Guatemala (est. 1609)

Guatemala City •

Viceroyalty of New Granada (est. 1717)

Bogotá •

• Quito

Recife •

B R A Z I L

Cuzco •

Salvador •

Lima •

Pacific Ocean

Viceroyalty of Peru (est. 1542)

• La Plata (Sucre)

MINAS GERAIS

Rio de Janeiro •

Viceroyalty of the Río de la Plata (est. 1776)

• Córdoba

0   400   800   1200   1600
Kilometers

0   200   400   600   800   1000
Miles

2

Music, Conquest, and Colonialism

SUSAN THOMAS

Introduction

The "colonial period" in Latin America refers to four centuries of history, from Columbus's arrival on the shores of the Caribbean island of Hispaniola (now the Dominican Republic and Haiti) in 1492 to the final severance of colonial control in 1898. It encompasses the histories of hundreds of indigenous groups; the various colonizing projects of the Spanish and the Portuguese; the cultural, political, and economic influence of competing incursions led by the French, English, and Dutch; the active role of the Catholic Church; and the impact of the Atlantic slave trade, which included the forced integration of hundreds of thousands of African slaves and their descendants into distinct Latin American societies. "Colonial period" thus refers to the history of an entire hemisphere and its relationship with Europe and Africa over nearly half a millennium. Any effort to represent a complete trajectory of even one aspect of that history—such as music—would be impossible in the space available here. This chapter thus does not claim to represent a comprehensive survey of Latin American colonial music. Rather, it asks you to consider some of the extraordinary works composed and performed during this period within the context of conquest and colonization. The listening guides not only feature representative musical works, but also provoke inquiry into the colonial project itself. What meanings did music convey for people of different groups? How was music produced and performed? What kind of cultural and political work did music do and how did it help shape what we know today as Latin America?

LISTENING guides

"Hanacpachap cussicuinin"

Gutiérrez de Padilla, Credo, from *Missa Ego flos campi*

Fernandes, "Xicochi conetzintle"

Lôbo de Mesquita, Salve Regina

Nunes Garcia, "Cum Sancto Spiritu," from *Missa de Nossa Senhora de Conceição*

Zipoli, "In te spero," from *In hoc Mundo*

Torrejón y Velasco, "No sé, que a sombra me dormí," from *La púrpura de la rosa*

Murcia, "Jácaras por la E"

Murcia, "Fandango"

Cervantes, "Los delirios de Rosita"

◀ **FIGURE 2.1** Composite map of New World colonies established 1521–1776

For indigenous peoples, European colonizers, enslaved Africans, and the diverse hybridization of communities and cultures that these groups later produced, music represented more than mere entertainment. Music could show military and political force or display economic wealth. It served as a representation of religious faith and as an important tool of conversion. Perhaps most powerfully, music—whether pre-Columbian "flower songs," complex choral works performed in ornate cathedrals, boisterous street processions, or allegorical operas performed in colonial palaces—both reflected and influenced society. How music was performed and by whom; how it was taught, listened to, or danced to; the content of its lyrics; and even the sound of the music itself shaped the worldview of both the colonizer and the colonized.

Following a brief historical overview of colonial history and a discussion of music at the time of conquest, selected colonial musical practices are discussed through a number of thematic lenses. They include education, space and place, religion and ritual, material culture, entertainment, and cosmopolitanism. A summary of these themes follows.

Education: The Catholic Church initially embraced certain elements of indigenous culture as a means of evangelizing locals, and it incorporated these elements into a colonial music pedagogy that had the ultimate aims of religious conversion and the stable and unified growth of the church in the New World. In the process, indigenous and Afro-Latin concerns and aesthetics also entered into dialogue with European musical expressions of religion. Music education's power as a colonizing force extended beyond the initial conquest. As the Spanish extended their empire in the eighteenth century in both North and South America, the missionary presence expanded in both regions, as did the music's use as a tool of conversion and **acculturation**.

Space and Place: Where was music performed, and what significance did those spaces hold culturally and politically? Key to this discussion will be the role of the cathedral as the de facto center of the colonial soundscape, as well as how processions and outdoor celebrations strengthened colonial authority.

Religion and Ritual: Highly organized ritual, in which music figured prominently, was a central part of many of the indigenous societies encountered by European colonizers, as it was to the Europeans themselves. This chapter pays particular attention to the primary ritual of the Roman Catholic Church, the Mass, and its relationship to indigenous ritual practices.

Material Culture: This chapter draws your attention to the material aspects of music-making, such as the availability and manufacture of instruments and the influence of indigenous and African instruments on colonial-era music. Additionally, the practical realities of evangelization and the sometimes-competing directives of church officials in Rome influenced the types of instruments used in religious practice.

Entertainment: Secular music for entertainment was an important part of colonial life. Theater music, dance music, and popular songs entertained at the same time that they helped negotiate new Latin American identities. Because secular music was transmitted orally and often improvised, there are fewer surviving sources of it than there are of sacred music. Its influence, however, is undeniable. The secular songs and dances of the colonial era set the stage for many of the prominent genres discussed in later chapters in this book.

Cosmopolitanism: Latin American musical culture did not develop in isolation, nor did it merely borrow from sources elsewhere. Rather, it developed in dialogue with Europe and, by the end of the colonial period, with the United States as well. The latest musical trends from France and Italy, as well as Spanish and Portuguese styles, sounded in Latin American cathedrals, theaters, and ballrooms. Additionally, new Latin American rhythms as well as novel variations on European forms crossed back over the Atlantic. The Atlantic slave trade continued until the 1860s (albeit illegally), and along with human cargo it brought continuous infusions of African cultures, languages, and musical traditions, elements of which found their way into local musics. Several genres that became popular on both sides of the Atlantic, such as the *zarabanda* (sarabande), contradanza (contradance), and habanera, had their origins in colonial Latin America's unique cosmopolitanism.

The Colonization of Latin America: Historical Overview

Columbus's inadvertent landing in the Caribbean in 1492 soon led to a burst of exploration from Spain and its neighboring competitor, Portugal. Spanish monarchs Ferdinand and Isabella asked Pope Alexander VI for official ownership of the territories (still believed to be part of Asia) in exchange for undertaking the task of Christianizing local inhabitants. The resulting Papal bull granted Spain title to the "Western parts of the Ocean Sea, toward the Indies," and a later version clarified and expanded Spanish dominion to include all the lands west of a north–south demarcation line one hundred leagues west of Cape Verde and the Azores. The Portuguese, feeling that this limited their possibilities for expansion, threatened war. The two kingdoms eventually signed, in 1494, the Treaty of Tordesillas, which created a new line of demarcation some 370 leagues west of the Cape Verde Islands. Spain would control all lands to the west of this line, and Portugal those to the east, allowing the Portuguese to claim Brazil following their "discovery" of the territory in 1500.

The desire for precious metals and other resources and the enslavement of native populations to extract those resources compromised the Spanish crown's commitment to evangelization, as the project of true conversion (rather than just mere baptism) conflicted with the demands of wealth generation. Harsh labor conditions and abuse combined with unfamiliar European diseases had a disastrous effect on native populations. Estimates of the island of Hispaniola's population at the time of Columbus's arrival range from several hundred thousand to more than one million. By 1518 the population had already been decimated to about 30,000. The Spanish soon began to look elsewhere for labor and natural resources, conquering Puerto Rico in 1508 and Cuba in 1511. The native populations suffered tremendous losses there as well, and in neighboring islands. The Spanish responded by importing increasing numbers of African slaves and they also began to explore the Latin American mainland.

Africans arrived in the New World almost as soon as Europeans did. Free black sailors accompanied the earliest expeditions in 1492. Not all arrived in the Americas of their free will, however. The Portuguese capture of the strategically located North African city of Ceuta in 1415 led to increasing Portuguese exploration of, and trade with, the West African coastline. Although initial trading between the Portuguese and West African groups focused on the acquisition of African goods (including gold, iron, copper, textiles, and salt), by the 1480s it became more common for European goods to be traded for slaves. In the final decades of the fifteenth century, Portuguese traders bought and exported more than two thousand slaves annually. Over the next century the slave trade grew and continued to do so for more than three hundred years, eclipsing all other relations and trade between Europe and Africa. From 1513 until the 1860s, Africans forcibly brought to the Americas maintained, to varying degrees, elements of their religions, languages, and cultures—and their musics.

The conquest of the mainland began with Hernán Cortés's overthrow of the **Mexica** (Aztec) empire from 1519 to 1521. (Most historians prefer to use the term Mexica, rather than the popularly used term Aztec, to describe the collection of Nahuatl-speaking peoples who formed the Mesoamerican empire in place at the time of Cortés's arrival. Some writers use Mexica to refer to the empire itself and Nahua to refer to the people of this linguistic group and their cultural practices. This text uses Mexica broadly, to cover both meanings.) Spurred by discoveries of gold and other precious commodities, Spanish control over the continent quickly spread. In 1526 Francisco Pizarro made first contact with the Inca; six years later he overthrew and executed the Inca leader Atahualpa and seized control of Cuzco. With Latin America's two great urban empires thus defeated, an age of European colonization began in earnest.

Colonialism developed differently in Latin America than it did in the English colonies. While English colonies were governed remotely from overseas, Spain gave its Latin American satellites considerably more local control. Initially, Spain divided its Latin American holdings in two primary administrative divisions: the **Viceroyalty** of New Spain, which included what is now Mexico, Central America, and much of the southern United States, as well as the Philippines and the Caribbean; and the Viceroyalty of Peru, which included the entire western third of South America. The Spanish split up this large territory in 1717 and created a new jurisdiction, the Viceroyalty of New Granada, corresponding to present-day Panama, Colombia, Ecuador, and Venezuela, and parts of Brazil and Peru, as well as Trinidad and Tobago. A smaller jurisdiction was the Captaincy General of Guatemala (sometimes referred to as the Kingdom of Guatemala), an autonomous region that encompassed much of Central America including present-day Guatemala, Costa Rica, Honduras, El Salvador and the southern Mexican state of Chiapas. Finally, in 1776, Spain established the Viceroyalty of Río de la Plata, containing present-day Argentina, Bolivia, Paraguay, and Uruguay (Figure 2.1). A local viceroy, who functioned as a surrogate for the Spanish crown, governed each of these jurisdictions.

Many historians prefer the term viceregal period to colonial period when discussing these centuries of European control, as it emphasizes the considerable autonomy that the viceroyalties enjoyed from Spain. However, the degree of autonomy varied greatly by region. Cuba and Puerto Rico, for instance, experienced much stronger direct economic, military, and cultural ties with Madrid than they ever did with Mexico City, owing in large part to Cuba's strategic military location and Havana's important role in maritime trade. In rural and remote regions such as the Southern Cone, the administrative and cultural imperatives of missionary groups often had a greater impact than overarching viceregal experience. In order to broadly address all of these cases, the term "colonial period" will be used throughout this chapter. In addition, the slightly more political nature of the latter term calls our attention to the power relationships that fundamentally shaped new musical cultures.

Unlike the Spanish, the Portuguese initially approached their new territory as a material resource but not as a colony for settlement. The crown leased out rights to a number of companies who extracted the rich, red-grained Brazilian wood known as dyewood (the favored wood for making violins and other musical instruments), caught parrots and other exotic animals, and captured some indigenous slaves. Spain for the most part accepted the juridical basis for Portugal's claim on Brazil, arguing only about boundaries, but other emerging colonial powers did not recognize the validity of the original Papal bull. Eventually King João III of Portugal determined that the only way to stake a lasting claim on the new territory was to settle it. The first four hundred settlers arrived on the mainland in 1530, and Brazil was a remotely governed colony until 1763, when it gained the status of a viceroyalty. Brazil's status changed again from 1808 to 1821 when the Portuguese royal family moved the seat of the throne to Rio de Janeiro to escape Napoleon's advancing troops.

The Roman Catholic Church permeated colonial life. In the Spanish colonies, church officials' loyalties extended to both Rome and the Spanish Crown. In 1508, just before the Conquest of the mainland began in earnest, a Papal bull established the **patronato system**, which gave the Crown authority to control the clergy in its American territories. While the Pope continued to be the spiritual leader of the church, the Spanish king and his representatives coordinated religious activities. The religious orders administered educational and charitable institutions such as schools, hospitals, and orphanages. Lay (nonclergy) brotherhoods, or confraternities, known as **cofradías** in Spanish and **irmandades** in Portuguese, arranged for music to accompany church services and helped to organize local religious festivals, funerals, and other special occasions. All of these institutions became important sites for music-making.

The church calendar, with its periods of penance (Lent), celebration (Easter, Christmas), anticipation and reflection (Advent), and individual feast days, mapped itself onto daily life throughout Latin America, merging European practices with local traditions (Figure 2.2). South America's location in the Southern Hemisphere causes religious holidays there to be seasonally inverted from the way they are experienced in the Northern Hemisphere (i.e., Christmas takes place during the hottest summer months, Easter in the fall, and so on), which helped to foster new traditions. Feast days such as the celebration of Corpus Christi, discussed later in this chapter, became sites for the negotiation

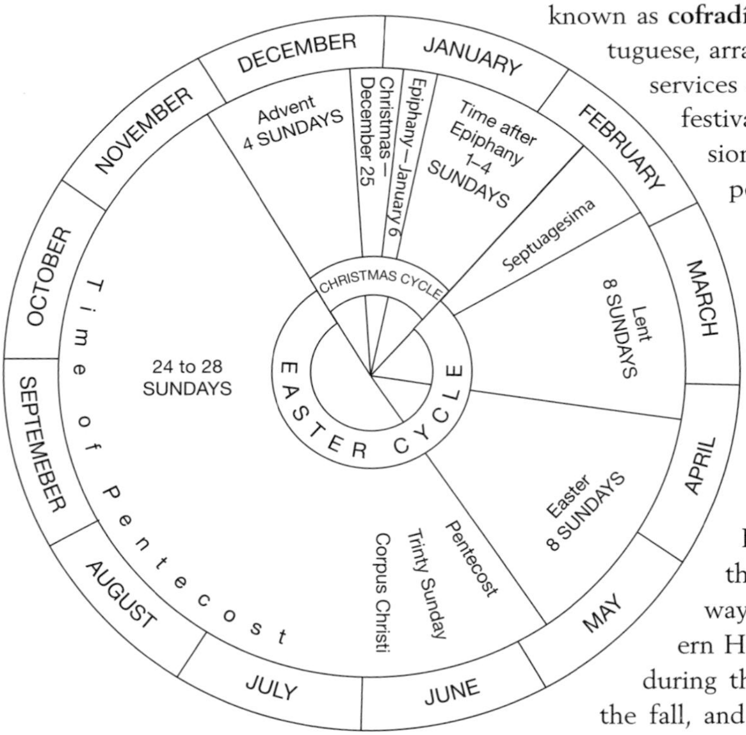

FIGURE 2.2 Roman Catholic Church calendar

of local identities and religious beliefs, as the descendants of Europeans, Africans, and indigenous groups created new forms of religious expression, often expressed in musical terms. Such feast days have continued to shape religious and musical culture throughout Latin America into the present, as will be discussed in subsequent chapters.

In their new territories, the Spanish (and later the Portuguese) pursued a development model that replicated Renaissance ideals for both urban planning and civic government. Just as European cities asserted their identities through musical displays in architecturally impressive cathedrals and palaces, the two new viceregal capitals, Mexico City and Lima, as well as other prominent cities, such as Puebla, Oaxaca, Cuzco, Sucre, and Bogotá, proclaimed their status not only through elaborate new architecture, public works projects, and the transformation of preexisting indigenous monuments, but also through the musical use of civic spaces. Elaborate multivoiced, or polyphonic, compositions resounded from cathedrals and churches, and musicians sang and played the latest compositional styles from Europe. By the eighteenth century, Latin American cities hosted performances of new Latin American operas and other repertoire. Such music powerfully asserted identity—an identity not merely Spanish, Portuguese, or Catholic, but increasingly local.

Indigenous Musical Culture at the Time of the Conquest

In the 1490s, the indigenous population of the Caribbean and mainland Latin America is estimated to have numbered between 35 and 55 million people. This population varied widely, comprising more than 350 major tribal groups and more than 160 distinct languages. European explorers encountered—and developed strategies to conquer—three different types of indigenous societies: (1) nomadic groups who relied on hunting and gathering for subsistence; (2) small, sedentary groups who relied on agriculture; and (3) densely populated and urbanized societies with highly stratified religious and governmental hierarchies, organized militaries and advanced architectural, and scientific expertise. Groups such as the Inca, Maya, and Mexica correspond to the latter category. Although these urbanized societies represented only a fraction of the overall indigenous population, we know considerably more about them and their musical activities than we know about other groups, as Europeans documented contact with them. Of course, the European invaders or missionaries who wrote about indigenous culture viewed it through the bias of their own preconceptions, leaving us with many questions. Surviving instruments and pictorial evidence provide further resources to help reconstruct elements

FIGURE 2.3 Photo of teponaztli (reproduction carved by master carver Agustín Rodiles)

of preconquest music cultures. This section primarily examines Mexica music-making, using available sources while recognizing that the urban musics of Mesoamerica represented only one music culture flourishing in Latin America at the time of the conquest.

Music constituted an important part of social, civic, and religious life in the Americas long before the arrival of Europeans. In Mexica society, musicians enjoyed high social status. They trained in special schools, known as *cuicacalli*, dedicated to the performing arts. As in modern Western conservatories, expert faculty taught specific instruments and, while students received general training in all aspects of the performing arts, advanced students would specialize in a chosen instrument. In Mexica culture, musicians were an important part of public and ritual life. They accompanied the most sacred rituals, performed for dances, celebrated births and mourned deaths, and accompanied soldiers into battle. Although we can never know how pre-Columbian music sounded to those that created and consumed it, archeological evidence and descriptions written by early Spanish explorers stress an enormous diversity of musical expression.

Prior to contact, indigenous groups across Latin America made vocal music and played a wide variety of percussion instruments and wind instruments. In Mesoamerica, for example, the Mexica used two types of ritual drums, a split log drum called **teponaztli** and the single-headed **huehuetl**. The sound of the teponaztli, an idiophone, was produced by rubber-tipped mallets that drew two pitches from the tongues of wood created by the H-shaped slit carved into the drum (Figure 2.3). Extant copies of the instrument suggest that the most common tuning for the teponaztli was an interval a fourth or a fifth apart. The huehuetl (Figure 2.4) was a membranophone; a jaguar skin stretched across the top of the upright cylinder could be tightened and tuned so that the player, striking the membrane with his bare hands, could produce two tones a fifth apart. Pictorial evidence (Figure 2.5) as well as sixteenth-century written accounts confirm that the two instruments were commonly played together. Spanish explorers described the drums' dramatic power, and the threatening din they produced may have led Spanish soldiers to slaughter Mexica drummers in the massacre at

FIGURE 2.4 Photo of huehuetl (reproduction carved by master carver Agustín Rodiles)

Tenochtitlán in 1520 (In Depth 2.1). Yet while Spanish explorers wrote about the impact of such drums and described their use in both battle and in human sacrifice, their descriptions of the music itself are vague. Therefore, neither the actual rhythms produced nor the meanings such rhythms generated can be known to us today. Furthermore, it is likely that what the Spanish identified as individual pieces or songs were actually part of much longer and complex compositions and music dramas that may have lasted hours or even days. The *Cantares Mexicanos*, a sixteenth-century compilation of 91 *xochitl/cuicatl*, or "flower songs," provides a tantalizing glimpse into the Mexica's spiritual worldview and their adaptation to Christianity. One of the most striking elements of the *Cantares* is that it is the only sixteenth-century source that provides extensive notation for drumming, using a syllabic notation, or **solfège**, that appears to refer to both pitch and rhythm. Using four syllables—ti, to, qui (pronounced "ki"), and co—the manuscript notates patterns at

FIGURE 2.5 Image from the *Florentine Codex* showing huehuetl and teponaztli players at a feast for a newborn child

The Massacre at the Templo Mayor

On May 10, 1520, Hernán Cortés left the Mexica city of Tenochtitlán to deter rival Spanish explorers who had arrived on the coast with the attention of arresting Cortés and exploiting the continent's riches for themselves. Cortés left the city to fight them, putting his deputy governor Pedro de Alvarado in charge. During Cortés's absence, the Mexica celebrated the festival of Toxcatl, dedicated to Tezcatlipoca and Huitzilopochtli, both gods associated with war. Perhaps because Alvarado recognized the martial undertones of the festival, or perhaps merely because he and his soldiers were eager to get their hands on Mexica gold, he unleashed his soldiers on all those in attendance at the height of the ceremony. Friar Bernardino de Sahagún (1499–1590), a Franciscan missionary, provides a contemporary account of the event.

> [W]hen already the feast was being observed, when already there was dancing, when already there was singing, when already there was song with dance, the singing resounded like waves breaking. When it was already time, when the moment was opportune for the Spaniards to slay them, thereupon they came forth. They were arrayed for battle. They came everywhere to block each of the ways leading out and leading in […] No one could go out.

> And when this had been done, thereupon they entered the temple courtyard to slay them. […] Thereupon they surrounded the dancers. Thereupon they went among the drums. Then they struck the drummer's arms; they severed his hands; then they struck his neck. Far off did his neck [and head] go to fall. (*Florentine Codex*, Book 12, Chapter 20)

Historians estimate hundreds died in the massacre. It represented a defining moment in

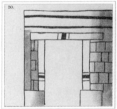

FIGURE 2.6 Images from the *Florentine Codex* documenting the massacre at the Templo Mayor

Spanish/Mexica relations, accelerating hostilities. In Figure 2.6, taken from the sixteenth-century *Florentine Codex*, panels 66–69 document the massacre that took place, with panel 70 showing the Templo grounds devoid of life. Panel 71 (not shown) depicts news of the massacre being spread. When Cortés returned, the Mexica attacked (panel 72, not shown). Cortés sent their captured ruler, Moctezuma, onto the rooftop to try to calm them, but considering Moctezuma a traitor, Mexica warriors stoned him as he tried to speak. He died a few days later.

the beginnings or sectional divides of individual texts. Thus the syllables are grouped into patterns such as "tocotico tocoti" or "toco tico tocoto, tiqui tiqui tiquiti." Some scholars have suggested that such notation uses vowels to refer to pitch, with "i" being the higher pitch and "o" the lower, while consonants and their use in combination could refer to rhythmic pattern. Such readings are largely conjecture, but many scholars of pre-conquest music have tried their hand at interpreting this notation and providing contemporary listeners with an idea of what the drums may have sounded like.

Sixteenth-century explorers extensively described the use of aerophones, both in Mesoamerica and the Andean region. Archeologists have documented a variety of flutes in Mesoamerica, and surviving aerophones from the Andean region are especially diverse, including conch-shell *qqepa* trumpets, *antara* panpipes, and the end-blown kena (p. 329) and *pingullo* flutes. Many of these instruments are still used today (see Chapter 8). As with the Mexica, Incan music accompanied all aspects of social, religious, military, and civic life.

Music of the Conquest and Early Colonial Period

In conquering the territories of the New World and its inhabitants, Spanish colonizers used strategies that had already served them effectively in the expulsion of the Moors from the Iberian peninsula and the conversion of those that remained. They seized and destroyed sites with significant religious and political significance and often repurposed them, building Christian churches and civic buildings in the same location. The Spanish viewed the saving of indigenous souls as justifying their control of the region, and music became a key part of this campaign.

In his earliest explorations, Hernán Cortés traveled with both clergy and musicians, and he would direct them to sing Mass in every new town and settlement that they entered. The urban civilizations of Mesoamerica and the Andes placed a high value on ritual spectacle, a trait that they shared with the European invaders. The instrumental and vocal music-making that characterized the Roman Catholic Mass thus represented a powerful ritual aesthetic that resonated with local expectations. Cortés's savvy awareness of the importance of musical ritual may have helped him conquer the Mexica; he even interrupted his early negotiations with Moctezuma to construct an altar and have a priest sing the Mass. Cortés's prioritization of music may have gone too far, however, when he insisted on bringing a contingent of musicians along with him on a failed expedition to control territory to the

explore

Listen to the San Antonio Vocal Arts Ensemble's (SAVAE) intriguing, if not necessarily authentic, reconstruction of "Teponazcuicatl," on their 1999 album, *El Milagro de Guadalupe*. In their reconstruction, SAVAE sets a text found in the *Cantares Mexicanos* with a newly composed melody that uses a pentatonic scale found on surviving *huilacapitzli* (clay flutes). The group interprets the *Cantares*'s percussion solfège to set the rhythms and uses the manuscript's remarks on performance practice to help determine the overall formal structure.

south. The undersupplied group ran out of food and resorted to eating their horses and then to eating each other!

As increasing numbers of missionaries arrived in the new territories, they established music instruction along with basic religious instruction. Indigenous converts, or **neophytes**, learned singing, solfège, and instrumental music. An important figure in this process was a Franciscan friar named Pedro de Gante who worked in New Spain from 1523 to 1572. Fluent in Nahuatl (the main language of the Mexica), Gante came to understand the important role that singing and dancing played in indigenous belief systems, and he indulged local preferences for elaborate rituals while overlaying them with Christian theology. "Upon [...] realizing that all their songs were composed to honor their gods," he wrote, "I composed a very elaborate one myself." Gante adapted many aspects of indigenous culture in his campaign to convert and educate natives, staging ornate ritual processions in which the locals danced in costumes painted with Christian symbols or depicting religious figures. He focused much of his educational efforts on children, who often proved more receptive than adults. Gante set up schools in which he translated biblical themes into Nahuatl and set them to familiar liturgical melodies, known as **plainchant** (often referred to as "Gregorian chant"). In these early years of the conquest, the Vatican directly supported missionaries' appropriation and adaptation of local cultures—and even local religious expression—as long as it did not directly conflict with Christianity.

The teachings of Gante and other like-minded missionaries had an enormous impact. Many local inhabitants rapidly converted and learned European music. Wind instruments (such as **shawms**, **sackbuts**, and flutes) held a particular attraction, perhaps because they most readily corresponded to indigenous preferences for bright-sounding aerophones. Neophytes quickly mastered the skills necessary to play these instruments and to sing European polyphony. In a relatively short time, even the smallest towns had their own church musicians. By 1576, only 57 years after the conquest began, an estimated one thousand church choirs existed in New Spain, and elaborate music programs had been established in major urban centers. As early as 1530, the neophyte choir in the Mexico City cathedral impressed visitors so much that it earned the reputation of rivaling the chapel choir of the Holy Roman Emperor Charles V. Most cathedrals preferred to employ organists and chapelmasters from Europe, yet there simply were not enough of these musicians to fill the necessary posts. Many cathedrals thus hired indigenous singers and instrumentalists. Later, mestizo musicians as well as musicians of African descent joined their ranks.

As mentioned, priests occasionally employed indigenous languages, rather than Latin, in religious music. While many of these compositions sound purely European in everything but language, scholars believe that some composers used actual indigenous melodies as the basis of European-style works, particularly in areas with heavily indigenous populations, such as the Peruvian city of Cuzco. The anonymous Quechua hymn "Hanacpachap cussicuinin" (The Bliss of Heaven) exemplifies this trend (Listening Guide 2.1). Published in 1631 as part of a manual for priests, it served as a processional entrance hymn, or Introit, to honor the Virgin Mary, and it is the first published polyphonic work in the New World. The original manuscript is set for four voices and comprises 20 verses, each containing five eight-syllable lines followed by a four-syllable phrase. In the original manuscript, this last four-syllable phrase is printed in italics and often forms a poetic link to the text of the next verse. The poetry itself contains metaphoric imagery that refers to both Christian and indigenous belief systems. Verse 2, for example, refers to the Virgin Mary as the bearer of the Christ Child, using common Christian metaphors of the lily, the "white shoot," and the long wait of Advent.

Uyarihuai muchascaita	*Hear my prayer,*
Diospa rampan Diospa maman	*Litter of God, Mother of God,*
Yurac tocto hamancaiman	*White shoot of the lily,*
Yupascalla, collpascaita	*Worshipped, my barren state,*
Huahuaiquiman suyuscaita	*Show me your son,*
Ricuchillai.	*Whom I await.*

The thirteenth verse, however, speaks of life-giving sustenance in local terms—the corn harvest and palm fruit—and it specifically refers to images with powerful ritual significance to the Inca. These include the color red, reserved for royalty, and references to the paving stones of the temple (rather than the church).

Ñucñu ruruc chunta mallqui allqui	*Sweet fruit of the chonta palm,*
Runacnap munai callcha	*Fine corn harvest of the people,*
Pucai pucai çumacpallcha	*Fair gentian flower crimson red,*
Sutarpu tutuchec callqui	*Paving stones for the temple,*
Titu huachec ñauillaiqui	*Sustenance from the gaze of your eyes*
Quespi huampu.	*Translucent wave.*

The four-voice setting is homophonic, meaning that all of the voices move together; they pronounce the syllables simultaneously, much as in the four-part setting of a church hymn today. The meter is slow and regular, appropriate for processional music; you can imagine a procession slowly winding its way through the streets and into a church as each of the 20 verses are sung to the same music.

⊚ "Hanacpachap cussicuinin" (The Bliss of Heaven)

Composer/lyricist: Anonymous

Date of composition: 1631

Date of recording: 2008

Performers/instruments: Ex Cathedra Baroque Ensemble; Jeffrey Skidmore, conductor (Baroque strings, winds, organ, and percussion; choir)

What to Listen for:
- Two-part musical form with three phrases in each part
- One note per syllable, or syllabic text setting
- Syncopation at 1:01 and 1:11

Time	Text	Translation	Description
0:00			Instruments play through entire verse
1:10	Hanacpachap cussicuinin	The bliss of Heaven	Homophonic and syllabic; phrase ascends by a fifth
1:17	Huaran cacta muchas caiqui	I will worship you a thousandfold	Melody begins a fourth higher, then descends
1:25	Yupai rurupucoc mallqui	Revered fruit of a mature tree	Phrase begins with faster eighth notes on beat 2, creating light syncopation
1:35	Runacunap suyacuinin	Long awaited by your people	Eighth-note pattern continues; phrase ascends by a third
1:43	Callpannacpa quemicuinin	Protection of spiritual strength	Eighth-note pattern continues; phrase descends to resolve
1:50	Huacyascaita.	Heed my call.	Slow closing, or cadential phrase; resembles "amen" of hymn settings

The music itself is quite straightforward. The first two lines of text are set in a melodic arc, with the first line ascending and the second gently descending. While the verses consist of five eight-syllable lines, followed by the four-syllable ending phrase, the musical phrases divide into two halves, with each half being made up of 3 + 3 + 4 bars. Just as the final four-syllable phrase of text acts as a linkage to the poetry of the following verse, the internal four-bar phrase connects with the musical material of the second half by setting up a light syncopation that is heard again in phrases four and five. The final four-bar phrase, which coincides with the final four-syllable verse line, stands out for its slower, declamatory setting. In the recording that accompanies Listening Guide 2.1, the entire verse is played through once on instruments. A choir then sings the first verse (of 20) of the hymn.

Instruments, especially wind instruments, were widely used in Catholic religious music in Europe and in the colonies. Musicians played the louder wind instruments, such as the shawm and trumpet, for outdoor religious processions and celebrations, but they also played them in indoor celebrations of the Mass alongside bowed strings, harps, flutes, and drums. The vibrant and occasionally boisterous use of instruments eventually attracted the attention of Vatican officials. The Council of Trent, a conference of church authorities that met in the Alpine city of Trent (now in Italy) from 1545 to 1563, outlined the church's response both to the Protestant Reformation and to perceived abuses and extravagances within the church itself. The council also had a direct impact on colonial music-making. The council issued directives curtailing polyphonic practices and instrumental performance that detracted from the solemnity of the Mass. It banned instruments considered loud or shrill (shawms, trumpets, sackbuts) from liturgical use, along with instruments associated with popular music such as flutes and **viols**. In their place, the council advocated that organs be used to accompany the liturgy. The council's instrumental ban, and particularly its singling out of "shrill" wind instruments, prohibited precisely the type of musical expression in which indigenous musicians were most visible (and audible). It signaled a radical shift in the approach towards colonization, rejecting the syncretic, "anything goes" approach to indigenous culture that characterized early evangelism. This hard-line attitude culminated in 1577 when the Spanish Crown forbade further inquiry into native history and religion and banned the publishing and distribution of materials by Catholic friars that contained such information.

The church's initiatives met with spotty success; instrumental music continued to be an important part of colonial religious activity. Efforts to introduce the organ, however, proved hugely successful. By the end of the sixteenth century, large churches and cathedrals had two or even three of the instruments as well as a smaller, portable one used for outdoor processions. The demand for organs, and the expense of importing them, gave rise to local manufacturers who produced them in both New Spain and Peru. Many independent organ makers were indigenous artisans who had been taught instrument-making skills by missionaries, especially the Jesuits, who arrived in Latin America in the mid-sixteenth century. Over the next two centuries, until their expulsion in 1767, Jesuit missions spread across the less-populated regions of the continent, including what is now Argentina, Brazil, Bolivia, Uruguay, and Paraguay.

The Mass

The Mass is the central religious ritual of the Catholic Church. It consists of prayers and readings organized around a ritual reenactment of the last supper, known as the celebration of the Eucharist. The texts spoken or sung during the Mass are of two types: those present in every Mass and those that change according to the occasion. Some prayers, such as the Kyrie (Lord have mercy), Gloria (Glory to God in the highest), Credo (Nicene Creed), Sanctus (Holy, holy, holy), and the Agnus Dei (Lamb of God), are present in every celebration; that is, they are performed daily. These five unchanging texts are part of what is known as the **Ordinary** of the Mass. Other texts were intended to draw attention to, and underscore the importance of, specific days in the church calendar, such as Christmas, Easter, or Pentecost, feast days for particular saints, or even the visit of a dignitary. These more "custom" texts formed what is known as the **Proper** of the Mass and include the Introit (Entrance hymn), Gradual, Alleluia, Offertory, and Communion.

Most frequently, the Mass was sung in plainchant. Monophonic and metrically free, plainchant conformed well to the conditions of the New World and could be performed by the priest alone or with a choir, if one was available. In medieval Europe, plainchant had been categorized according to the scale utilized for each melody, known as mode, and chant melodies utilized preexisting melodic figures and formulas in a process known as centonization. Such processes made learning and retaining chant melodies easier, aiding the Roman Catholic Church in unifying religious practices across Europe. They proved similarly useful in the New World colonies. Once trained choirs had been established, they could move beyond plainchant to sing polyphonic compositions, allowing Latin American cathedrals to resound with the same sophistication as their European contemporaries.

In the first century after the conquest, choirs typically performed polyphonic Masses *a cappella*, without instrumental accompaniment. If instruments did play along, they merely doubled or reinforced the vocal line. In the seventeenth century, composers often juxtaposed and intermingled works for two separate choirs in what is known as **polychoral style**. Occasionally instruments such as organ, harp, or bassoon accompanied these polychoral works.

A key composer of the polychoral style was Juan Gutiérrez de Padilla (ca. 1590–1664). Born in Málaga, Spain, Gutiérrez de Padilla emigrated to New Spain by 1622, where he served in the Puebla cathedral (Figure 2.7) as assistant to chapelmaster and composer Gaspar Fernandes. He took over the position following Fernandes's death in 1629. Gutiérrez de Padilla composed in all of the important sacred genres of the day and also composed

FIGURE 2.7 Interior of the Puebla Cathedral

secular villancicos (p. 45). Some of his liturgical works are polychoral and create a great variety of sound by juxtaposing one group of singers and instruments against another. One of his Masses, the *Missa Ego flos campi*, dramatically illustrates this type of writing.

Gutiérrez de Padilla's *Missa Ego flos campi* is based on a pre-existing polyphonic work, a setting of the Christmas song, "Ego flos campi" (I am the flower of the field), now lost. The Mass is impressively beautiful and surprising, and features two choirs that sometimes sing back and forth to one another in what is known as **antiphonal** style. At other moments, the four parts of each choir (eight parts in all) weave in and out in overlapping patterns, creating a tapestry of sound that recalls the multicolored play of light coming through a stained glass window. At particularly important moments in the text, Gutiérrez de Padilla marshals both choirs and has them deliver the text together, in the same rhythm. This change in delivery, and the sheer, sonic power behind it, can be truly dazzling.

The *Missa Ego flos campi*'s text settings are unusual for the Mass Ordinary. Remember that texts from the Ordinary are unchanging. In the Middle Ages, composers could make a setting of the Ordinary "Proper" by adding text specific to a particular occasion. By the second half of the sixteenth century, however, such practices fell into disuse, having been largely banned by the Council of Trent. Here, however, Gutiérrez de Padilla doesn't tailor the Mass for a special occasion; rather, he creates refrains out of parts of the original text that stress the celebratory and evangelical aspect of Catholic theology. In the Credo, for instance, he creates a choral refrain with the word, "credo" (I believe). In typical settings of the Mass, this word is not sung by the choir, but is instead intoned once by the priest. Here, however, the word serves as a repeated profession of faith, providing a sense of evangelical zeal. At the end of the composition, Gutiérrez de Padilla creates a similar refrain out of "confiteor" (to acknowledge/accept), which is repeated three times.

Far from being a rote iteration of religious doctrine, the Credo is highly expressive, using particular textures or melodic or rhythmic gestures to bring out the meaning of individual words, a technique referred to as word painting. For instance, at the words, "et descendit de coelis" (and descended from heaven), we hear the antiphonal choirs sing a falling melodic figure, or motive. Although this type of gesture is common in European polyphony of this period, it also resonates powerfully with the Mexica belief that both divine spirits and songs descended from the heavens. For the Mexica, the act of singing represented the physical expression of a spirit presence descending to earth through the lips of the singer. Song 70 of the *Cantares Mexicanos* begins, "In this place of scattering flowers I lift them up before the Ever Present, the Ever Near. Delicious are the root-songs, as I, the parrot corn-tassel bird, lift them through a conch of gold, the sky songs passing through my lips." Gutiérrez de Padilla's use of the descending motive represents accepted European compositional practice, a practice performed in cathedrals across New Spain. There is no evidence that he was aware of the metaphoric connections to indigenous theology. However, recognizing these resonances in the *Missa Ego flos campi* offers us an opportunity to consider how similarities in religious metaphor might have aided the syncretic appropriation of Christianity by indigenous cultures.

Note Gutiérrez de Padilla's use of a slow homophonic declamation at critical theological points, "et incarnatus est" (and he was made flesh) and "et homo factus est" (and he was made man). The work's presentation of the crucifixion is surprisingly lively: the dancelike rhythms of the choirs already look past the death and burial (passus et sepultus est) to the resurrection. The text, "et resurrexit … et ascendit in caelum" (he was resurrected … and he ascended into heaven), bursts out with joyous, ascending lines that seem to spiral up to the heavens.

A shift in the composition of liturgical music took place in the early eighteenth century, mirroring European trends. Composers highlighted textural contrasts, especially between solo singing and choral sections, and they divided settings of the Mass Ordinary into smaller fragments, which included elaborate and virtuosic **arias**, much in the style of Italian opera. The instruments in the orchestra became increasingly independent. They no longer served merely to support the vocal lines, but increasingly became more active and interesting, adding new colors, movement, and texture to the music. In New Spain, much of this shift can be witnessed in the polychoral Masses of Ignacio de Jerusalem y Stella (1707–1769), an Italian-born composer and violoncello virtuoso. Many consider Jerusalem's work to exemplify the arrival of the modern, **galant** style of composition in New Spain. This style is characterized by contrasting segments that showcase lightly accompanied homophony, rhythmic variety, delicate and refined ornamentation, and an overall sense

explore

For examples of the galant style, listen to Jerusalem's *Matins for the Virgin of Guadalupe* recorded by Chanticleer (Teldec, 1998) and the Coro Exaudi de La Habana's *Esteban Salas: Un barroco cubano* (Jade, 2005).

⊚ Gutiérrez de Padilla: Credo, from *Missa Ego flos campi* (I Am the Flower of the Field)

Composer: Juan Gutiérrez de Padilla

Date of composition: ca. 1650

Performers/instruments: The Harp Consort; Andrew Lawrence-King, conductor (double choir with Baroque guitars, harp, sackbut, and organ)

Date of recording: 2002

What to Listen for:

- Antiphonal, polychoral texture
- Interjections of the word "Credo"
- Instances of word painting
- Use of homophony and syllabic text setting to draw attention to certain words
- Instruments playing along with voices

Time	Text	Translation	Description
0:00	Credo en unum Deum	I believe in one God	Intonation by solo voice, sung by priest or other ordained official
0:07	Patrem omnipotentem, factorem caeli et terrae,	Father almighty, maker of heaven and earth,	
0:27	**Credo** visibilium omnium et invisibilium;	**I believe** of all that is seen and unseen;	"Credo" interrupts the text and musical flow. Dancelike syncopations on "visibillum" follow. Primarily homophonic text setting adds emphasis to the statement of faith
0:34	**Credo** et in unum Dominum Iesum Christum,	**I believe** and in the Lord Jesus Christ,	
0:40	**Credo** Filium Dei unigenitum,	**I believe** the only Son of God,	
0:45	**Credo** et ex Patre natum ante omnia saecula:	**I believe** eternally begotten of the Father:	
0:51	**Credo** Deum de Deo, **Credo** lumen de lumine, **Credo** Deum verum de Deo vero,	**I believe** God from God, **I believe** light from light, **I believe** true God from true God,	

(continued)

Time	Text	Translation	Description
1:26	**Credo** genitum non factum, consubstantialem Patri, **Credo** per quem omnia facta sunt; **Credo** qui propter nos homines et propter nostram salutem descendit de caelis;	**I believe** begotten, not made, of one being with the Father, **I believe** through him all things were made; **I believe** for us and for our salvation he descended from heaven;	"Descendit" features a scattered, falling melodic line.
1:35	**Credo** et incarnatus est de Spiritu Sancto ex Maria Virgine	**I believe** was made flesh by the Holy Spirit and the Virgin Mary	Softer, slower, and almost tender repetition of "Credo," emphasized by the homophonic setting of the text
2:48	**Credo** et homo factus est; crucifixus etiam pro nobis	**I believe** and was made man; for us he was crucified	Pause after final reiteration of "et homo factus est". "Crucifixus" set to lively and syncopated music
2:58	**Credo** sub Pontio Pilato, passus et sepultus est;	**I believe** under Pontius Pilate, he died and was buried;	Syncopation ends with the announcement of Christ's death. Slow and somber setting with a descending run on "sepultus" to depict burial
3.07	**Credo** et resurrexit tertia die secundum Scripturas;	**I believe** [and that] he was resurrected on the third day according to Scriptures;	Syncopation returns with the resurrection
3:16	**Credo** et ascendit in caelum, sedet ad dexteram Patris; **Credo** et iterum venturus est cum gloria iudicare vivos et mortuos; **Credo** cuius regni non erit finis;	**I believe** [and that] he ascended into Heaven, seated at the right hand of the Father, **I believe** he will come again in glory to judge the living and the dead; **I believe** his kingdom will have no end;	Word painting on "ascendit" and "sedet"
4:13	et in Spiritum Sanctum, Dominum et vivificantem:	and in the Holy Spirit, the Lord, the giver of life,	Pause after final repetition of "finis"

(continued)

Time	Text	Translation	Description
4:26	**Credo** qui ex Patre Filioque procedit; **Credo** qui cum Patre et Filio simul adoratur et conglorificatur; **Credo** qui locutus est per Prophetas; **Credo** Et unam sanctam catholicam et apostolicam Ecclesiam.	**I believe** who proceeds from the Father and the Son; **I believe** who with the Father and the Son is worshipped and glorified; **I believe** who has spoken through the prophets; **I believe** [and also] in the holy catholic and apostolic Church.	Overlapping lines stress oneness of the holy trinity
4:57	**Credo** **Confiteor** unum baptisma **Confiteor** in remissionem peccatorum; **Confiteor** et expecto resurrectionem mortuorum,	**I believe** **To acknowledge** one baptism **To acknowledge** the forgiveness of sins; **To acknowledge** and I await the resurrection of the dead,	Declamation of "Confiteor"
5:24	**Credo** et vitam venturi saeculi. **Credo** Amen.	**I believe** and the life of the world to come. **I believe** Amen.	Return of "Credo"

of simple—and often lighthearted—elegance. Jerusalem's masses, written for the cathedral in Mexico City, juxtapose block chordal movement in the choir, rapid embellishments in the orchestra that provide a sense of motion, and lyrical and expressive solo writing. In these respects, Jerusalem's music closely resembles that of his Brazilian contemporary, José Joachim Emerico Lôbo de Mesquita (1746–1805), discussed next. Another fine example of the galant style is found in the music of Esteban Salas y Castro (1725–1803), a Havana-trained composer who became the music director of the Santiago de Cuba Cathedral in 1764. There he enjoyed a prolific career, composing over ninety liturgical works plus a large number of lighter works known as villancicos (discussed next) for the Christmas season.

THE VILLANCICO

The **villancico** represents one of the most prominent musical genres through-out the colonial era. Most often performed by a chorus with instrumental accompaniment, villancicos are lively and often feature rhythmic groupings of two against three, recalling popular dance music. Typically, they exhibit a two-part form made up of quatrains (coplas) and a choral refrain (estribillo), although the genre absorbed a variety of formal deviations (Fernandes, "Xicochi conetzintle," Listening Guide 2.3). Latin American villancicos used religious, nonliturgical texts that often referenced elements of secular life, such as drumming or dancing, or the sounds of the street. Especially popular at Christmastime, they often accompanied processions that reenacted Mary and Joseph's journey to Bethlehem.

By the seventeenth century, the villancico played a fundamental role in the religious life of New Spain. Performers in convents or monasteries often grouped them into suites of eight or nine pieces to be included in the daily cycle of monastic prayers and ritual known as the **Divine Office**. Villancicos could be worked into the Mass as well, and bishops often solicited the composition of new villancicos for church services. Whereas music for the liturgy sounded awe-inspiring and removed from the realities of daily life, the villancico, and its dancelike and boisterous relative the **jácara** (**xácara**), sought to represent popular culture. Sung after the responsories and intended to enliven the service, villancicos featured comic plays on words, caricatures of local racial or ethnic groups, and the use of dance instrumentation, hand percussion, and drums. On occasion, they also included viols or organs as well as wind instruments such as recorders, shawms, cornettos, **crumhorns**, and sackbuts. The blend of secular and religious elements present in villancicos made them particularly adaptable to local tastes. In manuscripts across Latin America we find them composed in a variety of languages including Nahuatl, Quechua, Catalan, Galician, Spanish, and African-influenced dialects. The power of villancicos to entertain congregations alarmed church authorities as much as it attracted them as a tool for moral instruction.

The poet, musician, intellectual, and nun Sor Juana Inés de la Cruz (1648/51–1695; In Depth 2.2), was a prolific writer of villancico texts, and she grouped them into sequences of eight or nine to coincide with the sections of Matins (the first of eight daily prayer services comprising the Divine Office). Each villancico honored a particular saint. From her biographers we know that Sor Juana largely taught herself to compose. Evidence of her relationship with music can be found in the sizeable body of literary works that she produced during her lifetime. She used musical metaphors and musical imagery continuously in her poetry, philosophical writings, theater works, and in texts actually meant to be set to music, such as villancicos. She followed current fashion by including references to the various dialects and customs of New Spain. Because of the villancico's connection with popular culture, Sor Juana could include controversial elements in her texts and assert her politics in a way that evaded censorship by church officials. The following text, for example, recalls the Virgin Mary as well as the erotic allegory of the biblical Song of Songs. However, Sor Juana recasts these Christian themes in

Sor Juana Inés de la Cruz

Sor Juana Inés de la Cruz was born Juana Ramírez de Asbaje in either 1648 or 1651 near Mexico City. Due to her grandfather's extensive library and her strong intellectual drive, she received a thorough education, unusual for a woman of her day. Her grandfather died when she was an adolescent, and she moved to Mexico City where her musical and literary talents endeared her to the viceregal court. Courtly intrigues were not to her liking, however, and at the age of 18 she joined the Convent of San Gerónimo, where she remained for the rest of her life. The convent had a rich musical life. The sisters practiced and studied the musical arts daily and gave performances. In the relative absence of male authority, they had near total autonomy over the musical environment. Additionally, the rather liberal order allowed Sor Juana to continue to her studies and writing, and she is considered by many to have been the most prominent author of New Spain, male or female. Sor Juana's exceptional status as an educated and exceptionally talented woman may have enabled her to produce more controversial writings than most men, as authorities did not initially view women as a possible source of dissent. In her insistence that women should be valued equally with men, she directly clashed with the church. At the same time, she cloaked her feminism within religious expressions of Marian devotion, a practice that

FIGURE 2.8 Sor Juana Inés de la Cruz

may have spared her from the Inquisition. Sor Juana wrote prolifically over a short life span; she died in 1691, in her early forties. While her theological writings have garnered considerable study and critique, her many villancico texts are less well known. Between 1676 and 1692, she published at least 22 sets of villancicos in Mexico City and Puebla. Churches performed the works throughout New Spain, with music provided by a separate composer.

a local fashion, describing the bride as a brown-skinned woman tanned by the sun. In this way she created solidarity with indigenous, black, or mestizo congregants and evoked the locally powerful image of the Virgin of Guadalupe. In the following excerpt, you can clearly see both the villancico's formal structure as well as the author's woman-centered theology.

Estribillo

Morenica la Esposa está
Porque el Sol en en rostro le da.

Dark-skinned is the Bride
because the Sun shines in her face.

Coplas

Del Sol, que siempre la baña,	*from the Sun, that always bathes her,*
está abrasada la Esposa;	*the Wife is seared/embraced;**
y tanto está más hermosa	*and thus is more beautiful*
cuanto más de Él se acompaña:	*the more He accompanies her:*
nunca su Pureza empaña,	*her Purity is never tarnished,*
porque nunca el Sol se va.	*because the Sun never goes away.*

Estribillo

Morenica la Esposa está	*Dark-skinned is the Bride*
porque el Sol en en rostro le da.	*because the Sun shines in her face.*

Coplas

Negra se confiesa; pero	*She acknowledges she is black; but*
dice que esa negregura	*says that such blackness*
le da mayor hermosura:	*gives her greater beauty:*
pues en el Albor primero,	*for at the first Dawn*
es de la Gracia el Lucero	*it is from its Perfection*
el primer paso que da.	*that the Morning Star first shines.*

*The participle "abrasada" makes a phonetic pun between the verbs, *abrazar* (to embrace) and *abrasar* (to sear).

Portuguese-born composer Gaspar Fernandes (1565–1629) was also a celebrated composer of villancicos. He began his professional career in the New World in 1599 as organist of the Guatemala cathedral. Seven years later, he became chapelmaster of the Puebla cathedral, where he remained until his death in 1629. While in Puebla, Fernandes wrote a number of villancicos that demonstrate his stylistic diversity and his ability to work with multiple languages, including Spanish, Portuguese, Afro-Spanish dialects, and Nahuatl. Of the latter, "Tleycantino choquiliya" and "Xicochi conetzintle" (Listening Guide 2.3) exemplify the villancico's strong association with the Christmas season.

A lullaby to the Christ Child, Gaspar Fernandes's "Xichochi conetzintle" is a short, simple, and expressive work. Only 21 measures long, it deviates from standard villancico form in that it lacks an estribillo, making it technically a *chanzoneta*, one of the many formal structures absorbed into the villancico genre. It shares with other villancicos its syncopation, its mixing of religious themes with the local vernacular, and its sense of graceful, ebullient joy.

The repeated short–long rhythmic pattern blends the familiar rocking motion of a lullaby with the dance-inflected expectations of the genre, creating a lilting accent on beat 3 within the ⅜ meter, as can be seen in the alto-line excerpt (Example 2.1).

Additionally, Fernandes arranges the text so that natural stress accents (which in compound words tend to be on the antepenultimate syllable) fall

⊚ Fernandes: "Xicochi conetzintle" (Sleep Revered Baby)

Composer: Gaspar Fernandes

Date of composition: ca. 1610–1615

Performers/instruments: Estampas de Mexico (*a capella* choir)

Date of recording: 2008

What to Listen for:

- Contrasts between solo statements and choir
- Lilting syncopation
- Contrast between soloist and chorus

Time	Text	Translation	Description
0:00	Xicochi, xicochi conetzintle	Sleep, sleep, revered baby	Entrance of soloist, echoed by chorus. Dancelike syncopations continue throughout piece
0:11	Caomiz huihui joco in angelos me	The angels already rocked you	Entrance of soloist, echoed by chorus; both join together and declaim text homophonically
0:27	Aleloya	Alleluia	All voices sing the same rhythm
0:32	Xicochi, etc.	Sleep, etc.	Performance repeats

on longer notes, preserving the quality of the language and working against the Spanish tendency for penultimate syllabic stress. Aligning itself with early **Baroque** preferences for homophonic texture rather than elaborate counterpoint, the setting contrasts solos by the contralto voice with full choral responses in **concertato style**.

Villancicos written on texts that pretended to mimic the dialects spoken by African slaves entertained audiences throughout Latin America (and Spain as well). Known as **villancicos de negros**, such pieces pose a quandary for performers today who must weigh the highly racialized and often belittling lyrics against the works' enduring popularity. An example of this genre can be found in the work Juan de Araujo (1646–1712), a La Plata–born composer who held choirmaster posts at the cathedrals of Lima and La Plata (now Sucre) after spending some years in Panama. His "Los coflades de la estleya" is a Christmas villancico sung from the perspective of members

EXAMPLE 2.1: Excerpt from Gaspar Fernandes, "Xicochi conetzintle"

xi - co - chi xi - co - chi, xi - co - chi co - net - zin - tle

explore

For an example of a villancico de negros, listen to "Las coflades de la estleya" in the *Norton Anthology of Western Music, vol. 1, Ancient to Baroque (6th edition)*. The anthology also includes detailed commentary.

("*coflades*" or "brothers") of the "Confraternity of the Star," a lay-religious brotherhood similar to the Brazilian irmandades discussed in the following section. The Spanish lyrics are written in a dialect that mimics the accentuation and slang of the black vernacular. The text carries a dual meaning. First, the characters' proposed journey to Bethlehem implies that they might be North Africans, strengthening their allusions to kinship with the three wise men (who the text suggests have come from Angola) and particularly to "Gasipar" (Gaspar), one of the three who was frequently represented in Spanish popular culture as being from Africa. At the same time, the overtly New World quality of the black Spanish dialect, along with the shifting syncopations that occur within the $\frac{6}{8}$ meter, merge the tale of the original Christmas journey with the spectacle of local Christmas processions and festivities.

Music and Colonialism in Brazil

While the first two centuries of Spanish colonization saw the active conquest and suppression of one civilization and vibrant efforts to construct another in its place, Portuguese colonial endeavors in Brazil proceeded quite differently. Portugal initially concerned itself less with evangelization than did Spain, and as a result religious organization got off to a slower start in the new colony. Brazil did not create elaborate networks of cathedrals with schools to train indigenous converts in music. Additionally, the Portuguese more systematically adopted the antimusical reforms indicated by the Council of Trent than did the Spanish, and that may account for a relative lack of written music from the early colonial period. Although it appears that Brazilian chapelmasters did include polychoral and polyphonic works in their repertoire, they preferred simple, four-part harmonizations of Gregorian chant. Finally, Portugal fell under the influence of Hapsburg Spain from 1580 and only regained its independence in 1668, with clashes continuing until 1713. This political instability caused considerable economic weakness, which helps to account for a rather low musical output. In the eighteenth century, increasing political stability and the growth of both the economy and the population corresponded with an increase in musical activity.

Colonial musical activities in Brazil were largely overseen by lay brotherhoods, or irmandades. Organized along lines of class and race, irmandades existed for each sector of Brazilian society and had tremendous influence. They built churches and hospitals, maintained clergy, oversaw funerals and feast days, and supplied music. Within cities and regions, irmandades competed to have the highest quality music, engaging in bidding wars for musicians and composers.

The southern mining region of Minas Gerais became an important site for musical activities after colonists found gold there in the late seventeenth century. Far from other sites of musical production, such as Salvador (capital of Brazil from 1549–1763) and Recife, Minas Gerais provides a powerful example of the connection between local economic production and the culture industry. The gold rush led to rapid population growth and colonizers brought African slaves to work in the mines, where they joined a population that included indigenous peoples and mestizos. By the middle of the eighteenth century, black and mixed-race inhabitants formed the majority of the population, some enslaved and others free. The makeup of the irmandades reflected the demographics of the population, with individual brotherhoods representing distinct groups. Some irmandades, particularly those with mixed-race membership, became strongly associated with music-making. In spite of restrictions that limited advanced study in composition to white students, nearly all of the prominent composers of the region were mixed race, or mulato, a phenomenon that has been termed *mulatismo musical*. There has been considerable scholarly debate in recent years surrounding the reasons underlying the racialization of professional music-making in colonial Brazilian society. Much work remains to be done, but it seems clear that the rise of a musical artisan class offered new opportunities for black and *mulato* musicians whose access to other forms of economic advancement had previously been restricted.

FIGURE 2.9 Schnitger Organ, Cathedral de Nossa Senhora da Assunção, in the town of Mariana, Minas Gerais, Brazil

The wealth generated in the mines financed a musical boom in Lisbon that rebounded to Minas Gerais. Local composers imported and reinterpreted the mix of Portuguese and Italian Baroque and pre-Classical musical styles enjoyed by the Portuguese court. They saw their works performed in ornate churches and theaters and on newly imported instruments, including a Schnitger pipe organ bought in 1752 that survives to this day (Figure 2.9).

Financed by its new material wealth, Minas Gerais produced an incredible amount of music and supported almost a thousand active musicians from 1760 to 1800. Among the most prominent was José Joaquim Emerico Lôbo de Mesquita. The son of a Portuguese colonist and an Afro-Brazilian slave, Lôbo de Mesquita was, like most Brazilian composers of African descent, largely self-taught. Renowned as an organ virtuoso and improviser as well as a composer, he contracted his services to various irmandades in the region. In 1801 he moved to Rio de Janeiro where he worked as a chapel organist.

Lôbo de Mesquita's surviving compositions include two masses, a Te Deum, a Salve Regina, several motets and litanies, and music for the Office of the Dead. His music reflects the hybrid style that typified music in eighteenth-century Minas Gerais, blending Baroque and galant elements. His Salve Regina, for example, owes a debt to the Neapolitan composer Giovanni Battista Pergolesi, whose compositions were popular in Lisbon and who had himself composed a Salve Regina that bears an uncanny resemblance to Lôbo de Mesquita's later composition. Lôbo de Mesquita stretches this Neapolitan model, however, using a four-part chorus to interact with his emotive setting for solo voices. The piece is constructed of relatively short, contrasting sections. This concertato style looks back to established Baroque practice, while the independent colors and textures in the orchestra reflect an awareness of contemporary European trends. The variety in this short piece is striking; Lôbo de Mesquita even includes a self-contained, "mini aria" for soprano in the middle.

Rio de Janeiro (capital of Brazil from 1763–1889) produced the most celebrated composer of colonial Brazil: José Mauricio Nunes Garcia (1767–1830). Little is known about Nunes Garcia's early life and musical training. The son of free, mixed-race parents, he was born in Rio de Janeiro shortly after the capital shifted to that city. A gifted boy soprano, Nunes Garcia participated in the city's most influential musical irmandades and he joined the priesthood in 1792. Six years later, at the age of 31, he became chapelmaster of the Rio de Janeiro cathedral, the most prominent musical appointment in the city. As chapelmaster, he not only composed and played the organ, but also served as music director, impresario, and music teacher. Nunes Garcia's career took an unexpected turn in 1808, when the arrival of the Portuguese royal family transformed Rio de Janeiro from the capital city of a colonial outpost to the epicenter of a thriving Portuguese empire. The Portuguese Prince Regent, Dom João, strongly supported music and upon discovering the gifted composer immediately appointed him director of the Royal Chapel.

Nunes Garcia composed prolifically. More than 230 of his works survive, including sacred repertoire, instrumental compositions, and secular songs. His music is marked by its eclectic style, blending the innovations of Italian composers like Rossini with Classical-era approaches of composers like Mozart, Haydn, and Cherubini. He kept up with the music of his European contemporaries and in 1819 even conducted the first performance in Brazil of Mozart's Requiem. Most of his sacred works are written for four-part chorus (with or without soloists) and orchestral accompaniment. His appointment to the Royal Chapel allowed him to expand the orchestra, and he regularly wrote for strings, paired woodwinds, trumpets, and occasionally trombone or timpani. He composed at

⊚ Lôbo de Mesquita: Salve Regina

Composer: José Joaquim Emerico Lôbo de Mesquita

Date of composition: 1787

Performers/instruments: Cantoría de la Basílica de Nuestra Señora del Socorro, Camerata Rio de Janeiro (soloists, choir, chamber orchestra)

Date of recording: 2006

What to Listen for:
- Short sectional contrasts, or concertato style
- Contrasts between solo voices and the chorus

Time	Text	Translation	Description
0:00			String introduction with sighing motive
0:40	Salve Regina Mater misericordiae	Hail Queen Mother of mercy	Entrance of tenor soloist accompanied by strings a third below
1:02			Chorus enters in layers, beginning with tenors
1:21	Vita, dulcedo et spes nostra, salve	Our life, sweetness and hope	Soprano soloist enters
1:39			Chorus echos soprano's text
1:56			String interlude
2:04	Ad te clamamus exules filii Hevae ad te suspiramus gementes et flentes in hac lacrimarum valle.	We cry to you Exiled children of Eve We sigh to you Mourning and weeping In this valley of tears.	Soprano soloist sings a "mini aria." Dissonances against the strings on "gementes" (mourning, 2:44) and "flentes" (weeping, 2:49) create tension.
3:16	Eia, ergo advocata nostra, illos tuos misericordes oculos ad nos converte;	Hurry, therefore Our advocate, turn the Illumination of your Merciful eyes towards us;	Chorus introduces new musical content. Homophonic and lively setting with an active **continuo**, creating movement in the bass
4:07			Pause
4:10	Et Jesum, benedictum fructum ventris tui, nobis post hoc exsilium ostende.	And show us Jesus, The blessed fruit Of your womb After our exile is past.	New section features homophonic text setting with expressive tension on "exsilium ostende"
4:40	O Clemens, O pia, O dulcis Virgo Maria.	Oh mild, Oh pious, Oh sweet Virgin Mary.	Final, poignant prayer voiced by chorus and orchestra in unison

least 32 masses, 19 of which survive. The *Missa de Nossa Senhora da Conceição* (Mass of Our Lady of Immaculate Conception, 1810) demonstrates Nunes Garcia's hybrid style. In Listening Guide 2.5, the movement "Cum Sancto Spiritu" is performed by the University of Texas Chamber Singers and records the first performance of the *Missa* in more than two hundred years! In 1998, a young Brazilian musicologist named Ricardo Bernardes found parts of the manuscript for the *Missa*, and he created a performance edition of the work, often having to deduce what Nunes Garcia would have done and fill in missing instrumental parts. Bernardes went on to pursue a doctorate at the University of Texas, and it is his performance edition that the University of Texas used for this performance. In the example, you'll hear the "Cum Sancto Spiritu" that occurs near the end of the Gloria portion of the Mass. The text is set twice, first with soloists in a "modern," classical style and then in a full choral fugue that recalls an earlier Baroque style. Nunes Garcia uses this two-part approach to set this text in several of his masses.

LISTENING guide 2.5

◎ Nunes Garcia: "Cum Sancto Spiritu," from *Missa de Nossa Senhora de Conceição* (Mass of Our Lady of Immaculate Conception)

Composer: José Mauricio Nunes Garcia

Date of composition: 1810

Performers/instruments: University of Texas Chamber Singers; James Morrow, conductor (soloists, choir, orchestra)

Date of recording: 2005 (released 2009)

What to Listen for:
- Expressive use of the orchestra, especially the winds
- Contrasts in texture between soloists and chorus
- Changes in orchestral style and texture
- Repetition of the same melodic idea, or subject, by each voice in the fugue section

Time	Text	Translation	Description
0:00	Cum Sancto Spiritu In Gloria Dei Patris, Amen	With the Holy Spirit In the Glory of God the Father, Amen	Sustained horn and arpeggiated strings introduce a duet, answered by the full chorus; expressive wind section and independent violin line
0:37			Instrumental interlude builds in volume and intensity before the tenor's entrance
0:43	Cum Sancto Spiritu ...	With the Holy Spirit ...	Tenor sings a fanfare-like melody, doubled by the brass a fifth above

(continued)

Time	Text	Translation	Description
0:49			Chorus repeats tenor's melody
1:15			Orchestral cadence leads into fugue
New Track			
0:00			Fugue Sopranos enter with the fugue subject Altos answer
0:12			Tenors enter with new cadential motive
0:16			Altos take the subject
0:31			Tenors take the subject
0:42			All four voices take the cadential motive
0:47			Basses take the subject; tenors take the countersubject
1:03			Sopranos take the subject; basses take the countersubject
1:37	In Gloria Dei Patris, Amen	In the Glory of God the Father, Amen	Switch to homophonic texture
1:46			Brief return to fugal texture
1:58	In Gloria Dei Patris, Amen	In the Glory of God the Father, Amen	Homophonic, cadential formula
2:14			Return of fugue
3:31	In Gloria Dei Patris, Amen	In the Glory of God the Father, Amen	Coda; fugue ends and a separate thought begins. Instruments are more independent, and the music is in a more modern galant style, like the opening "Cum Sancto Spiritu" section

Music in the Streets: The Feast of Corpus Christi

Not all colonial-era religious music was liturgical in nature, allowing the musical evangelization of the New World to spill out of the cathedrals. Urban streets became a site where people from different social, linguistic, and racial groups saw and heard each other, literally and figuratively. To the Spanish, religious processions offered an opportunity to display the fruits of colonization: repurposed precolonial buildings, newly built colonial architecture, and a society organized on a European model. For the colonized, processions reinforced this new order; their journeys through civic space highlighted the new sites of political and religious power: the cathedral, the *cabildo* (town hall), and military fortifications.

Across Latin America, processions constituted a major component of Corpus Christi, an important religious and civic holiday. Established by church officials in the fourteenth century as an obligatory feast celebrating the central Catholic doctrine of transubstantiation (the belief that the sacred host used in the Mass became the literal body of Christ), the feast took place on the ninth Thursday after Easter. Following the expulsion of the Moors from the Iberian Peninsula, the Spanish observance of Corpus Christi took on a decidedly martial tone, with those who celebrated the feast characterized as victors, and those that did not (such as the Moors) characterized as vanquished enemies. In 1551, the Council of Trent declared Corpus Christi a "triumph over heresy," and it became common in Spanish towns and villages for processions to take place with the host—the body of Christ—carried through the streets. Processions tended to be elaborate, with music and dance, banners and tapestries, and all sorts of civic pageantry.

These themes of victory, vanquishing, and proselytizing resonated strongly with the colonial project, and Corpus Christi quickly became one of the most important festivals in Latin America. The Peruvian city of Cuzco held particularly lavish festivities. Visitors described the visual impact of indigenous costumes, the city's ornate architecture, and the procession of residents from parishes both within and outside of the city, each group holding the statue of its patron saint. "The entire course of the procession is a continuous altar," remarked an eighteenth-century observer, noting the church officials who stopped to pray at designated sites. Written sources suggest that church officials processed to the singing of chant alone, but paintings show musicians accompanying them on "loud" wind instruments (Figure 2.10). Other paintings show musicians singing while holding sheets of music, suggesting that they are performing polyphony.

FIGURE 2.10 Painting depicting Corpus Christi procession in Cuzco, Peru, 1674–1680

Indigenous performers not only played European instruments, but also marked the festivities with displays of indigenous culture, singing in local languages and playing traditional flutes, conch shells, and drums.

Corpus Christi coincided roughly with the Inca festival of Inti Raymi, the "Festival of the Sun," and early observers suggested a syncretism between the two events on the part of indigenous participants, although recent scholars, particularly Carolyn Dean, have suggested that the conflation of the two events was more important to Spanish colonialists than to the Inca as the feast represented a triumph of Christianity over pre-Hispanic religion. The fact that Cuzco had been the capital of the Inca Empire made the festivities even more significant in this sense. In Cuzco, the pageantry of Corpus Christi enacted the defeat of Inca rulers at the hand of the Spanish. The presence of both indigenous and European participants powerfully symbolized the shift from an old world order to a new. Although Spanish authorities made the training of indigenous musicians in European music a central strategy of colonization, they simultaneously required the performance of some indigenous music at civic celebrations. Thus, as ethnomusicologist Geoffrey Baker has shown, indigenous, "pagan" music could be overcome and replaced by European sounds.

Similar rites took place elsewhere in Latin America. In Cuba in 1573, the Havana City Council ordered all free blacks to take part in the procession of Corpus Christi, bringing with them their "inventions and games," referring to music and dance. Afro-Cubans did indeed participate, with some donning West African raffia masks of the *íreme*, or *diablito* (little devil), causing the festival in Cuba to become known as the Festival of Devils. The participation of Afro-Cubans, with drums, songs, and dances, added to the grandeur of Corpus Christi and contributed to the festival's narrative of Christianity's triumph over the infidels. The strength of this narrative may help to explain why the dominant Afro-Cuban festival was not Corpus Christi, but Kings' Day (Epiphany), a carnivalesque holiday that momentarily inverted local power hierarchies, with high and low classes, slaves and slave owners symbolically performing the other's identity.

In Brazil, as in other parts of Latin America, outdoor celebrations provided an environment where European musical aesthetics could commingle with African and indigenous musics, giving rise to the development of hybrid forms. Churches, civic leaders, and irmandades hired musicians to perform at outdoor festivities such as Corpus Christi, bringing together formally trained musicians with those who performed popular music or played in military bands. Performers of double reed instruments, such as the shawm or **chirimía** (an ancestor of the oboe), along with the other loud wind instruments, performed together in raucous ensembles called **charamelas** that processed through the streets. Played by Afro-Brazilian musicians as well as by whites, the sounds of the charamela loudly proclaimed the cultural mixing that pervaded colonial Brazil.

Mission Music

Missionary activities not only accompanied the conquest but also continued to exert an important influence throughout the colonial period. Jesuit and Franciscan missionaries traveled to the far reaches of the Spanish Empire to convert new souls to Christianity. Much of the mission music of the Jesuits in Bolivia and Paraguay or of the Franciscans in California is, like that of the earliest missionaries, designed to be utilitarian and accessible. At the same time, however, surviving repertories from both mission traditions illustrate that music could also dazzle the listener with sophistication; some of the most captivating music from the eighteenth century is found in these repertories.

Two important collections of music from South American missions survive, both of them in Bolivia. The first, held in Concepción, Bolivia, contains music from the mission churches of San Rafael and Santa Ana. A more recently discovered collection contains music manuscripts used by Jesuits who worked with the Moxos Indians. The variety of the music held in both collections is remarkable. Unaccompanied choral repertoire is present, but so are also vocal pieces with instrumental accompaniment and pieces for instruments alone. While many of the compositions are written in Latin, others appear in a variety of indigenous languages, including Guaraní, Moxa, Chiquitana, and Baure. It is difficult to determine whether these pieces were written by indigenous composers trained in the European style or by missionaries themselves. Works by European composers also appear, including 14 compositions by Domenico Zipoli (1688–1726), an Italian-born Jesuit who came to Argentina in 1717 and worked as the Córdoba chapelmaster until his death. His works became famous as far away as the Viceroyalty of Peru.

Zipoli's aria "In te spero" (Listening Guide 2.6) is the central movement of the **motet** *In hoc Mundo* (On This Earth), written for tenor, two violins, and continuo. The work is a full-blown **da capo aria** in operatic style, complete with elaborate vocal **coloratura** that alternates with instrumental refrains, or **ritornelli**. "Da capo" translates as "from the head," and the term is used for an aria with an **A** section followed by a contrasting **B** section (usually in a different tempo and another key), then a return of the **A** section. The da capo aria offered ample opportunities for singers to display their skill, especially in the return of the **A** section, in which they embellished upon the written score.

The aria uses the full expressive possibilities of opera. Listen, for example, to how the dramatic denunciation of the "inimici" (enemies) contrasts with the tender expression of faith, "spero, in te confido" (I hope, in you I trust), at 0:49. Similarly, the staccato treatment of "non timebo naufragare" (I do not fear shipwreck) takes a device straight out of Italian comic opera: individual syllables set to short, staccato notes like this is a classic representation of fear, timidity, or even sneakiness. Zipoli contrasts that staccato articulation with a strong and aggressive delivery of the same text, suggesting that in the face of strong faith, fear is laughable. In Listening Guide 2.6, repetitions of the **A** section text are printed in brackets to aid your listening comprehension.

The legacy of Spanish colonialism is evident to anyone who has spent time in the southwestern United States, and it is particularly visible in the

⊚ Zipoli: "In te spero," from *In hoc Mundo*

Composer: Domenico Zipoli

Date of composition: early eighteenth century

Performers/instruments: Florilegium and Bolivian Soloists; Henry Villca, tenor (tenor soloist with strings and continuo)

Date of recording: 2004

Genre: da capo aria

What to Listen for:

- Word painting at key moments in the text
- Instrumental ritornelli serving as both a structural frame and an expressive tool
- The formal "da capo" structure of the piece

Time	Text	Translation	Description
0:00			**Instrumental introduction**
0:24	In te spero, In te confido Omnes fraudes, Omnes insidias	In you I hope, In you I trust All the deceits, All the plots	**A Section**
0:35	Inimici superare	Of the enemy I will overcome	
0:42			**Instrumental ritornello**
0:49	[In te spero, In te confido Omnes fraudes, Omnes insidias Inimici superare]	[In you I hope, In you I trust All the deceits, All the plots Of the enemy I will overcome]	
1:07			Strings
1:20 1:25 1:30 1:39	Et in portu malefido Inter fluctus, Et inter undas, Non timebo naufragare	I put no trust in the harbor Amid storms, And amid waves, I do not fear shipwreck	**B Section** "Inter fluctus" is repeated at a higher and higher pitch, leading to descending staccato articulation with large gaps between notes at "Non timebo naufragare." Final repetition of text is aggressive and in tempo, similar to earlier setting of "inimici"
1:41			**Instrumental ritornello**
1:48	Et in portu malefido Inter fluctus, Et inter undas,	I put no trust in the harbor Amid storms, And amid waves,	Repetitive "shaking" motive precedes the staccato articulation heard earlier.
2:00	Non timebo naufragare	I do not fear shipwreck	Ornamentation on "non" simulates fear

(continued)

Time	Text	Translation	Description
2:11			Da capo—return of instrumental introduction
2:20			Return of A section The singer uses subtle vocal ornaments to differentiate the return of **A** from the first time he sang it

string of missions that dot the West Coast. In 1767, Franciscan friar Junípero Serra set out from Mexico City on an evangelical enterprise that brought him first to the missions in Baja California and then to San Diego in 1769. From there he helped found 9 of 21 new missions extending up the coast of what the Spanish called "Alta California." Serra's endeavors coincided with King Carlos III's expulsion of the Jesuits from the Spanish Empire (providing opportunities to the Franciscan and Dominican orders) and a general reduction of the influence of Rome within Spain and its territories. The Crown feared that increasing Russian exploration of North America might imperil Spain's claim to its west coast holdings (extending up to what is now southeast Alaska), so the king ordered the immediate colonization of the previously ignored territories.

California's mission history and the role played by Serra and other friars has frequently been a source of controversy. Serra remains well known in California. His statue stands in Golden Gate Park, and generations of school children learned of the hardships that missionaries faced in their efforts to "civilize" the new territory. In recent decades, however, Serra has been the subject of debate. The Vatican's decision in 1987 to beatify Serra led to angry protests by Native Americans, who pointed to the decimation and maltreatment of native populations following the arrival of the Spanish.

For many years, scholars believed that music-making served a merely pedagogical and rudimentary function. However, John Koegel's 1992 rediscovery of manuscripts of complex polyphonic works, including three Masses (at least two have been attributed to Mexico City choirmaster Ignacio de Jerusalem y Stella) offers compelling evidence of the highly skilled performances that took place in California. Such evidence corroborates reports by eighteenth- and nineteenth-century visitors who commented on the high quality of the music-making there and on the skill of indigenous instrumentalists and singers.

In Alta California, the training of indigenous musicians in European and European-style music remained an important part of the evangelical process. As in the early days of the conquest, many friars studied indigenous

explore

Listen to the vocal group Chanticleer's recording *Mexican Baroque,* which features a performance of Jerusalem's Mass in D, reconstructed by musicologist Craig Russell from the scores found by John Koegel in the Los Angeles archives.

language and culture and became fascinated by indigenous musical practices. Juan Bautista Sancho, for example, a Mallorcan-born friar who came to the California Mission of San Antonio de Padua in 1804, eventually learned several indigenous languages and translated catechisms into local dialect. His musical activities have been studied by musicologist Craig Russell. In written documents, Sancho not only describes the neophytes' skill at learning European instruments and musical practices but also comments on their own music, noting the presence of an open-ended flute and a one-string musical bow. His description of contemporary indigenous singing practices is especially valuable, as it provides more details than those left to us by earlier missionaries.

> They have many songs to sing in their dances, and outside of them as well [...] they sing using various final pitches and with different scales; they rise and fall in intervals of seconds, thirds, fourths, fifths, and octaves; and they never sing polyphonically, and when they do sing all together some of them sing an octave above.

At the Mission of San Antonio, Sancho directed a large choir and orchestra, and introduced compositions from both Europe and New Spain, many of which he had copied himself and brought with him. The Jerusalem Masses, discussed previously, may have been among these works. He also composed Masses himself, as well as polyphonic arrangements of plainchant.

Understanding the role of mission music in Alta California not only helps us to understand the artistic and cultural history of New Spain but also enriches our understanding of the cultural heritage of what later came to be the United States. That such a musical infrastructure existed in California at the end of the eighteenth century is remarkable considering the still rather rustic cultural conditions that existed in the fledgling British colonies far to the east. Recognizing colonial California's musical culture forces us to expand our historical understanding of the United States to include Hispanic, as well as English, cultural heritage.

explore

Listen to Juan Bautista Sancho's Misa en sol, on Chanticleer's album, *Mission Road* (2008). The recording includes an interesting documentary about the group's reconstruction of California mission music.

Opera

In Spain, Philip IV's ascension to the throne in 1621 transformed the role of the arts in Spanish society, ushering in a new "Golden Age" of theater, music, and art. Although opera grew in popularity during that same period, the Italian style of **recitative** (dialogue sung in a speech-like manner) and aria (more-elaborate and melodic songs) did not have much immediate influence. Spanish composers and audiences instead preferred **zarzuelas**: Spanish-language, sung dramas that fused chains of strophic songs, allegorical plots, and dance with spoken dialogue. In the second half of the seventeenth century, however, composers and librettists revisited the idea of opera, experimenting with recitative and merging elements of the newer Italianate style with more traditionally Spanish sensibilities. Staged musical dramas debuted in the Viceroyalty of Peru as early as 1672, with a performance of *El arca de Noé* (Noah's Ark). The performance included elaborate stage machinery, scene changes, costumes, and lighting. Sponsored by the viceroy himself, the musical spectacle was a huge success.

The first opera produced in Latin America was Tomás de Torrejón y Velasco's *La púrpura de la rosa*, which premiered in Lima in 1701. Based on Pedro Calderón de la Barca's 1659 libretto, it commemorated the Peace of the Pyrenees between Spain and France, and Spanish composer Juan Hidalgo had already set the text in 1660 in one of the first successful and well-received Spanish operas. Torrejón y Velasco's setting celebrated the birthday of Philip V, the first Bourbon king of Spain. In Torrejón y Velasco's version of *La púrpura de la rosa*, the composer avoided Italian-style recitative, instead structuring the opera around chains of strophic songs over a spare continuo (accompaniment) played by plucked strings, such as guitar or harp. Focusing on Ovid's amorous tale of Venus and Adonis, the opera features well-known characters from Greek mythology in a morality drama that stresses prudence and reason over emotion. Groups of professional female actresses typically performed dramas such as this; the only male roles in Torrejón y Velasco's score are for the *villano* (ruffian) and the role of Chato, both comic, lower-class (and lower-voiced) male characters.

While the musical form and texture are relatively simple, the composer achieved tremendous expressive variety in setting Calderón's text, bringing out the libretto's erotic tension through suggestive dance rhythms, insistent repetitions, and expressive ornamentation and vocal dissonances. Contemporary performance practice allowed singers to embellish upon, or ornament, the written score, adding small runs or additional dissonances to draw attention to key moments in the text. The music might seem tame to modern ears, but some present at the 1701 Lima production protested the "immorality" of the amorous plot as well as some of its Enlightenment-oriented ideas. These included having the wives in the audience sit in chairs next to their husbands rather than on pillows at their feet.

Beginning in the 1990s, *La púrpura de la rosa* has enjoyed something of a renaissance. This is due partly to the availability of a modern critical edition of the score edited by musicologist Louise K. Stein as well as to the commitment of performers of early music to revive the work. *La púrpura de la rosa* has been performed in professional opera houses, recorded by a number of word-class ensembles, and performed by young singers in universities, where the work's preponderance of female roles often suits the available performers. As a result, the opera has been performed and heard more in the last two decades than in the previous three and a half centuries!

In the excerpt included here, Adonis (sung by soprano Ellen Hargis) details to Venus the contents of a rather erotic dream from which he has just awoken. After a brief introduction in which Adonis says that images keep reappearing in his dreams, the music engages in a kind of circular repetition, much like a dream from which one can't awake. Each poetic couplet, or copla, is set to the same melodic formula, but the music changes subtly in performance. Much of what you hear in Listening Guide 2.7 represents the

Torrejón y Velasco: "No sé, que a sombra me dormí," from *La púrpura de la rosa*

Composer: Tomás de Torrejón y Velasco

Librettist: Pedro Calderón de la Barca

Date of composition: 1701

Performers/instruments: The Harp Consort; Andrew Lawrence-King, director; Judith Malafronte and Ellen Hargis, sopranos (two soprano soloists, Baroque double harp)

Date of recording: 1999

What to Listen for:
- Spare texture created by solo voice and continuo
- Melodic repetition of coplas
- Subtle variations in melodic repetition

Time	Text*	Translation*	Description
0:00	**Venus:** ¿Qué ha sido esto? **Adonis:** No sé, que a sombra me dormí destos troncos, y como se suelen repetir	What has happened? I don't know Because I was asleep Beneath the shade of these trees; And because the impressions	Introductory, "framing" material. The word "repetir" (to repeat) establishes formula for music that follows
0:14	en fantasmas del sueño de aquello que antes vi las especies, soñé que el fiero jabalí	Tend to repeat themselves Of what I saw earlier, I dreamed that the Fierce wild boar	**Copla 1** Singer's rapid ornamentation on "fiero" highlights the attack
0:26	que a ti te daba muerte, volviendo contra mí las aceradas corvas, navajas de marfil,	That had tried to kill you Returned and charged at me Its steel-hard tusks, Razors of ivory,	**Copla 2** Ornamentation highlights "aceradas corvas" (sharp knives)
0:35	con mi sangre manchaba las rosas, que hasta aquí de nieve fueron, para que fuesen de carmín.	Stained the roses with my blood, Roses that, until now, Were white as snow, So that they would be crimson.	**Copla 3** Expressive use of pauses and vocal *sostenuto* stresses sensory experience rather than action
0:50	Y no sólo a este susto del sueño me rendí, pero sañudo áspid, que debió de encubrir	And not only did I find myself Overcome by this nightmare, But a cruel asp That must have hidden	**Copla 4**

(continued)

Time	Text*	Translation*	Description
0:59	de su traidor veneno, de su ponzoña vil, la astucia entre uno y otro macilento alhelí,	Its treacherous poison, Its vile venom, All of its cunning there Between one withering vine and another,	**Copla 5** Performer links this copla with the previous one to give a sense of continuous action
1:09	el corazón me ha herido, pues al restituir el sentido, aún no cesa el sentimiento en mí;	Wounded my heart; Because even upon awakening And recovering my reason, still the Feelings persist in me,	**Copla 6**
1:21	de suerte que despierto duran en afligir ansias que fabriqué, temores que fingí,	So that, although I am awake The anxieties that I invented And the fears that I imagined Still afflict me,	**Copla 7**
1:35	pasando ¡ay infeliz! la sombra a luz, el pasmo a frenesí.	Ah, alas! Transforming shadows Into light and wonder into madness	**Closing frame**

*Edition of Spanish text and English translation by Louise K. Stein.

singer's expressive interpretation of Torrejón y Velasco's score. The performer embellishes the pitches in the original coplas, adding additional vocal flourishes, or **ornaments**, to the composition. Notice, for example, how the run on "fiero" (fierce) dramatizes the attack of the wild boar, and how the singer's expressive pauses when discussing blood staining the white roses seem to stop time and turn the tale from one of action to one of sensory experience.

Operatic entertainment soon reached New Spain as well, where the local viceroy commissioned Manuel Sumaya (1678–1755), then a musician in the Mexico City cathedral (he would become chapelmaster there in 1715), to write an opera. Sumaya composed his *La Partenope* (1711) on a libretto by Italian poet Silvio Stampiglia, making it the first opera composed by a New World composer. Sadly, the music, composed sometime between 1700 and 1711, does not survive.

While operatic entertainments graced the homes and palaces of the elites, and theatres were later built to showcase European operatic works, *La púrpura de la rosa* and *La Partenope* are exceptional musical occurrences of their time; Latin American operatic production in general got off to a sporadic start. It would be nearly a century before Brazil saw the composition of its first opera, *Le due gemelle* (composed sometime between 1813 and 1821, also lost). Although European opera maintained its dominance over Latin America throughout the colonial period, Torrejón y Velasco's and Sumaya's compositions stand out as important developments, followed by the emergence of regional and national operatic styles in later centuries.

Popular Dance Music

Dance flourished at every level of Latin American colonial society. From stately and refined European-derived figure dances popular in aristocratic circles to boisterous and physical popular dances that were enjoyed across class lines, dance music was consumed across the continent, with many local styles making their way back to Europe. Guitarists, harpists, and violinists formed the core ensemble of colonial dance music, although hand percussion such as tambourines, *palmas* (hand clapping), or castanets might also be heard.

Although both written and iconographic sources attest to the prominent role musical entertainment played in the New World, we know less about the repertoire and its performance practice than we do about music written for religious purposes. This is because secular music-making was primarily an oral tradition. Tunes passed from performer to performer, and skilled players and singers improvised melodic and rhythmic variations on existing melodies and newly composed themes alike. Thus, understanding what dance music and other secular musical entertainment sounded like requires a fair amount of musicological detective work. Two of the primary sources of colonial-era dance music available to us today are collections for guitar and harp by Santiago de Murcia and Lucas Ruiz de Ribayaz, Spaniards who traveled to the Americas along with their music. The books include popular tunes of the day, and because the voyages of Ruiz de Ribayaz (who arrived in Lima in 1667) and Murcia (believed to have arrived in New Spain sometime after 1717) fell 50 years apart, they provide a glimpse into the development of popular music over several decades. Murcia's source book came to the notice of music scholars by chance. In 1943, Gabriel Saldívar, one of Mexico's earliest musicologists, found the manuscript (now referred to as the Saldívar Codex) in an antique shop in León, Guanajuato. Recognizing its value, he spent much of his remaining life uncovering its secrets. Chief among more recent "musicological detectives" has been Craig Russell, whose edition and study of the Saldivar Codex has made the music widely available to contemporary scholars and performers.

The jácara (xácara) was one of the most popular dances of the Baroque period. A boisterous *baile* that had its origin in Spanish theater (the *jácaro* was a stock character, a ruffian or a trickster), the jácara developed on both sides of the Atlantic. It is recognized by its emphasis on the minor mode and its alternation of two primary harmonies, such as D minor and A major, and by its incessant and energizing hemiola pattern, which can be seen notated in Example 2.2.

This jácara rhythm is found in many forms of music besides dance music, such as the villancico genre, where it referenced popular culture. "A la

EXAMPLE 2.2: Hemiola pattern

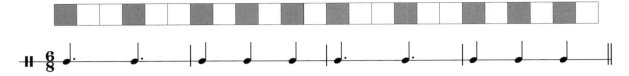

explore

Listen to "A la jácara jacarilla" on Ars Longa de la Habana's recording, *Juan Gutiérrez de Padilla: Música de la Catedral de Puebla de los Ángeles* (2006).

xácara, xacarilla" by Juan Gutiérrez de Padilla is an example of just such a fusion. The villancico seems to goad the musicians on, suggesting that joyful dance is the only appropriate response to the Christmas story, calling out, "¡Vaya de xácara!" (On with the jácara!) Not only does Gutiérrez de Padilla engage with dance rhythms, but the work's text is a medley of sorts, with each stanza containing the first line of a popular **romance**, or secular poem, that would have been well known to contemporary listeners. Thus, while the subject of the villancico is ostensibly sacred (the birth of the Christ Child), its delivery is highly secular.

In Santiago de Murcia's "Jácaras por la E" (Listening Guide 2.8), you can hear a performance of an instrumental jácara found in the composer's compilation for guitar. The recording begins with percussionist Pedro Estevan clapping the 2-3 division. The *palmas* (hand claps) continue throughout the recording, making the guitarist's rhythmic play especially audible. Throughout the recording, you'll hear guitarist Paul O'Dette alternate between two primary articulations on the guitar, a plucked style (**punteado**) derived from lute performance in which every note sounds individually, and the strummed (**rasgueado**) style that took hold on the newly invented five-course guitar with each **course** (pair) of strings tuned in unison. While some jácaras are through-composed, this one features a refrain that alternates with melodic variations in a more improvisatory style. The variations get more intricate and virtuosic as the piece goes on. It is important to realize that performance practices, such as the use of hand percussion or particular strumming techniques, are decisions made by historically informed performers. They are not included in the manuscript or in more recent editions.

A **fandango** "craze" swept the New and Old Worlds in the early eighteenth century. Unlike the dances of the previous generation, which had strong class affiliations, the fandango was open to all. Danced by a couple rather than a group, the fandango incorporated zapateo (foot stomping), and its choreography mimicked sexual pursuit. The dance's eroticism led Casanova to describe the man's motions as "visibly representing the action of satisfied love" while those of the woman celebrated "consent, ravishment, and the ecstasy of pleasure."

The origins of the fandango are unknown. Some suggest it has Native American origin, while others claim it originated in the Caribbean. One of its

◎ Murcia: "Jácaras por la E" (Jácara on E)

Composer: Santiago de Murcia

Date of composition: mid-eighteenth century

Performers/instruments: Paul O'Dette with Pedro Estevan, Pat O'Brien, Steven Player (Baroque guitars, percussion)

Date of recording: 1998

Genre: jácara

What to Listen for:

- Hemiola, rhythmic play
- Alternation between major and minor harmonies
- Strumming (rasgueado) and plucking (punteado) techniques
- Alternation of structured refrains with variations in an improvisatory style

Time	Description
0:00	Hand percussion (*palmas*) claps the two-against-three hemiola rhythm that pervades the entire piece
0:12	**Refrain** Rasgueado-style articulation, outline of harmonic and rhythmic structure
0:42	**First variation** Rasgueado articulation blends with punteado plucking
1:12	**Refrain**
1:27	**Second variation** Scalar patterns with rasgueado articulations
1:49	**Refrain**
2:04	**Third variation** All punteado
2:26	**Refrain**
2:42	**Fourth variation**
3:12	**Refrain** Ends on A major

most characteristic features is use of a repeating harmonic progression, often referred to as the **Andalusian cadence**, that comprises four chords built on a descending bass line (three whole steps followed by a half step). This is also referred to as a minor **descending tetrachord** (Example 2.3a), and results in a progression that begins on a minor chord (usually D minor) and ends on a major chord a fourth below (usually A major—Example 2.3b). This fluctuation between major and minor gives fandangos a sense of tonal ambiguity.

EXAMPLE 2.3a: Minor-descending tetrachord

dm   CM   B♭M   AM

EXAMPLE 2.3b: Andalusian cadence

Murcia's "Fandango," found in the *Saldívar Codex*, is the first known arrangement of the dance genre to appear in manuscript form (Listening Guide 2.9). In the recording, the harmonic ambiguity, the lack of clear cadences, and the relentless indefatigability of both the harmonic

---

LISTENING guide 2.9

◉ Murcia: "Fandango"

Composer: Santiago de Murcia

Date of composition: mid-eighteenth century

Date of recording: 1998

Performers/instruments: Paul O'Dette with Pedro Estevan, Pat O'Brien, Steven Player, and Andrew Lawrence-King (Baroque guitars, percussion, Spanish double harp)

What to Listen for:
- Interplay between major and minor tonalities
- Repeated descending four-chord pattern, or Andalusian cadence
- Changes in the melodic/rhythmic gesture
- Interplay between the guitar and the castanets

Time	Description
0:00	**Primary statement of harmonic framework** Guitar introduces harmonic framework played in an aggressive, rasgueado style. First three chord articulations stress D minor; more rapid, strummed chords immediately follow, outlining A major material until 0:28. All material until 0:28 highlights these two harmonies within the descending chord pattern
0:28	**First melodic variation** Melody articulated with a punteado style punctuated by occasional strummed chord accents
0:44	**New melodic gesture introduced** New gesture played punteado; some pitches outline the melody, while others ornament it
1:01	**New melodic gesture** Accompanied by castanets
1:26	**New melodic gesture**
1:39	**Return of rasgueado chordal pattern** Rasgueado chords alternate with a punteado melodic gesture featuring rapid descending runs
2:04	Extended rasgueado chordal alternation highlights the dance rhythm along with the castanets
2:38	**The piece repeats** Castanets accompany the guitar through the repeat, highlighting the rhythmic play

progression and the triple meter create a sense of open-endedness. Over this cyclic framework, the melody spins out in improvisational-sounding variations, each developing a different melodic or rhythmic gesture. This provides enormous variety in spite of the harmonic constraints. The recording uses castanets to provide the rhythms that in a different context might have been added by a dancer's feet.

The Contradanza

The Spanish-Caribbean **contradanza** offers another example of a genre that traveled back and forth across the Atlantic, adapting to local circumstances and tastes. It derives from the English country dance of the seventeenth and early eighteenth centuries, originally popular among the lower classes, in which dancers in ring or double-line formation performed a series of figures, often announced by a caller. Over time, the genre gained popularity across the social spectrum and spread to France, where it challenged the dominance of the more elite minuet. It became so popular in France that many believed the dance originated there. In its "longways" format, with men and women standing in a double row, the French *contradanse* quickly spread to France's colonies. French influence in the Spanish Bourbon court as well as intra-Caribbean contact helped it spread to Spain's Caribbean colonies by the early nineteenth century where it developed many variants. In Cuba, for example, the white elite employed professional black and mulato musicians to form small dance orchestras typically containing violins, clarinets, trumpets, bass, and percussion. Military-style brass bands also entertained mixed social gatherings with the same music, often outdoors. Some musicians wrote contradanzas as salon music in the form of small-scale piano works. One of the interesting aspects of the contradanza is that although the compositions of Cuban composers like Ignacio Cervantes or Manuel Saumell were intended for solo piano, such works could be arranged for dance orchestras and played in other settings.

The Cuban contradanza maintains the simple, two-part structure of the original European dance while introducing African-derived syncopations or repeated rhythmic ostinatos, especially in the bass line. The most notable ostinato is the so-called **habanera rhythm** (Example 2.4)

EXAMPLE 2.4: Habanera rhythm

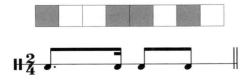

EXAMPLE 2.5a: Cinquillo rhythm

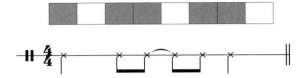

EXAMPLE 2.5b: Cinquillo rhythm followed by quarter notes

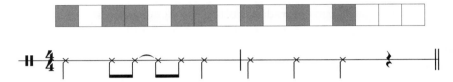

Another fundamental rhythm is what Cubans call the **cinquillo** (Example 2.5a); its presence in Cuban popular music at the turn of the nineteenth century derives in part from the arrival of refugees from Haiti following the Haitian Revolution. Cinquillo rhythms figure prominently in the melodies of Cuban contradanzas. The "long-short-long-short-long" cinquillo pattern typically alternates with a measure of two or three quarter notes (Example 2.5b), creating coherence with the Cuban "three-two" *clave* pattern, discussed in Chapter 5. Found throughout the Caribbean, the cinquillo later became a distinguishing feature of Dominican merengue.

Listening Guide 2.10 is an example of a Cuban contradanza: Ignacio Cervantes's "Los delirios de Rosita." In the Spanish Caribbean, the contradanza and its variants facilitated the transition from group figure dancing to independent couple dancing, a transition facilitated in Europe by the waltz. Thus the contradanza served as the precursor to many of the well-known couple dances from Latin America discussed later in this volume, such as *danzón*, son, merengue, and even the tango.

The End of the Colonial Era

Spain's hold in the New World began to weaken, if only symbolically, with its ceding of the Louisiana Territory to France in 1802. By the early nineteenth century, however, Spanish dominance became increasingly challenged by her subjects as well as by other colonial powers. The Bourbon

⦿ Cervantes: "Los delirios de Rosita" (Rosita's Deliriums), from *Danzas cubanas* (Cuban Dances)

Composer: Ignacio Cervantes

Date of composition: 1875–1895

Performer/instrument: Frank Fernández, piano

Date of recording: 2001

Genre: contradanza

What to Listen for:

- Use of the habanera rhythm
- Syncopated play between the right and left hand of the piano
- Form enlivened by sectional changes in rhythm, melody, and texture

Time	Description
0:00	**A** Left-hand bass plays a habanera rhythm, while the right hand plays a lightly syncopated melody. The **A** section is made up of two similar phrases; each begins the same, but the second, which begins at 0:07, is slightly different
0:14	**Return of A material**
0:26	**B** The left hand continues with a variation on the habanera rhythm, but the right hand has new melodic material played with parallel pitches a third apart; syncopations much more pronounced
0:39	**C** Bell-like motive alternates at the octave, followed by a lightly syncopated descending pattern that bears a resemblance to the opening melodic material, bringing the piece to a close

takeover of Spain in the early eighteenth century led to a series of reforms that aimed to tighten the Crown's control over the colonies and their resources, and to reduce the power of the viceroys and other local authorities. The Crown also distrusted the growing influence of the Jesuit order, and in 1767 King Charles III expelled the Jesuits from the colonies, effectively dismantling many of the communities that the order had built. Many colonists viewed these actions unfavorably and, like their counterparts in North America, saw their economic interests to be at odds with the Crown. Discontent and calls for self-governance followed the French occupation of Spain in the early nineteenth century and increased further when the British attempted to seize control of the Viceroyalty of Río de la Plata in 1806. Those calls led to action over the next decades. The Mexican *grito* or "cry" for independence (1810) led to the first of a series of revolutionary wars that resulted in the independence of Paraguay (1811), Uruguay (1815 but ruled by Brazil until 1828), Argentina (1816), Chile (1818), and Peru (1821). From 1810 to 1825, Simón Bolívar successfully expelled the Spanish from much of the Viceroyalty of New Granada, including what is now Venezuela, Colombia, Panama, Ecuador, and Bolivia. Santo Domingo declared independence in 1821, though Haitian forces (free since their own revolution in 1791) occupied it until 1844. Mexico's long independence war concluded in 1821 and Brazil gained its independence in 1822. Thus, for the second half of the nineteenth century, only Cuba and Puerto Rico remained Iberian colonies. They constituted the last remnants of Spain's power in the Americas until Spain's defeat by the United States and Cuba in 1898. What had once been an enormous political, economic, linguistic—and musical—empire slowly transformed into a diverse array of regional and national identities.

Conclusion

Today, Latin America's colonial history is most clearly evidenced by the period architecture and streetscapes at the center of many of Latin America's modern cities. Skyscrapers and sixteenth-century *cabildos* stand side by side. Ornate Roman Catholic cathedrals neighbor contemporary Pentecostal sanctuaries, while surviving Baroque organs share church space with microphone stands and amplifiers. The ubiquity of such juxtapositions is perhaps a fitting metaphor for the colonial past's continued influence on the present.

Divisions within Latin American society based on class and ethnicity have outlasted colonialism as is revealed in the following chapters. The Roman Catholic Church, though no longer inseparable from affairs of state, continues to be a dominant force throughout the region. Lay religious organizations continue as musical intermediaries between the church and the community, in some cases performing colonial-era music, as occurs during some Holy Week celebrations in Minas Gerais, Brazil.

Our knowledge of Latin American colonial music is largely dependent on the material record: scores and manuscripts left in archives, surviving instruments, the architectural spaces where music was performed, and so on. The choral polyphony of sixteenth-century cathedrals, the lavishness of the Brazilian galant, and the large orchestras marshaled within the flourishing mission enclaves of Alta California reveal an artistic and musical culture that flourished according to the whims of local commerce. Rapid economic expansion, such as during the Brazilian gold rush, inevitably led to more expansive music-making. Patrons, whether state, religious, or private, supported musicians as a means to advertise their social status as well as to promote particular religious or cultural world views. Of course, music's relationship to economic prosperity and its use as an ideological tool did not end with independence. Today, for example, the Venezuelan music education program known as El Sistema draws from state oil revenue in order to foster a vision of equity and social uplift through the arts (see Chapter 4). Likewise, profits from the international drug trade have been used to sponsor musicians whose songs laud the invincibility of their patrons (see Chapter 10).

The themes discussed in this chapter—education, space and place, religion and ritual, material culture, entertainment, and cosmopolitanism—are particularly pertinent for understanding how the competing interests of power, creativity, faith, and subjugation created the unique circumstances under which colonial musical culture flourished. An awareness of such themes and the issues they raise can provide insights not only into the historical past, but into the present as well.

KEY TERMS

acculturation	descending tetrachord	Proper
Andalusian cadence	Divine Office	punteado
antiphonal	fandango	rasgueado
aria	galant	recitative
Baroque	habanera rhythm	ritornello
charamela	huehuetl	romance
chirimía	irmandades	sackbut
cinquillo	jácara (xácara)	shawm
cofradías	Mexica	solfège
coloratura	motet	teponaztli
concertato style	neophytes	viceroyalty
continuo	Ordinary	villancico
contradanza	ornaments	villancico de negros
course	patronato system	viols
crumhorn	plainchant	zarzuela
da capo aria	polychoral	

FURTHER READING

Baker, Geoff. *Imposing Harmony: Music and Society in Colonial Cuzco*. Durham, NC: Duke University Press, 2008.

———. "Latin American Baroque: Performance as a Post-Colonial Act?" *Early Music* 36, no. 3 (2008): 441–48.

Dean, Carolyn. *Inka Bodies and the Body of Christ: Corpus Christi in Colonial Cuzco, Peru*. Durham, NC: Duke University Press, 1999.

Knighten, Tess, and Alvaro Torrente, eds. *Devotional Music in the Iberian World (1450–1800): The Villancico and Related Genres*. Aldershot, UK: Ashgate, 2007.

Manuel, Peter. *Creolizing Contradance in the Caribbean*. Philadelphia: Temple University Press, 2009.

Olsen, Dale. *Music of El Dorado: The Ethnomusicology of Ancient South American Cultures*. Gainesville: University Press of Florida, 2002.

Reily, Suzel Ana. "Remembering the Baroque Era: Historical Consciousness, Local Identity, and the Holy Week Celebrations in a Former Mining Town in Brazil." *Ethnomusicology Forum* 15, no. 1 (June, 2006): 39–62.

Russell, Craig. *From Serra to Sancho: Music and Pageantry in the California Missions*. New York: Oxford University Press, 2009.

———. *Santiago de Murcia's Códice Saldívar No. 4: A Treasury of Guitar Music from Baroque Mexico*, vol. 1. Urbana–Champaign: University of Illinois Press, 1995.

Stein, Louise K. "'La música de dos orbes': A Context for the First Opera of the Americas." *The Opera Quarterly* 22, nos. 3–4 (Summer–Autumn 2006): 433–58.

Stevenson, Robert. *Music in Aztec and Inca Territories*. Berkeley and Los Angeles: University of California Press, 1977.

FURTHER LISTENING

El Milagro de Guadalupe. San Antonio Vocal Arts Ensemble (SAVAE). Iago Records, 1999.

Esteban Salas: Un barroco cubano. Coro Exaudi de La Habana. Jade, 2005.

Juan Gutiérrez de Padilla: Música de la Catedral de Puebla de los Ángeles. Ars Longa de la Habana. Almaviva, 2006.

Matins for the Virgin of Guadalupe. Chanticleer. Teldec, 1998.

Norton Anthology of Western Music, vol. 1, Ancient to Baroque (6th ed.). W. W. Norton, 2010.

NEVADA
UTAH
COLORADO
KANSAS
MISSOURI
ILLINOIS
INDIANA

CALIFORNIA
•Los Angeles
Santa Fe
•Albuquerque
OKLAHOMA
KENTUCKY
TENNESSEE

Tijuana
ARIZONA
NEW MEXICO
United States
ARKANSAS

BAJA
CALIFORNIA
•Tucson
TEXAS
MISSISSIPPI
ALABAMA

SONORA
Ciudad Juárez
Rio Grande
Rio Bravo
Austin•
LOUISIANA

CHIHUAHUA
COAHUILA
Houston•

BAJA
CALIFORNIA
SUR
Gulf of California
SIERRA MADRE OCCIDENTAL
DURANGO
SIERRA MADRE ORIENTAL
NUEVO
LEÓN
Monterrey•
Gulf of Mexico

SINALOA
ZACATECAS
TAMAULIPAS
Mexico

AGUASCALIENTES
SAN
LUIS
POTOSÍ
QUERÉTARO

NAYARIT
GUANAJUATO
FEDERAL DISTRICT
YUCATÁN
QUINTANA ROO

Guadalajara•
JALISCO
HIDALGO
TLAXCALA
CAMPECHE

Morelia•
Mexico City◉
Veracruz
Belize

COLIMA
MICHOACÁN
Puebla•
PUEBLA
VERACRUZ
TABASCO

Pacific Ocean
MORELOS
GUERRERO
OAXACA
Guatemala

Acapulco•
Oaxaca•
CHIAPAS
Honduras

El Salvador

0 100 200 300 400
Kilometers

0   100   200   300
   50   150   250
Miles

Mexico

JOHN KOEGEL

Introduction

Mexico's history and musical traditions are among the richest and most varied in Latin America. Mexico is the second-largest Latin American country, with more than 111 million inhabitants; its capital, Mexico City, has become one of the largest cities in the world. Migration within Mexico from the countryside to the cities accelerated greatly in the twentieth century, and about 77 percent of the population now lives in urban areas. As in the case of other Latin American countries, Mexican music draws heavily from its rural past, yet increasingly dialogues with modern, international influences. One of the most dynamic areas of musical experimentation in recent years has occurred in the northern region bordering the United States, and new forms of music have developed there, as well as among Mexican Americans living in states such as California, Texas, and Illinois.

Mexico is a land of great geographic diversity. Its total physical area is about 12.5 million square miles, and its two main mountain ranges divide the country north to south. Images of the two imposing volcanos in the vicinity of Mexico City (Iztaccíhuatl and Popocatépetl) have long served as symbols of national pride. The narrowest point in the mainland part of the country is the Isthmus of Tehuantepec, long a trade route linking the Gulf of Mexico and the Pacific. The almost eight-hundred-mile-long Baja California peninsula is separated from mainland Mexico by the Gulf of California.

Mexico has a sizable indigenous population of about ten million with its own unique languages—more than 50 of them, including

LISTENING guides

"Huistan, Fiesta of San Miguel, 1974. Three Drums and Small Flute"

"La bruja"

Olmos, "El Siete Leguas"

"El son de la negra"

Esperón, "¡Ay! Jalisco no te rajes"

Lara, "Solamente una vez"

Café Tacuba, "Eres"

Ponce, *Concierto del sur*, third movement

Chávez, *Sinfonía india*

Revueltas, *Sensemayá*

◄ **FIGURE 3.1** Map of Mexico

Nahuatl, Maya, Tzotzil, Mixtec, Zapotec, Otomí, and so on—and cultural forms, with the largest concentration of indigenous Mexicans in the southern states. Of the total population of Mexico, roughly 9 percent is of Indian heritage. Entire civilizations rose and fell prior to the European conquest; the cultural legacies of groups such as the Olmecs, Toltecs, Mayas, and Aztecs warrant independent investigation on your part. Many important figures of Mexico's past have been of indigenous ancestry, including president Benito Juárez, revolutionary war hero Emiliano Zapata, and composer Juventino Rosas. In recent years, indigenous uprisings in Chiapas and elsewhere led by the EZLN (Ejército Zapatista de Liberación Nacional/the Zapatista Army of National Liberation) have made international headlines. Mexican politicians and cultural leaders, and indigenous groups themselves, have struggled for many years to integrate local influences fully into national culture, overcoming biases inherited from the colonial period.

The largest part of the Mexican population today is of **mestizo** or mixed-race ancestry, in this case primarily indigenous and Spanish, with some African and other influences. Most styles of traditional Mexican music can be considered mestizo, in that they combine elements of European, indigenous, and African heritage, as well as transnational influences. The term mestizo originated as part of the *casta* or caste system employed during Spanish colonial control. Under this system, mixed-race individuals had more legal rights than Africans or native peoples, but considerably fewer rights than Spaniards and their descendants (known as criollos or creoles). However, it is important to consider that citizenship was granted to Mexico's indigenous peoples long before it was granted to indigenous peoples in the United States. In Mexico and elsewhere, the notion of mestizo-ness or mestizaje initially had negative associations, but became central to a new national identity as the country struggled for independence from Spain in the early nineteenth century.

Mexico is intricately bound to the United States by a common history, geography, and through immigration; and the two countries share a two-thousand-mile border. The states of California, Arizona, New Mexico, and Texas once belonged to Mexico, and Mexican cultural traditions are strongly represented there today. Individuals of Mexican heritage constitute the largest U.S. Latino group by far. Continued difficult economic conditions have forced many Mexicans north in search of better opportunities, and Mexican settlement in the United States has expanded in recent decades to include the Southeast, Chicago, the Northeast, and elsewhere. California continues to have the largest Latino population in the United States, and Los Angeles County now has the second-largest Mexican population in the world after Mexico City.

A Brief History

Mexico's contact with the European world began in 1519, the year Spanish *conquistadores* arrived and began to colonize the region. Having encountered primarily small groups of native peoples previously, the Spanish found to their amazement that a large, urban civilization existed in central Mexico, with expertise in architecture, astronomy, a system of pictographic writing, and libraries. The Aztec empire, with a population of hundreds of thousands, extended from coast to coast and south into what is now Central America; its capital, Tenochtitlán, ranked among the largest cities in the world at the time (see Chapters 1 and 2). At first unsuccessful in their attempt to conquer the region, the Spanish returned and subdued the Aztec forces with firearms in 1521. The capture of Tenochtitlán marked the beginning of a three-hundred-year-long colonial period in which what is now Mexico and large parts of the southwestern United States became part of Nueva España or New Spain. Spanish authorities burned Aztec documents and killed members of the educated classes, making it difficult to reconstruct their social and cultural life in detail today. European-styled cities were established throughout central Mexico including Mexico City, Puebla, Guadalajara, Valladolid (now known as Morelia), Oaxaca, and Veracruz, some on the sites of indigenous settlements that existed long before the arrival of the Spanish. Cathedrals were established in many colonial cities, and parish churches built in towns and villages throughout New Spain. Music for religious services was given an important role in the ceremonial life of both the parish church and cathedral.

Political unrest in the early nineteenth century led to independence movements in many Spanish colonies. On September 16, 1810, the priest Miguel Hidalgo y Costilla (1753–1811) first declared Mexican independence in the small town of Dolores (now in the state of Guanajuato). The struggle for an independent Mexico lasted 11 years, concluding in 1821 when General Agustín Iturbide declared himself emperor of newly independent Mexico. Ongoing political upheaval followed as different factions vied for power. General Antonio López de Santa Anna, one of the dominant figures of the period, served as president numerous times between 1833 and 1855. His attempt to keep Texas as part of Mexico failed when his forces surrendered to those of Sam Houston in 1836; in 1845 the United States annexed the independent Texas Republic (1836–1845). The U.S. victory in the Mexican–American War of 1846 to 1848—instigated by President Polk under the aegis of U.S. expansionism—resulted in the forced cession of a large portion of Mexican territory (now the states of California, Arizona, Colorado, and New Mexico) to the United States.

In the first half of the ninteteenth century, Mexico experimented with monarchical, federal, and centralized forms of government; liberal, moderate, and conservative factions alternated in power. In the second half of the nineteenth century, new conflicts developed that challenged the fledgling Mexican nation. Attempts to reign in the far-reaching power of the Catholic Church led to a civil war known as the War of Reform (1857–1861). Victory by liberal forces in this conflict led in 1861 to the first presidency of Benito Juárez (1806–1872) and the confiscation of church property. Juárez suspended Mexico's foreign debt payments that year because of an economic crisis, angering European creditor nations. Shortly thereafter, French military intervention forced Juárez from Mexico City and led to the crowning in 1864 of a new magnate, Austrian Archduke Maximilian (1832–1867), as emperor. He retained the throne for four years, but eventually lost in battle to Juárez's forces, was captured, and executed in the city of Querétaro. Juárez then resumed the presidency.

Political tranquility generally reigned during the dictatorship of Porfirio Díaz (1830–1915), a military leader who forcibly took over the government in 1876 and ruled the country imperiously for many years, serving as president from 1876 to 1880 and 1884 to 1911. Under Díaz, foreign investment supported rapid growth in the country's infrastructure. Many beautiful European-style civic buildings date from this period; the railroad expanded significantly; communication throughout the country improved greatly; and trade increased. But this period of industrialization carried a high social cost as many people continued to suffer from poverty. Large numbers of disenfranchised rural *campesinos* (peasants), many illiterate and of indigenous heritage, served the interests of a relatively small number of wealthy *hacendados* (large property owners). Large disparities of wealth existed between the urban elite and middle classes and the rural population. All of this, in combination with a lack of democratic rule, led to political unrest and ultimately armed rebellion.

The violent Mexican Revolution of 1910 to 1920 resulted from these inequities and radically changed Mexican society. In its aftermath, the government broke up many *haciendas* (large rural properties) and redistributed the lands to individuals and communities. The 1920s and 1930s also brought a flowering of the arts. The Mexican mural painting movement, supported by the government and headed by artists such as Diego Rivera, José Clemente Orozco, and David Alfaro Siqueiros, celebrated Mexican indigenous culture consistently for the first time, as well as the heroes of the Mexican Revolution. Artists of the period attempted to symbolically unify a country heavily divided along lines of class and ethnicity and whose leadership had never fully come to terms with the country's indigenous heritage.

The Mexican film industry gained international stature from the 1930s, and Mexican entrepreneurs established radio stations throughout the country. Both film and radio had a tremendous influence on national and international music-making. Mexico City's XEW, "La Voz de la América Latina" (The Voice of Latin America)—broadcasting first in 1930 and featuring prominent musicians such as Agustín Lara—became one of the most influential radio stations in the western hemisphere. After suffering through the Great Depression of the 1930s, Mexican society rebounded during the 1940s and the post–World War II economic boom, in no small part due to the nationalization of Mexico's large oil reserves. This prosperity ushered in a "golden age" of Mexican film that lasted through the 1960s. Musical films from this period achieved broad international popularity, and contributed to the popularization of mariachi repertoire, the bolero, mambo, *cha-cha-chá*, and other genres.

Social and political trends in more recent decades have continued to shape Mexico's cultural life. The rapid growth of Mexico City, now home to nearly a third of the country's population, has made it central to musical life. And yet, as northern states such as Baja California, Sonora, Sinaloa, Chihuahua, and Nuevo León have become important as conduits of trade with the United States, they have influenced the rest of the nation musically as well, especially with the musical genres of banda sinaloense and música norteña. The strong influence of popular culture from the United States and Europe has led to the emergence of a vibrant rock scene in Mexico. NAFTA, the North American Free Trade Agreement, implemented in 1994, has not been a resounding success, especially for communities reliant on agriculture for their sustenance; agricultural products imported from abroad without tariffs have had a negative impact on Mexican farmers. The assertion of indigenous rights continues to take many forms, and immigration from Mexico to the United States remains a topic of urgency on both sides of the border, as does the war against drugs.

Traditional and Popular Music

Indigenous Traditions

Indigenous Mexican communities have been able to maintain many unique traditions because they have adapted to changing circumstances, despite forced servitude, the devasting effects of European diseases, land expropriation, and marginalization. In spite of significant efforts to integrate indigenous groups into the nation in recent decades, they often remain socially disadvantaged. The states with the largest indigenous representation include Oaxaca, Chiapas, Veracruz, Yucatán, and Puebla, as well as the area around Mexico City. Each of the scores of distinct indigenous groups has its own rich music and dance traditions; countless styles of music are performed in these communities, making it difficult to characterize the repertoire in general. However, the music of various indigenous communities does share common functions, especially music for entertainment and for ritual celebrations: marriages, wakes and funerals, fiestas for locally venerated Catholic saints, and other commemorations.

Important efforts have been made to preserve and study indigenous music, culture, and languages in recent decades, and local and national governmental patronage supports a wide range of projects: the teaching of native culture and history in schools, bilingual education, radio programs in Zapotec, Mixtec, and other indigenous languages, research and publications on indigenous topics and history, competitions for the best literature in indigenous languages, subsidies for native wind bands, and so on.

Some Mexican indigenous music sounds very different from Western music, other pieces sound modern and cosmopolitan; a majority blend newer and older influences. Few examples of indigenous music as performed before European colonization exist today, however. Most native communities have adopted at least some European-derived instruments (violins, guitars, harps, etc.), often altering their construction, tuning, or performance practice in some way. Indigenous groups also perform well-known genres including the son (discussed shortly) and form ensembles such as wind bands, as do other segments of the population. Much native Mexican music is instrumental, performed

FIGURE 3.2 A Totonac musician plays an indigenous flute before performing the dance of Los Voladores (The Flyers) at Chapultepec park in Mexico City on September 30, 2009

on drums or other percussion such as rattles or shells, and flutes. As in the case of U.S. native traditions, dance and movement, as well as the use of masks or costumes, are often closely linked to music-making; ceremonial performances often enact beliefs and legends about the supernatural world. This is certainly true of some of Mexico's more spectacular indigenous musical traditions such as the performances by the Totonac *voladores* of Papantla from the state of Veracruz (see Figure 3.2). The four fliers ("bird men") launch themselves from the top of a high pole and descend slowly, circling the pole with their feet attached to the pole by a rope. They represent the four cardinal directions and the four elements of earth, air, fire and water; their descent is accompanied by the music of a pipe and drum played by the *caporal*, who stands on the top of the pole.

The southern state of Oaxaca, with the largest number of native peoples, had an advanced civilization well before European contact, as evidenced by the archeological sites at Monte Albán and Mitla. Many leading figures in Mexican history have come from the state, including Benito Juárez and Porfirio Díaz, and the artist Rufino

Tamayo. The dominant native languages spoken there are Zapotec and Mixtec. Oaxaca is also known for its many other contributions to Mexican society and culture: piquant *moles* (sauces made of ground spices) and other regional foods, colorful indigenous dresses for women, local fiestas (especially the Guelaguetza ceremonies in Oaxaca City), and the dominance of women in market life in the Isthmus of Tehuantepec.

"Huistan, Fiesta of San Miguel, 1974. Three Drums and Small Flute" (Listening Guide 3.1) comes from the neighboring southern state of Chiapas

"Huistan, Fiesta of San Miguel, 1974. Three Drums and Small Flute"

Performers/instruments: anonymous field recording; three drums and small flute

Date of recording: 1974

Form: varied binary

Tempo/meter: lively simple triple

What to Listen for:

- Melody consisting of two contrasting musical phrases, one high and one low, played in alternation and varied improvisationally each time by the flutist
- Musical phrases unequal in length that also vary throughout the performance
- A constant, recurrent drum pattern
- Melodic ornamentation similar to that of traditional Irish music, and a tonic note that sounds slightly high (or "sharp") to Western ears

Time	Description
0:00	First presentation of the high melody, played alone
0:06	Drum enters, gradually becomes louder
0:08	First presentation of lower melody
0:13	Second presentation of high melody, without highest notes
0:19	Variation of lower melody
0:26	High melody variant
0:33	Low melody variant
0:40	A second low melody played here, breaking the alternation
0:48	High melody variant
0:55	An especially long, low melody variant

Indigenous Culture in San Juan Chamula, Chiapas

More than a fourth of the population of the southern state of Chiapas identifies as indigenous. The largest groups include the Tzeltales, Tzotziles, Choles, and Zoques, while the region surrounding San Juan Chamula, Chiapas, has a predominantly Tzotzil Maya-speaking population. Located at an elevation above 7,200 feet, the town of San Juan Chamula is a popular tourist destination because of the beauty of its surroundings and its colorful celebrations, especially during carnival season and the feasts of San Juan Bautista (Saint John the Baptist, after whom the town is named) between June 24 and 26, San Sebastián, and Santa Rosa. Local handicrafts include woven textiles and various forms of folk art. Residents of San Juan Chamula have a long history of resistance to outside governmental authority. The area was a site for the Tzeltal Rebellion of 1712 to 1715 and the Guerra de las Castas (War of the Castes) of 1869. In the 1990s, it was a center of Zapatista guerrilla activity.

The church of San Juan Chamula vividly demonstrates the syncretic approach local indigenous peoples take towards Catholic ritual and Maya religious beliefs. The Tzotziles come as families and in other small groups at all hours, light candles on the floor covered in pine needles, and recite prayers in Tzotzil that move between song and spoken phrases. Catholic saints are venerated alongside indigenous religious symbols, showing how conversion to Catholicism is far from complete here. Musicians play harps and other forms of music outside the church door on important feast days. Although the area is predominantly Catholic, evangelical Protestant groups have gained converts in recent years, creating conflict with local community leaders, who seek to maintain their authority and general adherence to traditional religious beliefs.

In addition to indigenous vocal and instrumental music, especially on marimbas, many different styles are heard in the area: rock, accordion-based música norteña from northern Mexico, and other popular genres. The town of San Juan Chamula is also noted as a center for the manufacture of musical instruments, especially harps and violins. The rock fusion group Sak Tzevul (meaning "lightning"), founded in the 1990s, comes from Zinacantán, Chiapas, near San Juan Chamula. It performs throughout Mexico and Central America and releases innovative commercial recordings. Leader Damián Martínez (singer, guitarist, composer) and other band members sing in Tzotzil, Spanish, and other languages, and describe their music as *música tradicional/progresivo* (traditional/progressive music).

where most communities are Maya descendants. The piece was recorded in the 1970s as performed by the Huistan people—known for their resistance to external cultural influences—during a festival for a patron saint. Many of their musical forms (including this one) are associated with folk Catholicism, the blending of Catholic and indigenous practices. A three-hole cane flute provides the principal melody in the example, accompanied by several single-headed drums played with sticks. Note the recurrent rhythmic pattern supporting the principal melody, a characteristic of much indigenous repertoire, as well as the melodic ornamentation, the constant improvisation or variation of melodic themes, and the subtle differences between the pitches used and those characteristic of Western music. Listening Guide 3.1 provides some feel for contemporary indigenous musical practices, although these continue to change. Even many of the "traditional" flutes and drums used by the Huistan and others are patterned after European instruments brought to the Americas centuries ago rather than those used before the conquest.

Though indigenous music like that in "Huistan, Fiesta of San Miguel, 1974. Three Drums and Small Flute" can be characterized as traditional, most Mexican music straddles the boundary between traditional and popular. Through the mid-twentieth century, Mexico remained a relatively rural society with countless musical forms rooted in local communities. Today the situation has changed. Traditional forms persist, yet have been transformed through performance in urban contexts, dissemination in the mass media, "folklorization" (being placed on stages in formal concert settings), and fusion with other national and international genres. Many forms of Mexican music evoke the rural past stylistically or lyrically, but are equally tied to modern urban experience.

Traditional Dance Repertoire

Dance has been important to Mexican society for many centuries, and dance music is heavily represented in its traditional repertoire, mestizo and indigenous. In the eighteenth and ninteenth centuries, common European dances included the contradanza (contradance), minuet, **waltz**, **mazurka**, and **polka**. Orchestras made up of strings and wind instruments, or of combinations of harp, guitar (and various guitar types), violin, and piano supplied dance music. Earlier dance styles also included the **zapateado** (a dance that featured fancy heel work, rhythmic striking of the feet against the ground), fandango, and *seguidilla*. The Mexican **jarabe** was also well known. Dance often attracted the attention of the Catholic Church, which at first condemned the jarabe and other genres because of their allegedly indecent nature (too much close physical contact, flirtation, bawdy lyrics, etc.).

The jarabe consists of a series of different-but-connected short dance pieces played in succession as a single unit, often with contrasting tempos, rhythms, keys, and choreography. Although solo harpists and guitarists frequently performed the music of the early jarabe, larger groups such as mariachis continue to play it today. In the early twentieth century, the jarabe from the state of Jalisco, the *jarabe tapatío* (known in English as the "Mexican Hat Dance"), came to be viewed as representative of Mexican musical folklore on a national level. Grade-school children are taught to perform it today, along with other regional styles. Mexican classical composers have published arrangements, especially for piano, that preserve old jarabe melodies.

explore

Listen to the CD *Tzotziles: Psalms, Stories, and Music* (Sub Rosa SR17) for traditional syncretic ceremonial music of the Tzotziles. Listen to indigenous Mexican music on the Smithsonian Folkways website, and compare this music with modern commercial releases by Sak Tzevul or artists such as Lila Downs, a mixed-race performer from Oaxaca who records frequently in indigenous Mexican languages.

Typical songs used in the jarabe include pieces such as "El atole" (A hot, sweet corn beverage), "El perico" (The Parakeet), "El durazno" (The Peach), and "Los enanos" (The Dwarfs). Some of these titles refer to the choreography used in the dance, especially those that imitate the subjects of the song titles. Some, such as "El durazno," contain sexual or erotic double entendres. "El perico" plays on the sound of the repeated words "pica" (to peck) and "perico" (parakeet). It discusses birds as a metaphor for a young couple and is clearly intended to be flirtatious. "El atole" contrasts the sweetness of the beverage with the bitterness of the the atole seller; the song seems to suggest that she also needs to be "sampled" before she "goes bad."

"El perico"	"The Parakeet"
Pica, pica, pica, perico,	*Peck, peck, peck, parakeet,*
pica, pica, pica la rosa.	*Peck, peck, peck at the rose.*
Quisiera ser periquito	*I would like to be a parakeet*
para volar en el aire	*So that I could fly in the air*
y allí decirte secretos	*And tell you secrets there*
sin que los oyera nadie.	*Without anyone else hearing them.*

"El atole"	"The Atole"
Vengan a tomar atole	*Come and drink atole*
todos los que van pasando.	*All of you who are passing by.*
Que si el atole está bueno	*For if the atole is good*
la atolera se está agriando.	*The atole seller is becoming bitter.*
De este atolito de leche	*From this atole made of milk*
y tamales de manteca	*And tamales made with lard*
todo el mundo aproveche	*Everyone benefits*
que por esto no se peca.	*Because this way no one sins.*

References to animals, fruit, and flowers are common in the poetry of rural communities, and can be seen as anthropomorphized symbols of human activities, including courtship. Figure 3.3, Casimiro Castro's mid-nineteenth-century lithograph *El fandango*, shows a couple dancing to the sound of traditional dances.

Dance is perhaps not as widespread as it once was among the total population because of competition from more passive forms of entertainment, and because of modern lifestyles that limit individual free time. Nevertheless, Mexicans have eagerly embraced dance styles such as reggaeton (p. 209), salsa, and cumbia (p. 143) that originated in other areas of Latin America, especially the trans-Caribbean region, and also create their own local versions. Other social dances such as the *danzón* (imported from Cuba) and European ballroom dancing are still practiced, especially in the state of Veracruz and in Mexico City.

FIGURE 3.3 Casimiro Castro, *El fandango*, nineteenth-century print

Son jarocho

One of the most important kinds of traditional Mexican music is the **son**. The term son is a cognate of the English word "song"; it can be used in a general sense by Spanish speakers in various countries to mean song or tune, but can also refer to specific regional or national styles of music. Mexican son styles are especially diverse: at least a dozen distinct forms exist in individual areas, all with unique characteristics. The son jalisciense (Jalisco-style son) and the son huasteco or huapango are among the best-known subgenres, and are discussed next. Sones (the plural form of son) have become closely tied to national identity and national representations of Mexico. They emerged as distinct musical forms by the eighteenth century, the result of fusions of influences from Spanish, indigenous, and West African musical practices.

One example of a regional son variant is the **son jarocho** from the state of Veracruz, along the coast of the Gulf of Mexico. Instruments in the jarocho ensemble typically include the *arpa jarocha* (Veracruz-style harp), various types of **jarana** (a small guitar), and the requinto (another guitar-like instrument), along with voices. The jarocho harp has between 32 and 36 strings, stands about five feet high, and plays all the diatonic notes in the key of the song, but cannot play chromatic notes because it does not have pedals to raise or lower the pitch of individual strings. A change to another key can require the retuning of the instrument. Considerable proficiency is needed to play the *arpa jarocha*, which provides a bass line (played by one hand) and the chords and melody (played by the other). The typical jarana has frets and

FIGURE 3.4 A traditional son jarocho ensemble. Veracruz, 1956

between eight and twelve strings arranged in five courses (sets or pairs of strings), usually three doubled courses and two single strings. The jarana is strummed and provides the chordal and rhythmic accompaniment. The requinto usually has four single strings, and is played with a pick. It provides melodic lines that complement those played on the harp.

Son jarocho repertory consists of regional sones from Veracruz as well as dances and songs from other parts of Mexico and from abroad. Those that are particularly associated with Veracruz and the son jarocho include lively dances with sung verses and that alternate between ¾ and ⁶⁄₈ meter. Well-known examples include "La bamba" (the most famous), "La iguana" (The Iguana), and "La guacamaya" (The Macaw). These are played and sung as dance music, or performed separately. They allow for vocal dialogues, with singers alternating verses back and forth, often improvising them as they go.

Jarocho dancers typically perform as couples on a slightly raised wooden platform (*tarima*), creating a percussive effect with their rapid footwork. Women often dance, rather than singing or playing. Famous son jarocho groups include the ensemble of Afro-Mexican *jarocha* harpist Graciana Silva, "La Negra Graciana" (Black Graciana), and, more recently, Tlen Huicani, Son de Madera, and Chuchumbé (this last group is named after an erotic dance banned by the Catholic Church). Son jarocho has made an impact outside its own world, with rock groups such as Café Tacuba and Los Lobos incorporating its sounds and instruments into their performances.

"La bruja" (The Witch, Listening Guide 3.2) is a son jarocho with lyrics in the typical form of paired four-line stanzas. As described, performers can freely change the order of the verses or improvise new ones. When this son is performed as a dance, it is customary for women to balance lit candles on their heads. The lyrics of "La bruja" present an image of a bewitching and beautiful woman who captures the attention of a man. The term *jarochito* refers to a person from the gulf coast of Mexico in the state of Veracruz. Note that "La bruja" is performed in a waltz rhythm, and thus represents an interpretation by a son jarocho group of a European-derived form. Search for examples of pieces such as "La iguana" on your own in order to compare "La bruja" with the livelier, up-tempo and syncopated pieces that feature prominently in son jarocho repertoire.

⊚ "La bruja" (The Witch)

Performers/instruments: José Gutiérrez y Los
Hermanos Ochoa (harp, jarana, requinto, voices)

Date of recording: 2003

Genre: son jarocho

Form: copla/verse form

Tempo/meter: waltz tempo; moderate triple meter

What to Listen for:

- Harp melody playing high notes during instrumental passages such as the introduction, as well as requinto countermelodies played simultaneously at a lower pitch

- Bass notes of the harp on the downbeat of each $\frac{3}{4}$ measure, and the jarana strumming on beats 2 and 3

- Lead harp melody complicates the basic pulse of the music through **arpeggiation**, melodic ornamentation, and playing slightly earlier or later than expected

Time	Text	Translation	Description
0:00			**Introduction** Instrumental introduction; harp accompanied by requinto, spoken interjection
0:18	¡Ay!, qué bonito es volar a las dos de la mañana, a las dos de la mañana, ¡Ay!, qué bonito es volar. Volar y dejarse caer en los brazos de una dama. ¡Ay!, qué bonito es volar a las dos de la mañana, ¡Ay, mamá! Me agarra la bruja, me lleva a su casa, se sienta en mis piernas, me muerde y me abraza.	Oh, how wonderful it is to fly At two in the morning, At two in the morning, Oh, how great it is to fly. To fly and let yourself fall Into the arms of a lady. Oh, how great it is to fly At two in the morning, Oh, mama! The witch grabs me And takes me home, She sits on my lap, And bites and hugs me.	**Stanzas** Vocals alternate between lead and chorus; bass runs are played on the harp, as well as short melodies that fill in breaks in the vocal line and complement the vocal line (for instance beginning at 0:51); jarana strumming; requinto drops out initially, but is audible beginning at 1:09
1:22			**Instrumental interlude** Harp solo; requinto plays countermelody and jarana the chordal accompaniment

(continued)

Time	Text	Translation	Description
1:38	A una bruja me encontré que en el aire iba volando, que en el aire iba volando. A una bruja me encontré, ¡Ay, mamá! Y al verla le pregunté: ¿A quién andaba buscando? Busco a un señor como Ud, pa' que me cante un huapango, ¡Ay, mamá! Me lleva la bruja, me lleva al cuartel, se sienta en mis piernas y me empieza a morder.	I spotted a witch Flying in the sky, Flying in the sky. I spotted a witch, Oh, mama! When I saw her I asked: For whom were you looking? And she said, a man like you, To sing me a huapango, Oh, mama! The witch took me To the barracks, She sat on my legs And started to bite me.	**Stanzas** Musicians sing stanzas 4–6, alternating in solo and harmony; other musicians interject spoken encouragement. Prominent harp countermelody throughout

The Corrido

The **corrido** is one of the most enduring forms of Mexican song. It is both a traditional genre with a long history and part of contemporary commercial repertoire. Corridos are narrative ballads about particular people, groups, or events of social or historical importance. The stories they tell might have occured in the past, or can be about current events. Common themes include the exploits of outlaws or military men, the extraordinary experiences of common people, and natural disasters or other newsworthy happenings. Corridos have been widely popular at least from the time of the Mexican Revolution of the 1910s. Many songs deal with conflicts along the U.S.-Mexico border, generally between English- and Spanish-speaking groups or individuals. Indeed, the history of the corrido is closely linked to the border, and scholars such as Américo Paredes have argued that it first developed there rather than in central Mexico. One of the most famous of all corridos is "El corrido de Gregorio Cortéz," about the conflict between Texas Mexicans and Anglo-American Texans at the turn of the twentieth century. The corrido today is as favored a musical genre among Mexican immigrants in the United States as it was a century ago, and many corridos have dealt with the mistreatment of immigrants by U.S. authorities, as well as the clash between cultures along or near the border. There is a sense of empathy in corridos for the oppressed individual who has become an outlaw or has been rejected as a result of political and social repression. A probable predecessor of the genre is the Spanish romance, a narrative ballad form that also told stories of heroic events or deeds, typically by the aristocracy.

Corrido texts usually consist of four-line stanzas, each line having eight syllables. The melodies to which they are sung are simple, easy to remember, and strophic in form (each stanza of text is sung to the same melody), which makes them easy to perform and to pass along from one community to the next. The harmonies used are also simple. Acoustic guitars traditionally accompany corridos, though full mariachis also perform them, as do música norteña groups (the northern Mexican accordion-based style) and other ensembles.

In the past, many corrido lyrics were sold as printed broadsides, single sheets of paper with striking images that illustrated the events described. Figure 3.5, "Corrido de la cucaracha" (Corrido of the Cockroach), presents a well-known piece from the 1910s with an image drawn by the famous artist José Guadalupe Posada. The lyrics discuss General Francisco "Pancho" Villa (1877–1923), a central figure of the Mexican Revolution. Corridos have also been published as sheet music or in songbook collections without music notation known as *cancioneros*. Some of Mexico's most famous popular singers, such as Lucha Reyes, Ana Gabriel, Vicente Fernández, and Juan Gabriel, have recorded corridos.

Listening Guide 3.3, "El Siete Leguas," is a famous corrido written by Graciela Olmos (ca. 1895–1962), which has been sung by Pedro Infante, Antonio Aguilar, and Los Alegres de Terán, among others. It tells another story about Villa, who served as commander of the División del Norte (Northern Army Division), and his favorite horse, "El Siete Leguas" (Seven Leagues). The song recalls the fight of the Bracamontes brigade at the Irapuato (Guanajuato) train station and the singing of the wandering group known as "Los Horizontes." The narrator reminds Pancho Villa of his attacks on the village of Paredón and the city of Torreón (Coahuila), bids farewell to the beautiful towers of Chihuahua, and tells listeners that Villa came to liberate the border. Known as "la bandida" (the female bandit), Olmos reportedly served alongside Villa's army as a *soldadera* (female camp follower). Her corrido "El Siete Leguas" inspired the 1955 film *Siete Leguas*, loosely based on the events in the corrido and starring singer-actor Luis Aguilar. In the film, Villa sends Rodolfo (Aguilar) to the village of "Paredones" to prepare the people for an upcoming siege. Olmos's corrido became so famous that a brand of Mexican tequila was even named after Villa's horse!

FIGURE 3.5 "Corrido de la cucaracha," traditional broadside sheet, 1915

explore

The CD set *The Mexican Revolution* (see Further Listening) contains many historic and more-recent recordings of corridos about the revolution. This also includes a very extensive program booklet with lyrics and translations.

⊚ Olmos: "El Siete Leguas" (Seven Leagues)

Composer/lyricist: Graciela Olmos

Date of recording: late 1940s or 1950s

Performers/instruments: Pedro Infante with mariachi

Genre: corrido

Form: strophic

Tempo/meter: moderate triple meter

What to Listen for:

- Waltz-like rhythm with the bass instrument marking the downbeat of each measure, while guitars and other instruments strum on 2 and 3, as in "La bruja"
- Violins filling in between stanzas and melodic phrases; their entrances frequently alternating with the trumpets
- Pedro Infante's smooth style vocal style in this sophisticated instrumental arrangement (other singers of corridos often use a less polished timbre and perform in smaller groups)

Time	Text	Translation	Description
0:00			**Introduction** Instrumental introduction by mariachi; a brief quotation of the overture to Rossini's famous opera *William Tell* in the trumpet part; *gritos* (shouts) of enthusiasm
0:13	Siete Leguas, el caballo que Villa más estimaba . . . En la estación de Irapuato cantaban los Horizontes . . .	Seven Leagues was the horse That Villa loved best . . . At the train station in Irapuato The "Horizontes" sang . . .	**Stanzas 1–2,** with softer accompaniment; violins and trumpets interject with countermelodies
1:15			**Instrumental Interlude** Similar to introduction
1:25	Oye tú, Francisco Villa: ¿qué dice tu corazón? . . . Como a las tres de la tarde silbó la locomotora . . .	Hear this, Francisco Villa: What does your heart tell you? . . . At three in the afternoon The train blew its whistle . . .	

Mariachi Music

Mariachi music, the form of Mexican music best known abroad, first developed in the state of Jalisco in west-central Mexico by the mid-nineteenth century. Early mariachis were string band ensembles known only to local residents that played at parties, weddings, and other events. At first their repertoire included local styles from the state of Jalisco, as well as European-derived repertoire; later, as the ensembles gained popularity throughout the country, they incorporated musical forms from other regions of Mexico (and Europe), becoming more representative of the country as a whole. Mariachis first gained national recognition in the early twentieth century when they toured to Mexico City and to the United States. Cinematic portrayals were central to their mass acceptance, and many films from the 1930s onward featured their music.

❊ In Depth 3.2

Contemporary Corridos

The corrido is a living musical form. As in the past, corrido composers today deal with themes of immediate interest to their public: immigration, social inequity, poverty, political corruption, and so on. The corrido has a journalistic purpose, and composer Paulino Vargas (d. 2010), accordionist of the group Los Broncos de Reynosa, believed that creators of this genre should be considered reporters, even if they sometimes exaggerate contemporary events. Corridos present a history from the popular viewpoint, not that of the official record. Vargas's "Las mujeres de Juárez" (The Women of Juarez City), recorded by música norteña group Los Tigres del Norte on their 2004 *Pacto de Sangre* (Blood Pact) album, for instance, condemns the murder of innocent women in the northern border city, many of them factory workers: "Humillante y abusiva la intocable impunidad/los huesos en el desierto muestran la cruda verdad/las muertas de Ciudad Juárez son vergüenza nacional" (Humiliating and abusive, the untouchable impunity [the government's failure to act]/The bones in the desert show the raw truth/The dead women of Ciudad Juárez are a national shame). Vargas also wrote "La crónica de un cambio" (The Chronicle of a Change), charging Mexican President Vicente Fox to effect real reform during his term of office (2000–2006), and "La banda del carro rojo" (The Red Car Gang), about cross-border drug smuggling (a film of the same title recounts this story).

Los Tigres del Norte is one of the leading popular groups performing corridos today. However, they have been criticized for their performances of narcocorridos (corridos that may glorify drug culture, p. 411) such as "Contrabando y traición" (Contraband and Betrayal). The group also recorded Enrique Franco's "El corrido," whose lyrics sum up the essence of the form: "Como la corriente de un río crecido/que baja en torrente impetuoso y bravío/voz de nuestra gente un grito reprimido/un canto valiente eso es el corrido" (Like the current of a gushing river/That flows turbulently, impetuously, and bravely/Voice of our people, repressed cry/A courageous song, that is the corrido).

Mariachi music served at that time as a marker of rural, working-class culture. After the Mexican Revolution, mariachi music helped to unify a country torn apart by revolutionary war and class divisions, symbolically bridging the gap between rural and urban areas. Its commercial form since the 1940s has adopted complex instrumental arrangements and a *bel canto* (quasi-operatic) vocal style, adding an element of urban sophistication to earlier practice. The post-revolutionary government adopted mariachi music as representive of populist *mexicanidad* (Mexican national pride).

Early mariachi instrumentation consisted of one or two violins, guitar, regional guitar variants such as the five-string *vihuela*, and harp. By about 1900, the **guitarrón** (a large guitar-like instrument tuned a fifth lower than the standard guitar) was added, frequently replacing the harp as the ensemble's bass instrument. Standard mariachi ensembles today consist of seven to fifteen musicians, with two trumpets (common since about the 1940s), three to six violins, guitars, *vihuela*, and guitarrón. The first mariachi to make recordings (in 1908) was the Cuarteto Coculense (Cocula Quartet), named after the town of Cocula, Jalisco, which claims to be the birthplace of mariachi. Mariachi Vargas de Tecalitlán, in existence for more than one hundred years, is the most famous mariachi in the world. It is named after its founder Gaspar Vargas and the city of Tecalitlán in the state of Jalisco, which also claims to be the birthplace of mariachi.

Each instrument in the marachi has its own role. Violins and trumpets play melodies and are featured in sections and in the form of musical dialogues against one other. The guitar and *vihuela* provide chordal accompaniment, often by means of flashy, complex strumming patterns. The guitarrón plays the bass line, plucking its notes in octaves to create a louder sound. When harp or other instruments are used, they provide special instrumental color. Musical interest in mariachi music is created mostly through rhythmic shifts, and by contrasting various instruments, as chord progressions tend to be relatively simple.

The term **compás** is used in much of Latin America to describe the rhythmic structure of a piece of music, but has specific meanings in conjunction with mariachi repertoire. Most commonly, it references recurrent rhythms that serve as the structural basis of certain genres, especially son variants. Most Mexican sones are written in a fast triple meter and are intended for dancing, zapateado-style. The basic compás or rhythmic cell associated with them consists of two halves, each with six beats. The first half of the rhythm emphasizes particular groupings of notes, for instance beats 1, 3, and 5, while the second half emphasizes different beats such as 1 and 4 or 2 and 5. Guitars and other strummed instruments foreground these rhythms in the ensemble, and the guitarrón usually plays two-measure bass patterns that correspond to them as well. The constant alternation in successive measures

EXAMPLE 3.1: Basic strumming pattern for the first half of the son jalisciense compás

EXAMPLE 3.2: Alternate strumming pattern for the first half of the son jalisciense compás

between contrasting accents lends a highly syncopated feel to Mexican sones. Such rhythmic play in triple-meter compositions is common to other kinds of Latin American music as well and may represent the influence of West African traditions on the region's development. One common word in Spanish for such syncopation, alternating groupings of two and three notes in triple-meter compositons, is **sesquiáltera**.

The **son jalisciense** (son from Jalisco), a prominent genre of mariachi music, serves as a means of further exploring the notion of compás. The basic compás associated with this genre consists of a measure of strumming that emphasizes beats 1, 3, and 5 of the § measure followed by another that emphasizes beats 2 and 5. The first measure, especially, can be interpreted various ways. The guitars and *vihuela* may strum only on beats 1, 3, and 5, as indicated in Example 3.1. Alternately, they may strum on all six beats but accent beats 1, 3, and 5 more strongly (Example 3.2).

Most commonly, however, they play only on beats 1, 3, and 5, but "dress up" beat 3 with a flourish (a fast series of three strums) known as a **redoble**. Following this, the second half of the measure involves constant strumming in a "down-down-up down-down-up" pattern over the six beats, with emphasis on strokes two and five. Finally, the guitarrón plays a complementary pattern, with the first half marking beats 3 and 5 of the measure and the second half beats 2 and 4. Note that the guitarrón patterns tend to avoid beat 1, increasing the syncopated feel of the music.

The complete compás schema of the son jalisciense is provided in Example 3.3. For simplicity's sake, all transcribed examples have been written with the less syncopated measure first, but in practice compositions might begin on either side of the pattern.

Mariachi repertory is large and consists of many older traditional sones jaliscienses such as "El carretero" (The Cart Driver), "La mariquita" (The Ladybug), and "El gavilancillo" (The Little Sparrow Hawk), as well as newer pieces. "El son de la negra" (The Tune of the Dark Woman, Listening Guide 3.4), is one of the most famous of all traditional pieces in this style, performed here by Mariachi Vargas de Tecalitlán (Figure 3.6). The recording

EXAMPLE 3.3: Complete compás for son jalisciense strumming

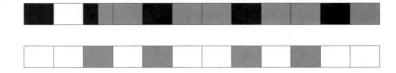

son jaliscience ♩ = 120

Guitar

Guitarrón

provides an excellent opportunity for hearing the rhythms of the son jalisciense in context. Listen as the performers begin strumming the son jalisciense compás and see if you can tell which side of the pattern they enter on.

It is instructive to compare the rhythms of the son jalisciense with another prominent type of son in the mariachi repertoire, the **son huasteco** or **huapango**, and to consider their similarities and differences. The son huasteco is another musical form in a syncopated triple meter, traditionally intended for dancing, and is typically played by a trio of musicians performing on violin, *jarana huasteca* (a small guitar), and *guitarra huapanguera* (guitar). The term *huasteco* refers to the Huastec region in northeastern Mexico, inland from the city of Tampico, including interior towns like San Luis Potosí. The

FIGURE 3.6 Mariachi Vargas de Tecalitlán

◎ "El son de la negra" (The Tune of the Dark Woman)

Composer/lyricist: anonymous (arranged by Silvestre Vargas and Rubén Fuentes)

Performers/instruments: Mariachi Vargas de Tecalitlán (violin, trumpet, guitar, *vihuela*, guitarrón)

Date of recording: 1997

Genre: son jalisciense

Form: strophic (with variations)

Tempo/meter: brisk compound duple, with many syncopated accents (sesquiáltera)

What to Listen for:

- Compás of the son jalisciense, focusing on the standard alternating pattern played by guitars and *vihuela*, as well as on the moments when they deviate from the standard pattern
- Guitarrón lines up with and complements the strumming
- *Gritos* (stylized shouts of enthusiasm), characteristic of much Mexican music, perhaps representing indigenous influence on contemporary music

Time	Text	Translation	Description
0:00			**Introduction** Long instrumental introduction begins slow and speeds up, and includes *gritos*. Strumming instruments play a fairly straight rhythm, with the occasional redoble. The son jalsciense compás begins at 0:25
0:41	Negrita de mis pesares, ojos de papel volando, negrita de mis pesares ojos de papel volando. A todos díles que sí, pero no les digas cuándo, así me dijiste a mí, por eso vivo penando.	Little dark woman of my sorrows, With her flashing eyes, Little dark woman of my sorrows With her flashing eyes. Tell everyone yes, But don't tell them when, So you said to me, And because of this I suffer.	**Stanzas** A softer section; instrumentalists play and sing, while the trumpets are silent
0:57	Hablado: ¡Claro que sí!	Spoken: But of course!	**Interlude** Instrumental section with long *gritos*; strumming variations by the guitars and *vihuelas*, deviations from the standard compás

(continued)

Time	Text	Translation	Description
1:46	¿Cuándo me traes a mi negra? Que la quiero ver aquí con su rebozo de seda que le traje de Tepic. [Repeats]	When will you bring me my love? Because I want to see her here With the silk shawl That I brought her from Tepic.	**Final stanza** Trumpets and violins play during instrumental breaks
2:20	Hablado: ¡Así se baila en Tecalitlán, sí señor!	Shouted: That's how they dance it in Tecalitlán, yes, sir!	**Ending** Instrumental coda section with *gritos*, and additional deviations from the standard compás

name derives from the Huastec people, a Nahuatl-speaking indigenous group in the area. *Huapango*, an alternate name for the same music, is the Nahuatl word for the raised wooden platform on which dancers frequently perform. As in the case of the son jalisciense, the son huasteco has made a transition from regional to national popularity, primarily through its adoption by mariachis. Today, sones huastecos as played by mariachis may be written in a fast, dancelike tempo, or at a slower tempo for listening only.

The compás associated with the son huasteco is similar to that of the son jalisciense in that it consists of a two-measure repeated pattern, each half with a distinct rhythm. As before, one side of the pattern is straighter or less syncopated, the other more so. The primary element making the son huasteco sound unique is the use of *topes* (literally, "bumps"), percussive slaps the performer executes with the palm of his or her hand against the deadened strings of the guitar at particular moments while fanning out the fingers. Also characteristic of the son huasteco are frequent falsetto breaks in the vocal melody, a shift from chest voice to head voice when singing high notes.

In the following transcription (Example 3.4), note that the bass pattern (here played by the guitarrón in the mariachi version of the son huasteco) is the same as in Example 3.3, and that only the guitar style sets this genre apart. An "x" in the transcription indicates a tope or slap. As you can see, they occur every fourth beat, marking off groupings of three beats. Other notes (shaded in the TUBS transcription) indicate the strumming pattern. Search for recorded examples of well-known son huasteco pieces such as "La malagueña" (Woman from Málaga), "Serenata huasteca" (Huastec Serenade), and "El crucifijo de piedra" (The Crucifix of Stone) on your own, and listen for the rhythmic patterns described.

Mariachis frequently play salon dances such as waltzes, polkas, and even a few well-known nineteenth-century opera and Spanish zarzuela (operetta) overtures. The bolero and Colombian-derived cumbia are an important part of the repertory as well. However, **música ranchera** is the dominant

EXAMPLE 3.4: Son huasteco compás

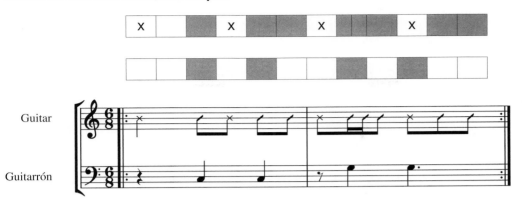

genre associated with mariachis. It emphasizes full-throated, emotional singing on a wide range of themes strongly felt by ordinary people such as pride of country and region, love, marital infidelity, nostalgic memories, and loss through death or abandonment. North American country music is thematically similar in many ways. The most common form of música ranchera, also known simply as ranchera, is a slow song in either duple or triple meter, usually featuring a solo singer. It appears to have developed as a working-class variant of an earlier urban song form known as the *canción*. In the same way that the corrido appears to have reworked the romance to reflect the perspective of the poor, the ranchera represents a transformation of middle-class song styles to reflect working-class tastes.

José Alfredo Jiménez (1926–1973) is the best-known composer of rancheras, including "El rey" (The King), "El hijo del pueblo" (The Son of the People), and "Cuando lloran los hombres" (When Men Cry), usually backed by mariachi groups. José Alfredo's songs, which are often quite romantic in sentiment, seem to speak to the Mexican psyche. One reason why they are so well received is that they reflect the experiences of the ordinary person. Jiménez was a somewhat controversial figure to the Mexican musical establishment of the mid-twentieth century. Not only did he not read music, but he could not play an instrument, and frequently wrote about topics such as heavy drinking. And yet he demonstrated amazing musical talent, composing hundreds of beloved songs by setting his poetry to melodies and singing them to his musician friends. They in turn would write the melodies down and arrange them for mariachi or other ensemble.

The lyrics to "El hijo del pueblo" provide a good introduction to Jiménez's work. In them, the singer expresses his pride in being a poor Mexican and an Indian ("a descendent of Cuauhtémoc") and the pleasure he receives in love, drinking, and singing. Since he has nothing, he has nothing to lose, unlike members of high society. "Cuauhtémoc" in the lyric refers to the last Aztec ruler of Tenochtitlán prior to its capture by the Spanish in the 1500s.

"El hijo del pueblo" (The Son of the People)

1. Es mi orgullo haber nacido,
   en el barrio más humilde,
   alejado del bullicio
   de la falsa sociedad.

   I am proud to have been born,
   In the humblest neighborhood,
   Far from the bustle
   Of pretentious high society.

5. Descendiente de Cuauhtémoc,
   mexicano por fortuna,
   desdichado en los amores,
   soy borracho y trovador.

   I am a descendent of Cuauhtémoc,
   A Mexican by fortune,
   Unhappy in love,
   I am a drunkard and a troubador.

6. Pero cuántos millonarios,
   quisieran vivir mi vida,
   pa' cantarle a la pobreza
   sin sentir ningún temor.

   But how many rich men,
   Would want to live my life,
   To sing to poverty
   Without fear.

8. Yo compongo mis canciones,
   pa' que el pueblo me las cante,
   y el día que el pueblo me falle,
   ese día voy a llorar.

   I write my songs,
   So that the people will sing them to me,
   And the day that the people fail me,
   On that day I will cry.

FIGURE 3.7 Jorge Negrete and María Elena Marques, *Cinema Reporter*, 1945 (Mexico City), cover photograph

Jorge Negrete (1911–1953) was arguably the greatest *charro* (horseman/cowboy) singer to perform in the música ranchera style in films, accompanied by mariachis. Negrete originally trained as an opera singer, but later turned to popular music where he made a strong impact throughout the Americas. Early in his career, he appeared on Mexico City radio stations and sang in New York nightclubs. In the 1930s, Negrete became a motion picture idol, playing characters that varied from rural *charros* to urban sophisticates. "¡Ay! Jalisco no te rajes" (Jalisco, Don't Back Down! Listening Guide 3.5), written as a polka and accompanied by a mariachi, is the title song from a famous film of the same name from 1941. It expresses pride in the state of Jalisco and compares its capital city of Guadalajara to a beautiful girl. The song is an example of música ranchera in the broader sense: a composition in any rhythm or style that lyrically references the countryside or local imagery and is performed to mariachi accompaniment.

Mariachis today play in a very wide range of contexts, from informal *al talón* (wandering, on-foot) performances at restaurants to formal events such as fiestas, parades,

⊚ Esperón: "¡Ay! Jalisco no te rajes" (Jalisco, Don't Back Down!)

Composer: Manuel Esperón

Lyricist: Ernesto M. Cortázar

Performer/instruments: Jorge Negrete, voice, with mariachi ensemble

Date of recording: 1940s

Genre: música ranchera

Form: verse–refrain form

Tempo/meter: quick duple meter

What to Listen for:

- Negrete's semiclassical vocal style and the sophisticated harmonized choral arrangement in the introduction reflecting urban influence

- The guitarrón's strong downbeats and the strumming instruments' backbeats

- The trumpet's running countermelody in the refrain

Time	Text	Translation	Description
0:00	¡Ay!, Jalisco, Jalisco, Jalisco, tú tienes tu novia que es Guadalajara.	Oh, Jalisco, Jalisco, Jalisco! You have your lover, and she is Guadalajara.	**Introduction** Vocal introduction, first two lines of stanza 1; sung by Negrete and chorus; unaccompanied
0:27	¡Ay, Jalisco, Jalisco, Jalisco! Tú tienes tu novia que es Guadalajara, muchacha bonita, la perla más rara de todo Jalisco es mi Guadalajara. Y me gusta escuchar los mariachis, cantar con el alma sus lindas canciones; oír como suenan esos guitarrónes y echarme un tequila con los valentones.	Oh, Jalisco, Jalisco, Jalisco! You have your lover, She is Guadalajara A beautiful girl, the rarest pearl Of all of Jalisco is my Guadalajara. I like to listen to the mariachis, To sing from my heart their beautiful songs; To hear how these guitarrónes sound, And to drink tequila with the brave ones.	**Stanzas 1–2** Negrete sings solo; trumpet and violins fill between vocal phrases with fragments of the melody
1:20	¡Ay, Jalisco no te rajes! Me sale del alma gritar con calor, abrir todo el pecho pa' echar este grito: ¡Qué lindo es Jalisco, palabra de honor!	Oh, Jalisco! Don't back down! A burning cry comes from my soul, I open my heart to give this shout: How beautiful is Jalisco; my word of honor!	**Refrain** Trumpet countermelody
1:44			**Interlude** Brief instrumental interlude separates verses

(continued)

Time	Text	Translation	Description
1:56	Pa' mujeres, Jalisco primero . . . En Jalisco se quiere a la buena . . .	For women, Jalisco is the best . . . In Jalisco one loves good girls . . .	**Stanzas 4–5** Same accompaniment as for stanzas 1–2
2:48	¡Ay, Jalisco no te rajes! . . .	Oh, Jalisco! Don't back down! . . .	**Refrain** Full mariachi with Negrete

explore

Many recordings by the major mariachis are readily available, including those by Mariachi Vargas de Tecalitlán, Mariachi Los Camperos, Mariachi Cobre, and other leading groups.

baptisms, political rallies, marriages, *quinceañeras* (celebrations for a girl's fifteenth birthday), and *serenatas* (serenades). They also give formal concerts, including performances with symphony orchestras. International mariachi festivals are held in places such as Guadalajara and Tucson, Arizona, and mariachi musicians now come from outside Mexico and the United States—Japan and Bulgaria, for instance. In the past, almost all mariachi musicians were male, but now professional women mariachis perform as well, such as in the Mariachi Reyna de Los Ángeles in California. This tradition has changed significantly over time, from an informal, regional practice to a highly polished and stylized commercial form. Mexico's famous mariachis often back superstar vocalists such as Vicente Fernández and Ana Gabriel in live performances, films, recordings, and on radio (Figure 3.8).

FIGURE 3.8 Vicente Fernández and Ana Gabriel performing in San Jose, California, 2004

Agustín Lara and the Bolero

Leading Mexican songwriters brought the bolero to a high point of popularity beginning in the late 1920s. Agustín Lara (1897–1970), a pianist, singer, and film actor, is probably the most famous. He wrote hundreds of songs, and is especially known for his evocative boleros, reflecting a sense of urban modernity. The Latin American bolero first developed in Cuba (see Chapter 5), but took on new musical characteristics and eventually reached wider international audiences after being adopted by Mexican composers and performers. Lara is a pivotal figure in the "Mexicanization" of the genre and its incorporation into film. He usually wrote for the piano rather than the guitar and for single voices rather than two or three, and he composed pieces that reconciled the bolero sound with international popular music of the period, especially mainstream jazz and crooner repertoire from the United States.

Lara's boleros are often in duple or quadruple meter and usually consist of two contrasting musical sections, which can be repeated. Some works from the 1930s typically incorporate the cinquillo rhythm found in older Cuban boleros. His lyrics present a bittersweet view of unfulfilled, lost, or idealized love, often from a male perspective. However, many women have sung his bo-

FIGURE 3.9 Agustín Lara, ca. 1940

leros, most notably Toña la Negra (María Antonia del Carmen Peregrino Álvarez, 1912–1982). Lara's works contribute to what some writers have called the "cult of the idealized woman." He tended to portray them either as saintly (as in the song "Santa") or as sinners (the song "Pecadora"), rarely in a more realistic or nuanced fashion. Lara sang many of his own songs, usually accompanying himself on the piano, in a flexible way that allowed the meaning of the poetry to be emphasized without always following a strict pulse.

Performers who have recorded Lara's famous bolero "Solamente una vez" (Only Once, Listening Guide 3.6) include Nat King Cole, Luis Miguel, Julio Iglesias, and Bing Crosby. The Trío Los Panchos recorded one of the best-known renditions. This ensemble, which formed in New York in 1944, consisted of two Mexicans and one Puerto Rican. They recorded the accompaniment of "Solamente una vez" (discussed later) on two guitars and **requinto** (here a small guitar tuned a fourth higher than a regular guitar). Two harmonizing voices support the lead vocal part to create a smooth blend, one that proved highly influential on future generations of Latin American

◎ Lara: "Solamente una vez" (Only Once)

Composer/lyricist: Agustín Lara

Date of composition: 1941

Performers/instruments: Trío Los Panchos (guitars and requinto, bass, bongo drum, maracas)

Date of recording: ca. 1950

Genre: bolero

Form: sung stanzas alternating with instrumental interludes

Tempo/meter: moderate simple quadruple

What to Listen for:

- The smooth, high tenor of the lead vocalist against the backup vocals, often performing complex rhythms in unison against the basic pulse of the song
- The percussion instruments laying down straight time, with the requinto playfully "fighting" the basic pulse, speeding up or slowing down at will
- Caribbean-derived percussion such as the bongo drum and maracas that accompany this bolero, common internationally by the 1940s

Time	Text	Translation	Description
0:00			**Introduction** Instrumental introduction played by guitars, requinto, bass, and percussion
0:19	Solamente una vez amé en la vida, Solamente una vez y nada más. Una vez nada mas en mi huerto brilló la esperanza, la esperanza que alumbra el camino de mi soledad. Una vez nada más se entrega el alma, con la dulce y total renunciación. Y cuando ese milagro realiza el prodigio de amarse hay campanas de fiesta que cantan en el corazón.	Only once did I love in my life, Only once and never again. Only once in my orchard Did hope shine, the hope That lights up the pathway of my solitude. Only once is one's soul delivered With sweet and total renunciation. And when this miracle Realizes the marvel of loving you Festive bells Sing in my heart.	**Stanzas 1–2** Solo voice with two lower voices singing in harmony, accompanied by the instrumental ensemble
1:29			**Interlude** Instrumental solo
1:48	Una vez nada más en mi huerto brilló la esperanza . . .	Only once in my orchard Did hope shine . . .	**Stanza** Repeat second part of stanza 1
2:04	Una vez nada más se entrega el alma . . .	Only once is my soul delivered . . .	**Stanza** Repeat stanza 2, performed as in stanza 1

singers. The *trío* is not only a trio (a group of three musicians), but also a very particular and Mexican type of vocal ensemble. Although the bolero is a song genre from the past, along with the ranchera it is still a well-appreciated form and the romantic music of Mexico par excellence.

Lara's contemporary, María Grever (María Joaquina de la Portilla Torres, 1894–1951), was the first Mexican woman to achieve significant fame as a composer and as a lyricist. Though she lived in the United States for many years, Grever composed more than 450 Spanish-language pieces. Like Lara, she wrote in several popular forms including the bolero, tango, waltz, and *canción*. Many of Latin America's most famous singers performed her music, including the tenors Alfonso Ortiz Tirado and José Mojica. Among her most famous songs are "Júrame" (Promise Me) and "Cuando vuelva a tu lado" (When I Return to Your Side). The latter was also sung in English as "What a Difference a Day Makes" by Frank Sinatra and Bing Crosby. Her songs are sophisticated, urbane evocations of both melancholy and passionate love.

Wind Bands

Wind instruments have long been important in Mexican music. From at least the mid-nineteenth century, ensembles boasted complete families of wind instruments, including woodwinds (flutes, clarinets, saxophones), brass (trumpets, trombones, tubas), and percussion (snare and bass drum, cymbals, timpani). The growth in the number of military and municipal bands brought such music to many areas of Mexico, even small villages, often providing the majority of secular musical entertainment. Wind band repertory reflected both European and Mexican musical tastes, including popular dance music and arrangements of operatic excerpts. The Banda de Policia (Police Band) of Mexico City, led for more than forty years by composer and conductor Velino M. Preza (1866–1945), was one of the most notable ensembles, and made many recordings (Figure 3.10). Some Mexican

FIGURE 3.10 Banda de Policia, directed by Velino M. Preza, in New York City, ca. 1900

wind band compositions, such as Genaro Codina's well-known *Marcha de Zacatecas* (Zacatecas March), dedicated to the city and state of the same name, maintain worldwide fame.

Today other types of wind bands, often regional in nature, now attract the kind of attention that earlier military bands enjoyed. The more than five hundred wind bands from the southern state of Oaxaca are central to everyday life in the region. Wind bands are featured at the annual Guelaguetza festival, held on two Mondays in July in Oaxaca City. The term Guelaguetza derives from a Zapotec word for offering; the ceremony was originally held to propitiate the gods in return for sufficient rain and a good harvest. Many Indian villages and towns in the state of Chiapas also sponsor wind bands, which serve an important ceremonial role in civic and religious fiestas.

Three wind band styles from the northernwestern states of Sinaloa, Zacatecas, and Durango are especially prominent today: **tamborazo** (Zacatecas), **pasito duranguense** (Chicago and Durango), and **banda sinaloense** (Sinaloa). They share a common repertory, feature similar instruments, and emphasize music for dancing. Though these bands are connected with urban areas, the themes of the songs they play and their costumes (cowboy hats, outfits, and boots) represent a rural, working-class sensibility. Percussion instruments such as snare and bass drums feature prominently in this music against the brass. The tuba plays a prominent bass line, with strong emphasis on the downbeat in either duple- or triple-meter pieces, and also executes rapid solo passages. Some groups incorporate an electric keyboard or synthesizer. Others stress a strong division between the parts: melody instruments (clarinets, trumpets, and saxophones), harmonic accompaniment playing on the "off-beat" (trombone and alto horn), bass line (tuba or other bass instrument), and percussion. All of these northern Mexican regional popular bands favor a strong, brassy sound.

Many regional variants of the wind band format can be heard today. Tamborazo from Zacatecas is named after the bass drum used in the ensemble. Banda Jerez de Zacatecas is one of the best-known groups. It features three singers and uses the following instrumentation: three clarinets, three trumpets, three trombones (with valves instead of the usual slide), tambora (a bass drum, p. 203), *tarola* (snare drum), cymbals, tuba, and two *armonías* (E-flat alto horns). The relatively new wind band genre called pasito duranguense originated in Chicago, where many Mexicans from the state of Durango have migrated. Groups playing this style are often smaller than those from Zacatecas or Sinaloa. Grupo Montez de Durango, from Chicago, is one of the leading ensembles; it often performs songs whose lyrics speak of the immigrant experience in the United States. Banda, or banda sinaloense, from the northern state of Sinaloa, is also called tambora after the large drum featured in the ensemble. It has attracted national and international attention. Banda Sinaloense "El Recodo" de Cruz Lizárraga, from the town of El Recodo, Sinaloa (near Matzatlán), founded and originally led by Cruz Lizárraga, is the most famous group. As with other popular ensembles, their repertory and performance styles have changed significantly over the years since Lizárraga founded the group in the early 1950s. Tambora instrumentation today is similar to that of the bands from Zacatecas, and they usually have about 15 members. *Technobanda*, a modern amplified and electrified version of banda sinaloense, is performed at an accelerated tempo by an ensemble consisting of electric bass (used in place of the tuba), electric guitar, keyboard, percussion, saxophone, trumpet, and vocalists.

FIGURE 3.11 A member of the Banda Sinaloense "El Recodo" de Cruz Lizárraga playing *armonía* (E-flat horn), 1999

Música Norteña

While the northwestern states of Mexico listen avidly to wind band repertoire of various kinds, northeastern border states favor accordion-based repertoire known as **música norteña** or norteño (similar to conjunto repertoire in Texas, p. 410). The typical música norteña ensemble includes a three-row diatonic button accordion, a stripped-down drum set consisting primarily of high hat and floor tom, a large guitar-type instrument with doubled courses of strings known as a **bajo sexto**, and either an acoustic or electric bass. Sometimes saxophone or other wind instruments are used in these groups, along with electric keyboard. Prominent bands include the previously mentioned Los Tigres del Norte, Ramón Ayala, and Los Invasores de Nuevo León.

Música norteña developed as a discrete musical style at the turn of the twentieth century on both sides of the border. It resulted from multiple influences including the broad dissemination of the button accordion internationally and the presence of many German and Czech settlers along the border. Accordionists in this style perform flashy right-hand melodic lines, downplaying the bass keys and harmonic possibilities of the instrument, as the bajo sexto and bass fill that role. In polka-influenced music, the mainstay of the repertoire, the bass plays on strong beats while the bajo sexto alternates strumming on backbeats with the execution of melodic runs and fills. Other genres performed by música norteña groups include Mexican versions of the **cumbia** (Example 10.2; "Mi gente," Listening Guide 10.6), as well as boleros, rancheras, and waltzes. In recent decades, a more commercial-sounding version of música norteña has developed in the United States, known as música tejana, which is characterized by prominent use of synthesizers and drum machine rather than acoustic instruments. Search on your own for videos and recorded music of the música norteña artists just mentioned and compare them with tejano (p. 409) performers such as Little Joe y la Familia, Jay Pérez, La Mafia, and Selena.

Rock and Roll and Rock Music in Mexico

In the 1950s and 1960s, Mexican youth began to listen to British and American rock and roll and rock music, which they associated with sophisticated, international fashion. The Mexican media initially viewed rock and roll positively and promoted the youth trend. Local talent developed as a response, with emphasis on the *refrito* or cover tune; groups such as Los Locos del Ritmo and Los Blue Jeans initially performed Spanish-language versions of standard North American hits. The emergence of *rocanrol* coincided with the rise of the Mexican urban middle class, enabled by postwar political and economic stability and growth.

In the 1960s, Mexican rock increasingly adopted an attitude of defiance, reflecting trends in American and British rock, and attracted governmental scrutiny and censorship. The audience for rock also expanded significantly to include the urban poor, not just the middle class, which contributed to the music's increasingly oppositional tone. The arrival of U.S. *jipis* (hippies) and drug culture created controversy as well. Despite the fact that the genre had been imported from abroad, rock came to be viewed as the "authentic" voice of Mexican youth within a surprisingly short period of time. Students adopted it as they staged protests calling for government reform. In response, government spokesmen began characterizing rock as dangerous to Mexican society and an affront to traditional values and culture, and on several notorious occasions government forces clashed violently with protesters, including the infamous massacre at Tlatelolco in 1968.

From the late 1960s, influential rock groups such as La Revolución de Emiliano Zapata, Peace and Love, Reforma Agraria, and Three Souls in My Mind (now called El Tri) spearheaded a movement called La Onda (The Wave), which advocated against governmental repression of current popular youth culture such as rock music. Some of these names refer to major figures and initiatives of the Mexican Revolution of the 1910s (Zapata, agrarian reform) and suggest the revolutionary cultural experiments being undertaken by youth of the 1970s and 1980s. El Tri has remained active and put a particularly Mexican stamp on their music. Their song "Abuso de autoridad" (Abuse of Authority) still evokes a sense of opposition: "Vivir en Mexico es lo peor/nuestro gobierno está muy mal/y nadie puede desvariar/porque lo llevan a encerrar" (To live in Mexico is the worst/Our government is very bad/And nobody can protest because they'll be taken to jail). New rock music figures appearing from the 1980s include Julieta Venegas and the bands Café Tacuba, Maná, Molotov, Jaguares (previously Caifanes), and Maldita Vecindad. They mix a wide range of musical influences in their repertory: standard rock, samples of traditional Mexican music, funk grooves and ska grooves (the latter especially associated with Maná), hip-hop, electronic music, punk, heavy metal, and others.

Café Tacuba, founded in 1989, is one of the leading Mexican rock en español (Spanish-language rock, p. 152) bands today; it is named after the famous restaurant of the same name on Tacuba Street in Mexico City. The group presents an eclectic mix of styles that blends elements of Mexican folk music (incorporating genres from Veracruz, for example), punk and electronic music (the group used a drum machine instead of a live drummer until about 2002), rock, and música norteña. Café Tacuba's very popular song "Chilanga Banda" (Mexico City Gang) is a partly sung, partly spoken recitation of Mexico City slang—over a funk/hip-hop beat—that plays on the sounds of the Spanish consonant "ch" and the word *chilanga* (meaning someone or something from Mexico City). It refers to modern life among a sector of the working class: "Ya chole chango chilango/que chafa chamba te chutas/no checa andar de tacuche/y chale con la charola" (Cut it out, Mexico City dude/What an uncool job you have!/You don't look good in a suit/And what's with the badge?). Café Tacuba's music has been used in the prominent Mexican films *Amores perros* (2000) and *Y tu mamá también* (2001). Argentine composer Gustavo Santaolla, who wrote the critically acclaimed musical score to *Amores perros*, has produced most of Café Tacuba's albums (see Chapters 9 and 10).

"Eres" (Listening Guide 3.7), the song , comes from their album *Cuatro Caminos* (Four Roads) of 2003, inspired by the name of a Mexico City subway station. "Eres" discusses the passion of all-consuming love, reinforced by the frequent repetition of the word *eres* (you are). The song is a carefully crafted studio product, typical of urban popular music. Most of the song is written over a four-measure recurrent harmonic pattern in

FIGURE 3.12 Café Tacuba performing at the Latin Grammy awards. Houston, Texas, 2008

⊚ Café Tacuba: "Eres" (You Are)

Composer/lyricist: Café Tacuba

Date of composition: 2003

Performers/instruments: Café Tacuba (rock band with voices)

Genre: rock en español

Tempo/meter: moderate duple meter

What to Listen for:

- Very "empty," sparsely orchestrated sections featuring acoustic guitar contrasting with the louder, full rock sound
- Two-measure bass pattern, reminiscent of the compás in the Mexican son, frequently complementing the recurrent two-measure rhythmic figure played on the drum set during the verse
- Use of studio techniques (instrumental layering, altered vocal production, synthesizer)

Time	Text	Translation	Description
0:00			**Introduction** Instrumental introduction
0:27	Eres lo que más quiero en este mundo, eso eres . . .	You're the one I love the most in this world, this you are . . .	**Stanza 1** A sparse section featuring primarily acoustic guitar and voice, along with electric bass and drums
0:52	Eres cuando despierto lo primero, eso eres . . .	You are [the first thing I see] when I awaken, this you are . . .	**Stanza 2** Entrance of electric guitar, layering over other instruments
1:18	Qué mas puedo decirte, tal vez puedo mentirte sin razón . . .	What more can I tell you, perhaps I can lie to you without reason . . .	**Bridge** A constrasting **B** section, harmonically distinct, louder, bringing the music to a climax; ends with break and return to acoustic guitar, intimate sound
1:43			**Interlude** Instrumental interlude, similar to introduction, featuring acoustic guitar picking, strummed electric guitar, and synthesizer melody
2:13	Eres el tiempo que comparto, eso eres . . .	You are the time that I share, this you are . . .	**Stanza 3** Section sung over a single strummed chord on the electric guitar, creating a sense of dissonance and tension; drums and bass drop out

(continued)

Time	Text	Translation	Description
2:38	Soy él que quererte quiere como nadie soy . . .	I am he who in loving you loves like no one else . . .	**Stanza 4** Full instrumentation enters once again
3:04	Aquí estoy a tu lado y espero aquí . . .	Here I am at your side and I wait here . . .	**Bridge** Same accompaniment as in the previous bridge
3:48			**Ending** Full instrumentation; vamp continues, but with a new altered chord

A minor: $Am–C–E^7–E^7$, occasionally with more extended and jazz-influenced chords. Note the use of both electric and acoustic guitars in the recording, at times used separately, at other times layered on one another, as well as the use of synthesizer and the studio-altered vocals toward the end.

Classical Music

Classical music on the European model was first introduced in colonial-era Mexico soon after European conquest in 1521 and has had a significant presence ever since. After independence from Spain in 1821, sacred art music continued to be performed in Mexico's many cathedrals and parish churches, as it had since the arrival of Christianity. Secular instrumental and vocal music particularly flourished after independence in public theaters, as well as in the salons (private homes) of the upper and middle classes. Before independence, the Church had been the principal patron of formal musical events. Subsequently, private and governmental initiatives played a greater role, and by the mid-twentieth century a large infrastructure for classical music existed in Mexico. Some of the important components of this musical establishment included music conservatories; professional orchestras, chamber music ensembles, and opera companies; and governmental patronage of music, including support for composers, performers, and music scholars. This section investigates several important topics among many relating to classical music in Mexico—piano music, music for theater and film, and symphonic music—and features three of Mexico's most important twentieth-century composers: Manuel M. Ponce, Carlos Chávez, and Silvestre Revueltas.

FIGURE 3.13 Sheet music, Julio Ituarte, *Écos de México*, title page

Piano Music

The piano had a significant impact in Mexico from the end of the colonial period. Many middle- and upper-class Mexican families owned pianos, which were often played by women. An ability to play the piano was considered a sign of sophistication and of good upbringing, much as in the United States at the time. Preferred repertory included arrangements of works from the musical theater, Mexican and Cuban **danzas** (two-part, 32-measure solo piano works based on the Caribbean habanera rhythm; see Chapter 2 and Listening Guide 2.10), as well as classical pieces. From the nineteenth century onward, Mexican and visiting foreign virtuosos performed works by Franz Liszt (1811–1886), Frédéric Chopin (1810–1849), and other European and Mexican composers in public performance venues throughout the country.

Composer-pianists such as Julio Ituarte (1845–1905), Ernesto Elorduy (1853–1913), and Ricardo Castro (1864–1907) wrote many works for solo piano in the standard European forms. They also composed nationalistic pieces that reflected their interest in Mexico's rich local heritage. In his *Écos de México: Aires nacionales* (Echoes of Mexico: National Tunes), Ituarte incorporated numerous well-known son melodies. His work is an elegant musical homage to Mexico that shows the melodic richness of the folk music on which it is based, as well as Ituarte's harmonic inventiveness, grasp of balanced musical form, and melodic ingenuity in quoting and reworking the traditional sones in novel ways. Mexican composers also wrote many piano pieces based on nineteenth-century social dance forms such as the waltz or mazurka. The best-known example is probably the world-famous waltz "Sobre las olas" (Over the Waves) by the indigenous Mexican composer Juventino Rosas (1868–1894).

Music for Theater and Film

In nineteenth-century Mexico, comic and serious operas in Italian became increasingly prominent forms of expression, as did operas by Mexican composers and Spanish theatrical forms such as the zarzuela. Among Mexican composers writing operas on Italian models at the time was Melesio Morales (1838–1908). Morales studied composition in Europe and wrote four operas in Italian that were performed at the National Theater in Mexico City, the most famous being *Ildegonda* (1865). Foreshadowing later developments,

Aniceto Ortega's (1825–1875) *Guatimotzin* (1871) was one of the first Mexican operas to deal with a local subject. It told the story of the defense of Tenochtitlán by the Aztecs against the Spanish.

Mexican composers have continued to write operas. *La mulata de Córdoba* (1948) by José Pablo Moncayo (1912–1958) retells the Mexican legend of a mulata enchantress who vanished in a puff of smoke when called to appear before the Spanish Inquisition. The most successful Mexican opera composer, however, may be Daniel Catán (1949–2011), whose operas include *Florencia en el Amazonas* (Florencia in the Amazon, 1996); *La hija de Rapaccini* (Rapaccini's Daughter, 1990), based on Mexican writer Octavio Paz's play warning of the dangers of blind science; and *Salsipuedes, a Tale of Love, War and Anchovies* (2004). Catán's Spanish-language opera *Il Postino* (The Postman), based on the 1994 film about the life of Chilean poet Pablo Neruda, premiered in Los Angeles in 2010, starring the world-famous Spanish tenor Plácido Domingo as Neruda.

explore

Recordings of Morales's *Ildegonda* and Catan's *La hija de Rapaccini* and *Florencia en el Amazonas* are commercially available.

In contrast to operatic repertory with its universal themes, zarzuela of the nineteenth and early twentieth centuries frequently based its stories on Spanish (or Mexican) topics. It also incorporated spoken dialogue instead of the recitative (declamatory, speech-like singing) used in opera, and prominently featured popular dance rhythms and song forms. Popular zarzuelas include Tomás Bretón's *La verbena de la paloma* (The Festival of the Dove, 1894), from Spain, and Luis G. Jordá's Mexican work *Chin-Chun-Chan* (1904). Musical revues, known as **revistas**, also held the stage in Mexico during the first half of the twentieth century. These were similar in many respects to Broadway musical revues such as the Ziegfeld Follies of the 1910s and 1920s. The shows had a minimal plot and stressed songs (often with erotic lyrics), dances by scantily clad chorus girls, and comic skits. However, Mexican revistas were often more politically charged and satirical than their Broadway counterparts, which sometimes led to their suppression or censorship by governmental authorities.

In the twentieth century, music to accompany film assumed an important role. From about 1900 through the 1920s, piano, organ, or orchestral music almost always accompanied silent films. From the 1930s, Mexican motion picture studios produced films with sound tracks and employed some of Mexico's leading songwriters and composers; their films utilized scores featuring full orchestras, as well as mariachis and other Mexican ensembles. A notable documentary film that included an important classical score was *Redes* (The Wave, 1936), with music by Revueltas. The motion picture industry enjoyed a golden age between the 1930s and 1950s. Sound tracks with a variety of musical styles were featured in many film genres: the sentimental tearjerker; the romantic swashbuckler; the *comedia*

explore

DVDs of the following classic Mexican motion pictures in various genres, all of which include musical scores, are available: the *cabaretera* film *Aventurera* (Adventuress, 1950); the rural dramas *María Candelaria* (1944) and *Flor Silvestre* (Wild Flower, 1943), with Dolores del Río and Pedro Armendáriz; and the comedy *Dos tipos de cuidado* (Two Careful Fellows, 1953), with Jorge Negrete and Pedro Infante.

ranchera (rural comedy); *cabaretera* films, dark tales of urban deception and redemption, often dealing with cabaret girls, nightclubs, and prostitutes; and comedies featuring the antics of Cantinflas (Mario Moreno Reyes, 1911–1993) or Tin-Tan (Germán Valdés, 1915–1973). A fair number of film releases continued to center around song and orchestral music through the 1970s. Films from past decades continue to air on television and circulate on DVD, and songs from the cinema retain an important place in the Mexican musical imagination.

Classical Repertoire in the Twentieth Century

Like their counterparts in the United States, Mexican classical composers embrace international models while also referencing local musical, literary, and historical elements in their works. During the *Porfiriato*, or rule of Porfirio Díaz, the Mexican government gave subsidies to musicians to study in Europe with master teachers. Paris was an attractive location for study for composers such as Ricardo Castro and Manuel M. Ponce. When they returned to Mexico, they opened their own private music schools, and many taught at the National Conservatory in Mexico City.

The Mexican Revolution (1910–1920) disrupted but did not end concert life. In its aftermath, the Mexican government's interest in encouraging representations of indigeneity and Mexican themes encouraged stylistic innovation in many artistic fields, including music. Diego Rivera painted his famous murals on Mexican subjects at this time. With her paintings representing indigenous themes, especially the *tehuana* (woman from the Isthmus of Tehuantepec), Frida Kahlo, Rivera's wife, also contributed to this trend. Concert activity increased significantly from the 1920s. In 1928, composer Carlos Chávez founded the Orquesta Sinfónica de México (Mexican Symphonic Orchestra, now the Orquesta Sinfónica Nacional—the National Symphony Orchestra), which he directed for many years. Under Chávez's leadership, the ensemble performed numerous works by Mexican composers, North Americans such as Aaron Copland, and Europeans. Chávez also performed his own pieces regularly, as well as those of Ponce, Revueltas, José Rolón, and other Mexican composers.

The opening of the Palacio de Bellas Artes (Palace of Fine Arts) in Mexico City in 1934 stimulated the growth of classical music. This important performance

FIGURE 3.14 Palacio de Bellas Artes, Mexico City

space is located in the city center, near the Zócalo (the main plaza), the Cathedral, and the National Palace, and is the venue for orchestral, chamber music, choral, operatic, theater, and dance performances, including the Ballet Folklórico de México, the professional folkloric dance troupe.

The number of professional and conservatory orchestras grew significantly from the 1950s, as did public appreciation for orchestral music. Some of the techniques used by recent generations of composers—tonality, atonality, **electroacoustical** music, musical style crossovers, and so on—are discussed in greater detail in Chapter 9 and in the appendix "Elements of Music." The final section of this chapter explores music by the three best-known Mexican composers of the first half of the twentieth century: Ponce, Chávez, and Revueltas. Of course, many others also contributed to the development of Mexico's musical life. Julián Carrillo (1875–1965), a microtonal composer and the inventor of the Sonido Trece (Thirteenth Sound) method of composition, was of the same generation as Ponce. Other important twentieth-century and contemporary composers include Blas Galindo (1910–1993), José Pablo Moncayo, Mario Lavista (b. 1943), and Ana Lara (b. 1959).

Manuel M. Ponce

Manuel María Ponce (1882–1948) wrote in many genres, but is especially noted for his art songs (many based on traditional Mexican melodies), works for solo guitar and piano, and orchestral music. He was born in Fresnillo, Zacatecas, but grew up in the city of Aguascalientes. Between 1904 and 1907 he studied music in Italy and Germany. After his return to Mexico, he composed, performed, taught music, and developed an interest in his own country's musical heritage. His 1913 lectures on the **canción mexicana** (traditional Mexican song) encouraged interest in musical nationalism among other Mexican composers. Ponce went into self-imposed exile between 1915 and 1917 during the Mexican Revolution because his personal circumstances put him at odds with the political faction then in power. After his return, he continued his earlier musical activities until 1925, when he moved to Paris to study composition with Paul Dukas; he returned permanently to Mexico in 1933.

Ponce's friendship with Spanish guitarist Andrés Segovia (1893–1987) led to multiple artistic collaborations: Segovia encouraged Ponce to write works for the guitar, which Segovia then edited, performed, and promoted. These became cornerstones of the modern classical guitar repertory. Ponce was also an outstanding pianist. His output represents an ecclectic mix of compositional styles, ranging from late **Romanticism** in his early works, to **impressionism** in the **symphonic poem** for orchestra *Chapultepec* (1934),

explore

Blas Galindo's *Sones de Mariachi* and José Pablo Moncayo's *Huapango* (both for orchestra), based on Mexican traditional *sones,* are attractive pieces. Mario Lavista's *Cinco danzas breves* (Five Short Dances) is a set of short, modern pieces. Recordings of all of these works are available.

explore

Ponce's most-famous song is "Estrellita" (Little Star); his arrangements of traditional Mexican songs for classical guitar such as *Tres canciones populares mexicanas,* played by Andrés Segovia, are well known. All have been recorded.

to atonality in the Sonata for Violin or Viola (1939). His guitar and piano **sonatas** are particularly noteworthy. Ponce's symphonic poem *Ferial* (1940) uses Mexican indigenous and mestizo melodies when referencing fiestas in a Mexican village. Listening Guide 3.8 is the third movement

LISTENING guide 3.8

◎ Ponce: *Concierto del sur*, third movement

Composer: Manuel M. Ponce

Date of composition: 1941

Performers/instruments: Alfonso Moreno and Orquesta Filarmónica de la Ciudad de México; Enrique Bátiz, conductor (solo guitar, orchestra)

Genre: guitar concerto

Tempo/meter: *allegro moderato*, triple meter

What to Listen for:

- Eclectic style of the guitar writing, with some sections containing flashy strumming, pedal notes, and arpeggios, and other sections that are more melodically or harmonically oriented and that blend easily with the orchestra

- Ponce's tonal harmonic language, and his melodic themes influenced by Spanish and Mexican traditional music; most of the orchestral texture is homophonic, with the accompaniment supporting a single prominent melody

Time	Description
0:00	Orchestral introduction: a lively string melody in counterpoint, followed by winds and percussion
0:08	Guitar enters with strummed chords, first alone, then supported by bass and flute; themes from the introduction enter again thereafter
0:35	Running sixteenth-note passages in guitar part supported by light orchestral accompaniment
1:01	Three-measure "Spanish-tinged" melodic fragment introduced and developed; strummed chords interrupt periodically
1:36	Orchestral section, foregrounding the strings
1:45	Guitar reenters with new melody that includes a pedal or sustained bass tone
2:14	Variation on a previous melodic theme is heard, but supported by different chords; followed by a three-note motive on the guitar, supported by the orchestra
2:57	Guitar plays another new theme in a major key, cycling through many chords in succession; later begins to develop and vary the same musical motive; finally, arpeggiates rapidly, ceding the melody to the orchestra, which picks up the same theme
4:17	Orchestral interlude leads into a second section of guitar arpeggiation, supporting orchestral melodies; tambourine enters during a new iteration of the central theme in the orchestra; moments of intense guitar strumming and back-and-forth interaction between guitar and ensemble conclude the piece

of his *Concierto del Sur* (Concerto of the South, 1941) for guitar and orchestra. It presents a carefully balanced musical dialogue between the guitar soloist and the orchestra and shows an inventiveness of original musical ideas. Ponce wrote it for a reduced ensemble (strings, woodwinds, timpani, and tambourine, but no brass instruments) so as not to cover the softer-sounding guitar.

Carlos Chávez

Carlos Chávez (1899–1978), who studied with Ponce in the 1910s, was another of Mexico's leading composers. He also wielded great power over Mexico's musical establishment as an arts administrator and conductor. The orchestral pieces *Sinfonía india* (Indian Symphony, 1935) and the ballet score *Caballos de vapor [H.P.]* (Horse Power, 1926) are among his most important works. He also wrote five other symphonies, string quartets, and a great deal of piano music. Much of his music is modernist and experimental and is abstract—that is, without descriptive references, unlike the music for *Caballos de vapor*, for instance, which was used to accompany choreographed movements titled "Dance of Man," "Boat to the Tropics," "The Tropics," and "Dance of Men and Machines."

Chávez's *Sinfonía india* (Listening Guide 3.9) was composed in New York in 1935 for a radio concert. It is a one-movement orchestral piece in five sections and uses an expanded percussion section. The latter includes several indigenous instruments: butterfly cocoons, deer hooves, and a re-creation of an Aztec drum (the teponaztli; see Figure 2.3). It is one of few works by Chávez to quote genuine indigenous Mexican musical themes, in this case from the Cora and Seri tribes. Example 3.5 reproduces a Cora melody; it appears at various points in the piece, for instance at 0:39.

EXAMPLE 3.5: Cora melody as it appears in Carlos Chávez's *Sinfonía india*, mm. 42–47

◎ Chávez: *Sinfonía india* (Indian Symphony)

Composer: Carlos Chávez

Date of composition: 1935

Performers/instruments: Orquesta Sinfónica de Xalapa; Luis Herrera de la Fuente, conductor (orchestra)

Genre: one-movement symphony

Form: five sections

Tempo/meter: varies

What to Listen for:

- "Busy" texture of the piece, which uses looped melodic fragments as an ostinato against which to contrast other melodies

- Strong rhythmic accents used in unconventional ways; cannot be said to have a set beat or pulse, but instead shifts the pulse frequently

- Pentatonic melodies, constructed from a scale consisting of five notes rather than the seven typically found in Western music. Pentatonic melodies appear frequently in Mexican indigenous music, and Chávez seems to be referencing "Indianness" in this way

Time	Description
0:00	**Section I:** *Vivo* (very fast) Layers of melodic motives and rhythmic ostinatos; trumpet and piccolo prominent; indigenous percussion used frequently, and insistent, driving rhythms heard throughout; Cora melody ("The Course of the Sun") at 0:39, and in variation thereafter, along with other pentatonic melodies
2:06	**Section II:** *Allegretto cantabile* (somewhat quickly in a singing style) A contrasting slower section; broad, lyrical theme repeated many times; prominent use of indigenous percussion, especially deer hooves and the teponatzli; subsections within the main section present variations on the Cora melodic and rhythmic material through 3:46; at 3:47, a new theme introduced based on a Seri melody ("The Joyous Wind") and presented in variation through 5:50
5:50	**Section III:** *Allegro* (fast) Returns to Cora theme, in variation, accelerating the tempo; indigenous and classical percussion used forcefully in tandem; high flute sounds referencing prominence of flutes in native traditions; at 6:42 second theme presented, more syncopated and accented with maracas and other percussion
7:15	**Section IV:** *Andante con moto* (slower with motion) Second contrasting slower section; Seri melody from section II repeated and varied; broad, lyrical mood reestablished
8:07	**Section V:** *Vivo* (very fast) Very fast ending section, similar to section I with small, looped melodies; tempo accelerates, and a few new melodic themes presented (for instance at 8:35), also in looped form

As part of the generation that came to artistic maturity in the 1920s, Chávez took inspiration from indigenous Mexican themes. He recognized that the strength of indigenous music was "rooted in its intrinsic variety, in the freedom and amplitude of its modes, and scales, in the richness of its instrumental and sound elements, and in the simplicity and purity of its melodies." Besides *Sinfonía india*, Chavez's native-inspired works included *Los cuatro soles* (The Four Suns, 1925) and *Xochipilli* (1940), named after a deity associated with art and beauty, and subtitled "An Imagined Aztec Music." Idealized representations of indigeneity by musicians such as Chávez, as well as by the painters Rivera and Orozco, represented an important step toward valorizing indigenous culture within Mexico.

Silvestre Revueltas

Composer and violinist Silvestre Revueltas (1899–1940) (Figure 3.15) lived in a number of locations before settling permanently in Mexico City (he was born in the state of Durango). Because of the Mexican Revolution, Revueltas moved as a young man to the United States, studying and working as a musician in Austin and San Antonio, Texas; Chicago, Illinois; and Mobile, Alabama. By the time that Chávez called him home to Mexico in 1928 to be assistant conductor of the Orquesta Sinfónica de México, Revueltas was a fully formed musician. During the last ten years of his life, he composed a series of very original compositions. These mature works demonstrate the composer's love for and understanding of his country; they also represent Revueltas's own personal eclectic compositional style and sense of humor. For instance, his music for the puppet play *El renacuajo paseador* (The Strolling Tadpole, 1933, based on a poem by Columbian Rafael Pombo), the film scores to *Redes* (The Wave, 1935) and *La noche de los Mayas* (Night of the Mayas, 1939), the chamber piece *Ocho por Radio* (Eight for Radio, 1934), and String Quartet No. 4 (1932, subtitled *Música de feria*, Festival Music) all have strikingly original rhythmic, melodic, and harmonic elements. Some of the devices he used in these pieces include sesquiáltera (here the alternation between triple and compound duple meter), innovative orchestration techniques (the juxtaposition of

FIGURE 3.15 Silvestre Revueltas, 1930s

instruments such as tuba and piccolo), and the quotation of traditional Mexican repertoire.

Sensemayá (1938), a **programmatic** piece (i.e., based on a specific theme or idea) for orchestra, is Revueltas's most famous work; it is inspired by Cuban poet Nicolás Guillén's poem of the same name, one that

---

LISTENING guide **3.10**

◎ Revueltas: *Sensemayá*

Composer: Silvestre Revueltas

Date of composition: 1938

Performer/instruments: Los Angeles Philharmonic; Esa-Pekka Salonen, conductor (orchestra)

Genre: symphonic poem

Form: four sections

Tempo/meter: primarily $\frac{7}{8}$ $\left(\frac{2}{4} + \frac{3}{8}\right)$, but with occasional alternating meters

What to Listen for:
- Prominent tuba solo, brass and woodwind solos
- Irregular, shifting meters, low ostinatos in a minor key, and chromatic melodies
- Contrasting blocks of orchestral sound (low brass, trumpets, woodwinds, etc.)

Time	Description
0:00	**Section I** starts in $\frac{7}{8}$ meter with a low drone in the woodwinds and a low ostinato in the percussion
0:22	Tuba solo
0:55	Muted trumpet doubles the principal melody
1:25	Woodwinds join, accompanied by accents in low horns and percussion
1:51	Trumpets and strings play their own repeated patterns; melodies become more agitated as the segment climaxes
3:00	Trumpet leads again; volume decreases; drones and ostinatos become more audible as the texture thins
3:43	**Section II** begins with a loud chord, then moves to $\frac{2}{4} + \frac{3}{8}$ meter. Prominent eight-note melody played by the trombones and later the trumpets imitates the eight-syllable "Mayombé-bombe-mayombé" incantations and evokes the confrontation with the snake
4:18	**Section III** opens with a drop in volume. Section I material returns, and pulse reverts to $\frac{7}{8}$ meter. Clave sticks heard prominently
4:35	Brass instruments used to create loud, contrasting blocks of sound
4:59	Flute, clarinet, and marimba take the principal melody
5:26	Brass and percussion dominate once more
5:52	Climactic segment based on section II with brass and cymbal crashes
6:03	**Section IV** builds tension and volume to a climax with theme from section I; heavy use of percussion

describes the ritual killing of a snake. The strong rhythmic accents of the poem's refrain, "¡Mayombé—bombe—mayombé!" referencing Bantu religious culture, are mirrored in the irregular accents of the musical composition, and in particular its melodic phrases. The killing of the snake here can be viewed metaphorically as an exorcism of slavery, as well as a broader struggle between good and evil. *Sensemayá* creates a hypnotic spell with its rhythmic, serpentine ostinatos and repeated solo tuba lines. It stresses the irregular meter of $\frac{7}{8}$ and builds gradually to a climax, as does the poem; towards the end of the work the main themes are combined in a complex, **contrapuntal** manner.

CONCLUSION

This chapter has introduced many important genres of Mexican music. Other styles and traditions have been omitted for lack of space, including the influence of North American jazz and hip-hop, dance dramas with music and other music of indigenous communities, the activities of current composers of classical music, the varied marimba traditions of southern Mexico, the characteristics of other regional son genres, protest song, most sacred music traditions, and so on. Chapter 3 has emphasized forms of Mexican music that are known both nationally and globally, and notes the ongoing give-and-take between Mexican and North American society and musical forms. More information on the latter theme is available in Chapter 10. Mexican performers and composers operate internationally, with an especially strong presence in the United States and elsewhere in Latin America, yet especially look within their own borders to develop musical repertories and institutions that fulfill artistic needs. Mexico's most important musical contributions include Mariachi Vargas de Tecalitlán, its vast bolero and romantic song tradition, its rancheras that reminisce nostalgically on past loves and the experiences of rural life, the corrido with its recounting of epochal tales, harp traditions from Veracruz and other states, musical film performances by Jorge Negrete and other stars, and the repertoire of recent rock en español groups. Likewise, the classical compositions of Manuel M. Ponce, Carlos Chávez, Silvestre Revueltas, and other Mexican composers reverberate in concert halls throughout the world.

KEY TERMS

arpeggiation	jarana	sesquiáltera
bajo sexto	mariachi	son
banda sinaloense	mazurka	sonata
canción mexicana	mestizo	son huasteco
compás	música norteña	(or huapango)
contrapuntal	música ranchera	son jalisciense
corrido	pasito duranguense	son jarocho
danza	programmatic	symphonic poem
electroacoustic	redoble	tamborazo
guitarrón	requinto	waltz
impressionism	revista	zapateado
jarabe	Romanticism	

FURTHER READING

Bitrán, Yael, and Ricardo Miranda, eds. *Diálogo de resplandores: Carlos Chávez y Silvestre Revueltas*. Mexico City: CONACULTA, 2002.

Burr, Ramiro. *The Billboard Guide to Tejano and Regional Mexican Music*. New York: Billboard Books, 1999.

Parker, Robert. *Carlos Chávez: Mexico's Modern-Day Orpheus*. Boston, MA: Twayne Publishers, 1983.

Pedelty, Mark. *Musical Ritual in Mexico City: From the Aztec to NAFTA*. Austin: University of Texas Press, 2004.

Ragland, Cathy. *Música Norteña: Mexican Migrants Creating a Nation between Nations*. Philadelphia, PA: Temple University Press, 2009.

Russell, Craig. *From Serra to Sancho: Music and Pageantry in the California Missions*. New York: Oxford University Press, 2009.

Simonett, Helena. *Banda: Mexican Musical Life Across Borders*. Middletown, CT: Wesleyan University Press, 2001.

Stevenson, Robert. *Music in Mexico*. New York: Crowell, 1952.

Zolov, Eric. *Refried Elvis: The Rise of the Mexican Counterculture*. Berkeley: University of California Press, 1999.

FURTHER LISTENING

La Bamba: Sones Jarochos from Veracruz. José Gutiérrez and Los Hermanos Ochoa. Smithsonian Folkways, 2003.

The Mexican Revolution: Corridos about the Heroes and Events 1910–1920 and Beyond! Arhoolie, 1997

Revueltas: The Centenial Anthology. RCA Red Seal, 1999.

¡Viva ed Mariachi!: Nati Cano's Mariachi Los Camperos. Nati Cano and Los Camperos. Smithsonian Folkways, 2002.

FURTHER VIEWING

Chulas Fronteras. Les Blank, director. Brazos Films, 2003.

Gulf of Mexico

Cuba

Mexico

Belize City
CHIAPAS
Belize

Jamaica

Guatemala

La Ceiba
San Pedro Sula
Quetzatelnango
Honduras
Guatemala City
Santa Ana
Tegucigalpa

Caribbean Sea

San Salvador
San Miguel
El Salvador

Chinandega
Nicaragua

"ATLANTIC" COASTAL REGION

León
Managua
Masaya

Pacific Ocean

Costa Rica
Puntarenas
Alajuela
San José

Panama City
DARIÉN MTS.

Panama

Colom

0   100   200   300   400
Kilometers

0   50   100   150   200   250
Miles

4

Central America, Colombia, and Venezuela

T.M. SCRUGGS

Central America

The more than 42 million inhabitants (2009 estimate) of this relatively small isthmus correspond to the highest nation state density in Latin America per square mile, forming seven contemporary countries, from northwest to southeast: Guatemala, Belize, Honduras, El Salvador, Nicaragua, Costa Rica, and Panama. Although it is a relatively small geographical area—a narrow arc measuring less than 202,000 square miles and about 1,140 miles end to end—this zone encompasses a variety of ecosystems. Central America can be roughly divided into Pacific Ocean– and Caribbean Sea–bordering zones. The northeastern Caribbean region consists mostly of low-lying tropical plains and savannahs, crossed by several major rivers in Honduras and Nicaragua. The southwestern Pacific region contains a more mountainous central area, from the large Guatemalan highlands through to southern Costa Rica, together with the coastal plains and hills that hold the bulk of the population in El Salvador and Nicaragua. As its name implies, Central America is a meeting ground between two large continents, and shares flora and fauna from both. It contains the narrowest land division between the Atlantic and Pacific Oceans—only 30 miles in one part of Panama—which has made it a focus of outside economic and political interest since the conquest.

◄ FIGURE 4.1 Map of Central America

A Brief History

The Caribbean region was inhabited by peoples related through a shared Chibcha language prior to European contact. The remoteness of much of the terrritory and a lack of easily exploitable natural or human resources worked against intensive Spanish development; by the seventeenth century, the English had greater contact throughout much of the eastern coastal area. The inability of the Spanish to extend their control from coast to coast in Central America meant that the eastern zone's primary cultural and economic relationship with the outside has been with the greater Caribbean basin.

In the west, the Spanish quickly subdued local indigenous peoples. To the north, Mayan city-states had collapsed only a couple of centuries earlier for reasons still not fully understood. The coastal Chorotega-Mangue peoples of Nicaragua suffered a rapid 90 percent depopulation resulting from murder, disease, and forced deportations to Peru as slaves. Musical performances of native repertoire were prohibited and native documents burned to eliminate cultural resistance to European rule. Similar fates befell the Lenca communities in north-central Honduras, the Pipil in El Salvador, and other peoples. During the colonial period, a widespread process of racial and cultural mixture along the Pacific Coast region formed a majority **mestizo** ethnicity and culture south of Guatemala. In mountainous Guatemala (like the state of Chiapas in neighboring Mexico), the Mayan people's relative inaccessibility aided their cultural survival. K'iche, Kaqchikel, Mam, and other Mayan groups still number almost half of Guatemala's contemporary population of more than 13 million; almost all of the other half is mestizo (often called **ladino**.)

The western zone did not allow for the cultivation of crops (like sugarcane) that led to the mass importation of Africans elsewhere in Latin America. A relatively small African presence was established in the late 1700s on the Honduran coast by the arrival of the Garífuna or Garinagu, mixed Carib and Arawak Indian and African slaves deported from St. Vincent Island by the British after an unsuccessful rebellion. A small number of slaves and escaped slaves also arrived on the coast. West Indian immigrant laborers settled in the region from the late 1800s onwards. A lack of contact, and even a segregation of the two zones, continued well into the 1950s; Afro–Costa Ricans were actually barred by apartheid laws from entering San José, the highland capital. Distinctions between the Pacific and Caribbean areas began to break down significantly when various mestizo political leaders moved to more fully integrate them. The spread of popular music from the northeast Afro–Central American Caribbean zone to the mestizo southwest has been key in this process, introducing citizens of the same country to one another for the first time, though integration remains far from complete.

The more European-descent ruling elite has utilized crude and violent policies to maintain a divide between themselves and the poor indigenous, mestizo, and rural populations. The U.S. government, unfortunately, bears responsibility for training and maintaining some of Latin America's worst tyrannical military regimes that have enforced this social order. In 1932, for instance, near-starving indigenous peasants in El Salvador tried to unseat their military rulers but failed. Soldiers and landowners slaughtered more than thirty thousand people within days, an event still called La Matanza (The Massacre.) In the aftermath, fearful indigenous people stopped speaking their languages or wearing traditional clothes; musicians burned their marimbas.

Around the same time in Nicaragua, Augusto Sandino organized a peasant militia to combat the nation's corrupt military, and occupying U.S. Marines. Sandino's murder in 1934 brought in the Somoza dictatorship that lasted over four decades. Not until the 1970s did social movements in Guatemala, El Salvador, and Nicaragua finally grow enough to challenge oppressive social conditions. The people's attempts to defend themselves spiraled into full-scale war. At great human cost, the Somozas were defeated by the leftist Sandinista (from Sandino) Front in 1979, but the immense weight of U.S. government power shored up right-wing forces, and the region was plunged into a bloodbath that subsided only in the early 1990s. Peace accords achieved the U.S. government goal of keeping Central America's ruling strata on top, but North American promises of investment and rebuilding never materialized. Economic conditions since then have decimated the popular classes, and a huge human migration to the United States, Europe, and within the region has ensued. Remittances from abroad are now the biggest "industry" in El Salvador, and more than a half million Nicaraguans have relocated to Costa Rica (which has avoided the destruction of previous decades). Ongoing economic crises throughout most of the region has negatively impacted musical performance, from traditional repertoire to chamber orchestras to local popular music.

Traditional Music

The Maya

There are nearly three million Mayan descendants, almost all in Guatemala and in Chiapas, Mexico. Many communities have continued precontact religious beliefs and rituals, though they have absorbed some outside influence over centuries. Probably the largest cultural change has been the recent intrusion of Protestant evangelism, sponsored by North Americans. Ancient and contemporary Mayan beliefs do not adhere to a rigid division between religious and secular aspects of life, including music; rather, all

FIGURE 4.2 Elaborately carved tun used by the Mayan elite

things, such as nature, have at least some degree of sacred significance. An important musical example is the linkage of the sun deity with the **tun** (or *tun-tun*), an onomatopoetically named two-note instrument formed by cutting an "H" into the top of a suspended hollow log that is struck with mallets (Figure 4.2). The same instrument is called teponaztli among Nahuatl speakers in both their original region of central Mexico (see the discussion of composer Carlos Chávez in Chapter 3) and in western Nicaragua to where many emigrated centuries ago.

Other instruments are documented in accounts of contact-generation Spaniards or archeological iconography, such as the amazing mural at Bonampak in Chiapas. Painted in 790 for royalty, the mural depicts a large musical ensemble performing for a ritual sacrifice of a captive. The musicians play long trumpet-horns, various drums, tortoise shells, and large rattles. Music continues to play a central role in Mayan life. Examples include song cycles and dance-dramas that recount origin myths, accompanied by trumpets and the tun; ancestor songs to invoke spirits of the departed; songs of healing; and a corpus of music determined by the Mayan calendar that relates to agricultural cycles. A well-balanced world requires music to be performed as dictated by ancestors and supernatural forces, and encompasses many forms, such as solo singing; cane flute repertoire, often paired with small double-headed drums; guitar pieces on modified local instruments; and tun music, sometimes played together with long valveless horns or European-style trumpets. Following Mayan belief, most Mayan instruments are gendered, that is, classified as either male or female. Actual musical performance, however, remains limited to men.

The Marimba

The marimba serves as both a signifier of a musical unity as well as a prism into the wide cultural diversity on the isthmus. Marimbas consist of a series of wooden keys in increasing size attached to a frame and struck with mallets. No one knows exactly when or precisely where, but this instrument first appeared in several places in Latin America when captive Africans began to recreate them. In some places, like Brazil, the marimba has disappeared, but they are very much in use in African American communities along the Pacific Coast of Colombia and Ecuador. The indigenous population adopted them from the few Africans brought into Central America, a group so small that they mixed with the indigenous and mestizo population and eventually disappeared as a distinct group. The first written mention dates to 1680 in Guatemala. Over time, the marimba has become associated exclusively with indigenous peoples, leading to unfounded assumptions about its Mayan ancestry. My own speculation is that the similarity of using a mallet to strike a tun or teponaztli made for easy Amerindian adoption of wooden-keyed African marimbas.

Over the last two centuries, social pressures and the desire to perform more urban and European-based music led to experiments by Central Americans and Mexicans to enlarge and change the form of the marimba. There are three main types, and Guatemala provides a useful showcase because all three types are still in use there: the **marimba de tecomates**, the **marimba sencilla**, and the **marimba doble**.

Marimba de Tecomates

Marimbas have various names in Mayan languages. The Spanish name comes from the term used for the resonators under each key (Figure 4.3). This earliest form of marimba has a hoop, or an arc, of wood attached on each end of the frame; a single performer sits inside and on top of the hoop. The instrument has a single straight row of 28 large keys that are **diatonic** (like the white notes on a piano). Keys are cut from a heavy, dense type of wood; their weight usually obliges the *marimbista* to prop up the front of the marimba with a stick. This marimba is rarely seen outside of Mayan villages deep in the countryside, sometimes accessible only by foot. It provides music at rituals, such as the blessing of seeds before planting, as well as in secular contexts like recreational dancing. Often it is accompanied by a small drum and vertical cane flute.

FIGURE 4.3 K'iche Mayan musician plays a marimba de tecomates (he sits atop the arc). Chichicastenango region, Guatemala

Marimba Sencilla

This instrument was created to play popular music beginning in the 1800s. Besides being *sencilla* (simple, single) with one row of keys, it is also diatonic. Urban Mayans and mixed-race mestizos expanded its range to four to five octaves (33 to 40 keys), so the arc had to be abandoned in favor of legs to support the increased weight. Multiple musicians can play on a marimba sencilla: one carries a bass line, and others produce chords and harmonized melodies. Gradual deforestation of the region led builders to design rectangular wooden boxes to replace the tecomates. In Guatemala, Honduras, and parts of El Salvador and Costa Rica, these marimbas play alone or together with drums and

FIGURE 4.4 The house band at a hotel, consisting of a standard duo of Guatemalan marimba dobles, or grandes (missing the usual fourth player on the bass keys of the largest marimba). Antigua, Guatemala, 1993

other percussion. The growth in instrument size reflects the parallel growth of small towns and cities and increased Mayan contact with musical influences outside traditional village life.

Marimba Doble, or Grande

Unbeknownst to one another, Sebastián Hurtado of Quetzaltenango, Guatemala, in 1894, and then Corazón Borraz Moreno of Chiapas, Mexico, in 1897 added an upper row of keys like the black keys on a piano to the marimba sencilla (Figure 4.4). This innovation eventually changed the attitude of the well-heeled elite when they heard marimbas reproduce music previously only heard in the parlors of wealthy homes. The marimba doble soon became very popular in urban areas throughout Central America, and musicians toured the United States and Europe as novelty acts. In the mid-twentieth century, this marimba was adopted and transformed outside Central America. Substituting metal cylinder resonator tubes (with no buzzing sound) created the marimba currently used in jazz, new age, and Euroclassical music.

In Central America, musicians often combine a four-person lead marimba with a smaller three-person one to produce a "wooden wall of sound." Lyrical melodies result from precise repetitions on the same keys by expert musicians to produce the effect of sustained notes and smooth, legato phrases. Note that all African and Latin American marimbas have a distinctive "buzzing" sound. A hole near the bottom of each resonator is surrounded with thick, black bee's wax, and some kind of membrane stretched across it (Figure 4.5). Traditionally, the thick webbing around spiders' eggs were used, but now dried pig intestine is preferred, following the same principle that makes a kazoo buzz.

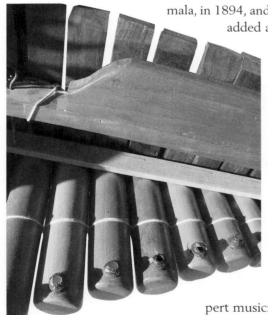

FIGURE 4.5 Dried pig intestine membrane held by bees wax on marimba de arco resonators that replace gourds (tecomates) in Nicaragua

The Nicaraguan *baile de la marimba* and Its Music

The Nicaraguan **marimba de arco** offers a clear example of how closely tied dance often is to marimba music. In Nicaragua's traditional repertoire practically all pieces are in a major key. The tempo is quick, usually in ⅝, though some sections switch to ¾. The standard format is that of a trio: a guitar strums a triple pattern and sits by the bass keys of the marimba, and a small, high-pitched four-metal stringed **guitarilla** sits by the treble keys and strums a quick ⅝ rhythm. The *marimbero* plays two musical roles: in his left hand, a single mallet (sometimes two) alternates primarily between two notes in a four-beat pattern, and the right hand continually changes the position of two mallets between thirds, sixths, octaves, or even a single note to play and harmonize the usually syncopated melody based on a pattern of six beats. You can feel this metric duality by following Example 4.1. First, try the main beats with both hands; then change just the right hand in groups of three beats; then back to both hands on the main beats; then try the left hand in groups of two. Whenever you feel ready for your first step, add them together to beat twos against threes.

With few exceptions, the form of the pieces is either **ABAB**, or **ABABA**. Dances are performed by couples, for fun in private homes or more publicly on saint's day celebrations. During the latter, groups of four to eight couples approach the dance as a serious religious commitment and practice their steps for weeks. During processions, the marimba is carried, and couples line up by gender and face each other, trying to move sideways down the street as they dance. Groups go from one sponsor's house to another, and one pair

EXAMPLE 4.1: Basic rhythmic pattern on the marimba de arco

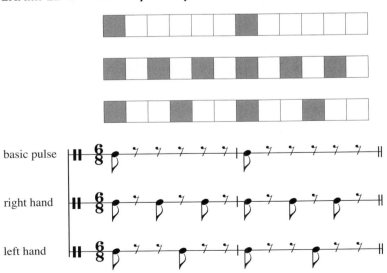

at a time dances in the living room. The marimba trio may be jammed behind a wall of spectators, but the structure of each piece is so standardized that they don't require eye contact with the dancers. This didn't used to be the case: the musical structure used to be quite flexible and marimba players would cue each section. Constraints of recordings and demands of new semiprofessional dance troupes codified the repertoire into its current form. The cues still remain in the music: Example 4.2 shows the marimba de arco's playing at the point that cues the next section, and the chords that change at this point (at 0:38 to 0:46, and 1:45 to 1:50 in "El sapo," Listening Guide 4.1.)

LISTENING guide 4.1

◎ "El sapo" (The Toad)

Composer: unknown

Date of composition: unknown

Performers/instruments: Jacinto Cano, marimba de arco; other Cano family members, guitar and guitarilla

Date of recording: 1985

Form: introduction, then **ABAB**

Tempo/meter: quick compound duple

What to Listen for:
- Two basic sections, each accompanying a different dance step and choreography
- Different strumming patterns for guitar and high-pitched guitarilla
- Harmonies in marimba de arco player's right hand against constant left-hand patterns

Time	Structure and Description
0:00	*Zapateado* music, used as introduction to begin dance: with short, *zapateado* (from *zapato*, meaning "shoe") steps, a man invites a woman to enter the dance
0:22	**Section A:** first theme Woman enters; both man and woman following an open, *suelto* (loose) pattern of slowly circling around facing each other
0:48	**Section A:** second theme *Suelto* steps and choreography
1:07	**Section B** Dancers approaching with shorter *zapateado* steps, facing same direction, with man behind and to left side of woman, flirting with her
1:25	**Section A:** first theme Return to *suelto* steps and choreography
1:52	**Section A:** second theme
2:11	**Section B** Return to zapateado steps and choreography

EXAMPLE 4.2: Section from "El sapo" played by Jacinto Cano

tonic chord (shown as C) ⎿_____⏌ dominant (G⁷)

dominant (G⁷) ⎿_____⏌ tonic (C) ⎿_____⏌

musical cue to dancers that a different section is coming ⎿_____⏌

Women are equal in dance participation, but never play the music past adolescence. The explanation usually given is that female musicians would be inappropriate in the heavily male-dominated world of fiestas and parties. One daughter of a famous Masaya dancer mastered the instrument and even appeared on television, yet the nature of alcohol-infused social scenes far from home deterred her from pursuing a professional career as a marimba de arco musician.

The Triumph of an "Inferior" Instrument?

If you could visit mid-twentieth century Nicaragua, you would find marimba de arco trios, mostly in certain regional towns, and full marimba doble groups in larger cities. If someone told you that only one instrument survived to the end of the century, wouldn't the larger chromatic instrument seem the obvious choice? Yet the opposite occurred. The close identification between the marimba de arco and the traditional dance it accompanies led to its increasing visibility (or audibility), especially after the 1979 Sandinista revolution. The public's identification with feelings of *nicaragüanidad* ("Nicaraguan-ness") granted the 22-key marimba a symbolic power that allowed it to persevere while larger marimbas were marginalized. This provides us a lesson that what is important about music is its social meaning, not the complexity of its formal structure. Nicaraguans have access to the world's many technological sonic devices, yet the marimba de arco still holds a special place in contemporary culture and in people's hearts.

explore

Compare "El sapo" (Listening Guide 4.1) with selections on *¡Nicaragua Presente!: Music from Nicaragua Libre*, as well as compilations such as *Music From Honduras, Vol. 1* and *Music from Guatemala, Vol. 1* (on the Caprice label). Large Guatemalan ensembles of marimbas grandes abound, and some bands cover seemingly every type of music possible to play on wooden keys.

Popular Music

Countless popular musical styles that have developed over the last hundred years in this region. In Guatemala the marimba has retained a place of national prominence where it is heralded as the "national instrument." Mayan-Guatemalans, now about half the population, still intensely identify with the marimba. Additionally, a singular piece of legislation helped cement the instrument's place among mestizos. In the 1950s, the government decreed that all radio stations had to play a significant block of national marimba music every morning. Although at first some chafed at this rule, in time the law had its desired effect. Today, Guatemalan marimba doble ensembles, often expanded with drum, bass, and horn sections, remain very popular and interpret all kinds of musical styles.

Central American popular music has had three major waves of exposure outside the isthmus: the previously mentioned tours of marimba groups in the early twentieth century; the spread of protest music in the 1970s and 1980s; and the popularization of Garífuna (or Garinagu) music since the 1990s. The violent social upheavals of the 1970s produced at least one positive result: a prolific outpouring of new music and its dissemination internationally. Music with social or political content played a key role in mobilizing the population for more social equality and democracy. The 1979 overthrow of the Somoza dictatorship and the extended warfare throughout the 1980s in the northern half of the region focused the world's attention on Central America as never before. Exiled music groups from El Salvador and bands in Sandinista-led Nicaragua (1979–1990) toured Latin and North America and Europe; several albums were released on labels outside the region.

Nicaragua

Far and away the best-known musical artist from Nicaragua is Carlos Mejía Godoy. It would be hard to overestimate the fundamental importance of his music in motivating compatriots first to overthrow the dictatorship and then to work to transform the nation in the 1980s while simultaneously defending it from attacks on civilians by the U.S.-funded contra (counterrevolutionary) forces based in Honduras. Mejía Godoy's primary medium was a song style created as recently as the 1930s known as the *son nica*. The *son nica* borrows its defining rhythm from the marimba de arco trio's guitar triple-stroke strumming pattern, as well as from melodic patterns and consistent choice of a major key.

Following two hugely popular albums, Carlos Mejía Godoy composed a Catholic mass based on the tenets of **liberation theology** entitled *La misa campesina nicaragüense* (The Nicaraguan Peasant Mass). As in his other

⊚ Godoy: Credo from *La misa campesina nicaragüense*

Composer/lyricist: Carlos Mejía Godoy

Date of composition: 1974

Performers/Instruments: Carlos Mejía Godoy: voice, accordion, and marimba; members of Los de Palacagüina: voices, guitar, electric bass

Date of recording: 2007

Genre: *son nica*

Form: verse and chorus

Tempo/meter: moderate triple meter

What to Listen for:

- Slightly delayed second of three beats of the *son nica* rhythm
- Intimacy and sincerity expressed by the various vocalists
- Inclusion of marimba, though lack of "buzzing" gives away that it is not a Nicaraguan marimba de arco

Time	Text	Translation	Description
2:47			Instrumental interlude; Melody in accordion and marimba
2:58	Yo creo en vos, compañero, Cristo humano, Cristo obrero, de la muerte vencedor. Con tu sacrificio inmenso engendraste al hombre nuevo para la liberación.	I believe in you, compañero,* Human Christ, worker Christ, Victor over death. With your immense sacrifice You brought forth the new man For [our] liberation.	Solo voice; light electric guitar in left channel
3:12	Vos estás resucitando en cada brazo que se alza para defender al pueblo del dominio explotador. Porque estás vivo en el rancho, en la fábrica, en la escuela. Creo en tu lucha sin tregua creo en tu resurección	You come back to life In each arm that stretches out To defend the people From exploitation. Because you live in every little farm, In the factory, in the school. I believe in your constant struggle, I believe in your resurrection.	Chorus with marimba; Carlos joins for the second verse
3:30	Porque estás vivo en el rancho, en la fábrica en la escuela. Creo en tu lucha sin tregua creo en tu resurección.	Because you live in every little farm, In the factory, in the school. I believe in your constant struggle, I believe in your resurrection.	Carlos sings with chorus
3:42	Creo en vos, arquitecto, ingeniero, artesano, carpintero albañil y armador. Creo en vos, constructor de pensamiento, de la música y el viento, de la paz y del amor. [repeats]	I believe in you, Architect, engineer, Craftsperson, carpenter, Bricklayer and builder. I believe in you, Inventor of thought, Of music and wind, Of peace and love.	First two notes held, then all sing chorus; hand claps added, marimba sounds last notes

Compañero means comrade, and in other contexts pal, colleague, and so forth. The lyricist chooses this word to view Christ as accompanying us in a personal way, and not above us out of reach.

explore

Compare the rest of this recent rerecording of *La misa campesina nicaragüense* against both the original recording and an electrified pop version that was recorded in Spain in 1978. Listen also to the almost entirely *son nica*–based *La misa popular nicaragüense* versus the variety of regional styles used in *La misa campesina nicaragüense.* You may enjoy other songs by Carlos Mejía Godoy, as well as those by his younger brother Luis Enrique Mejía Godoy.

explore

Regrettably, this and other CDs by Rómulo Castro are very difficult to obtain outside of Panama. The cover by Rubén Blades on his Grammy-winning CD *La rosa de los vientos* also features other songs by Panamanian composers.

works, he masterfully drew from the everyday speech and local cultural manifestations of western Nicaragua. Recordings of the mass included many types of traditional repertoire, such as brass bands for the celebratory Gloria section, but in practice, the mass was usually sung by congregations with just guitar accompaniment. Somoza's military violently broke up the first public celebration of the mass in 1977, but cassettes of the studio recordings and printed lyrics circulated widely underground, and of course later openly during the Sandinista-led government.

Other Central American Popular Music

In the late 1990s the dance music called *punta* gained some musical exposure outside the isthmus. *Punta* is a modern genre created by musicians of the Garífuna, or Garinagu, people that dot the Caribbean coastline from Belize to Nicaragua. One of the most accomplished musicians, Andy Palacios, seemed poised to become a major world music star when he tragically died young. Look for his album *Watina*, an amazing blend of traditional songs and modernized dance styles, and current star Aurelio Martínez.

Panama remained a Colombian province until the United States literally created the country in order to occupy it and construct an interoceanic canal. Finished in 1914, the canal project attracted large numbers of Jamaican and Trinidadian laborers who reinforced Afro-Panamanian elements of the nation's culture. One of the first stars of modern reggaeton (p. 209) was Panamanian El General (Edgardo A. Franco). Other Panamanians made their mark in New York earlier during the explosion of salsa in the 1960s and 1970s. The best known of these is Rubén Blades, a greatly admired composer, singer, and band leader. He revitalized salsa toward the end of its boom with lyrics that spoke to social issues and ethnic and national pride. When the height of salsa's popularity subsided, Blades relaunched his career with music that reflected his renewed interest in his home country. He even ran for president in 1994; though unsuccessful, he later served as Minister of Culture from 2004 to 2009.

Blades's return hit was a cover of "La rosa de los vientos" by the talented singer-songwriter Rómulo Castro. Castro has composed and performed in politically oriented New Song groups, his current and most enduring being Grupo Tuira (a river). Just as Panama is a crossroads of many cultural influences, Rómulo Castro draws from a wide palette of musical styles. His lyrics can stand alone as poetry; their beauty defies foreign translation. In fact, Rubén Blades reworked a good part of the lyrics shown to be more broadly accessible—or more pedestrian, depending on one's point of view. The song was composed just after the U.S. military invasion

◎ Castro: "La rosa de los vientos" (The Rose of the Winds)

Composer/lyricist: Rómulo Castro
Date of composition: 1996
Performers/instruments: Rómulo Castro y Grupo Tuira
Date of recording: 1996
Genre: popular song/cumbia
Form: verses and chorus
Tempo/meter: moderate, a bit too slow for dancing, designed more for listening; quadruple meter

What to Listen for:
- Introduction, ending, and echoing of voices creating an epochal mood that befits the gravity of the moment Panamanians had just experienced
- Layers of Afro-Panamanian drumming combine with rhythms that draw from salsa and popular song
- Pianist adding blues licks in the accompaniment

Time	Text	Translation	Description
0:00			**Instrumental introduction** Distorted guitar chords; foreboding sounds suggest thunder and jet planes
0:28	E-ye-ya, e-ye-ya, Cada hombre lleva encima la huella de su tiempo. [2x]	[vocables (nonsense syllables)], Each man carries the mark of his own time. [2x]	Sung by children, the inheritors of a future Panama; echo effect suggests time depth
0:51			**Instrumental break** Texture interrupted by brass; main rhythmic background set
0:58			**Verse 1**
1:36	¿Quién dice que perdimos la facultad de amar, o que estamos perdidos entre tanto signo de brutalidad? Seguimos respirando también por los demás, y es una carga noble que me agobie su pesar.	Who says that we lost the ability to love, Or that we're lost surrounded by so much brutality? We keep breathing, for others as well, And it's a noble cause whose burden weighs me down.	**Verse 2** An appeal to optimism The singer urges us to speak for the disenfranchised who cannot be heard
2:12	E, a-je ayombe, ah-je-a-je, mi tierra llore. E, a-je ayombe, ah-je-a-je, mi patria llore.	[vocables and "ayombe"] My land is crying. [vocables] My homeland cries.	"Ayombe": an interjection in songs to mark a heartfelt feeling (also found in Colombian vallenato)

(continued)

Time	Text	Translation	Description
2:33	¿Quién dijo que la vida se puede apuntalar con la historia mañida de lo sacrosanta libertad de atar? Puedes negar un nombre o un ghetto desecar, decir que el polo norte está en el sur y delirar.	Who said that life can be underpinned with a well-worn history of sacrosanct liberty to tie people down? You can erase a name or desiccate a ghetto, Say the North Pole is South and talk nonsense.	**Verse 3** Ghetto: Chirinos, a poor and heavily African American part of Panama City that was partially destroyed by U.S. bombings. Speaker of "nonsense": the U.S. government
3:10	E, a-je ayombe, ah-je-a-je, mi tierra llore. E, a-je ayombe, ah-je-a-je, mi patria llore.	[vocables] My land is crying. [vocables] My homeland cries.	Addition of echo suggests voice echoing throughout Panama
3:30	**Coro:** Yo soy de dónde nace la rosa de los vientos, La azota el vendaval, pero crece por dentro.	**Chorus:** I come from where grows the wind-blown rose, The gale winds lash it, but it grows back from within.	The singer suggests that, though Panama is small, it is indomitable in its independent spirit
4:11			**Instrumental break with electric guitar solo** Cries of "saloma" by a campesino in the background
4:32	E-ye-ya, e-ye-ya,	[vocables]	Repeat of first section: a point in time recedes into history
4:55	Saloma		Isolated cry of "saloma" marks the song as Panamanian

that overthrew corrupt general Manuel Noriega, once a close ally of U.S. intelligence services. Most Panamanians were glad to be rid of Noriega but regretted the lack of U.S. support for earlier Panamanian resistance to him and the invasion's indiscriminate destruction. As mentioned in the song, entire working-class neighborhoods in Panama City were targeted. A Grammy winner and a hit throughout the continent, the lyrics of "La rosa de los vientos" appealed to many concerned with national and regional sovereignty.

European and European–American Classical Music

The historical record of music in the Euroclassical tradition, much of it housed in churches, has suffered from the destruction of earthquakes and the ravages of wars following the independence struggles of the 1820s. Central America still lags far behind most of the continent in careful, systematic research on all types of music; hopefully more scholarship will appear in the future. Spanish Colonial authorities' efforts to reproduce Europe's elite music favored Guatemala, the center of political authority for the isthmus (outside of Panama, governed from Bogotá), and the largest church ensembles developed there.

In the mid-nineteenth century, secular compositions and the first conservatories dedicated to the classical idiom began to appear. Composers with some formal training typically wrote sacred works for church ensembles, especially choruses, as well as sacred and secular works for brass and wind bands. These bands featured the best-trained musicians within their respective countries and often developed over time into symphony orchestras. One of the most important brass and wind bands has been the Honduran *Banda de los Supremos Poderes* (Band of the Supreme Powers). Composer and director Manuel Adalid y Gamero (1872–1947) established its fame throughout the region, and it remains a leading ensemble.

As Central Americans had little contact with contemporary compositional practices in Europe, waltzes and other dance forms typify the secular works of the later nineteenth and early twentieth centuries. Nicaragua is a representative example. Like others of his generation, José de la Cruz Mena (1874–1907) adopted a European academic style reminiscent of Franz Joseph Haydn for his masses, but his most famous pieces are instrumental waltzes like those of Johann Strauss. Band and chamber orchestra director Pablo Vega Raudes (1850–1919) founded the nation's first school of music. His son Alejandro Vega Matus (1875–1937) wrote sacred masses and led the most celebrated dance and orchestral band of the day, a vehicle for his many fox-trots, one-steps, *pasodobles*, and other songs.

Symphonic orchestras have suffered from a lack of consistency, forming, disbanding, and reorganizing according to the vagaries of government and upper-class financial underwriting. However sporadic their existence, symphonic orchestras and the gradual expansion of formal musical education spurred nationalist compositional currents. Almost all composers relocated for a time to Europe to advance their studies and then relied on their own research into local traditional music for nationalist material. For instance, the most prominent early nationalist composer in Panama, Narciso Garay (1876–1953), was also one of the nation's most prominent folklorists.

Unhappily, the embryonic state of ethnomusicology and folklore research has often led composers to a very uneven and often erroneous grasp of traditional music. Salvadoran María de Baratta (1894–1978) and Nicaraguan Luis A. Delgadillo (1887–1962), for instance, studied in Italy and upon returning based several works on imagined indigenous music before and after the conquest. Baratta and especially Delgadillo's notions of indigenous music may have been inaccurate, but that did not hinder the music's acceptance: their fellow middle- and upper-class audience members were not so interested in authenticity as in demonstrating that their country was just as capable of creating a national elite style as the rest of the world. One of the best composers in the first half of the twentieth century was Guatemalan Ricardo Castillo (1891–1966). He wrote several short orchestral works of nationalist character inspired by Mayan religion.

Many composers in the European-based classical tradition continued conservative approaches that harked back several decades, but more-recent compositions parallel the most avant-garde cosmopolitan currents. Guatemalan Joaquín Orellana (b. 1937) is one of the region's most original composers. He has experimented with the sonorous possibilities of the marimba and created several unique instruments that he integrates into nontonal and minimalist compositions, sometimes combined with electronic tape. His crescent-shaped *imbaluna* combines "im" from "marimba" and "luna" (moon.) His *ciclo im* faces keys inward, so that when spun, a ball randomly hits the inverted keys (Figure 4.6).

Other major composers include Salvadorans Gilberto Orellana Sr. (b. 1921), the first Salvadoran to use **serial** techniques in the early 1960s, and German Cáceres (b. 1954) who led the national symphony for many years; Honduran Sergio Suazo Lang (b. 1956), pianist and composer; and Nicaraguan Juan Manuel Mena Moreno (1917–1989), founder and director for many years of the Nicaraguan National Chorus, whose creative settings of traditional music remain well known. Panamanian Roque Cordero (1917–2008,) remains probably the best-known Central American composer (in part because he relocated to the United States) and one whose nonnationalist work is most easily available.

FIGURE 4.6 Several instruments created by Joaquín Orellana, including in the foreground the serpentine *imbaluna* and on the ground two versions of the circular *ciclo im*

Colombia

Colombia constitutes the northwest corner of South America, almost twice the size of Texas (at 440,000 square miles). Its contrasting geographical zones can be grouped into five major regions (moving from northwest to southeast):

1. The Pacific coast, tropical lowlands west of the Andes mountains. Historically isolated, its heavily African-descent population is famous for marimba-centered music and dance (see Chapter 8).

2. The Atlantic/Caribbean coast, known simply as La Costa. It contains the nation's beach destinations and major city Cartagena. Its population is of mixed European, African, and indigenous ancestry.

3. The Andes. This region contains agricultural and industrial production, is a center of political power, and is home to a majority of the country's population. Major cities include the capital, Bogotá, as well as Medellín and Cali.

4. The Colombian Amazon, in the far south, is a tropical lowlands populated with isolated indigenous groups. More than one hundred distinct Amerindian languages are spoken within Colombia, most in the Amazon region.

5. The Llanos or prairie, in the southeast.

Colombia's total population of 44 million is estimated to be 58 percent mestizo, 20 percent fully European, 18 percent predominantly African descent, and only 1 percent fully indigenous.

A Brief History

During the colonial period, the Spanish invested significantly more in what is now Colombia than in neighboring Venezuela. The discovery of gold and other valuables in Colombia supported the development of European musical practices in the churches of Bogotá and Cartagena. Most of Spanish-speaking South America broke ties with Spain in the early 1820s during prolonged wars of independence, led by Simón Bolívar and other European-descent elites. Bolívar's dream of creating a Greater Colombia failed, but Ecuador, Colombia, and Venezuela still have similar national flags. Independence soon consolidated emancipation for African-descendant slaves, though economic systems in both countries concentrated resources in the hands of a small ruling class.

Colombia has received comparatively little immigration since independence due to the general weakness of its economy. Coffee exports

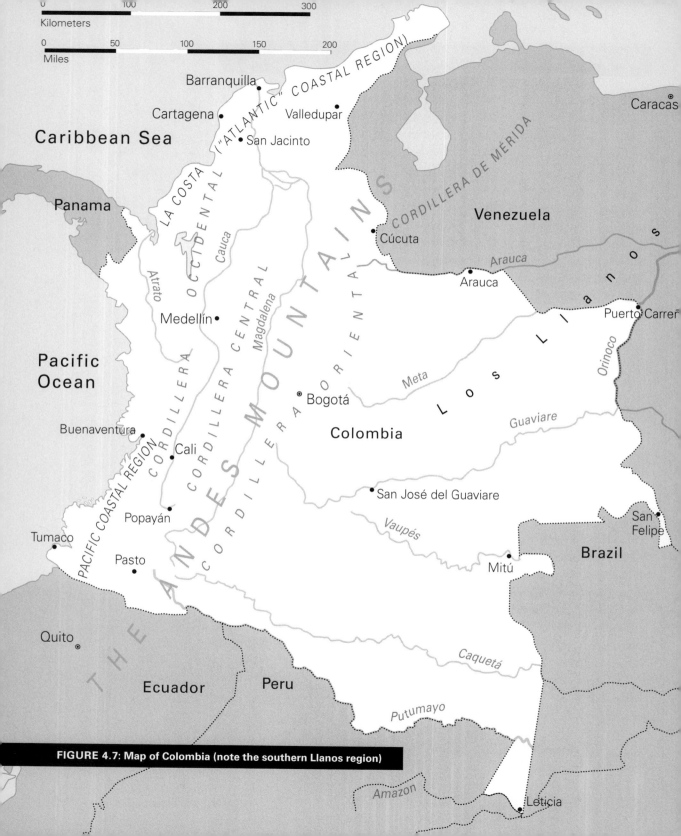

FIGURE 4.7: Map of Colombia (note the southern Llanos region)

represented the only source of modest export revenue through the 1970s, and much of the rural population still lives in poverty. Attempts at socio-economic reform literally died with the assassination of progressive President Jorge Gaitán in 1948. His murder plunged Colombia into a protracted civil and ideological war, often referred to as "La Violencia."

The tremendous revenues generated through cocaine and heroin production have corrupted both the once-populist guerrilla movement and the military-dominated government. Despite recent gains in industrialization and agricultural development, drug production still strongly influences politics and the national economy. Struggles to control the supply of cocaine (to satisfy demand mostly in the United States) have thwarted Colombia's democratic process and led to terrible violence, most of it committed by the military and its affiliated "civilian" paramilitary units. The same drug wars that have restricted cultural development contributed directly to the salsa "boom" in Cali and the spread of vallenato music (discussed later), with drug lords frequently sponsoring their favorite artists or groups. For better or (mostly) worse, the recreational drug industry remains a major player in Colombia's destiny.

Traditional Music

If one had to single out the one Colombian musical form that has achieved widest popularity, it would have to be the **cumbia**. The basic commercial version's dance is easy to master, and the music so infectious that for many decades, in its various local interpretations, it reigned as the dance music of choice in Mexico, most of Central America, and Peru (where it was renamed *chicha*.)

The traditional cumbia sounds quite different, though its African-based rhythms have influenced all subsequent permutations of the genre. The traditional dance is performed at night by couples standing in a circle around the musicians. Women illuminate the scene with bundles of candles wrapped together in cloth. The traditional ensemble **conjunto de gaitas** clearly demonstrates the tripartite indigenous, African, and European cultural formation of the Caribbean coastal area of Colombia. The flutes are of Amerindian origin; the drums are of African derivation; and the language of any lyrics used and the music's melodic form and tonal harmony trace back to Europe. The term **gaita** refers to a flute, a musical genre, and also a traditional ensemble. Some twentieth-century urban popular music continues to be called gaita, but most of the music derived from the conjunto de gaita, together with other styles from the Atlantic coastal region, are now subsumed under the umbrella term cumbia.

The conjunto de gaitas consists of two long, vertical gaita flutes made from *cardón*, a type of cactus tree. The ones heard in "Fuego de Cumbia" (Listening Guide 4.4) are *gaitas largas*, almost three feet long. Players blow across a quill from a turkey that has been carefully embedded in a mass of

FIGURE 4.8 Conjunto de gaita with maraca, *gaita macho*, *gaita hembra*, *tambor llamador*, and *tambor alegre*

beeswax mixed with some ground-up coal on the top end of the flute. The sound is breathy, rich with many overtones. The *gaita hembra* (female) has five holes about halfway down the flute, and the slightly longer (and therefore lower-pitched) *gaita macho* (male) two holes. The *gaita hembra* takes portions of the melody that the *gaita macho* complements by doubling or constrasting, with the two flutes exchanging short phrases back and forth. Accompanying **maracas,** filled with dried seeds and usually made from large gourds, accentuate offbeats.

Cumbia percussion comes from three distinct kinds of drums. The highest-pitched is the *tambor llamador* that, as its name implies, "calls" by holding the group solidly in rhythm with a consistent pattern. It has a single head, is cylindrical in shape, and is held between the legs. The *tambor alegre* (literally, "happy drum") is about two feet long in a cone shape, much like a conga drum. The *tambor alegre* drummer often enters into an improvised dialogue with the *gaita hembra*. The tambora is a large double-headed drum that is hit with drumsticks on the head and the shell. This drum has a deep, bass sound, and represents a more recent addition to the ensemble (Figure 4.8 and Example 4.3).

For decades Los Gaiteros de San Jacinto have been the best-known conjunto de gaitas in Colombia. They formed in the 1930s in the region known as Montes de María near the Caribbean. Folklorists first helped to promote them in the 1950s, and they toured internationally and made recordings that cemented their national status. In recent years Los Gaiteros have obtained more international success as a world music group. This international

EXAMPLE 4.3: Basic cumbia rhythms in a traditional conjunto de gaita

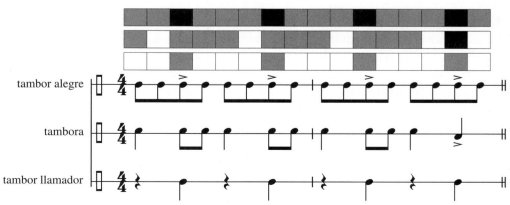

recognition has helped inspire a revival of interest in traditional gaita music among urban performers and audiences in Colombia, the most influential example being Carlos Vives (p. 152).

The lyrics of the title song of their CD *Fuego de Cumbia* (Cumbia Fire) refer to laments, for the conjunto de gaitas traditionally perform for funerals as well as dances. The singer mentions the combination of ethnicities that form

⊚ Los Gaiteros de San Jacinto: "Fuego de Cumbia" (Cumbia Fire)

Composer/lyricist: Rafael Pérez García

Date of composition: 2003

Performers/instruments: Los Gaiteros de San Jacinto: Fredys Arrieta, *gaita hembra*; Joaquín Nicolás Hernández, *gaita macho*; Rafael Castro, *voice*; Gabriel Torregrosa, *tambor alegre*; Rafael Rodríguez, *tambor llamador*; Joche Plata, tambora (drum); chorus

Date of recording: 2003

Genre: cumbia

Tempo/meter: moderate; simple quadruple meter

What to Listen for:

- Two gaita flutes intertwining to create harmony, counterpoint, and unison melodies
- Breathy, thin timbre of gaitas
- Notes of the gaitas not exactly in Western tunings
- Call-and-response vocals
- Frequent improvisation on drums, especially during breaks

Time	Text	Translation	Description
0:00	Un pueblo de sangre pura, Que con lamentos se canta.	A people of pure blood, Sung in laments.	Opening call
0:08			**Instrumental introduction** Gaitas combine phrases to state main melody
0:18	(Cumbia, cumbia, [a] Carlos, a tí Maria en Barranquilla)	(Cumbia, cumbia, [to] Carlos, to Maria in Barranquilla)	Singer dedicates song
0:48	Se encienden noches oscuras Como un jolgorio que encanta. Los repiques de tambores, La raza negra levanta, Y el indio pasivamente Con su melódica gaita, Interrumpen el silencio Cuando una fogata baila, Y yo siento por mi venas Un fuego que no se apaga.	Dark nights light up in fire Like a feast that enchants. The beating of the drums, The black race rises up, And the Indian, passively With his melodic gaita, Interrupts the silence When a bonfire dances, And I feel through my veins A fire that never goes out.	**Verse 1** Moderate rhythm creates space between singers and instrumentalists

(continued)

Time	Text	Translation	Description
1:23	Es el fuego de mi cumbia, es el fuego de mi raza, Un fuego de sangre pura, Que con lamentos se canta.	It's the fire of my cumbia, It's the fire of my race, A fire of pure blood, Sung in laments.	Solo vocalist sings chorus, gaitas play a melody that cues the chorus
1:50	¡Wepa-je! (Oye, Maribel, en Bogotá)	[vocal interjection] (Listen up, Maribel, in Bogota)	**Instrumental interlude** Gaitas repeat melody, short solo on *tambor alegre*
2:13			**Verse 2**
2:48	Con el fuego de mi pueblo, con el fuego de mi raza, Un fuego de sangre pura, Que con lamentos se canta.	With the fire of my people, With the fire of my race, A fire of pure blood, Sung in laments.	Solo singer states chorus line, gaitas state melody that cues singers in second part
3:14	Guepajé!	[exclamation]	**Instrumental interlude** One gaita solo in high register
3:55			**Verse 3**
4:31			**Chorus and ending**

Colombian culture, with stereotypical attributes for each: animated African influences from the drums and "passive" (stoic) Indian melodies on the flute. The phrase "sangre pura" (pure blood) refers both to the connectedness of the population through bloodlines and to the strength and courage it takes to survive in this zone of armed conflict. Fighting and land mines have endangered farming and even the harvesting of the *cardón* to make flutes.

Popular Music

Música Tropical

As in many other parts of Latin America and the Caribbean, urban military brass and woodwind bands in the latter half of the nineteenth century inspired ensembles in Colombian towns and small cities that adapted local musical forms into new formats. The first to achieve national diffusion was the **bambuco**, labeled at first simply *canción colombiana* (Colombian song). This music transformed guitar and other repertoires from the country's interior into arrangements appropriate for large bands that performed in city ballrooms. In the 1930s and 1940s, the predominantly European-descent upper and middle classes in Bogotá and elsewhere found the reworked bambuco easier to accept than music from the African-influenced coastal regions.

Ever-larger orchestras introduced non-Colombian styles such as waltzes, fox-trots, and tangos into their repertoire. By the 1940s, musicians incorporated Caribbean dance music influences as well (mambo, *son*, merengue) and increased the size of ensembles to become like jazz orchestras in the United States and elsewhere. These influences helped smooth the way for the successful adaptation of the Afro-Colombian coastal *porro*, which is rhythmically quite similar to the cumbia, followed by the acceptance in elite circles of other dance-band transformations of traditional musical forms.

By the 1950s, these Afro–Atlantic Coast styles, collectively termed **música tropical**, had become the most popular form of national dance music. Lucho Bermúdez led one of the most innovative and successful orchestras of this type. Dressed in suits or swanky uniforms and following elaborate arrangements, Bermúdez's band and other musicians helped to make coastal music suitable for "high society" ballrooms and social clubs.

While Afro-Cuban popular music impacted música tropical, the repertoire was undeniably Colombian and featured the smooth sound of the woodwind section (imitating traditional reed instruments). In the following selection, "Gaita de las flores" (Gaita of the Flowers), note how the horn section often plays repeated short phrases, a trait taken directly from the traditional cumbia as heard on the gaita flutes in the previous example.

LISTENING guide 4.5

Bermúdez: "Gaita de las flores" (Gaita of the Flowers)

Composer/lyricist: Lucho Bermúdez

Performers/instruments: La Orquesta de Lucho Bermúdez (Bermúdez on clarinet)

Date of recording: late 1940s

Genre: gaita

Form: alternates short chorus with instrumental breaks and solos

Tempo/meter: upbeat simple quadruple

What to Listen for:
- Much of the rhythm of the traditional gaita retained, despite faster tempo
- Short phrases function like melodic cells in large horn sections
- Bermúdez's clarinet

Time	Text	Translation	Description
0:00			**Instrumental section** Full orchestra presents main material; alternation between brass and clarinets and saxophones

(continued)

Time	Text	Translation	Description
0:40			Rhythmic foundation established; unison horn melody; clipped, staccato notes drive the rhythm forward
0:50	Esta es la gaita de las flores, Oyela, que sabrosita está. Gaita que lleva mis amores, Oyela, que sabrosita está.	This is the gaita of flowers, Listen to it, it's so tasty. Gaita that carries along all my loves, Listen to it, it's so tasty.	**Verse** Lead singer alternates with chorus
1:00			"Blast" of brass section, then clarinet featured in melodic fragment related to main melody
1:10			**Instrumental section** Full orchestra enters; the wavering attack of trumpets is typical of 1940s Latin big bands
1:21			Foregrounding of rhythmic foundation; relative calm setting the stage for next section
1:31			Parts of instrumental introduction repeated and expanded; brass answered by winds, winds answered by brass
2:10			Music from 1:21 repeats
2:20			**Verses** Short verses make the lyrics comment on the instrumental music, rather than focusing attention on vocals
2:30			**Instrumental section** Repeat of first part of piece
2:52			Same horn figure as in 0:40 to 0:49; then long "blasted" final brassy chord. Decrescendo quiets the music almost to a whisper, then the song ends on a note played as loud as possible (typical of many endings in Afro-Caribbean popular music)

Vallenato

The origin of **vallenato** is contained in its name: *nato*—"born in," *valle*—"valley." This hugely popular music and dance form emerged as a distinct style around the 1940s in the city of Valledupar, in the rural northeast region. A typical early vallenato band consisted of a button (not piano keyboard) accordion, a small single-headed drum called a *caja* (literally, box), and a *guacharaca*, a scraper usually made from a dry gourd. Around the 1970s, vallenato bands added an electric bass, and this quartet created new versions of traditional Colombian music (including cumbia). Unlike some música tropical, in vallenato lyrics are an indispensable element. The lead singer is always joined by another who harmonizes a good part of the song in thirds. Lyrics tend towards romantic themes. Two common genres performed by vallenato groups are the merengue in $\frac{6}{8}$ meter (not to be confused with the Dominican merengue) and the *paseo* in $\frac{4}{4}$ meter.

During the heyday of música tropical, most of the nation disdained vallenato as the music of hicks from the countryside. Nevertheless, it slowly gained popularity, also crossing the border to become a favored style in western Venezuela. Rafael Escalona's compositions and talent helped propel vallenato out of its regional base. Some ensembles tried to enhance their appeal by adding synthesizers and more percussion. Central to the music's ascension was the rise of the marijuana industry in the region that expanded exponentially from the 1970s onwards. Drug cartels patronized bands and underwrote their recordings and tours. By the 1990s, vallenato began to

FIGURE 4.9 Vallentano goes international: Hugo Carlos Granados, winner of the "King of Kings" contest in Colombia, on accordion at a festival in Guadalajara, Mexico, in 2007, with gaita, tambor, and a hat typical of Colombia's northeastern region

By the 1970s, salsa music—the "Nuyorican" transformation of Cuban popular dance music— quickly expanded to four principal cities: New York; San Juan, Puerto Rico; Caracas, Venezuela; and Cali, Colombia, which has sometimes promoted itself as the "salsa music capital." Some of the biggest names in salsa—Joe Arroyo, Fruko y los Tesos, and Los Carruseles—have come from Colombia and orchestras continue to flourish there.

eclipse música tropical nationally with talented band leaders as Diomedes Díaz, Binomio de Oro, and Lizandro Meza. Meza was an especially amazing accordionist and singer who broke into the international world music market. Vallenato attracted a new generation when pop musician and actor Carlos Vives broke sales records with his rock interpretations of vallenato and other traditional forms, as discussed in the following section.

The classic quartet of accordion, *caja*, *guacharaca*, and bass is still the mainstay of vallenato music (Figure 4.9, the bass player is not shown). When the Smithsonian-Folkways label went to Colombia to record in 2008, it is not surprising one group's offering was the song "Cadenas" (Listening Guide 4.6). Composed by one of vallenato's most respected composers, Rosendo Romero Ospino, the first recording (by Los Black Stars) in 1969 became such a sensation that some credit it as the most important song in establishing vallenato's popularity in Colombia.

This *vallenato-paseo* is modified with the addition of a repeated chorus, indicative of the plasticity of form of many modern vallenatos. The lyrics tie the composer's feelings of despair from personal mistakes to the loneliness of the narrow streets in small towns in the northeastern mountainous region of Colombia.

LISTENING guide | **4.6**

⊚ Ospino: "Cadenas" (Chains)

Composer/lyricist: Rosendo Romero Ospino

Date of composition: 1969

Performers/instruments: Ivo Díaz y su grupo; Ivo Díaz, vocals; Orangel "El Pangue" Maestre, accordion; Daniel Castilla, *caja*; Jaine Maestre, *guacharaca*; José Vásquez, bass; Luis Ángel "El Papa" Pastor, guitar; Jesús Cervantes, *congas*; Eder Manjarrez and Jesús Saurith, chorus

Date of recording: 2008

Genre: vallenato

Form: *paseo*; verse and chorus

Tempo/meter: moderately fast simple quadruple

What to Listen for:
- Accordion employing its full melodic range
- Solo singer's voice invoking the anguish of being shunned
- Harmonized chorus serving as a moral commentary by others

Time	Text	Translation	Description
0:00			**Instrumental introduction** Accordion states main theme

(continued)

Time	Text	Translation	Description
0:20	Yo que creí que me soñaban las mujeres y que podía enamorarme de cualquiera, siempre egoísta me burlé de sus quereres pero el corazón, me puso cadenas. Carga del alma por parrandas y placeres pero la aventura me ensanchó una pena.	I thought that women dreamed of me That I could get any to fall in love with me, Always stuck-up, I made fun of their love But my heart put chains on me. I was all partying and good-timing But these adventures filled me with sorrow.	Melody outlines a chord in the first, second, and fourth lines; the third line contrasts by being legato, stepwise, and harmonized
0:42	Cosa increible, yo que fui el gran ruiseñor y que creí ser el rey de los amigos, creí sincero a todo el mundo, y la traición hizo mil fronteras sobre mis caminos. Yo fui el galán que hoy vive de cualquier manera sufriendo a la espera de cualquier cariño.	Incredible, me who was the big nightingale And I thought myself the king of all friends, I thought I was sincere with everyone, and insincerity Placed a thousand roadblocks across my path. I was the big shot that now can barely get by Suffering with the hope for any kind of affection.	Here, and in all verses, the accordion improvises an accompaniment
1:01	Y la niña que mi alma adoró, la perdí sin poder hacer nada, de esa vivencia brotó esta canción cadenas tristes, cadenas del alma. ¡Qué vida tan triste! ¡Qué pueblo tan solo! Me muero mil veces, en cada recodo. [2x]	And the girl whom my soul adored, I lost her, unable to do anything about it, From that experience sprouted this song Sad chains, chains of the soul. What a sad life! What a lonely town! I die a thousand times in each turn [of the streets].	Section mostly sung by harmonized chorus; relatively new to the vallenato
1:24			Accordion-led break, with use of sustained high notes, somewhat like crying
2:39			**Verse 2** Moral message: avoid these mistakes
3:44	¡Ayombe!	[vocal interjection]	Shaking of the accordion on last chord creates an effect similar to a studio echo

FIGURE 4.10 Carlos Vives, in concert, playing harmonica with T-shirt of his album "Rock of My People"

Regional Musics Plug In: Carlos Vives

Colombian musicians, always in competition the international Latin and Anglo pop-music industry, received a game-changing boost when Carlos Alberto Vives Restrepo (b. 1961) turned his talents from portraying a vallenato musician on a runaway hit *telenovela* (TV soap opera) to concentrate on actually playing music (Figure 4.10). Some vallenato purists were taken aback, but no one can deny that when Carlos Vives released his album *Clásicos de la provincia* (Classics from the Provinces/Regions), it not only reminded Colombian musicians and audiences of the depth of their nation's musical riches, but also introduced his reworking of vallenato and other Colombian genres to the rest of the continent in a tremendously successful way. The embrace by thoroughly urban audiences of musical sounds like actual gaita flutes showed that city dwellers now feel far enough removed from their rural origins to not fear losing social status from association with such music. In Figure 4.10 note the juxtaposition of an electric guitar (played by Luis Ángel "El Papa" Pastor) and a three-row, button accordion used in vallenato with the accordionist's (Egidio Cuadrado) traditional indigenous bag prominently slung by his side. Vives's fusion of local forms with rock, pop and some Caribbean musical elements garnered Billboard and Grammy recognition and encouraged Colombians to draw from national sources for inspiration. Vives opened the door to compatriots Juanes and Shakira, both of whom performed in a similar stylistic vein before moving into more generically Latin American and North American crossover pop stardom respectively (see Chapter 10). Following Vives, the Latin American **rock en español**

![explore]

The artists mentioned remain very popular; for more-recent vallenatos, try compilations such as *Lo mejor de la música Vallenata, Vol. 3* (Discos Fuentes), or Carlos Vives's "rockified" vallenatos on *Clásicos de la provincia* and *El amor de mi tierra*.

movement took off and groups around Latin America rode a new wave of creativity and commercial success.

European and European–American Classical Music

After subduing the indigenous peoples and suppressing their musical life, Spain transferred their own musical practices into the Nueva Granada colony, which would become independent Colombia. By the early 1600s, Bogotá's cathedral boasted the largest collection of written music in the Americas. This efflorescence in the religious realm of the European art tradition continued apace for a century, when it began a slow decline. By the 1820s, church organs were in disrepair, and few professional singers could be found. The rest of the nineteenth century saw the slow development of secular Euroclassical music, overwhelmingly centered in Bogotá. Early attempts at nationalist composition by José María Ponce de León (1846–1882), like pieces based on bambucos, failed to generate widespread interest.

Only as the twentieth century progressed did determined efforts at institutional European classical education begin to bear fruit. Guillermo Uribe Holguín (1880–1971) founded the Orquesta Sinfónica Nacional (National Symphonic Orchestra) in Bogotá in 1936, and conservatories and permanent performing ensembles established themselves in Cali and other cities. Uribe Holguín studied with the Panamanian composer Narciso Garay. Holguín's work, also strongly influenced by studies in Paris, has recently enjoyed a certain revival. A notable composer in the latter twentieth century is Jesús Pinzón Urrea (b. 1928), the founding director in 1967 of the Orquesta Filharmónica de Bogotá, currently the most prestigious Colombian symphony. He has written pieces without set forms and using chance composition. He also attempted to adapt indigenous music from the far south Amazon in his cantata *Goé Payari* or *Bico anamo* of 1982, and traditional music in his symphonic piece *Canción vallenata*.

There are many active contemporary composers, and most experiment with integrating national musical material. Blas Emilio Atehortúa (1943), who studied with Alberto Ginastera in Argentina, gained international attention beginning in the 1960s. Francisco "Pacho" Zumaqué (b. 1945) must be one of the continent's most eclectic musical talents: he first worked with his father's Afro-Caribbean band and wrote the pop-salsa hit "Colombia Caribe"—which was chosen as the theme song for the national soccer team—as well as establishing himself as a composer of electroacoustic avant-garde Euroclassical pieces. Luis Pulido Hurtado (b. 1958) twice won the annual Ministry of Culture's composition prize, in 2006 with a woodwind quintet entitled *Diosa Chía*, named from a mythical female figure of the indigenous Chibcha people. Historically, financial support has fallen short of that necessary to expand the understanding and popularity of this genre; perhaps the success of El Sistema in neighboring Venezuela (p. 171) will inspire similar support in Colombia as well.

The Llanos

The **Llanos** qualifies as a bi-national region with an identity all its own (Figures 4.7 and 4.12). "Llano" means flat, and the associations with this large swath of plains parallel those of the mythic West in United States culture. As in the Old West, the main occupation in the Llanos is cattle raising. This South American region floods during the rainy season, however, and cowboys with water all the way up to the bottom of their horses have to herd cattle onto dry areas where they can feed. Ethnically, *llaneros* (Llanos residents) are a mixture of Europeans, indigenous peoples, and Africans, the last including many escaped slaves that made their way from coastal plantations south to the Llanos to freedom. In Colombia and Venezuela, mestizo refers to any combination of this tripartite ethnic makeup.

Though an important region in Colombia as well, the Llanos hold a special place in the Venezuelan imagination. In the twentieth century, Venezuela's elite promoted the Llanos as a touchstone of national identity. As the nation urbanized, images of open land and rugged individualism comforted those moving into concrete buildings with city noise and pollution. To this day, the novel *Doña Bárbara* by Rómulo Gallegos, set in the Llanos, is required reading for all Venezuelan high school students. *Música llanera* has played a role similar to that of country music in the United States, closely associated with a earlier, more rural time. Overall it remains the music most commonly identified with Venezuela.

Música Llanera

The hallmark music from the Llanos is the **joropo llanero** genre, and often a specific subgenre known as *pasaje*. The word joropo probably stems from the Arabic *xörop*, the same root for the English word "syrup," a reference to something sweet and pleasing. Writers in the early nineteenth century used the word joropo to describe celebrations with music and dancing. Currently, the term mostly references a specific musical style and the couple dance that accompanies it.

The joropo found in the Llanos consists of a singer, a four-stringed **cuatro** (not to be confused with the Puerto Rican cuatro; see Chapter 5), maracas, and the **arpa llanera**, a 32-stringed harp (Figure 4.11). The cuatro is strummed, not plucked. Joropo maraca players are probably the most virtuosic in the world. They often hold a pair of small, high-pitched maracas vertically and execute complex rhythmic improvisations, moving their arms in an amazing display. The harp is a diatonic instrument, derived from traditional instruments brought by Spanish settlers. Its strings were made originally from animal gut, but now are of plastic. Harpists play a bass line on lower strings with their left hand and chords or melodies simultaneously with their right, often using both hands melodically during solos. Recently, performers have added an electric bass guitar, and sometimes the larger guitar-like *bandola* also joins in, but the basic iconic quartet continues to represent llanera culture.

FIGURE 4.11 Joropo llanero trio in 1955, with arpa llanera, cuatro, and maracas, the same ensemble used today

Joropo music is in a ⁶/₈ or ¹²/₈ meter, usually at a moderate tempo, but sometimes is very quick and therefore musically challenging. Singing is prominent in this style, and lyrics often recount historical events in a manner similar to that of Mexican corridos (see Chapter 3). Vocals have a high, pinched, nasal quality. A true llanera singer must not only have an extensive repertoire of memorized songs, but, most importantly, he or she must also be able to improvise four-line coplas (rhyming sets of verses) on the spot. There are a good number of female singers, but this is a male-dominated tradition. Like the *desafíos* or duels of central and southern Spain, and like the acerbic commentary in traditional music from western Africa (and therefore like rap), an accomplished llanera singer locked in competition with another singer will try to "one up" his compatriot with biting comments. Hailing from an impoverished small town in the western Venezuelan Llanos, president Hugo Chávez Frías grew up in such an environment that prized verbal dexterity. He still publically sings joropos, a proud acknowledgment of his humble roots that valorizes a tradition no previous president would "stoop" to associate themselves with.

Singer-songwriter Reynaldo Armas is one of the best-known and most prolific masters of *música llanera* since his first album in 1977.

The song "El indio" was a major hit for Armas and speaks to the pride people of the plains maintain in their mestizo heritage. Probably the

Ⓢ Armas: "El indio" (The Indian)

Composer/lyricist: Reynaldo Armas

Date of composition: 1981

Performer/instruments: Reynaldo Armas, singer; arpa llanera, cuatro, maracas, electric bass

Date of recording: 1981

Genre: *música llanera*

Form: strophic, each set of verses with an **ABB** melodic pattern (no chorus), separated by short instrumental breaks

Tempo/meter: moderate (slower than most songs in the genre), compound duple

What to Listen for:

- Harp providing harmony, and then melody during breaks
- Nasal vocal quality specific to *música llanera*
- Repetitive, compressed lyrics at beginning of section B
- Semispoken word "indio," similar to spitting an insult

Time	Text	Translation	Description
0:00			**Instrumental introduction** Harp solo
0:17	Indio me dice la gente, y para mi es un honor, y además soy complaciente, popular y jugetón.	Indian, the people call me, And for me it's an honor, I'm also easy to get along with, Well liked and playful.	**Verse 1** **Music section A**
	Me gusta vivir mi vida de acuerdo a la situación no tolero la injusticia porque me causa dolor, debe ser porque en el cuerpo solo tengo corazón.	I like to live my life as it comes I don't tolerate injustice for it hurts me inside, The reason is because I am full of heart.	**Music section B** Tension of very short phrases in the first part. first part, then release with "me causa…"
0:51	Llevo sangre del cacique aquel que no doblegó, aquel que perdió sus tierras pero no se resignó, combatiendo hasta morir con nobleza y con valor.	I carry the blood of a chief The one that never gave in, The one that lost his lands but never gave up, Fighting to the death with honor and courage.	**Music section B** Similar tension and release (with "pero no se resignó…")
1:07			**Instrumental break** Harp solo

(continued)

Time	Text	Translation	Description
1:24	Indio me dice la gente es porque hay una razón, criollo de tierra caliente de mi pueblo un sevidor.	Indian, the people call me It's for a good reason, [I'm] a native from the hot Lands, servant to the people.	**Verse 2** **Music section A**
1:39	Mi madre una hermosa india, mi padre de buen color, cuatro hermanos piel canela más yo que soy el menor, de una misma descendencia y una misma religión.	My mother: a beautiful Indian, my father: good and dark- skinned, Four brothers with cinnamon- colored skin Plus myself the youngest, All from the same ethnic Background and religion.	**Music section B** Tension and release (with "más yo que…")
1:57	El campo donde nacimos nos fue llenando de amor: sus flores, sus mariposas su fragancia y su color, detalles que siendo humildes no se mustian con el sol.	The land we were born in Filled us with love: Its flowers, butterflies Its fragrant smells and color, Details that, being of humble origins The sun could not wither away [though poor, nothing could take from us the beauty of the Llanos.]	**Music section B** Tension and release (with "su fragancia…")
2:15			**Instrumental break** Harp solo
2:32			**Verse 3**
3:22			**Instrumental ending** Harp solo

majority of llaneras are in a major key, though many are in minor, as in this example. Perhaps Armas chose this slow tempo and minor key because of the contemplative nature of the lyrics. Notice how at the beginning of section B he declaims several lines using only two or three notes, almost like talking. Sometimes singers emphasize this technique when improvising, especially in duels with other singers.

Venezuela

Venezuela, about twice the size of California (352,000 square miles), is one of the most ecologically diverse nations on the planet. The continents of Africa and North and South America first separated along a line in the

explore

Look for videos of *música llanera* **or joropo llanero. The CD** *Sí, soy llanero* **(Smithsonian-Folkways) contains recently recorded Colombian musicians and demonstrates how the style is shared across the Colombia–Venezuela border.**

spectacular southeast region where today tropical mesas still yield new discoveries of plant and insect life (this region inspired the book *The Lost World*). The southeast is inhabited by scattered indigenous groups and a steady stream of tourists that flock to see the earth's tallest waterfall. The far southeast overlaps with Amazonian Brazil. Venezuela's immense Llanos make up over a fourth of the country, shared with Colombia to the west. Southwestern Venezuela contains the most northern tropical Andes, farmed by people of European and indigenous descent. In the far northwest of Venezuela lies Lake Maracaibo, the largest freshwater lake in South America, resting atop tremendous oil reserves. A strong African-descendant presence remains in several towns around the lake and has contributed to racial mixing in the nation's second largest city, Maracaibo. Other heavily African-Venezuelan pockets dot the northern coast where cacao has been cultivated, especially the eastern Barlovento area. The indigenous Wayu'u live both in the arid Perijá peninsula, shared with northeast Colombia, and in neighborhoods of Maracaibo. The bulk of the population of 27 million lives in the northern third of the national territory and is one of the most urbanized in the world at 93 percent (compare with 74 percent of Colombians.)

A Brief History

Venezuela takes its name from the Amerindian houses on stilts that reminded the first Spanish of Venice. The colonial era brought only minimal economic development to this region, mostly agricultural. "The Liberator," slaveholder Simón Bolívar (1783–1830), eventually realized that emancipation was key to mobilizing the African American and mixed-race population against Spain. He allied with the fierce mestizo horsemen of the Llanos who carried the day in the final 1821 clash with colonial forces. The landed aristocracy, however, soon reasserted control, marginalizing other groups from power. Despite various rebellions since independence, near-feudal conditions continued until oil was discovered in the early twentieth century. Oil production generated considerable revenue. Sadly, for the bulk of the population the oil wealth circulated only among a small professional class while successive dictatorships perpetuated one of widest economic gaps between rich and poor in the Americas.

Several campaigns in the twentieth century to "whiten" the nation succeeded in attracting (in order of number) Spaniards, Italians, Portuguese, and (Christian and Muslim) Lebanese to Venezuela. The creation of affluent mini-cities surrounding oil production sites contributed to a

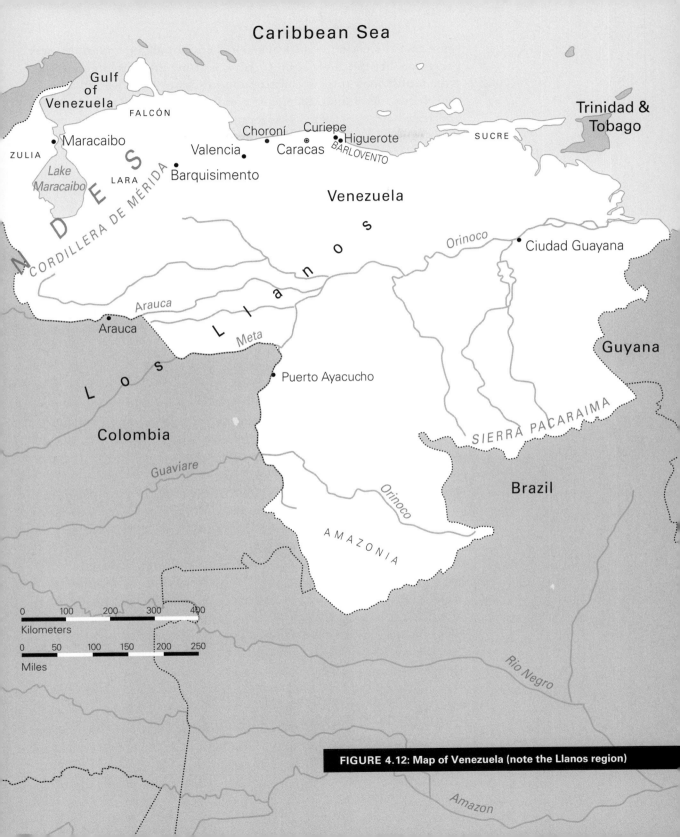

FIGURE 4.12: Map of Venezuela (note the Llanos region)

sense that the nation was advanced and cosmopolitan, and in this way exceptional to much of Latin America. Cutting-edge architecture gave a modernist look to new construction in Caracas. Oil wealth allowed the pioneering ethnomusicologist couple Luis Felipe Ramón y Rivera and Isabel Áretz (originally Argentinian) to systematically document many musical traditions and to host intensive training workshops for music folklorists and ethnomusicologists from throughout Latin America, the only continent-wide initiative of its kind. Caracas also became a magnet for the nation's poor, who constructed shantytowns in the surrounding hills. At night, hundreds of thousands of light bulbs continue to twinkle from small houses and shacks on the periphery. It is a captivating sight, but also a visible indicator of still-disproportionate divisions of wealth.

Economic "neoliberalism" consists of the privatization of public institutions and industries to roll back national programs and increase profitability of private holdings. The developed world increasingly imposed neoliberalism on the underdeveloped or "Third World" beginning in the 1970s. Such policies resulted in declining living standards for the vast majority. This worldwide scheme met its first serious public challenge in Venezuela in 1989. The newly elected government promised to change the neoliberal economic direction, but when it reversed course and drastically raised prices on public services, a huge rebellion erupted in Caracas and elsewhere. Though disturbances ended after a few days, the government ordered military reprisals in poor residential areas, and a series of massacres resulted. Called the "Caracazo," this violence spurred a mass movement that eventually brought its charismatic candidate, Hugo Chávez, to elected office in 1998. In 2002, a right-wing coup overthrew the government and dissolved all elected offices, but a massive outpouring of grassroots support dismantled the conspiracy within 48 hours.

This same ferment helped radicalize the direction of the Chávez administration. Since 2003, oil revenues have been redirected into a series of social programs that have significantly reduced poverty. Nationwide access to primary health care, educational opportunities, various community initiatives, new legal protections for indigenous peoples, and other programs have further stimulated progressive social change. The new desperately needed social services exist side by side with the previous economic system and an entrenched and resentful ruling class. To further its accomplishments, the new social movement will need to overcome its own weaknesses, such as cronyism, inefficient government bureaucracies, and an overreliance on Chávez's personality.

Traditional and Popular Music

European-Based Musics

Heritage from Spain remains vital in the great variety of traditional forms within the nation, though of course many genres have changed over time from interaction with African and indigenous aesthetics, and traditions vary widely. In the Tuy valley region just south of Caracas, for instance the *joropo tuyero* uses a harp with metal strings that produces a completely different sound from the joropo llanero. The cuatro is not used, and song lyrics incorporate a complicated Iberian rhyming scheme. The hilly state of Lara, between Lake Maracaibo and Caracas, is often thought of as the most musical region of the country. The best cuatros are handcrafted in Lara, and some cuatro variants have additional strings. The Spanish-derived cuatro is so widespread within Venezuela that it is considered the national instrument.

FIGURE 4.13 Daisy Gutiérrez with cuarto. Caracas, 2008

One of the numerous song forms that utilize a cuatro is the **polo**, now distinct from the Spanish flamenco variant of the same name. Polo is found in the far northeastern state of Sucre, named for José Antonio Sucre, a young compatriot of Bolívar. Listening Guide 4.8, "Los dos titanes" (The Two Titans), is a *polo sucrense* (from the state of Sucre) written in the early twentieth century and still well known. Polos are characterized by a moderate tempo in ¾ or ⁶⁄₈ meter. Their accompaniment consists of four sections that alternate between major and minor. The particular repeated pattern of "Los dos titanes" is shown in Example 4.4:

Daisy Gutiérrez is from the eastern part of the country and struggles to make a living as a professional musician. "Los dos titanes" (The Two Titans) comes from the album she and her husband produced themselves. She accompanies herself on the cuatro and has added a flute and mandolin played in a manner similar to the Euroclassical tradition. This type of arranged traditional material came to prominence in the 1970s and is discussed shortly.

explore

Look for videos of Daisy Guitiérrez, as well as the version of "Los dos titanes" by María Rodriguez, one of Sucre's artistic treasures who continues to perform in her late eighties. The eastern variant of the joropo is well represented on *¡Y Que Viva Venezuela! Maestros del joropo oriental* (Smithsonian-Folkways.)

EXAMPLE 4.4: Typical chordal pattern of a *polo sucrense*

F	C⁷ A⁷	d	B♭	A⁷	d C⁷
major ⌐___⌐ ⌐_____ minor _____⌐ ⌐_major

⊚ Guitiérrez: "Los dos titanes" (The Two Titans)

Composer/lyricist: Félix Calderón Chacín

Performers/instruments: Daisy Guitiérrez y Su Grupo: Daisy Guitiérrez, voice and cuatro; unknown musicians on flute, mandolin, and acoustic bass

Date of recording: 2006

Genre: *polo sucrense* (polo from Sucre)

Form: sets of verses, last two lines repeated each verse.

Tempo/meter: moderately quick compound duple

What to Listen for:

- Steady cuatro accompaniment (on left channel)
- Variation of melodic line between repeated notes and outlining the chord, bringing out the contrast between major and minor modes
- Flute and mandolin share short precomposed sections and solo improvisations, often intertwining in counterpoint akin to the Euroclassical tradition

Time	Text	Translation	Description
0:00			**Instrumental introduction** Flute and mandolin in precomposed melodic lines
0:28	Hay dos gigantes, genios que la historia con mil laureles coronó de fama: Bolívar adalid de la victoria, Sucre de mi tierra soberana.	There are two giants, Geniuses that history Crowned with a thousand laurels: Bolivar, victorious leader, Sucre from my sovereign homeland.	**Verses 1 and 2** Only string instruments accompany singer
0:47	Los dos lucharon por el más fecundo ideal, de inefable providad, y alcanzaron la gloria de este mundo dándole medio mundo libertad. [repeat last two lines]	The two struggled For the most fecund [deepest] Ideals of ineffable probity [virtue], And achieved glory in this world Giving liberty to half the world.	
1:16	Bolívar, cual Jesús el peregrino, Sucre, como Abel sacrificado, los dos forman el alma del soldado, que a América brindó mejor destino.	Bolivar, [like] Jesus on a pilgrimage,* Sucre, like a sacrificed Abel,† The two form the soul of the soldier that gave America a better destiny.	**Verses 3 and 4** "Bolivar..." in major; "Sucre..." in minor fits his martyrdom. Flute and mandolin accompany with improvised melodic lines; synchronized endings precomposed
1:36	Ellos son ideal bolivariano que nos conduce hacia las obras buenas, y la fe que circula por las venas, de nuestro corazón venezolano. [repeat last two lines]	They are the Bolivarian ideal That leads us To do good work, And the faith that flows in the veins of our Venezuelan heart.	

(continued)

Time	Text	Translation	Description
2:05			**Instrumental break** Flute and mandolin; short mandolin solo
2:45			**Verses 3 and 4 repeat** Flute and mandolin continue melodic accompaniment
3:35	Por eso, esta tierra capitana donde no prosperó la tiranía, y si veo flamear otra bandera ufana yo respondo orgullusa con lamía. Y si un día el pie del extranjero profana el suelo del Libertador, con el ejemplo suyo lucharemos hasta poner en fuga el invasor. [repeat last two lines]	That's why, this land of captains‡ [exists] Where tyranny could not prosper, And if I see another [foreign] flag wave in arrogance I'll respond proudly with my own. And if some day a foreigner's foot Profanes the soil of the Liberator,§ With his example will will fight Until we put the invader to flight.	**Verses 5 and 6** Flute and mandolin continue same type of accompaniment
4:22			**Instrumental ending**

*The phrase "on a pilgrimage" refers to Bolívar's travels to fight the Spanish from what is now Venezuela across the Andes to Bolivia (named after him).

†Sucre was assassinated soon after independence as he championed peasants and laborers against the landed gentry.

‡The term "captains" means people in charge of their destiny.

§Simón Bolívar.

African-Based Musics

The many enclaves of African-descent communities in Venezuela exist in relative isolation from each other and have generated a wide variety of musical styles. It would be impossible to do justice here to the impressive number of instruments and rhythms unique to these groups. The following section focuses on two regions that have produced nationally known music of African origin: (1) the gaita from the western state of Zulia; and (2) music from Barlovento on the coast east of Caracas.

Gaita

African-Venezuelan communities along the southern and eastern shoreline of Lake Maracaibo have contributed to various versions of folk-rooted

El canto necesario

El canto necesario (Necessary Song) is the Venezuelan name for socially conscious music more commonly called nueva canción (new song) in most of Latin America. Venezuela has produced many songs protesting unjust conditions and recounting struggles to remedy them, but in the 1960s a new wave of singers and songwriters developed. This outpouring coincided with the upsurge of socially engaged compositions elsewhere in Latin America.

The towering individual within this movement remains singer-songwriter Alí Primera (Rafael Sebastián Primera Rosell, 1942–1985) (Figures 4.14 a and b). Alí grew up dirt-poor in the dry central northern Falcón state. He began singing in universities, where his impressive performances eventually led to a full-time musical career and earned him the title "El cantor del pueblo" (The People's Singer). His lyrics sharply underscored the hypocrisy of a country whose petroleum wealth was siphoned off by the wealthiest segment of the population, leaving the rest to deprivation. The establishment strongly repressed Alí's music. Several attempts were made on his and his family's life, and he died in a car crash some consider suspicious. His music was banned from both TV and radio, so he cultivated relationships with open-minded radio DJs and appeared on live shows to disseminate his music. Alí eventually created the record label Cigarrón (Big Cigar) since commercial labels refused to sign him. One of his songs, "Las casas (or techos) de cartón" (The houses [or roofs] of cardboard), describes the misery of migrants from the countryside in the slums of Caracas. To this day, the song is well known throughout Latin America.

With Alí's passing, the canto necesario movement receded, but in the late 1990s his music began to circulate again. Hugo Chávez aided this resurgence when he quoted and sang his songs in election speeches. In the early 2000s Alí Primera's music achieved airtime on community radio stations, and his music may have better exposure now than during his lifetime.

FIGURE 4.14 Alí Primera: (a) in concert, in 1983 and (b) memorialized on a small town's mural in 2004

gaita. The contemporary commercial gaita developed from the *gaita de fulia*. The iconic instrument associated with this genre is the **furro** friction drum: a wooden stick protrudes from the drumhead that the musician moves to produce a deep, resonant "grunting" sound. In the 1960s the group Guaco began to integrate salsa and rock with gaita and vaulted this new hybrid to national popularity. Noncommercial gaita of earlier years had been part of Christmas celebrations, primarily in Maracaibo. Despite admonitions from the Catholic hierarchy, the lively new popular music and its sensual dance have increasingly surpassed other Christmas repertoire in popularity. Traditionally, gaitas are also vehicles for social commentary, though these are not the ones that became nationally famous and are used around Christmas.

Barlovento

The largest region with a strong African musical heritage is called Barlovento (Where the Wind Blows), a flat, tropical coastal area between Caracas and Sucre. The annual celebrations around the San Juan festival are a major tourist attraction, drawing migrants back home to Caracas.

FIGURE 4.15 Children playing culo'e puya, or redondo drums, on a street in Curiepe, Barlovento

The small saint's image is paraded around town to an outpouring of joy and celebration during a week punctuated with music and dancing. All kinds of dance music are played, but traditional acoustic drumming is heard this week like no other. There are two sets of drums: the large **mina** and the trio of thin **culo'e puya** or **redondo** (cylinder) drums (Figure 4.15). The mina can be traced to Dahomey region of West Africa, and the *redondo* and some of its accompanying dance choreography is similar to Central African forms, possibly from the Mnagbele people from the Congo. Made from a hollowed tree trunk, the mina drum is over six feet in length. One player hits the skin on the top, while one or more other players play on the side of the drum.

The culo'e puya or *redondo* drums are held by straps around the neck of three players. These three drums (called *pujao*, *cruzao*, and *corrío* or *prima*) form a typical rhythmic interlocking pattern (Example 4.5).

Afro-Venezuelan music and dance enjoyed new exposure from the late 1960s onwards with the formation of groups dedicated to reproducing traditional genres in various reworked formats for

EXAMPLE 4.5: Pattern of culo'e puya, or *redondo* drums

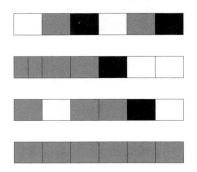

stage presentations. This coincided with the move of people from African-descent communities to larger cities, especially Caracas. For instance, the nationally famous Un Solo Pueblo (A Single People) band popularized the **tambor**, a dance and music from coastal Choroní and elsewhere. Motivated by the impact of salsa's popularity, other groups formed in the African-descent communities of Sarría and San Augustín in Caracas to learn various Afro-Caribbean rhythms. Percussionist Orlando Poleo, now active in Europe, and Miguel Urbina began their performance careers by learning Afro-Cuban drumming styles, then turned to studying African-Venezuelan repertoire, especially from Barlovento. Urbina's current group, Mina, is named after the large mina drum as well as in homage to Francisco Mina, an individual who for several years led a community of escaped slaves until he was killed in 1771. Urbina created an innovative fusion of salsa and Barlovento rhythms. The lyrics of "Sueños de Guillermo" (Dreams of Guillermo, Listening Guide 4.9) show the growing racial consciousness of the *Afro-descendiente* (Afro-descendant) movement in Venezuela. For decades, an official myth maintained that "there is no racism in Venezuela." However,

Grupo Mina: "Sueños de Guillermo" (Dreams of Guillermo)

Composer/lyricist: Miguel "Miguito" Urbina
(arranged by Miguel Urbina and Alfredo Naranjo)

Date of composition: 2003

Performers/instruments: Miguel "Miguito" Urbina,
mina (modified, smaller version) and culo'e puya;
Alfredo Naranjo, vibraphone; Palbo Gil, tenor
sax; Gerán Quintero, trumpet; Morocho Vázquez,
flute; Luis Pacheco, piano; Marcos Romero bass;
Héctor Chastre, solo voice; Jhonny Rudas, culo'e
puya; Kenny Quintana culo'e puya; Juan Carlos
Figueredo, trap drums

Date of recording: 2004

Genre: *malembe* (with salsa and jazz elements)

Form: binary: verse, and montuno (p. 190)

Tempo/meter: moderate duple (slower than most
salsa tempos), compound duple with simple
quadruple swing section

What to Listen for:

- Structural similarities with salsa
- Culo'e puya and mina drums combine to create a unique Barlovento-based rhythmic foundation
- Jazz elements in chords and section in swing tempo
- Moderately slow tempo compared to most salsa tunes, as the *malembe* accompanies the solemn return of a saint or the last part of a funeral procession

Time	Text	Translation	Description
0:00	A la le le le, a la loa	[Vocables of African derivation]	**Introduction** Chorus alternates with horns
0:26	Lugar de donde viene el viento humedecido de esperanzas, en las nubes, la confianza moral en el firmamento.	Land where the wind blows Humid with hope, In the clouds a firmament Of moral confidence	**Verse 1** Solo male voice over percussion; distinguished from salsa by the timbre and rhythmic patterns of Venezuelan druming
	Donde el mar atestiguó una historia transitada, que no ha sido bien contada por aquel que la escribió.	Where the sea witnessed A history transpire That has not been well told By those who wrote it.	
	Lugar de donde viene el viento esfuerzo de lo vivido, si tuve un sueño sagrado fué porque soñé contigo. [repeat twice the first time]	Land where the wind blows Strength of lived history, If I had a sacred dream it Was because I dreamed of you.	**Verse 2** Singer's plaintive rise in melody calls out to departed spirit of Guillermo Rivas
	Si vivieras más allá de un destino prefijado a todo tiempo esperado un sentido le darás.	If you live in the beyond In a predetermined destiny You give meaning to all the time We have waited [for liberation].	

(continued)

Time	Text	Translation	Description
1:32			**Instrumental break** Swing jazz rhythm (in 𝄴)
1:52			**Verse 1** repeats
2:18	**Chorus response:** A la le le le, a la loa **Solo call:** Allá en el Cumbé de Ocoyta una historia se vivió, cimarrón Guillermo Rivas su fuerzo no se perdió. Noches de estrellas y lunas un sueño que transcurría mujeres niños y hombres que en el monte se perdían. Ay lo-o-o-o, Ay lo-o-o-a cimarrones del saber que tuvieron corazón. Ay lo-o-o-o, Ay lo-o-o-a si ellos lo hicieron ayer ¿qué haremos nosotros hoy?	**Chorus response:** [vocables] **Solo call:** There in the Cumbé Ocoyta A history was lived out, Escaped slave Guillermo Rivas, Your power has not been lost. Nights of stars and moons A dream became reality Women, children and men That lost themselves in the countryside. [vocables] Escaped slaves With a strong heart. [vocables] If they did this yesterday What should we do today?	**Montuno section 1** Set choral response alternating with solo call; singer's voice becomes more assertive for an assured recounting of history leading up to a final challenge to be courageous in the present
2:57			**Instrumental break**
3:24	[more lyrics in style of montuno section 1]		**Montuno section 2**
3:44	**Chorus response:** A la le le le, a la loa	**Chorus response:** [vocables]	Instruments take on "verse" role with precomposed lines that vary
4:11			**Coda** Mina and other drums solo; piano montuno

the new empowerment of the darker-colored majority has brought ugly racist attitudes out into the open. Urbina strives to promote an awareness of the African-Venezuelan experience that until recently had been largely ignored in official history. The name of the slow-tempo *malembe* song form

❀ In Depth 4.2

Recent Media Initiatives

Historically, the commercial music industry in Venezuela has offered little support to local music. The progressive social movement that began to win elections in the late 1990s pushed for changes, and in the early 2000s various cultural initiatives took shape. These can be broken down into four main areas:

1. New national television channels, VIVE-TV and TEVES, offer new space for Venezuelan musicians.

2. The government has provided support for the creation of community radio and more than four hundred new stations have been launched since 2003. Participants are volunteers, and each station reflects the local needs of their communities. The community broadcasts represent a significant counterbalance to conservative corporate media, both culturally and politically.

3. In 1999, Internet access was a privilege of the wealthy, accessed by less than 6 percent of the population. Access has increased substantially, including free Internet centers, often connected to free health care clinics, that allow even some of the poorest sectors of society to surf the net.

4. Different nations throughout the Americas have attempted to level the playing field for national artists who must compete with the multinational corporate music industry by guaranteeing them a certain percentage of airtime on the radio. Usually these laws failed for lack of follow-through. Venezuela passed such a law in the 2002 that requires half of what stations play to have some connection with Venezuela, be it through performers, composers, the style of music, lyrical references, and so on. Imagine this: the morning the law took effect, the manager of one of the largest radio stations in Caracas announced to his employees that they literally had no Venezuelan music in the studio! It was just such disdain for and ignorance of Venezuela's own music that this law attempted to redress, and the results soon became apparent. As audiences heard Venezuelan music they began to request it in stores as never before.

Together, these four cultural initiatives have raised the profile of national music, but it still suffers from lack of coherent and consistent support.

traces from a deity of protection in the Congo region of Africa and is associated with the tenderness of returning the consecrated statue of San Juan Congo, the most important religious figure in Barlovento, back to his church after days of joyous—and highly musical—celebrations.

As the musical style of "Sueños de Guillermo" suggests, there has been a strong jazz scene in Caracas for decades. Many jazz musicians move between the United States and Venezuela, including pianist Luis Perdomo

Compare the urban and jazz-inflected sound of Grupo Mina with one of the earliest and most important bands to champion Afro-Venezuelan music, Un Solo Pueblo.

and vibraphonist Alfredo Naranjo, both featured in Listening Guide 4.9, and others, such as pianist Prisca Dávila and Leo Blanco.

Any overview of recent African-Venezuelan music would be remiss without pointing out the important place Caracas played in the salsa "boom" of the 1960s and 1970s. Caracas can claim the first salsa radio show and the first published LP that used the term salsa. Major international salsa groups regularly toured to packed stadiums in Caracas and its importance is evident in the many compositions dedicated to the city by top figures such as Ray Barretto (see Chapter 5.) *Salsa dura* (hard salsa,) hardcore salsa from the 1970s, remains amazingly popular in Venezuela. When I took a public bus in 2006 from Caracas to Barlovento, I thought I had entered a time machine: the speakers blared out classic hits and everyone sang and drummed along.

Salsa now competes with hip-hop and other genres in the mixed-race neighborhoods of Caracas. Early in the 1980s, a Spanish-language ska revival produced a major band that remains the best-selling national group outside the country, Desorden Público (Disorderly Conduct) (a law from the 1960s used to harass youth of color). While most commercial radio remains unimaginative and ignores many musical treasures at home, alternative Venezuelan musicians and progressive audiences keep in touch via the Internet with trends in global popular music and create vibrant and experimental musical mixtures.

European and European–American Classical Music

Despite Venezuela's lack of economic resources during the colonial period, a group of classically trained composers, including several young mestizos, emerged in the late 1700s and into the independence period. They produced mostly religious music, and, with the onset of the anticolonial struggle, many patriotic pieces. The latter includes the hymn "Gloria al bravo pueblo" (Glory to the Brave/Proud People), now the national anthem. Later in the nineteenth century, Teresa Carreño (1853–1917) gained an international reputation as a pianist; the national theater in Caracas is named after her. The discovery of oil brought the economic development necessary to support more activity. Vicente Emilio Sojo and Juan Bautista Plaza emerged as nationalistic composers in the first half of the twentieth century when symphony orchestras and music conservatories began to flourish. One of Sojo's students was José Antonio Abreu (b. 1939) who would establish **El Sistema** (The System), a network of youth orchestras based in working-class communities. In the 1960s, an avant-garde movement emerged in various artistic realms as symbolic of progress and modernism. One of the few electronic music studios in Latin America was founded in Caracas at this time.

El Sistema is an experiment that has blossomed into a tremendous success story. Abreu tirelessly cajoled major businesses in the 1970s to donate to the effort of bringing Euroclassical music into impoverished neighborhoods in Caracas and elsewhere. The talent young children exhibited in the flagship National Youth Orchestra garnered accolades and transformed it into a prestigious national institution. With strong government support in recent years, the program has redoubled its efforts. On international tours, the orchestra astonished audiences with their precision and exuberance. Its star conductor, Gustavo Dudamel (b. 1981), is now music director of the Los Angeles Philharmonic (where he is affectionately nicknamed "The Dude") and hopes to initiate a similar system of musical instruction there. The social benefits of access to such a well-run educational program have been touted internationally. Yet some now question its exclusive focus on elite European music and refusal to consider other musics in achieving the same positive social and artistic goals.

One unexpected result of El Sistema has been what could be termed an urban traditional music revival. Ensembles, many containing El Sistema graduates, combine traditional instruments, especially the cuatro, with string bass and an eclectic array of symphonic instruments, especially clarinet and flute. The resulting semiclassical instrumental music is similar in many ways to choro in Brazil (see Chapter 6). In 2009 some of these artists set up a collective website under the name **Movimiento Urbano Acústico** (Urban Acoustical Movement). The emphasis on instrumental virtuosity and arrangements of folkloric repertoire with a Euroclassical sound makes one wonder how to draw the line between "classical" and "traditional." As in other parts of Latin America, Venezuelans do not feel bound to separate these repertoires and their creative talents draw from multiple sources. Cheo Hurtado's compositions for cuatro and Claudia Calderón's adaptation of joropos and other genres for the piano are excellent examples that straddle this divide. The groups C4 Trío and Ensamble Gurrufío have albums and websites.

Aldenaro Romero is another musician known for an eclecticism that spans popular and classical idioms. In the mid-1960s he combined *bossa nova* with Venezuelan elements to create what he called *Onda nueva* (New Wave). He has written in the classical vein, relying on a tonal foundation and often direct references to traditional or regional musics. Probably his

EXAMPLE 4.6: Theme from "Fuga con pajarillo"

best-known classical work is the "Fuga con pajarillo" from his *Suite para cuerdas No. 1* (String Suite No. 1). A *pajarillo* is a rapid couple dance, similar to the joropo llanero. In this work, Romero conveys the feeling of improvisation of the harp, maracas, and cuatro parts against the rigor inherent in a composed fugue. The first part of the main them is notated in Example 4.6.

LISTENING **guide** 4.10

⊚ Romero: "Fuga con pajarillo" (Fugue with *pajarillo*), from *Suite para cuerdas*

Composer: Aldenaro Romero

Date of composition: 1975

Date of recording: 2008

Performer: Simón Bolívar Youth Orchestra; Gustavo Dudamel, conductor

Genre: orchestral suite

Form: through-composed

Tempo/meter: quick simple triple

What to Listen for:

- $\frac{3}{4}$ meter, sometimes suggesting contrasting $\frac{6}{8}$ meter; $\frac{3}{4}$ with accent on the latter two beats (2 and 3)
- Sharp attack of strings, imitative of attack of harp and voice of joropo
- Fugal treatment intermittent and not always fully executed

Time	Description
0:00	Statement of main theme, intertwined in fugal fashion
0:34	Long held notes (at the fifth) reference the way singers often begin joropos vocally
0:47	Further restatements and fugal treatment of theme
1:48	New contrasting material introduced
3:10	New melodic figure introduced
3:45	Fugal treatment of fragments of main theme; restatements of thematic material
5:50	Final statement; variants of theme presented over consistent rhythmic foundation

Conclusion

This chapter has provided only the briefest of introductions to the musics of nine different nations; hopefully it will whet your appetite to learn more on your own. Many musical styles could not be covered here: Panamanian *tamborito*, Costa Rican *calypso*, Nicaraguan *palo de mayo*, Guatemalan *son chapín*, Colombian *champeta*, bambuco, Venezuelan tambor, *parranda*, and so many others. The rise to national prominence of the many diverse, regional musics in Colombia, Venezuela, and Central America belies any claims that a single style could possibly be said to be *the* national music of a country.

With increased communication through the Internet, no one can predict exactly what the hybridized music will sound like from so many different communities. Yet the discussion of music and community presented in this chapter demonstrates that the power of music will continue to influence and support the lives of its creators and those that listen and dance to it.

KEY TERMS

arpa llanera

bambuco

canto necesario

conjunto de gaitas

cuatro

culo'e puya or redondo
　drums

cumbia

diatonic

El Sistema

furro

gaita

guitarilla

joropo llanero

ladino

liberation theology

maracas

marimba de arco

marimba de tecomates

marimba doble (grande)

marimba sencilla

mestizo

mina drum

Movimiento Urbano
　Acústico (Urban
　Acoustical
　Movement)

música tropical

polo

rock en español
　movement

serial

tambor

tun

vallenato

FURTHER READING

Brandt, Max. "African Drumming from Rural Communities around Caracas and its Impact on Venezuelan Music and Ethnic Identity." In *Music and Black Ethnicity: The Caribbean and South America*, edited by G. Béhague, 267–84. Miami: University of Miami North-South Center, 1994.

The Garland Encyclopedia of World Musics: South America, Mexico, Central America, and the Caribbean. Edited by D. Olsen and D. Sheehy. New York/London: Routledge, 1998. See the entries on each nation.

List, George. *Music and Poetry in a Colombian Village*. Bloomington: University of Indiana Press, 1983.

Navarrete Pellicer, Sergio. *Maya Achi Marimba Music in Guatemala*. Philadelphia: Temple University Press, 2005.

Scruggs, T.M. "Central America: Marimba and Other Musics of Central America." In *Music in Latin American Culture: Regional Traditions*, 80–125. New York: Schirmer Books, 1999.

Scruggs, T.M. "The Rise of Afro-Venezuelan Music to the Present Day Hugo Chávez Era." 2007. http://afropop.org/hipdeep/HipDeep .html#programId=690&view=1

Sider, Ronald R. "Contemporary Composers in Costa Rica." *Latin American Music Review* 5, no. 2 (1984): 263–76.

Wade, Peter. *Music, Race and Nation: Música Tropical in Colombia*. Chicago: University of Chicago Press, 2000.

FURTHER VIEWING

El Sistema: Music to Change Life. Simón Bolívar Youth Orchestra. Paul Smaczny and Maria Stodtmeier, directors. Euroarts, 2009.

Shotguns and Accordions—Music of the Marijuana Regions of Colombia. Nafer Durán, director. Shanachie, 2001.

Gulf of Mexico

Atlantic Ocean

Spanish-speaking
French-speaking
English-speaking
Dutch-speaking

U.S.
FLORIDA

Mexico

Havana ○
● Matanzas

Bahamas

Cuba

N

0 100 200 300 400
Kilometers

0 50 100 150 200 250
Miles

Cayman
Is.

Jamaica
Kingston

Santiago de Cuba ●

Santiago de los Caballeros

Haiti

Port-au-Prince ○

Dominican Republic
Santo Domingo ○

San
Juan ●

Puerto Rico

Virgin
Is.

Belize City
Belize

Honduras
○ Tegucigalpa

Nicaragua
○ Managua

Anguilla
St. Martin
St. Eustatius
Antigua &
Barbuda

St. Kitts & Nevis
Montserrat
Guadeloupe
Dominica
Martinique
St. Lucia

Caribbean Sea

Costa Rica
○ San José

Panama
Panama City ○

Aruba
Curaçao
Bonaire

St. Vincent &
○ Grenadines

Granada

Barbad

Pacific Ocean

Caracas ○

Colombia

Venezuela

Trinidad &
Tobago

Bogotá ○

Quito ○

Georgetown ○

Guyana

Ecuador

Surir

Peru

Brazil

5

Cuba and the Hispanic Caribbean

ROBIN MOORE

Introduction

The Hispanic Caribbean is a vibrant area both culturally and musically. This relatively minor region, with its small population, has proven to be a cultural force rivaling or even surpassing wealthy countries of the developed world. Commercial music from Cuba, Puerto Rico, and the Dominican Republic is now listened to around the globe. Of course, the Hispanic Caribbean supports many noncommercial forms of traditional African- and European-derived music as well. It boasts classical music performance, everything from music for the Catholic Mass to avant-garde electronic composition. And external musical influences from rap to flamenco continue to influence local practices, resulting in new hybrid forms.

In geographic and cultural terms, the boundaries of the Caribbean are difficult to define. The Atlantic coastal regions of South and Central America have a great deal in common with the islands discussed in this chapter. The music and lifestyle of Cartagena, Colombia, for instance, resemble those of Havana, Cuba, or San Juan, Puerto Rico, much more than those of Bogotá. For this reason, scholars tend to refer both to the Caribbean as such and to the "circum-Caribbean" area as related. Recent years have witnessed massive numbers of Caribbean immigrants moving abroad to New York, Miami, Madrid, and elsewhere, further complicating notions of Caribbean geography. Several factors do tie the Caribbean together, however, related to the common experience of colonial domination and exploitation, as discussed in the introduction, and the gradual emergence of cultural forms in the context of West African slave labor.

◄ **FIGURE 5.1** Map of the Caribbean

Concepts of mestizaje or creolization are central to scholarship on Caribbean music. As discussed in the introduction, these terms refer to the fusion of different racial and cultural groups over time—in the case of the Caribbean primarily West Africans and Spaniards—and the creation of something new and unique. Mestizaje may be evident in the color of people's skin and other aspects of their physical appearance, but it is also manifest in local languages, cuisines, religious expression, and in music. Of course, hybridized music exists side by side with other forms that may not be as hybrid, for instance music that continues to employ African languages or that derives from Spanish heritage, such as the música guajira tradition described later. One might conceive of a continuum of Caribbean music in this sense, with some genres more culturally blended than others; residents of the region move with ease among a dizzying array of different styles of music. After discussing the history of the Caribbean, this chapter provides examples of various styles of traditional music, then moves on to consider more fundamentally hybrid popular genres, and classical music.

A Brief History

Early missionary accounts tell us that several indigenous groups lived in the Caribbean when Christopher Columbus first sailed into the area, believing he was in Asia. Natives there included the Arawaks, Siboneys, and Taínos. Though most greeted the newcomers as friends, it quickly became apparent that Spaniards wished only to subjugate them. During the first decades of the conquest, conquistadors ruled their new possessions in the Americas from the island of Hispaniola (now divided into Haiti and the Dominican Republic). Within 150 years, they had killed off most of the original inhabitants through open warfare, disease, and starvation.

Regrettably, little information remains about the culture of most of these indigenous groups. Some native foods like cassava (similar to the potato) are still cultivated; practices such as sleeping in hammocks and smoking tobacco also persist. The names of many Caribbean islands derive from indigenous languages (e.g., Cuba from *Cubanacan*, Taíno for "central place"). One type of communal music event is mentioned in early accounts as well, involving as many as a thousand participants who danced in circles around a group of musicians. Some of these ceremonies were religious, while others took place after the death of a community member or in preparation for war. They could last several days. Dancers would sing chants in a responsorial style, following a lead singer and accompanied by various percussion instruments. These included hollowed-out logs, maraca-like instruments, and gourd scrapers similar to the modern **güiro**. Small hand percussion of this sort may represent an indigenous musical influence on the present.

From the late 1490s through the mid-seventeenth century, Spain alone controlled the Caribbean region; Caribbean countries that speak Spanish today thus reflect the earliest phase of European colonization. Beginning in the seventeenth century, Britain, France, and the Netherlands began to contest Spanish authority and to attack various islands. In 1650, the British succeeded in taking the island of Jamaica. France controlled much of Hispañola by 1664. Trinidad and Tobago passed hands at various times between the British, French, and Dutch.

The Atlantic slave trade greatly influenced modern Caribbean history and culture. The slave trade accelerated in the late seventeenth century as colonial powers established plantations to cultivate sugar and other crops. Following massive slave revolts in the French Caribbean of the 1790s, other islands including Cuba began importing slaves in larger numbers to meet the European demand for sugar. By the late 1880s, when slavery was finally abolished in all of Latin America, three or four million Africans and African descendants lived in the Caribbean region.

African descendants in the Americas derive from three major West African cultural groups: (1) Muslim-influenced peoples originating in the Sudan, the Gambia, and Sierra Leone; (2) Bantu-Kongo tribes from the area that now comprises Angola, Central African Republic, and the Democratic Republic of Congo; and (3) groups associated with the coastal rainforest regions of present-day Cameroon, Nigeria, and Benin, especially the Yoruba. Bantu groups are prominent in all former Portuguese and Spanish colonies. Yoruba-derived traditions are strongly represented in countries such as Cuba and Brazil whose slave trade peaked in the final decades before abolition.

(a)

(b)

FIGURE 5.2 African-derived drums from the Hispanic Caribbean: (a) Dominican *palo* drummers performing in a local festival, Sainaguá, Dominican Republic; and (b) Puerto Rican bomba drummers playing in Chicago, Illinois

Spanish-derived music has strongly influenced traditions throughout Latin America as well. Musicians accompanied the conquistadors on their very first visits to the Americas. Likewise, Catholic priests incorporated music into their efforts to "civilize" and convert indigenous groups and later Africans. The legacy of Spain is evident in the many epic ballads and songs still sung in the region, as well as their poetic forms. European-derived instruments abound as well. Virtually all string and keyboard instruments in the region come from Spain or were based on European models. Even though they represented a demographic minority in the Caribbean, Europeans controlled local societies and influenced them profoundly. They brought elite musical traditions—that is, classical music of various sorts and church music performed by conservatory-trained instrumentalists—as well as traditional music. This split reflects the divisions between the poorer, common people who emigrated from Europe and the smaller circle that controlled political and business interests.

Traditional and Popular Music

Spanish-Influenced Music

Cuba is the largest and most populous island of the Caribbean and lies less than 100 miles south of the Florida coast. Christopher Columbus visited the island during his first voyage across the Atlantic; it remained a Spanish colony for more than four hundred years. Following a series of wars of independence, Cuba became a nominally independent republic, though heavily influenced by the business interests and foreign policy of the United States. In 1959, the island entered a new period of revolution, left-leaning politics, and alignment with the Soviet Union. Since 1989, Cuba has struggled to survive without the assistance from its former Soviet allies and continues to be constrained by the U.S. economic embargo.

Música guajira is the term used in Cuba to denote traditional music associated with rural farmers, often of Spanish ancestry. Música guajira is most frequently heard on the western end of the island (known for its tobacco farms) and in the center, specifically the area stretching from Santa Clara to Camagüey. It is music for entertainment, performed at parties and other informal gatherings, as well as at annual competitions such as the Festival Cuculambé. Spanish-derived string instruments predominate in this repertoire and come in a bewildering number of shapes and sizes. One of the most common instruments used is the **tres**, an instrument similar to the guitar but smaller, and with three double sets of metal strings. A similar Puerto Rican instrument is the **cuatro**, a folk guitar with four or five

Cuba and the United States

The proximity of Cuba to the United States has caused many tensions between the two countries. By the late nineteenth century, only two Spanish colonies remained in the Americas: Cuba and Puerto Rico. Many North Americans sympathized with the independence movement in Cuba, led by José Martí (1853–1895). The U.S. government, however, saw in the conflict a chance to annex the island from Spain; this eventually led to the Spanish-American War of 1898, after which both Cuba and Puerto Rico came under U.S. influence. Despite Cuba's independence in 1902, its economy and government remained in the grip of the United States, which still retains a naval base at Guantánamo Bay. Puerto Rico became a U.S. commonwealth in 1917, a status it still retains.

Fidel Castro (b. 1926) led a new revolutionary effort in the 1950s and wrested control from dictator Fulgencio Batista. Castro had communist sympathies and soon allied himself with the former Soviet Union, nationalizing or evicting foreign companies and threatening to spread leftist revolution throughout Latin America. This alarmed the U.S. government and led to attempts to assassinate him and to overthrow his government (the Bay of Pigs Invasion); it also led to a crisis over the stationing of Soviet nuclear weapons in Cuba in 1962 and to the imposition of an economic embargo. The embargo has increased the hardships on the Cuban people without weakening the revolutionary leadership.

FIGURE 5.3 Cuban leader Fidel Castro (center) delivering a speech in Havana next to Camilo Cienfuegos (right) and Ernesto "Che" Guevara (left) in 1959

During the first half of the twentieth century, Cuba became a playground for vacationing Americans, and especially in the 1950s a center for gambling and organized crime. Since 1959, relations between the countries have entered a deep freeze, with severe restrictions on travel and no formal diplomatic relations. Cuban expatriates who fled the Castro revolution have congregated in Miami and elsewhere, where they exert a strong influence on North American politics, especially as regards maintaining the embargo. Politics within the exile community have been changing, however, and hopefully improved relations with Cuba will be possible in the coming years.

doubled strings. Iberian-derived string repertoire of a similar nature exists in Mexico, Brazil, Argentina, and throughout the hemisphere.

Cuban música guajira is usually performed in a major key and in triple meter. It emphasizes sung poetry, with instruments in a secondary or supportive role. In many cases, singers and instrumentalists use precomposed melodies or chord progressions rather than creating new ones. Singers tend

(a)   (b)

FIGURE 5.4 Two virtuoso performers: (a) Puerto Rican Yomo Toro with his cuatro and (b) Cuban Pancho Amat on tres

to improvise their lyrics on the spot, just as rappers in the United States might do.

Música guajira lyrics are expected to follow strict and difficult rhyme sequences. One common pattern, known as a quatrain, uses a four-line "internal" rhyme scheme in which line 1 rhymes with line 4 and line 2 with line 3 (i.e., an **ABBA** structure). A more extended variant of the same idea consists of two five-line units: the first half adopts the structure **ABBAA**, a quatrain with an extra A line; the second half follows the same pattern, but with different rhymes, **CDDCC**. In Latin America, the generic name for this sort of poetry with ten lines is **décima** poetry.

A recent example of décimas from Puerto Rico is provided on the CD *Ecos de Borinquen: jíbaro hasta el hueso*, by Smithsonian Folkways. It exemplifies the way many Caribbean performers emphasize local identity and images of rural life in such music. Another interesting aspect of virtually all compositions on the release is that they include a "forced foot" (*pie forzado*), a poetic line the singer is obliged to work into the last phrase of every décima. The pieces on the CD are precomposed, but a forced foot may also be given to singers in competitions to see how effectively they can incorporate it as they improvise. The Smithsonian Folkways website provides video clips of the *Ecos de Borinquen* performances as well.

Listening Guide 5.1 presents improvised décima poetry from Cuba. It is called simply "Controversia" or "Controversy," the name for an improvised poetic duel. Note that the pulse of the song is not strict, but instead slows down and speeds up at various points. Musicians perform slowly and out of time in the background as singers improvise new verses. When singers finish a given segment, the musicians suddenly break into a lively tempo, playing repeated stock phrases in variation until one of the singers begins again.

In some cases, while one singer is in the process of inventing a line, the other may actually jump in and "steal" the composition away with a different line than his or her opponent was planning, but one that nevertheless rhymes appropriately within the décima. This sort of intervention takes place in "Controversia" during the last minute or two of the track as indicated. A partial guide is provided because the full transcription is rather long. Bold letters outline the décima rhyme scheme.

◎ Alfonso and Vega: "Controversia" (Controversy)

Composer/lyricist: Adolfo Alfonso and Justo Vega

Date of composition: 1980s

Date of recording: 2002

Performers/instruments: Conjunto Palmas y Cañas, directed by Miguel Ojeda; instruments include Ojeda on laúd, accompanied by guitar, Alfonso and Vega on vocals, as well as claves and conga drums during the introduction and finale

Genre: música guajira/*controversia*

Form: varied strophic

Tempo/meter: brisk compound triple, punctuated by pauses

What to Listen for:
- Music supports the poetry, slowing to give singers time to think of their next line
- Music features stock phrases and melodies that repeat in variations
- Witty singers, following preestablished rhyme schemes, ridicule their opponent in a good-natured way in an attempt to "win" the musical improvisation

Time	Structure and Text	Translation	Description
4:21	**A** Tratas de ser ocurrente **B** Festivo, irónico y ducho [2x] **B** Porque a tí te gusta mucho **A** Todo lo que no es decente **A** Busca la luz del presente **C** Que a todos nos ilumina **C** Porque con esa rutina **D** Esa guasa, y esa cosa **D** Estás negando la hermosa **C** Superación campesina	You try to be slick Festive, ironic, smart You so enjoy What isn't decent Find the light of the present That shines on us all 'Cause with that routine Those jokes, You deny the beautiful Progress of the farmer	Vega sings. Most instruments stop playing, but the laud player continues slowly outlining chords while the guitarist plays a bass line, occasionally strumming a chord.
4:51	**A** No puedo negar la hermosa **B** Superación campesina **B** Que a toda Cuba ilumina **A** En su marcha victoriosa **A** Por tu forma caprichosa **C** Me pintas como no soy **C** Y más que seguro estoy **D** Que lo haces para engañar **D** Procurando desvirtuar **C** Los palos que yo te doy	I can't deny the lovely Farmers' progress It illuminates all Cuba In its victorious march In your capriciousness You describe me falsely I'm more than sure You're doing it to deceive Trying to deflect The blows I'm giving you	Alfonso sings; instrumentalists play stock chord progressions in C major (most often C–Dmin–G⁷–C or E⁷–Amin–Dmin–G⁷–C) to accompany. At 4:58, the band plays to offer Alfonso more time to invent his décima, but it stops when he begins reciting.

(continued)

Time	Structure and Text	Translation	Description
5:16	**A** Cuando te expresas así **B** Insolente renacuajo [2x] **B** Es cuando te miro abajo **A** Muy por debajo de mí **A** Pretendes negar aquí **C** Mi capacidad humana **C** Cuando tú eres tarambana **D** Antes la presencia mía **D** Por cobarde una jutía **C** Y por miedoso una rana	When you talk like that Insolent tadpole I see you down below Far below me You try to deny My humanity When you are a rascal In my presence A cowardly rodent A frightened frog	Vega repeats lines of verse in order to construct his next rhyme within the décima, but both singers respond to each other almost immediately without needing the band to play between verses
5:46	**A** Compárame a la jutía **B** Y compárame a la rana [2x] **B** Porque a mí no amilana **A** En nada esa tontería **A** Lo terrífico sería **C** Mi querido compañero **C** Es que en un tono ligero **D** Cualquiera sin meditar **D** Me quisiera comparar **C** A este esqueleto rumbero	Compare me to a rodent To a frog It doesn't scare me All that silliness What would be scary My dear friend Is that casually Anyone might without thinking Compare me to This skeletal rumba player	Alfonso refers to Vega as a "skeletal *rumbero*" since he is an older, thin man
6:16	**A** Esa falta de respeto **B** Una vez más ha probado [2x] **B** Que eres un maleducado **A** Un bruto, un analfabeto	Your lack of respect You've proven again You're uneducated A brute, illiterate	Vega
6:28	**A** Hay que ver que a este sujeto **C** Siempre la ira a lo ciega **C** Mas cuando el momento llega **D** A pesar de su recato **D** El viejo se pone sato **C** Lo que pasa es que lo niega	This subject Always rages blindly Yet when the moment comes Despite his modesty The old guy gets crafty But he always denies it	Alfonso jumps in and steals away the décima
6:42	**A** Eso es mentira, mentira **B** Hipócrita deslenguado	That's a lie, a lie Insolent hypocrite	Vega tries again
6:47	**B** Para no verte agitado **A** Toma jarabe de güira	Don't get too excited Take some güira syrup	Alfonso jumps in a second time
6:55	**A** Cállate la boca, mira	Shut your mouth, listen	Vega doing the same to Alfonso
6:57	**C** Déjate de ser gruñón **C** Poeta mariposón	Don't be a whiner You gay poet	Alfonso, with an inappropriate slur

(continued)

Time	Structure and Text	Translation	Description
7:00	**D** No me vuelve a ofender **D** Porque te voy a romper **C** La boca de un pescozón	Don't offend me Or I'm going to break open Your mouth with a punch	Vega finishes the décima to applause
7:05			Brief instrumental coda in time; percussion enters again, emphasizing compound triple meter

African-Influenced Traditions

The scope and diversity of Afro-Caribbean musical traditions is nearly overwhelming, and much research remains to be done on their countless variants. African musical heritage is strongest in religious repertoire. In many countries, African slaves and their descendants managed to reconstruct their ancestral beliefs, using religious worship to retain a sense of common heritage. Indeed, some colonial authorities encouraged the creation of Afro-Caribbean religious institutions; they hoped slaves would maintain both their distinct identities and also the ethnic rivalries that some harbored, making them less likely to revolt en masse.

Batá Music

"Elegguá, Oggún, Ochosi II" (Listening Guide 5.2) comes from Cuban Yoruba-derived traditions associated with the religion known as **Santería** or *Regla de Ocha*; Santería means worship of saints or deities, but in this case African deities as well as Catholic ones. Traditional West African religion is based on ancestor veneration, including the spirits of deceased parents and other family members. Even the most powerful deities (**orichas**) of Santería are believed to be ancestors as well, figures who lived centuries ago but whose spirits still influence the present. They represent fundamental elements of human life in a metaphorical sense: wisdom, motherhood, beauty, skill in warfare, and aspects of nature. Perhaps most important for our purposes, both music and dance are fundamental to worship of the orichas.

Each deity in this religion has many specific praise songs, rhythms, and dance movements dedicated to him or her. Santería involves spirit possession; practitioners believe that the gods want to advise those on earth and will take over the body of an initiate in specific contexts in order to interact with the community. Yoruba-influenced religious music in Cuba has multiple ensembles; here there is time to discuss only one representative example: **batá** drumming, considered the most sacred.

Batá drumming typically takes place in the homes of individual believers. Worship may be organized to celebrate a particular saint's day, to become an initiate, to mark the anniversary of becoming an initiate, or for other reasons. The traditional ensemble consists of a set of three hourglass-shaped, double-headed drums (batás) played together. The largest drum leads the others, performs the most extended improvisations, and (together with the lead singer) provides cues to transition between rhythms. The middle drum also performs considerable improvisation and elaboration as it complements the rhythms of the lead drum. The smallest drum functions as a metronome, providing a basic pulse and playing a relatively static rhythms.

FIGURE 5.5 Master percussionist Francisco Aguabella (1925–2010), performing here on the largest of the three batá drums during a show in New York City, 2008

Sacred batás used in ritual contexts must be constructed and consecrated through an elaborate ritual process. They are believed to contain a divine force that aids in communication with the orichas. Since the 1930s, unconsecrated drums have also been made for use in secular contexts (such as in Figure 5.5). Recently, such drums have appeared in jazz and popular music ensembles, as well as in more traditional settings.

Each batá drum has a large head and a small head. The larger heads generate the prominent open and closed tones that, in combination with other drums, create characteristic aggregate melodies specific to each rhythm. The smaller head is more often slapped, providing rhythmic accompaniment. The large drum usually has a net of brass bells draped around the outside; the jingling creates a complementary sound to that of the drumheads. A lead singer and a chorus complete the performance ensemble. Vocalists sing praise songs in a fragmented, two-hundred-year-old form of Yoruba as brought to the island by slaves in the nineteenth century; the exact meanings of some songs have been lost.

Formal religious events often begin with unaccompanied drumming in front of an altar hours before most guests arrive; this serves to purify the space. Drums play a series of rhythms dedicated to particular orichas in prescribed order that takes roughly half an hour. A second kind of drumming begins after most guests have arrived, providing accompaniment for dancers and singers during the main event. This is the kind of music that has been re-created in the recording studio by the performers of "Elegguá, Oggún, Ochosi II" (Listening Guide 5.2). The second section of most ceremonies also begins by praising major orichas (there are about 20 of them) in a

⊚ Abbilona: "Elegguá, Oggún, Ochosi II"

Composer/lyricist: anonymous

Date of composition: traditional

Performers/instruments: Abbilona; Irián López, Manley López, and Eduardo Aurelio on batá drums; Jesús Lorenzo, Juan Carlos Rey, and Jesús Gilberto on lead vocals; chorus

Date of recording: 1999

Genre: traditional/devotional

Form: structured around a series of praise songs in call-and-response form

Tempo/meter: moderate triple

What to Listen for:

- Chants repeat a few times in variation before a new melody is heard
- Lead singer performs more elaborate versions of each chant than the chorus
- Batá drums play the same rhythm for extended periods, but vary it considerably
- Chorus sings text in italics

Time	Structure and Text	Translation	Description
0:00	Ago Elegguá abukenke [2x]	Praise to Elegguá, he takes so he can be rich	Track fades in with the lead vocalist singing the first song; drummers play a variant of a rhythm called *latopa*
0:09	*Ago Elegguá abukenke [2x]*		Chorus responds with same chant
0:15			Lead singer varies the melody
0:21			Chorus, same chant
0:28	Abukenke, abukenke Amila topa loko	This chant mentions a particular incarnation of Elegguá	Lead singer begins second chant; drummers switch to a rhythm called *abukenke*
0:34	*Abukenke, abukenke*		Chorus responds
0:37	Elegguá de mas sankio, etc.	Translation unknown	Lead singer continues improvising phrases against the chorus; at about 1:12 drums switch to *ñongo*
1:20	*Beni beni mabe echuo bene mabo, bene bene*	Translation unknown	The lead singer calls a third chant, and chorus responds; chorus and soloist continue in alternation
2:04	*Oba keyen keyen Elegguá*	Elegguá the child king	Fourth chant begins, introduced by the lead singer; larger batás improvise frequently
2:55	*Chenche mabo*	Translation unknown; "chenche" means spiritual work	Final chant in this segment begins; tempo of the piece increases, and drums improvise freely, imitating the "hotter" final sections of a religious event

prescribed order. Following this, the lead singer is at liberty to choose songs with greater freedom and to invoke a particular oricha repeatedly as necessary in order to induce spirit possession. In all, ceremonies last many hours.

Our example of batá music comes from the CD *Tambor Yoruba: Elegguá, Oggún, y Ochosi. Tambor* is the word for "drum" in Spanish, and the final three words in the CD's title refer to particular orichas, all of them warriors. Elegguá is known as a messenger, "guardian of the crossroads" (or of important moments involving choice), and also as an opener of doors, spiritual and otherwise. He is always worshipped first in any event in order to facilitate communication with the other divinities. Oggún is an oricha of the forge and metalworking, known for his dogged determination. Ochosi is a wise woodsman whose symbol is the bow and arrow. All major orichas in Afro-Cuban religions are associated with particular Catholic saints as well. In this hybrid form of devotion, for instance, Ochosi is believed both to be an incarnation of the Catholic angel Santiago and of an African deity.

The rhythms associated with batá drumming are complex, and, with six heads sounding at once, it takes time to learn to distinguish between them. Example 5.1 is a transcription of one rhythm heard in this excerpt, called **ñongo**; it is one of about 30 standard batá rhythms used to accompany religious ceremonies, and is heard in our example beginning at 1:10. In the Western notation provided, high notes represent hits on the small head on each drum and low notes on the large head. A slash-style notehead indicates a slap, an "x" means a muffled tone, and a round notehead indicates an open tone.

EXAMPLE 5.1: *Ñongo* **rhythm**

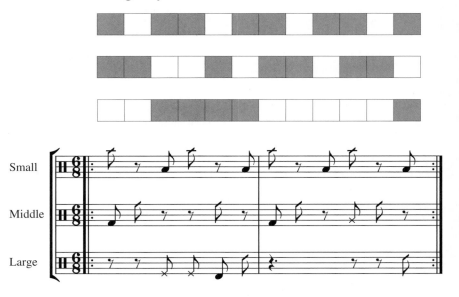

EXAMPLE 5.2: Santería melodies

Song 1

A - go E - leg - guá   a   bu - ken - ke   A - go E - leg - guá   a   bu - ken - ke

Song 2

Ken - ke,   a - bu - ken - ke   (E - leg - guá de mas san - kio)   *A - bu*

Try to reproduce the rhythmic patterns given, and then sing a couple of the melodies in this piece. You can learn them by ear, like performers in the Caribbean do, or, if you read music, refer to the transcription of the melodies (Example 5.2). Note that in cases where the melody is divided, Roman text indicates the part sung by the lead singer and italics indicate the response by the chorus. Remember that the lead singer improvises and changes his melody constantly, so the transcription represents only one way he might sing it.

Rumba

To contrast this piece with a different African-influenced tradition from Cuba, consider the **rumba**. Rumba music is secular, not religious; it developed in the late nineteenth century out of earlier forms associated with Cuba's rural Afro-Cuban population. With the abolition of slavery in 1886, many former slaves and agricultural workers moved to cities such as Havana and Matanzas in search of better jobs. In these cities, in large tenement buildings, rumba music and dance coalesced as a style. Like música guajira, rumba is a form of secular entertainment, traditionally performed among friends or community members. Many variants exist; Bantu/Kongo rhythms and culture are said to have been especially influential in rumba's formation, and in fact the "conga" drum (also known as a *tumbadora*) bears the name of this ethnic group.

Rumba can still be heard on the street corners of poorer neighborhoods and similar informal contexts (Figure 5.6). Because of widespread bias against drumming on the part of elites and its close associations with the black working class, laws existed to keep it from being performed in other areas for many years. Even today, some Cubans cannot see value in this music, or in African-derived religious repertoire, considering it backward or primitive. Nevertheless, rumba has been recognized as a bona fide part of Cuban culture; since the 1970s, the Ministry of Culture has

FIGURE 5.6 A rumba performance for locals and tourists in the Callejón de Hamel, Havana, featuring performers from the ensemble Yoruba Andabo, 2001

supported it through recordings and promotion, and finds places for rumba musicians to perform publicly on a regular basis. These include *Sábado de la Rumba* (Rumba Saturday) events hosted by the state-supported National Folklore Troupe (the Conjunto Folklórico Nacional).

Many instruments can be used to perform rumba, but the most common are a set of three conga drums of different sizes, a set of **claves** (short, resonant wooden sticks), and a pair of longer sticks used to strike a wood block or the side of a drum. The rhythm produced by the sticks is sometimes called a "shell pattern" (*cáscara*) because it is often performed on the shell of a drum; this pattern has been adopted by present-day salsa performers. Sometimes resonant boxes (Figure 5.6) or other percussion are heard as well. As in the case of batá drumming, a lead singer and chorus perform along with drummers and dancers. Unlike batá ensembles, however, the drum with the highest pitch improvises most in this style. The middle-pitched and lowest-pitched conga drums play somewhat more static patterns, though they also improvise frequently. By contrast, the claves and sticks play patterns that remain constant throughout the performance.

To many listeners, rumba sounds African-derived, but upon closer examination it also demonstrates European influences. Most songs are sung in Spanish, for instance. The first section of the music is strophic, with changing lyrics over a constant melody, a European concept. Some of the poetic forms employed are also Spanish-derived, including the décima described earlier. Rumba lyrics touch on many topics, including love, politics, famous rumba players of the past, and the like. As in the case of most traditional music, rumba tends to be performed in a single key and does not modulate.

Rumbas typically begin with a brief improvised melody or *diana* over the percussion rhythms, sung by the lead singer. This melody sets the key, so that other singers will know which pitch to enter on. Following the *diana* come the two major sections of the piece: the strophic verse, then a final section, the fastest and most improvisatory, known as the **montuno**. In the montuno, the lead singer improvises short vocal lines in alternation with the chorus, much like in the batá example (Listening Guide 5.2). The tempo speeds up a bit, dancers begin to dance, and the lead conga player improvises more aggressively. This spontaneous final jam can last as long as the participants feel inspired, anywhere from a few minutes to half an hour or longer. The montuno structure is cyclic, based on repeating loops of rhythms and interlocking sounds; its open-ended performance style derives from traditional West African aesthetics.

Before continuing, it is important to discuss the word "clave," which can refer to a percussion instrument, as mentioned, but also to a constantly repeated rhythmic figure that serves as the structural foundation for the rest of a piece's rhythms. Repeated patterns of this sort are found in many kinds of Afro-Caribbean music, and in West African music. They often contrast a more syncopated figure in one half of the clave rhythm (this side of the rhythm in the rumba's clave pattern is known as the "three-side," because it incorporates three beats) against a relatively straight figure in the other half (known in rumba as the "two-side"). As mentioned, the clave pattern should correspond with other rhythms in the song in particular ways; if such a correspondence does not occur, musicians may describe the song as being "out of clave" or having a "crossed clave." Distinct clave patterns exist for the son, rumba, Yoruba-derived religious music, and other genres.

"En opuestas regiones" (Listening Guide 5.3) provides a good introduction to Cuban rumba and to the notion of clave because it is fairly slow and the drum parts are relatively easy to hear. This piece is actually a remake of a song originally written for guitar and voice in the early twentieth century. The only unusual aspect of it is that it does not include a stick part (the *cáscara*). Try listening to the beginning of the track. It starts with a pair of claves playing the traditional rumba clave:

Next, a **chéquere**, a gourd shaker with a net of beads around it, enters at about 0:03 playing "and-*one*" at the very end of each measure into the beginning of the next. The middle conga drum enters simultaneously. Initially it plays soft, muted notes with rapid touches on the drumhead, then prominent open tones against the "two side" of the clave. Sometimes the middle drum plays several open tones in a row, sometimes a single tone. This first happens at about 0:07 and 0:09.

Against all this, the low drum enters as well, improvising for a moment about 0:05 and then playing a clear open tone on beat 4 of each measure (you can hear it at about 0:07 and 0:09, for instance). Finally, the high lead drum makes its first entrance at about 0:08 with a series of prominent

EXAMPLE 5.3: Rumba clave

open tones. Try listening to the drum patterns on headphones for clarity, focusing on their different pitches in order to distinguish them. A complete transcription of the percussion parts against one another during the first ten seconds or so of the song would look something like Example 5.4 in Western notation.

As you listen to the piece, you will begin to hear the characteristic melody in this subgenre of rumba, a melody created through the interaction of the open tones on the two lower conga drums. That constant low–high pitch alternation, with the open tones of the middle drum against the "two side" of the clave, forms the essence of the sound. Try to keep track of the

EXAMPLE 5.4: Initial section of "En opuestas regiones"

⊚ Garay: "En opuestas regiones" (In Opposing Regions)

Composer/lyricist: Sindo Garay

Date of composition: 1910s

Performers/instruments: Muñequitos de Matanzas; three conga drums, claves, chéquere, singers

Date of recording: 1999

Genre: *rumba yambú*

Form: binary—strophic section followed by montuno

Tempo/meter: moderate simple quadruple

What to Listen for:
- Lyrics mention two noteworthy figures in Cuba's wars of independence: José Martí and Antonio Maceo
- Accompaniment consists of percussive loops of rhythm, punctuated by solos on the high drum

Time	Text	Translation	Description
0:00			**Introduction** Percussion instruments enter in staggered fashion
0:10			Lead singer establishes the key, chorus responds
0:24	En opuestas regiones Dos almas grandes nacieron Siendo la Independencia Su único ideal	In two opposing regions Two great souls were born Independence being Their only ideal	Verse section of the song begins, sung as a duet; the two "opposing regions" are the eastern and western extremes of the island
	También en opuestas regiones cayeron Las dos almas templadas Dos héroes de gloria De nombre inmortal	And also in different regions fell silent Two beating hearts Two glorious, Immortal heroes	
	El apóstol de Cuba, El verbo elocuente En la inmensa Habana Fue donde nació	The apostle of Cuba [Martí] Of eloquent tongue In immense Havana He was born	
	El genio guerrero Maceo en Oriente Allá en Punta Brava Perdió su existencia Martí en Dos Ríos De cara al sol cayó	The brilliant warrior Maceo in the east There in Punta Brava He was lost to us Martí fell to his death In Dos Ríos facing the sun	
3:18	A estudiar cubano Cubano mi Cuba ya es libre	Start studying, Cubans Cubans, my Cuba is now free	**Beginning of montuno** Lead singer sets up the call-and-response vocals

(continued)

Time	Text	Translation	Description
3:22	*A estudiar Cubano* Somos libres y soberanos *A estudiar Cubano* Evacuen si, evacuen ya Ay pero evacuen si, evacuen ya, rumbero *Evacuen si, evacuen ya* Estamos evacuando a los de arriba Y también a los de abajo *Evacuen si, evacuen ya* Evacuen la rumba que me esta llamando Pero evacuen ya, yere *Evacuen si, evacuen ya*	*Start studying, Cubans* We're free and sovereign *Start studying, Cubans* We're getting them out, getting them now Oh, but get them out, get them *rumbero* *Get them out, get them now* We're taking out the elites And also those from below *Get them out, get them now* Leave the rumba, it's calling me But get out now, *yere* *Get them out, yes get out now*	Choral responses, indicated by italics; first chorus underscores the importance of knowing history, second alludes to the U.S., with anti-imperialist associations

clave as the piece unfolds, as well as the low drum and chéquere patterns, which are relatively constant. Then focus on the improvisations by the high conga drum, noticing how they become busier between vocals and at the end of the song. Listen for the beginning of the montuno and note the increase in tempo that ensues.

Traditional rumba has influenced many composers and musical styles. The two-part form of the rumba with its verse and montuno has served as the model for contemporary salsa, discussed shortly. The shell rhythms played by the sticks have been adopted by the timbales, also in modern dance music. And rumba rhythms are now used in various formats, from Latin jazz to classical chamber music to pop songs. If you can find the recordings, listen to pieces such as "Obsesión" (interpreted by Manny Oquendo and Libre) or "Camerata en guaguancó" (interpreted by the Camerata Romeu) and see if you can hear how they have incorporated elements of traditional rumba.

Popular Music

Cuban Son

The most widely known form of Cuban popular music is the son (not to be confused with other sones from countries such as Mexico). Son has become a national symbol, in large part because it effectively integrates African and European aesthetics. Although its lyrics are primarily in Spanish, African-derived terminology also appears at times. Son instrumentation includes both string instruments from Spain and percussion modeled on African traditions. It incorporates European harmonies but combines them with ostinatos—looped, repeated rhythmic or melodic patterns—in an African style. As in the case of the rumba, the structure of son music is hybrid, combining a strophic verse section and a call-and-response montuno, similarly demonstrating the fusion of African and European influences. Finally, the dance style is also hybridized, with a choreography derived from European-style couple dancing, but adding hip and shoulder movements inherited from West Africa.

Cuban son developed around 1890 in eastern Cuba, where it was performed by Afro-Cubans in the hills surrounding cities such as Santiago, primarily at parties and similar gatherings. In its earliest manifestations, the music consisted of only a repeated choral refrain supported by percussion and very simple tonic–dominant chords on a string instrument (usually the tres). Against this, a lead singer might improvise brief phrases, in alternation with the chorus.

The years following the wars of independence against Spain witnessed much demographic movement on the island. Eventually, performers brought the rural son to Havana where it began to fuse with the bolero (p. 206) and other popular music traditions, including North American jazz. By the 1920s an urban son style had developed and was first performed publicly in beer gardens, dance academies, brothels, and other sites of working-class entertainment (similar in this respect to early jazz, the tango, etc.). Its typical instrumentation included guitar; the smaller, guitar-like tres, maracas, claves, bongo drum, bass, and often a trumpet. Sones broke many racial barriers in subsequent years as they gained widespread acceptance, allowing working-class performers of color access to the mainstream music industry for the first time.

Various musical characteristics define the son. One is its clave rhythm, usually played on the claves themselves (Figure 5.7). Another is the unique

FIGURE 5.7 The Septeto Habanero (Havana Septet), a longstanding group that performs son as heard in the 1930s and 1940s

melodies played on the tres, outlining or implying chords but not actually strumming them. In the final montuno, especially, melodies on lead string instruments often correspond to the clave, with a syncopated half of the melody played against the "three-side" and a straighter rhythm played against the "two side." Another characteristic pattern found in son music, played by the bongo drum, consists of strong strokes on the smaller head of the drum on beats 1 and 3 of a $\frac{4}{4}$ measure, and then a hit on beat 4 on the larger drumhead. However, bongo players improvise frequently, deviating from this pattern and adding numerous flourishes.

Probably the most unique aspect of the son is its anticipated bass; bass notes are often played slightly earlier than one might expect. In many types of music, the bass pattern sounds on beats 1 and 3 of the $\frac{4}{4}$ measure, as in rock or U.S. country music. In the son, by contrast, the bass plays on the "and" of beat 2 (i.e., an eighth note before the "normal" spot on beat 3) and on 4 (a full quarter note before the "normal" spot on beat 1). This lends the music a syncopated feel and can make it hard to discern the downbeat.

Listening Guide 5.4, "Beso discreto" (Discreet Kiss), provides an example of traditional son as interpreted by a modern-day ensemble. The small quintet performing here includes only bass, a guitar that has been modified with doubled strings to sound like a tres, rhythm guitar, bongo, maracas, and voices. Yet musical elements are easy to hear in the smaller group, and the overall sound is quite similar to that of early son bands. The only unusual aspect of the piece is that some verses repeat after the chorus is heard; usually a longer montuno would follow the verses and end the song.

Salsa

In the 1940s, an expanded son music format that included a second and often a third trumpet became popular in Cuba. This in turn required written arrangements to coordinate melodies played by the entire section. As more performers joined son bands and music literacy spread, groups performed more structurally and harmonically elaborate pieces. Pianos became a standard part of son instrumentation at this time. A single conga drum was added as well, and by the 1950s, the **timbales** came to be played alongside the bongo and two congas. This expanded format contributed to the development of **salsa** music in the 1960s and 1970s as performed by Latin American immigrants in New York. Salsa musicians adapted the son style to their own needs and tastes, in some cases changing the original style markedly.

◎ Matamoros: "Beso discreto" (Discreet Kiss)

Composer/lyricist: Miguel Matamoros

Date of composition: 1941

Performers/instruments: Eliades Ochoa, lead voice and guitar, and the Cuarteto Patria; Humberto Ochoa, second guitar; Eglis Ochoa, maracas; William Calderón, bass; Roberto Torres, bongos

Form: two-part, strophic section followed by a brief montuno

Tempo/meter: brisk duple

What to Listen for:
- Modified guitar playing syncopated melodies rather than strumming
- Transition from verse to montuno marked by the entrance of the bell
- Anticipated bass rhythm "fighting" the basic pulse of the percussion

Time	Text	Translation	Description
0:00			**Instrumental introduction** Melody played on the guitar to the accompaniment of other instruments
0:09	Una niña enamorada Al novio con ilusión Le dice muy apurada "Bésame en este rincón" El novio dice: espera, "Deja que pase la gente Que miradas callejeras Son miradas imprudentes"	A girl in love To her boyfriend Says quickly: "Kiss me in this corner" The boyfriend says: "Let the people go by first Cause folks on the street Stare imprudently"	**Verse 1**
0:32			**Instrumental melody** Same melody as the introduction
0:43	¿Como quieres que te bese, mi amor, Si la gente está mirando de aquí? Esperemos un momento mejor Que quiero besarte así	How can I kiss you, my love, If everyone is looking over here? Let's wait for a better moment I want to kiss you like this	**Verse 2**
0:52			Transition to the montuno Bongo player switches to bell
0:53	[kissing sounds] *Así, así, así, así*	*Like this, like this, like this, like this*	**Chorus**
1:02			**Instrumental melody**

(continued)

Time	Text	Translation	Description
1:16	Nunca espera que te niegue mi amor Esos besos que son para tí Esperemos un momento mejor Que quiero besarte así	Never expect me to deny you my love Those kisses that are for you Let's wait for a better moment I want to kiss you so	**Verse 3**
1:25	[kissing sounds] *Así, así, así, así*	*Like this, like this, like this, like this*	Bongo player switches to bell again
1:33			**Guitar solo** Bongo player switches back to the drum
2:12			**Instrumental melody** Cues end of the solo
2:23			**Repeat of the second verse**
2:33	[kissing sounds] *Así, así, así, así*	*Like this, like this, like this, like this*	Return of chorus; bongo player switches to bell
2:41			**Instrumental melody** Bongo player switches back to the drumheads
2:55			**Repeat of third verse**
3:04			**Partial repeat of the chorus** Bongo player switches to bell
3:11			Sudden break and held note as song concludes

In New York, salsa first gained popularity in the context of social and political activism on the part of Latino immigrants. Many lived in the poorer neighborhoods of East Harlem and the Bronx. As they struggled to get by in their new home, they came to resent the disregard for Latin American history and the Spanish language within most public schools. Salsa thus became an important emblem of cultural identity as Latinos slowly asserted their rights. Many also associated the music with the movement in Puerto Rico for complete independence from the United States.

Partly for these reasons, early New York salsa has a raw, edgy sound. It tends to be performed at a much faster tempo than son, with percussion featured prominently. Its harmonies are more complex than that of earlier Cuban dance genres, reflecting the influence of jazz and other U.S. repertoire. The use of trombones also makes the music distinct. New York–based salsa performers may incorporate folk instruments, such as the cuatro, or percussion rhythms unique to Puerto Rico or elsewhere in Latin America as well.

Two well-known performers who lived in New York for many years collaborated on "Ritmo en el corazón" (Listening Guide 5.5): Celia Cruz and Ray Barretto (Figure 5.8). Celia Cruz (1925–2003) was one of the best-known vocalists during salsa's heyday in the 1970s and 1980s. Born in Havana, Cuba, to a modest family, Cruz first came to the attention of the public singing on local radio broadcasts in the 1940s. After she won several talent competitions, a dance band called La Sonora Matancera (The Matanzas Sound) offered her a job as a singer. Following the Cuban Revolution of 1959, Cruz and other Sonora Matancera band members left the island and resettled in the United States. She recorded subsequently with bandleaders such as Puerto Rican Tito Puente and Dominican Johnny Pacheco, becoming a star on New York's Fania Record label. Her death led to a major public event in Miami, with hundreds of thousands of fans taking to the streets in remembrance.

FIGURE 5.8 Celia Cruz and Ray Barretto

Conga player and bandleader Ray Barretto (1929–2006) is remembered as an award-winning musician and a prominent part of the U.S. salsa and Latin jazz scenes for many years. Born in New York to parents of Puerto Rican descent, Barretto grew up listening to mainstream music from the United States, jazz, and traditional music of the Spanish-speaking Caribbean. In the early 1960s, his music fused elements of Latin dance repertoire with rhythm and blues and he played conga on recordings for groups such as the Rolling Stones. In 1967 he too joined the Fania label, eventually becoming its musical director. In 1990, Barretto was awarded a Grammy for his *Ritmo en el corazón* CD, which features the piece in "Ritmo en el corazón."

Among the most prominent aspects of salsa are its bell patterns. The timbales player plays mostly on the side of the drum shells with the sticks during the verse, but switches to a driving bell pattern that locks together with

explore

In "Ritmo en el corazón" (Listening Guide 5.5), the musicians imitate a Puerto Rican rhythm called *bomba sicá* from 1:12 to 1:28. Research this rhythm on your own (and bomba music in general) to determine how it has influenced salsa.

ⓢ Barretto and Cruz: "Ritmo en el corazón" (Rhythm in the Heart)

Composer/lyricist: Juan R. Ortiz González

Date of composition: 1988

Performers/instruments: Ray Barretto, congas, and Celia Cruz, lead vocal; Ricky González, piano; Sal Cuevas, bass; Jimmy Delgado, timbales; Carlos Soto, bongo; maracas; Héctor Zarzuela, Steve Gluzband, and Ángel Fernández, trumpet; Jimmy Bosch, trombone

Date of recording: 1988

Genre: salsa

Form: binary; verse and montuno

Tempo/meter: brisk duple

What to Listen for:
- Initial section strophic, with two verses
- Brief change from son-based rhythms to a common rhythm played on the Puerto Rican bomba drum
- Entrance of bell patterns and chorus, indicating a switch to the montuno
- Multiple choruses getting increasingly shorter

Time	Text	Translation	Description
0:00			**Instrumental Introduction** Brass instruments introduce the melody, with punctuation by the timbales, keyboard, and bass; horn lines stack against each other at 0:07
0:10	Desde pequeña pude sentir Dentro de mí la guaracha Me prendía el corazón Cuando tocaban tambores Y luego al pasar el tiempo Sentimiento sonero Se apoderó de mi vida Y dije "eso es lo que quiero" Y así comenzó, señores Mi gran amor por la rumba	Since I was little I felt Within me the music My heart burned When I heard drums As time passed Son singing Took over my life And I said "this is what I want" That's how it began My great love for the rumba	**Verse section** Syncopated piano style of salsa music heard behind Cruz's voice, derived from tres playing; horns fill in between vocal lines; bongo riffs prominently; timbales play a stick pattern (*cáscara*)
0:36	Y solo podrá la tumba Arrancarme de mi son	Now only the grave Will take the son away from me	Montuno bells enter here briefly, on the timbales and bongo bell
0:41	Pues llevo en el corazón Como una llama candente Que quema para mi gente El fruto de su folclore Y soy rumbera de ataño Rumbera soy del presente	I carry in the heart Like a burning call It burns for my people The product of their folklore I'm a rumba player from way back, still am	**Continuation of the verse**

(continued)

Time	Text	Translation	Description
0:56	Porque al pasar de los años Sigue la rumba en mi mente	Because with the passing of time Dance music stays on my mind	Montuno bells enter briefly
1:02	Si hay ritmo en el corazón La música es para siempre	With music in the heart The music lasts forever	**Conclusion of the verse**
1:13			Instrumental interlude features a *bomba sicá* rhythm on the congas, highlighting Afro–Puerto Rican heritage
1:29	*Si hay ritmo en el corazon* *La música es para siempre* Y ya desde chiquitita me inspiró la rumba y entré en el ambiente La sigo cantando ahora en el presente porque mi rumbita la pide la gente Para siempre, para siempre, mi música es para siempre Yo tengo, tengo ritmo en el corazón porque he nacido en una tierra caliente	*With rhythm in the heart* *The music is forever* Since I was small the rumba inspired me, I sought it out I keep singing rumba now because the people ask for it Forever, forever, the music lives forever I have rhythm in my heart because I was born in a tropical land	Montuno begins, as well as chorus 1 (italics); Cruz improvises against it; bongo and timbales switch to bells
2:18			**Break** All instruments stop
2:22			**Instrumental interlude** Barretto improvises on the congas at 2:39
2:55	*Si hay ritmo en el corazon* *La música es para siempre* Tiene tradición, lo sabe la gente. La rumba se baila hasta en el Oriente Es muy contagiosa, no crean otra cosa, vino de Africa, hey, se hizo famosa Desde pequeña en mi corazón sentí ese ritmo con emoción Si hay ritmo en el corazón la música vive siempre	*With rhythm in the heart* *The music is forever* It's tradition, people know, they dance the rumba even in the East It's contagious, believe it, it came from Africa, hey, and became famous Since I was little I felt this rhythm in my heart If there is rhythm in the heart, music lives forever	Same chorus lyrics, but a slightly different melody

(continued)

Time	Text	Translation	Description
3:38			**Instrumental interlude** Two different horn melodies play against each other, as commonly heard in salsa montunos. The melodies, called **moñas** (literally, "ribbons"), add another level of excitement to the climatic section
4:11	*La música es para siempre* Ay, mi música es para siempre Si hay ritmo en el corazón Para siempre es, para siempre es	*The music is forever* Oh, my music is forever If there's rhythm in the heart Forever, forever, it's forever	Piece draws to a close with a shorter final chorus
4:31			**Coda** Similar to introduction

the bongo bell during the montuno. Example 5.5 is a transcription of typical bell patterns played by the timbales and bongo players against son clave. In the staff transcription, stems down on the bongo bell indicate a stroke on the larger end; stems up indicate a stroke on the smaller end.

EXAMPLE 5.5: Salsa bell patterns

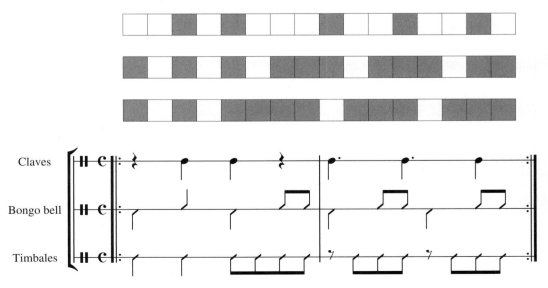

Merengue

Merengue has long been the most popular music in the Dominican Republic. It began as an Afro-Dominican variant of ballroom genres imported from Europe, such as the polka. Initially rejected by elite Dominicans as vulgar—because of its intimate dancing, its associations with the working classes, and its use of African-derived percussion—merengue slowly gained acceptance in the 1920s and 1930s. The instrumentation of the traditional rural merengue consists of button accordion, metal scraper (**güira**), a bass instrument of some sort (sometimes a large African-derived thumb piano), a double-headed drum called the **tambora**, and singers. Over the years, commercial merengue has adopted influences from jazz and international popular music, as in the case of son and salsa. In commercial merengues, the piano is now used instead of the accordion. Also, a larger horn section is incorporated that features saxophones and trumpets. Merengue became an international phenomenon in the 1980s, competing with salsa for airplay on Latin radio stations throughout much of Latin America and the United States.

Most merengues have a form similar to that of salsa: they begin with an instrumental introduction followed by a verse and finally a call-and-response section, interspersed with horn interludes. Horn lines in later sections often overlap just like the moñas of salsa music, fitting together in a manner similar to the percussion parts. The technique derives from West African musical structures (refer to the earlier commentary on batás and rumba).

FIGURE 5.9 Traditional merengue instruments: the three-row button accordion, tambora drum, and güira scraper

The tambora has its own unique rhythms to play. Percussionists place the drum across their knees and strike one head with a stick, the other with their hand. The end that is hit with the stick produces a louder sound, allowing the player to alternate high, sharp, syncopated cracks on the rim of the drum with open tones on the head. The metal scraper tends to emphasize either strong beats (1 and 3 of the $\frac{4}{4}$ measure) or backbeats (2 & and 4 &), but also improvises with virtuosic flourishes and variations. In larger dance bands, conga drummers play a characteristic two-measure pattern against other percussion.

A transcription of characteristic rhythms performed on these percussion instruments appears in Example 5.6. In the tambora line of the staff notation, round noteheads designate an open tone and slash heads indicate a rim shot. In both the tambora and conga lines, notes with upward stems are performed by the strong hand, downward stems with the weak hand, and an "x" designates a slap. In the conga transcription, the different levels denote drums tuned at different pitches; slash heads indicate a soft touch. Darker shading in the TUBS graph represents stronger, accented notes.

As you follow Listening Guide 5.6, you will recognize that one unique quality of this genre is its speed: unlike other Latin dance music, merengue horn (especially saxophone) lines usually consist of many rapid notes. Frequently, merengues' overall tempos are quicker as well, though not in this case. The prominence of the saxophone is also striking. Saxophones play fast, repeated melodies, outlining the chords. Keyboard parts in modern merengue also tend to be fast and syncopated, similar to those in salsa. Bass

EXAMPLE 5.6: Merengue rhythms

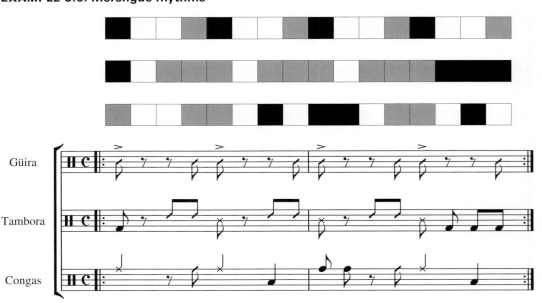

⊚ Crespo: "Píntame" (Paint for Me)

Composer/lyricist: Elvis Crespo

Date of composition: 1999

Performers/instruments: Elvis Crespo, lead vocal; José Díaz, Edgard Benítez, and José Santiago, saxophones; Jan Duclerc, Tommy Villariny, and Luis Aquino, trumpets; Moisés Nogueras and Antonio Vásquez, trombones; Luis Ángel Cruz, piano; Miguel González, bass; Ito Colón, drum set; Héctor Herrera, congas; Richard Mercado, güira; chorus

Date of recording: 1999

Genre: merengue

Form: strophic, followed by call-and-response

Tempo/meter: fast duple

What to Listen for:

- Saxophone and trumpet melodies interact throughout the piece
- Modern-style bass
- Heavy, constant pulse provided by floor tom of the drum set

Time	Text	Translation	Description
0:00	"Píntame," Le dije yo al pintor Píntame la carita De la niña más bonita Dentro de mi corazón *Pinta, pinta* *Pinta su carita* Sin esa carita Hoy me muero yo	"Paint for me" I said to the artist Paint the face Of the loveliest girl Inside my heart *Paint, paint* *Paint her face* Without that face Today I will die	Introduction, played slowly and without percussion; chorus parts in italics
0:21			**Instrumental interlude** Percussion and rhythm instruments enter in time; trumpets play the main melody, with saxophones outlining chords
0:37	Quiero su carita Pintada en mi corazón...	I want her face Painted in my heart...	**Verse 1**
1:26	*Píntame su nariz* *Para respirar su aire* *Píntame su boquita* *Para yo poder besarle...*	*Paint me her nose* *To breathe in her air* *Paint me her mouth* *So I can kiss her...*	Chorus repeats part of the verse
1:47	Pinta su carita [*pinta*] Que yo quiero sentir...	Paint her face [*paint*] I want to feel...	Chorus sings "pinta" (paint) in between lead vocals, which begins the call-and-response section

(continued)

Time	Text	Translation	Description
2:13			Instrumental interlude with trumpets on lead melody. Saxophones play at 2:28 and the trumpets at 2:37
2:53	Amigo pintor [*pinta*] Píntame la carita...	Artist, my friend [*paint*] Paint me her face...	Call-and-response continues
3:09	Le dije yo al pintor Píntame la carita...	I said to the artist Paint the face...	
3:26			Final moña-like instrumental section with interlocked saxophone and trumpet melodies
4:13	Pequeña... *Píntame*	Hey little girl... *Paint me*	

FIGURE 5.10 Elvis Crespo, composer of "Píntame," appearing at the 8th Annual Latin Grammy Awards in Miami, 2007

parts vary. In the past, the most common beat was a straightforward pulse on beats 1 and 3. However, in the last fifteen years a drum set's floor tom has taken over this role, and the bass has been used more to add color or "punch" at various moments. Sliding and slapping sounds are common, and bassists stop and start rather than playing consistently.

The Bolero

The term **bolero** is used in Spain to refer to a genre of music played in triple meter to the accompaniment of string instruments and castanets, but the Latin American bolero is an urban romantic song form influenced by European parlor music. It first developed in eastern Cuba in the late nineteenth century. Performers there, relatively affluent Afro-Cubans, used the term to describe songs in a slow duple meter, usually performed by two singers and accompanied by two guitars and claves. One guitar played a bass line and provided basic harmonic accompaniment, the other improvised melodies between vocal phrases. These Cuban boleros were slow and harmonically complex, intended for listening, with refined lyrics reflecting middle-class taste. Musicians played them in private homes, in cafés, and similar venues for their friends. By the mid-1920s, a trio format had developed for interpreting boleros that would prove influential throughout the region (Figure 5.11).

Beginning in the 1930s, the genre spread internationally, and Mexico became the most important center of bolero performance. Composers in that country (María Grever, Agustín Lara, etc.) fused the Cuban idiom with influences from jazz and popular music of the day. The appeal of recordings made in Mexico and disseminated through record sales, radio, and film resulted in the proliferation of new bolero composers and performers throughout Latin America. The mid-twentieth century represents a veritable heyday for the bolero in which it dominated popular music recording throughout the region. A sampling of thousands of well-known boleros have been collected in Jaime Rico Salazar's *Cien años de boleros* (Bogotá: Panamericana Press, 2000).

Since the 1950s, the bolero has continued to change. In the 1940 and 1950s, bolero music accompanied by large big-band orchestras became

❀ In Depth 5.2

Bachata

In the Dominican Republic, bolero repertoire from Mexico and elsewhere inspired the music now referred to as **bachata**. The history of this bolero variant demonstrates the ways in which international music traditions often become localized over time. As documented by Deborah Pacini Hernandez, bachata emerged in shantytowns on the edges of Santo Domingo in the 1970s. Early artists performed for dances and parties on acoustic guitars with small ensembles featuring the bass, bongo, and maracas or metal scraper. At that time, the term bachata was used to refer to all music performed by the urban poor, including boleros and acoustic merengues.

Since the mid-1980s, however, bachata has come to represent a distinct genre, developed in part by musician Blas Durán. Modern bachata is performed at a slightly faster tempo than standard boleros and adopts a more percussive sound, although its harmonies tend to be simpler. Bands now feature electric guitars and additional percussion, including drum set and drum machine. An electric guitar with a flange-effects box typically plays instrumental melodies, often outlining

chords in quick runs. A unique dance step has developed as well that involves taking three steps to each side in alternation followed by a distinctive hop-like motion. Couples perform the bachata while holding each other in a tight embrace and swinging their hips.

Bachata lyrics for many years employed colloquial forms of expression—"street slang"—rather than the refined lyrics of earlier boleros and reflected a decidedly male perspective on love and relationships. They often still express despair, suffering, indignation, and longing; bawdiness and sexual double entendre are common as well. As one might imagine, the repertoire initially struck middle-class listeners as rather crude. Of course, since the music has gained a broader public, its lyrical content has conformed more to that of other international popular music. The Bronx-based Dominican group Aventura (see Chapter 10) represents one of the most successful recent groups, performing at the White House in 2009 and modernizing the image of the genre. Consult the Internet and library resources to learn more about bachata's history, the sound of the music, and its dance style.

FIGURE 5.11 The influential Trío Matamoros, photographed here in about 1930; left to right: Rafael Cueto, Miguel Matamoros, Siro Rodríguez

explore

As an introduction to the bolero, listen to "Dos gardenias" (Two Gardenias) or "Veinte años" (Twenty Years) from the Buena Vista Social Club releases of the mid-1990s, or Puerto Rican favorites such as "Perdón" (Forgive Me) or "Obsesión" (Obsession) by Pedro Flores.

popular. Perhaps the most influential innovation of the 1960s was the fusion of elements from the earlier classic bolero with elements of international pop music (the drum set, synthesizer, electric guitar, string arrangements, etc.). Mexican Armando Manzanero and Brazilian Roberto Carlos were early exponents of this variant. Some critics consider their songs "watered-down" Latin American culture, not "Latin" enough, yet they have proven very successful commercially. In the 1990s, bolero (with a somewhat "rocki-fied" backtrack) made a strong come back across Latin America with the wildly successful recordings of Mexican Luis Miguel.

Political Song

Socially engaged protest song first became popular within Latin America in the 1960s and 1970s; the most common term for it is **nueva canción** or "new song." The genre first emerged in South America, specifically Argentina and the southern cone region (see Chapter 7), but it soon caught on in the Caribbean and developed a loyal following there. Early enthusiasts tended to be young adults, primarily college-educated, and they performed in coffeehouses, on campuses, small theaters, and sometimes at political rallies. These enthusiasts sought an alternative to music dominating the media that they perceived as overly commercial. Some nueva canción artists created new kinds of high-quality music, often by incorporating elements of local repertoire that earlier generations considered of little interest. Others co-opted international genres (rock, blues, the bolero) and adapted them to their own purposes. Nueva canción lyrics have touched on many subjects, drawing attention to social injustice or discussing more-conventional themes such as romance in fresh, unconventional ways.

Cuban youths who grew up in the aftermath of the revolution (1959) have been strong advocates of nueva canción (though Cubans refer to it as nueva trova). The government there actively encourages artists to comment on social issues and to avoid slavish imitation of music from the United States and Europe. Among prominent first-generation figures associated with the nueva trova movement are Pablo Milanés (b. 1943) and Silvio Rodríguez (b. 1946, Figure 5.12). Milanés, an Afro-Cuban, has consistently demonstrated an interest in traditional genres (son, bolero, rumba), and many of his songs demonstrate such influences. For his part, Silvio Rodríguez has more typically taken inspiration from international rockers including Bob Dylan and the Beatles. His musical output is extensive and quite varied; many songs are noteworthy for their harmonic complexity. Rodríguez's lyrics are highly sophisticated and metaphorical. He was the first nueva trova musician recognized as such, appearing on Cuban television in 1968, and continues to be a prominent composer today.

FIGURE 5.12 Cuban singer-songwriter Silvio Rodriguez performing in Havana, 2004

"En estos días" (Listening Guide 5.7) is a good introduction to Rodríguez's repertoire. The composition can be read as a love song, as commentary on the country's political leadership, or as a critique of Cuba itself in the 1970s. Regarding the latter, the song's at times apocalyptic statements apparently refer to momentous events that framed the revolution's initial decades such as the October missile crisis, the Cold War, the ongoing embargo and isolation of Cuba, and tense international relations. Though a believer in socialism, Rodríguez had numerous conflicts with government officials early in his career; perhaps for this reason, he has tended not to comment on the specific inspiration for many of his early songs. The multiple readings of the music increase its appeal to diverse audiences.

Puerto Rico has many of its own nueva canción singers, including Roy Brown (b. 1945), Andrés Jiménez (b. 1947), and Antonio Cabán Vale (b. 1942). Some compose in a style similar to that of Silvio Rodríguez; others work with local Puerto Rican traditional genres. Their music is worth exploring on your own, as it references important political tensions between Puerto Rico and the United States. And the *plena*, an important musical genre from the Afro–Puerto Rican community, has for many years served as a grassroots form of protest in its own right.

Reggaeton

Reggaeton is one of the most popular forms of music from the Hispanic Caribbean today, especially among younger listeners. The genre emerged in the early 1990s. It is fundamentally transnational, with roots in the modern

explore

Search for recorded examples of the Puerto Rican protest singers mentioned and for further information on the *plena*. The short film *Plena Is Work, Plena Is Song* (New York: Cinema Guild, 1989) provides a good introduction to the *plena* and its associations with protest; the book *Music in the Hispanic Caribbean* (Oxford University Press, 2010) contains information on both.

⊚ Rodríguez: "En estos días" (In These Times)

Composer/lyricist: Silvio Rodríguez

Date of composition: 1978

Performer/instruments: Silvio Rodríguez (guitar, voice)

Date of recording: 1995

Genre: nueva trova

Form: strophic

Tempo/meter: moderate simple quadruple

What to Listen for:

- International style of the music, influenced by the bolero, but not specific to Cuba, reflecting Rodríguez's tastes
- Early sections of the lyrics appear to discuss romance, but later sections make veiled political references
- The lines "how many stay" and "how many go" allude to the exile of tens of thousands of Cubans in the 1960s and 1970s

Time	Text	Translation	Description
0:00			**Instrumental introduction** Prominent descending bass line, complex harmonies
0:16	En estos días Todo el viento del mundo Sopla en tu dirección La Osa Mayor corrige La punta de su cola Y te corona con la estrella Que guía: la mía	In these times All the winds of the world Blow in your direction The Great Bear curls The end of its tail And crowns you with the star That it guides: mine	**Verse 1** Verse sung over the same chords as the introduction
0:32			Brief return of introductory theme
0:35	Los mares se han torcido Con no poco dolor Hacia tus costas La lluvia dibuja En tu cabeza la sed De millones de árboles Las flores te maldicen Muriendo, celosas	The seas have writhed In no little pain Toward your coasts The rain traces On your face the thirst Of millions of trees Flowers curse you As they die, jealous	**Verse 2**
0:55	En estos días No sale el sol Sino tu rostro Y en el silencio Sordo del tiempo Gritan tus ojos ¡Ay!, de estos días terribles ¡Ay!, de lo indescriptible	In these times The sun does not rise But instead your face And in the deaf Silence of time Your eyes scream Oh, what terrible days Oh, unspeakable days	Contrasting **B** section with new chords

(continued)

Time	Text	Translation	Description
1:14			Full introductory theme
1:30	En estos días no hay Absolución posible Para el hombre Para el feroz La fiera que ruge Y canta ciega Ese animal remoto Que devora y Devora primaveras	In these times there is No absolution possible For men For the fierceness The fury that bellows And sings blindly That distant animal That devours and Devours springtimes	**Verse 3**
1:45			Brief return of introductory theme
1:49	En estos días No sale el sol Sino tu rostro Y en el silencio Sordo del tiempo Gritan tus ojos Ay, de estos días terribles Ay, del nombre que lleven Ay, de cuantos se marchen Ay, de cuantos se queden Ay, de todas las cosas Que hinchan este segundo ¡Ay!, de estos días terribles Asesinos del mundo	In these times The sun does not rise But instead your face And in the deaf Silence of time Your eyes scream Oh, what terrible days Oh, how can they be described Oh, how many are leaving Oh, how many stay Oh, all the things That burden this moment Oh, these terrible days Assassins of the world	Extended **B** section
2:35			Brief instrumental finale

dance music of Jamaica as well as in black U.S. genres. Characterized by segments of spoken or sung lead vocals and a constant, syncopated beat, reggaeton might be thought of as a form of Spanish-language rap that uses a rhythm known in Jamaica as "Dem Bow" under most tracks. Lyrics tend to focus on partying and romance, but some also reference issues of pan–Latin American and pan-Latino pride, racial consciousness, and other social concerns.

Aside from the music, fans also are also attracted to reggaeton dance moves, often of a provocative and sexually explicit nature. Probably the best known of these is **el perreo** (roughly, "doggy-style"), which seems to derive from Jamaican dances of the 1980s. The overt sexuality of many moves and the vulgarity of some reggaeton lyrics became the focus of considerable controversy for a time among those who preferred salsa, merengue, or other more traditional forms of music and dance.

EXAMPLE 5.7: Basic reggaeton beat

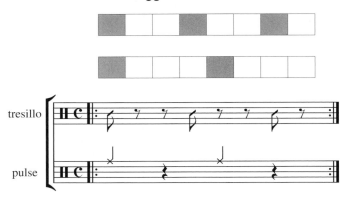

The reggaeton beat is created through the combination of a low drum playing a steady pulse on beats 1 and 3 of the $\frac{4}{4}$ measure and a **tresillo** rhythm played against it by a contrasting instrument (Example 5.7). The tresillo figure is found in virtually all of the Caribbean, as well as in other parts of Latin America influenced by African heritage. It is centuries old, with roots in the music of Kongo cultures and those of the Middle East.

Jamaican artist Shabba Ranks first popularized the reggaeton beat as modern dance music in his song "Dem Bow" from the 1991 CD *Just Reality*. "Dem Bow" circulated in several countries and influenced releases by numerous Spanish-speaking artists. By the mid-1990s, Puerto Rican producers had created entire albums based on the Dem Bow groove, relabeling it reggaeton. The music can take many forms depending on who records it. Although it utilizes the same beat, it may also include introductions or interludes of entirely different rhythms. Artists often change the timbre of the instruments playing the tresillo and may add in new harmonies, background melodic figures, and so on. Current stars of the genre include Puerto Ricans Don Omar (William Omar Landrón, b. 1978) and Daddy Yankee (Ramón Ayala, b. 1977).

"Loíza" (Listening Guide 5.8) comes from Tego Calderón (b. 1971), an Afro–Puerto Rican performer. His music often incorporates insightful social commentary and in some instances blends Puerto Rican traditional rhythms with electronic sounds. Calderón took the name for this composition from a small beachside neighborhood outside of San Juan known for its Afro–Puerto Rican population and its preservation of bomba drumming. Listening Guide 5.8 includes a partial transcription.

FIGURE 5.13 Tego Calderón performing at the Copacabana Club, New York City, 2004

◎ Calderón: "Loíza"

Composer/lyricist: Tego Calderón

Date of composition: 2003

Performers/instruments: Tego Calderón, voice; studio-generated percussion, electric bass, electric guitar, and synthesizer; studio-produced with the help of DJ Adam

Date of recording: 2003

Genre: reggaeton

Form: Rapped vocals over cyclic percussion

Tempo/meter: moderate duple, tresillo pulse against downbeat

What to Listen for:

- Almost the entire piece features a studio-generated variant of traditional bomba drumming (compare with the bomba segment in "Ritmo en el corazón," Listening Guide 5.5)
- The standard reggaeton beat stops and starts in order to vary the texture
- The complete lyrics include multiple references to Puerto Rican politicians and social issues

Time	Text	Translation	Description
0:00	Oye, esto es Pa' mi pueblo Con cariño Del "Abayarde" Con DJ Adam Y Cachete, el majadero de los cueros Pa' mi pueblo Que tanto quiero De Calderón, Pa' Loíza entero, oye	Listen, this is For my town With affection From the "Stinging Ant" With DJ Adam And Cachete, the guy with the drums For my people Whom I love so much From Calderón, For all of Loíza, listen	Brief percussive introduction, in a rhythm based on *bomba sicá*, over which Calderón speaks
0:18	Ando sin prisa Pero tu lentitud me coleriza Y él que no brega con Loíza (No, no llores) Me quiere hacer pensar Que soy parte de una trilogía racial Donde to' el mundo es igual Sin trato especial Sé perdonar Eres tú quien no sabe disculpar *So,* ¿cómo justifica tanto mal? Es que tu historia es vergonzosa Entre otra cosas Cambiaste las cadenas por esposas	I'm not in a hurry But your torpor angers me Those who ignore Loíza (No, don't cry) Try to make me think That I'm part of a racial trilogy And that everyone is equal No special treatment I know how to forgive It's you that doesn't So, how to justify so much evil? Your history is shameful Among other things You exchanged chains for wives	Initial verse; above a variant of a traditional bomba rhythm, entrance of a synthesized reggaeton beat enters; electric piano and bass playing a sparse four-measure chord vamp

(continued)

Time	Text	Translation	Description
0:38	No todos somos iguales En terminos legales Y eso esta proba'o en los tribunales En lo claro la justicia Se obtiene con cascajos, oye Por eso estamos como estamos (Que se joda) Que si no hay chavo' pa'l abogado Te provee uno el estado Pero hermano Te llevó quien te trajo Te matan y no desenfundan La jaula se te inunda Sentencia legal es defensa de segunda	Not everyone is equal In legal terms And that's proven in the tribunals Clearly justice Is obtained with grit, hey That's why we are how we are (Screw them) If you don't have money for a lawyer The state will get one But brother They'll get you one way or the other They kill without pulling a gun The lockup gets you A legal sentence is a second-rate defense	Continuation of same percussive and chordal vamp
0:58	Nunca va a haber justicia sin igualdad Maldita maldad que destruye la humanidad Porque protesta va a quitarme la libertad Si yo no reconozco su autoridad Nunca va a haber justicia sin igualdad Maldita maldad que destruye la humanidad Porque protesta, va a quitarme la libertad Si yo no pertenezco a su sociedad...	There's no justice without equality Evil that destroys humanity Why protest, they take away my liberty If I don't recognize their authority There's no justice without equality Evil that destroys humanity Why protest, they take away my liberty I don't belong to their society...	Entrance of a new synthesizer line over the existing vamp, adding a new layer of complexity

Classical Music and Latin Jazz

Classical Music

Cuba and the Hispanic Caribbean have a long history of classical music performance, with the earliest forms of the repertoire associated with the Catholic Church. As early as 1540, organists at the cathedral in Santo Domingo offered instruction to aspiring performers; by 1600, other cathedrals had been built in the region and the post of chapelmaster was established, one that involved the coordination of all musical activity. As mentioned, colonial authorities used church music to convert indigenous and African peoples to Catholicism. For this reason, mixed-race and non-European members of society figured prominently in the performance of European religious music from the earliest years. In Cuba, for instance, Esteban Salas, of mixed black and white ancestry, began composing in the 1750s; his substantial body of Baroque compositions consists of Masses, psalm settings, motets, and Christmas music for church choir.

Secular forms of classical music took longer to develop. Their earliest manifestations, dating from the eighteenth century, involved music accompanying events of state such as the celebration of a new Spanish king or the performance of minuets and other light classical dance forms. Public concerts of classical music began to appear consistently only in the nineteenth century, owing to the growing wealth of colonial populations, primarily the result of profits from slave labor. A one-peso tax on the importation of each new slave brought to Cuba, for instance, provided Spanish governor Miguel Tacón with ample funding to create Havana's Teatro Tacón in 1838, the largest opera and symphony house in North America or Latin America at the time. This and other theaters hosted artists from France, Spain, Italy, the United States, and elsewhere.

By the mid-nineteenth century, Cuban composers such as Laureano Fuentes Matons (1825–1898) began composing symphonies, operas, and chamber music in a European classical style. Nicolás Ruiz Espadero (1832–1890) established himself as one of Cuba's first piano virtuosos, writing pieces modeled after those of Franz Liszt. Ignacio Cervantes (1847–1905), probably the most important Cuban composer of his era, wrote short, stylized dance pieces for piano that were considered the epitome of local expression. In this sense he perfected a tradition established by his predecessor, Manuel Saumell (1817–1870). In Puerto Rico, Felipe Gutiérrez Espinosa (1825–1899) began composing operas and religious music beginning in the 1850s, and Manuel Gregorio Tavárez (1843–1883) and Juan Morel Campos (1857–1896) composed salon repertoire based on dance music. Music conservatories were established in the Dominican Republic following its independence from Haiti in 1844, training composers such as José Reyes (1835–1905) and José María Arredondo (1840–1924).

In the final decades of the nineteenth century, the habanera song genre became popular internationally. The habanera rhythm on which it is based, virtually the same one heard in modern reggaeton, soon found its way into light classical compositions. Visitors to Cuba learned popular habaneras and performed them in other Latin American countries and in Europe. The rhythm contributed to the emergence of the Argentine tango and was featured in European operas of the day such as Georges Bizet's *Carmen* (1875). Other European classical composers who have used the habanera rhythm in their works include Claude Debussy, Maurice Ravel, Isaac Albéniz, and Manuel de Falla.

Composer and violinist Amadeo Roldán (1900–1939) became director of Havana's municipal conservatory in the 1920s, as well as director of the Philharmonic Orchestra, one of two symphonies in that city. In 1930, Roldán, a bold experimenter and modernist, wrote the first piece of classical music exclusively for percussion as part of a chamber work called *Ritmicas*. He and his contemporary Alejandro García Caturla (1906–1940) promoted an artistic movement called *afrocubanismo*, attempting to reconcile influences from Afro-Cuban percussion and/or song with classical traditions. Movements 5 and 6 of *Ritmicas*, for instance, feature claves, bongo, güiro, and other traditional Afro-Cuban instruments. This work generated considerable controversy among conservative listeners of the day who did not feel that such instruments were appropriate in the concert hall.

One of the most famous and commercially successful Caribbean classical composers of all time is Ernesto Lecuona (1896–1963). His career reflects Cuba's strong tradition of classical piano performance. In the 1950s, Lecuona's name was well known even to many North Americans. He grew up in a fairly affluent family outside of Havana and developed a reputation as a child prodigy; most who heard him believed that he was destined for a career as a concert soloist. After the premature death of his father, however, Lecuona began playing music in theaters to support himself, often for silent films, blackface sketches, or other comedy acts. Later, as the result of successful compositions such as his *Andalucian Suite* for piano, he returned to the concert stage and toured internationally, fulfilling his childhood ambitions.

Lecuona's music represents a sophisticated fusion of classical and popular elements, straddling the boundary between the two repertories. Often his works take inspiration from traditional sources of various kinds, including *música guajira* and Afro-Cuban music. He was one of the first classically trained performers to create works based on Afro-Cuban themes. Lecuona should also be remembered as an internationalist, someone open to styles from many countries. His compositions are amazingly diverse; they include pieces inspired by Spanish dance music, *zambas* from Argentina (see Chapter 7), and fox-trots and blues-inspired music from the United States. He gained greatest recognition within Cuba for his musicals (zarzuelas), often based on life in the colonial past.

The best-known experimental composer living in Cuba today is Leo Brouwer (b. 1939). Also renowned as a guitarist, conductor, and arranger, Brouwer came from a musical family (his great uncle was none other than Ernesto Lecuona!). He took classical guitar lessons from an early age and later studied in the United States, both at Juilliard and at the Hartt School of Music. Since the late 1960s, Brouwer has gained international recognition as a composer of many kinds of music (symphonic repertoire, chamber pieces) but especially guitar works. His **études**, for instance, are idiomatically suited to that instrument—beautiful, challenging, and innovative.

Brouwer's harmonic language is expansive and varied, incorporating everything from references to traditional or popular music from the Caribbean to extreme avant-garde timbres and unusual sonorities. More than virtually any other Cuban composer, he has demonstrated an interest in world music, adopting traditional Andean melodies, North Indian *ragas*, and African rhythmic patterns as sources of inspiration. Since 1981 he has been a principal conductor of the Havana Symphony Orchestra.

Brouwer's work demonstrates his interest in expanding the sonic possibilities of the guitar. He has developed innovative ways of playing chords, for instance by using the thumb of his left hand on the fretboard in addition to the fingers. He adapted muted **pizzicato** plucking techniques originally associated with violins (and developed by Béla Bartók) to the guitar. He sometimes specifies that performers employ harmonic overtones as part of melodic sequences or play on unusual parts of the guitar string, such as between the bridge and the tuning pegs. He has written guitar works to be played with a bow, typically used only on a cello or acoustic bass. **Pedals** (sustained notes) and ostinatos of various kinds are common in his work. He has developed alternate guitar tunings for some compositions. On occasion, he has also used the body of the guitar as an instrument, instructing instrumentalists to rap or tap on the wood. In addition to writing for the concert stage, Brouwer has set music to some of the most famous Cuban films of all time, including *Death of a Bureaucrat*, *Lucía*, *Memories of Underdevelopment*, and *The Last Supper*.

Among his most distinctive and original works is *La espiral eterna* (The Eternal Spiral, Listening Guide 5.9) for solo guitar, an atonal, avant-garde work. Its music suggests an endless spiral in its rapid alternation of notes, and it is a virtuoso showpiece that reveals Brouwer's remarkable talents as a performer as well as a composer.

FIGURE 5.14 Leo Brouwer (right), along with former Beatles producer George Martin (left), thank the audience after the Havana Symphony's 2002 performance of two well-known Lennon and McCartney songs, "Hey Jude" and "Yellow Submarine"

Latin Jazz/Michel Camilo

The final artist discussed in this chapter is Michel Camilo (b. 1954), a Dominican whose work has consistently straddled the boundary between the worlds of classical music, popular music, and jazz. In this sense, his music is indicative of tendencies toward the fusion of elements from many kinds of music within and beyond the Caribbean in recent years. Camilo

⊚ Brouwer: *La espiral eterna* (The Eternal Spiral)

Composer: Leo Brouwer

Date of composition: 1971

Performer/instrument: Elena Papandreou, guitar

Date of recording: 2002

Genre: classical guitar repertoire

Form: free form, based on a succession of circular motives played very fast

Tempo/meter: ametrical, without clear tempo

What to Listen for:

- As in many of Brouwer's works, development of musical motives without employing conventional harmonies or chords
- Sections in this piece are defined only by the changing use of musical material, rather than by contrasting keys or themes
- Minimalist musical material, with only small changes occurring between gestures

Time	Description
0:00	**Opening section** Quiet but rapid spiral-like alternations between a cluster of notes a half step apart in a variety of patterns; gradual downward movement in pitch
1:50	**Conclusion of opening section** **Tone cluster** dissolves into a striking unison, ending with a "Bartok snap," in which a string is pulled upward and released to percussively snap against the fretboard
2:05	**Second section** Discontinuous sounds featuring "white noise" produced by rubbing the fingers on the wound bass strings, more snaps as well as muted sounds produced by dampening the strings with the fingers while playing the spiral motive; ascent to uppermost register of guitar
4:03	**Third section** Sounds produced by percussively depressing the strings onto the fretboard with fingers of either hand
4:54	**Fourth section** Arpeggios of dissonant chords in upper register, with a disjointed melody woven into the middle register; concludes with chord combining a snap with harmonics
6:01	**Fifth section** Muted clusters of notes alternate with percussive plucking of strings
6:30	**Sixth section** Return of spiral motive, now in lower register; fades away into eternity

first trained at the National Conservatory in Santo Domingo, where he studied classical piano and percussion, and shortly thereafter he took a job as percussionist in the National Symphony Orchestra (at age 16!). In 1979, Camilo moved to the United States, studying music at the Juilliard School and Mannes College. In 1987 he made his debut as a conductor of the Dominican National Symphony, interpreting works by Ludwig van Beethoven, Antonín Dvořák, and others. Camilo has appeared as a piano soloist with the Atlanta Symphony, the Copenhagen Philharmonic, the BBC Symphony Orchestra, and many other world-class classical ensembles.

In addition to his classical focus, Camilo has long demonstrated interest in both jazz and Caribbean traditional music. He took part in the International Montreal Jazz Festival in 1982 as a member of Puerto Rican Tito Puente's band. Between 1982 and 1986 he performed regularly with Cuban jazz saxophonist Paquito D'Rivera and shortly thereafter collaborated with Cuban percussionist Ignacio Berroa as well. Camilo has composed prolifically both in the classical and jazz idioms, writing scores for television and film. One of his best-known pieces, "Why Not," is heavily influenced by North American jazz and helped win him a Grammy in 1983. Other works, such as Listening Guide 5.10, "Caribe," have been interpreted by jazz great Dizzie Gillespie and others.

Because Camilo's work contains elements of both classical repertoire and Latin jazz, it would be useful to define the latter term briefly. As a general rule, the complexity of jazz lies in its harmonies and in sophisticated arrangements, while the complexity of much Afro-Latin music lies in its rhythms, its varied timbres, and the ways in which it layers particular melodic or rhythmic elements. Latin dance music tends to be harmonically simpler than jazz and to consist of shorter formal structures (often two-, four-, or eight-measure phrases) that are repeated many times in variation; it is closer to its West African roots in this sense. Styles of soloing often differ between jazz and Latin artists as well. Because they cannot necessarily count on frequent harmonic changes to generate interest, Latin jazz performers rely more on innovative uses of rhythm, on repeated melodic shapes known as **sequences,** and on other techniques.

The significant differences that exist between jazz and traditional Caribbean music made the two genres somewhat difficult to reconcile with one another. Probably the most common means of fusing them has involved reliance on jazz harmonies and big-band jazz instrumentation supporting rhythmic patterns, anticipated bass lines, and syncopated melodies derived from Cuban son, salsa, and other genres. Michel Camilo builds on earlier Latin

FIGURE 5.15 Michel Camilo (left) alongside Cuban jazz saxophonist Paquito D'Rivera (right), in a photo from 1988

⊚ Camilo: "Caribe" (Caribbean)

Composer: Michel Camilo

Date of composition: 1988

Date of recording: 2002

Performer/instrument: Michel Camilo, solo piano

Genre: based loosely on traditional Caribbean genres

Form: sectional

Tempo/meter: varied duple, with frequent **rubato**

What to Listen for:

- Performance freely re-creates on piano a piece originally composed for jazz combo
- Three melodic ideas heard and presented in variation
- Similarities audible between the syncopated "Caribbean" melodies played in the right hand and U.S. ragtime music

Time	Description
0:00	Introduction in a free tempo; initial motive in two different keys (0:01 and 0:06), ending with a contrasting melodic idea (0:09)
0:22	The first section in time, labeled Bomba on the score; syncopated bass line emphasizes beat 4 of the ⁴⁄₄ measure, imitating bomba in this sense; upper melody also quite syncopated
0:46	A slower interlude over the same chords, though the syncopated bass continues for a time
1:09	Return of bomba theme an octave higher, and in variation; ends in a loud cadence with fast runs
1:54	Beginning of a new, up-tempo section, labeled "Rumba" on the score, presentation of a new melodic theme and chords between 1:54 and one 1:58, then improvisation on them; returns to a simple version of the theme at 2:05 and at 2:17. Salsa-style anticipated bass from 2:24 to 2:42, more syncopated than earlier in the piece
2:49	Return of introduction's melody, but more forcefully and in tempo
3:02	Bomba theme returns over a low pedal tone hammered in octaves with the left hand
3:17	Return of rumba theme, initially (3:17–3:23) played in a syncopated salsa style
3:31	Syncopated bass pattern and implicit chords of the rumba theme with Camilo's left hand, but free improvisation with his right
4:07	Return of rumba theme in variation
4:19	More free improvisation, salsa keyboard-style, over pedal notes in the left hand
4:32	Return of rumba theme, played in contrasting octaves, and a final cadence

jazz experimentation, molding it to his personal tastes and infusing the already hybridized idiom with elements from light classical repertoire such as the compositions of Ignacio Cervantes and Juan Morel Campos mentioned earlier.

CONCLUSION

This brief introduction to Spanish Caribbean music should serve as a point of departure for a more extended exploration of the traditions of various islands, regions, and composers. There are countless styles of music that we have not covered well here, and that deserve mention: the danza and *danzón*, the *cha-cha-chá* and mambo, carnival music of various sorts, Latin rock and rap, Afro-Dominican drumming, and so on. Though the overview has not been comprehensive, it provides some insights into the diversity and complexity of the region. It offers frames of reference for thinking about the interrelations between various styles and the cultural influences that have given rise to them. Finally, the chapter has emphasized the fundamentally hybrid nature of Caribbean cultures and music. Most West African- and Spanish-derived traditions performed today have blended over time, resulting in genres that reflect a uniquely New World reality. And hybridized culture as it exists today continues to assimilate new external influences from the hemisphere and beyond, leading to ongoing musical innovation and synthesis.

KEY TERMS

bachata	merengue	rumba
batá	moñas	salsa
bolero	montuno	Santería
chéquere	música guajira	sequence
clave	ñongo	tambora
cuatro	nueva canción	timbales
décima	orichas	tone cluster
el perreo	pedal	tres
étude	pizzicato	tresillo
güira	reggaeton	
güiro	rubato	

FURTHER READING

Allen, Ray and Lois Wilcken, eds. *Island Sounds in the Global City: Caribbean Popular Music and Identity in New York*. New York: New York Folklore Society, 1998.

Manuel, Peter. *Caribbean Currents*. 2nd ed. Philadelphia: Temple University Press, 2006.

Moore, Robin. *Music of the Hispanic Caribbean*. New York: Oxford University Press, 2010.

Rivera, Raquel, Deborah Pacini Hernández, and Wayne Marshall, eds. *Reggaeton*. Durham, NC: Duke University Press, 2009.

Waxer, Lise, ed. *Situating Salsa. Global Markets and Local Meanings in Latin Popular Music*. London: Routledge, 2002.

FURTHER LISTENING

Africa in America. Music from Nineteen Countries. Cambridge, MA: Rounder Records, 1993.

Latin Jazz: La Combinación Perfecta. Smithsonian Folkways, 2002.

FURTHER VIEWING

In the Tradition. Miami: Warner Brothers, 1996.

Salsa: Latin Music of New York and Puerto Rico. BBC "Beats of the Heart" series. Newton, NJ: Shanachie Records, 1979.

Routes of Rhythm with Harry Belafonte, 3 vols. Cultural Research and Communication, Inc., 1989.

Brazil

CRISTINA MAGALDI

Introduction Brazil is the largest and most populous country in Latin America; it is also fifth in the world in terms of territory (3,287,597 square miles) and population (estimated at 191 million in 2010). This giant nation is the homeland of peoples from a variety of ethnicities and backgrounds and has a rich cultural fabric composed of European, African, Amerindian, Arab, Jewish, and Japanese heritages, among others. Within such a large and diverse country, music-making in Brazil has been particularly important as a tool for cultural enclosure as well as a channel for communal expression, helping people to articulate locality, regionalism, and nationality. Brazilian performers and composers have blended and transformed a myriad of traditions to produce commercial popular styles, like samba and bossa nova and, more recently, Brazilian country music, funk, rap, and rock. Alongside other Brazilian cultural icons such as soccer, music has served to showcase Brazilian culture abroad, helping to intensify Brazilians' pride in their country and traditions.

Brazil is the only Portuguese-speaking country in the Americas, and the language has served well over the years to unify the country's large and diverse population. Nonetheless, other languages have coexisted with the "official" Portuguese and are important parts of Brazil's cultural diversity. While descendents of immigrants have maintained German and Italian dialects in Central and Southern regions, some 180 Amerindian languages are still spoken. West African dialects are also kept alive in Afro-Brazilian religious ceremonies in the Northeast and recently Japanese has started to reappear as a resource for community building in central Brazil.

◀ **FIGURE 6.1** Map of Brazil and neighboring countries

FIGURE 6.2 Brazilian landscapes: (a) Rio de Janeiro, (b) Amazon forest, (c) Iguaçu Falls, and (d) Serra dos Brejões, Bahia

Similar in political structure and organization to the United States, Brazil is a Federal Republic divided into 26 states and one district capital. The country's extensive territory spans three time zones and several climate regions, and comprises a myriad of landscapes occupied by diverse flora and fauna. The country enjoys 4,650 miles of Atlantic coastline, hosts 60 percent of the Amazon forest, and has one of the world's most extensive river systems. Brazil's mesmerizing landscapes have always been an important symbol of Brazilian culture and have served as sources of inspiration for Brazilian composers of art music and continue as unifying themes in popular music.

While landscape and language have served to promote shared feelings of Brazilian nationality, they have also set the country apart from the rest of the continent. Although Brazil shares borders with most South American countries (Ecuador and Chile being the exceptions), the vast Amazon forest and the Andes Mountains in the West have historically hindered Brazilians' cultural exchanges with their Latin American neighbors. Furthermore, the majority of the Brazilian population lives in cities on or near the coast,

Learning Japanese Through Singing

Brazil hosts the largest Japanese population outside Japan—1.3 million people of Japanese descent. They are located mostly in the state of São Paulo and in Brazil's central areas, where Japanese families have traditionally settled as farmers. In the capital city of São Paulo, *nikkei* (Japanese immigrants and their descendents) have played an important role in growing small and large businesses and in transforming São Paulo into a leading city within the world's economy.

Nikkei cultural influences can be seen in a variety of areas, from agricultural techniques, to cuisine, to sports—for example, Brazilians are proud to have one of the world's leading judo teams. Brazil has also recently emerged as an important center for karaoke singing. For most young Brazilians, whether or not they have links to Japanese culture, karaoke is just another form of entertainment, but throughout the state of São Paulo, *nikkei* communities are energizing by reconnecting to Japanese traditions through karaoke.

The practice of karaoke has also proven to be a useful tool in the teaching and learning of the Japanese language. Japanese pop and traditional songs, as well as Brazilian pop songs translated into Japanese, figure prominently in karaoke competitions, which can gather as many as three hundred participants and thousands of fans in live karaoke marathons and on popular TV shows. A whole infrastructure is being built to support these karaoke competitions, including the construction of schools devoted to the teaching of the Japanese language through karaoke. Brazilians, of Japanese descent or not, are singing along, sometimes repeating Japanese words without knowing their meaning, as the karaoke phenomenon spreads to other states where Japanese culture and language have just started to penetrate.

---

where large ports maintain the country's economic, political, and cultural ties to Europe more than with its Spanish-speaking neighbors. Continuous migration from the countryside to coastal cities has further favored the connections with Europe, while fostering a constant cultural exchange between traditional and international popular musical styles.

It is also worth noting that Brazil is a young country: 50 percent of its population ranges from 20 to 40 years of age, the great majority living in large cities where advanced communications puts them side by side with other cosmopolitans around the world. Thus contemporary Brazilian musical life reflects its youthful population's desire to belong and to contribute to the new musical "global village."

A Brief History

The Portuguese first arrived in Brazil in 1500, and they ruled until 1822. Because Portuguese policies favored commerce and trade over settlement, colonial Brazil did not harbor strong European elite cultural and musical institutions, as did Spanish Latin America. That situation changed in 1808 when the Portuguese monarch João VI moved the court from Lisbon to the Brazilian capital, Rio de Janeiro, to avoid Napoleon's troops. After Napoleon's defeat in Europe, João VI returned to Portugal, leaving his son, Pedro I, as a regent in Rio de Janeiro. But tensions started to build between Rio de Janeiro and Portugal as Portuguese rulers attempted to restore Brazil's status as a colony. In 1822, Pedro I, the heir to the Portuguese Braganza family, declared Brazilian independence from Portugal and the monarchical regime continued when Pedro II ascended to the throne in 1840.

The presence of a European monarchy was a unique political and historical event and had a strong impact on Brazil's history and culture. While wars for independence in Spanish-speaking countries resulted in political and social unrest, during the nineteenth century, Brazilian independence began on a politically stable foundation that favored the development of European-style institutions and a constant flow of European musical trends to Brazilian cities.

Despite these differences, the Portuguese shared several practices with other European colonizers in the Americas. Like the Spanish, upon their arrival the Portuguese enslaved natives for agricultural work. Cultural conflicts, forced labor, and widespread disease led to the deaths of millions of indigenous Brazilians. It is estimated that about four to five million native inhabitants lived in Brazil when the Portuguese arrived; they belonged to four large ethnic groups—Tupi, Gê, Arawak, and Carib—and to some thousand different cultural groups. About 500,000 indigenous Brazilians from about 200 cultural groups remain today. Some communities were integrated into mainstream Brazilian society, and others have maintained indirect contact with the culture of the colonizers, while a few, living in remote regions, have managed to keep their cultural and musical heritages almost intact.

Like the Spanish, the Portuguese also imported Africans as slaves to work on sugarcane and coffee plantations. About four million Africans were brought to Brazil, more than to any other single country in the Americas, coming mostly from West African countries such as Nigeria, Benin, and the Portuguese colony of Angola. The majority belonged to the Yoruba and Bantu-Ewe cultural groups, who brought with them a wide gamut of cultural and musical traditions.

The large number of Africans taken to Brazil, the endurance of slavery until 1888—decades after abolition in most Latin American countries and the United States—and a close interaction between Africans and white Europeans in urban areas resulted in a strong and lasting influence of African culture on mainstream Brazilian society. According to the latest demographics, Afro-Brazilians, mulatos (descendants of Africans and Europeans), *cafusos* (descendants of Africans and indigenous Brazilians), and **caboclos** (descendants of Europeans and indigenous Brazilians) account for 44 percent of Brazil's population. African-derived traditions are particularly strong in the Northeast, an area with the largest concentration of people of African descent outside Africa. Brazilian culture is deeply marked by a long history of contrasts and clashes between the different cultures of the Africans, Amerindians, and Europeans. As in countries of the Caribbean, Brazilian culture is also distinguished by a conspicuous intermingling of these elements, a complex mix that characterizes the core of the country's musical scene.

With the proclamation of the republic in 1889, Brazil finally began breaking away from the Old World, although a strong cultural and commercial connection to Europe continues to this day. Growing industrial production, the rise of the local economy, and the growth of a middle class in large cities helped shape the path towards modern Brazil. As in many countries in the Americas, during the first part of the twentieth century, Brazil witnessed a strong wave of nationalism—a political and intellectual movement that supported artistic expressions symbolic of a new, unique, and unified nation. The movement celebrated the local mix of races, ethnicities, and cultures, with European and African elements as the main components. During this time, the idea of *Brasilidade* (Brazilianness), of something that identifies the uniqueness of Brazilian culture, became central to politicians, intellectuals, and artists, an idea that continues to shape music production and consumption in contemporary Brazil.

Late in the 1950s a new city, Brasília, was built in the middle of the country to serve as the capital and to bring economic development to the country's central region. A city planned by the famous architect Oscar Niemeyer, Brasília is considered an architectural wonder. Its concrete buildings and open green spaces mark Brazil's entrance into the modern world. In 1964, at the height of the Cold War, democratically elected President João Goulart was forced out of power by a military coup because of his left-wing political ideals. The military dictatorship held Brazil back politically, but the country reemerged as a democracy in 1985 and continues to grow as a major political and economic power. Today, Brazil's economy ranks seventh in the world, with wealth concentrated in the hands of a few. As a country of extreme richness and accentuated poverty, the harsh social divide has also become part of Brazilian culture. If hybrid popular musical styles have contributed to symbolize a unified country within a nationalistic political agenda, a rich variety of regional musics have also played a role in highlighting Brazil's regional, social, and ethnic tensions.

In exploring some of these musics, keep in mind Brazil's geography and history, its various cultures, shared national pride, cosmopolitan experiences, ethnic mix, and social divides. These elements overlap and interact in complex ways, resulting in a myriad of original musical styles and performance practices that successfully blend tradition and modernity.

Mercosul (Mercosur) Politics, Trade, and Culture

Although Brazil continues to be more connected to Europe than to its Spanish-speaking neighbors, recently this situation has begun to change. In the early 1990s, political leaders in Brazil, Argentina, Paraguay, and Uruguay joined forces to forge a free-trade agreement—a common market of the south, or Mercosul (Mercosur in Spanish)—following the models of the European Union and NAFTA in North America. The goals of Mercosul are to facilitate trade and political integration in the region and to form an economical and political bloc to respond to economic pressures from other large markets.

With Colombia, Bolivia, Chile, Ecuador and Peru joining as associate members, today the countries of Mercosul make up the fifth largest economy in the world and have begun to impact global trade. As common passports start to be issued for citizens of Mercosul countries and their citizens cross each other's borders more easily, local tourism has exploded. As a way of integrating Brazilian youths with other Mercosul members, the Brazilian Congress has approved a law requiring public schools to offer Spanish as a second language.

It is expected that a "cultural Mercosul" will soon emerge to cater to the local interests and shared traditions. Some concrete examples are easy to notice today. The gaucho culture of the south of Brazil and Argentina, for example (see Chapter 7), figures prominently in the Bienal do Mercosul, an art and cultural event in the Brazilian Southern State of Rio Grande do Sul. With a huge Spanish market ready to receive new products, Brazilian popular musicians have started to record in Spanish on a regular basis, while popular styles like Brazilian country and rock are now widespread in Spanish-speaking countries.

Traditional and Popular Music

Amerindian Music

In 1557, the French Calvinist missionary Jean de Léry ventured inland from the central Brazilian coast and lived among the Tupinambá people. In 1578 he published a book reporting on the lives of the Tupinambás; the third edition (1585) included the earliest transcriptions of songs in the Tupi language. The Tupinambá song "Canidé-ioune" transcribed by Léry (Example 6.1) is an homage to a bird with yellow feathers. The song, which has been a source of inspiration for several Brazilian composers over the years, continues to be performed in a variety of versions in contemporary Brazil, reminding Brazilians of their native roots.

During colonial days and into the nineteenth century, other explorers published reports on indigenous musical practices, but the culture and music of indigenous Brazilians only began to be studied with academic rigor in the last 50 years, when a new generation of ethnomusicologists set out to explore local musical practices. Even so, considering the wide range of indigenous cultures spread over an extensive territory, ethnomusicologists still have a lot of work ahead of them before we can fully comprehend such a rich musical culture that is, in some ways, very different from our own. This text can only sample the amazing variety of musics. Nonetheless, we can identify some commonalities among the Brazilian indigenous musical practices, especially among groups living in the large Amazon basin.

As with most world cultures, to indigenous Brazilians music-making serves to organize social interaction, and they enjoy a variety of repertories associated with celebrations, commemorations, fishing, hunting, work, religious rituals, and curing songs. Among groups in the Amazon basin there is a prevalence of communal singing and group instrumental performances in which no distinction exists between performers and audiences. Nonetheless, instances of solo performances are also found, often associated with rituals to connect with the supernatural. The music is passed down orally from generation to generation, a job often performed by the shaman, a religious and political leader.

The body is an essential part of indigenous musical expression, as there is an intrinsic link between musical performances, singing, and dance. Music-making is also a strong marker of gender roles. In several groups, for instance, women are not allowed to play flutes, and in some rituals, not even permitted to see the flute performed.

Indigenous Brazilians prefer musical instruments from the aerophone and idiophone families. Some scholars believe that chordophones were not introduced to indigenous culture until the arrival of the Jesuits during colonization. Membranophones are uncommon in the Amazon basin; instead hollow log drums serve to accompany celebratory and shamanistic rituals.

Aerophones like flutes and whistles are special instruments to many indigenous groups because they can be used to imitate birds and are believed to connect humans to their spiritual ancestors. Flutes are also essential in rituals associated with fish and fishing, a crucial activity to many communities in the Amazon basin. Idiophones come in a variety of forms, but shakers are the most common. Attached to the ankles, wrist, or waist as bracelets and belts, small shakers look like ornaments made out of seeds, animal teeth, or claws; they serve to expand the sound of foot stomping and, when attached to

EXAMPLE 6.1: "Canidé-ioune" (Jean de Léry, *Viagem à Terra do Brasil*)

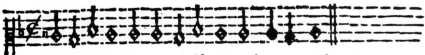

Canidé-ioune, canidé-ioune heura-oueh

FIGURE 6.3 Kamayurá playing the giant Uruá flutes: Upper Xingu (a tributary of the Amazon river)

stomping tubes or a wood stick, they help mark the rhythm as accompaniment to singing and dancing. The *maracá* (*maraká*, maraca), usually a gourd filled with seeds, is an essential shaker to accompany dance. It is used in shamans' rituals, in which the instrument symbolizes spiritual power. A great deal of work and care is put into the construction of musical instruments, which are often decorated with leaves and feathers in colorful designs drawn with paints extracted from seeds.

We can identify several musical characteristics common to groups living in the Amazon basin:

1. Melodic lines tend to move in descending and stepwise motion in a narrow melodic range. Two or three-note motives in chanting usually favor one pitch that is repeated several times and thus might be understood as a tonal center. The early transcription provided by Léry (Example 6.1) depicts a tune comprised of three notes that move in stepwise fashion.

2. There is a tendency towards a constant, regular pulse that is often marked by foot stomping and shakers.

3. Repetition of short sections helps to create larger musical structures that follow the lyrics and choreography of long rituals and celebrations. The integrated parts may be seen as a musical drama.

4. Sliding pitches and the resulting microtonal intervals are common in flute performances and in singing. As a result, the line between speech and singing is not clearly defined.

5. Monophonic singing is usually favored but vocal and instrumental drone accompaniments are also used.

6. Spontaneous individual performances lead to rhythmic/melodic variations that overlap during communal performances and create heterophonic textures. Indigenous musical performances can become so complex that it is difficult for outsiders to grasp the musical elements and vocal emissions and to capture them through traditional musical notation.

"Nhuiti ngrere" (Listening Guide 6.1) is a field recording (obtained by ethnomusicologists Max Peter Baumann and Linda K. Fujie) of the

Kayapó-Xikrin people, a community located by the Cateté River, a tributary of the Amazon in the State of Pará. The example is an excerpt of the *nhiok* female naming ritual, a rite of passage when young women learn about the group's hierarchy of kinship (relatives and friendship), and about their culture and society. In "Nhuti ngrere," the men are preparing, singing, and dancing before they move toward the female name-recipients' houses. The song and dance in this excerpt revolves around associations between

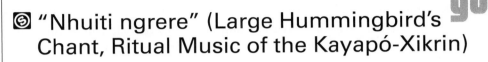

⊚ "Nhuiti ngrere" (Large Hummingbird's Chant, Ritual Music of the Kayapó-Xikrin)

Date of recording: 1995

Performers/instruments: male vocal ensemble; villagers of the Xikrin group of the Kayapó people

Genre: traditional ritual music

Form: two motives, **A** and **B**, repeated several times with variations

Tempo/meter: slow duple

What to Listen for:

- Constant, moderate rhythmic pulse articulated by vocal accentuation on every beat
- Spontaneous vocal interjections and vocal emissions imitating birds
- Vocal drone and heterophonic texture caused by individual variations of motives

Text	Description
A nhiuinhiuire a na kruoi Nhiok nhoikóré pari bê Ngo tó djua	**A** Text associates name-recipient with hummingbird, sung in a speech-like mode.
eae eae eae gu ga	**B** Vocables used as a refrain; two-note motive (a fourth) repeats, followed by a group interjection
Góra me mrãm boi ne Min kókótire ngo ató Mãna nhiok kóré kuman ibô ne	**A**
eae eae eae gu ga	**B**
Amin angró tutchi kamã Ne ba kamã kótó a bin Nhiui – mu nhiokóré pumu ketere Kumã ibônhodja	**A**
eae eae eae guga	**B**

the young women and hummingbirds, and it is easy to hear the sound relationships in the song. The Kayapo's *nhiok* is one of several native rituals with song and dance that link animals (especially birds and jaguars) as "guardian spirits" with humans.

The music of Brazilian indigenous groups may be perceived as simplistic or monotonous by those used to radios, mp3 players, computers, and an array of electronics that exponentially expand sounds and musical possibilities. Nonetheless, it should be viewed in a context marked by complex cultural relations founded on an intrinsic connection between human beings and nature that is expressed in a variety of different timbres, vocal emissions, and instrumental sounds specific to each indigenous community.

Some musical traits of indigenous Brazilians have blended with European and African traditions and are manifested in the caboclo culture and music of the North and the Northeast, discussed later in this chapter. Nonetheless, the idealized image of the indigenous Brazilian as pure and authentic, explored in nineteenth-century Romantic classical music, has been retained to this day in popular culture through a kind of native nostalgia. The figure of an idealized native, for example, is re-created every year by singers and dancers who dress in Indian "costumes" and parade during carnival celebrations throughout Brazil (p. 246).

Recent efforts to save the planet from global warming and pollutants have resulted in further blending of indigenous with outside musics. Popular musicians from all over the world have visited and performed with Amazon groups and brought them to perform in concerts for the preservation of rainforests. The most well-known example is the singer/composer Sting, who visited the Xingu reservation in the late 1980s and performed with the Xavante group. More recently, Brazilian jazz performer Egberto Gismonti has appeared in concert with the Kamayurás. In addition, the musics of Brazilian indigenous peoples have served as inspirations for contemporary musicians all over the world, from the Brazilian composer and performer Marlui Miranda, to the metal rock band Sepultura, to the minimalist U.S. composer Philip Glass.

European-derived Musics: Bumba-meu-boi, Baião, Música caipira/Música sertaneja

The Iberian Peninsula's long-held traditions of outdoor festivities, parades, and dramatizations with music and dance are alive and well in contemporary Brazil. Sacred music dramas recounting celebrations of the Catholic calendar were vital during colonization as a tool for converting natives and Africans to Catholicism and continue in today's Brazil in several regional

explore

You may want to learn about the project "Video nas Aldeias" by visiting their website. The goal of the project is to offer indigenous groups film equipment and training so that they can document their own traditions and show their world through their own eyes.

variations. In this text we will learn about secular dramatic dances, especially the **bumba-meu-boi**. A tradition that goes back to colonial days and that connects European, African, and Amerindian elements, the bumba-meu-boi plot metaphorically re-creates the agrarian cycle by enacting, in an outdoor parade with music and dance, the kidnapping, death, and resurrection of an ox. The plot, told in several regional variations, involves a Portuguese master and his wife, a slave (Pai Francisco) and his pregnant wife, and other Afro-Brazilians and native slaves. As the story goes, one day Pai Francisco's wife had a craving to eat ox tongue, in particular the tongue of her master's favorite animal. Pai Francisco killed the ox to satisfy his wife, but as a result fell in disgrace with his master. The master ordered Francisco to bring the ox back to life, which he did with the help of the *pajé* (shaman) who used native medicines and sacred rituals. The animal awakened and everyone celebrated with singing and dancing.

The bumba-meu-boi tradition is most prominent in the North and Northeast during the month of June. As the drama unfolds, the ox, the main character of the drama, makes an appearance as a dancer in the middle of the parade, covered by a colorful and ornate costume. The ox is killed, and then resurrected while participants sing **toadas**, strophic songs with refrains. They are accompanied by percussion, especially by the **zabumba** (bass drum), **pandeiros** (frame drums similar to a tambourine), and maracas, and sometimes also by *pífanos* (bamboo flutes), guitar, and a *sanfona* (accordion). In the northeastern state of Maranhão, bumba-meu-boi performances are famous for their large percussion ensembles, which include the *pandeirão* (a large frame drum ranging from 20 to 30 inches in diameter). Each parade group has its own performance style and rhythmic patterns, the *pandeirão* providing a characteristic bass sound as well as improvised rhythms.

One city known for its elaborate celebrations of the ox is Parintins, located in an island in the Amazon River situated between the Amazon state capital of Manaus and the city of Santarem in the state of Pará. With a population of some 100,000 inhabitants, recently Parintins has attracted businesses from all over the world due to its status as a commercial hub in the Amazon, but the city has also become a center of attention for outsiders because of its elaborate June celebrations of the ox. Known in Parintins as boi-bumbá, the celebrations highlight the Amazon River's natural environment and caboclo culture—the mix of indigenous and Afro-Brazilian traditions. The native motif is a constant presence in the dramatization, especially the *Pajé*'s role of resurrecting the ox through music and dance. Depictions of the Amazon landscape dominate the decorations of floats and costumes during the parade and the lyrics of songs recount myths of the Amazon forest, whether or not associated with the ox.

Over the years, the boi-bumbá dramatization has grown to gigantic proportions to become a mega folk event that attracts some 100,000 spectators to Parintins every year, doubling the city's population. In 1988, the celebrations moved to the *bumbódromo*, a stadium in the center of Parintins constructed in the shape of an ox, where some 35,000 spectators gather during three days at the end of June to see boi-bumbá groups compete in a lavish parade (Figure 6.4; compare with the carnival parade in Rio de Janeiro in the next section). In the *bumbódromo* the European, African, and indigenous elements are not only wedded but also modernized with laser light shows, amplifiers, and electric paraphernalia that bring the spectacle into the twenty-first century.

The focus of attention is on two groups: the Caprichosos, represented by the color blue, and the Garantidos, represented by the color red. With some four thousand members each, the groups parade singing toadas, accompanied by a large percussion section of about four hundred performers playing zabumbas, pandeiros, and maracas. Some toadas are part of a traditional repertoire passed down orally, but professional composers have begun writing and recording new toadas every year, adding brass, strings, and electronic instruments to percussive sounds and rhythms that resemble Caribbean merengues (see Chapter 5). These adaptations highlight the locals' interests led by advanced technologies and communication with surrounding regions, but also show conscious transformations motivated by an increasing touristic appeal of the boi-bumbá parade.

Listening Guide 6.2 is a toada written for the group Caprichoso, the blue team. The lyrics show the world of the caboclo weaving together indigenous, European, and African elements. In the song, the caboclo's dream is compared with that of a bird, a mythical figure to indigenous groups surrounding Parintins. The song presents the "blue ox" alongside textual images of the forest and the river with a percussion background. As in most traditional toadas, in this example one can note the traditional harmonic progression of I–VI–IV–V–I repeated several times to accompany a strophic song, the marching duple meter marked by the downbeats of the zabumba, while maracas playing sixteenth notes accentuate the offbeats, adding rhythmic and timbral variety. But the overall studio-produced sound

FIGURE 6.4 Boi-bumbá parade in the city of Parintins

◉ "Pássaro sonhador" (Dreamer Bird)

Composer/lyricist: Sidney Resende and
José Cardoso

Date of composition: 1995

Performer/instruments: Arlindo Junior; zabumba,
maracas, viola, guitar, keyboard, and electronic
instrumentation

Date of recording: 2007

Genre: toada (song)

Form: strophic

Tempo/meter: moderate duple

What to Listen for:

- Guitar, electronic instrumentation, and studio effects convey the idea of the caboclo's and bird's dreams
- Characteristic sound of the zabumba drum marking beats 1 and 2, and the maracas filling in with the sixteenth notes highlighting the offbeats
- Strophic song structure; repetition of the first line of the verse "Viaja caboclo viaja" serving as a refrain that is repeated extensively in the middle of the song

Time	Text	Translation	Description
0:00	Introduction		Guitar and keyboard; studio effects
0:24	Viaja caboclo viaja Viaja em seu pensamento A olhar no espelho das águas O azul do firmamento É azul a cor do céu É azul minha paixão É o azul do Caprichoso O Boi que me deixa orgulhoso No grito de guerra da nação	Feel free to travel, caboclo, travel Let your thoughts travel When you see the blue of the sky reflected on the water And at the blue of the horizon Blue is the color of the sky Blue is the color of passion Blue is the color of the Caprichoso The Ox that makes me proud When our Nation is called to war	**Verse 1** Percussion enters with the zabumba marking beats 1 and 2 of the marching rhythm, and the maracas fill in all sixteenth notes of the measure
0:50	Viaja caboclo viaja Braço forte na remada Como se ouvisse bem alto A batucada marujada A floresta na magia Despontando com explendor Mostra mais linda toada Caminho da ilha encantada A voz do caboclo sonhador	Feel free to travel, caboclo, travel With your strong arm ready to row As if you can hear the loud Sound of the *batucada* of the *marujada* [Caprichoso's percussion section] The forest and its magic powers Showing its splendor And its beautiful toada Shows the road to the enchanted isle [Parintins] The voice of the dreamer caboclo	**Verse 2**

(continued)

Time	Text	Translation	Description
1:16	Viaja caboclo viaja	Travel, caboclo, [let your thoughts] travel	**Verse 3**
	Vai chegando a seu chão	To arrive at your land	
	Como sonho de marujo	As a *marujo's* dream [a Caprichoso member]	
	Reascendendo a emoção	Lightening up his emotions	
	Ele esquece do remo	He forgets the paddle	
	Ele esquece da dor	He forgets about pain	
	Balançando as bandeiras	He shows his team's banner	
	Na arena seu mundo se revela	In the [*bumbódromo*] he reveals his world	
	Agora ele é um pássaro sonhador	He is now a dreamer bird	
1:43	Viaja caboclo viaja (group)	Travel, caboclo, [let your thoughts] travel	**Chorus**
1:54			**First verse repeats**
2:20			**Second verse repeats**
2:47			**Third verse repeats**
3:13			**Chorus repeats**

characterizes this toada as a modern rendition that shows the local interest in diversifying and enriching their performances, while projecting their tradition outward and capitalizing on its commercial potential.

In the Northeast of Brazil, instrumental groups consisting of zabumba, *sanfona*, and *pífanos* also play prominent roles as accompanying ensembles in dance gatherings called **forró**. A general word for "party," forró is also an umbrella musical term that includes various rhythmic patterns and dance choreographies. The popularity of forró has caused the *sanfona* and *pífano* ensemble to serve as a symbol of musical regionalism, one that separates the northeastern culture of small farmers and cattle ranchers from the more cosmopolitan population of central–south coastal areas. Forró lyrics describe in poetic terms the harsh migratory experiences of low-income groups who live on small farms and on the outskirts of cities in the Northeast and who move south every year in search of jobs and a better life in large cities. In this context, forró songs and instrumentation have served well as a means of cultural enclosure, as the music articulates the participation of northeastern workers and their musical culture as outsiders in the complex cultural mix of growing cities.

EXAMPLE 6.2: Baião: basic rhythm patterns

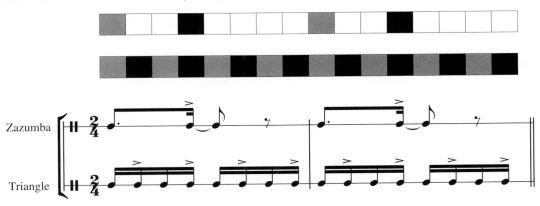

Nonetheless, the well-known composer, singer, and accordionist Luiz Gonzaga (1912–1989) built a large following for forró dances among blue-collar workers and college students in cities throughout the country. Gonzaga is known as "the king of the baião," a popular dance rhythm in forró gatherings. **Baião** is a dance with a fast-paced melodic line played on the accordion and a characteristic marchlike accompanying rhythm, with an emphasis on the syncopated first beat of the measure marked by the zabumba and the offbeats marked by a triangle.

Listening Guide 6.3 is one of Luiz Gonzaga's best known pieces, "Asa Branca" (White Dove), a song that has become popular enough to serve as an anthem for northeastern Brazilian culture. "Asa Branca" narrates the devastation of the *sertão* by drought, the pain of leaving home, and a dream of coming back. The main melodic motive—with the flatted seventh that is characteristic of traditional music in the Northeast—is played first by Gonzaga's *sanfona*. This serves as a characteristic introduction as well as an interlude that separates the verses, functioning as a refrain. The zabumba marks the downbeat followed immediately by syncopation, as in Example 6.2, while the shuffling triangle rhythmic pattern helps propel the dancers.

The rich tradition of sung improvised poetry of the Iberian Peninsula is found in several countries in Latin America, as discussed in Chapters 5 and 7. In the Brazilian Northeast, it is know as **cantoria**, a tradition that identifies itinerant peasant singers, or *cantadores*. Part of the daily scene in both rural and urban areas, cantadores improvise lyrics over the strumming of a **viola**, a string instrument smaller than the guitar with five double metal courses. The songs' short melodies are sung with a characteristic raspy and high-pitched vocal style. Verses cover a range of issues from the peasant world, such as agrarian life, but they can also be about contemporary social and political issues in Brazil and abroad.

explore

For a modern rendition of the song "Asa Branca," check out the performance by a young band from New York City, Forró in the Dark, featuring vocals by U.S. performer David Byrne.

⊙ Gonzaga: "Asa Branca" (White Dove)

Composer/lyricist: Luiz Gonzaga/Humberto Teixeira

Date of composition: 1947

Performers/instruments: Luiz Gonzaga and
Maria Helena, voice; Ivanildo Leite, zabumba;
Dominguinhos, *sanfona*; Toinho, triangle; Renato
Piau, electric guitar; and Porfírio Costa, bass,
cabaça (shaker), and *reco-reco* (scraper)

Date of recording: 2009

Genre: baião (song/dance)

Form: strophic song

Tempo/meter: moderate duple

What to Listen for:

- *Sanfona* introducing the tune **A** (a sequence of descending thirds, starting on the flat seventh degree of the scale)
- Baião rhythm with a strong downbeat in the zabumba followed by the accentuatuated syncopated note
- Triangle playing the sixteenth notes marking the offbeat
- Lyrics focusing on the loss of the homeland, the anxiety caused by the city, and the hope for the return to the countryside
- Strophic song structure with the last two sentences of each verse repeating as refrain

Time	Text	Translation	Description
0:00			**Instrumental introduction** *Sanfona* with tune (**A**)
0:06			Luiz Gonzaga hums the main part of the tune (**B**), then the *sanfona* repeats (**A**)
0:32	Quando olhei a terra ardendo Qual fogueira de São João	When I saw the land was burning Like the bonfire for St. John's celebrations	**Verse 1** Zabumba and triangle join the ensemble with tune **B**
0:38	Eu perguntei a Deus do céu Porque tamanha judiação Eu perguntei a Deus do céu Porque tamanha judiação	I asked God in heaven Why so much destruction I asked God Why so much destruction	The last two sentences repeat as a refrain followed by the instrumental tune (**A**)
1:00	Que braseiro que fornalha Nem um pé de plantação	What a blaze and heat Nothing left in the plantation	**Verse 2** Tune **B**
1:08	Por falta d'água perdi meu gado Morreu de sede meu Alazão Por falta d'água perdi meu gado Morreu de sede meu Alazão	Because of the drought I lost my cattle And my horse died of thirst Because of the drought I lost my cattle And my horse died of thirst	The last two sentences repeat as a refrain, followed by the instrumental tune (**A**)

(continued)

Time	Text	Translation	Description
1:29	Até mesmo Asa Branca Bateu asas do sertão	Even Asa Branca (a white dove) Flew away from the *sertão*	**Verse 3** Tune **B**
1:37	Então eu disse adeus Rosinha Guarda contigo meu coração Então eu disse adeus Rosinha Guarda contigo meu coração	So, I said goodbye to Rosinha Keep my heart with you So, I said goodbye to Rosinha Keep my heart with you	The last two sentences repeat as a refrain, followed by the instrumental tune (**A**)
1:57	Quando o verde dos seus olhos Se espalhar na plantação	When the green of your eyes Spreads over the plantation	**Verse 4** Tune **B**
2:07	Eu te asseguro não chores não viu Eu voltarei, viu, pro meu sertão Eu te asseguro não chores não viu Eu voltarei, viu, pro meu sertão	Please don't cry, I promise I will be back to my *sertão* Please don't cry, I promise I will be back to my *sertão*	The last two sentences repeat as a refrain, followed by the instrumental tune (**A**)

Since the 1960s, the cantoria and forró traditions have spread to large cities like São Paulo. Singers such as Elomar and Zé Ramalho have used the *cantadores'* style to appeal to large audiences and to break into the pop music industry. Interestingly, the similarity between the techniques of cantoria and U.S. rap, improvised poetry over a repetitive bass, has not escaped the attention of younger Brazilians and has created much debate about the "true" Brazilian origin of rap. Regardless, young popular musicians from Recife (the capital of the Northeastern state of Pernambuco) have been successful in exploring improvised rhymes accompanied by drum machines and mixing regional traditions with new international styles. One such group is Nação Zumbi, whose original *mangue beat* sound has revolutionized the Brazilian popular music scene in the 1990s.

The tradition of the wandering singer has also served as a symbol of rural identity in Central and Southern Brazil, where **música caipira**, or hillbilly music, has grown to become a best seller in the Brazilian pop music market. Música caipira can be understood as the music of the rural worker, but it has also crossed rural/urban boundaries due to the constant migration of workers to the cities. In música caipira, a duo sings in parallel thirds to the accompaniment a combination of violas, guitar, and accordion. Their verses are not improvised, but crafted strophic songs about romance and life in the country. Singers of música caipira do, however, sing with the same characteristic nasal, high-pitched vocal tones of the wandering *cantadores* and the sound of the viola is often present or implied. As música caipira

explore

Check out Chitãozinho & Xororó's music videos available on their website, where you can hear the duo's singing style and collaborations with well-known country music artists in the United States.

reached the air waives, it spawned hits in large cities and became known as **música sertaneja**, or country music. New duos have popped up in the growing market and have wedded the sound of the viola with electronic instrumentation and drums, string orchestras, and a whole new sound produced in state-of-the-art studios that are reminiscent of the Nashville sound in U.S. country music. The duo Chitãozinho & Xororó has sold millions of records in Central and Southern Brazil and has also reached the international market, recording songs in Spanish and English with famous U.S. stars like the Bee Gees and Reba McEntire. In several Chitãozinho & Xororó's songs, the metallic sound of the viola is softened by a string orchestra, drum set, and studio effects, giving the music a pop appeal. Still, the duo's singing style, with high-pitched vocals sung in parallel thirds, hallmarks their country roots, while their songs emphasize romance and nostalgia for life in the country.

Afro-Brazilian Musical Traditions: Candomblé and Capoeira

FIGURE 6.5 Women in Bahia carrying flowers to celebrate Yemanjá, the orixá of the seas

African traditions have exerted widespread influence in several Latin American countries. In the northeastern state of Bahia, the pervasiveness of African culture is such that the state's capital, Salvador, has become a national and international hub for African-derived culture and music. Salvador is particularly important for followers of Candomblé, a religion that has preserved direct links with its original West African Yoruba culture. **Candomblé** ceremonies, cultural patterns, and music are part of a larger set of African-derived religions of the African diaspora and shares several traits with other African-derived religions in Latin America.

In Candomblé ceremonies in Salvador, worshippers sing songs with lyrics derived from the Yoruba language and in responsorial style, with the religious leader calling out a line and participants responding in unison with short phrases and interjections. Worshippers sing and dance to the sound of sacred drums, *atabaques*, to evoke, or "call" particular *orixás*, or deities, and to eventually get the *orixás* to possess their bodies and communicate with the worshippers.

It is believed that about 1.5 million Brazilians are devoted to the Candomblé religion, and its practice is well known and acknowledged today. But this was not always the case. Until the beginning of the twentieth century,

Afro-Brazilians were prohibited by the white ruling classes from practicing their faith in the open. Nonetheless, African songs and drumming remain the most important symbols of Candomblé and a strong mark of the African traditions preserved in Brazilian music. Even when drumming mixes with other traditions, crosses over to the secular realm, and is performed in commercial popular musics, it never loses its symbolic power of communicating with the supernatural and of linking Brazilians with their African heritage. In Chapter 5 there is an extended discussion of these elements in both sacred and secular traditions in Cuba and the Caribbean.

African-derived secular practices are also very strong in the Brazilian Northeast. This chapter discusses **capoeira**, a fight/game/dance with movements similar to martial arts. During slavery, the performance of capoeira concealed fighting among African groups by disguising fights as dances. Today Afro-Brazilian capoeira is used as a dance and game that involves high degrees of physical strength and agility. However, what makes capoeira unique is the dance/game's dependence on music.

Capoeira performers are accompanied by *atabaques*, pandeiros, and **berimbaus**. The berimbau is a musical bow made out of wood in the shape of an arc; it is strung with a steel wire and is played by striking the wire with a small stick. A dried gourd is attached at the bottom of the bow and serves as a resonator. Berimbau performers hold a small rattle (*caxixi*) with the right hand and coordinate it with a rock held between the thumb and index finger.

Two or three berimbaus of different sizes are used in capoeira, each producing two pitches, one low and the other one step higher. The different combinations of these pairs of sounds; the characteristic instrumental timbre created by striking the wire when the rock is not used (open sound), when the rock is firmly pressing against it (closed sound), and when the rock is barely touching it (buzzing sound); plus the varying tempos make each capoeira *toque* (a rhythmic/melodic pattern) distinctive.

Capoeira is performed in a *roda de capoeira* (capoeira ring) where two players/dancers perform in the middle of a circle made up of observers and other participants. In the *roda de capoeira*, the leader sings the *ladainha*, a long, narrative song, and then follows with a section in responsorial style called *chula*, during which the participants join in by clapping and responding to the call with small phrases in unison.

Listening Guide 6.4 is an example of a capoeira in the Angola style, in a slow tempo; the basic rhythmic pattern of the *berimbau gunga* (bass berimbau) and atabaque appears in Example 6.3. Capoeira songs are learned orally and have lyrics that report, revive, and recount the experiences of

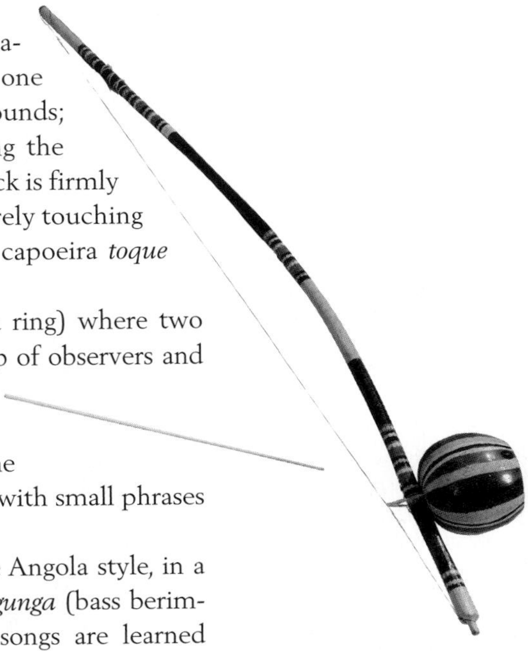

FIGURE 6.6 Berimbau

EXAMPLE 6.3: Capoeira rhythmic pattern

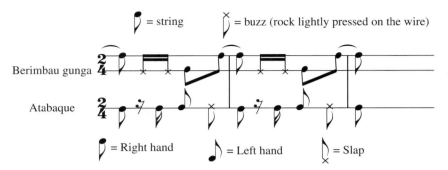

Afro-Brazilians. The music of Listening Guide 6.4 recounts the importance of Rei Zumbi in guiding slaves to freedom and Zumbi's role in the slave settlement of Palmares. The lyrics praise Zumbi as a leader who brought slaves to freedom and who continues as a hero for Afro-Brazilians today. The text also criticizes the established history of Brazil, noting that Afro-Brazilians continue to struggle for freedom.

During times of slavery, the white ruling classes disapproved of capoeira gatherings and repressed them by force and imprisonment. Although capoeira is no longer repressed, to this day the idea of resistance and liberation is ingrained in the minds of *capoeiristas*, regardless of their ethnicity or origin. People from all over the world now engage in capoeira for both its physical and spiritual benefits. There are several international competitions and capoeira academies spread across the continents. The practice of

FIGURE 6.7 *Roda de capoeira*, in Trancoso, a town in Bahia, where capoeira performers from Brazil and all over the world gather every year for the International Capoeira Congress

◉ Trinidade: "Rei Zumbi dos Palmares" (King Zumbi of the Palmares)

Composer/lyricist: Pedro Moraes Trinidade (Mestre Moraes)

Date of composition: unknown

Performer/instruments: Capoeira Angola (berimbaus, *caxixi, atabaques,* pandeiro, and *reco-reco* [scraper])

Date of recording: 1995

Genre: capoeira (song/dance)

Form: *ladainha:* long narrative verse followed by a section in call-and-response form (*chula* and corrido)

Tempo/meter: slow duple

What to Listen for:

- Distinctive *toque* in the introduction with three berimbaus, each playing two notes
- Long narrative section with a soloist singer (*ladainha*) followed by the responsorial singing in the *chula*, where the rest of the group in the roda joins in the performance
- Slow duple meter in capoeira Angola style

Time	Text	Translation	Description
0:00			**Instrumental introduction** Berimbaus enter one at a time, accompanied by *caxixi*; next, *atabaque* and pandeiro join the group
0:21	A história nos engana Diz tudo pelo contrário...	History deceives us It says everything the wrong way...	**Ladainha** Solo singer starts with a call and follows with narrative lyrics; instruments continue with the same *toque* as the introduction.
New Track			
0:00	lê vamos embora, camará lê pela barra fora, camara...	lê, let's go, camará lê, to barra, camará...	**Chula** Call-and-response, the group repeating the call made by the soloist; instruments continue with the same *toque*

capoeira also links several African-derived traditions in the Americas. For example, the moves of capoeira closely resemble those of African American break dancing in the United States.

Carnival, Samba, and Samba-Reggae

The celebration of carnival is not unique to Brazil, but an ongoing tradition throughout the Americas wherever the Catholic Church played a role in colonization. From Cuba to Trinidad and Tobago, from Colombia to Argentina, carnival marks the preparation for the season of Lent, a period of fasting and disregard for the pleasures of the flesh ("carnevale") that starts on Ash Wednesday, 40 days before Easter. The best-known North American equivalent is New Orleans's Mardi Gras celebration. During the week leading up to the beginning of Lent, usually at the end of February, communities revel with masquerade balls, outdoor parades, singing, and dancing. In colonial Latin America, servants and slaves were allowed to celebrate at the same time as, and sometimes together with, the European colonizers and white elite. Over the years, the celebration of carnival became a symbolic act of inclusion, a time of collective euphoria that blurs racial and social divides.

In Brazil, no other cultural expression achieves so well and so intensely the status of a national event as the celebration of carnival. However, not everyone celebrates the same way. Brazilian carnival occurs in various formats, from rural, informal gatherings, to larger, urban, organized events. Outdoor celebrations are more elaborate in large cities, where parades including music, song, and dance mark the event in an exquisite manner.

Rio de Janeiro hosts Brazil's most elaborate carnival parade, one that is arguably the world's most luxurious and extravagant celebration of this type. Since the nineteenth century, small groups from all social classes have paraded in the streets during carnival in costumes, singing and dancing popular marches and polkas accompanied by brass instruments and drums. But it was the participation of Afro-Brazilians in these celebrations that transformed an essentially European tradition into an expression of the Brazilian people. In less-privileged neighborhoods, where the population consists of a majority of mulatos, Afro-Brazilians, and low-income European immigrants, carnival has been celebrated with **samba**, an African-derived song/dance, accompanied by percussion.

Scholars believe that traditional samba music and dance have origins in the Angolan *semba* and involve a characteristic choreography, the *umbigada*, in which dancers move their navels and hips to suggest sexual pursuit and to invite others to dance. Samba has acquired a variety of formats and styles in different Brazilian regions, but we can highlight broad musical characteristics that describe most of them. Samba music is in duple meter and has an underlying 1-2 steady bass rhythmic pattern in the manner of a march. Several overlapping syncopated rhythmic patterns, performed by a variety of percussion instruments, interact with the bass, as a response to the guiding marching beat. Samba is also a strophic song form with refrain accompanied with a guitar and percussion. In the early twentieth century, with the migration of Afro-Brazilians from Bahia to Rio de Janeiro, samba gatherings with music and dance became a constant presence in Rio's central areas, serving as both social outlets and as tools for Afro-Brazilians and mulato cultural expression. Over time, samba music and dance mixed with popular duple-meter European dances, such as polkas and marches, to become the samba performed today during carnival parades.

As outdoor carnival celebrations became more elaborate in Rio de Janeiro, people felt the need to meet and rehearse. These meetings were transformed into neighborhood associations called *escolas de samba* (samba schools) where participants could learn to sing and dance samba and prepare for the parade. In the 1930s, carnival parades in Rio de Janeiro started to receive state supervision from the populist government of President Getúlio Vargas, who saw in the growing popularity of Rio's carnival celebration a potential to instill nationalist ideals. He offered state financial support that allowed the parades to become neighborhood competitions and grow to gigantic proportions. To host the parade, in 1984, Rio de Janeiro's government built the *sambódromo*, a mile-long street with bleachers on either side holding some 80,000 spectators. Today, some 60 samba schools, each with 2,000 to 4,000 dancers, parade to samba music and dance with luxurious costumes and floats during carnival season.

FIGURE 6.8 Floats and dancers from samba schools flow through the *sambódromo* during carnival in Rio de Janeiro

The complex social–racial interactions taking place in the organization of a samba-school parade provide a microcosm of the Brazilian social–racial reality. A showcase for national and international tourists, Rio de Janeiro's carnival parade is now a multimillion-dollar industry, an expensive enterprise that is financially dependent on the government and other moneyed individuals within each neighborhood. At the same time, samba schools are still headquartered in the neighborhoods where the schools' participants live, usually on the periphery of the city where there is a lack of basic infrastructure. The success of the parade depends on a large population of low-income and mostly mulato and Afro-Brazilians who work throughout the year as a community for their samba school to have a magnificent one-day carnival show; they rehearse performers, singers, and dancers, and design and manufacture floats and costumes. The more elaborate costumes are sold at top dollar to celebrities and tourists, allowing them to participate in the parade.

Every year each samba school chooses a theme (*enredo*), a plot that unfolds during the parade, and sponsors the composition of a new samba song—a **samba-enredo**—that narrates a story or theme related to the country's history and helps dancers make their way through the *sambódromo* in synchronization. The songs have catchy refrains that can be easily learned by participants whose enthusiastic singing helps their neighborhood do well in the competition. To coordinate a large group over a one-mile stretch of street, a *puxador*, or leader, sings from a strategic position with a microphone accompanied by a **cavaquinho**, a ukulele-like, four-string instrument.

Dancers and singers are accompanied by a huge percussion section of some 300 to 500 performers called the **bateria**, which includes European and African-derived instruments (Figure 6.9) as follows:

FIGURE 6.9 Bateria of samba carnival: Surdo, repenique, caixa, pandeiro, tamborim, cuíca, agogô, and shakers

1. **Surdo**: a bass drum that provides the basic marching rhythm that drives the samba.
2. **Repenique**: a high-pitched, double-headed drum that provides the calls that cue the entrances of the other percussionists.
3. **Cuíca**: a friction drum that produces both high- and low-pitched notes improvised on top of the surdo beats.
4. *Caixa* or *tarol*: a snare drum.
5. Pandeiro: a handheld, single-headed frame drum similar to a tambourine.
6. **Tamborim**: a high-pitched, small single-headed frame drum
7. **Agogô**: a double (sometimes multiple) bell of African heritage that provides a metallic sound and melodic quality to samba bateria.
8. *Ganzá*: a shaker.

Each of these instruments plays a short rhythmic ostinato that can be repeated incessantly or varied according to the skills of the performer. Example 6.4 illustrates some of these rhythmic patterns. In "Um a um" (Listening Guide 6.5), you can follow each instrument as it joins the group. In this example only the bateria is heard. During the parade, all members of the samba schools sing together in unison.

In the Northeast, distinctive carnival celebrations showcase Brazilian cultural richness. In the 1970s and 1980s, carnival in the city of Salvador

EXAMPLE 6.4: Bateria basic rhythmic patterns

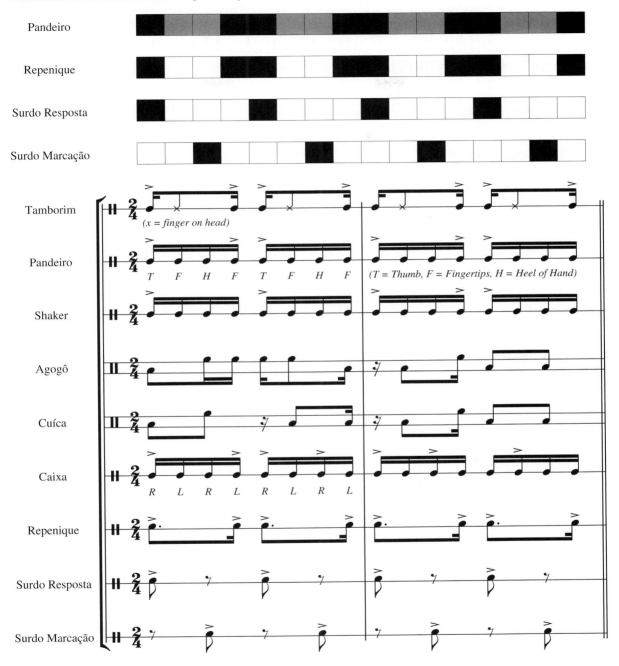

Escola de Samba Mocidade Independente de Padre Miguel: "Um a um" (One at a Time)

Performer/instruments: Escola de Samba Mocidade Independende Padre Miguel; percussion: surdo, repenique, cuíca, pandeiro, tamborim, agogô, shakers

Date of recording: 2005

Genre: samba (song/dance)

Form: improvisatory/open-ended

Tempo/meter: slow duple

What to Listen for:

- Distinctive timbres of each instrument that add interest to the ensemble and result in a fantastic conglomerate of sounds
- Repetition of small ostinato rhythms stacked one on top of the other
- Basic 1-2 beat in the surdos that helps synchronize the marching
- Syncopations and improvisations of the other instruments that fill each bar with varied ostinato rhythmic patterns
- Cuícas' "squeaking" calls interspersed throughout the performance and solos provided by the tamborims

Time	Description
0:00	**Pandeiro** Repeated rhythmic pattern emphasizes beats 1 and 2
0:11	**Cuíca** New rhythmic pattern and new timbre with high note on the offbeat for contrast
0:19	**Agogô** New rhythm and timbre (metal) adds interest to the group
0:32	**Repenique** New rhythmic pattern and new timbre contrasting with agogô
0:43	**Caixa** New rhythm and timbre adds interest
0:51	**Break and repetition** Cuíca and agogô improvise with contrasting high and low notes
1:21	**Tamborim** Addition of more timbre interest; cuíca improvises in the background
1:36	**Surdo and full ensemble** The surdo marks beats 1 and 2 in the marching duple meter; cuíca improvises in the background
2:12	**Tamborim** Tamborim (call) to anticipate the break
2:27	**Break and new tamborim call** Tamborim in call-and-response with the cuíca and full ensemble
2:56	**Full ensemble**
3:10	**Another break and full ensemble**

(state of Bahia) became an important channel for both the expression of Afro-Brazilian traditions as well as for the unification of African cultures in the diaspora. Less formal than the samba-school parades in Rio, in Salvador *blocos* (groups) gather thousands of participants to parade around town for a week before Ash Wednesday. The most traditional groups are the *Afoxés*, who celebrate their African roots by parading with Candomblé instruments and rhythms. The *blocos-Afro* parade to the sounds of Afro-Brazilian songs and percussion, adding Afro-Caribbean rhythms and instrumentation to create a mix that became popular in the 1980s as **samba-reggae**. The basis of the samba-reggae sound rests on a percussion ensemble with an extended surdo section, plus *caixas* and *repiques* (smaller repeniques played with two plastic sticks). The ensemble marks the duple-marching beat with the added emphasis on a shuffle rhythm that accentuates the sixteenth notes on the last beat of every other measure, while *repiques* stress the offbeats in a constant shuffle that creates a reggae feel solely with percussion. These patterns are summarized in Example 6.5.

The best-known *bloco-Afro* group, Olodum, has recently added saxophones, electric guitar, and keyboard to their percussion ensemble in concert performances to attract an international pop audience. Olodum and similar groups have also been active in social causes, creating schools in their communities and providing free entertainment to low-income populations. They have played a crucial political role, putting together rallies and speaking out about social activism and the role of Afro-Brazilians within the larger Brazilian society. Olodum has performed side by side with Michael Jackson in Salvador in the music video "They Don't Care About Us" (1996), a recording that projected the group's political stance internationally.

Another way carnival is celebrated in Salvador is with the *trios elétricos*. These are huge trucks onto which amplifiers, loudspeakers, and all manner of electronic apparatus are mounted to offer music to throngs of up to

EXAMPLE 6.5: Basic rhythmic patterns of samba-reggae

twenty thousand people who follow each *trío elétrico* dancing through the city's streets. Since the 1970s, *tríos elétricos* have become fantastic machines of sound and light, each truck equipped with guitars, bass, and several keyboards in addition to the traditional drums; they bring millions to the streets in a frenzy that lasts for several days. In the 1990s, the electrified carnival of Salvador gave rise to *Axé* music. *Axé*, a Yoruba word that can be translated as "good vibrations" or "power," became an umbrella term that refers to dance-like music that mixes Afro-Brazilian (Candomblé and samba) and Afro-Caribbean musics (reggae, merengue, rumba), with the electric sounds of the *tríos elétricos*.

Our example of *Axé* music is the song "O canto da cidade" (The Song of the City, Listening Guide 6.6) by Daniela Mercury, a versatile

FIGURE 6.10 Daniela Mercury performing at the Latin Grammy awards

---

LISTENING guide 6.6

⊚ Gira and Mercury: "O canto da cidade" (The Song of the City)

Composer: Tote Gira

Lyricist: Daniela Mercury

Date of composition: 1992

Performers/instruments: Daniela Mercury; electric keyboard, guitar, bass, drums, surdos, repenique, and pandeiro

Date of recording: 1998

Genre: samba-reggae (song/dance)

Form: several sections that repeat and alternate with a refrain (**A**)

Tempo/meter: duple, with moderate samba-reggae rhythm

What to Listen for:
- Keyboard, guitar, and bass alongside drumming
- Samba-reggae rhythms with the regular emphasis on beats 1 and 2 of the samba, the rolling sixteenth notes at the end of every second measure, and the accentuation on the offbeats
- Lyrics emphasizing race in the association between "the color of the city" and the predominance of Afro-Brazilians

Time	Text	Translation	Description
0:00			**Introduction** Electric keyboard, guitar, bass, and drums
0:04	A cor dessa cidade sou eu O canto dessa cidade é meu [repeats]	The color of this city, it's me The song of this city, it's mine	**A** Electronic instruments continue without percussion to emphasize Mercury's voice

(continued)

Time	Text	Translation	Description
0:22	O gueto, a rua, a fé Eu vou andando a pé Pela cidade bonita O toque do afoxé E a força de onde vem? Ninguém explica Ela é bonita (a) [repeats]	The ghetto, the street, the faith I go walking on foot Through the beautiful city The *afoxé* rhythm And its strength, where do they come from? Nobody can explain She is beautiful	**B** Full percussion ensemble enters; bass drum dominates, and repique accents offbeats recalling reggae
0:58	Uô ô, Verdadeiro amor Uô ô, Você vai onde eu vou [repeats]	Oh, truthful love Oh, you go where I go	**C** Short section closes the verse
1:16	Não diga que não me quer Não diga que não quer mais Eu sou o silêncio da noite O sol da manhã Mil voltas este mundo tem Mas tem um ponto final Eu sou o primeiro que canta Eu sou o carnaval	Don't say you don't want me Don't say you don't want more I am the silence in the night And the morning sun The world goes around But there is a final destination I am the first one who sings I am the carnival	**D** New melodic material and lyrics; percussion and rhythmic pattern continues as in **B** and **C**
1:35	A cor dessa cidade sou eu O canto dessa cidade é meu	The color of this city, it's me The song of this city, it's mine	**Refrain** Introduction of **A** with added percussion
1:52			**Instrumental Section** Keyboard accompanied by percussion; offbeats accentuated with a moderate tempo recalling reggae
2:11			**D**
2:28			**C**
2:46			**Refrain** Introduction of **A**
3:04			**Instrumental Section** Fades away

songwriter, arranger, and performer. The lyrics present Mercury as a diva of her heavily Afro-Brazilian city, equating her skin color, although very light, with the black "color of the city." Mercury's energetic singing style, samba-reggae rhythms, and electric sounds give the local Afro-Brazilian tradition an irresistible cosmopolitan appeal that has made her popular throughout Brazil.

Cosmopolitan Popular Musics: *Maxixe,* Choro, Samba canção, Bossa Nova, MPB, and Tropicália

In nineteenth-century Brazilian cities, theaters and dance halls were the main venues for popular music, where one could listen to arrangements for small ensembles of operatic arias, short songs in Portuguese called *modinhas,* and European dances such as polkas, marches, and waltzes. The polka was the most popular dance and spawned a variety of local variants throughout the Americas, such as the Brazilian tango, the two-step and ragtime (from the United States), and several others. These dances shared the lively duple meter of the polka, wedded to rhythmic traits believed to be derived from the African heritage, such as syncopations and dotted rhythms in the bass, the melody, or both. In Rio de Janeiro the most popular of these polka-derived pieces was the *maxixe.* Born in poor Rio de Janeiro neighborhoods where Afro-Brazilians and European immigrants lived in close proximity in cramped tenements, the *maxixe* was celebrated as the first truly Brazilian popular dance. Example 6.6 provides some illustrations of such rhythms found in *maxixes* and similar dances.

At the turn of the twentieth century, the most successful Brazilian composer of polkas, waltzes, tangos, and *maxixes* was Ernesto Nazareth (1863–1934), a virtuoso pianist who made a living playing in local cafés and early movie theaters in Rio de Janeiro. Popular musicians in military bands also performed these dances in the streets; their groups later added stringed instruments such as guitars, **bandolim**, and cavaquinho. These performers were known as *chorões,* probably because of their overuse of low guitar notes as countermelodies to their melodic improvisations in a style that was described as *chorar,* to lament or cry. *Chorões'* performances brought several urban musical experiences together, integrating the

EXAMPLE 6.6: Rhythms of Brazilian polkas, tangos, and *maxixes*

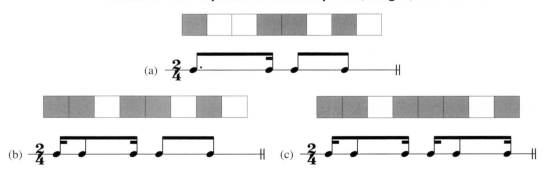

European and African heritages in the Brazilian urban context. Their music became known as **choro**, or *chorinho*, Rio de Janeiro's first instrumental popular music style and one that parallels the emergence of jazz in the United States (specifically, in New Orleans). A famous composer and performer who made significant contributions to the choro repertoire was Alfredo da Rocha Viana Filho (1896–1973), known popularly as "Pixinguinha." He left a long list of pieces that have become standards in the repertoire of Brazilian popular music.

FIGURE 6.11 Choro instruments: cavaquinho and guitar

In choro performances, operatic tunes, waltzes, and polkas are extended with improvised instrumental passages. The bandolim, cavaquinho, and flute are the preferred solo instruments, but the ensemble may also include a piano, a clarinet, and light percussion used to stress syncopated rhythms. Example 6.7, "Brejeiro," is a piece originally written for the piano by Ernesto Nazareth and performed in Listening Guide 6.7 by a choro ensemble with the virtuoso Jacob do Bandolim (1918–1969) as the soloist.

In the 1930s and 1940s the **samba-canção** (samba song) dominated the recording industry and radio. In samba-canção, the lively and syncopated rhythms of the traditional samba are softened by slower tempos, longer melodies, and romantic lyrics. Samba-canção performers favored the guitar and light percussion, and occasional accompanying flutes, clarinets, saxophones, and string orchestra. A prominent role was given to the solo singer, and samba-song crooners became national radio stars during the 1930s and 1940s.

Samba-canção singer/composer Ary Barroso (1903–1964) left memorable songs with sophisticated lyrics and melodies that appealed to a large middle class. Listening Guide 6.8 is a contemporary rendition of Barroso's "Aquarela do Brasil" (1939) (Watercolor of Brazil; known in the United States as "Brazil"). It became so popular that it has served as a second national anthem for Brazilians; it also became popular internationally

⊚ Nazareth: "Brejeiro" (Charming)

Composer: Ernesto Nazareth

Date of composition: 1893

Performer/instruments: Jacob do Bandolim; bandolim, cavaquinho, guitar, twelve-string guitar, pandeiro, and shakers

Date of recording: 1994

Genre: instrumental choro

Form: AABBABAA

Tempo/meter: fast duple

What to Listen for:

- Syncopated melody in the bandolim moving freely and rapidly from high to low notes and contrasting with the slow countermelody in the bass line played by guitars and cavaquinho

- Repetition of the **A** and **B** sections with elaborate improvisations

- Percussion emphasizes offbeats and upbeats in the sixteenth-note subdivision of each beat

- Chords of the top line in section **A** accent the offbeats

Time	Description
0:00	**Introduction** First two measures with guitars and mandolin; percussion and bass enter in measure 3; use of variations of rhythms in Example 6.6
0:06	**A** First theme
0:24	**A′** Repeat with variations; countermelody in the bass
0:42	**B** New tune
1:01	**B′** Repeat with variations and improvisations
1:20	**Introduction**
1:24	**A** (in minor) Added variations
1:42	**A′** (in minor) Added variations
2:00	**B** (in major) Added variations
2:19	**Introduction**
2:24	**A** (in major) Same as in initial **A**
2:42	**A′** Extended with improvisation; rhythm of the accompanying strings and the fade-out

EXAMPLE 6.7: Ernesto Nazareth's "Brejeiro"

⊚ Barroso: "Aquarela do Brasil" (Watercolor of Brazil)

Composer/lyricist: Ary Barroso

Date of composition: 1939

Performers/instruments: Rosa Passos (voice), Odair and Sergio Assad (guitar), Paquito D'Rivera (clarinet), and Yo-Yo Ma (cello)

Date of recording: 2004

Genre: samba-canção (samba song)

Form: Strophic form with two sections, **A** and **B**

Tempo/meter: moderate simple duple

What to Listen for:

- Syncopations in the melody and wide-ranging melodic line
- Nationalist lyrics praising the beauty of the country and its people
- Stereotypical representation of Afro-Brazilians ("*mulato inzoneiro*") in lyrics
- Hook ("Brasil, pra mim") at the end of sections **A** and **B** that functions as a short refrain

Time	Text	Translation	Description
0:00			**Introduction** Guitar and light percussion; clarinet, cello, and percussion improvise on the theme, emphasizing the syncopated rhythms

(continued)

Time	Text	Translation	Description
0:30	Brasil, meu Brasil brasileiro Meu mulato inzoneiro Vou cantar-te nos meus versos O Brasil, samba que dá Bamboleio que faz gingá O Brasil do meu amor Terra de Nosso Senhor Brasil! Brasil! Prá mim... prá mim...	Brazil, my Brazilian Brazil My sly mulato I'm going to sing about you in my verses Oh Brazil that gives us samba A swing that makes us sway My beloved Brazil Land of Our Lord Brazil! Brazil! For me... for me...	**A** Wide and long melodic line with syncopated rhythm; the cello, clarinet, and piano improvise a countermelody in the background
1:03	"Ô, abre a cortina do passado"... Brasil! Brasil! Prá mim...prá mim...	"Oh, open the curtain and look at our past"... Brazil! Brazil! For me...for me...	**B** Voice with cello, clarinet, and piano responding in the background
1:34			**Transition**
2:06	"Brasil, terra boa e gostosa"... Brasil! Brasil! Prá mim... prá mim...	"Brazil, such a good land"... Brazil! Brazil! For me... for me...	**A** Voice and cello emphasize the rhythmic aspect of the syncopated melodic line
2:40	"Ô, esse coqueiro que dá côco"... Brasil! Prá mim... prá mim...	"O! The coconuts from our coconut tree"... Brazil! For me... for me...	**B** Voice with cello, clarinet, and piano responding in the background
3:12			**Transition**
3:47	[scatting]		**Coda** The word "Brazil" is repeated several times with vocal and instrumental improvisation

when it was included in Walt Disney's movie *Saludos Amigos* (1942). Since then, "Aquarela" has been recorded in English and Portuguese with a variety of arrangements by famous artists like Frank Sinatra, Desi Arnaz, Dionne Warwick, and Chick Corea, among others. One of the most popular interpreters of Barroso's sambas was the Brazilian singer Carmen Miranda (1909–1955), whose voice, dazzling performing style, and outfits (recalling Afro-Brazilian Candomblé dancers) showcased samba songs as an international symbol of Brazilian and Latin American exotic music on Broadway and Hollywood during the 1940s.

In the 1960s and 1970s, Brazilian urban popular music diversified greatly as a result of industrial development and the empowerment of the middle and upper classes. In Rio de Janeiro's wealthy neighborhoods, young musicians created a new way of performing samba-canção, which they called **bossa nova** (new wave or new style). Singer/composer João Gilberto (b.1931) started the trend by singing in an intimate low tone and using the picking of guitar chords to emulate samba percussion. Gilberto was joined by highly educated musicians and poets, such as composer Antônio (Tom) Carlos Jobim (1927–1994) and poet Vinicius de Moraes (1913–1980). As in samba-canção, light percussion accompaniment is preferred in bossa nova, and the syncopated guitar is then brought to the forefront, resulting in the characteristic bossa nova sound and beat (Example 6.8). Jobim's classical music training allowed him to create well-crafted melodies that move easily and smoothly in wide intervals (as in the song "Vou te contar," "Wave"), or do not move at all (as in the song "Samba de ums nota só," "One-Note Samba"), but are supported by fast-changing harmonies in the bass enriched with chords borrowed from jazz.

The bossa nova style was associated specifically with the city of Rio de Janeiro and the lifestyle of its elite neighborhoods, dreamlike beaches, and upper-class life—elements that made the music attractive to cosmopolitan audiences worldwide. Jobim's tunes became international classics and are alive today in the repertoire of jazz musicians in Brazil and especially in the United States. The intimate, laid-back feel of bossa nova has also made it appealing as background music at cocktail parties and in waiting rooms.

FIGURE 6.12 Carmen Miranda

FIGURE 6.13 Cover of the 1942 musical score of "Brazil," with Donald Duck and his "tropical" friend Zé Carioca

EXAMPLE 6.8: One common rhythmic pattern of bossa nova guitar

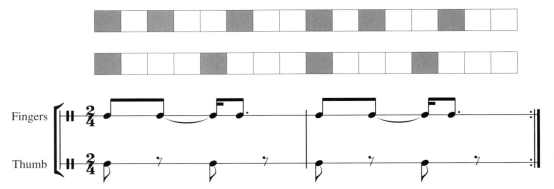

Bossa nova's most famous song, "A garota de Ipanema," tells the story of the poet's frustrated love for a beautiful woman living in the idyllic city of Rio de Janeiro, a typical bossa nova theme. The lyrics here are sung first in Portuguese by João Gilberto and then in English by Astrud Gilberto, followed by an instrumental version with improvisations by U.S. saxophonist Stan Getz (Listening Guide 6.9).

LISTENING guide 6.9

ⓢ Jobim: "A garota de Ipanema" (The Girl from Ipanema)

Composer: Antônio Carlos Jobim

Lyricist: Vinicius de Moraes (Portuguese lyrics); Norman Gimbel (English lyrics)

Date of composition: 1962

Performers/instruments: João Gilberto (guitar and voice), Astrud Gilberto (voice), Stan Getz (saxophone); guitar, bass, drums, piano

Date of recording: 1964

Genre: bossa nova (song)

Form: Strophic, **AAB′A**

Tempo/meter: slow duple

What to Listen for:
- João Gilberto's low tones and intimate singing style
- The strumming of the guitar as a percussive tool and the dominating syncopated beats
- Repeated motif in the **A** section ("Tall and tanned..." contrasting with the wide melodic range of section B ("Oh I watch her so sadly...")
- Jazz improvisations by Stan Getz

Time	Text	Translation	Description
0:00			**Introduction** João Gilberto improvises on the guitar to set the intimate mood for the song

(continued)

Time	Text	Translation	Description
0:25	Din, din, din…	Din, din, din…	Gilberto's vocal improvisation on the tune (**A**) with the typical bossa nova three-note descending motive repeated to emphasize the rhythm; guitar with syncopated bossa nova rhythmic pattern
0:43	Olha que coisa mais linda…	Look how beautiful…	**A** Descending sequence of the motive; constant guitar and light percussion in the background
1:00	Moça do corpo dourado do sol de Ipanema…	A girl with a golden tanned body from Ipanema's sun…	**A** Repetition of tune with second stanza of the verse
1:16	Ah porque estou tão sozinho?…	Ah why am I so lonely?…	**B** Contrasting section with a lyrical tune in an ascending harmonic sequence, concluding with a chromatic descending melodic line
1:49	Ah se ela soubesse…	Ah if she knew…	**A'** Concluding stanza back to short opening rhythmic motif
2:05	Tall, and tan, and young, and lovely…		**A** Repetition of the song with English lyrics
2:22	When she walks…		**A**
2:38	Oh but he watches her so sadly…		**B**
3:10	Tall and young…		**A**
3:26			**Saxophone solo** Stan Getz's improvisation on **A**
3:58			Stan Getz's improvisation on **B**
4:29			Stan Getz's improvisation on **A**
4:46	Tall, and tan, and young…		Repetition of song with English lyrics with saxophone improvising in the background

Today, there is a revival of bossa nova as young performers rework the music with added electronic instrumentation in a style called *bossatrônica* (bossa nova and *electrônica*). Interestingly, *bossatrônica* performers are mostly female singers who are helping to revive the style in Brazil and spread bossa nova all over the globe.

explore

Check out Bebel Gilberto's new, updated bossa nova sounds in her album *Tanto Tempo* (2000), which includes new and old bossa nova songs in English and Portuguese.

Soon after bossa nova reached the international music scene in the early 1960s, political turmoil erupted in Brazil after the military coup. During this time, the country witnessed another wave of nationalism, a movement led by intellectuals, artists, and musicians, who presented themselves as both critics of the regime and defenders of authentic Brazilian music. This new, politically oriented musical movement promoted a variety of styles that were grouped under the umbrella term **MPB,** an acronym for **Música Popular Brasileira** (Brazilian Popular Music). As with bossa nova, MPB musicians were middle- to upper-class artists who catered to the tastes of intellectuals and college students. But instead of bossa nova's laid-back lyrics dealing with beaches and easy life, in MPB the focus was on sociopolitical topics and stylized versions of Brazilian traditional musical styles. The best known MPB musician is Chico Buarque [de Hollanda] (b. 1944), whose music and lyrics reflect both his opposition to the military dictatorship and his criticism of Brazil's social and racial divides.

MPB's diverse musical scene also brought to prominence talented musicians, poets, and performers like Caetano Veloso (b. 1942) and Gilberto Gil (b. 1942). These musicians were part of *Tropicália*, a 1960s movement in Brazil that paralleled U.S. artistic movements such as rock, concrete poetry, and pop art. Tropicalists aimed at liberating Brazil from cultural isolation by creating hybrid sounds that mixed electronic instrumentation with traditional Brazilian styles and instruments. At a time when nationalistic feelings of the Brazilian middle class were acute, Veloso's and Gil's embrace of foreign sounds and ideas were not immediately accepted. Nonetheless, their well-crafted and provocative lyrics brought to the fore contemporary topics that spoke directly to cosmopolitan Brazilians, such as consumerism, mass media domination, and a general disillusion with the military regime.

A good example is Veloso's 1968 song "Tropicália." On the surface, the work is similar to MPB songs, with duple meter, moderate tempo, and strophic structure with a refrain. But Veloso's lyrics avoid the sentimentalism of samba-canção, superimposing images of airplanes, the Brazilian landscape, carnival instruments, bossa nova, Carmen Miranda, and other Brazilian musical icons. In the song, there is no sequential narrative, but elements that overlap tradition and modernity within the Brazilian context; what results is a collage of Brazil's varied landscape, history, culture, and music. These textual elements are highlighted by the simultaneous use of electrical guitar, keyboard, and drum set with brass, strings, and traditional Brazilian percussion.

explore

For Veloso's early version of "Tropicália," check out *Tropicália Essentials* (1999, UMG/ Hip-O Records).

By the early 1970s, the Tropicália movement was exhausted, but Veloso and Gil continued their careers as innovators in Brazilian popular music.

Today, they are two major forces on the Brazilian musical and artistic scene, representing a strong link between traditionalism and cosmopolitanism in popular music.

Brazilian Rock, Hip-hop and Funk

Early Anglo-American rock and roll entered the Brazilian music market in the 1960s and immediately inspired local compositions, although they were never as mainstream as MPB. This changed in 1985, the year of the first Brazilian rock mega-concert, "Rock in Rio." The event, which featured internationally acclaimed rock groups performing alongside Brazilian bands, helped propel rock music into the mainstream in Brazil. Significantly, 1985 also marked the end of the military regime and the return to democracy. For young Brazilians who were raised under the dictatorship, rock music provided an alternate outlet for the problems posed by the times. Instead of the traditional samba percussion and refined lyrics that had served MPB, the new generation moved to electric music exclusively and to a more direct language.

Today, *rockeiros* continue to enjoy a large audience of young, white middle-class Brazilians with whom they share the problems of their age and time. Their lyrics talk about urban lives in chaos and criticize the established values of contemporary urban society, but they also address social issues inherent to the country in which they live. Singing in Portuguese, they re-create a wide range of international styles in original ways, sometimes integrating elements of local traditions in their songs. The group Os Paralamas do Sucesso, for example, mixes reggae with soul and romantic pop to produce danceable music with cosmopolitan appeal. Their songs talk about love and youthful anguish but also comment on impoverished neighborhoods of Rio de Janeiro and social inequality. Another important group is the Brazilian metal band Sepultura, whose members sing in English and Portuguese (sometimes intertwined) and explore musics from Brazilian indigenous groups and Afro-Brazilian traditions in original ways.

In the mid 1980s other international music styles took the country by storm: rap and funk. Through the exposure of films, videos, and pictures on record sleeves with images of U.S. black ghettos, rap quickly made its way from the black neighborhoods of New York and Los Angeles to the *favelas* (shantytowns or slums) of São Paulo and Rio de Janeiro, where Afro-Brazilians live in neighborhoods stigmatized by racism, poverty, and violence.

Despite longstanding claims of racial equality in Brazil, Afro-Brazilians continue to suffer enormous social and racial discrimination. Their socio-economic position is hardly evident in the lyrics of romantic samba songs or in the celebratory nature of samba-enredos during carnival. Hip-hop, rap, and funk, however, have given the local youth a chance to deviate from the accepted channels of earlier musical expression. Through rap, young Afro-Brazilians aggressively combat the status quo, talking about misery, fights with police, and survival issues on the periphery. Recordings produced and distributed by the groups themselves have generated large revenues and have given them the means to provide their neighborhoods with basic infrastructure and services.

Listening Guide 6.10 is from a São Paulo rap group, Os Racionais MCs. Their music lacks reference to Brazilian traditional instrumentation; instead it includes samples by U.S. groups and artists such as Public Enemy, Curtis Mayfield, and Isaac Hayes, among others. Their lyrics imitate U.S. gangsta rap, serving as tools to "fight the power" and discrimination. In the 1997 hit song "Capítulo 4, versículo 3," the group uses samples from "Slippin' Into Darkness" by the U.S. funk band War, while making references to the Bible (Chapter 4, Verse 3). The use of religion here is quite important, since Brazil has one of the largest Catholic populations in the world, and thus the song's language reverberates right into the minds of Brazilians. At the same time, the lyrics offer realistic descriptions of the social and economic hardships of their Afro-Brazilian "manos" (Brothers). After a spoken introduction with data about the social status of Afro-Brazilians, Mano Brown's low voice emphasizes his power to disrupt the status quo. He does not avoid strong language that suggests confrontation and force.

In the 1990s, after the emergence of rap, a new generation of low-income Brazilians, mostly blacks and mulattos, started a new local craze in Rio de Janeiro: **bailes funk** (funk dances). Bailes gather thousands of young people in the city's most impoverished neighborhoods where they socialize and dance to the beat of electronic drum machines and sampled sounds. The word funk serves as an umbrella term to describe a creative local mix of U.S. African American styles of the 1970s and 1980s ranging from disco, soul, and funk, to Motown, rhythm and blues, and rap. Most influential is the now-passé 1980s Miami freestyle dance-pop sound, with a syncopated heavy bass, over which catchy pop vocals exhort the crowd to nonstop dancing. Creative DJs have learned to manipulate and add samples of percussion from samba bateria to this music in a mix they call the *tamborzão* (bass drum) sound.

Rio de Janeiro's bailes funk take place in local clubs, outdoors, or in samba school *quadras* (halls), where sound-system crews stack speakers and amplifiers to form a wall of sound that pumps out a loud, heavy bass. In the midst of disco lights and lasers, MTV-style screens, and *tamborzão* mixes, local DJs recycle English words and mix them with Portuguese

⊚ Brown: "Capítulo 4, versículo 3" (Chapter 4, Verse 3)

Lyricists: Edy Rock, Ice Blue, and Mano Brown

Producer: KL Jay

Date of composition: 1996

Performer/instruments: Mano Brown, voice; electronic sampling, drum machine

Date of recording: 2002

Genre: song, rap

Form: strophic with a hook at the end of each verse

Tempo/meter: moderate duple with emphasis on the backbeat

What to Listen for:

- Association of sound and lyrics: the high-pitched strings at the beginning contrast with bass lines (bass and keyboard) to help set the dramatic tone
- Introduction by the organ to help create the religious atmosphere of a church
- Realistic and aggressive tone of the lyrics

Time	Text	Translation	Description
0:00	60% dos jovens de periferia sem antecedentes criminais já sofreram violência policial. A cada 4 pessoas mortas pela a policia, 3 são negras. Nas universidades brasileiras apenas 2% dos alunos são negros. A cada 4 horas um jovem negro morre violentamente em São Paulo. Aqui quem fala é primo preto, mais um sobrevivente.	60% of youths from the periphery without police records have been victims of police brutality. Of every 4 people killed by the police, 3 are black. In Brazilian universities, only 2% of the students are black. Every 4 hours a black youth dies violently in São Paulo. This is "Primo Preto" [Black Brother] speaking, another survivor.	Section concludes with strong brass and drums call, emphasizing the tragic report
0:48	Minha intenção é ruim, esvazia o lugar…	I have bad intentions clear the place…	**Verse 1** Closes with the reference to the Bible: "And the prophecy has come as predicted" and the "black fury"
2:08	Hallelujah		**Chorus** Organ introduced to help create the religious atmosphere of a church
2:27			**Verse 2**

in improvised commentaries. They sing about parties and romance, but also compose narrative lyrics that recount the harsh reality of their daily scenes of violence and social exclusion. In some neighborhoods, bailes became scenes for drug lord confrontations, while explicit lyrics and choreographies in "funk sensual" highlight invitations for sex. Female DJs are particularly prominent in this area, creating the most popular sexually provocative songs and dance moves.

While life in the *favelas* has never been described in such a realistic way, the popularity of bailes funk is the result of complex social, racial, and gender dynamics and has generated both devoted fans and outspoken critics. New song lyrics highlight the gap between the white rich and the mostly black poor, where there is no room for traditional samba music that carries images of cordial Afro-Brazilians happily celebrating. Some believe that the emphasis on synthesized bass drums in funk music is an expression of political resistance that recalls local traditions, while others see the use of physical spaces once devoted solely to samba to host bailes as a reflection of new Afro-Brazilian identities. Either way, bailes funk and the music associated with them quickly became stigmatized by middle-class, white Rio de Janeiro residents. Even so, funk has started to gain a space in the music industry, as recording labels invest in "cleaning up" funk lyrics to market them to a larger audience eager for the novel, danceable music. Meanwhile, Rio de Janeiro's DJs have started to sell their attractive *tamborzão* mixes to European and U.S. clubs, some of which are available online.

explore

Listen to the CDs *Rio Baile Funk: Favela Booty Beats* and *Rio Baile Funk: More Favela Booty Beats* to hear some innovative Rio funk sounds.

Classical Music

Classical music flourished after the Portuguese royal family moved to Rio de Janeiro in 1808. Responding to the demands of the Brazilian aristocracy, the imperial government subsidized the construction of luxurious theaters, allowing the opera craze dominating Europe during the nineteenth century to take Rio de Janeiro by storm. The city became a major center for opera in Latin America and a mecca for European singers and impresarios in search of new audiences. To support Brazilian opera composers, emperor Pedro II subsidized an Imperial Conservatory and an Imperial Academy of National Opera (1857–1863). These institutions trained singers and performers, promoted the translation of European operas into Portuguese, and commissioned local composers to write operas with librettos on Brazilian subjects. The National Opera produced original operas by several Brazilian composers, including two works by a young musician who would become Latin America's most prominent opera composer in the nineteenth century: Antônio Carlos Gomes (1836–1896).

Born in the town of Campinas (state of São Paulo), Gomes moved to Rio de Janeiro in 1859 to study music at the Imperial Conservatory. He soon incorporated the operatic style into his compositions, which were very well received by local audiences. In 1863 Gomes received a grant from Pedro II and the directors of the National Opera to continue his studies in Milan, Italy, one of Europe's major centers for opera. In Italy, Gomes wrote his most famous work, the opera *Il Guarany* (1870) with a libretto based on the Brazilian nineteenth-century Indianist novel *O*

FIGURE 6.14 Theatro São Pedro de Alcantara in 1846

Guarani (1857), written by José de Alencar (1829–1877). The plot tells the story of the love of Peri, a Guarani Indian, for Ceci, the daughter of a Portuguese nobleman, and glorifies the formation of the Brazilian race through the union of the Amerindian and the European. *Il Guarany* premiered at the famous La Scala Theater in Milan on March 19, 1870, and later in the same year in Rio de Janeiro with great success. Soon after, the opera was performed in several cities throughout Europe and Latin America.

The plot of *Il Guarany*, the wedding of the European and the Indian, suggested that Brazil was a unified nation and served as an early expression of national pride. Written in the fashionable contemporary Italian style, *Il Guarany*'s charm lay also in Gomes's memorable melodies that became immediate successes inside and outside the opera house. One of the opera's most memorable tunes is the duet between the two major characters, Ceci and Peri; it became so popular that choro musicians soon performed it in the streets. Early in the twentieth century, it was published and recorded in a variety of arrangements, and ultimately the tune was used in carnival marches. *Il Guarany's* overture was also an immediate hit. Since the 1930s it has served as the musical opening of a government-sponsored radio program, *A hora do Brasil* (Brazil Hour). Heard daily on the radio from the coastal cities to the remote villages of the Amazon, *Il Guarany's* overture, with its brass introduction resembling a military call, has evoked sentiments of Brazilian civism as a substitute for the Brazilian national anthem.

With the advent of the Republic in 1889 and the decline of state patronage for classical music, the golden age of opera in Brazil came to an end. Nonetheless, several Brazilian composers continued to pursue classical music and the creation of a musical language that could symbolize the new, independent, Republican nation. The composer Alberto Nepomuceno (1864–1920) was key to this transition. He directed the National Institute of Music in Rio de Janeiro and organized several concerts in which he presented music by young Brazilian composers. Nepomuceno worked passionately to cultivate a nationalistic music school by defending the use of Portuguese in songs at a time when only Italian and French were deemed acceptable languages. He left a large body of work that shows the influences of German and French music, but he also used themes from Brazilian traditional music like in his famous *Batuque, Dança de negros* (1887) for orchestra, which is inspired by an Afro-Brazilian dance.

Nationalism in Brazilian classical music, the use of music to evoke notions of a Brazilian nation, became much in vogue in the first part of the twentieth century and is particularly evident in the works of composer Heitor Villa-Lobos (1887–1959, Figure 6.15). Born in Rio de Janeiro, Villa-Lobos was first introduced to music by his father, an amateur musician, and received a few private cello and composition lessons with local teachers. He was a quick learner and absorbed a variety of classical styles that were fashionable at the beginning of the century in Rio de Janeiro. To make a living as a musician, Villa-Lobos played the cello in theaters and cinemas and participated in popular choro groups, playing the guitar alongside influential popular musicians of his time. Villa-Lobos was also interested in folklore; he visited cities in the North and Northeast, and in the Southern state of Paraná, where he heard music he later used in his compositions.

Villa-Lobos's early work (1915–1922) shows the influence of late nineteenth-century French music. Nonetheless, living in an era in which defining Brazilianess became central for artists, Villa-Lobos made it a goal of his career to create a music that had international appeal but that also could also

FIGURE 6.15 Heitor Villa-Lobos

represent Brazil musically. With that in mind, he skillfully wed French musical nationalism and impressionism with local elements, using Brazilian traditional and popular musics as the main sources of his works.

In 1923, with the financial help of friends and a governmental stipend, Villa-Lobos went to Paris, where he met important figures of the European musical world and conducted several presentations of his works. When he returned to Brazil in 1930 his music had been performed throughout Europe and the Americas, his publications were circulating worldwide, and he was consecrated as the best composer the country had ever produced. Villa-Lobos first visited the United States in 1944 in the midst of President Franklin Delano Roosevelt's "good neighbor" policy, which aimed at strengthening U.S. political, economic, and cultural ties with its Latin American neighbors during World War II. Villa-Lobos's international reputation grew exponentially after the war, especially in the

United States and Europe, where he conducted important orchestras in various cities. Acclaimed as one of the most important composers of the Americas, Villa-Lobos lost his fight with cancer in 1959, when he died at age 72.

Villa-Lobos was an extremely prolific composer and left more than a thousand works. The influences of French descriptive music are already in evidence in the early ballet *Amazonas* (1917) and symphonic poem *Uirapuru* (1917), in which he shows originality in a musical exaltation of his country's flora and fauna. In *Uirapuru*, the traditional orchestra is enhanced by a large percussion section with Indian and Afro-Brazilian instruments that serve as a background to Villa-Lobos's story of an enchanted native bird transformed into a handsome youth. To the unusual instrumentation and extramusical elements, such as imitation of bird singing and sounds from the forest, Villa-Lobos adds harmonic devices such as note clusters and polytonality, demonstrating novel musical ideas on par with contemporary European music. Villa-Lobos left works for a variety of instruments and some of his piano music became standards in Brazilian literature. The guitar was another of Villa-Lobos's preferred instruments and his guitar works are mainstays in the repertoire of classical guitar.

During the 1920s, Villa-Lobos wrote the monumental cycle of 14 *chôros* inspired by urban popular music. From 1930 until 1945, he wrote a cycle of nine *Bachianas Brasileiras*, which remain some of his best-known pieces. The cycle was conceived as a series of Baroque suites, as homage to the eighteenth-century composer Johann Sebastian Bach (Bachianas), and was set to a variety of instrumental combinations. The most famous is his Bachiana No. 5 for soprano and orchestra of cellos, which has been recorded by prominent orchestras and singers worldwide.

Listening Guide 6.11 is the first movement of Villa-Lobos Bachianas Brasileiras No. 1 (1930), written for an ensemble of cellos. This introductory movement is entitled "Embolada," the name of a Brazilian musical style from the Northeast, in which singers duel with improvised songs similar to cantoria. Villa-Lobos's skill in wedding European Baroque music and local traditional styles is evident throughout the piece. In the opening section, the cellos' fast, repetitive rhythmic cells recalls both urban popular salon music and the rural, up-tempo embolada songs, while at the same time referencing the Baroque fast-paced instrumental **toccata** in the style of J. S. Bach. The cellos then introduce Villa-Lobos's characteristic long, lyrical melody, reminiscent of operatic arias much favored by Brazilians. Then a three-note theme follows, and is insistently repeated at different tonal levels, highlighting the dueling character of the embolada as each group of cellos presents the theme in sequence. While the initial rhythmic ostinato reappears as transitional material and accompaniment throughout the movement, the following sections introduce secondary thematic materials that are always derived from

◎ Villa-Lobos: Bachianas Brasileiras No. 1: Introduction (Embolada)

Composer: Heitor Villa-Lobos

Date of composition: 1930–1938

Performer/instruments: Pleeth Cello Octet, cello orchestra

Date of recording: 1987

Genre: suite for cello orchestra

Form: AB (with variations) CA

Tempo/meter: fast simple duple

What to Listen for:

- An orchestra of cellos, rather than a typical string orchestra
- Interaction between short, rhythmic ostinatos and long melodic lines, sometimes played by a section of cellos, sometimes by a cello solo
- Rhythmic and melodic variations that connect sections
- Rhythmic movement in the accompaniment that recalls both the Brazilian embolada and the Baroque toccata
- **Walking bass** in the cellos provides a countermelody to a tune constructed by note repetition (C), recalling Baroque music

Time	Description
0:00	**Introduction** Cello ensemble with a rhythmic motive serving as background throughout the piece
0:11	**A** Cello group entering with main theme while the rhythmic ostinato continues in the background
0:29	**A′** Solo cello with variation of main theme
0:47	**Transition to B** Duel: several entrances of the three-note theme at different pitches
0:56	**B1** Repetition; insistence and dueling
1:09	**B2** Continued dueling with repetitions of the three-note sequence
1:24	**B3** Full ensemble
1:46	**Transition** Transition with material from **B**
2:05	**B4** New long melodic line using rhythms from (**A**) and (**B**) with added syncopations, supported by the rhythmic and melodic ostinato in the background based on **B**

(continued)

Time	Description
2:28	**B5** New melodic cell with constant accompaniment
2:46	**B6** New, short melodic cell derived from (**A**) and (**B**)
3:08	**C** New theme with repeated notes and walking bass, in the Baroque style
4:17	**C'** Repetition
5:10	**Transition** With material from (**C**) and (**A**), anticipating the final return to the beginning; long lyrical melody first played by a group and then by a cello solo
5:59	**A (major)** Return of rhythmic cell played by whole ensemble as in the introduction, with a major-key ending

the initial themes, resulting in a sequence of sections that are interconnected through variation and melodic and rhythmic expansion, a compositional technique preferred by Villa-Lobos. At the end of the piece, there is a return to the beginning, and a triumphal end in a major key concludes the musical duel.

Two generations of composers followed Villa-Lobos's nationalistic ideals, refining and diversifying the nationalistic musical language. The list is long but we can single out Camargo Guarnieri (1907–1993), one of the most successful twentieth-century composers who merged traditional Brazilian music with classical European repertoire. Similarly to Villa-Lobos, Guarnieri's music exhibits a penchant for long, arched melodic lines characteristic of operatic music. He left memorable piano pieces and a long list of songs that are among the best in the Brazilian repertoire, but Guarnieri was also successful in writing full-scale orchestral works. Five symphonies and several concertos display his mastery of classical forms. Guarnieri conducted his music throughout the world, and at the age of 85 he received the Gabriela Mistral award by the Organization of the American States, recognizing him as one of the most accomplished Latin American composers of the twentieth century.

Guarnieri made it a goal of his career to defend musical nationalism against other musical languages that were attracting Brazilian composers in the middle of the twentieth century. Among his adversaries was the German-born composer Hans-Joachim Koellreutter (1915–2005), who was responsible for bringing the music of German composer Arnold Schoenberg to the attention of Brazilian composers during the 1950s and 1960s. Like Schoenberg, Koellreutter was an advocate of serialism, which broke with tonality and opened up the world of art music to much experimentation during the twentieth century. Koellreutter's influence on the Brazilian musical scene is felt to this day, especially his preference for abstract musical compositions that did not use any elements from local traditional or popular musical styles. Koellreutter groomed new Brazilian composers who, once freed from strict nationalism, were able to pursue new techniques and eventually revitalize the Brazilian musical language.

European music of the classical tradition is alive and well in contemporary Brazil. In the wake of strong influence from European centers of new music like Paris and Darmstadt (Germany), Brazilian composers have started to look toward compositional schools in the United States. Eclecticism and postmodern experimentations that blend a variety of languages characterize the contemporary musical scene. Important compositional schools in Rio de Janeiro, São Paulo, and Bahia have produced successful composers that use multimedia, electronic effects, and computer-generated sounds as their source of inspiration. Jocy de Oliveira (b. 1936) has been very successful wedding multimedia, computer-generated sounds, and music theater. She is the author of a music theater trilogy focusing on women's topics: in "Inori to the Sacred Prostitute" (1993) with texts in various languages including Japanese and native Bororo, she explores the myth of the sacred prostitute, the ancient archetypes of female sexuality; in "Illud Tempos" (1994), she deals with women's dreams and fairy tales; and in "As Malibrans" (1999–2000), she addresses the dark side of the Diva image.

Conclusion

Brazilians tend to recognize music as the most important emblem of their nation's identity, but no particular musical style can be claimed as representative of such a large and diverse nation. This overview has discussed numerous styles, an introduction aimed at showing the richness and diversity of the Brazil's music. Although certain genres like bossa nova and samba have been widespread internationally and as a result are claimed as representative of Brazil abroad, inside the country music and music-making have served as cultural delimiters. As in any other nation, music in Brazil has been a strong marker of generational gaps, as well as of regional factions, and especially of social and ethnic divides. Furthermore, like many other countries in the Americas, music-making inside Brazil has been shaped by historical connections with other countries, connections that link, rather than separate, music-making in Brazil with other places beyond its borders. Today, with the Internet and the availability of technology in remote areas, Brazilians are more aware of their own cultural diversity than ever before; they are also more responsive to musical trends from abroad. These connections, from within and from abroad, are the main forces that continue to reshape music in contemporary Brazil.

KEY TERMS

agogô	cavaquinho	samba-enredo
baião	choro	samba-reggae
bailes funk	cuíca	surdo
bandolim	forró	tamborim
bateria	MPB (Música Popular	toada
berimbau	Brasileira)	toccata
bossa nova	música caipira	Tropicália
bumba-meu-boi	música sertaneja	viola
caboclo	pandeiro	walking bass
Candomblé	repenique	zabumba
cantoria	samba	
capoeira	samba-canção	

FURTHER READING

The Brazilian Sound: Samba, Bossa Nova and the Popular Music of Brazil. Philadelphia, PA: Temple University Press, 1998.

Crook, Larry. Northeastern Traditions and the Heartbeat of a Modern Nation. Santa Barbara, CA: ABD-CLIO, 2005.

FURTHER LISTENING

Forró in the Dark, Bonfires of São João. Nublu Records, 2006.

Babel Gilberto, Tanto Tempo. Six Degrees, 2000.

Paralamas do Sucesso, Arquivo. EMI, 1990.

Rio Baile Funk: Favela Booty Beats and Rio Baile Funk: More Favela Booty Beats. Essay Recordings, 2005.

Chico Science and Nação Zumbi, Da lama ao caos. Sony Music, 1996.

Sepultura, Roots. Roadrunner Records. 1996.

Tropicália Essentials. Hip-O Records, 1999.

FURTHER VIEWING

Beyond Ipanema: Brazilian Waves in Global Music. Guto Barra and Béco Dranoff, directors. Beyond Ipanema Films, 2009.

Favela on Blast. Leandro HBL and Wesley Pentz, directors. Mad Decent, 2008.

7

Argentina and the Rioplatense Region

DEBORAH SCHWARTZ-KATES

Introduction This chapter focuses on the vibrant musical traditions of Argentina, the second-largest country south of the U.S. border, along with the musical practices of Uruguay and Paraguay, two smaller Latin American nations. Together these three countries belong to the **rioplatense** region—an area named after the Río de la Plata, an extensive waterway that begins in Paraguay and Uruguay and runs southward along the Argentine and Uruguayan borders into the Atlantic Ocean. The Río de la Plata is the widest river in the world, and on its northern and southern banks lie the cosmopolitan capitals of Montevideo, Uruguay, and Buenos Aires, Argentina. Musically, the rioplatense nations lay claim to a remarkable range of expressive forms and practices. The tango, which arose in the capital cities of Argentina and Uruguay, has captivated listeners throughout the world. Other local genres—the milonga, candombe, and chacarera, coupled with a wide array of commercial styles and classical idioms—contribute to the dynamic musical landscape.

Together, Argentina, Uruguay, and Paraguay occupy an imposing physical space of approximately 1.3 million square miles—a territory larger than the combined total sizes of Mexico, California, Arizona, and Texas. Yet, even though the rioplatense region encompasses a large and imposing landmass, it has a relatively small population. Today, Argentina has only slightly more than 41 million people (according to 2011 estimates). Compared to the two other territorially largest countries in

LISTENING guides

Yupanqui, "Malambo"

Zitarrosa, "Milonga para una niña"

Palavecino, "Chacarera del paisano"

Gardel, "Por una cabeza"

Piazzolla, *La camorra I*

Possetti, "Bullanguera"

Serú Girán, "Los sobrevivientes"

Ginastera, "La doma, from *Estancia"*

Ginastera, First Piano Sonata, first movement

Barrios, *La catedral*

◀ FIGURE 7.1 Map of Argentina and surrounding countries, including Paraguay and Uruguay

FIGURE 7.2 Skyscrapers
in the Retiro district of
Buenos Aires

Latin America—Brazil (population 191 million) and Mexico (population 111 million)—it remains an underpopulated nation. Yet, it is precisely this sparse rate of settlement within a proportionately large landmass that defines key characteristics of the rioplatense population.

A Brief History

Compared to other parts of Latin America, the rioplatense nations were slow to develop. A relatively sparse population of indigenous groups originally settled in the region. Their numbers declined rapidly upon the arrival of the Spaniards, who expelled, obliterated, and assimilated a large number of native communities. Other indigenous groups fell prey to European diseases. Today, Uruguay lacks a statistically sizeable indigenous population. In contemporary Argentina, less than 3 percent of the people belong to Amerindian groups, which have been forced into a marginalized existence along remote border regions. Paraguay differs from other rioplatense nations in that European settlement initially took hold in the eastern half of the country, which was inhabited by indigenous groups who spoke the native language, **Guaraní**. The Spaniards quickly subjugated and assimilated this group, giving rise to a predominantly mestizo (mixed-race) population. Today, the Paraguayan government recognizes both Guaraní and Spanish as official languages, but the original practices of preconquest groups remain outside the cultural mainstream.

European settlers moved slowly into the rioplatense region, which lacked the rich material resources of other areas such as Mexico and Peru. Yet, once faced with the threat of a Portuguese invasion (via Brazil), the Spaniards established a stronghold there. In 1776, they founded the Viceroyalty of La Plata, which included the present-day countries of Argentina, Paraguay, and Uruguay, as well as parts of southern Bolivia. The Viceroyal capital, Buenos Aires, exercised an imposing degree of power, controlling access to both the Atlantic and Pacific Oceans. Yet, after 1816, when the Viceroyalty declared independence, Argentina, Paraguay, Bolivia, and Uruguay formed as separate nations. These new countries faced similar dilemmas as they aimed to establish distinctive identities and differentiate themselves from Spain. Ultimately, the way that rioplatense nations used their music to define, contest, and negotiate their changing identities offers fundamental insights into our knowledge of the region.

The rioplatense area had a less pronounced West African cultural presence than many other parts of Latin America. During the Colonial period, both Montevideo and Buenos Aires emerged as major slave ports and absorbed thousands of Africans arriving into the New World. However, during the nineteenth century, a disproportionate number of slaves were forced into military service, where they lost their lives fighting for South American independence and in the following civil wars. In 1871, a yellow fever epidemic struck the southern *barrios* of Buenos Aires and had a devastating effect on the Afro-Argentine population there. Tragically, few traces of this community survive today, although in Montevideo and the surrounding areas an important Afro-Uruguayan presence remains. In Paraguay, a small but significant community of African descent emerged during the 1820s, when José Gervasio Artigas, the founder of Uruguayan independence, was forced into exile near Asunción and brought a company of Afro-Uruguayans troops with him. Today, as Afro-Paraguayans struggle against marginalization and aim to win back territories that the government has seized from them, they have received infusions of cultural support from Afro-Uruguayan communities in Montevideo.

As a whole, Argentina and Uruguay are considered two of the most Europeanized Latin American nations. This characteristic dates back to the time of Spanish settlement and was reinforced during the late nineteenth and early twentieth centuries, when millions of immigrants from Italy and Spain, as well as from France, Britain, Germany, Russia, and Eastern Europe, arrived on rioplatense shores—a tendency that coincided with immigration to Ellis Island in the United States. Around 1900, first-generation Europeans made up over one-third of the total Uruguayan and Argentine population. In large cities, this figure rose higher—to around 50 percent. This influx of new settlement had a pronounced impact on local expressive forms, not the least of which was music. As we shall see, two of the most significant rioplatense genres—tango and opera—received their impetus from Italian immigrants and the strong cultural imprint they left upon the region. Thus, immigration and its impact on local musics form another central theme of this chapter.

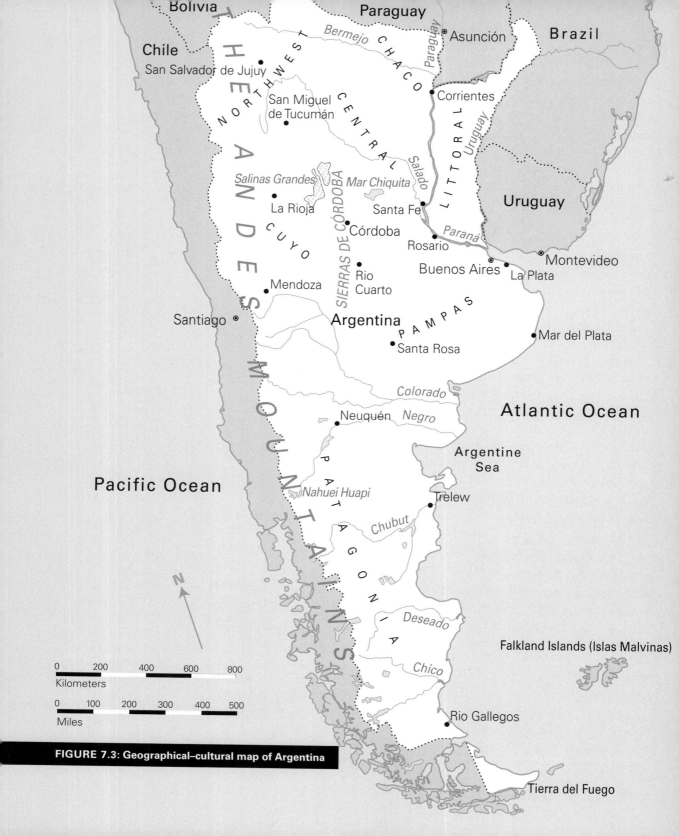

FIGURE 7.3: Geographical–cultural map of Argentina

Traditional Music

Panorama of Argentine Music

Argentina can be divided into seven areas, each with its own landscape and musical features (Figure 7.3). The **pampas** are a fertile farming and grazing region. The tremendous livestock and agricultural industries of this area have fortified the Argentine economy. This territory also holds great political sway because it includes the large and powerful capital of Buenos Aires, whose supremacy Argentines have challenged but have never successfully replaced. From Buenos Aires and the pampas come the tango, milonga, and many recent forms of urban popular music.

The **littoral**, to the northeast, occupies the space between the Paraná and Uruguay rivers. It is characterized by social dances of European origin and the use of the accordion, transplanted by immigrants. Further to the north is the subtropical Chaco, with its indigenous populations and cultural links to Paraguay. The central Argentine region, settled early during the Colonial period, is known for its Hispanic influences and is home to the chacarera, examined later in the chapter. The western area of Cuyo musically resembles that of nearby central Chile. Likewise, the northwestern Argentine territory has close cultural ties to surrounding Andean communities. As migrants from this region in search of better opportunities moved into Buenos Aires, their music gave rise to an incipient Andean folk revival movement, discussed in Chapter 8. Finally, the remote Patagonian area, extending to the tip of South America, remains sparsely inhabited. There the Mapuche tribe forms an important part of the local Argentine population, and this community has an even greater cultural presence in Chile.

In Argentina, scholars tend to classify traditional music into two categories. They use the term *indígena* (indigenous) to describe musical repertoires that predated the arrival of the Spaniards and that preserved preconquest languages, instruments, and practices. They apply the term criollo (creole) to music that uses the Spanish language and has a predominance of European features. Generally, throughout Latin America, the term criollo denotes traditions descended from European roots, while the term mestizo refers to blended cultural characteristics. However, in Argentina—a country profoundly shaped by European immigration—the term criollo also refers to the absorption and inclusion of indigenous elements within the mainstream population.

Common cultural and musical features extend across Argentine regional borders. One central characteristic is the **criollo** tradition in which

Contemporary Indigenous Communities

Indigenous communities in the rioplatense region have endured a harsh history of territorial conquest, military aggression, geographical displacement, and genocidal annihilation. Yet, despite centuries of hardship, surviving groups have proved remarkably resilient in finding ways to preserve traces of their traditional beliefs and practices. In recent years, the knowledge of indigenous repertoires has increased due to the activity of rioplatense scholars such as Irma Ruiz who have conducted extensive fieldwork among local populations. The Argentine National Institute of Musicology owns a vast collection of sound recordings, photographs, and instruments that document and preserve this heritage. The three Argentine regions with the largest contemporary indigenous populations are the Chaco, the littoral, and Patagonia.

The remote Chaco region, with its inaccessible geographical terrain, has a high density of indigenous communities, among them the Mataco and Toba. The cultural and musical practices of these groups converged during the late nineteenth century, when they were forced to work together under harsh labor conditions in sugar plantations and lumber mills. Another strong influence was the Protestant evangelical movement, particularly Pentecostal missionaries, who prohibited nonreligious music and forced members of indigenous communities to relinquish traditional instruments. Interestingly, the Toba responded by founding the United Evangelical Church (based on Pentecostal principles), and this religious movement later came to influence the Mataco. Although the new Toba religious music eliminated controversial elements that the missionaries strove to erase (such as the shaman or indigenous healer), it nevertheless contains allusions to older communal practices, which have ceased to exist in their original form today.

Guaraní-speaking people live in the northeastern Argentine province of Misiones, located in the littoral. The main indigenous community of this region, the Mbyá, originated in Paraguay, where some members of the group still reside today. Like the Mataco and Toba, the Mbyá came under pressure from Protestant missionaries to accept evangelical Christianity. Yet, unlike other groups, they ferociously guarded their religious and cultural identity. They have maintained an intensely private religious life, practicing ritual ceremonies inside the homes of spiritual leaders to avoid attracting attention. Yet, the Mbyá have adopted string instruments of European origin—a five-string guitar and a three-string *rebec* (folk violin)—that they consider their own. Even though they know how to play the six-string guitar, which is standard throughout the region, they reserve the five-string instrument for their own ritual music.

The Mapuche ("people of the land") inhabit the Patagonian area, as well as occupying large portions of central and southern Chile. This group maintained a strong and independent presence until the late nineteenth century, when Argentine and Chilean armies defeated them. The Mapuche are known for their complex religious beliefs and musical practices. Women play a leading role in performing sacred music. A central Mapuche ritual is *tayil*, which connects community members with the souls of their living and deceased ancestors. Today, as younger generations begin to lose their traditions and assimilate within surrounding communities, *tayil* endures as a reminder of the group's collective belief system and relation to a shared ancestral past.

Hispanic influences prevail. As in other Iberian-based repertoires, dance rhythms frequently center on the interplay between triple $\frac{3}{4}$ and compound duple $\frac{6}{8}$ meters, resulting in hemiola. One common pattern found in Argentine social dances such as the *zamba*, chacarera, and *gato* appears in Example 7.1. The first full measure of the upper part (representing the melody) is in $\frac{6}{8}$ time, with accents on the first and fourth eighth notes. These accents divide the six-beat pattern into two parts. The second measure emphasizes the first, third, and fifth eighth notes dividing the beat patterns into threes. This alternation between twos and threes creates hemiola from one measure to the next. At the same time, the accompaniment (shown in the lower part) implies triple meter, creating hemiola against the melodic part in the first measure. Try clapping and counting this pattern aloud with a classmate. Feel the rhythm pulling apart and coming back together again. This sense of convergence and divergence, of musical fission and fusion, gives Argentine music its compelling dance rhythms.

Criollo songs have a nostalgic and sentimental flavor. They tend toward slow tempos and nonaccented rhythms that ebb and flow freely along with the text. This expressive style differs markedly from criollo dance music and establishes a sharp contrast between local styles of singing and dancing. This duality extends beyond the traditional repertoire and encompasses other styles of Argentine music. For example, Astor Piazzolla's *La camorra I* illustrates these powerful expressive contrasts by juxtaposing nostalgic songlike sections with brilliant technical passages derived from the raw intensity of Argentine dance (see Astor Piazzolla, *La camorra I*, Listening Guide 7.5).

Melodically, most criollo music is based on European major or minor scales. Some pieces from the North or Northwest employ **tritonic** (three-note) or pentatonic (five-note) scale systems. Other examples fluctuate

EXAMPLE 7.1: Criollo rhythmic pattern

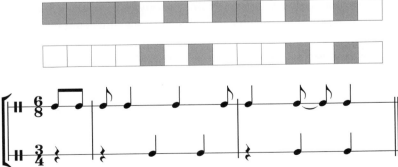

between major and minor keys. A large number of Argentine melodies use regular phrases and descending melodic lines. The traditional criollo repertoire relies largely on European harmonies, especially tonic, subdominant, and dominant triads (I, IV, and V) of major and minor keys (see Appendix). Usually, the music follows patterned harmonic progressions, with regular chord changes every one or two measures. The principal type of texture consists of accompanied melody. Frequently, the highest voice sings the main musical idea and a second part harmonizes three or six notes below it. This vocal style, known as singing in parallel thirds and sixths, is widespread throughout the world and has its roots in Iberian practices.

Traditional Argentine instruments include the violin, guitar, accordion, and **bombo** (large double-headed drum played with sticks). The **bandoneón**, an accordion-like instrument of German origin, arose in conjunction with the tango, but is also used in traditional ensembles throughout Argentina. Above all, the guitar is the preferred criollo instrument. Originally acquired from the Spaniards, it developed in various sizes and shapes throughout the rioplatense region. Today, the standard six-string instrument prevails. It is the national instrument of Argentina.

Criollo poetic forms also derive from Spanish traditions. Frequent subjects include patriotism, heroism, philosophy, and humor. One important group of poetic texts (found especially in *vidalitas* and milongas) focuses on emotional extremes. These poems mourn personal tragedies, dwell on thoughts of suicide and death, and convey a sense of hopelessness. When Argentine musicians perform such lyrics in an expressive criollo style (using slow tempos, free rhythms, minor scales, and descending contours), their sense of melancholy increases. Even as outsiders to the culture, we can identify with these sentiments because the same elements connote sadness in our own music, which likewise stems from European traditions. To get an idea of this expressive vocal style, listen to Alfredo Zitarrosa's "Milonga para una niña" (Listening Guide 7.2), examined in detail later in the chapter.

Most Argentine rural dances involve one or two non-embracing couples. Choreographic gestures include handkerchief-waving, finger-snapping, and hand-clapping, along with an agile foot-tapping motion known as **zapateo**. Some criollo dances derive from the principle of *cambio de sitio* (change of place). They consist of two complementary sections. In the first, *la primera*, the dancers end in opposite positions; in the second, *la segunda*, they come back to their original places. These two sections create a sense of symmetry that derives from Iberian roots and that forms the basis of Argentine criollo dance.

Music of the Pampas

Let us now take a more detailed look at a specific Argentine region. The pampas offer an excellent point of orientation as the geographic, economic, and political nucleus of the nation. A central folk figure is the **gaucho**, who works with native cattle and horses. The gaucho, who arose as a male mestizo, dates back to the colonial period, and his ethnic roots reflect the blending of Spanish, indigenous, and African populations. Yet, this figure was also recognized as a criollo because of the perceived dominance of his Hispanic heritage. More than a racial category, however, the gaucho is defined by his way of life. His existence centered around horses, which allowed for mobility across the plains; his cattle offered a steady food supply and provided a source of income. The gaucho lived off the land in a simple thatch and mud hut. He ate a diet of roasted beef cooked over an open flame that was accompanied by little other than *mate*, a highly caffeinated herbal tea that people from the rioplatense region still drink today. The gaucho worked at difficult and dangerous tasks—breaking horses, rounding up cattle, and managing livestock on commercial ranches known as *estancias*. Rugged masculinity and competition characterized his work and typified his music.

A related figure of the pampas was the *payador*, a gaucho singer and guitarist who performed, composed, and improvised music. In rural fiestas and *pulperías* (local bars and stores), he played music for his own enjoyment, provided an accompaniment for dancing, and competed in improvised song

FIGURE 7.4 Cattle in the Pampas region

explore

To view a modern performance of payada, search for "*payada de contrapunto*" (competitive payada). Pay special attention to José Curbelo, whose performances retain important links to the historical *payador* tradition.

contests known as **payadas** (which paralleled the Cuban *controversia* and Brazilian cantoria described in Chapters 5 and 6). Payadas involved two or more gauchos who performed improvised stanzas in ferocious contests of wits. In these spirited duels, gauchos hurled difficult questions and daring remarks at their opponents at the same time that they dodged the challenges leveled at them. They were expected to think quickly, maintain the speed of the music, and avoid hesitations that revealed signs of weaknesses. The contests lasted for hours until one of the gauchos was exhausted, defeated, or overwhelmed by the cries of the spirited crowd in attendance. Today, rioplatense musicians perform payadas competitively in folkloric festivals. National Payador Day takes place on July 23 in Argentina and August 24 in Uruguay.

Gauchos also competed in **malambos** (improvised dance contests). In these competitions, two male contestants took turns performing vigorous zapateo dance steps. Malambos lasted for hours until one of the dancers was exhausted or defeated. In 1871, Ventura Lynch described a malambo that lasted an entire night and consisted of 76 separate dance sequences. The malambo is accompanied by a strummed guitar accompaniment in § time. It uses simple progressions in major keys, such as the harmonies G–A–D (IV–V–I). As the malambo progresses, the guitarist improvises variations on the progression to coordinate with the dancers' changing steps. Today malambos are taught in national dance schools and performed in Argentine festivals. Modernized versions are staged in folkloric celebrations such as the Festival Nacional del Malambo in Laborde.

The example of a malambo (Listening Guide 7.1) was composed by Atahualpa Yupanqui (Héctor Roberto Chavero, 1908–1992)—a singer, poet, guitarist, and folk music collector who revived and promoted Argentine music. Yupanqui grew up in Buenos Aires Province and identified with the gaucho heritage. He composed around 1,200 pieces of folk music, and his performances show respect for the original tradition. In "Malambo," Yupanqui revitalizes the rural gaucho dance for modern urban audiences. This piece is based on traditional malambo harmonies (note the IV–V–I progression at 0:18). Yet, the composition also incorporates non-traditional features. Although rural malambos are strummed, Yupanqui's piece draws upon the full range of modern guitar techniques including plucking, slurs, arpeggios, muted strings, and *golpes* (strikes on the body of the instrument). These sounds enhance the piece for modern listeners, who experience the music outside its original context, but form a clear image of the original gaucho genre through the composer's creative additions.

Yupanqui forms part of a larger group of Argentine performers who created original music from traditional sources and who played in professional

⊚ Yupanqui: "Malambo"

Composer: Atahualpa Yupanqui

Date of composition: 1970s

Performer/instruments: Atahualpa Yupanqui, guitar (also used as percussion)

Date of recording: 2008

Genre: malambo

Form: Variations on two chord progressions

Tempo/meter: moderate compound duple

What to Listen for:
- First chord progression: G–A–D (IV–V–I)
- Second chord progression: A⁷–D (V⁷–I)
- Major key
- Extended techniques including *golpe* (strikes on the body of the guitar)
- Increasing rhythmic activity that parallels the heightened intensity of the dance

Time	Description
0:00	Introduction
0:18	Main progression: G–A–D (IV–V–I); played four times with muted strumming
0:27	Variations on the main progression; extended techniques (plucking, arpeggios, and slurs)
2:01	Second progression: A⁷–D (V⁷–I) and variations; uses syncopation, *golpe*, and strumming on muted strings
2:43	Free improvisation; based on D, G, and A⁷ (I, IV, and V⁷) chords
3:04	Return to the main progression; includes *golpe*
3:17	Return to the second progression; *golpe* continues
3:38	Final flourish

venues such as radio, television, and folk festivals. The most famous Argentine musician who continued in this style was Mercedes Sosa (1935–2009). Sosa was born in rural Argentina in the northwest province of Tucumán. In 1965, her professional career began when she sang at the most important national folkloric festival held in Cosquín. Inspired by Yupanqui's revival of traditional music, she championed a new Argentine song movement known as *nuevo cancionero*. Closely aligned with Cuban *nueva trova* and Chilean nueva canción (see Chapters 5 and 8), this movement combined traditional styles with left-leaning political lyrics that aimed to improve the socioeconomic conditions of poor workers. Sosa endured constant harassment during the years of the Argentine military dictatorship (1976–1983). The government arrested her during a concert in La Plata, intimidated her with death threats, and banned her music from the public media. Artistically silenced, she retreated

explore

To learn more about Mercedes Sosa, visit her online obituaries and explore her award-winning CDs: *Acústico* (Acoustic), *Corazón libre* (Free Heart), and *Cantora 1* (Singer 1).

FIGURE 7.5 Mercedes Sosa playing the bombo drum. Paris, 1973

to Europe, where she remained from 1979–1982. Upon returning to Argentina, she reached out to broader audiences by incorporating popular styles and joining forces with rock musicians in her critique of the regime. The recipient of several Latin Grammy awards, Sosa is remembered for her powerful alto voice and for her use of music to protest human rights abuses throughout Argentina and the world.

Transformation of the Pampas

Around the turn of the twentieth century, the gaucho's traditional lifestyle changed. As Argentine leaders promoted the financially beneficial exportation of livestock, ranchers fenced the open range and selectively bred their cattle in pens. This step eliminated the legendary independence of the gaucho, who previously had enjoyed great freedom of movement across the plains. The native horsemen now had to work within a commercialized system. Those who were unable to adapt were forced into the suburbs of Buenos Aires, where they found new work in slaughterhouses and meat-salting factories. There they mingled with a new group of immigrants, who were also marginalized and displaced. In the process, some traditional customs disappeared, while others assimilated into new ways of life. Accordingly, much of the gaucho repertoire that comes down to us today survives in this hybridized state.

One type of music that transitioned from the country to the city is the **milonga**. Although the term "milonga" can refer to popular urban performance spaces, more often it designates a genre—one of the most representative of the pampas today. There are several types of milongas, among them the *milonga pampeana*, an expressive solo song. Frequently, this genre uses eight-syllable lines arranged in ten-line stanzas known as *décimas* (which are also heard in the Cuban *controversia*). Textually, some milongas evoke the disappearing rural culture of the past, while others recall events from the lives of real or imagined gauchos. A considerable number dwell on intensely melancholy sentiments, heightened by slow to moderate tempos, minor scales, and descending melodic lines—all features identified with criollo repertoires.

Our example of a milonga, composed by Alfredo Zitarrosa (1936–1989), comes from Uruguay, which shares a common pampean culture with Argentina. Like Yupanqui, Zitarrosa promoted the traditional music of his nation and focused specifically on the pampas. His "Milonga para una niña" uses a typical *décima* rhyme scheme, **ABBAACCDDC**. The lyrics exemplify the criollo tradition by portraying music as a release from human suffering. This piece deals with a man who cannot return the love of a young woman who adores him. He offers her a milonga as the one lasting form of joy he can give her.

The "Milonga para una niña" begins with a guitar introduction in syncopated duple meter. Afterward, sung *décimas* alternate with instrumental interludes. Note how the vocal style contrasts with the rhythmically animated guitar sections. If we tried singing along with Zitarrosa, we would notice that the shape of his melody barely changes. This is because his entire range is limited to five notes of the minor scale, which makes it sound as if he is speaking the text rather than singing it. After the eighth line, Zitarrosa pauses dramatically, as guitar chords punctuate the vocal line, driving home the message of the text. Meanwhile, the melody, which lingered on the dominant (fifth note of the scale), descends to the tonic (first note of the scale) to complete the stanza.

LISTENING guide 7.2

◎ Zitarrosa: "Milonga para una niña" (Milonga for a Girl)

Composer/lyricist: Alfredo Zitarrosa

Date of composition: ca. 1960

Performer/instruments: Alfredo Zitarrosa, voice; three guitarists

Date of recording: 1980

Genre: milonga

Form: strophic

Tempo/meter: moderate duple

What to Listen for:

- Contrast between vocal and instrumental sections
- Speech-like vocal style with limited range
- Each *décima* following the rhyme scheme: **ABBAACCDDC**
- Dramatic pauses after the eighth line of each stanza

Time	Text	Translation*	Description
0:00			**Introduction** Guitar solo
0:15	**A** Él que ha vivido penando **B** por causa de un mal amor, **B** no encuentra nada mejor **A** que cantar y d'ir pensando. **A** Y si anduvo calculando **C** qué culpa pudo tener, **C** cuando ve que la mujer **D** no conoce obligaciones, **D** se consuela con canciones **C** Y se olvida de querer.	He who has lived in sadness, Disappointed in love, Will find nothing better Than to sing and wonder. And, if he tries to figure out How he was to blame, When he learns that women Have no sense of duty, He'll take comfort in song And forget about love.	***Décima 1***; speech-like vocal style

(continued)

Time	Text	Translation*	Description
0:41			**Interlude** Guitar solo
0:52	**A** Por eso niña te pido **B** que no me guardes rencor, **B** yo no puedo darte amor **A** ni vos podés darme olvido....	That's why I'm asking you, girl, Not to hate me. I can't give you love And you can't make me forget you....	Opening text of ***Décima 2***; speech-like vocal style
1:17			**Interlude** Guitar solo
1:28	**A** Yo no te puedo entregar **B** un corazón apagado....	I cannot give you A heart that's not beating....	Opening text of ***Décima 3***; speech-like vocal style
1:52			**Interlude** Guitar solo
2:03	**A** Cuando te vuelva a encontrar **B** nos podremos sonreír; **B** prefiero verte partir **A** como te he visto llegar. **A** Cuando vuelvas a pensar **C** que una vez te conocí **C** y que nomás porque sí **D** te compuse una canción, **D** cantará en tu corazón **C** lo poquito que te dí.	When we meet again We can smile at each other; I'd rather see you go Just as you came. Then you recall That I once knew you And wrote a song for you And that I did it just because, What little I gave you Will sing in your heart.	***Décima 4***; speech-like vocal style

*English translation by Tony Beckwith

Beyond the Pampas

Musical practices in traditional areas, such as the central province of Santiago del Estero, have greatly enhanced Argentine cultural life. The music of this region incorporates lyrics in the indigenous language of Quechua. It emphasizes the violin within ensembles that also include the guitar and bombo. One vibrant genre associated with the region is the **chacarera**, a lively couples dance that is frequently performed in *peñas* (folkloric clubs). Rhythmically, the dance features compelling offbeat accents and shifts between $\frac{6}{8}$ and $\frac{3}{4}$ meters. Note how the bombo creates the characteristic hemiola associated with the dance. While the rim part accentuates beats 1 and 4 (dividing the six-count measure into two), the head part emphasizes beats 3 and 5, suggesting triple meter. The guitar reinforces these patterns. A transcription of the signature chacarera rhythm appears in Example 7.2.

EXAMPLE 7.2: Chacarera rhythm, transcribed by Mitsuko Kawabata

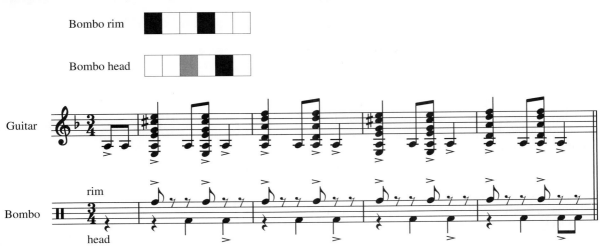

Today, most chacareras are sung, and their form derives from the alternation of vocal and instrumental sections. Normally, the music begins with an instrumental introduction as the singer announces the start of the first section ("la primera"). At the end of the section, the group takes a break until the leader cues the second section (in this recording we hear him call "otra vuelta," meaning "one more time"). Then, the music from the first section recurs, but with a different text. The form of the chacarera appears in the diagram below.

Form of the Chacarera						
I. La Primera						
Introduction	Stanza 1	Interlude	Stanza 2	Interlude	Stanza 3	Stanza 4
Break, Cue						
II. La Segunda						
Introduction	Stanza 5	Interlude	Stanza 6	Interlude	Stanza 7	Stanza 8

The "Chacarera del paisano" (Listening Guide 7.3), created and performed by the folk singer and violinist Sixto Palavecino (1915–2009), illustrates the traditional rhythms, instruments, and structure of the genre. Note how Palavecino represents the confrontation between the

⊚ Palavecino: "Chacarera del paisano" (The Villager's chacarera)

Composer/lyricist: Sixto Palavecino

Date of composition: unknown

Performer/instruments: Sixto Palavecino (vocalist), violin, guitar, bombo

Date of recording: 2006

Genre: chacarera

Form: two large sections (*primera, segunda*) separated by a break

Tempo/meter: lively alternation between compound duple and simple triple

What to Listen for:

- Rural–urban conflict in the lyrics
- Violin dominates the ensemble and harmonizes with voice
- All stanzas have the same music (strophic form)
- Use of the signature chacarera rhythm

Time	Text	Translation*	Description
0:00	**I. La Primera**		**Introduction** Instrumental (violin, guitar, bombo)
0:10	Tanto que lo han ponderado por fin resolví por conocer Buenos Aires hasta allá me fui.	People have wondered so much about it That at last I decided To see Buenos Aires So I went there myself.	**Stanza 1**: voice and violin harmonize; shift between major and minor keys
0:19			**Interlude** Instrumental (violin, guitar, bombo, same music as introduction)
0:25	Llegando en ese Retiro ahí no más bajé para donde iba la gente yo también rumbié.	When I arrived at Retiro Station I got off the train And then just Followed the crowd.	**Stanza 2** (same music as Stanza 1)
0:34			**Interlude**
0:40	Esos troles y los trenes a electricidad ¡mama mía! ay, que peligro son para viajar.	Those trolleys and trains Powered by electricity, Mama mía! How dangerous Traveling on them can be.	**Stanza 3**
0:49	Los autos pasan y pasan pasan sin cortar, me he quedado un día entero sin poder cruzar.	The cars drive past, one after another With never a break between them I have waited a whole day And not been able to cross.	**Stanza 4**

(continued)

Time	Text	Translation*	Description
0:57	Otra vuelta	One more time	**Break** Spoken voice
0:58	**II. La Segunda**		**Introduction**
1:08	En ese subte que dicen Fui a mosquetear, Unas cosas como trancas Empecé a pechar.	In the subway, as they call it, I want to look around, And found some kind of barriers That I pushed against.	**Stanza 5**
1:16			**Interlude**
1:23	Cualquiera puede pensar Trancas de corral, Si no le largan moneda No deja pasar.	You might think They were corral gates, But if you don't give them your money They won't let you through.	**Stanza 6**
1:31			**Interlude**
1:38	Trenes hay en ese hoyo Como pa' no creer, Vieran son como balazos Estos pa' correr.	There are trains down in that hole Like you wouldn't believe, You should see them Moving as fast as bullets.	**Stanza 7**
1:47	Eso quién lo habrá inventado Zupay ha de ser, Inteligencia de hombre Yo no puedo creer.	Who could have invented that? It must have been Zupay (the Devil), I can't believe that it was Human intelligence.	**Stanza 8**

*English Translation: Tony Beckwith

countryside and the city. The word "paisano" in his title refers to someone who comes from an Argentine village or rural area. This country-dweller recalls his trip to Buenos Aires, where he encounters the modern lifestyle of the city. Overwhelmed, frustrated, and amused, he meets city life on his own terms. The paisano uses the rural term *rumbear* (to make one's way) to describe his arrival at Retiro Train Station. Later he compares the subway turnstile to the familiar "trancas de corral" (corral gates). He attributes the frightening speed of mass transit to Zupay, the Quechuan term for the Devil. This conflict between urban and rural values characterizes many Argentine expressive texts.

Another traditional Argentine genre is the **chamamé**, which began in the littoral. This dance mixes the Czech polka, brought over by immigrants, with local criollo features. Yet, unlike the original polka, which uses duple meter, the chamamé is based on a combination of $\frac{6}{8}$ and $\frac{3}{4}$ time.

explore

If you liked the traditional chacarera, you might enjoy modern examples, such as the electronic "Chacarera for Argentina" by Angelini Music or the jazz fusion "Chacarera de la esperanza" (Chacarera of Hope) by the Pablo Ablanedo Octet.

explore

For a documentary that traces cultural influences on the chamamé and includes vibrant performances by contemporary artists, see *Argentina: Chamamé crudo* (Films Media Group 39528, 2007). You may also enjoy listening to recordings of Chango Spasiuk, an iconic chamamé musician who is featured in the documentary.

It has a romantic character, sentimental lyrics, and is danced cheek-to-cheek. It frequently uses texts in Guaraní—an important linguistic marker of the region. The chamamé features the accordion as the main melodic instrument within an ensemble that can also include a bandoneón, two guitars, and an upright bass. Although this dance originally developed in rural areas, it achieved widespread popularity through the mass media, beginning with "Corrientes poty" (Corrientes in Bloom), which RCA Victor recorded in 1931 in Buenos Aires.

The Paraguayan Harp

The folk music of Paraguay parallels the Argentine littoral in important ways. Both traditions employ song lyrics in Guaraní and embracing couple dances. Yet, as opposed to the focus on the accordion in northeastern Argentina, Paraguayan music emphasizes the harp. Traditionally this was a diatonic instrument, meaning that it could not play outside a given key without having to retune the strings or adjust the mechanism. Transplanted from Europe, it was modeled on the Spanish harp used to accompany liturgical music and play for court celebrations during the medieval and Renaissance periods. Initially, in the New World, the harp fulfilled a religious function. Yet as Alfredo Colman, an authority on the Paraguayan harp, points out, during the twentieth century, the government symbolically promoted the instrument to foster a sense of Paraguayan identity. Today, the harp plays a vibrant role in defining the musical culture of the nation (Figure 7.6). It functions as both a solo and ensemble instrument and can be fitted with a special lever to access the chromatic notes and perform the international repertoire.

FIGURE 7.6 Paraguayan Harp Day

The most famous traditional Paraguayan harpist was Félix Pérez Cardozo (1908–1952). He established a professional standard of harp playing as well as collecting, arranging, and composing folk music for the instrument. His most popular arrangement, "Pájaro campana" (The Bell Bird), imitated birdcalls with onomatopoeic instrumental effects. In addition, the harp assumes a central role in performing traditional Paraguayan genres, the most important of which is the *polca paraguaya* (Paraguayan polka). Like the Argentine chamamé, the *polca paraguaya* features syncopated rhythms in $\frac{6}{8}$ and $\frac{3}{4}$ time. It bears no resemblance to the European genre of the same name, which is in duple meter.

Afro-Uruguayan Candombe

Uruguay shares important musical features with Argentina, especially the traditional pampean repertoire. Yet, one key difference revolves around the Afro-Uruguayan presence based in Montevideo. This vibrant community contributes central expressive forms that have shaped the cultural identity of the nation.

The most significant musical contribution of the Afro-Uruguayan population is **candombe**, which has recently received worldwide recognition from UNESCO as Intangible Cultural Heritage of Humanity. The term candombe (which differs from Brazilian candomblé) dates back to the colonial period and refers to a dramatic dance of African origin. Historically, candombe used a stock cast of symbolic characters that were believed to represent important authorities in African society. These characters included: a king, a queen, a *gramillero* (young dancer disguised as an old man), an *escobero* or *escobillero* (broom maker), and a *mama vieja* (old woman). Although this dance lost certain aspects of its original pantomime, important characters survive in performances today. Figure 7.7 illustrates several of these figures in a modern candombe performance. On the right is the *gramillero*, who has a false white beard, a pair of glasses, and a top hat. He walks with a cane and can be seen with a bundle of herbs, since he is portrayed as an herbalist or medicine man. On his left is his female counterpart, the *mama vieja*, who has a head cloth, wears a long flowing skirt, and holds a parasol. Behind the *gramallero* and *mama vieja* are two of the characteristic drums associated with the candombe tradition—the *chico* and piano tamboriles, which are described in detail in the following paragraph.

The main instrument associated with candombe is the **tamboril**, a single-headed drum that also appears elsewhere throughout Latin America. Musicians carry this instrument over

FIGURE 7.7 Modern candombe performance. Montevideo, 2004

explore

To learn more about candombe, watch the DVD: *Afro-Uruguayan Rhythms: Candombe* (Surmenages, 2006). You may also enjoy listening to music by Cachila and his group, Cuareim 1080.

their shoulders and play it with two hands, one of which holds a stick. Originally, four sizes of *tamboriles* participated in candombe. From the highest to the lowest, they were the *chico*, *repique*, *piano*, and *bajo* or *bombo*. Recently, the lowest part has disappeared. The three remaining instruments produce a drum call known as the *llamada*, which is polyrhythmic, meaning that each instrument has its own independent beat pattern. The *llamada* is the defining musical element of the dance.

A rhythmic transcription of a *llamada* is shown in Example 7.3. The notes above the line are played by the left hand and, the notes below it, by the right hand using a stick. The accent marks represent slaps, and the letters "x" on the noteheads indicate muffled strokes. Because the *repique* part is improvised, this example shows only one of many possible rhythms that can occur in a candombe performance. Additionally, any instrument may improvise a Caribbean clave pattern known as *madera* (wood) on the body of the drum at any time.

One remarkable thing about candombe is the way that the genre has reinvented itself throughout history. It began as a modest expression of a culturally vibrant but impoverished community. During the early twentieth century, the *conjuntos lubolos*, or societies that maintained the tradition, instituted the dance in Montevidean carnival. Within this new context, the emphasis shifted toward a commercialized style of performance in lavish parades and competitions. While certain traditional practices continued, candombe came under the influence of Brazilian carnival and added new personalities and attractions drawn from show business. Once candombe

EXAMPLE 7.3: Candombe rhythm

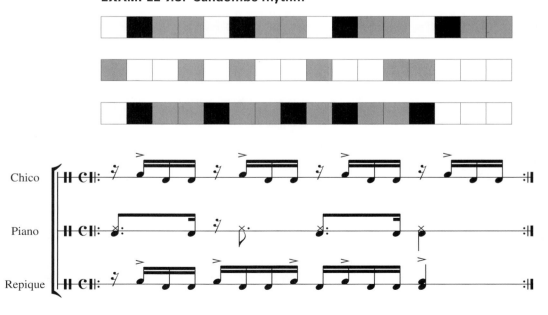

entered into a commercially mediated space, it mixed with other popular styles, upon which it juxtaposed its signature *llamada* rhythm. Some musicians used the guitar to replace the tamboril parts, which previously had anchored the genre throughout its many stylistic transformations. These fascinating developments raise a provocative set of questions. Is candombe still an Afro-Uruguayan form, even though it has interacted significantly with other types of music? And can it still be considered a form of traditional music, since its performers now operate within an urban popular space, where artistic decisions are mediated by commercial concerns?

Other genres explored throughout the chapter touch on similar issues. Although the chacarera originally had close ties with Santiago del Estero, it has since been assimilated within a broader national repertoire, where it is taught in the public schools and performed in folkloric shows as one of many Argentine dances. Contemporary musicians have added new instruments, such as the saxophone and electric guitar, and have used the chacarera rhythm to create urban hybrid fusions. In the littoral, the chamamé has grown popular through its dissemination in the mass media, beginning with its earliest recordings produced in Buenos Aires. In Paraguay, questions about the local versus the global have led to debates about whether musicians should chromatically alter their instruments to accommodate international repertoires. These cases raise questions about the connections between local genres and their original performance settings. These cases, which raise questions about the connections between local genres and their original performance settings, lead us to ask how performers have modified their aesthetics (that is, their ideas about how music should sound and what it should mean) when representing works to an international community. In this way, the genres we have examined can be seen as dynamic cultural fields through which musicians negotiate conflicting ideas about tradition and modernity. Although the future of such genres remains unclear, one thing is certain: rioplatense musicians have drawn upon a wide variety of regional traditions as a source of creative inspiration. They will continue to find innovative ways to celebrate their heritage in the years ahead.

Popular Music

The Rioplatense Tango

Among the many styles of Latin American music, the **tango** has fascinated audiences throughout the world. Nostalgic, melancholy, sensual, and dramatic, it has captivated the public with its compelling rhythms and dance steps. Today, international audiences experience the tango in different ways. They attend popular stage shows and musicals; they listen to Astor Piazzolla's recordings;

they watch street musicians in the subways of Paris, Helsinki, and Tokyo; and they learn to dance the tango in nightclubs and dance studios. Most of all, for the people of Argentina and Uruguay, tango is a deeply embedded symbol of rioplatense culture.

The word "tango" is of probable African origin. It once referred to popular music and dance celebrations performed by slaves throughout the Caribbean and Atlantic coastal regions. Initially, the genre overlapped with the milonga and candombe, as well as with the Cuban habanera (see Chapter 5). By the turn of the twentieth century, however, tango emerged as an independent dance genre (around the time that the urbanized samba took hold in Brazil). The rioplatense tango arose on the outskirts of Buenos Aires and Montevideo in poverty-stricken districts known as **arrabales**. The **compadrito**, a quintessential early figure associated with the genre, emerged out of this social setting. He assumed the pose of an arrogant bully; his dress and behavior mocked the elite. The compadrito blended gaucho and immigrant characteristics. He spoke **lunfardo**, a dialect tinged with references to the criminal underworld that combined Italian idioms with rioplatense speech. Most people considered him vulgar and disreputable, but others secretly admired his provocative sensuality. Indeed, he was the one figure who captured the mythical space that the gaucho once held in the Argentine imagination.

Originally, the compadrito danced the tango with prostitutes in brothels. (However, due to a shortage of women in an environment dominated by young male immigrants, two men could also perform the dance.) The risqué choreography, which showed couples locked in a tight embrace, disturbed modest citizens outside the arrabal. Some construed the dance as a representation of compadrito knife fighting, or *duelo criollo*, while others interpreted it as an enactment of sexual intercourse itself. Eventually, the tango began to lose its stigma when professional musicians introduced it into more-reputable social spaces, such as the theater, radio, and cinema. A turning point came after 1911, when Camille de Rhynal (a Parisian dancer and choreographer) modified the steps into an elegant ballroom dance that the French aristocracy embraced. (Figure 7.8 illustrates the gentrified Parisian choreography.) Once the tango received its endorsement from France, upper-class Argentines had no choice but to accept it, since they upheld Paris as the model of cultural refinement. Technically, the tango never represented all of Argentina, as the original genre was associated with Buenos Aires. Yet, acceptance from Paris guaranteed its status as an iconic national dance.

FIGURE 7.8 French ballroom version of the tango from a drawing by Xavier Sager, 1914

The first stage of tango history, known as *La Guardia vieja* (Old Guard), lasted until 1920. During this period, the tango emerged as a genre of instrumental music based on a three-part form with different sections (ABC). Usually, *Guardia vieja* ensembles had four instruments: violin, flute, guitar, and bandoneón (In Depth 7.2). Arguably the most famous tango ever written, Gerardo Matos Rodríguez's "La cumparsita" ("The Little Carnival Procession"), recorded in 1917, dates from this period. Initially, early tangos used rhythms related to the habanera and milonga in duple meter (Example 7.4a). Yet, during the 1910s, bandleaders began to slow the tempo and adopt a quadruple meter with sharp accents. Two new patterns, marcato and *síncopa* (Examples 7.4b–c), characterized the bass line of these more recent tangos and established their harmonic and rhythmic foundations.

As the tango gained prestige, it entered into a second phase called *La Guardia nueva* (New Guard), which lasted from 1920–1955. People from all social classes experienced the genre on the radio, in the movies, in nightclubs, and in cafés. As the tango moved into these upscale social spaces, it underwent a rags-to-riches transformation. Because listening to the music was now just as important as dancing, a new style evolved called the *tango canción* (tango song). This genre emphasized the voice, which skillfully used rubato (that flexible sense of rhythmic ebb and flow) to highlight the expressive accents of the text. The instrumental accompaniment became smoother and more polished as piano and strings enhanced the ensemble, which eventually

EXAMPLE 7.4A: Habanera and milonga rhythm

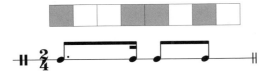

EXAMPLE 7.4B: Marcato

EXAMPLE 7.4C: *Síncopa*

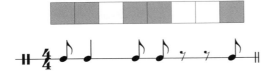

The Bandoneón

The bandoneón once dominated the tango ensemble; its sound and style still define the genre today. Transported to Argentina by German immigrants, this instrument visually resembles the accordion. Its 38 right-hand buttons play in the upper and middle ranges, and its 33 left-hand buttons produce the low register. Originally designed as a diatonic folk accordion that played in only a few keys, the bandoneón evolved to include more buttons, which allowed it to substitute for the organ in small German churches. Normally on keyboard instruments, neighboring tones occupy adjacent keys, but because of the haphazard way that the *bandoneón* evolved, its complex physical layout defied logical explanation. Fiendishly difficult to play, it has attracted a core group of performers who have built the core repertoire of the tango around this impractical (but fascinating) instrument.

FIGURE 7.9 The bandoneón

FIGURE 7.10 Carlos Gardel sings on the radio, 1934

employed professional performers and arrangers. No single instrument stood out, and the bandoneón, which had once dominated the ensemble, blended seamlessly with the other instruments. The *tango canción* used a standardized form with two equal and balanced sections, which highlighted the new features of the genre and allowed audiences to hear them more clearly.

The rioplatense singer and composer, Carlos Gardel (1884?–1935) is upheld as a legendary idol in tango history. He created the earliest *tango canción* with his 1917 recording of "Mi noche triste" (My Sad Night). Gardel's exquisite sense of delivery is still a model for tango singers. His life is cloaked in mystery, making it difficult to differentiate the fact from the myth. According to one account, he was born the illegitimate son of a French washerwoman who immigrated to Buenos Aires. Yet, another story claimed him as the unwanted child of an Uruguayan colonial, who was adopted by his maid! Despite these uncertainties, we do know that Gardel had a remarkable voice that allowed him to break out of the arrabal and establish an international career. He moved in elite social circles, befriending movie stars and appearing in motion pictures himself. Above all, Gardel convinced rioplatense immigrants that they too could achieve great success. The nation mourned Gardel when he died tragically in a plane crash over Medellín, Colombia, at the height of his career. His lifestyle and music brought legitimacy to the genre worldwide.

Just as the arrabal brought gauchos and immigrants together, Gardel's tangos combined rural and urban elements. Gardel himself personified this cultural fusion. In early performances, he dressed in gaucho clothing and sang to the accompaniment of the guitar. His songs combined the polished *Guardia nueva* style with signature features of traditional criollo music (including rubato, descending melodies, and a dramatic style of singing that verged on speech). Like the rioplatense milongas, Gardel's tangos favored emotional extremes. The text of "Por una cabeza" unfolds in fatalistic terms, as the singer compares his thrilling but destructive love affair to a poorly timed horse race, in which he loses everything just barely "By a Head."

LISTENING guide 7.4

◎ Gardel: "Por una cabeza" (By a Head)

Composer: Carlos Gardel

Lyricist: Alfredo Le Pera

Date of composition: 1935

Performer/instruments: Gardel (vocalist), strings, piano, two bandoneones, and backup singers

Date of recording: 1935

Genre: tango

Form: introduction **ABAB**

Tempo/meter: moderate simple quadruple

What to Listen for:

- Contrast between **A** and **B** sections
- Speech-like **A** section in a major key with rubato
- Lyric **B** section in a minor key with descending melodies
- Marcato quadruple rhythms in the orchestra
- Similarity of the vocal style to Zitarrosa's milonga

Time	Text	Translation*	Description
0:00			**Introduction** Based on **B**
0:15	Por una cabeza de un noble potrillo que justo en la raya afloja al llegar y que al regresar parece decir: no olvidés, hermano, vos sabés, no hay que jugar.	By a head, As when a noble racehorse Slackens off Just short of the finish line, And on the ride back Seems to be saying: "Remember, brother, You know you shouldn't gamble."	**A** **Stanza 1;** Speech-like; major key; rubato (music lingers on the opening syllables); marcato rhythms

(continued)

Time	Text	Translation*	Description
0:49	Por una cabeza, metejón de un día de aquella coqueta y risueña mujer, que al jurar sonriendo el amor que está mintiendo, quema en una hoguera todo mi querer.	By a head, My one-day infatuation With that flirtatious, Dazzling woman, Who lies about the love That she's promised with a smile, Then incinerates All the love I have to give.	**Stanza 2**
0:49	Por una cabeza todas las locuras, Su boca que besa borra la tristeza, calma la amargura….	By a head All the craziness, And her kisses That banish my sadness And ease my misery….	**B** **Stanza 3**; Lyrical; minor key; background vocals; soaring strings
1:04	Por una cabeza si ella me olvida qué importa perderme, mil veces la vida para qué vivir.	By a head, If she leaves me What would it matter To lose my life a thousand times over, Why go on living?	**Stanza 4**
1:20	Cuántos desengaños, por una cabeza….	So many sad affairs Lost by a head….	**A** **Stanzas 5–6**; Speech- like style continues
1:53			**B** Stanzas 3 and 4 repeat

*English Translation: Tony Beckwith

explore

To learn more about
Guardia nueva
orchestras, listen to De
Caro's "Boedo" (after
a *barrio* in Buenos
Aires), Pugliese's
onomatopoeic "La
Yumba," and Troilo's
"Sur" (South).

New forms of dance music also developed during the *Guardia nueva* period. Standard tango orchestras now used two violins, two bandoneones, piano, and bass. The bandleader Julio de Caro (1899–1980) applied an expressive rubato style known as *arrastre* (to drag) that delayed the arrival of the first beat. De Caro's orchestras featured virtuosic solos, bridges, and fills, along with percussive instrumental effects. Later bandleaders, such as Osvaldo Pugliese (1905–1995), Aníbal Troilo (1914–1975), and Horacio Salgán (b. 1916), elaborated upon this "Decareano" style of playing by intensifying the sense of *arrastre* and by enhancing the music with their own rhythmic and technical innovations.

By 1955, the genre entered into a third phase, *Nuevo tango* (New Tango), which emphasized experimental extremes. The leader of this movement, Ástor Piazzolla (1921–1992), mastered the styles of both tango and classical music. He took composition lessons from

Alberto Ginastera, the most influential Argentine classical musician of his day, and he studied in Paris with Nadia Boulanger, a remarkable teacher of students such as Aaron Copland. Coming from this background, Piazzolla produced a large number of classical works, including the chamber opera, *María de Buenos Aires* and the twelve-minute virtuoso showpiece, *Le Grand Tango*, which he dedicated to concert cellist Mstislav Rostropovich. Yet, ultimately Piazzolla found his original voice by integrating Argentine popular idioms with the intellectual structures of classical music. Through this synthesis, his music exemplified a level of technical sophistication that no tango musician before him had achieved.

FIGURE 7.11 Ástor Piazzolla plays bandoneón at the Olympia Music Hall in Paris, 1974

With his Octeto Buenos Aires (1955–1957) and Quinteto Nuevo Tango (1960–1971), Piazzolla rejected established tango traditions. His experimental approach provoked controversy, and his confrontational attitude only made matters worse. He once remarked that Matos Rodríguez's famous "La cumparsita" was "the worst of all tangos, the most dreadfully poor piece in the world" (although he still made multiple recordings of the piece). Piazzolla's performances of the standard tango repertoire alienated traditional fans. His introduction of the electric guitar scandalized the musical establishment because previous ensembles had only used acoustic instruments. His complex rhythms caused audiences to complain that they could no longer dance to his music, which was his deliberate intent. Harmonically, Piazzolla's use of harsh sounds, known as **dissonances**, pushed fans beyond their comfort zone, since they listened to the tango for enjoyment, not for a challenge to their ears. He further antagonized traditional listeners by eliminating the polished tango orchestra and emphasizing the strident sound of the bandoneón—an instrument that he played with an aggressive physicality that would soon become legendary.

La camorra I (Fight No. 1) is a remarkable composition that illustrates Piazzolla's experimental innovations (Listening Guide 7.5). This piece is scored for bandoneón, piano, violin, electric guitar, and bass—the composer's classic quintet that became the standard for new tango musicians. In the powerful rhythmic sections of *La Camorra I*, Piazzolla's syncopated patterns fall behind or get ahead of the main beats. These sections use prominent dissonances, even at the beginning of the piece, which is normally one of the most stable sections. Example 7.5 illustrates the opening piano part of *La camorra I*. The

EXAMPLE 7.5: Dissonant notes (ninths, flatted fifths, and elevenths) in Piazzolla's *La camorra I*

D minor: i   °6

ⓢ Piazzolla: *La camorra I*

Composer: Ástor Piazzolla

Date of composition: 1988

Performer/instruments: Ástor Piazzolla, bandoneón; Fernando Suárez Paz, violin; Pablo Ziegler, piano; Horacio Malvicino, Sr., electric guitar; Héctor Console, bass

Date of recording: 1989

Genre: tango

Form: sectional

Tempo/meter: moderate simple quadruple with rubato in the slow sections

What to Listen for:

- Alternation between fast rhythmic sections (with a clear beat) and slow nostalgic sections (with rubato)
- Complex dissonant polyphony
- Beginning of a three-voice fugue
- "The grunt"
- Improvised solos in the slow sections

Time	Description
0:00	**Fast rhythmic section** Full ensemble; dissonant chords
1:07	**Slow nostalgic section** Bandoneón and violin duet; improvisational style
3:00	**Fast rhythmic section including the opening of a three-part fugue** Full ensemble; fugue theme in the bandoneón (3:09), violin (3:26), and electric guitar (3:42); includes "the grunt" (4:22)
4:23	**New fast rhythmic theme, followed by transition** Full ensemble with güiro scrapes
4:40	**Slow nostalgic section** Bandoneón and violin duet joined by cello (5:07); improvisational style
5:46	**Fast rhythmic section** Full ensemble; rhythmically precise until bandoneón solo (6:16)
6:40	**Final rhythmic section** Repetition of eight-measure idea (6:40, 6:58) with variations

notes that are circled (E and G) represent dissonances that do not belong to the main chords of the piece.

Another daring feature is Piazzolla's use of polyphony (multiple independent musical lines). Previously, tangos used homophony (i.e., they were based on a simple melody and accompaniment, as in the *tango canción*). Yet, because Piazzolla studied classical music, he could write complex polyphonic textures. One of the most intricate types of polyphony he used was the fugue (literally "flight"). Fugues involve two or more independent lines based on the same theme that artfully imitate each other. *La camorra I* includes the opening of a three-part fugue in which the bandoneón (3:09), violin (3:26), and electric guitar (3:42) successively present versions of a shared musical idea. One final touch is Piazzolla's visceral grunt at 4:22. Before that time, no one had ever uttered such a guttural sound in a tango before, and his listeners were shocked beyond belief. Indeed, it is this gesture, along with many others, that demonstrate how far Piazzolla would push the limits of a genre that he deeply respected, yet forever changed.

explore

If you enjoyed *La camorra I*, you may also like Piazzolla's *Tres minutos con la realidad* (Three Minutes with Reality), *Adiós Nonino* (Farewell, Nonino), and *Balada para un loco* (Ballad for a Madman).

Contemporary Tango

Since the turn of the millennium, tourism has emerged as one of the most profitable Argentine industries. It has affected the cultural production of the tango, because one of the main tourist attractions in Buenos Aires is attending commercialized tango shows in local nightclubs. Promoted by large hotels, these shows represent a virtuosic but superficial image of the dance, which often appears combined with elements of Broadway musicals and Argentine folk genres. Nevertheless, the tourist boom has opened up new employment opportunities for performing musicians, some of whom may disagree about the way that tango is artistically represented, but who still reap sizeable profits from the tourist industry.

Tourism aside, the contemporary tango movement has entered into a new creative phase as younger musicians engage with innovative projects that renew classic tango styles, repertoires, and practices. Modern tango artists have sought to recuperate historical knowledge of the genre, which reached a low point during the seventies and eighties and, at one point, verged on extinction. Their reconstructions of the tango have allowed them to celebrate a specific local identity and resist subjugation to foreign-dominated popular musics. Some groups, such as the Orquesta Típica Fernández Fierro, have revived the golden-age orchestras in the style of Osvaldo Pugliese. Other ensembles, such as *34 Puñaladas* (34 Stabs) have updated the image of the Gardelian *tango canción*, incorporating old and new lunfardo lyrics and portraying themes of poverty, bitterness, and injustice that resonate with Argentine socioeconomic problems. Still other musicians, like Daniel Melingo, perform original compositions that combine tango elements with electronic instruments and sampling techniques, along with international rock styles and Latin American popular idioms. The creative possibilities for tango innovation seem limitless.

A leading contemporary tango musician is the pianist-composer Sonia Possetti (b. 1973), who studied with the golden-age bandleader Horacio Salgán. In 1998, Possetti formed a duo with her husband, the violinist Damián Bolotín. Four years later, she established a quintet (that has since expanded into a sextet with the unusual addition of a trombone). Possetti is fully aware of the political implications of creating and performing tango in a country controlled by globalized economic and cultural interests. On the stage of a 2004 Boston concert, the contemporary tango scholar Michael O'Brien heard her say: "Our music is what we do so that they cannot invade us," referring to the global music industry. Nevertheless, Possetti is receptive to the possibility of assimilating outside influences. In addition to standard percussion, she incorporates instruments such as the *djembe* (a large African hand drum), cymbals, bongo, and wood block. Her "Bullanguera" is based

LISTENING guide 7.6

⊚ Possetti: "Bullanguera" (Lively)

Composer: Sonia Possetti

Date of composition: 2003

Performers/instruments: Sonia Possetti, piano; Federico Pereiro, bandoneón; Damián Bolotin, violin; Adriana González, double bass; Fabián Keoroglanian, percussion

Date of recording: 2003

Genre: tango

Form: introduction **AB** Coda

Tempo/meter: rapid duple

What to Listen for:
- Milonga rhythm (first heard in the *djembe*)
- 3 + 2 clave
- Brief Piazzolla-style fugue
- "Blue notes" and jazz-like solos
- Sixteen-bar melodies in the **A** section

Time	Description
0:00	Piano solo
0:15	*Djembe* introduces the milonga rhythm; entire ensemble plays
0:30	**A theme (stanziac)** Violin and bandoneón

(continued)

Time	Description
0:45	Violin variation with blue notes
1:00	**Varied reprise of the introduction** New instrumentation and syncopated accompaniment
1:16	**Long varied reprise of the introduction** Piano solo based on the introduction with blue notes
1:38	**Varied reprise of the introduction** Ensemble plays syncopated variant of the introduction
1:53	**Transition to B**
2:17	**B theme** Percussion section; 3 + 2 clave rhythm; includes Piazzolla-style fugue with the theme in the violin (2:18), bandoneón (2:33), and piano and bass (2:48)
3:03	**Coda**

on a milonga rhythm (Example 7.4a) first sounded in the *djembe*. Later, she layers a salsa clave pattern in the percussion over the milonga foundation (2:17). Jazz techniques, such as the addition of "blue notes," improvised solos, and sixteen-bar progressions, add new dimensions to the piece. Taken as a whole, Possetti's creative conception remains true to the roots of the tango, yet engages with a sophisticated range of current popular musics.

Argentine Rock Nacional

Rock music began in Argentina during the 1950s and 1960s, as international popular styles spread through the mass media. Gradually, local songwriters created new forms of original music that incorporated Argentine characteristics. Beginning in the 1960s rock music engaged with national politics, as young people increasingly drew upon popular expressive forms to create a culture of resistance. The roots of this movement (1946–1955) date back to the charismatic leadership of Juan D. Perón and his wife "Evita," whose dynamic yet controversial political styles contributed to the crisis. The Peróns' policies of social justice for the poor provoked harsh criticisms among the upper and middle classes, who suffered in the resulting redistribution of power. The army, which alternately supported and conspired against Perón, staged a 1955 coup, shortly following Evita's death. From 1955 to 1973, the Argentine people endured instability in the extreme, with a fragmented electorate of more than 20 political parties and frequent military takeovers. Many believed that the only hope of stability would come with the reinstatement of Perón to power. The former leader returned from exile to assume the Argentine presidency in 1973. Yet, he died that same year, bequeathing a precarious political legacy to his inexperienced third wife, Isabel Perón, who lost control of the government in 1976 when the military removed her in a bloodless coup. What followed was one of the most infamous periods in Latin American history.

For the next eight years, during the *Guerra sucia* (Dirty War), the government arrested, tortured, and executed its opponents, causing thousands of innocent people to "disappear" (see In Depth 7.3). According to Pablo Vila, an Argentine sociologist specializing in music of the period, the regime leveled most of its violence against Argentine youth between the ages of 18 to 30, who represented more than two-thirds of the missing population. Some young people belonged to activist groups that the government wished to suppress. Yet, others were university students and members of the intelligentsia, whose only "crime" consisted of thinking critically, which the regime perceived as a threat. Terrified by daily disappearances of friends and classmates, young people gathered together to listen to music and allay their fears. They attended concerts in Luna Park, the largest stadium in Buenos Aires. They subscribed to underground magazines that voiced the words that they could not speak. To Argentine youth, *rock nacional* meant more than listening to a favorite singer or following a popular band—it had become a way of life.

The iconic Argentine group, Serú Girán, headed by the multitalented popular musician Charly García (b. 1951), defined the *rock nacional* movement during the Dirty War. The four members of the group came from eclectic musical backgrounds. García, who played keyboards and studied classical music, favored acoustic instruments. Guitarist David Lebón came from an electric rock and blues background. Pedro Aznar, the bass player, fused folk, rock, jazz, and tango styles together. Oscar Moro, the drummer, drew upon influences of the 1960s. As a group, Serú Girán defied classification. Yet, the musicians' eclecticism appealed to a broad fan base that might otherwise have disagreed about the ideal way to convey their youthful voice of resistance.

The 1979 LP titled *La grasa de las capitales* (The Grease of the Capitals) exemplifies Serú Girán's approach to the musical poetics of political engagement. The song "Los sobrevivientes" (The Survivors) expresses the alienation of Argentine youth, who will "never have roots" since they have no safe place to live. The last two lines of the poem refer to Christ's death in a metaphor that brings to mind the victims of the dictatorship. In the comforting instrumental music that follows, Serú Girán offers *rock nacional* listeners a sense of solace. By banding together in the memory of those who suffered a Christlike martyrdom, they can continue as the "survivors."

In Depth 7.3

The *Guerra sucia*

The *Guerra sucia* (Dirty War) began on March 24, 1976, when the ruling military junta imposed a state of martial law. Headed by Generals Videla, Viola, and Galtieri, the authorities used extreme terrorist tactics to silence their opponents. Today, the number of lives the government claimed is unclear. At least nine thousand deaths have been confirmed, and it is believed that the real number is much higher. Some human rights groups have estimated the total as high as thirty thousand.

In 1983, after the fall of the military dictatorship, the new Argentine president, Raúl Alfonsín, created a fact-finding commission to investigate human rights abuses and uncover the fate of the *desaparecidos* (missing persons). Headed by the influential Argentine writer, Ernesto Sábato, the commission produced a document titled *Nunca más* (Never More), which revealed some of the most atrocious human crimes conceivable. The commission discovered that the Argentine military had carried out a deliberate campaign of terror, with systematic rituals of kidnapping, torture, detention, and execution. Secret police abducted their victims at night, ransacking their homes and seizing them in front of their families. They took the captives to secret locations throughout the city, where they subjected them to extreme forms of torture. In one abhorrent practice, known as "submarine," they covered prisoners' heads with hoods and submerged them in water to the point

of unconsciousness. Psychological torture and sexual abuse ran rampant. Those prisoners who survived the ordeal were taken to detention centers where they endured substandard medical care and unhygienic conditions. The final step involved ritualized execution by death squads, drowning in the river, or burial in unmarked graves that the victims were forced to dig. This system of oppression, which controlled society through extreme terrorist tactics, stands as one the most notorious cases of human rights abuse in recent history.

Although few Argentines had the courage to resist, a group of courageous mothers who had lost their loved ones in the Dirty War held weekly Thursday vigils in the Plaza de Mayo. Their public protest called international attention to the plight of the *desaparicidos*. As tensions mounted, the military regime appealed to nationalist sentiments by invading the nearby Falkland Islands, which, since 1833, had fallen under the disputed territorial ownership of the British. This move resulted in a humiliating defeat, with a death toll of thousands of British and Argentine lives. After the fiasco, the military had no other choice than to agree to free elections. With the restoration of democracy under President Raúl Alfonsín (1983–1989), the Argentine people demanded justice. They established public tribunals that convicted Generals Videla, Viola, and Galtieri. Weekly vigils in the Plaza de Mayo continue to this day.

Because the musicians of Serú Girán lived in fear of government reprisals, they avoided delivering this message directly. Faced with threats of censorship, repression, and arrest, the group used lyrics with cryptic meanings that escaped the uninitiated, but that insiders to the movement could interpret as political critique. Like most *rock nacional* groups, Serú Girán employed long sections of instrumental music, since the dictatorship could not censor a song

EXAMPLE 7.6: Serú Girán, "Los sobrevivientes," opening vocal melody

Es-ta-mos cie-gos de ver____   can-sa-dos de tan-to an-dar____

without words. As you listen to "Los sobrevivientes" (The Survivors) in Listening Guide 7.7, imagine how Argentine university students—themselves the "survivors"—felt. Note the fragile effects of the opening A section, with its use of falsetto (high, male register) and its tentative melody that sweeps upward in the shape of a question (Example 7.6). Compare this sound to the instrumental return of A (2:07), set to a powerful electric guitar melody. The song progresses from weakness to strength as the musical protagonists—along with the real-life survivors—experience this transformative journey.

LISTENING guide 7.7

⊚ Serú Girán: "Los sobrevivientes" (The Survivors)

Composer/lyricist: Charly García

Date of composition: 1979

Performers/instruments: Charly García, keyboards; David Lebón, electric guitar; Pedro Aznar, electric bass; Oscar Moro, drums

Date of recording: 1992

Genre: *rock nacional*

Form: sectional

Tempo/meter: moderate quadruple

What to Listen for:
- Opening **A** section that matches the fragility of the poem with a hesitant melodic line, falsetto singing, and the use of a minor key
- Hymnlike **B** and **C** sections in major keys that evoke religious imagery
- Instrumental conclusion that features a powerful return of **A**, reinforced by electronics (with reverb)

Time	Text	Translation	Description
0:00			**Introduction** Piano
0:32	Estamos ciegos de ver, cansados de tanto andar, estamos hartos de huir en la ciudad. Nunca tendremos raíz, nunca tendremos hogar y sin embargo, ya ves, somos de acá.	We are blind from seeing, Weary from so much wandering, We are fed up with fleeing in the city. We'll never have roots, We'll never have a home And yet, as you can see, we are from here.	**A** Complex melody; weak upper range in falsetto; minor key

(continued)

Time	Text	Translation	Description
1:04	Vibramos como las campanas, como iglesias que se acercan desde el sur, como vestidos negros que se quieren desvestir. Yo siempre te he llevado bajo mi bufanda azul, por las calles como Cristo a la cruz.	We vibrate like the bells, Like churches that approach from the south, Like black dresses that want to undress. I have always carried you Under my blue scarf. Through the streets like Christ to the cross.	**B** Major key and bell-like effects evoke religious imagery; at 1:34 a single voice in the style of **A** references the Crucifixion
1:41			**C** Instrumental; hymnlike theme with a firm chordal structure, major key, and crescendo
2:07			**A′** Instrumental restatement of **A** with electric guitar, keyboard, and added reverb
2:38			**D** Free-form conclusion

*English Translation: Tony Beckwith

After 1983, with the return to Argentine democracy, *rock nacional* changed. As young people no longer united behind a common political cause of resistance, the movement grew fragmented. Some groups, such as Serú Girán, dissolved as individual members pursued solo careers. Meanwhile, new pop-rock bands used lighter, more-commercialized styles and took advantage of freer access to the mass media to promote their works to international audiences. One of the top Spanish-language bands of the eighties was Soda Stereo. This group's appealing mixture of pop, reggae, and new wave, combined with a polished marketing image, was widely imitated. Soda Stereo's *Signos* (Signs, 1986) was the first *rock nacional* album released on CD.

During the 1990s, as the Argentine economy deteriorated due to hyperinflation, unemployment, and devaluation of the national currency, young people grew increasingly resentful. Working-class Argentines, who were most strongly affected, responded with music that reflected life on the margins and that glorified crime, gangs, drugs, and violence. Their music was known as *rock chabón* (after the Argentine slang for "dude"). Groups like Almafuerte, Dos Minutos, and Attaque 77 used punk rock and heavy metal to convey their confrontational positions. At the same time, *rock chabón* musicians aligned with right-wing ideologies, performing with Argentine flags as backdrops and incorporating native traditions drawn from tango and folklore. By the late 1990s, as the economy deteriorated, a new type of music called *cumbia villera* (cumbia from the ghetto) took hold in the same marginalized sectors. It combined images associated with gangsta rap and rhythms of the Colombian cumbia, which had circulated widely throughout Latin America. The titles of the songs—"Gatillo fácil" (Quick Trigger), "La canción del yuta" (Cops' Song), "Entre cuatro paredes" (Inside Four Walls), and "Tumberos" (Prisoners)—referred to themes of urban street life, as did the names of the groups themselves: Los pibes chorros (The Thieving Kids), El punga (The Pickpocket), and Yerba Brava (referencing marijuana). Although *cumbia villera* may not appeal to everyone, this genre figured as one of the most popular expressive forms to capture Argentine listeners during the early twenty-first century.

Another popular genre associated with working-class Argentines is *cuarteto*, which has been studied in depth by the ethnomusicologist Jane Florine. *Cuarteto* first developed in Córdoba among uprooted immigrants who had no other common music. At first, this style consisted of arrangements of international dance genres, such as fox-trots, *pasodobles*, *rancheras*, *tarantellas*, and waltzes that were performed by small economical ensembles. *Cuarteto* used duple meter with a characteristic bass line that emphasized tonic and dominant chords on strong beats. Later, it maintained this pattern but incorporated larger ensembles, faster tempos, electronic instruments, and Afro-Caribbean music features. Although initially viewed as lowbrow, *cuarteto* has since acquired a type of reverse snob appeal that draws significant numbers of fans from the upper and middle classes.

Popular Music in Uruguay and Paraguay

In Uruguay, the development of popular music closely paralleled that of Argentina. The tango arose on both sides of the Río de la Plata, where it experienced an equally vital existence. In 2009, UNESCO acknowledged the binational contribution to the genre by declaring the tango an Intangible Cultural Heritage of both countries. Like Argentina, Uruguay suffered a neofascist military coup (1973–1985), preceded by an economic crisis and destabilization of the political system. The military seized control of the government and imposed an authoritarian regime that arrested, tortured, and killed thousands of people. Rigid artistic censorship and repression forced popular musicians into exile and their works underground. Uruguayans endured this terror by preserving their collective cultural memories and reviving an acoustic song tradition known as *canto popular* (popular song). The Montevidean singer-songwriter and leader of the movement, Daniel Viglietti (b. 1939), faced imprisonment and exile before returning to his homeland toward the end of the dictatorship. After the restoration of democracy, Uruguayan musicians cultivated eclectic styles. During the late 1980s, *rock de arrabal* (similar to *rock chabón*), appealed to unemployed youth with its aggressive combination of punk and heavy metal. In the 1990s, young Uruguayans who had spent much of their childhood abroad came home to form groups that reflected their bicultural experiences. One band, *Peyote Asesino* (named after the Mexican comic strip character), juxtaposed elements of hip-hop and hard rock; another, La Vela Puerca (The Pig-Like Marijuana Joint), mixed ska, funk, rap, and punk. Both groups signed deals with major record labels, through which they engaged with transnational music markets.

FIGURE 7.12 La Vela Puerca performing at Club Ciudad, Buenos Aires, 2009

In Paraguay, considerable continuity exists between traditional and popular musics. Much of the popular music repertoire is based on contemporary updates of national dances such as the *polca paraguaya*. For almost 35 years (1954–1989), the Paraguayan people suffered under a repressive military regime. General Alfredo Stroessner maintained rigid control over the country and suppressed all political opposition. He treated indigenous groups inhumanely and was charged with frequent human rights violations. During the 1970s, rock music arose as a voice of social and political resistance. Yet, the local music scene developed slowly because Paraguayan bands lacked the resources to record their music and communicate with fans. The turning point came in 1983, when the Pro Rock Ensamble issued its first LP of *rock nacional paraguayo*, marking the official birth of the movement. Since the fall of Stroessner's regime, rock music has flourished free of censorship and has achieved a wider distribution through the popular media. Today, eclectic mixtures of hybrid styles attract Paraguayan youth and play a vital role in social settings.

As this chapter has shown, strong similarities connect the popular expressive forms of the rioplatense region. These connections date back to the tango, which initially pursued a parallel course on both sides of the Río de la Plata. Another shared reality stems from the devastating military dictatorships that took hold throughout the region. In Argentina, Uruguay, and

Paraguay, popular music served as a powerful weapon in the struggle against political injustice and oppression. After the return to democracy, popular musics of these three nations experienced greater freedom because of the relaxation of censorship regulations. Rock bands openly distributed their works to the public through the mass media. Once rioplatense musicians entered into the global music marketplace, they came under its influences. Since the 1990s, popular groups have absorbed and combined international styles in a wide array of hybrid musical genres. At the same time, the constant presence of imported music has stimulated local musicians to redefine their identity as they seek recognition within the powerful economic space of transnational music markets.

Classical Music

Argentina in the Nineteenth Century

The rioplatense region has richly contributed to the tradition of Latin American classical music. Initially, this activity centered around the city of Buenos Aires, whose citizens embraced fashionable genres such as zarzuelas (operettas), operas, piano pieces, guitar music, and songs. Beginning around 1880, a generation of professionally trained musicians delved deeply into their roots, as the musicians sought to convey their identity. These composers cultivated the figure of the gaucho, whom they upheld as a symbol of the nation. Countries throughout the world all acknowledge their own types of horsemen, whether the *charro* from Mexico or the cowboy from the United States. During a period when Argentine composers sought recognition for their music abroad, the gaucho established their identity within an international community of nations.

Two early composers who based their music on the gaucho were Alberto Williams (1862–1952) and Julián Aguirre (1868–1924). Both figures studied in Europe, where they came under the spell of **musical nationalism**, a movement that encouraged composers to draw upon their own cultural resources as a source of creative inspiration. Williams's compositions closely resembled European Romantic models, but incorporated themes based on traditional Argentine genres. His talented colleague, Julián Aguirre, came from Basque roots and received his musical training in Spain. Aguirre's works combined a delicate approach that resembled the piano music of Chopin, with an intuitive empathy for criollo rhythms and harmonies. His songs and piano pieces, such as the *Huella* and *Gato* (named after traditional Argentine genres), set the standard for many years.

explore

A representative sampling of Aguirre's music can be found on the mp3 collection *Julián Aguirre y Carlos López Buchardo* performed by pianist Emilio de la Peña.

Opera in Buenos Aires

Argentina has long prided itself on its splendid operatic productions—an achievement that dates back to the population of Italian immigrants who settled in the rioplatense region. Because opera originally had its home in Italy and has flourished there ever since, the Italo-Argentine population promoted this tradition as a symbol of its identity. Opera also attracted enthusiastic support from the criollo elite, which amassed enviable fortunes in the agricultural and livestock industries and

FIGURE 7.13 Interior of the Teatro Colón

had ample time to devote to leisure activities. Theaters and opera houses sprang up all over Buenos Aires; each one had its own singers, repertoire, and concert season.

The leading opera house of Buenos Aires is the Teatro Colón. When the building first opened in 1857, it was a state-of-the-art theater. The original building closed in 1888, in order to build an even more lavish theater, which opened 20 years later in a new location. Typical of turn-of-the-century theaters, the new Colón blended a variety of influences, including "general characteristics of the Italian Renaissance, solid German construction, and French ornamental grace and variety," according to Víctor Meano, one of its chief architects. The Colón achieved international acclaim for its opulent physical surroundings, stellar productions, and faultless acoustics. Its performers have included the singer Enrico Caruso and the conductor Arturo Toscanini, along with Luciano Pavarotti, Plácido Domingo, and José Carreras ("The Three Tenors"). Clearly, the Colón was and is one of the great opera houses of the world.

The Teatro Colón emphasizes international opera, especially the standard Italian repertoire. However, since the new theater opened in 1908, it has produced a number of important national operas. Of these, Boero's *El matrero* (The Gaucho Bandit, 1929) is regarded as the consummate work of the Argentine lyric stage. Its story centers on the death of an idealistic *payador*, whose failure to integrate into Argentine society resonated with contemporary audiences, who experienced some of the same social changes.

The Renovation Movement

In 1929, a group of young composers banded together to found the **Grupo Renovación** (Renovation Group), through which they aimed to modernize

Argentine music. Three key members of the group included: Juan José Castro (1895–1968), Juan Carlos Paz (1897–1972), and Luis Gianneo (1897–1968). Together, they studied the latest international trends and applied them to Argentine music. They championed dissonant atonal music (which lacked a tonality or key, see Appendix) along with serialism (which organized music around a prearranged series of 12 chromatic tones encompassing the black and white notes of the piano). They employed neoclassicism, reviving traditional forms of the past, but viewed from a contemporary perspective. These developments laid the foundation for the music of Alberto Ginastera—the leading composer of the next generation and one of the most original creative voices of South America.

Alberto Ginastera: South American Musical Spokesman

Alberto Ginastera (1916–1983) was born in Buenos Aires into a family of Italian and Catalan descent. After graduating from the National Conservatory, he established his reputation as a brilliant young composer with works like *Estancia* (The Ranch, 1941). Following a trip to the United States on a Guggenheim Fellowship (1945–1947), where he came into contact with the North American composer, Aaron Copland, Ginastera returned to Argentina. There he founded and directed three visionary music schools and produced some of his major compositions. Of these, his First Piano Sonata

FIGURE 7.14 Alberto Ginastera, 1968

(1952) stands as one of the most popular works of the contemporary piano literature. Ginastera is also known for his string quartets, orchestral music, operas, and cello repertoire. His second opera, *Bomarzo* (1966–1967), revolves around themes of torture, abuse, obsession, homosexuality, and sexual impotence. The Argentine reaction to this work provoked a scandal when the right-wing Onganía government banned it from the Teatro Colón despite its triumphant premiere in Washington, D.C., months earlier. By 1971, a combination of personal and professional circumstances caused Ginastera to make his home in Geneva, Switzerland. Ten years later, he received a prestigious award from UNESCO in honor of his lifetime of creative achievement.

Ginastera's music reveals an imaginative synthesis of Argentine and international techniques. Early in his career, the composer conveyed his national identity through his memorable representations of the gaucho. He described how his trips to the pampas evoked feelings in him that were "now joyful, now melancholy, some full of euphoria, and others replete with a profound tranquility, produced by its limitless immensity and by the transformation that the countryside undergoes in the course of the day." Out of these sentiments emerged his ballet *Estancia*.

To convey his identification with the pampas, Ginastera employed a wide range of expressive resources. He included sung and spoken lyrics from the national epic poem *Martín Fierro*. In addition, he represented the gaucho malambo in a contemporary classical context. Although a more traditional

⊚ Ginastera: "La doma" (Horsebreaking), from *Estancia*

Composer: Alberto Ginastera

Date of composition: 1941

Performers/instruments: London Symphony Orchestra; Gisèle Ben-Dor, conductor

Date of recording: 2006

Genre: malambo

Form: Introduction **AA'** Coda

Tempo/meter: rapid simple triple and compound duple with syncopation and hemiola

What to Listen for:

- Multiple bass ostinatos, beginning with the six-beat pattern at 0:07
- New melodies layered above the ostinatos
- Large contemporary orchestra, with full brass and percussion
- **AA'** form (with intro and coda)

Time	Description
0:00	**Introduction**
0:07	**A** **First Ostinato:** Six complete statements of a six-beat pattern in the bass
0:21	**Second Ostinato:** Brass melody above the ostinato
0:28	**Third Ostinato:** New chordal ostinato with a melody in thirds above it
0:37	Several short ideas in irregular rhythms
1:05	**A'** **First Ostinato: A** varied with an expanded orchestration featuring timpani
1:19	**Second Ostinato:** Return of the brass melody above the ostinato
1:26	**Third Ostinato**
1:34	**Coda** Elaborates material heard at 0:37 combined with a new idea featuring hemiola
1:50	Final statement recalling the introduction

composer might have imitated the folk genre exactly, what mattered most to Ginastera was the rough and unpolished quality of the dance. He used dissonant contemporary chords to bring out the raw athleticism of the music. His tempos moved in dizzying speeds that verged on spinning out of control. His orchestration emphasized brass and percussion instruments, which had no relation to original gaucho music. Nonetheless, the strong associations of these instruments with military bands evoked the masculine quality the composer ascribed to the dance. "La doma," one of several malambos from *Estancia*, exemplifies Ginastera's imaginative representation of the gaucho.

After *Estancia*, Ginastera changed artistic directions. He avoided overt references to Argentine folklore, preferring to evoke a national character in an atmosphere "populated by symbols." In his works of the late 1940s and 1950s, the composer demonstrated his mastery of classical forms and techniques. The opening movement of his First Piano Sonata (1952) uses a traditional sonata form with two contrasting themes.

The sonata begins with a percussive theme in the low-middle range of the piano that recalls Argentine criollo music with its doublings in thirds. Yet, because Ginastera employs different doubled thirds in the melody and the harmony, his music is polytonal (a contemporary style of music using more than one key at once). The second theme sounds in the high register and contrasts with the opening idea (Example 7.7). This melody uses four notes of the Andean pentatonic scale, B–D–E–F♯, set to modern harmonies. Throughout the passage, Ginastera alternates § and ⅝ time signatures, which gives the piece its modern rhythmic edge.

Structurally, the movement follows a three-part **sonata form**. Formally, it uses balanced classical proportions. After the **exposition**, which presents the two main themes in an opening statement, Ginastera embarks on the **development**, which manipulates the two ideas. Toward the end of the piece, the opening material returns in the **recapitulation**. Taken as

EXAMPLE 7.7: Ginastera, First Piano Sonata, first movement, mm. 52–55

a whole, the jagged rhythms and modern harmonies of Ginastera's First Piano Sonata create a spontaneous sense of freedom. Yet, the structure of the work is meticulously planned, achieving that perfect balance between form and content to which the composer aspired.

Ginastera: First Piano Sonata, first movement

Composer: Alberto Ginastera
Date of composition: 1952
Performer/instrument: Barbara Nissman, piano
Date of recording: 2001
Genre: piano sonata
Form: sonata form
Tempo/meter: rapid with changing meters

What to Listen for:
- Exposition, development, and recapitulation of the sonata form
- Polytonal first theme with doubled thirds in the low-middle register
- Pentatonic second theme in the upper register
- Fusion of Argentine elements with contemporary classical techniques

Time	Description
0:00	**Exposition** Presentation of the main themes **First theme** Loud, rhythmic, and irregular; favors the low-middle register; uses polytonal doublings in thirds
0:37	**Bridge** Transitions to the second theme
1:02	**Second theme** Soft and lyrical; favors the upper piano register; uses a pentatonic melody with contemporary harmonies
1:16	**Development** Elaborates the main themes **First part** Develops the second theme in new keys
1:31	**Second part** Uses ideas from the bridge and first theme
1:51	**Third part** Features syncopated polytonal chords
2:03	**Fourth part** Presents the second theme in a major key and transitions to the recapitulation

(continued)

Time	Description
2:32	**Recapitulation** Restates the main themes **First theme**
3:09	**Bridge**
3:30	**Second theme** Uses thick chords and forceful dynamics
3:43	**Coda** Music intensifies and ends powerfully

Argentina: The Last 50 Years

Beginning in the 1960s, Ginastera forged experimental paths with his educational innovations. In 1962, he founded and directed the Latin American Center for Advanced Musical Studies at the Instituto Torcuato di Tella, which was a state-of-the art institution that trained new generations of Latin American musicians. Under Ginastera's leadership, the center arose as the model for new music in Latin America. It awarded two-year scholarships to promising young composers, who studied with specialists in avant-garde music. The center boasted an electronic music studio—a costly (and therefore rare) institution during the 1960s in Latin America. Although in 1971 the center closed its doors, it offered a remarkably high level of contemporary music instruction during its brief but influential existence.

Since that time, avant-garde music has flourished in Argentina. A leading composer is Gerardo Gandini (b. 1936), a brilliant piano virtuoso who studied with Ginastera and performed new tango with Piazzolla. Another major figure is Francisco Kröpfl (b. 1931), who founded the first permanent Latin American electronic music studio at the University of Buenos Aires. Marta Lambertini (b. 1937) is a prolific composer with an inclination toward stage music. One of her renowned works is the chamber opera, *Hildegard* (2002), which pays tribute to women composers whose voices were historically suppressed. Alicia Terzián (b. 1934) spends much of her time in Europe. She is one of the earliest Argentine musicians to use microtones (i.e., intervals smaller than the distance between the notes of the chromatic scale). Terzián directs an internationally recognized performance group that is dedicated to contemporary Latin American music.

Not all composers have pursued experimental paths. Some have written in a more conventional style that is accessible to concert audiences.

Carlos Guastavino (1912–2000) is known for composing over two hundred songs. Some of his vocal collections, such as *Pájaros* (Birds) and *Flores argentinas* (Argentine Flowers), evoke the Argentine landscape, while others, such as *Doce canciones populares* (Twelve Popular Songs) draw upon criollo influences. Guastavino studied classical music, but also came under the spell of folk artists such as Yupanqui. His music blends classical and vernacular idioms, causing doctrinaire members of the Argentine musical establishment to reject his works completely. Nevertheless, audiences have consistently warmed to Guastavino's lyric melodies and expressive poetic settings. Over time, the number of his followers can only increase.

explore

To learn more about Guastavino, listen to two of his most popular songs, "Se equivocó la paloma" (The Dove Was Deceived) and "La rosa y el sauce" (The Rose and the Willow).

Classical Music in Uruguay

Uruguay developed an important postcolonial tradition of classical music. As in Argentina, a sweeping Italian immigration movement resulted in an enthusiasm for opera. The 1856 inauguration of the Teatro Solís, which opened one year before the Teatro Colón, marked a key event in Uruguayan music history. Like the Colón, the Solís boasted brilliant performances and fostered the creation of native opera.

Nationalism played a leading role in twentieth-century Uruguayan music. Like Argentina, Uruguay aimed to establish a distinctive identity in response to immigration. Yet, because Uruguay came under the spell of Spain, Portugal, Brazil, and Argentina at different points in its history, composers had a wider spectrum of sources to draw upon as inspiration for their works. These materials primarily centered on the gaucho and the pampas, as in Eduardo Fabini's *Campo* (Countryside, 1922), but could also include elements of Brazilian music and Afro-Uruguayan candombe. Some composers cultivated avant-garde approaches; one such composer was Carmen Barradas (1888–1963), who was known for her early experiments with alternative ways of notating music. Héctor Tosar (1923–2002) was a talented composer who cultivated classical forms and received acclaim for his music abroad. León Biriotti (b. 1929), Antonio Mastrogiovanni (b. 1936), Coriún Aharonián (b. 1940), José Serebrier (b. 1938), and Sergio Cervetti (b. 1940) represent more recent Uruguayan musical currents.

Agustín Barrios Mangoré

In Paraguay, the best-known classical musician was Agustín Pío Barrios (1885–1944), also known under the stage name, Agustín Barrios Mangoré. Barrios was a guitar prodigy who concertized abroad and resided for years outside his native country. He composed hundreds of guitar showpieces that reflect the diverse Latin American countries where he lived. In addition to Paraguayan sources, Barrios's music is modeled on the Brazilian choro, Argentine *zamba*, rioplatense tango, as well as on European dances. Another major influence was the music of Johann Sebastian Bach, whose compositions were well known to Latin American guitarists through popular transcriptions and arrangements.

La catedral (Listening Guide 7.10) is one of Barrios's most celebrated compositions and a staple of the guitar literature. The composer is said to have received his inspiration for the work after hearing a performance of Bach's organ music at the San José Cathedral in Montevideo. *La catedral*

LISTENING guide 7.10

⊚ Barrios: *La catedral* (The Cathedral)

Composer: Agustín Pío Barrios

Date of composition: 1938

Performer/instrument: John Williams, guitar

Date of recording: 1995

Form: I. Prelude; II. Chorale, III. Rondo (**AABCAB'AB** coda)

Tempo/meter: I: moderate simple duple; II: slow simple quadruple; III: fast simple triple

What to Listen for:

- Differentiated tempo, form, and character of each movement
- Broken chords and improvisational style in the first movement
- Block chords, contrasting themes, and a **cadenza** (virtuosic solo passage) in the second movement
- Rondo form (**AABCAB'AB** coda) in the third movement

Time	Description
0:00	**I. Preludio saudade (prelude)** Broken chords underneath an expressive melody
2:21	**II. Andante religioso (chorale)** Block chords **First theme** Presented in upper (2:21) and lower (2:39) registers
3:01	**Second theme** Shares the marchlike character of the first theme
3:38	**Cadenza**
3:43	**Coda** Marchlike rhythm returns

(continued)

Time	Description
4:06	**III. Allegro (rondo)** **A: main theme** Broken chords
4:21	**A: (repeated)**
4:35	**B: first contrasting theme** Scales, broken chords
4:51	**C: second contrasting theme** Melody in the lower register
5:16	**A**
5:30	**B': with development**
6:08	**A**
6:22	**B**
6:33	**Coda** **B:** extended; soft chords at the end

consists of three movements. The first is a **prelude**, an introductory piece in an improvisatory style. The second uses block chords that suggest the sound of a **chorale** (hymn melody). The third is a virtuosic tour-de-force that recalls Bach's keyboard toccatas. It uses a rondo form, based on a memorable theme (A) that alternates with contrasting musical sections (B, C).

 **explore**

To explore one of Barrios's compositions based on folk themes, listen to his *Danza paraguaya* (Paraguayan Dance).

Conclusion

The end of this musical tour through the rioplatense region is at hand. Our time there has been all too short, especially when considering the large geographical scope of the area and all it has to offer. This brief survey has emphasized certain core themes: the centrality of the guitar, the influence of immigration, the importance of the pampas, the significance of the tango, the interrelationship between politics and popular musics, the globalization of local repertoires, and the connections between nation-building and contemporary classical music. Yet, if rioplatense music shares so many common features, why are the pieces all so different? And how can such diverse meanings be ascribed to them? The answer resides in the cultural plurality of the region, which remains one of its defining features. As you continue to explore the musics of Latin America, it is important to remember that the concept of diversity applies not only to the specificity of individual regions, but also to the wealth of musics within them.

KEY TERMS

arrabal	dissonances	pampas
bandoneón	exposition	payada
bombo	gaucho	prelude
cadenza	Grupo renovación	recapitulation
candombe	Guaraní	rioplatense
chacarera	littoral	sonata form
chamamé	lunfardo	tamboril
chorale	malambo	tango
compadrito	milonga	tritonic
criollo	musical nationalism	zapateo
development	neoclassicism	

FURTHER READING

Collier, Simon. ¡Tango! The Dance, the Song, the Story. New York: Thames and Hudson, 1995.

Florine, Jane L. Cuarteto Music and Dancing from Argentina: In Search of the Tunga-Tunga in Córdoba. Gainesville: University Press of Florida, 2001.

Gorín, Natalio. Astor Piazzolla: A Memoir. Translated, annotated, and expanded by Fernando González. Portland, OR: Amadeus, 2001.

Ruiz, Irma. "Musical Culture of Indigenous Societies in Argentina." In Music in Latin America and the Caribbean: An Encyclopedic History, edited by Malena Kuss, vol. 1, 163–80. Austin: University of Texas Press, 2004.

Schwartz-Kates, Deborah. "The Popularized Gaucho Image as a Source of Argentine Classical Music, 1880–1920. In From Tejano to Tango: Latin American Popular Music, edited by Walter Aaron Clark, 3–24. New York: Routledge, 2002.

Trigo, Abril. "The Politics and Anti-Politics of Uruguayan Rock." In *Rockin' las Américas: The Global Politics of Rock in Latin/o America*, edited by Deborah Pacini-Hernández, Héctor Férnández L'Hoeste, and Eric Zolov, 115–141. Pittsburgh: University of Pittsburgh Press, 2004.

Vila, Pablo. "Argentina's *rock nacional*: The Struggle for Meaning." *Latin American Music Review* 10, no. 1 (Spring–Summer 1989): 1–28.

_____. "*Rock nacional* and Dictatorship in Argentina." *Popular Music* 6, no. 2 (May 1987): 129–48.

FURTHER VIEWING

Afro-Uruguayan Rhythms: Candombe. Surmenages, 2006.

Argentina: Chamamé crudo. Films Media Group, 2007.

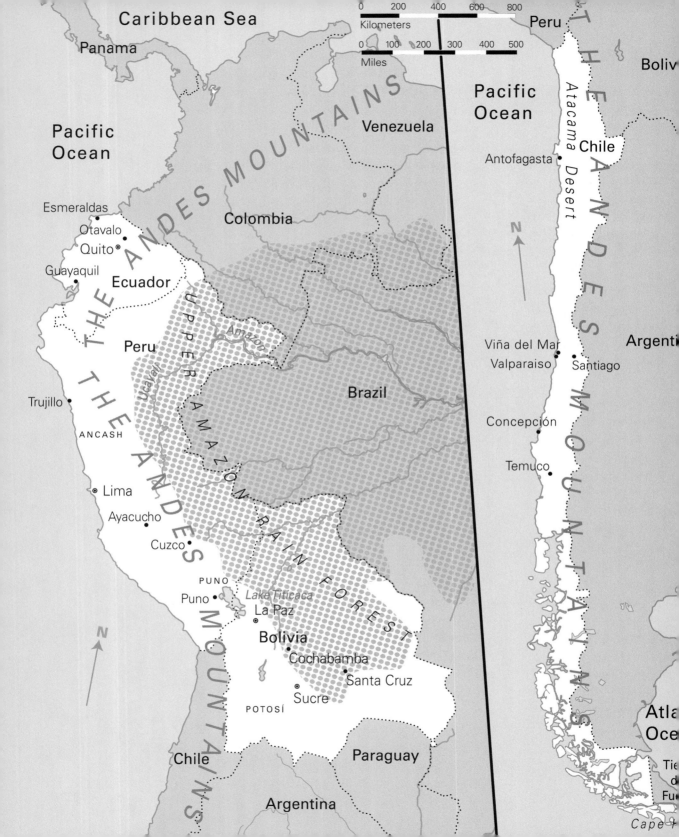

8

Peru and the Andes

JONATHAN RITTER

Introduction

In the early twenty-first century, one may hear something called "Andean music" nearly anywhere in the world. For decades, musicians playing stylized versions of indigenous Andean music have populated the subway stops and festival stages of major cities throughout Europe, Asia, and the Americas. Instruments once tied to distinct indigenous communities and seasonal practices in the Andes—such as panpipes or the **charango**, a small stringed instrument similar to a tiny guitar—can now be heard on Hollywood movie sound tracks, sampled into popular rock and rap hits, and found for sale at import shops and online music stores in the United States. More often than not, such music is accompanied by images of llamas and towering mountains, or the Inca ruins at Machu Picchu, linking ideas about Andean music with rural indigenous lifeways and the ancient past in the global imagination.

This sort of music represents only a small and relatively recent part of the extraordinary musical and cultural diversity of the Andean region. For nearly five centuries, the Andes have been a site of significant cultural mixing between indigenous, Spanish, and African peoples. This mixture, or mestizaje, however, is distinctive from that of many other areas in Latin America, due in part to the enduring and vibrant legacy of the region's indigenous heritage. **Quechua-** and **Aymara**-speaking peoples, two of the largest indigenous linguistic groups in Latin America, have constituted an outright majority of the population in the countries of Ecuador, Peru, and Bolivia throughout much of their history, and more than ten million people continue to speak these languages

◄ **FIGURE 8.1** Map of the Andes

325

on a daily basis. To the east, in the upper reaches of the Amazon basin, and farther south in the Chilean Andes, dozens of other distinct indigenous groups preserve their own languages and cultures. These groups have rarely held significant political or economic power in the region since the Spanish conquest, but their large numbers have nonetheless made them a dominant flavor in the cultural stew of Andean societies.

Urbanization, emigration, and the transnational media also play an important role in the formation of contemporary Andean musical cultures. The last 50 years have witnessed a tremendous demographic shift as people in rural areas have left their villages and resettled in larger cities in search of work and opportunity. A majority of the Andean population today is thus more likely to live within sight of a skyscraper than a snow-capped peak—or, in some places, both simultaneously. Whether urban or rural, most residents of the Andes now dress in Western clothing, watch television, and listen to the radio, and increasing numbers of them use the Internet for communication and commerce. Not surprisingly, these developments have further diversified musical practices. Young people especially find new ways of expressing their identities, fusing indigenous, mestizo, and Afro-descendant traditions with rock, rap, and other Latin American popular musics, even as those traditional forms continue to be valued and performed on their own. Indeed, one of the striking features of musical traditions in the Andes is that nothing ever seems to be abandoned completely; newer forms exist alongside older ones, all changing and evolving together, in a process of continual layering.

The very diversity of peoples and cultures in the Andes makes defining the region, musically or otherwise, difficult. Geography has played an important role in creating this diversity. The Andes Mountains, with their endless deep valleys, high plateaus, and snow-capped peaks and volcanoes, stretching for thousands of miles along the western edge of South America, constitute an imposing barrier to the movement of people and goods, and many cultural microregions have consequently emerged within this rugged landscape. On the Andes's northeastern flanks lie the equally forbidding rainforests of the Amazon basin, while to the west, the mountains descend to a narrow strip of coastal land along the Pacific Ocean, marked by dense vegetation and rain forest in the north (contemporary Ecuador and Colombia) and stark desert in the south (Peru and northern Chile). This coastal region is where many of the largest cities are located, and in Peru, it is now home to a majority of the population.

A Brief History

Numerous civilizations have united broad stretches of the Andean region over the last two thousand years. Of all of the empires to emerge prior to the arrival of the Spanish, however, none compared in size or power to the

Incas. Centered in Cuzco, the Incas grew from a small regional state in the fourteenth century to a massive empire a century later, dominating an area that stretched from northern Ecuador to central Chile. Known in Quechua as Tawantinsuyo ("Four *Suyos*," representing the quartal division of the empire), the rapid expansion of the empire was facilitated by an innovative blend of military ruthlessness and cultural flexibility. Although the Incas forcibly resettled those who resisted their control, they also demonstrated remarkable tolerance to certain cultural and religious differences among their subjects. Consequently, though Quechua was imposed as the official language of the realm, musical practices varied widely, which helps to explain some of the continued musical diversity found in the region.

The arrival in 1532 of Francisco Pizarro and his *conquistadores* to the shores of Peru initiated a slow transition away from indigenous rule in the Andes. Aided by lingering resentment of Inca control among some conquered subjects, the Spanish executed Atahualpa, the last Inca emperor, and began to build a new colonial regime literally on the remains of the one it defeated. Over the course of several decades, Spaniards made use of roads and other Inca infrastructure to establish their control and authority over the region; new Christian churches and cathedrals, for instance, were constructed directly on top of former Inca temples (Figure 8.2), and the Spanish even had new "Inca" walls built in several locations. The Spanish colony also built upon Incaic or otherwise indigenous cultural practices. The conversion of Andean peoples to Christianity, for instance, was often accomplished—at times by Andean peoples themselves—by inserting Catholic elements into preexisting indigenous festivals, and many religious and musical practices retain an essentially hybrid character today.

European colonization also ushered in a new period of racial and ethnic differentiation in the Andes. Early mixing between indigenous and Spanish populations produced a substantial class of mestizos, who formed an important intermediate social class between elites and peasants. The Spanish also introduced African slaves to the Andes in the sixteenth century. Though Afro-descendant peoples make up only a small percentage of the current Andean population, they constituted a sizeable presence during the colonial era, outnumbering Europeans in some areas, and strongly impacted the region's music. Afro-Andeans also intermarried with the local indigenous

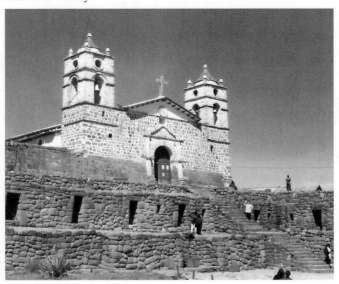

FIGURE 8.2 Catholic church in Vilcashuaman situated atop Inca ruins

population, producing yet another racial category: *zambos*, people with combined indigenous and African ancestry.

Over time, these terms came to describe social position more than biological heritage, and by extension, a set of cultural practices that included music. After independence from Spain in the early 1820s, for instance, *criollos*—descendants of Spanish settlers—took over from Spaniards at the top of the social order. Though the term *criollo* maintained an implicit association with lighter skin, in practice it referred to any member of the elite class with a European cultural orientation. Similarly, by the nineteenth century, most people identified as *indio* ("Indian") or mestizo could likely trace their background to both indigenous and Spanish forebears; individuals were identified as one or the other based less on physical appearance than on where they lived, their social position, and their cultural practices. The growing presence of other ethnic groups in the later nineteenth century, including small but significant populations of Japanese, Chinese, and Arab immigrants to certain Andean regions, and their consequent intermarriage with local mestizos and others, only reinforced the social (as opposed to strictly racial) nature of these identities.

In the twentieth century, a number of political, economic, and social forces combined to further diversify local identities. As already noted, massive migration from rural to urban areas at midcentury produced a new class of urbanized indigenous people, often known derisively as cholos, even as efforts to combat the discrimination faced by the indigenous population surged. Progressive and populist governments in Peru and Bolivia sought to valorize the contributions of indigenous cultures to national identity, while simultaneously emphasizing class over ethnicity in official discourse, for instance replacing the derogatory term *indio* with *campesino* ("peasant"). Indigenous peoples themselves also took the lead in asserting their rights in the latter twentieth century, particularly in Ecuador and Bolivia, where social movements of *indígenas*—their preferred term—have become a powerful political force.

The remainder of this chapter explores some of the musical practices of the people who inhabit and define the social and cultural landscape of the contemporary Andes. It focuses particularly on Peru, the largest and arguably most diverse of the central Andean countries. With a population of thirty million people—divided between the cosmopolitan cities of the coast, the smaller villages and towns located in the Andes mountains themselves, and the vast expanses of the upper Amazon—Peru provides a reasonable cross section, both geographically and culturally, of the Andean region as a whole. The first section surveys a broad range of traditional and popular music, beginning with indigenous genres deeply rooted in the colonial and pre-Hispanic past, proceeding through mestizo and criollo practices, and ending with an examination of popular music genres of more recent, cosmopolitan derivation. The chapter concludes by considering the history of art music in the Andes since the nineteenth century.

Traditional and Popular Music

Indigenous Musical Practices

Andean indigenous peoples have hardly lived "outside" of history; the forces of colonial and postcolonial rule have had a tremendous impact on their social and political organization and are reflected in many of their most important cultural and religious practices, from festivals celebrating Catholic saints to the adoption of European instruments like the harp and violin. Nonetheless, indigenous peoples continue to hold on to many spiritual, ritual, and musical practices whose roots date to the precolonial era. Certain instruments, such as panpipes or the end-blown **kena** flute, have had a continuous existence in the Andean region for millenia. Other ideas about music also clearly predate the arrival of the Spanish, including a widespread preference for dense, high-pitched sounds and the use of paired musical structures.

Taken as a whole, indigenous musical practices vary tremendously. In some places, a walk of an hour from one village to another may present a listener with an entirely different set of instruments, genres, and musical events. Certain instruments and practices, however, are associated with broader regions. The latter is true of the two contrasting examples focused on here: the singing of songs called **harawis** in a Quechua-speaking village in Ayacucho, a region in south-central Peru, and the playing of panpipes called **sikus** in the area surrounding Lake Titicaca, along the Peruvian/Bolivian border.

The Harawi

The harawi is one of the oldest musical forms practiced in the Andes, a vocal genre dating to the period of Inca rule. According to early Spanish chroniclers, the Incas sang harawis on many occasions: during the harvest season, as love songs, and as epic sung poetry performed at Inca festivals (Figure 8.3). Unfortunately, the chronicles provide few clues about what such songs actually sounded like. We do know that the meanings and performance practice of the genre evolved over the intervening centuries. Harawis today are sung in Quechua-speaking communities primarily to accompany agricultural work or ritual occasions, such as the roofing of a house or the burial of a deceased infant.

FIESTADELOSINGAS
VARICZA·ARAVI·DEL
INGA·CANTACON·SV·PVCA·LLAMA·

FIGURE 8.3 The *Waricza Araui*, a ritual in which the Inca monarch imitated the cry of a llama, to which a female chorus responds by singing a harawi. From Guamán Poma de Ayala (1615)

Musically, perhaps due to their roots in the pre-Hispanic era, harawis are distinctive even in comparison with other kinds of indigenous Andean music. Sung a cappella, they are performed exclusively by older women in a high vocal range, and are usually limited to a three-note or tritonic scale. Though residents of small villages in the Andes are increasingly bilingual, harawis are still sung exclusively in the Quechua language, with lyrics derived from long-standing oral tradition. Verses are usually repeated, and lyrics alternate with **vocables** (syllables like "la-la-la"). The latter are especially prominent at phrase endings, when the women sing a high "ay yah!" or "ya ooh!," then let the melody slide down in a long glissando—one of the defining characteristics of the genre. The performers include any capable female singers who happen to be present; harawis thus often have a heterophonic texture, with each woman varying her melody slightly in accordance with her own preferences and knowledge of the song. This type of slightly varied repetition, in which a single musical phrase is performed repeatedly with minor variations, is typical of indigenous Andean music.

The harawi in Listening Guide 8.1 was recorded in the village of Alcamenca, a small town in the Ayacucho region, at the beginning of a long day of work planting corn. Periodically throughout the year, members of the community come together for *faenas*, or communal work parties, to clean an irrigation canal, fix a road, or in this case, plant a communally owned field. Work at the *faena* is usually separated by gender, with men working in the field, while women sing, prepare food, serve periodic glasses of chicha (homemade corn beer) or a handful of coca leaves to each worker, and in between these tasks work in the field themselves.

In Alcamenca, agricultural harawis are sung at the beginning, middle, and end of the workday. On this occasion, as the men begin to work, the women gather in a corner of the field to perform the morning harawi, modestly placing their hands over their mouths and following the lead of the most experienced singer.

The harawi is the only genre performed in this region without instrumental accompaniment. During other times of the year, or at other musical

 Harawi

Date of recording: 1997

Performers/instruments: Unaccompanied female singers from the village of Alcamenca

Genre: harawi

Form: varied repetition of single melody, with each couplet separated by a short pause

Tempo/meter: nonmetrical

What to Listen for:
- High vocal range
- Melody based on a three-note scale
- Descending glissandos at the end of each verse
- Heterophonic texture

Time	Text	Translation	Description
0:00	Wawallallay, wawallallaway [2x] Ya ooh!	Children, children, children [2x] Ya ooh!	Sounds of the men's hoes and their shouts of encouragement to the singers
0:22	Tatayllakuna, Señorllaykunallay, Sumaqchallata araykuyanki, Ya ooh!	Fathers, sirs Plow very well Ya ooh!	Heterophonic performance style evident as some singers enter slightly before or after the others
0:42	Yanqa punchawllan, Nillaspaykichunllay Qawan ukunya, labraykuyanki Ya ooh!	On whatever day, As they say, Don't plow too quickly Ya ooh!	Informal nature of the performance highlighted by singers' comments and nearby conversation

1:01	Manam yanqallay,
	    punchawllapichullay
	Almidorunaspa
	    punchawchallampi
	Ya ooh!
		Today is not just any day
		
		It is the day of starch
		
		Ya ooh!
			"Day of starch"—the growth cycle of the corn, when tassels appear on the top of corn stalks

1:21	First verse repeats		

or ritual events, one may hear harp and violin duos, brass bands, saxophone orchestras, cow-horn trumpet duos, six- or twelve-string guitars, and more—sometimes, during major festivals, all at once! As with most regions dominated by Quechua-speaking peoples, though, people in Alcamenca place heavy emphasis on vocal genres and songs. Even in the case of instrumental performances, the melodies played often come from songs with lyrics. Moving farther south to the Peruvian–Bolivian border, however, to the high arid plateau known as the *altiplano*, songs diminish in importance and purely instrumental genres come to the fore.

Music and Shamanism

Numerous indigenous groups throughout lowland South America practice forms of **shamanism**, in which ritual specialists (shamans) communicate with spirit and/or animal worlds for purposes of healing, prophecy, and more. Though found as far south as central Chile, among the Mapuche people, shamanism is particularly prevalent among groups in the upper Amazon. In this region, bordering the eastern Andes, shamans play an important role in the ritual life of indigenous peoples such as the Shuar and Napo Runa in Ecuador and the Asháninka in Peru.

Music forms a key part of shamanic practices, structuring phases of a ritual while acting as a bridge between human, spirit, and animal worlds. Among the Napo Runa, for example, shamans called *yachaj* (Quichua for "one who knows") are believed to travel via song between this world and the spirit world in the context of healing ceremonies. In addition to providing a vehicle for metaphysical travel, songs offer commentary on the healing process itself, identifying sources of illness and narrating their resolution.

Musically, most Amazonian shamanic practices involve chanting, primarily by the shaman (typically a man in this region) who sings in a limited melodic range. He may also whistle, and accompany himself with various instruments including shaken leaf bundles, different types of rattles, a mouth bow, or among the Napo Runa, a cane flute and/or a modified version of the European violin. Among tribes of the upper Amazon, music is also frequently used in conjunction with a hallucinogenic tea called *ayahuasca*. Perceived as a beautiful female spirit, *ayahuasca* produces visions and enables the shaman's entry into the spirit world.

Look for the CDs *Music of the Jívaro of Ecuador* (Folkways FE 4386, 1973), which include several tracks recorded by a Shuar *uwishin* or shaman, and *Soul Vine Shaman* (Polar Fine Arts, 2007), featuring a field recording of an *ayahuasca* ceremony among the Napo Runa.

The Sikuri

The use of wind instruments (aerophones) has a long history in the Andes, with archeological remains of flutes dating back more than four thousand years. Indigenous communities of the *altiplano* still play dozens of different wind instruments, including **tarkas** (block duct-flutes); kenas (end-notch flutes); and, perhaps most famously, different types and sizes of panpipes such as the siku (Figure 8.4). While it is standard practice in Western societies to combine different types of instruments in a single ensemble—such as a saxophone, trumpet, piano, bass, and drums in a small jazz group—most indigenous wind instruments are performed exclusively in groups of similar instruments, accompanied by drums or other percussion. This practice derives in part from the association made between certain instrument types and the season in which they are played. Panpipes are considered a "dry season" instrument, for instance, and many believe that playing them during the growing season could attract a drought or frost. Even in places where such beliefs no longer hold, dry season instruments are simply not played with their wet-season counterparts.

Though all members of a siku ensemble play the same instrument, they do not necessarily play the same part; this is a crucial component of the community-based nature of this music. Sikus are constructed in pairs, with the complete notes of a diatonic scale alternating between the two halves of the instrument (Figure 8.5). A different musician plays each half in a practice of interlocking notes called hocketing. Though similar techniques existed in medieval and Renaissance Europe, evidence suggests that hocketing has been used in the Andes since at least the Inca era, and perhaps as far back as the Moche civilization (400–1000 CE). Hocketing requires a great deal of coordination between two mutually dependent players or groups of players,

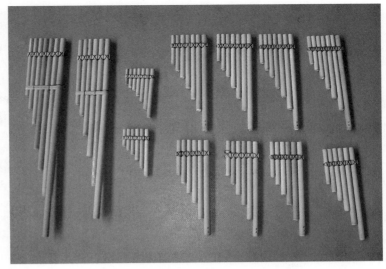

FIGURE 8.4 A set of siku panpipes with low-, middle-, and high-octave pairs

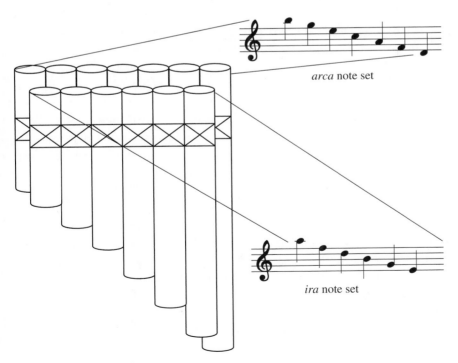

FIGURE 8.5 Diagram of a siku

arca note set

ira note set

who play parts identified as *ira* and *arca* ("leader" and "follower," respectively, in the Aymara language). There is no place for a solo performer in this music, reflecting a general emphasis on communal solidarity and cooperation as defining social values in most rural Andean communities.

Siku ensembles typically include 10 to 15 pairs of musicians, or 20 to 30 people, whose instruments are further differentiated by size, with several pairs of sikus tuned an octave or fifth above or below the main melody instrument. Three sizes of sikus, tuned to a low, middle, and high octave are most common, but here again great variation exists from one community to the next. In the **sikuri** (music and dance associated with sikus) tradition of Conima, Peru, studied by the ethnomusicologist Thomas Turino, for instance, no less than nine different voicings are used, including fifths and thirds, spread out over more than three octaves. Instrument makers also allow for slight variances in tuning from one octave or pair of instruments to the next, which produces a shimmering acoustic effect when the entire ensemble plays together. Virtually all pieces follow a similar formal structure, consisting of three individually repeated phrases (**AABBCC**).

Given the number of people and instruments required, the performance of sikuri music is restricted to large-scale festival contexts celebrated by the entire community, or sometimes multiple communities. Such festivals typically honor a particular Catholic saint or event in the Christian religious calendar. As noted, however, the roots and significance of a given festival may go beyond its surface Christian elements. Many festivals align with important moments in the agricultural cycle, such as planting or harvesting, and incorporate symbols from the pre-Hispanic past such as representations of the sun and moon, alongside Catholic iconography. In the region around Lake Titicaca, the largest annual festival, dedicated to the Virgin of Candelaria, takes place on February 2. "Mamacha Candelaria," as she is affectionately known in Quechua, is also associated with the lake itself—the birthplace of the Incas, according to legend—as well as Pachamama, the feminine Earth Goddess or "Mother Earth" of Inca mythology, who is still widely revered throughout the Andes.

Sikuri music constitutes an important tradition on the island of Taquile, located twenty miles from the shores of Puno on the Peruvian side of Lake Titicaca. Like most communities in the vicinity of the lake, people on Taquile perform a variety of instrumental traditions, including flute ensembles, siku panpipes, and various string instruments, each played for a particular festival. Traditionally, Taquileños play sikuris during festivals held in the months of May and June. During these events, two different sikuri ensembles, representing the social division of the island into "upper" and "lower" halves, engage in an informal competition with one another by playing and dancing together in the central town square. Each group consists of roughly

30 male musicians, with several female dancers, drawn from their respective side of the island. Each ensemble maintains its own set of instruments and performs tunes specific to the occasion and to each group. The result—as the two groups play different tunes simultaneously in close proximity, each trying to sonically overpower the other amidst shouts of encouragement from community members—is sheer cacophony. From a Taquileño perspective, all the "noise" is a major part of the fun!

In order to comprehend this performance, you must also understand some of the ways in which the residents of Taquile are quite unlike any other indigenous community in the region. Beginning in the 1970s, drawn by the beauty and mystique of Lake Titicaca, foreign travelers began touring the lake on boats. These tourists were particularly attracted to Taquile, which had a reputation as a source for exquisite handmade textiles and offered tourists a chance to experience what they imagined to be "uncorrupted" indigenous Andean life. Seeking to capitalize on this interest, Taquileños began shuttling tourists back and forth to the island on their own boats, and a booming tourist industry was born. By the year 2000, this small island with only around nine hundred inhabitants hosted up to twenty-five thousand tourists annually and became one of the most popular destinations in all of Peru for foreign visitors. Island residents now make a majority of their income providing services like food and lodging for tourists, as well as selling textiles. Not surprisingly, these developments have had a major impact on virtually every aspect of Taquileño life.

"Sikuri taquileño" (Listening Guide 8.2) was recorded on Taquile during the Fiesta of Santiago in 2000. Traditionally, residents celebrated the fiesta on July 25 with groups of transverse flutes (called *pitus*) and string bands, followed eight days later with dances accompanied by kena flutes and percussion. Beginning in the 1980s, however, authorities began sponsoring a crafts fair during the festival in order to attract more tourists, taking advantage of the high season for tourism, as well as the proximity of Peruvian Independence Day on July 28. Organizers then altered festival customs further to present a variety show featuring all of the island's music and dance traditions, drawn from the annual ritual calendar, performed in succession on a single afternoon. By the year 2000, traditional eighth-day activities had been supplanted entirely by the crafts fair, which spread out over two full weeks, and performances of dances and music were scheduled for every day.

LISTENING guide 8.2

⊚ "Sikuri taquileño" (Panpipe music from Taquile)

Date of recording: 2000

Performer/instruments: roughly 40 male siku players, playing three different sizes of siku panpipe with *wankara* (bass drum) accompaniment

Genre: sikuri

Form: AABBCC, repeated

Tempo/meter: brisk duple

What to Listen for:
- Repeated, circular **AABBCC** form
- The low, middle, and high octaves of the panpipes
- Hocketing between ira and arca

Time	Description
0:00	Short, melodic introduction, indicates to performers and the audience that the music is beginning
0:08	The formal composition begins (section **A**) with only a few experienced players who are soon joined by the other musicians
0:22	The **B** section of the melody; repeated
0:36	The **C** section; repeated
0:48	Repeat entire **AABBCC** form; midway through this repetition, announcements to crowd by master of ceremonies over the din of the performance
1:30	Repeat **AABBCC** form
2:09	Form begins again, and recording fades out (in a festival performance, even a staged version like this, a single piece may be played for 15 to 20 minutes without a break)

Though sikuris were not originally part of the Santiago festival, they now constitute the most important component of crafts-fair performances. In this particular recording, even the obligatory competition between lower and upper halves of the island has been eliminated. In order to give all performers some time off to get other work done, different groups perform serially on a rotating basis during the two weeks of the fair. The lack of a second, competing group, however, is the only notable change to the sound of this performance. In all other aspects, from the three-octave voicing of instruments to the **AABBCC** structure of the piece, it reflects typical performance practice.

Rather than competing with one another in an event of local religious significance, Taquileños now stage representations of their own traditions for foreign audiences, altering them to better accommodate audience expectations. Folklorists and ethnomusicologists often refer to this process of decontextualization and staged representation as **folklorization**. This should not, however, be simply dismissed as the corruption of a local tradition by foreign audiences. All traditions change, and in this case the people of Taquile have been active participants in altering their musical practices to meet contemporary needs. Indeed, thanks to income generated by tourism to the island, Taquileños are now among the wealthiest "peasants" in Peru. They have managed to accomplish this while holding on to—indeed, by *promoting*—some of the oldest and most "traditional" aspects of their culture.

Mestizo Musical Practices

Mestizos, as noted earlier, are identified today less by their mixed Spanish and indigenous ancestry than by their relative social position and cultural practices, which vary from region to region. In many parts of the Andes, mestizos are characterized as middle- to upper-class people who speak Spanish as their primary language, live in larger towns and cities, and engage in more "refined" pursuits and professional occupations. Many mestizo families are descended from *hacendados*, or hacienda owners, who formed the rural aristocracy until the early twentieth century. Upwardly mobile individuals from poorer or indigenous sectors of society might also achieve mestizo status through education, urban employment and—importantly—by adopting mestizo cultural practices, including music. Conversely, in other areas, such as Peru's Mantaro valley or Bolivia's Cochabamba region, most residents self-identify as mestizo, whether rural or urban, and the term connotes working-class rather than elite identity.

Defining "mestizo music," then, has less to do with mapping a combination of Spanish and indigenous musical influences—though it may include these, and others—than it does with identifying the diverse kinds of music

explore

For a sense of the extraordinary diversity of Andean indigenous music, peruse the discs in the eight-volume *Traditional Music from Peru* series published by Smithsonian Folkways Recordings, as well as their earlier two-volume release, *Mountain Musics of Peru.* The films *Dancing with the Incas* and *Mountain Music in Peru*, both by John Cohen, also present compelling portraits of indigenous music. Beyond Peru, numerous recordings are available commercially from the Otavalo region in northern Ecuador and North Potosí in Bolivia, both renowned for their vibrant indigenous musical life.

The Charango

Indigenous music in the Andes today is not limited to flutes, drums, and vocal genres with pre-Hispanic origins. One of the most popular Andean instruments today is the charango, a small strummed or plucked lute that developed during the colonial era, representing a unique hybrid of European and Andean practices. Lutes, the instrument family to which both the charango and the guitar belong, arrived in the Andes in the sixteenth century. Attracted to this type of instrument, indigenous peoples invented their own version, altering several important features in accordance with their own musical sensibilities. Most prominently, the charango is much smaller than the guitar, similar in size to a mandolin. This gives the charango a higher "voice," reflecting the general Andean preference for high-pitched sounds.

Charangos vary from region to region, depending in part on what materials are available locally. In parts of the southern Andes, instrument makers often construct the charango body out of the shell of the *kirkinchu* armadillo. In other areas, performers construct the instrument entirely out of wood, more closely resembling a small guitar. The number and type of strings on a charango also vary, reflecting both local custom as well as individual aesthetic choices. Mestizo versions of the instrument since the early twentieth century have tended to use gut or nylon strings, but indigenous groups almost invariably utilize metal strings, producing a "tinnier" tone. Similarly, while the standard mestizo charango today has ten strings (tuned in five double courses: G–G–C–C–E–E–A–A–E–E, low to high, with a split octave in the middle E course) and is often plucked to produce

FIGURE 8.7 Charango player performing during carnival in southern Ayacucho, 2002

individual notes, indigenous charangos may have as few as four or as many as 15 strings, all generally strummed together.

Among indigenous groups in Southern Peru and Bolivia, the charango is often associated with courting practices, and the belief that charangos have a power to attract and seduce women. Indeed, in some regions men play the charango almost exclusively to attract women. Related to the instrument's role in courtship activities is its relationship with mythical beings called *sirenas* ("mermaids" or "Sirens") who inhabit rivers and lakes and are believed to imbue the charango with its seductive power.

viewed as emblematic of a mestizo identity in a given locale. The discussion here focuses again on the Ayacucho region of Peru. The dominant mestizo instrument in Ayacucho is the six-string guitar, played with tremendous skill by men from the region, and often accompanied by other string instruments such as the mandolin. Many people believe that playing the guitar well is one of the hallmarks of a true Ayacuchan mestizo, and they refer to the region as the cradle of Andean guitarists. In keeping with their social position, however, most mestizos also believe that playing the guitar should remain an amateur pursuit, kept separate from an individual's more reputable, and presumably more lucrative, profession. Even Ayacucho's most famous musician, the world-renowned guitarist Raúl García Zárate, continued to work as a lawyer even after his national and international performance career could have supported him financially. Being a professional musician, with very few exceptions, carries lower-class associations in the Andes.

Nonetheless, part of the pride exhibited in the prominence of the guitar in Ayacuchan music is the technical difficulty of the regional style. One of its key features rests on the ability of the guitarist to simultaneously play a syncopated bass line, called the **bordón**, on the lower strings, while the other fingers pluck out a melody or strum on the upper strings. In the hands of a skilled guitarist, one guitar can sound like two or three playing at the same time. Other traits of the Ayacuchan mestizo style include extensive rapid passages in the introduction to most songs, or during instrumental breaks between verses, and frequent harmonization of the melody played on the upper strings, paralleling the vocal harmony (Example 8.2). Mastery of this style is complicated by the presence of multiple guitar tunings corresponding to different genres that make playing their respective bordones (bass lines) easier.

Though the guitar may be played in public during certain festivals in Ayacucho, especially carnival, and at staged presentations of folkloric music, mestizos most frequently play it informally in private house parties. During such parties, a group of friends may gather for hours—sometimes, all night—to eat, drink, dance, and make music. Indigenous musicians, especially harpists, may also be hired to entertain at important mestizo family occasions such as a birthday or anniversary; part of their role is to accompany any mestizo guests who wish to play or sing, and to keep the festivities going between such moments. Until the mid-twentieth century, serenades were also a popular activity, in which a soloist or small group of musicians would visit another house, performing outside for the enjoyment of those who would come out to listen. This was a classic manner of courting, with a young man singing love songs to his intended bride.

Among the different genres of mestizo music, the **wayno** (also *huayno*, *huayñu*) is by far the most important and frequently performed. Found prominently throughout the central and southern Andes of Peru and Bolivia, the wayno originated early in the Spanish colonial era as a couple dance, and remains the most popular genre in the region today. One remarkable aspect of the wayno's diffusion is that it is performed and enjoyed by indigenous peoples and mestizos alike, though usually with significant variations in instrumentation, tempo, and lyrical themes. Indeed, these differences are important indicators of class distinctions. Indigenous waynos generally reflect the musical aesthetics of native communities, including a preference for high-pitched women's voices, instrumental ensembles such as panpipes or harp and violin, texts in Quechua, and fast tempos for dancing. Mestizo waynos are comparatively slower; sung in a lower key or octave, often by men; typically address more sentimental lyrical themes; and may be sung in Spanish or a mix of Spanish and Quechua. Unlike genres such as harawis or sikuris, performed at set times of the year and in particular contexts, the mestizo wayno may be performed at any time for secular entertainment.

All waynos share several musical features. Rhythmically, the genre is identified by a repeated long-short-short figure (bar A in Example 8.1), which musicians may vary substantially in the course of a performance (see bars B and C for examples of standard variations). This pattern is especially evident in the strumming patterns heard on instruments like the guitar and charango, or in the bass notes of the harp when a wayno is performed by a harp and violin. In the latter scenario, a third musician often reinforces the rhythm by striking the body of the harp with his knuckles. All waynos are strophic and follow a binary form in each verse (commonly **AABB**), and most rely on predominantly pentatonic (five-note) melodies set in minor keys. The prevalence of minor tonalities in Ayacuchan waynos have led many people to erroneously believe that they are inherently "sad." Although some song texts do indeed address tragic or deeply sentimental themes, these are not related (as in Western music) to the minor key. On the contrary, many wayno texts address joyful and even mildly erotic themes and frequently engage in amusing wordplay. Finally, waynos typically incorporate a concluding section known as a *fuga* ("flight," not to be confused with a "fugue" in the classical music definition of the term), in which the melody is shortened and the tempo may speed up slightly.

The wayno heard in "Adiós pueblo de Ayacucho" (Listening Guide 8.3) is a classic of the Ayacuchan mestizo wayno repertoire. Written by an unknown composer around 1900, it was first recorded in the 1920s by a young harpist

EXAMPLE 8.1: Wayno rhythmic patterns

named Estanislaus "Tany" Medina on one of the earliest recordings of Andean music. The song's lyrics reflect the painful emotions aroused by its protagonist's departure from his hometown and family, questioning whether he will ever return. At the time it was written, migration away from Ayacucho's endemic poverty to the coast had just begun in earnest, and this song, along with others, emerged as an expression of longing for homes in the highlands. The song's theme resonated in a poignant way at this performance in the 1990s, as many people had recently fled the Ayacucho region once again as a result of a decade of horrific political violence (In Depth 8.3). Nonetheless, when played at a brisk tempo in the context of an evening party or other festive occasion, "Adiós pueblo de Ayacucho" can just as easily prompt a crowd to dance.

"Adiós pueblo de Ayacucho" (Listening Guide 8.3), a live concert recording made at a prestigious concert hall in Lima and featuring two renowned contemporary Ayacuchan musicians, Manuelcha Prado and Carlos Falconí, captures all of the distinguishing characteristics of the Ayacuchan mestizo wayno. The performance begins with an instrumental introduction marked by heavily ornamented guitar lines played by both players (with a third guitarist providing strumming accompaniment), giving way to a less ornamented style during sung verses. Rhythmically, the

---

✺ In Depth 8.3

The Shining Path and Testimonial Song

On May 17, 1980, a Maoist faction of the Peruvian Communist Party known as the "Shining Path" launched a guerrilla war from rural Ayacucho in hopes of toppling the Peruvian government. The guerrillas' calculated use of extreme violence, coupled with a brutal counterinsurgency campaign by the Peruvian military, soon plunged the region into chaos. According to the final report of the Peruvian Truth and Reconciliation Commission in 2003, nearly seventy thousand people were killed or "disappeared," and hundreds of thousands forced from their homes between 1980 and the end of the conflict in the 1990s following the capture of Shining Path leader Abimael Guzmán.

In the midst of the violence, musicians in Ayacucho turned to their art as a way of bearing witness to the brutality of the conflict. Using traditional music forms, including the wayno, singers and songwriters built upon a deep tradition of social commentary in Andean music to forge a new song movement, one that spoke with a powerful voice of outrage, and at times, hope, in a climate otherwise marked by fear and silencing. Cassette tapes of *canciones testimoniales* (testimonial songs) soon circulated between Ayacucho and its scattered refugee population, while new star performers of this music emerged, including Carlos Falconí, Manuelcha Prado, and many others. Their songs continue to be performed and recorded today, providing a forum for the remembrance of those deadly years.

⊚ Falconí and Prado: "Adiós pueblo de Ayacucho"

Date of composition: ca. 1900

Date of recording: 1990

Performers/instruments: Manuelcha Prado, guitar, vocals; Carlos Falconí, guitar, vocals; Victor Angulo, guitar; Chano Díaz, kena

Genre: wayno

Form: strophic

Tempo/meter: moderate duple

What to Listen for:

- Intricate, improvised plucked guitar lines, especially between verses
- Harmonized vocals sung in Quechua and Spanish (Quechua lyrics are in italics)
- Alternating major and minor chords
- Distinctive bordón bass patterns

Time	Text	Translation	Description
0:00			Guitar introduction; see transcription
0:24	Adiós pueblo de Ayacucho, *perlaschallay* Ya me voy, ya me estoy yendo, *perlaschallay* [2x] Ciertas malas voluntades, *perlaschallay* Hacen que yo me retire, *perlaschallay* [2x]	Goodbye, Ayacucho town, my little pearl I'm leaving now, I'm going, my little pearl Bad luck and circumstances, my little pearl Force me to leave, my little pearl	**Verse 1** Lead guitarist doubles the song melody and adds harmony, while the second guitarist switches to playing a bordón bass line; third guitarist strums the typical wayno accompaniment pattern to provide a rhythmic foundation
0:59			Brief guitar interlude between verses, referred to as a *floreo* or "flourish"
1:05	*Paqarinmi ripuchkani, perlaschallay* *Tutay tuta tutamanta, perlaschallay* [2x] *Mana pita adiosnispay, perlaschallay* *Mana pita despedispay, perlaschallay* *Kawsaspayqa kutimusaq, perlaschallay* *Wañuspayqa manañacha, perlaschallay*	Tomorrow I'll be leaving, my little pearl Early, very early, my little pearl With no one to say goodbye to, my little pearl With no one to say farewell to, my little pearl I'll return if I live, my little pearl If I die, I won't, my little pearl	**Verse 2** Two lead guitarists (Prado and Falconí) also perform the vocals, with one singing the main melody and the second performing harmony, generally a third below that of the main melody
1:38			Guitar interlude
1:44			A repetition of the verse without vocals, to highlight the virtuosity of the guitarists; kena player also audible in parts of this verse, doubling the melody

(continued)

Time	Text	Translation	Description
2:22			**Verse 3**
2:55			Guitar interlude
3:01	Brilla la luna, brilla el sol [2x] Viva mi tierra Huamanga Viva mi patria peruana	Shining moon, shining sun Long live my homeland, Ayacucho Long live my Peruvian fatherland	*Fuga* or concluding verse, with a shorter, contrasting melody
3:12			*Fuga* repeats and song concludes

EXAMPLE 8.2: Guitar introduction to "Adiós pueblo de Ayacucho"

syncopated bordón emphasizes the upbeat and often omits the downbeat altogether, typical of the Ayacuchan wayno. Spanish musical influence can be heard in the style of vocal harmonization, with a second vocalist frequently singing a third below the melody, while indigenous influence is apparent in the bilingual text, alternating between Spanish and Quechua. Finally, the performers end the wayno with a *fuga*, a short concluding verse. Though some waynos include a *fuga* composed specifically for that song, performers often draw upon a repertoire of relatively interchangeable ending verses that may be appended to any song. In this case, the musicians opt to include a short, patriotic verse as a *fuga* in order to provide a more ringing and definitive conclusion to their concert.

This section has examined one of the emblematic musical genres of mestizo music from Ayacucho; in other regions, different influences have prevailed. To the north of Ayacucho in the Mantaro valley of central Peru, for instance, the most important mestizo musical ensemble since the mid-twentieth century has been the saxophone orchestra, or *orquesta típica*, playing waynos and other regional styles of mestizo folk music. Farther south, in the Cuzco region, mestizo musicians have appropriated indigenous instruments such as the kena and charango and altered the way they are played to better fit mestizo aesthetics, as part of an ideological movement known as **indigenismo** ("Indianism"). In all cases, however, musical tastes and practices have been a crucial way of asserting a mestizo identity.

Afro-Andean Traditions

Afro-descendant peoples constitute a relatively small portion of the central Andean population today, and are concentrated in just a few key locations: the Yungas valley in northern Bolivia, the coastal region of central Peru, and the Chota River valley and the Esmeraldas Province in northern Ecuador. In all of these places, they have mixed racially and culturally with the surrounding mestizo, criollo, and/or indigenous populations. Nonetheless, people who self-identify as black have had a significant impact on the musical cultures of their respective countries in recent decades, and thus merit more discussion here than their small numbers might otherwise suggest. This commentary focuses on Ecuador, the smallest of the Andean countries, but the one with the largest Afro-descendant population.

Two distinct black population centers exist in Ecuador, both with their own representative musical traditions. African slaves were first brought to the highland Chota River valley by Jesuit priests in the seventeenth century, and their descendants continue to live in the valley today. Given their small numbers and their close relationship with surrounding mestizo and indigenous Quichua-speaking communities (an Ecuadorian dialect of Quechua), their musical traditions exhibit a mix of cultural influences. This is especially prominent in the musical genre for which they are most known, a dance music known as bomba. The typical musical ensemble for bomba includes one or more guitars, a smaller guitar known as a requinto, the small two-headed bomba hand drum, plus other percussionists and vocalists. Beyond these obvious Hispanic and African influences in instrumentation, the harmonic and melodic language of bomba music closely resembles the alternating minor–major tonality of indigenous music, as does the Quichua-inflected Spanish in which most bomba songs are sung. In recent years, this music has become popular with a wider class of Ecuadorians, especially in fusion versions that combine this already-hybrid music with more mainstream and commercial popular music styles.

Several hundred miles to the west, the coastal Esmeraldas Province is home to the largest African American population in the Andes, part of a larger cultural and geographic region that extends northward along the Pacific coast into Colombia. It is a green and verdant area, marked by dense mangrove swamps, numerous rivers, and a temperate rain forest that extends inland for more than a hundred miles. It is home to the marimba, a type of xylophone with African roots that is played together with several other drums and percussion instruments, accompanying a lead singer and chorus. Neither the instruments nor the music played by the marimba ensemble are exact copies of any particular African tradition. Unlike Afro-Cuban *Santería* or Brazilian candomblé, which can trace aspects of their musical and religious practices to the Yoruba people of Nigeria, Afro-Ecuadorian musics are essentially creative hybrids, containing both Hispanic elements and a strong pan-African character.

The marimba ensemble typically includes a number of different percussion instruments: one or more marimbas, two *cununos* (a conical, single-headed hand drum), one or more bombos (a double-headed bass drum played with sticks), and numerous tubular bamboo shakers called *guasás* (all shown, except the *guasás*, in Figure 1.5). While the marimba and drums are usually played by men, the shakers are often played by women known as *respondadoras*, who sing in "response" to the lead singer, known as a *glosador*. The latter may be a man or woman. Call-and-response relationships mark virtually all aspects of the music. Marimba parts are divided between the bordón, here referring to a repeated ostinato bass line, above which the *tiple* part improvises. *Cununos* are similarly divided between *macho* and *hembra* (male and female) parts that respond to one another.

Historically this music occupied a specific place in the lives of Afro-Ecuadorians, played at Catholic saint festivals and for secular entertainment

FIGURE 8.8 Petita Palma in performance with Tierra Caliente. Esmeraldas, Ecuador, 2010

at weekly dances, but today it is performed almost exclusively by amateur and professional folklore groups at large festivals and at beach resorts. These folklore groups first began forming in the early 1970s, when an elder generation of musicians grew concerned that not enough young people were learning to sing and dance marimba repertoire, due in part to mestizo antipathy towards Afro-Ecuadorian traditions, as well as to the slow incursion of foreign popular musics. Petita Palma formed one such group, Tierra Caliente, in 1972, and set out to train young singers and dancers through participation in her ensemble (Figure 8.8). Hundreds of local performers have now passed through the ranks of her group (and others), and many have gone on to found their own folklore troupes, both in Esmeraldas and in other towns and cities. Thanks to their collective efforts, the marimba has emerged in recent years as one of the principal symbols of a resurgent sense of ethnic and racial pride among Afro-Ecuadorians. One of the largest public celebrations in Esmeraldas is now the annual marimba festival held during carnival in February, drawing thousands of spectators.

Urban Popular Music in Lima

With a population of more than eight million people, more than a quarter of the population of Peru, Lima is one of the largest and most culturally vibrant cities in South America. Founded in 1535 as the seat of Spanish colonial power on the continent, for centuries it served as an enclave for Spanish elites and their criollo offspring, who remained culturally oriented to the fashions of Europe. This would not change significantly until the late nineteenth century, when a distinctive popular culture began to emerge from Lima's working-class neighborhoods, followed in the mid-twentieth century by a massive wave of immigration from the Andean highlands that irrevocably changed the social makeup of the city. Today, Lima is home to a thriving and diverse popular culture, reflecting influences from all of Peru and beyond—from indigenous and mestizo music from the highlands to upscale nightclubs featuring jazz, salsa, and rock. The following section explores some of these distinct musical scenes.

Criollo and Afro-Peruvian Music

Despite its reputation as a center for Spanish and European culture, Lima has always been a multicultural and multiethnic city. For much of the seventeenth and eighteenth centuries, Afro-Peruvians outnumbered the Spanish and criollo population, and smaller but still significant numbers of mestizo and indigenous Andean peoples have also resided in the city since its founding. Although the aristocracy maintained its European cultural orientation following Peruvian independence in 1821, new cultural currents began brewing in working-class neighborhoods where other segments of the population lived and worked together. Concentrated in the *callejones* of central Lima—narrow alleyways with shared washing and cooking facilities, surrounded by rows of cheap dwellings—a new, syncretic popular culture emerged that combined African as well as Hispanic influences. One of the primary contexts for the development of this new hybrid culture was the **jarana**, a festive gathering filled with music, dancing, and food that sometimes went on for days.

Though musicians played many types of music at jaranas, including the **marinera**, a syncopated § couple dance widely regarded today as Peru's national dance (closely related to the Chilean and Bolivian *cueca*), the most popular genre at the turn of the twentieth century was the **vals**. A modified version of the European dance, Peruvian valses (as with their northern cousin, the Ecuadorian *pasillo*) maintained the genre's ¾ meter, but unlike the primarily instrumental European waltz, the vals was meant to be sung. Singers performed with one or more guitarists who played variations on a stock rhythm known by the onomatopoeic term **tundete**. Beginning with the thumb playing a bass note on beat one (the "tun"), guitarists then pluck and quickly dampen a chord on the top strings on beats two and three ("de-te"; Example 8.3). Later in the mid-twentieth century, performers added the Afro-Peruvian **cajón** (wooden box drum; Figure 8.9) as standard accompaniment for the vals.

The vals figured prominently in the musical life of the poorer working-class neighborhoods of the city. Paradoxically, though the genre today is recognized as quintessentially criollo, many of its most prominent innovators

explore

For a fascinating audio document of jarana musical practices, especially the marinera and associated traditions of improvised singing, look for the CD *Jarana's Four Aces* (Topic Records, TSCD926, 2005), based on recordings made in Lima in the 1950s.

EXAMPLE 8.3: Guitar tundete pattern and cajón accompaniment

were Afro-Peruvian, or even of Chinese and Japanese descent. The criollo elite, for its part, initially shunned the genre as a debased version of the European original. Some of these class tensions were expressed in the music itself; while the lyrics of the "Old Guard" that pioneered the genre around 1900 primarily addressed romantic themes, a new generation of composers in the 1920s used the genre as a vehicle for more overt social commentary. Felipe Pinglo Alva (1899–1936), today hailed as one of the most important figures in the history of this music, penned his biggest hit with "El plebeyo" (The Plebian), which narrates a poor man's lament over the impossibility of love for an upper-class woman:

FIGURE 8.9 Afro-Peruvian cajón player Freddy "Huevito" Lobatón in performance in Lima, Peru, 2010

Mi sangre, aunque plebeya	My blood, although poor
También tiñe de rojo	Also stains red
El alma en que se añida	The soul in which nests
Mi incomparable amor	My incomparable love
Ella de noble cuna	She of noble birth
Yo un humilde plebeyo	I, a humble working man
No es distinta la sangre	Our blood is no different
Ni es otro el corazón	Nor our hearts distinct
¡Señor! ¿Por qué los seres	Lord! Are all people
No son de igual valor?	Not of equal value?

Pinglo notably incorporated influences from foreign genres (then popular) into his music, ranging from Argentine tangos to North American jazz, further contributing to the developing sound and harmonic language of the vals.

By the 1930s, middle- and upper-class audiences in Lima gradually accepted the vals. Early commercial radio played an important role in this process, as it began featuring music programs that helped legitimize the vals and associated genres. A second reason for the wider acceptance of this music was a surge in Peruvian nationalism and a consequent search for national symbols. This current swept across Latin America in the early twentieth century, as the challenges brought on by economic modernization, industrialization, and urbanization left governments and citizens scrambling to redefine themselves.

Not surprisingly, the search for a national culture brought old social rifts to the fore. Mestizo intellectuals and elites in the highlands turned to indigenous references, especially those dating to the Inca Empire, as a way of defining "Peruvian-ness." Collectively, their efforts gave birth to the movement known as indigenismo, though it rarely acknowledged or even engaged with the indigenous population itself. Middle- and upper-class elites in Lima, on the other hand, sought symbols that could represent a culture that was at once "Peruvian" as well as "coastal," in order to justify their economic and political control over the country. The vals, marinera, and associated forms of criollo music fit the bill, despite the poor opinion many elites previously held of such genres. By the 1940s and 1950s, they were being promoted in the capital as the national music of Peru, and the Peruvian Congress even declared a national annual "Day of Criollo Song" in 1944.

The most celebrated singer and songwriter of criollo music during this era was María Isabel Granda Larco, better known as Chabuca Granda (1920–1983; Figure 8.10). Raised in an upper-middle-class family in Lima, she formed a lifelong association with the city and its popular culture. Her most famous composition, the vals "Flor de la canela" (Cinnamon Flower), captures both the spirit of *criolloismo* (criollo-ism) in mid-twen-

FIGURE 8.10 Chabuca Granda in a studio portrait from the 1970s

tieth century Lima, as well as the evocative and sensual poetry that was Granda's trademark. "Flor de la canela" offers a nostalgic and romanticized view of an older (and more exclusively criollo) Lima, evoking specific places such as the bridge that passes over the Rimac River in the center of the city. Granda personifies the city as a young, *mulata* woman with "jasmine in her hair and roses in her face," a genteel allusion to the Afro-Peruvian influences on criollo music.

The immediate and sustained popularity of "Flor de la canela" among criollo audiences represented a reaction against Lima's rapidly changing social and musical environment. Uncontrolled population growth and industrialization altered the very face of the city, erasing many signs of its colonial past and its historically criollo identity. Members of the elite viewed such changes with alarm, and the idealized vision of their city's past as expressed in songs like "Flor de la canela" undoubtedly comforted them.

Importantly, Afro-Peruvian musicians, who played such a critical role in the development of criollo music (and who remain some of its most popular performers today) also began reclaiming their own musical heritage in the 1950s. The Afro-Peruvian revival, led by the siblings Nicomedes and Víctora Santa Cruz, demanded recognition for Afro-Peruvian contributions to criollo music, even as it promoted more exclusively Afro-Peruvian genres such as the *festejo* and the *landó* as symbols of a separate identity. Chabuca Granda—who was not Afro-Peruvian—also

⊚ Granda: "Flor de la canela"

Composer/lyricist: Chabuca Granda

Date of composition: 1951

Date of recording: unknown

Performer/instruments: Chabuca Granda, vocals; guitarist unknown

Genre: vals

Form: strophic

Tempo/meter: slow triple with several unmetered pauses

What to Listen for:
- Extended harmonies in the guitar accompaniment
- Periodic use of tundete pattern by the guitarist
- Dramatic use of unmetered sections and pauses

Time	Text	Translation	Description
0:00			Guitar introduction, introducing pieces of the melody and establishing key via arpeggiated chords
0:30	Déjame que te cuente limeño Déjame que te diga la gloria Del ensueño que evoca la memoria Del viejo puente, el río, y la alameda	Allow me to tell you *limeño* Let me tell you about the glory Of the dream evoked by memory Of the old bridge, the river, and the poplar grove	**Verse 1** Granda sings in a quiet, almost conversational way, heightening the intimate, nostalgic character of the song
0:52	Déjame que te cuente limeño Ahora que aún perfuma el recuerdo Ahora que aún se mece en un sueño El viejo puente, el río, y la alameda	Allow me to tell you *limeño* Now while the memory is still perfumed Now while in a dream are shimmering still The old bridge, the river, and the poplar grove	**Verse 2**
1:12	Jazmines en el pelo y rosas en la cara Airosa caminaba la flor de la canela Derramaba lisura y a su paso dejaba Aromas de mixtura que en el pecho llevaba Del puente a la alameda menuda pie la lleva por la vereda	Jasmine in her hair and roses in her face Gracefully walked the cinnamon flower She exuded innocence and with each step The perfume of the blend she carried in her breast From the bridge to the poplar grove her tiny foot is taking her	**Chorus** Guitar switches to the tundete pattern for the first two lines of this verse

(continued)

Time	Text	Translation	Description
	Que se estremece al ritmo de su cadera Recogía la risa de la brisa del río y al viento La lanzaba, del puente a la alameda	On the path that quivers to the rhythm of her hips She picked up the laughter of the river breeze and threw it to the winds From the bridge to the poplar grove	
1:53			**Verse 3** As the song develops, increase in emotional intensity of both the lyrics and Granda's performance
2:38	Y recuerda que . . . [repeat chorus]	And remember . . .	Just prior to the final chorus, Granda includes a dramatic pause on the phrase "Y recuerda que . . .," typical of how the song is still performed today

championed these genres later in her life, and her song "Maria Landó" became famous internationally in the 1990s as performed and recorded by Afro-Peruvian singer and folklorist Susana Baca. Indeed, Afro-Peruvian music has proven far more successful than criollo music in so-called world music markets in the United States and elsewhere in recent years, and Baca herself won a Latin Grammy for Best Folk Album in 2002 for her CD *Lamento Negro* (Black Lament).

Though the Afro-Peruvian revival presented a challenge to Lima's criollo exclusivity, the biggest change in Lima in the 1950s was the explosive growth of the Andean immigrant population. This "Andeanization" of Lima ushered in a new era in the city's popular music and added yet another layer to the texture of Peru's musical cultures. Though criollo music continues to be viewed as the national music of Peru in certain contexts, its historic claim to that title has been challenged repeatedly with the advent of a sustained Andean music scene in the capital.

The Commercial Wayno

Between 1940 and 1960, Lima's population nearly tripled, jumping from just 650,000 residents to more than 1.8 million; it almost doubled again in the following decade and has continued to grow ever since. Most of this growth resulted initially from migration from the rural Andean highlands. Migrants came for many reasons, but their principal motivation was financial: Lima held the best prospects for employment as well as education. Migrant hopes for a better life, however, often met a bitter end in Lima's shantytowns,

explore

The Afro-Peruvian compilation CD produced by David Byrne, *Afro-Peruvian Classics: The Soul of Black Peru* (Luaka Bop, 1995), first spurred international interest in Afro-Peruvian music, and it remains useful for its selection of historic tracks by key artists. Look also for solo CDs by musicians including Susana Baca, Eva Ayllón, and the group Perú Negro.

or *pueblos jóvenes* (young towns). Marginalized in their new surroundings and dismissed as **cholos** (a derogatory term for urbanized Indians), migrants turned to one another for support, and decades passed before they achieved middle-class status in significant numbers.

Along with their meager possessions, migrants brought music and musical tastes to the capital. Nostalgia for the highlands and for family and friends left behind, coupled with an emergent sense of identity as *provincianos* (provincials), provided the impetus for creating new forms of urban Andean repertoire. In the 1950s, an entire industry developed around this new music. Entrepreneurs organized Sunday afternoon concerts in *coliseos* (outdoor sports arenas or large tents) in which hundreds of spectators gathered to listen to music, eat typical highland food, and socialize. AM radio stations began broadcasting early morning shows dedicated to highland music, as well as announcements and news directed at the migrant community. Finally, and perhaps most importantly, a national recording industry developed that recorded and distributed Andean music, which accounted for half of national sales between 1950 and 1980.

Musically speaking, the Andean music that first developed in Lima built upon mestizo traditions from the highlands, with several adaptations. The most prominent change was an emphasis on solo singers who performed with a band in a staged environment. As previously discussed, in the highlands great emphasis is often placed on the group nature of performance. In Lima, however, a star system emerged among performers, most of whom adopted folksy stage names that stayed with them throughout their careers, such as Jilguero de Huascarán (The Goldfinch of Mt. Huascarán), El Picaflor de los Andes (The Hummingbird of the Andes), and Pastorita Huaracina (The Little Shepherdess of Huaraz). Literally thousands of such figures emerged in the midcentury.

These names reflected the kind of rural persona promoted in the music—similar to that of urban country music in the United States—and also reflected the continued importance of regional identities among migrants. Singers chose specific places from their home areas as part of their stage names, and reinforced that association by wearing folkloric clothing. Most importantly, they also chose their backup ensemble to reflect a particular region. El Picaflor de los Andes (Víctor Alberto Gil, 1929–1975), for instance, came from the Mantaro valley, located east of Lima, and employed a saxophone orchestra from that region. Pastorita Huaracina (María Alvarado Trujillo, 1930–2001) migrated from the Ancash region, and performed with a string band representative of mestizo practices there (Figure 8.11), while the trio Lira Paucina (The Lyre from Pauza) played the guitars and charangos associated with southern Ayacucho. Audiences for such groups, however, came from areas all over the highlands.

FIGURE 8.11 Maria Alvarado Trujillo, "Pastorita Huaracina," performs at a *coliseo* in the 1960s

The wayno dominated the repertoire performed by these singers and musicians. Though certain new performance practices emerged in the city, such as the interjection of verbal comments by the singer during instrumental interludes (a practice developed in radio broadcasts), the formal structure of the wayno remained intact, with its characteristic rhythm, tonality, and pentatonic melodies. This fidelity to the wayno's original form and regional styles also helped to popularize migrant singers back in their home provinces, where recordings began circulating soon after being released in the city.

The performance of a commercial wayno from the 1970s featured in Listening Guide 8.5 gives a sense of such changes and continuities, as well as some concerns expressed in the lyrics of Andean migrant music. "Neblina blanca" (White Fog) is a **chuscada**, a regional wayno variant from Ancash, recorded by Basilia Zavala Camones, "La Huaracinita" (The Little Woman from Huaraz). On this recording, she is backed by a traditional Ancash string band, including guitar, violin, harp, and an accordion. The song follows the typical **AABB** form of most waynos, concluding with a *fuga* section, and harmonically alternates between the usual minor and relative major.

Lyrically, "Neblina blanca" (Listening Guide 8.5) typifies many waynos in lamenting a lost love, but also contains elements of social critique reflecting the difficulties of migrant life. It begins with a statement of despair: "White fog of the month of May/It is you who steals the hopes of my passionate heart." "White fog" is a specific reference to life in Lima, where a mist hangs over the

⊚ La Huaracinita: "Neblina blanca"

Date of composition: unknown, probably 1960s–1970s

Date of recording: unknown, probably 1960s–1970s

Performer/Instruments: Basilia Zavala Camones "La Huaracinita," vocals; accompanied by violin, guitar, harp, and accordion

Genre: wayno

Form: strophic

Tempo/meter: fast duple

What to Listen for:

• String ensemble, typical of the Ancash region

• Two formal sections, including the initial wayno verses and the faster, concluding *fuga*

• The characteristic wayno rhythm, clapped during the *fuga*

Time	Text	Translation	Description
0:00			Instrumental introduction; violins carry the introductory melody, with rapid note passages in the guitar
0:12	Neblina blanca del mes de mayo [2x] Tú eres quien robas las esperanzas De mi corazón apasionado [2x]	White fog of the month of May It is you who steals the hopes Of my passionate heart	Wayno verse; **AABB** structure, with the two clauses of the melody each repeated
0:43			First verse repeated (spoken), with the violin playing the melody
1:14	Por muchos pueblos he recorrido Por todo el mundo he dado vuelta Pero en ningunos los he hallado Igual cariño como el tuyo [2x]	Through many towns I have traveled I've gone around the world But nowhere have I found Similar affection as yours	An insistent, upbeat bass line played by the guitarist throughout all of the vocal verses
1:45	Cerveza negra tomarás tú con tus amigos millonarios Chicha de jora tomaré yo con mis amigos provincianos [2x]	You will drink dark beer with your millionaire friends I will drink *chicha de jora* with my *provinciano* friends [2x]	*Fuga* section; increase in tempo; studio audience claps the wayno rhythm; repetition of entire verse a second time
2:04			Instrumental repetition of the *fuga*; in performance, during this instrumental verse, the singer dances at the front of the stage
2:22	Cerveza negra tomarás tú con tus amigos millonarios Chicha de jora tomaré yo con mis amigos provincianos	You will drink dark beer with your millionaire friends I will drink *chicha de jora* with my *provinciano* friends [2x]	Final repetition of the *fuga* verse by the singer, and a ringing V-I conclusion by the ensemble

city for nearly nine months a year, thanks to the cold Humboldt Current that runs just off its shores. On a more subtle level, the "white fog" of this song could also be a metaphoric reference to Lima's criollo (i.e., "white") culture, and the demoralizing climate of prejudice faced by highland migrants to the city.

In the second verse, the singer bemoans the loss of an unnamed love, noting that she has traveled "around the world" but has never found "similar affection as yours." Although on its surface this is a straightforward romantic lament, when heard in the urban context it echoes the kind of nostalgia felt by many migrants for the familiarity of highland life they left behind. Finally, in the *fuga*, nostalgia turns to a condemnation of those migrants who forget where they are from and turn their back on their heritage. Much like musical taste, an individual's choices in food and drink are often indicative of social identity. In this case, the singer condemns her old lover for drinking "dark beer," an expensive beverage in Peru, with his "millionaire friends," while she remains true to the migrant community by drinking *chicha de jora*, homemade corn beer.

By the 1980s, the golden era of the Andean wayno in Lima drew to a close. Competition from foreign genres, including Latin pop and salsa, and the development of variations of cumbia that appealed to second- and third-generation migrants (In Depth 8.4), contributed to the wayno's decline. Nonetheless, classic recordings by stars from the earlier era continue to sell well today, and two new styles of wayno have emerged in the last decade. Beginning in the 1990s, younger musicians from Ayacucho introduced synthesizers, drum set, electric bass, and pan-Andean instruments like the kena and panpipes into the traditional guitar-based mestizo Ayacuchan sound, and forged a style—simply called *música ayacuchana*, "Ayacuchan music"—performed by stars like Max Castro and the Duo Gaitán Castro, that remains popular today. A second style of contemporary wayno—featuring the strident, high vocal style of indigenous Andean music accompanied by amplified steel-string harp and drum machine, sometimes called *wayno con arpa* (harp *wayno*)—has also become tremendously popular among working-class listeners. In a sign of the changing social perception of Andean peoples in the capital, a 2004 television series about the life of wayno singer Dina Paucar captivated Peruvians of all social classes and catapulted Paucar into the national limelight.

Nueva Canción and Andean Music Abroad

At this point, you might reasonably be asking how the music examined thus far connects with the "Andean music" you are most likely to have heard before. Peruse your local CD store's music bins or search on the Internet for "Andean music," and you will undoubtedly find recordings of bands wearing ponchos or colorful handwoven vests, playing a combination of instruments that includes panpipes, the kena flute, a charango, a bombo bass drum, and one or more guitars. The music might include stylized versions

Chicha and Technocumbia

Commercial recordings of the Colombian cumbia burst onto Peru's musical scene in the 1960s. Within a decade, Peruvian bands were playing their own versions of the genre, experimenting with instrumentation and musical forms, and creating what would eventually coalesce into discernable "Peruvian" variants. Cumbia held a special appeal for the children of Andean migrants in Lima. Caught between a city that refused to fully accept them, and a highland culture they had never truly known, second-generation *provincianos* found in cumbia a modern, cosmopolitan genre with which they could identify. Given the similarity of the basic rhythms underlying both the wayno and cumbia, influences from the former were easily incorporated into the latter, and a number of early hits borrowed wayno melodies. The resulting music, fusing electric guitars and bass, Latin percussion like bongos and timbales, Andean melodic motifs, and lyrics about working-class migrant life in the city, became known as cumbia *andina* or chicha (after the fermented corn drink). The band Los Shapis and the singer Chacalón (Lorenzo Palacios) were two of the biggest chicha stars of the 1980s, and their recordings still circulate today.

Cumbia also took root in Peru's Amazon region. This "tropical" variant, centered at first in cities like Iquitos, had few of chicha's Andean influences. The style spread to the rest of the country in the 1990s, where it eventually became known as **technocumbia**. In contrast to chicha, which had never gained the approval of Lima's middle and upper classes, technocumbia captivated a broad cross-section of the listening public; according to ethnomusicologist Raúl Romero, this was arguably the first time that a single musical style had achieved such popularity in Peru across social, class, and ethnic lines. In place of Andean

FIGURE 8.12 Rossy War, backstage before a performance in 2001

influences, technocumbia referenced pan-Latin American popular dance music forms and included strictly romantic lyrical themes. This contributed to its broad appeal, as did the provocative dress and suggestive choreography of its mostly female performers. The singer Rossy War (Figure 8.12)—a playful translation of her legal name, Rosa Guerra Morales—catalyzed the technocumbia

(continued)

boom with her 1998 hit "Nunca Pensé Llorar" (I Never Thought to Cry). Her most common stage outfit is a modified version of the revealing black leather attire worn by Selena, the Mexican-American performer of tejano music (see Chapter 10). Rossy War's hoarse, alto vocals are modeled after that of another Mexican musical icon, the popular singer Ana Gabriel. If earlier versions of chicha emphasized ways to "localize" cumbia and make it meaningful on Peruvian terms, technocumbia took it in the opposite direction, attempting to "globalize" it by incorporating disparate elements and influences from abroad.

Technocumbia artists continue to perform and record, while recent years have also witnessed a resurgence of older chicha artists from the 1980s, as well as the popularization of salsa-influenced cumbia orchestras from Peru's northern coast. Some of the bigger Peruvian cumbia stars have recently been the subject of biographical miniseries on national television in the country—a true sign of changing attitudes and audiences for this formerly "lowbrow" music.

of indigenous or mestizo music repertoire, but probably also includes covers of other Latin American popular music, hits from the United States, and even new age compositions emphasizing breathy panpipes over synthesized sounds. Where did this music come from, and how did it come to represent "the Andes" for international audiences?

According to ethnomusicologist Fernando Rios, the "Andean music ensemble" of today emerged primarily in Buenos Aires and Paris, rather than in the Andes themselves. As explored in Chapter 7, rural folk music styles in Argentina were performed in *peñas* (folk music clubs) in Buenos Aires as early as the 1920s, where Andean genres also had a limited presence. By the 1940s, Andean influence had grown, bolstered in part by the presence of Bolivian and Peruvian musicians. Attracted to indigenous repertoire, but not bound by the practices of any specific tradition or community, these groups experimented with new combinations of instruments. One of the most prominent Argentine groups, Los Hermanos Ábalos (The Ábalos Brothers), performed with a lineup that incorporated the kena, charango, bombo, and guitar, standardizing a model for "neo-Andean folklore"—another example of folklorization—that would influence the presentation of Andean music internationally for many decades.

By the 1950s, recordings of artists like Los Hermanos Ábalos had traveled, along with a number of Argentine musicians themselves, to Paris, where their stylized repertoire captured the interest of listeners in the bohemian clubs of the Latin Quarter. Folk music clubs that programmed Andean groups became trendy nightspots. One, L'Escale (The Stopover), became famous for both its Andean music and as a hangout for celebrities like actress Brigitte Bardot. Few musicians who played there, however, had any personal connection to Andean music cultures. Indeed, the most prominent band of the Andean music craze, Los Incas, consisted of two Argentine and two Venezuelan musicians who had never played Andean music at all before moving to France. Nonetheless, the virtuosic way in which they and others performed appealed to international audiences, and contributed to the dissemination of this new sound.

Recordings and tours by such groups eventually made their way back to the Andean region itself, where they met with varied reactions. In rural communities and among urban migrants, this music never became popular. Among middle-class audiences, however, especially college students and other urban mestizos, neo-Andean folkloric music steadily grew in popularity from the 1960s onward. In Bolivia, groups like Los Jairas, founded by Swiss kena player Gilbert Favre, became a national sensation and played regularly at their own club in La Paz when not on tour internationally. In the 1970s, the Bolivian group Los Kjarkas emerged as arguably the most influential folklore group of the region. Their song "Llorando se fue," based on the rhythms of a Bolivian genre known as *caporal-saya*, circulated worldwide in the late 1980s as accompaniment for the *lambada* dance craze.

One of the performers at the L'Escale club in Paris in the 1950s and early 1960s was the noted Chilean folklorist and songwriter Violeta Parra. When she and her two children, Ángel and Isabel, returned to Chile in 1965, they helped launch one of the most influential musical movements in the history of Latin America. Known as **nueva canción** ("new song"), this movement fused Latin American folk music styles, especially the influences the Parras brought back from Paris, with leftist political sentiments then surging among students in Southern Cone countries.

As in many parts of the world, the 1960s and 1970s were a turbulent time in the Andes. Student groups, labor unions, and peasant federations took to the streets and, in some cases, took up arms in attempts to address widespread poverty and severe social inequalities. In the context of the Cold War, many adopted explicitly Marxist politics and goals, viewing the Cuban Revolution of 1959 as a model for the rest of Latin America. Alarmed by such developments, conservative political forces sought to protect their economic interests and limit the gains made by these groups. Though the confrontation varied in its details and intensity from one country to the next, its polarizing effects were most striking in Chile, where conflicts between right and left reached their peak during the presidency of Salvador Allende in the early 1970s.

Nueva canción grew out of this struggle. Just prior to the Parras's return to Chile, in 1963, a group of poets, musicians, and writers in Mendoza, Argentina, including a young Mercedes Sosa (see Chapter 7), published a manifesto in which they called for a *nuevo cancionero*, or "new songbook," that drew inspiration from that country's folkloric music but without being limited by its traditional canons. The group hoped to create a new, socially and politically conscious form of folk music. Inspired by their model, as well as by North American singers like Bob Dylan and Joan Baez, young Chilean musicians began creating songs that conspicuously incorporated Andean

FIGURE 8.13 Nueva canción group Inti-Illimani performing in Milan, Italy, in 1973. Inti-Illimani is a hybrid Quechua and Aymara term meaning "Sun of the Illimani," referring to a prominent mountain in Bolivia

instruments and influences (Figure 8.13). These musicians played a crucial role in the election of Salvador Allende, candidate of the leftist Popular Unity coalition, who took office as the president of Chile in 1970.

One of the most influential figures of the nueva canción movement was Víctor Jara. A theater director and singer-songwriter, Jara taught at the University of Chile in Santiago in the 1960s, where he came into daily contact with students and leftist intellectuals. Unlike many of these students, however, who came from middle-class backgrounds, Jara himself came from a working-class family and drew upon that experience when writing his material. In contrast with the neo-Andean folklorists, Jara usually performed alone, with only a guitar to accompany himself, and his musical style remained rooted in the Hispanic musical traditions of central and southern Chile.

FIGURE 8.14 Víctor Jara, ca. 1970

One of Jara's most famous songs is "Plegaria a un labrador" (Listening Guide 8.6), which he debuted at the First Festival of New Chilean Song in Santiago in 1969. Reflecting the political idealism of the moment, Joan Jara, Víctor's wife, later wrote that this song "was a call to the peasants, to those who tilled the soil with their hands and produced the fruits of the earth, to join with their brothers to fight for a just society. Its form, reminiscent of the Lord's Prayer, was a reflection of Víctor's newly awakened interest in the Bible for its poetry and human-ist values, at a time when a deep understanding was growing between progressive Catholics and Marxists in Latin America." Víctor Jara's theatrical sense is evident in how he constructed the music, which builds in intensity from a slow, arpeggiated introduction in a minor key, abruptly transitions to a faster and more hopeful section in major, and ends with a furiously strummed conclusion that returns to minor. This recording, from a recent live concert in Barcelona, Spain, features the nue-va canción group Quilapayún (Mapuche for "Three Bearded Men"), who accompanied Jara at the song's premiere.

Jara: "Plegaria a un labrador" (Prayer to a Worker)

Composer/lyricist: Víctor Jara

Date of composition: 1969

Date of recording: 2003

Performers/instruments: members of Quilapayún, including three guitarists with all members performing vocals

Genre: nueva canción

Form: strophic, with three distinct sections

Tempo/meter: compound duple, increasing in tempo with each section

What to Listen for:

• Dramatic increases in tempo and intensity

• Changes from tonality to major minor and back again

• Biblical references in the lyrics

Time	Text	Translation	Description
0:00			Introduction, with slow arpeggiated guitar chords, which accompany the melody, plucked by the lead guitarist
0:31	Levantáte, y mira la montaña De donde viene el viento, el sol y el agua Tú que manejas el curso de los ríos Tú que sembraste el vuelo de tu alma	Arise and look at the mountain Origin of the wind, the sun and the water You who directs the course of the rivers You who have sown your soul's flight	Solo voice, accompanied by arpeggiated guitar chords
1:08	Levántate, y mírate las manos Para crecer, estréchala tu hermano Juntos iremos, unidos en la sangre Hoy es el tiempo, que puede ser manaña	Arise and look at your hands So as to grow, reach out to your brother Together we will go, united by blood Now is the time that can become tomorrow	Entrance of other band members with backup vocals
1:43			Abrupt transition to major key, faster tempo, and strummed chords on the guitar
1:49	Líbranos de aquel que nos domina en la miseria Traenos tu reino de justicia e igualdad	Deliver us from the one who dominates us in misery Bring us your reign of justice and equality	New melody in a higher register, sung in a brighter vocal style

(continued)

Time	Text	Translation	Description
	Sopla como el viento la flor de la quebrada Limpia como el fuego el cañon de mi fusil	Blow like the wind the flower of the canyon Clean like fire the barrel of my gun	
2:13			Faster tempo again, with new strumming pattern
2:16	Hágase por fin tu voluntad aquí en la tierra Dános tu fuerza y tu valor al combatir Sopla como el viento la flor de la quebrada Limpia como el fuego el cañon de mi fusil	Let your will at last come about here on earth Give us your strength and valor to fight Blow like the wind the flower of the canyon Clean like fire the barrel of my gun	Increasingly complicated vocal harmonies, with all members singing in unison on last two lines
2:37			Increase in tempo, return to minor key
2:41	Levántate, y mírate las manos Para crecer estréchala tu hermano Juntos iremos, unidos en la sangre Ahora y en la hora de nuestra muerte Amen.	Arise and look at your hands So as to grow, reach out to your brother Together we will go, united by blood Now and in the hour of our death Amen.	Sense of urgency builds to the final lines sung in unison, then new harmonies ring out in the repeated "Amen"

On September 11, 1973, after three years of turbulent rule, General Augusto Pinochet led a brutal military coup that toppled the Allende government. Pinochet assumed control of the country for the next 17 years. Because of their close association with Allende, nueva canción musicians experienced severe persecution under the new regime. Soldiers tortured and executed Víctor Jara in the very stadium where he had performed "Plegaria a un labrador" just a few years before, and others, like Ángel Parra, spent years in prison camps. Quilapayún and Inti-Illimani, two of the most popular and influential nueva canción groups, were on tour in Europe at the time of the coup and remained in exile for nearly two decades. One unexpected outcome of these tragic circumstances was a further popularization of "Andean music" in Europe, as exiled groups performed their neo-Andean repertoire and political songs for crowds of fans and sympathizers throughout the 1970s and 1980s. The political triumph and tragedy of nueva canción in Chile also inspired other musicians in Latin America, who adopted its repertoire and ideology to create similar, politically engaged folk music movements in their own countries.

Beyond political activism, thousands of other musicians from the Andes also sought to capitalize on the international popularity of Andean music at this time by migrating to major cities in Europe, the United States, and Asia in hopes of making a living. Forming bands with the now-classic "Andean ensemble" instrumentation, they played on street corners, in subway stops, and, when possible, on concert stages, establishing a migratory circuit that continues to this day. The music that such bands perform is usually based on arrangements of Andean melodies that have now bounced back and forth across the Atlantic Ocean several times—from the folk music *peñas* of Buenos Aires to the Left Bank clubs of Paris, from the nueva canción movement in Chile to the subways of London and Frankfurt. Such "ponchos and panpipes" music, as British ethnomusicologist Jan Fairley has called it, now defines "Andean music" for much of the world, however distant in sound, execution, or aesthetic from the indigenous and mestizo genres it claims to represent.

Classical Music

Despite significant Western art-music composition and performance in the colonial Viceroyalty of Peru (see Chapter 2), the countries of the central Andes began importing much of their art music from Europe following independence from Spain in the 1820s. Italian opera ruled the day, usually performed by touring artists from Europe, though zarzuelas, Spanish "light operas," became quite popular in the late nineteenth century. Elites throughout the region embraced salon dance music from Europe, particularly the Viennese waltz, as home entertainment. As in much of Latin America, however, enduring art-music institutions and definable national styles of musical composition did not emerge until the twentieth century.

In the early 1900s, the sensibilities of European Romanticism gave way to a newfound sense of nationalism in Latin America, sparking a generation of composers to begin incorporating folkloric elements into their works. This nationalist awakening was particularly acute in the Andes, where military and territorial disputes led to bloody conflicts between Ecuador, Peru, Bolivia, Paraguay, and Chile, and prompted a search for cultural narratives that could better unite fragmented populations.

One of the first composers to channel nationalist sentiment into his music in Peru was José María Valle-Riestra (1859–1925). Born in Lima and educated in London, Paris, and Berlin, Valle-Riestra composed numerous works that reflected European trends of the time in their harmonic language and form. His major contribution to nationalist repertoire was the opera *Ollanta*, composed in 1900 and revised to great acclaim in 1920. Based on an eighteenth-century Peruvian tale of forbidden love between the title character, a lower-caste chief, and a daughter of the Inca emperor, the opera successfully fused the sounds of Italian opera with a romanticized vision of the Peruvian past. This created a paradigm for indigenista composition throughout the

Andes. The leading Ecuadorian composer of the early twentieth century, Luis Humberto Salgado (1903–1977), followed a similar model in his symphonic suite *Atahualpa* (1922), named after the last Inca ruler, while the Bolivian composer José María Velasco-Maidana utilized Quechua and Aymara mythical subjects in his ballet *Amerindia* (1934–1935) and other symphonic works.

Daniel Alomía Robles (1871–1942) stands out as the composer most associated with the indigenista school. Born in the highland city of Huánuco, Peru, Alomía Robles was the quintessential nineteenth-century gentleman-scholar. Trained as a naturalist, he read widely, maintaining professional interests in medicine, zoology, and botany, but also cultivating an interest in the nascent field of folklore. During his travels throughout Peru, Ecuador, and Bolivia collecting medicinal herbs, he encountered the region's variety of musical traditions. Alomía Robles eventually transcribed hundreds of indigenous and mestizo songs, systematically categorizing them and noting basic information about their places of origin. As part of this work, he became an early proponent of the theory that the Inca musical system was based upon a pentatonic scale, an issue that dominated Peruvian musicology for many decades.

Alomía Robles's lack of formal musical training restricted his musical output to smaller-scale compositions, primarily piano pieces and songs, but it also insured his originality. Rather than simply setting the hundreds of melodies he had collected to harmonic accompaniment—a popular method of "Indianist" composition in North America—or echoing European trends, he attempted to re-create the flavor of indigenous and mestizo tunes by writing his own, based on the melodic, harmonic, and rhythmic structures of the originals. The piece of this sort that made Alomía Robles famous, and the tune which has become synonymous with "Andean music" all over the world, is "El cóndor pasa."

FIGURE 8.15 Daniel Alomía Robles

Written in 1913 as part of the score for a zarzuela of the same name, "El cóndor pasa" proved immensely popular from the outset. With a libretto by Julio Baudouin (under the pseudonym Julio de la Paz), the zarzuela enjoyed more than three thousand performances during a five-year run at the Mazzi Theater in Lima. In contrast to other indigenista works of the period, the subject matter of "El cóndor pasa" was contemporary and quite political. Set in a small mining settlement in the highland Peruvian region of Cerro de Pasco, the story focuses on the exploitation of indigenous workers by the mine's North American owners. Led by the rebellious Frank, who, unbeknownst to him, is the illegitimate child of one of the owners, the miners eventually kill their bosses, and the play ends with a condor circling overhead as the symbol of their newfound freedom. Alomía Robles never published the zarzuela's score, and the only segment that has survived to the present is entitled "Cashua" (an indigenous genre with pre-Hispanic roots). This movement contains the melody now known as "El cóndor pasa," which the composer later acknowledged to have based in part upon an existing **yaraví** (a slow, romantic mestizo song form), entitled "Soy la paloma que el nido perdió" (I Am the Dove Lost by the Nest).

Alomía Robles himself contributed to the eventual international popularity of "El cóndor pasa," publishing a piano arrangement in New York after relocating there in 1919. It included three contrasting sections: a slow, ethereal introduction in which a single pentatonic motif is repeated against an arpeggiated E minor chord; a setting of the now-famous melody as a **pasacalle**, a heavy, downbeat-oriented genre of Andean music intended to accompany street processions or public dancing; and a final section set to the lively rhythms of a wayno. This version of "El cóndor pasa" resurfaced in the Parisian music clubs of the 1950s, where it formed part of "Andean folklore" repertoire, often without attribution to Alomía Robles. North American folk music star Paul Simon first heard the tune there in 1965 after meeting the band Los Incas, and eventually wrote his own lyrics to the melody. Recorded with Art Garfunkel and superimposed on the recording given to him by Los Incas, Simon's version appeared to worldwide acclaim on the 1970 LP *Bridge Over Troubled Water*. Since that time, there have been literally thousands of recordings of "El cóndor pasa" (iTunes currently lists more than 150!) ranging stylistically from salsa to mariachi to new age, including an inimitable version by Peruvian semiclassical soprano Yma Sumac. It remains standard repertoire for all Andean folkloric ensembles (Listening Guide 8.7), and in 2004 the Peruvian National Institute of Culture declared it "national cultural heritage."

Other composers in the early to mid-twentieth century followed nationalist-indigenista agendas similar to those of Valle-Riestra and Alomía Robles, though drawing on distinct regional traditions. Best known of the indigenista composers of this epoch in Peru was Teodoro Valcárcel (1900–1942), from Puno, who wrote numerous works for piano as well as for orchestra, including *Suite incaica* (Inca Suite, 1929). The Bolivian composer Eduardo Caba (1890–1953) drew upon the pentatonic melodies and **modal** structures of the traditional music of his native Potosí in numerous works, including the tone poem *Potosí*, his ballet *Kollana*, and a set of 18 works for piano, *Aires indios* (Indian Airs). In Ecuador, Pedro Pablo Traversari (1874–1956) pursued a similar path, writing numerous programmatic works based on indigenous legends, including *Cumandá*, *La profecía de Huiracocha* (The Prophecy of Wiracocha), and *Hijos del sol* (Children of the Sun).

⊚ Robles: "El cóndor pasa" (The Condor Passes)

Composer: Daniel Alomia Robles

Date of composition: 1913

Date of recording: 1992

Performers/instruments: Inca: The Peruvian Ensemble, with *pututus* (conch-shell trumpets), kena, charango, guitar, bombo, and *shacshas* (goat-hoof rattles)

Genre: Andean folklore (pasacalle and wayno)

Form: multiple contrasting sections, each increasing in tempo until the conclusion

Tempo/meter: unmetered introduction and conclusion; slow, medium, and fast duple meters in the **A**, **B**, and **C** sections

What to Listen for:

- Contrasting sections evoking different Andean genres
- Neo-Andean folklore ensemble format

Time	Description
0:00	**Introduction** Begins with two sustained blasts on conch-shell trumpets, an instrument utilized by the Incas
0:12	Sustained chords begin on the guitar and charango, accompanying an unmetered pentatonic motif played on the kena
1:14	**A** The famous "condor" melody played by the kena and accompanied by guitar and charango in the style of a very slow wayno
2:12	Entrance of a second kena, playing a harmonic accompaniment to the main melody; charango at harmony's beginning, as the performer switches to a sustained tremolo characteristic of charango playing in this folkloric style
2:59	**B** Repetition of the "condor" melody, this time at a faster tempo and set as a pasacalle; single, strummed downbeats in the guitar and charango
3:36	**C** Increase in tempo again and introduction of a new, two-part melody, played now in the style of a rapid tempo wayno; different strumming patterns played by the guitar and charango, which are typical for a wayno
4:18	Repetition of melody
4:53	Brief conclusion, marked by sustained chords on the string instruments and a cadenza-like kena solo, echoing the introduction

European musicians and composers who settled in Andean countries also made important contributions to indigenista repertoire and musicological literature at this time. The Spanish Franciscan monks Francisco María Alberdi (1878–1934) and Agustín de Azkúnaga (1885–1957) composed sacred music as well as secular works with indigenista themes, while their fellow Franciscan Manuel Mola-Mateau (1918–1991) directed the National Conservatory in Quito and founded a school for church music. Belgian composer Andrés Sas (1900–1967) settled in Lima in 1924 and eventually incorporated popular and folk melodies into his works, including the third movement of his String Quartet (1938). Sas also wrote the first major study of art music in Lima during the colonial period. Similarly, the German composer Rodolfo Holzmann (1910–1992), who moved to Peru in 1938 to teach oboe, wrote orchestral suites in an indigenista style, and made important contributions to Peruvian musicology, including the first survey of twentieth-century art-music composers and a study of the music of the Q'eros people in rural Cuzco.

Since the mid-twentieth century, Andean composers have alternated between nationalism (in the model of their indigenista forebears) and participation in more broadly transnational art-music trends. Some incorporate folk and popular melodies, others have embraced serialism and atonality, and still others have drawn on both. One prominent example of the latter approach, and arguably the most celebrated art-music composer in the Andes today, is Celso Garrido-Lecca (b. 1926). Born in the northern Peruvian city of Piura, Garrido-Lecca was a student of both Holzmann and Sas before continuing his composition studies in Chile and with Aaron Copland in the United States. Most of his early work bears a European modernist orientation, with the frequent use of **serial** techniques. In the 1960s and early 1970s, however, Garrido-Lecca taught at the University of Chile in Santiago, where he became involved with the developing nueva canción movement and collaborated with Víctor Jara and Inti-Illimani, among others. His compositional work ever since has incorporated both the formalism of his early training as well as Andean folkloric or popular elements. His String Quartet No. 2 (Listening Guide 8.8, 1988) offers a striking example, modernist in aesthetic but written in memory of Víctor Jara, and including variations on the melody of "Plegaria a un labrador" in its fifth movement.

In 1973, like many people associated with the nueva canción movement, Garrido-Lecca fled the Pinochet regime in Chile, eventually settling back in Lima. As director of the National Conservatory, Garrido-Lecca worked both to increase the stature and presence of art-music in Peru as well as connect the country's small art-music establishment with its thriving popular culture. Toward that end, he ran a "Popular Song Workshop" at the conservatory, offering classes in Andean instruments and even the Quechua language to conservatory students and poorer youth with no prior access to (or interest in) the institution. Despite his efforts, the worlds of art music and popular culture remain distant today in Peru, and classical music has at best a marginal presence in the region.

⊚ Garrido-Lecca, String Quartet No. 2, "Epilogue," fifth movement

Composer: Celso Garrido-Lecca

Date of composition: 1988

Performers/instruments: Cuarteto Latinoamericano, two violins, viola, and cello

Date of recording: 1992

Genre: string quartet

Form: sonata form

Tempo/meter: slow compound duple

What to Listen for:
- Use of Jara's "Plegaria a un labrador" melody as a main theme
- Sonata form, with exposition, development, and recapitulation

Time	Description
0:00	**Exposition**
0:06	**First theme** A sprightly, up-tempo theme drawing on material from the first movement of the string quartet
0:44	**Second theme** Opening melody of Jara's "Plegaria" played by first violin (Example 8.4)
1:17	**Development** **First section** Development of second theme, transposing it to new keys and altering fragments of the melody over a changing rhythmic foundation
2:11	**Second section** Development of the first theme, again transposing and altering fragments of the melody, then transitioning to the recapitulation
	Recapitulation
2:48	**First theme**
3:44	**Second theme** Played in the lower octave by the cello
4:28	**Coda** Slow fade to quiet murmur of string harmonics

EXAMPLE 8.4: Celso Garrido-Lecca, String Quartet No. 2, "Epilogue," mm. 24–32

Conclusion

This chapter has explored just a few of the many diverse musical traditions of the Andes. Many more merit discussion, from the elaborate dance-dramas of Cuzco's Sacred valley to the contemporary hip-hop of Chile's indigenous Mapuche population. Nonetheless, our focus on Peruvian musical practices demonstrates some of the important ways that Andean peoples use music to articulate class, ethnic, and national identities, and the key role that music has played in regional political developments. The chapter has also traced the process by which musical traditions move into new performance contexts, or have their meanings reconfigured, through engagement with the world far beyond the Andes—from foreign tourists listening to a sikuri on an island in Lake Titicaca, to Andean musicians playing "El cóndor pasa" on a street corner near you. More than the use of panpipes or pentatonic scales, it is that adaptability and layering of old and new sounds that defines Andean music today, and ensures that this region will continue to have a distinctive place in the panorama of Latin American musical styles.

KEY TERMS

Aymara	indigenismo	siku
bordón	jarana	sikuri
cajón	kena	tarka
charango	marinera	technocumbia
chicha	modal	tundete
cholo	nueva canción	vals
chuscada	pasacalle	vocables
folklorization	Quechua	wayno
harawi	serial	yaraví
hocketing	shamanism	

FURTHER READING

Bigenho, Michelle. *Sounding Indigenous: Authenticity in Bolivian Music Performance*. New York: Palgrave, 2002.

Bolaños, César, et al., eds. *La música en el Perú*. 2nd ed. Lima: Fondo Editorial Filarmonía, 2007.

Feldman, Heidi. *Black Rhythms of Peru: Reviving African Musical Heritage in the Black Pacific*. Middletown, CT: Wesleyan University Press, 2006.

Mendoza, Zoila. *Shaping Society through Dance: Mestizo Ritual Performance in the Peruvian Andes*. Chicago: University of Chicago Press, 2000.

Romero, Raúl. *Debating the Past: Music, Memory, and Identity in the Andes*. New York and Oxford: Oxford University Press, 2001.

Stobart, Henry. *Music and the Poetics of Production in the Bolivian Andes*. Aldershot, UK: Ashgate, 2006.

Turino, Thomas. *Music in the Andes: Experiencing Music, Expressing Culture*. New York: Oxford University Press, 2007.

Wibbelsman, Michelle. *Ritual Encounters: Otavalan Modern and Mythic Community*. Urbana and Chicago: University of Illinois Press, 2009.

FURTHER LISTENING

Traditional Music of Peru, vols. 1–8. Smithsonian Folkways Recordings, 1995–2002.

FURTHER VIEWING

Ciudad chicha ("Chicha City"). Omar Ráez and Raúl Romero, directors. Instituto de Etnomusicología, Pontificia Universidad Católica del Perú, 2005.

El derecho de vivir en paz ("The Right to Live in Peace"). Carmen Luz Parot, director. Warner Music Chile, 2003.

Latin American Impact on Contemporary Classical Music

WALTER AARON CLARK

Throughout this textbook, we have noted European influences on Latin American classical music, not only in terms of the importation of the music itself but also the many European musicians who have emigrated to and worked in Latin America. European-derived classical music remains a vital force in Latin American culture, as reflected in the music curricula of Latin American conservatories and universities. These emphasize classical music, while local traditional and popular styles are generally taught and practiced in other contexts. For example, while there are major conservatories of music in Mexico City and Buenos Aires, more than a thousand students are enrolled in the state-supported Universidade Livre de Música (Free University of Music) in São Paulo, where they study all kinds of popular music.

Classically trained performers and composers in Latin America get plenty of exposure to traditional and popular musics outside of the university or conservatory environment and frequently incorporate those influences into their music. In fact, nationalistic works by composers like Carlos Chávez, Alberto Ginastera, and Heitor Villa-Lobos draw heavily from vernacular musical traditions. Such composers are thoroughly embraced by the conservatories and universities in Latin America, and their music has acquired an almost official status as representative of their respective nations. In short, the European classical tradition has become a Latin American tradition as well, and governments and state agencies frequently support music written in this style even more enthusiastically than traditional or popular repertoire.

It is important to emphasize that cultural influences flow in multiple directions and that Latin America has had a great impact on the classical

LISTENING guides

Frank, *Sonata andina*, fourth movement

León, *Horizons*

Desenne, "Piazzolaberintus" from *Tango Sabatier*, Three Tangos for Arpegina and Piano

Sierra, "Agnus Dei," from *Missa Latina "Pro Pace"*

Ortiz, Five Micro Études for Solo Tape, No. 5

Davidovsky, *Synchronisms No. 10* for Guitar and Electronic Sounds

Chagas, *RAW*, a Multimedia Opera

Santaolalla, Overture to *Diarios de motocicleta*

music traditions of Europe, as well as the United States. That impact continues unabated today. Indeed, just as Latin America has historically imported composers from Europe, it now exports many composers to Europe and the United States; moreover, many U.S. composers with Latin American ancestry embrace their heritage in composing classical music. This chapter briefly surveys the history of Latin American influence in classical music beyond Latin America, and then focuses on the lives and creative work of eight prominent Latin American and Latino/a composers of today.

Historical Background

Europe

Not long after the conquest, hybridized Latin American songs and dances blending European, African, and indigenous elements were taken back to the Old World, where they underwent further changes and found their way from the streets of Spain to the courts of the European nobility. Dances of this sort included the *zarabanda* and *chacona*. Although no detailed information exists about their origins in the New World, we know that by the late sixteenth century they had become fashionable in Spain. These dances were lively and licentious, and the clergy at times attempted to suppress them, especially the *chacona*, notorious for its explicitly sexual movements.

During the early seventeenth century, versions of the *zarabanda* and *chacona* gained a following in other parts of Europe, especially Italy, where Girolamo Frescobaldi (1583–1643) wrote *ciaconnas* for harpsichord. Just as court musicians began to include this mestizo music in their repertoire and compose new pieces inspired by it, so dancers also adapted the steps to make them suitable for performance at court. Over time, the character of the genres changed, so that by the early eighteenth century, the Frenchified sarabande and chaconne had become stately and dignified rather than raucous. They were among the most prominent genres of music and dance during the entire Baroque period.

In the nineteenth century, the Latin American habanera (see Chapter 5) gained widespread popularity among European audiences. One of the most influential composers of habaneras abroad was Sebastián Iradier (1809–1865), a musician from the Basque region of Spain. His many habaneras include such hits as "La paloma" (The dove) and "El arreglito" (The little arrangement). "La paloma" is among the most popular songs ever written, in Latin America and around the world; indeed, many people mistakenly think it is a folk song. Iradier composed it after visiting Cuba in 1861 but died in obscurity a few years later, never to learn how successful his composition would become. The French composer Georges Bizet (1838–1875) made "El arreglito" famous in his 1875 opera *Carmen*, which tells the story of a Spanish Gypsy who lures an army officer to a life of crime, ultimately sealing her own fate as well as his. In the first act, Carmen sings her song "L'amour est un oiseau rebelle" (Love Is a Rebellious Bird). Thinking "El arreglito" was a folk song, Bizet freely used it as the basis for his aria; however, he soon realized his error and gave Iradier credit in the score. Several other French composers wrote pieces in the style of the habanera, especially Emmanuel Chabrier (1841–1894) and Maurice Ravel (1875–1937).

The habanera achieved popularity in Spain as well, and many composers there wove its characteristic rhythms into their instrumental and stage works. Several piano pieces by Isaac Albéniz (1860–1909) are in the style of the habanera, including "Tango" from *España: Seis hojas de álbum* (1890). As late as 1932, Federico Moreno Torroba (1891–1982) composed the lovely "Habanera del Saboyano" for the first act of his zarzuela (Spanish operetta) *Luisa Fernanda*.

United States

The Latin impact in classical music has also been noticeable among composers in the United States. One of the first to utilize Latin rhythms in concert music was the piano virtuoso and composer Louis Moreau Gottschalk (1829–1869). Born in New Orleans, Gottschalk studied in Paris and then spent considerable time concertizing in Cuba and Puerto Rico, where he came under the spell of the Caribbean's musical charm. Many of his works exhibit the syncopated rhythms of Afro-Cuban and Puerto Rican music and dance, especially his *Souvenir de Porto Rico, Marche des Gibaros*, op. 31, for piano and orchestra.

In the twentieth century, leading American composers borrowing from the treasure trove of Latin music included Aaron Copland (1900–1990), a close friend of Carlos Chávez. Some of Copland's most famous compositions evoke the sights and sounds of Mexico, where he spent time traveling and establishing connections with local musicians during the 1930s and 1940s. *Danzón cubano, El salón México*, and *Rodeo* are three orchestral works that utilize the sounds of Mexican traditional music.

A student and friend of Copland was the conductor and composer Leonard Bernstein (1918–1990), whose score for the 1957 hit Broadway musical *West Side Story* includes some of the most celebrated evocations of Latin American music, particularly the mambo that sets the scene for the dance party during which the star-crossed lovers first meet. Another number, "America," uses the *sesquiáltera*, or hemiola, rhythms that are a hallmark of Hispanic music. The lyrics express in an acerbic and even sarcastic manner the ambivalent feelings the Puerto Ricans harbor towards their new home, a land of promises not yet fulfilled.

Latin American Impact Today

Clearly, Latin American music of various kinds has had a continuous impact on classical music for hundreds of years. Commentary in the preceding chapters has also noted that, starting in the twentieth century, Latin American musical styles and Latin American composers themselves entered the mainstream of classical music and achieved international renown. Indeed, Villa-Lobos, Chávez, and Ginastera rank among the most prominent composers of the last century. That trend certainly persists today, and thus this chapter considers actual composers who are making their presence felt abroad through their music and their teaching. This discussion includes one composer who was born in the United States but has Peruvian ancestry and has spent considerable time in the Andes, and another who continues to work in Mexico but has spent years in Britain and the United States. The others all live and work in the United States or divide their time between the United States and their native countries. They are living proof that the impact of Latin America results not only from its vast musical heritage but also its outstanding composers.

One finds a great multiplicity of approaches to music composition among these composers, though many of them retain some element in their work that reflects their roots in Latin America. Latin American classical composers write tonal music, music reflecting the influence of popular culture, atonal and serial music, music for voices and for acoustic instruments, electronic music generated by synthesizers and computers, and multimedia works that bring together electronic and acoustic sounds as well as dance, theater, and the visual arts. They write this music for concerts, theater, film, and the church. Thus, their compositions reach a wide and diverse audience;

❀ In Depth 9.1

Composers in Latin America Today

The European-derived tradition of classical music is ubiquitous throughout Latin America, and numerous composers not only create new music but also teach in the region's many conservatories and universities. It serves a useful purpose here to list some of the leading figures, several mentioned in earlier chapters, before focusing on a select few whose careers have had international resonance. Although this list is far from exhaustive, it reveals the large numbers of contemporary composers in Latin America, most of whom continue to work in their native countries.

(continued)

Contemporary Composers in Latin America

Country	Composer
Argentina	Mario Davidovsky, Mariano Etkin, Gerardo Gandini, Osvaldo Golijov, Francisco Kröpfl, Marta Lambertini, alcides lanza, Graciela Paraskevaídis, Salvador Ranieri, Gustavo Santaolalla, Daniel Teruggi, Julio Viera
Bolivia	Augustín Fernández Sánchez, Oscar García, Cesar Junaro, Juan Antonio Maldonado, Willy Pozadas, Cergio Prudencio, Alberto Villalpando
Brazil	Jorge Antunes, Paulo Chagas, Rodrigo Cicchelli Velloso, Rodolfo Coelho de Souza, Paulo Costa Lima, Luis Carlos Csekö, Vânia Dantas Leite, Cirlei de Hollanda, Felipe Lara, José Augusto Mannis, Chico Mello, Flo Menezes, Marlos Nobre, Ilza Nogueira, Jamary de Oliveira, Jocy de Oliveira, Tim Rescala, Marisa Rezende, Agnaldo Ribeiro, Ricardo Taccuchian, Roberto Victorio
Chile	Juan Allende-Blin, José V. Asuar, Gustavo Becerra, Gabriel Brncic, Eduardo Cáceres, Eduardo Maturana, Juan Orrego Salas, Abelardo Quinteros, León Schidlowsky, Claudio Spies, Darwin Vargas
Colombia	Rodolfo Acosta, Blas Emilio Atehortúa, Mauricio Bejarano, Roberto García, Andrés Posada, Jesús Pinzón, Luis Pulido, Francisco Zumaqué
Costa Rica	Jorge Luis Acevedo, Mario Alfagüell, Alejandro Cardona, Luis Diego Herra, Mauricio Pauly, William Porras
Cuba	Cálixto Alvarez, Efraín Amador, Héctor Angulo, Juan Blanco, Leo Brouwer, Carlos Fariñas, Sergio Fernández Barroso, Jorge Garciaporrúa, Tania León, José Loyola, Carlos Malcolm, José Angel Pérez Puentes, Juan Piñera, Magaly Ruiz, Roberto Valera, Aurelio de la Vega
Dominican Republic	José Antonio Molina, Miguel Pichardo-Vicioso
Ecuador	Milton Estévez, Gerard Guevara, Diego Luzuriaga, Mesías Maiguashca, Arturo Rodas
El Salvador	Hugo Calderón, Jr., Víctor Manuel López Guzmán, Gilberto Orellana Castro
Guatemala	William Orbaugh, Joaquín Orellana
Honduras	Norma Erazo, Sergio Suazo Lang
Mexico	Manuel de Elías, Julio Estrada, José Luis Hurtado, Federico Ibarra, Ana Lara, Mario Lavista, Arturo Márquez, Gabriela Ortiz
Panama	José Luis Cajar, Florentin Giménez, Marina Saiz Salazar
Paraguay	Nicolás Pérez González
Peru	Luis David Aguilar, Teófilo Alvarez, César Bolaños, José Carols Campos, Walter Casas Napán, Pozzi Escot, Celso Garrido-Lecca, Leopoldo La Rosa, Pedro Malpica, José Malsio, Alejandro Núñez Allauca, Francisco Bernardo Pulgar Vidal, Edgar Valcárcel, Pedro Seiji Asato, Douglas Tarnawiecki, Jorge Villavicencio Grossmann
Puerto Rico	Luis M. Álvarez, Rafael Aponte-Ledée, Ernesto Cordero, Ignacio Morales Nieva, William Ortiz, Francis Schwartz, Roberto Sierra, Raymond Torres Santos
Uruguay	Miguel del Águila, Coriún Aharonián, León Biriotti, Sergio Cervetti, Diego Legrand, Antonio Mastrogiovanni, Rene Pietrafresa, José Serebrier
Venezuela	Miguel Astor, Jorge Benzaquén, Tulio Cremisini, Paul Desenne, Carlos Duarte, Carlos García, Emilio Mendoza, Alfredo del Mónaco, Alfredo Rugeles, Ricardo Teruel

however, very experimental, avant-garde works, especially atonal music, usually appeal to a rather select group of listeners who have both the openness and background to approach and appreciate this repertoire, which is often very challenging in its complexity.

The freedom a contemporary composer has to create according to his or her own vision is nearly complete and certainly greater than at any other time in music history. This freedom is made all the more noteworthy because of the emancipation of women in the world of professional music and their full participation as performers, conductors, and composers, something that had never before been the case in the male-dominated world of classical music from the Middle Ages onward (In Depth 9.2).

The following survey of the contemporary scene in Latin American classical music considers the principal developments of the last 20 years or so, focusing on representative composers who work in the major media and genres of contemporary music, including acoustic, electronic, electroacoustic, multimedia, and film music.

Acoustic Music

It should come as no surprise that a majority of contemporary composers continue to write for traditional instruments. First of all, they usually play these instruments themselves, especially piano, and feel a special rapport with them. Second, there is a continuing demand from performers and audiences alike for new acoustic music that can be presented in traditional concert venues. Composers have relatively few difficulties finding excellent pianists, violinists, or guitarists to play their new compositions. Finally, the resources of instruments like the piano, violin, and guitar have by no means been exhausted, and they present an ongoing challenge to composers to explore the sounds they can produce. **Extended techniques** are a crucial part of this exploration, as they represent nontraditional ways of playing traditional instruments, such as striking, blowing, plucking, or otherwise generating sound on them in ways earlier composers did not. Along with this increase in the resources available on acoustic instruments has come an expansion in the musical language itself, with the advent of **microtonality**, atonality, and new methods of notation.

I now consider a few composers whose acoustic compositions are on the cutting edge of contemporary music.

Gabriela Lena Frank

Gabriela Lena Frank (b. 1972) is a Bay Area composer whose mother is Chinese-Peruvian and father, American, of Lithuanian-Jewish extraction. She was raised in the United States but retains a close cultural and spiritual

In Depth 9.2

The Rise of Women Composers

FIGURE 9.1 (a) Gabriela Lena Frank, (b) Tania León, and (c) Gabriela Ortiz

Women have not occupied a central place in this textbook's survey of classical music, largely because of the marginalized position they traditionally held in society and the very limited professional opportunities available to them in the past. In the Middle Ages and well into the colonial period, women were normally not permitted to sing in church when men were present. This was in obedience to Paul's injunction in I Corinthians 14:34, stating that "women should keep silence in the churches." Thus, women were restricted to composing and performing sacred music for their own use, in convents and orphanages. Their music was almost never presented outside those contexts or published. This effectively eliminated women from the ranks of Renaissance composers whose music we know and perform today. Noblewomen could, of course, take private music lessons, but only to enhance their social graces. With the rise of opera in the seventeenth and eighteenth centuries and the increasing commercial demand for female voices, women began to appear more prominently

in professional musical circles and to obtain the training they needed to write music. But they were seldom accepted as professional composers. In the nineteenth century, female performers, such as Venezuela's Teresa Carreño (see chapter 4), gained celebrity status on both sides of the Atlantic, and they composed and even published piano pieces, songs, and chamber works; however, they were not taken seriously as composers of larger works, like symphonies and operas. Women were not thought to possess the intellectual gifts necessary for writing works of such complexity. In fact, the world most women inhabited remained bounded by domestic responsibilities until well into the twentieth century, when a rising tide of equal rights gave them greater access to musical education and professional opportunities, in both performance and composition. Today, some of the leading composers of our time are women, and they write in all genres, including symphonic works, and for all media, electronic as well as acoustic. Three such composers are featured in this chapter.

connection with Peru, where she has spent considerable time studying Andean folklore. In fact, her music frequently incorporates Andean mythology, archeology, art, poetry, and music into Western classical forms, reflecting her Peruvian American heritage.

Frank received her doctorate in composition from the University of Michigan in 2001. Although many composers today find it necessary to have a teaching position at a university in order to make a living, Frank has been able to support herself mostly by composing and performing. The roster of renowned concert artists who have played her music is large and includes such names as the Kronos Quartet; Cuarteto Latinoamericano; Chanticleer; the San Francisco, Chicago, Boston, Atlanta, Baltimore, and Philadelphia symphonies; and cellist Yo-Yo Ma. In 2009 she received a Guggenheim fellowship to work on an opera with Pulitzer Prize–winning playwright Nilo Cruz about Frida Kahlo and Diego Rivera. Her list of honors also includes a Latin Grammy (2009) for Best Contemporary Classical Composition, *Inca Dances*, written for guitarist Manuel Barrueco and the Cuarteto Latinoamericano.

Frank continues to demonstrate that it is possible for modern composers to connect with concert audiences without compromising their artistic vision. Her *Sonata andina* (Andean Sonata, Listening Guide 9.1) for solo

LISTENING guide 9.1

◎ Frank: *Sonata andina* (Andean Sonata), fourth movement

Composer: Gabriela Lena Frank

Date of composition: 2000

Performer/instrument: Gabriella Frank, piano

Date of recording: 2000

Genre: programmatic piano solo

Form: free alternation of various themes and sounds derived from Peruvian folk music

Tempo/meter: variable meters and complex rhythms drawing both on folklore and the classical avant-garde

What to Listen for:

- Virtuosic piano playing requiring excellent technique
- Suggestion of folk instruments, such as the charango (small lute), tambor (drum), and zampoñas (panpipes)
- Use of hemiola (*sesquiáltera*) rhythms typical of Latin American folk music

Time	Description
0:00	**Opening vamp** Impression of a group of guitarists, *charanguistas* (charango players), and *tamboristas* (drummers) strumming and drumming to signal the opening of the piece. Open strings of the guitar appear in the first couple of bars and then the harmony changes, displaying a wide variety of chords for the rest of the piece. At 0:26, *charanguistas* gradually die out, just as a rhythmic groove begins to enter at 0:38

(continued)

Time	Description
0:38	**_Golpe_ section 1** Quickly repeated chords in the right hand support a melody line that is punctuated by a simulation of guitar _golpes_, when a guitarist strikes the strings with the flat of the hand. _Golpes_ occur at roughly two-second intervals from 0:43 to 0:56
1:08	**Transition 1** Arpeggio figure in the left hand reoccurs throughout the movement
1:11	**Zampoña melody 1** First appearance of _sesquiáltera_; notes of this melody correspond to the pipes of some varieties of zampoña: E–G–A–B–D–E, against the left-hand arpeggio from transition 1. It is repeated, with new ornamentation, at 1:19
1:28	**_Zumballyu_ section** Spinning figure in the left hand inspired by a child's top from the Andes, the _zumballyu_ (will return later in the _vendaval_ section). At 1:34, another zampoña melody (zampoña melody 2) in the right hand, a skipping light phrase; parts of the melody mimick sliding the mouth over several pipes in one breath. At 1:53, repetition of the whole idea, with new harmony
2:08	**Transition 2** _Sesquiáltera_ that will return later
2:11	**Marimba-inspired section** Peruvian musicians also play the marimba, striking the same keys over and over again, with both mallets at once or alternating the notes and rhythms. Two basic rhythmic patterns appear here: the first at 2:11–2:17 and 2:24–2:31, and the second at 2:17–2:24 and 2:31–2:38
2:46	**Reprisal of first _golpe_ section** Return of the first _golpe_ section in a different key
3:11	**Reprisal of Zampoña melody 1** Melody from before, now in G minor and in strict imitation between the two hands
3:17	**Reprisal of transition 2** Same as before but transposed to another key
3:22	**_Vendaval_ section** A gusty storm (_vendaval_) inspired this section. Moving line in the right hand echoes the left-hand _zumballyu_ figure from before; left hand features the figure from transition 1 and the zampoña melody 1 sections; excerpts spliced in from the zampoña melody
4:04	**Long transition into coda** Inspired by the marimba patterns presented earlier, which build up to the return of the opening guitar-charango-drum vamp
4:11	**Reprisal of opening vamp** Very last dying figure in the final bar echoes zampoña melody 2, originally accompanied by the _zumballyu_ but now only accompanied by a low **trill** in the left hand, a final drum roll

piano is an excellent example of her skill in suggesting the sounds of folk instruments like the **zampoñas** (another common term for sikus in the Andes) and charango. The last movement draws inspiration from various live performances the composer heard in Peru during her first extended visit to the country. She spins these impressions in a way that is exciting to her personally, yet still preserves a distinctly Latin spirit. She intends to stretch the definition of a "Latin sound" through everything she composes.

Tania León

In the post–World War II era, composers in the Americas increasingly wrote music in the avant-garde style, without a tonal center or strong sense of pulse. It would seem that such a musical environment would not be conducive to the influence of Latin melodies and rhythms, but some contemporary composers have found a way to affirm their *hispanidad* in works that are otherwise quite rigorous in their modernity.

Tania León typifies a generation of composers determined to bridge a growing gulf between modern composers and audiences by writing music that is uncompromising in its originality and virtuosity while maintaining a profound connection with their musical roots. León (b. 1943) has African, Asian, and Spanish ancestry; originally from Cuba, she has lived and worked for many years in New York. A prolific composer, she writes for a wide range of genres, including orchestral works, ballets, opera, percussion ensemble, and chamber music.

León is not only a composer but an accomplished conductor as well, having led orchestras in the United States and throughout Europe. She has taught at Harvard and Yale and is currently a Distinguished Professor at City University of New York. She has received numerous prestigious appointments, grants, and awards, including a Guggenheim fellowship (2007). The range of her activities is truly impressive and indicative of the way that Latinas are having an increasing impact on the cultural life of the United States. For this reason, she has been featured on all the major networks, as well as Univision and Telemundo. In 2010 she was inducted into the American Academy of Arts and Letters.

Her orchestral composition *Horizons* (Listening Guide 9.2) skillfully combines avant-garde techniques—complex rhythms and atonal passages—with elements of Latin American music: imitation of the claves in the piano part, and use of the harp to suggest folk music. Though the harp is not common in Cuba today, León is clearly adopting a pan-Latin approach in her music. The same is true of her use of piano "claves," which play rhythms of her own invention and are meant, like the harp, to suggest Latin America in general, insofar as instruments similar to the claves appear in many regional traditions, not just in Cuba.

⊚ León: *Horizons*

Composer: Tania León

Date of composition: 1999

Performers/instruments: North German Radio Symphony, conducted by Peter Ruzicka

Date of recording: 1999

Genre: orchestral work

Form: free form based on evolving melodic ideas

Tempo/meter: lively tempo using complex, repeating rhythm patterns as basis for melodic overlay; juxtaposition of different tempos between piano "claves" and orchestra; sophisticated alternation and juxtaposition of meters

What to Listen for:

• Use of harp to evoke Latin American traditions of harp playing

• Complex rhythms in the piano imitating claves; these rhythms often move at a different tempo from the orchestra, suggesting African polymeters

• Brilliant palette of orchestral colors

Time	Description
0:00	**First section** Very brief clarinet solo, followed by lively outbursts in other woodwinds, suggesting bird songs; raucous brass lines add to the excitement
1:03	Bird trills initiate a calmer mood
1:25	Violent outburst in brass and percussion
1:48	Piano plays repeated rhythms in imitation of claves, followed by loud and dense writing for brass, percussion, and piano
2:29	Timpani solo
2:56	Piano introduces another clave rhythm over complex and strident rhythms in the percussion, followed by melodic ideas in winds and strings
3:25	Explosion of brass and percussion
3:37	Folklike melody in flute, performed with an extended technique called flutter tonguing
3:53	Further outburst in brass and percussion interrupting flute solo
4:04	**Adagio section** Serene slow passage in shimmering strings, consisting of long, drawn-out harmonies, played softly; piano, joined by brass, interjects dissonant notes at various points and with increasing frequency
5:57	**Transition** Serene atmosphere disintegrates as dissonant outbursts in piano and brass take over
6:24	**Quasi return to main section** Birdsongs in woodwinds reappear over a clave figure in piano

(continued)

Time	Description
6:49	Lengthy clarinet solo develops opening idea
7:11	Wild eruptions in strings, winds, brass, percussion, and piano
7:40	Reappearance of clave rhythm in piano
7:50	Tapering off of intensity; shimmering strings
8:03	**Conclusion** Appearance of harp over piano clave rhythm and percussion, playing chords in imitation of Latin American folk harp
8:18	Gyrating birdsong clarinet solo over piano, percussion, and harp, brings work to a colorful finish

FIGURE 9.2 Paul Desenne

Paul Desenne

Paul Desenne (b. 1959) is a native of Caracas, Venezuela. The son of a French father and an American mother, he demonstrated unusual talent for music at an early age and eventually made his way to Paris, where he studied cello, composition, and music history, and won prizes for his cello playing. It was in Paris that he began to compose, and even his early works are infused with the rhythms and melodies of South American music, particularly his native Venezuela, as well as neighboring Colombia and the Caribbean. In addition, Desenne's compositions reflect his love of Renaissance and Baroque music.

He returned to Caracas in 1986 and established himself as a leading performer, teacher, and composer in the Venezuelan capital, which he used as a base for advancing what would become an international career. Indeed, his works have been performed throughout the Americas and Europe, and the list of ensembles and performers that have performed his music is impressive and includes the Orquesta Simón Bolívar, Boston Classical Orchestra, Bogotá Philharmonic, I Musici de Montréal, Miami Symphony, and Nederlands Blasers Ensemble, as well as the Fodor Quintet and Verdehr Trio. Among the eminent musicians who have conducted his music is Tania León. In the fashion typical of most leading composers of our time, he has relied on various foundations for financial support of his creative activities, and he has received many prestigious grants, including one from the Guggenheim Foundation (2009).

Desenne's list of works is dominated by pieces for acoustic instruments, including chamber ensembles and symphony orchestra. Though evocations of the tango do not figure prominently in his output, still, among his most effective and evocative compositions is "Piazzolaberintus" from *Tango Sabatier*, Three Tangos for **Arpegina** (five-string viola) and Piano (Listening Guide 9.3), which reflects his strong sense of identity with South America in general, not just Venezuela. It is clearly intended as a tribute to the great tango performer and composer Astor Piazzolla (see Chapter 7) in its expressive use of dissonance, varied rhythms, and in its introspective mood, though its formal structure is quite distinctive.

LISTENING guide 9.3

◎ Desenne: "Piazzolaberintus" from *Tango Sabatier*, Three Tangos for Arpegina (five-string viola) and Piano

Composer: Paul Desenne

Date of composition: 2003

Performers/instruments: Jean-Paul Minalli, arpegina; Veronique Goudin, piano

Date of recording: 2003

Genre: chamber music

Form: free form with repetition and development of melodic ideas

Tempo/meter: moderate duple, characteristic of the tango

What to Listen for:

- General abstraction of the tango through elastic rhythms, variable tempos, and dissonance
- Pervasive melancholy mood, introspective and mournful, with occasional bursts of violent energy
- Dialogue between arpegina and piano as equals, rather than as soloist and accompaniment

Time	Description
0:00	Arpegina and piano present the main theme in the opening section; slow and mournful beginning in subdued tempo; tonal, with very dissonant elements
0:47	Both instruments present a new idea in the opening section; strong tango rhythm in the bass register of the piano; increasing sense of direction in the melodic line
1:51	Development of themes; strident chordal interjections in piano signal new section; jagged, angular rhythms in both instruments
2:20	New section based on new melodic ideas, though clearly related to earlier themes; sudden decrease in tension and dynamic level; mellow, more introspective, lyrical, relatively consonant; dialogue between arpegina and piano
3:40	Development of ideas; increase in rhythmic agitation and dissonance
3:57	Decrease in agitation and return to introspective mood
4:47	Return of opening section and reappearance of tango rhythm
5:41	Development of main theme and acceleration in tempo and rhythms
6:02	Mournful and languid conclusion

FIGURE 9.3 Roberto Sierra

Roberto Sierra

Roberto Sierra was born in Vega Baja, Puerto Rico, in 1953. After completing studies at both the Conservatory and University of Puerto Rico, he did advanced work in composition with György Ligeti at the Musikhochschule in Hamburg, Germany. He first rose to prominence with his orchestral work *Júbilo*, performed by the Milwaukee Symphony Orchestra at Carnegie Hall in 1987 (though the work had been premiered two years earlier by the Puerto Rico Symphony Orchestra in Puerto Rico). His compositions have since been performed throughout the United States and Europe, at festivals in New Mexico, Virginia, Puerto Rico, France, and Germany, by such ensembles as the New York Philharmonic, Los Angeles Philharmonic, Royal Scottish National Orchestra, BBC Symphony, as well as Spanish orchestras in Madrid, Galicia, Castilla-León, and Barcelona. In 2003, he received the music award from the American Academy of Arts and Letters.

Sierra's *Missa Latina "Pro Pace"* (Latin Mass for Peace, Listening Guide 9.4) was commissioned by the National Symphony Orchestra and the Choral Arts Society, both in Washington, D.C. It is scored for SATB chorus and orchestra, with soprano and baritone soloists. This expansive work is evidence of the enduring appeal of the texts of the Roman Catholic Mass and their ability to inspire composers to interpret and express the meaning of the texts through music. As the composer himself has stated,

> My concept of the mass came from my own experience growing up as a Catholic in a particular time and place. I still recall vividly hearing the mass in Latin in my own town in Puerto Rico when I was a child. From the beginning, there was for me a strong impression, which only deepened through the years: a sense of mystery combined with both power and compassion in the ritual involving this "dead language," and hearing the Gregorian chants intoned by the priest.

Though the title signals that Sierra has indeed used the traditional Latin texts of the Mass, his setting is a very personal plea for peace, written during an especially difficult time of war in Iraq. It is basically tonal but makes highly expressive use of dissonance, orchestral color, and dramatic vocal writing to express its theme. Passages suggesting anguish and uncertainty contrast with others that very effectively convey the peace for which this Mass constitutes an extended prayer. Throughout the work, Sierra employs Afro-Caribbean percussion and syncopated rhythms, including 3 + 2 clave, giving this Mass a distinctly Latin flavor. As Sierra himself points out, "The orchestration reflects my interest relating to my ethnic background merged

⊚ Sierra: "Agnus Dei," from *Missa Latina* "*Pro Pace*" (Latin Mass for Peace)

Composer: Roberto Sierra

Date of composition: 2003–2005; premiered 2006

Performers/instruments: Milwaukee Symphony Orchestra and Chorus, conducted by Andreas Delfs; Heidi Grant Murphy, soprano; Nathaniel Webster, baritone

Date of recording: 2008

Genre: mass movement

Form: binary

Tempo/meter: moderate triple, but without a strong sense of beat until the "alleluia" (in quadruple meter)

What to Listen for:

- Strident dissonance conveying sense of discord and conflict; consonant harmonies to express peace; and special attention given to the words "peccata" (sins), "miserere" (mercy), "pacem" (peace), and "alleluia"

- Kaleidoscopic variety of contrasts in timbre between voice and instruments, and within the orchestra itself

- Use of Afro-Caribbean rhythms and percussion at the end to express a distinctively Latin sense of rejoicing

- Tonally and metrically ambiguous setting of the Agnus Dei, followed by a contrastingly tonal and upbeat "alleluia"

Time	Text	Translation	Description
0:00	Agnus Dei, qui tollis peccata mundi, Miserere nobis;	Lamb of God, who takes away the sins of the world, have mercy upon us;	**First Agnus Dei** Baritone sings an extended melisma on the opening syllable, while winds and brass weave lines around the voice; pervasive air of mystery, especially in the use of Middle Eastern–sounding minor scales
0:52			Soprano and choir join baritone in completing the first line of text
1:11			Choir repeatedly intones "miserere nobis" (have mercy upon us), soon joined by orchestra, and swells to a climax, followed by a sudden drop in tension to prepare for line two
1:38	Agnus Dei, qui tollis peccata mundi, Miserere nobis;	Lamb of God, who takes away the sins of the world, have mercy upon us;	**Second Agnus Dei** Soprano sings Agnus Dei, accompanied by orchestra and chorus
1:58			Soprano and chorus repeatedly intone "peccata" (sins)
2:08			Baritone enters, singing "miserere nobis," which is taken up by the choir and soprano, accompanied by orchestra
2:34	Agnus Dei, qui tollis peccata mundi,	Lamb of God, who takes away the sins of the world,	**Third Agnus Dei** Chorus sings last statement of Agnus Dei

(continued)

Time	Text	Translation	Description
2:50	Dona nobis pacem.	Grant us peace.	Baritone concludes with the words "dona nobis pacem" (grant us peace), soon joined by the choir
3:10	Pacem relinquo vobis, pacem meam do vobis, dicit Dominus.	My peace I leave you, my peace I give you, saith the Lord.	Rapturous and dramatic soprano solo, eventually accompanied by chorus, presents the additional line of text, emphasizing the word "pacem"
5:19			**Transition** Piano notes in low register, with timpani and suspended cymbal, sound an ominous note but in fact herald the "alleluia," announced in the baritone and soon joined by the choir and brass instruments
5:30	Alleluia	Alleluia	Afro-Caribbean percussion and syncopated rhythms, now in quick duple meter, accompany the soloists, chorus, and orchestra in an upbeat celebration of praise
6:57			**Conclusion** Dance-like "alleluia" becomes a triumphal hymn, with soloists and chorus singing together

into the fabric of my music." In 2009, the Naxos recording featured in Listening Guide 9.4 was nominated for a Latin Grammy for Best Contemporary Classical Recording.

With the exception of the Introitus, Offertorium, and concluding "Pacem relinquo vobis . . . Alleluia," Sierra's Mass is a setting of the Ordinary, that is, those texts that do not change from one liturgical season to the next. The seven movements of this Mass are as follows:

1. Introitus (Introduction or Entrance, utilizing Sirach 36:18 and Psalm 121:1)

2. Kyrie eleison (Lord, have mercy; Christ have mercy; Lord have mercy)

3. Gloria (Glory to God in the Highest . . .)

4. Credo (I believe in one God . . .)

5. Offertorium (Offertory, utilizing Psalm 121:6–9)

6. Sanctus (Holy, Holy, Holy)

7. Agnus Dei (Lamb of God) (pronounced *Ahn-use Day-ee*)

We focus on the final movement, where the text consists of a three-fold statement of the same plea, with an important change in the third statement:

Agnus Dei, qui tollis peccata mundi, miserere nobis;
Agnus Dei, qui tollis peccata mundi, miserere nobis;
Angus Dei, qui tollis peccata mundi, dona nobis pacem.

Lamb of God, who takes away the sins of the world, have mercy upon us;
Lamb of God, who takes away the sins of the world, have mercy upon us;
Lamb of God, who takes away the sins of the world, grant us peace.

Sierra follows this with an additional text, the Communion of the Votive Mass for Peace,

Pacem relinquo vobis, pacem meam do vobis, dicit Dominus. Alleluia.
My peace I leave you, my peace I give you, saith the Lord. Alleluia.

An elaborate and extended setting of "alleluia," featuring Afro-Caribbean syncopated rhythms and percussion instruments, brings this mass to a joyous and uplifting conclusion.

Electronic and electroacoustic music

Tape recorders, synthesizers, computers, and electronic varieties of traditional acoustic instruments require specialized skills and knowledge to manipulate, but they offer virtually unlimited possibilities in sound generation and control. Many composers have written music using either purely electronic means or combining electronic instruments with traditional acoustic ones, to create electroacoustical works. The following segment considers two leading composers in this fascinating area of musical creativity.

Gabriela Ortiz

Gabriela Ortiz is among Mexico's leading composers today, one whose style combines elements of classical and folk music, as well as rock and jazz. Highly versatile, she writes for acoustic instruments as well as electronic media, concert music, music for modern dance, and even a recent "video-opera," *Unicamente la verdad* (Only the Truth). Ortiz was born in Mexico City in 1964, and her parents were both musicians in Los Folkloristas, a famous ensemble devoted to traditional music. After completing music studies at the Universidad Nacional Autónoma de México and Escuela Nacional de Música, she received a scholarship in 1990 to further her studies in England, where she obtained her doctorate in composition at City University London.

Her music exhibits a high degree of sophistication and complexity, yet through its connection with vernacular music it possesses the sort of immediacy and spontaneity that make it accessible and appealing to a larger public. Her compositions have been commissioned, premiered, or performed by ensembles throughout the Americas and Europe, such as the Los Angeles Philharmonic, Kronos Quartet, Orquesta Simón Bolívar, Cuarteto Latinoamericano, Mexico City Philharmonic, and the BBC Scottish Symphony, to name a few. She has won numerous awards, including a Guggenheim fellowship (2004) and grants from the Rockefeller and Ford Foundations. She has taught at the University of Indiana and is now on the composition faculty of the Universidad Nacional Autónoma in Mexico City.

Ortiz writes principally for acoustic media, and one of her most outstanding recent contributions to that repertoire is the string quartet *Altar de muertos* (Altar of the Dead), composed for the Kronos Quartet. However, one of her electronic works will be examined here, Five Micro Études for Solo Tape (Listening Guide 9.5). An **etude** is historically a piece of music intended to explore and develop particular aspects of instrumental technique. Continuing this tradition, Ortiz's *Micro Études* represent a novel exploration of the potential of electronically generated and recorded sound. Sounds are produced on a synthesizer and then recorded and manipulated on tape to create completely distinctive textures, colors, and rhythms. The fifth and final *Étude* in this collection evokes the sounds of wind chimes and bells.

Mario Davidovsky

Mario Davidovsky (b. 1934) is a U.S. composer of Argentine birth. He was born in the province of Buenos Aires, the son of Lithuanian-Jewish parents.

At the age of seven he began his musical studies on the violin, and he started composing at age 13. After graduating from the University of Buenos Aires, he emigrated to the United States in 1960 to pursue his studies and career, settling in New York City and becoming associate director of the Electronic Music Center run by Columbia and Princeton. His electroacoustical compositions earned him an international reputation, especially his series of *Synchronisms*, the sixth of which won a Pulitzer Prize in 1971. He became a professor of music at Harvard in 1994 and has taught at other leading music schools.

For Davidovsky, electronic generation of music allowed him to control the basic elements of musical sound, such as the beginning, duration, and end of each sound, along with tone color and intensity. Moreover, he could splice magnetic tape to assemble sounds in any order or sequence he desired. Each composition represented a new universe of sound that he himself created.

FIGURE 9.4 Mario Davidovsky

⊚ Ortiz: Five Micro Études for Solo Tape, No. 5

Composer: Gabriela Ortiz

Date of composition: 1993

Performers/instruments: Gabriela Ortiz, using synthesizer and magnetic tape

Date of recording: 2001

Genre: electronic composition

Form: free form exploring various sounds suggestive of everyday life

Tempo/meter: freely expressive and complex, without any sense of beat

What to Listen for:

- Introduction and alternation of different types of sounds
- Use of increasing or decreasing intensity to create transitions from one type of sound to another
- Wide variety of electronically generated sounds, including some suggestive of bells and wind chimes

Time	Description
0:00	**Introduction** Strident opening sounds taper off into silence
0:07	**Sound 1** Wind-chime–like sounds create a pleasantly whimsical effect, joined by the tinkling sound of small bells at 0:22
0:29	**Transition** Increasing intensity leads to a crash-like climax at 0:41
0:42	**Sound 2** Sound resembling the pealing of church bells becomes prominent, then fades out
0:59	**Sound 1** Return of sound of wind chimes and tinkling bells, growing in intensity
1:16	**Transition** Entrance of a straight tone heralds the arrival of a new sound
1:24	**Sound 3** Ping-pong–like sound, with sudden increase in intensity at 1:34
1:34	Deepening of the ping-pong effect and increasing rapidity of sounds, preparing for arrival of a new effect
1:47	**Transition** Climax and rapid decrease in intensity
1:49	**Sound 4** Drawn-out, sonar-like pings, with rapid cricket-like sounds in the background
2:04	**Transition** Intensity increases, with cricket-like sounds coming to the fore along with a sound that resembles a small gong
2:11	**Conclusion** Complex rhythms of the cricket sound begins to resemble castanets and travel from left to right speakers; sound gradually fades to nothing

In the 1970s, however, Davidovsky returned to writing music for traditional instruments and voice, and most of his works since that time have been acoustic, not electronic. His *Synchronisms No. 10* (Listening Guide 9.6), composed in 1992, is an exception to this trend, as it brings together guitar with prerecorded electronic sounds. Not only does the tape present many distinctive electronic elements, but the guitarist is also called upon to use extended techniques to increase the range of the guitar's expressive potential. These techniques include striking the instrument and rapidly brushing the strings with the fingers. The musical language is atonal, without a discernible meter or definite beat. In these respects, it is characteristic of much postwar avant-garde music.

LISTENING guide 9.6

⊚ Davidovsky: *Synchronisms No. 10* for Guitar and Electronic Sounds

Composer: Mario Davidovsky

Date of composition: 1992

Performer/instruments: guitarist David Starobin with prerecorded electronic sounds

Date of recording: 2000

Genre: electroacoustic composition

Form: free form, with basically two sections, the first featuring guitar alone, followed by a longer section introducing taperecorded sounds

Tempo/meter: freely expressive and complex, without any sense of beat

What to Listen for:

- Use of extended techniques on the guitar—striking the instrument and lifting up a string to allow it to slap against the fingerboard, creating a percussive effect; rapid brushing of strings with the flesh of the right-hand fingers

- Atonal harmony and use of silence to frame musical ideas

- Use of hemiola rhythms typical of Latin American folk music

- Wide variety of electronically generated sounds featured on the tape recording

Time	Description
0:00	Guitar alone; points of sound in free rhythm, including use of strumming, plucking, harmonics, and strings slapping against fingerboard; atonal and dissonant throughout
2:28	Silence
2:30	Guitar alone; rhythmically animated melodic line
2:40	Silence
2:44	Guitar alone; more isolated points of sound, strident and percussive at times, starting out agitated and becoming increasingly calm and reflective at 3:02
3:33	Silence
3:36	Guitar alone; continued reflective mood with use of flesh of right-hand fingers to brush the strings rapidly
4:30	Silence; longest silence yet punctuated by a single chord at 4:33

(continued)

Time	Description
4:37	Taped electronic sounds begin and interact with the guitar; sustained sounds in the tape recording, gradually becoming agitated
6:25	Guitar and tape; rapid escalation from soft to loud, with violent outburst in both tape and guitar starting at 6:35
6:40	Return to relative calm with occasional outbursts in taped sound; use of repeated rhythmic patterns
7:25	Peaks and valleys of loud, dissonant sounds, building to the climax
8:00	Explosion of rhythmic agitation and dissonance at intense dynamic level
8:17	Tapering off in intensity, then building up again
9:17	Final climax and dying out

Multimedia

Multimedia is a largely self-explanatory term. It refers to the use of multiple media to create a total work of art, comprising music and other arts such as dance, film, visual art, speech, acting, and electronic media.

Paulo C. Chagas

Paulo C. Chagas (b. 1953) has had a distinguished international career, beginning in his native Brazil, where he received bachelor's and master's degrees in music, then moving on to Germany and Belgium, where he received his doctorate in musicology. He is now in California, as professor of composition at the University of California, Riverside. He has composed over one hundred works, for multimedia, orchestra, instrumental and vocal ensembles, as well as electronic and computer music. In fact, he specializes in the use of digital technology in music composition. His works have been performed in Europe, the United States, and Latin America to both public and critical acclaim.

FIGURE 9.5 Paulo Chagas

Chagas worked for ten years (1990–1999) as sound director of the Studio for Electronic Music of the WDR (West German Radio and Television Broadcasting), where he conducted extensive research into electronic and computer music, algorithmic composition, interactivity, multimedia, and the spatial arrangement of recorded sound. He has also written music software and special computer applications for musical analysis and composition; in addition, he researches gesture and interactivity, which involves the use of sensors and the relationship between sound, image, and movement.

His techno-opera *RAW* (Listening Guide 9.7) was premiered by Opera Bonn in 1999. The title is WAR spelled backwards, and in this ambitious work, Chagas brings together a wide range

⊚ Chagas: *RAW*, a Multimedia Opera

Composer: Paulo C. Chagas

Date of composition: 1999

Performers/instruments: Opera Bonn

Date of recording: 1999

Genre: techno-opera

Form: free form, following the meaning and structure of the texts themselves

Meter/tempo: free and complex rhythms, usually without a definite sense of the beat, except in passages based on repeated patterns derived from West African drumming; variety of tempos

What to Listen for:

• Use of electronic media, including synthesizers, computers, and televisions

• Atonal harmony and freely expressive melodic lines

• Use of complex rhythms in free meter as well as rhythmic ostinatos derived from the $\frac{12}{8}$ bell pattern of the Ewe people in southern Ghana

Time	Description
0:00	**Scene 20** Soldier sings of the barbarity of war, while Ogun (a dancer in blue) dominates the scenery on his platform; televisions tuned to real-time programming, which just happened at the time to be showing the NATO bombing attack on Serbia; persistent syncopated rhythm throughout this scene derived from West African drumming
1:29	**Scene 21** General sings texts taken from the writings of Carl von Clausewitz, who is famous for remarking that "war is a continuation of politics by other means" (this quote actually appears in the text of scenes 55–57 and 59); percussive rhythm changes in this scene from the pattern in scene 20

of electronic and acoustic instruments, as well as various other media, to explore themes of violence. Chagas was himself the victim of violence when, at age 17, he was arrested and tortured by the military dictatorship in Brazil in 1971 for collaborating with opposition groups fighting for democracy. He described his ordeal to me in the following way:

> I was put in the "fridge," a small room, refrigerated and acoustically isolated, and completely dark and cold. Various noises and sounds—howling oscillators, rumbling generators, distorted radio signals, motorcycles, etc.—shot from loudspeakers hidden behind the walls. Incessantly, the electronic sounds filled the dark space and overwhelmed my body for three long days. After a time, I lost consciousness. This auditory and acoustic torture was then a recent development, partially replacing traditional methods of physical coercion that killed thousands in Latin American prisons between the 1960s

and 1990s. Such sounds injure the body without leaving any visible trace of damage. The immersive space of the torture cell, soundproofed and deprived of light, resonates in my memory as the perfect environment for experiencing the power of sound embodiment.

He was freed from prison only after the intervention of a military officer who was a friend of his parents. His works continue to explore themes of power, violence, and control, using the latest technology and theoretical approaches.

The main characters in the opera are the Yoruba god of war, Ogun, and his three wives, as well as a general and a soldier. Their respective texts are taken from traditional Yoruba poetry, the writings of the nineteenth-century Prussian general Carl von Clausewitz, and three books by author Ernst Jünger dealing with World War I. Chagas is clearly drawing on his personal experience in this work, as he grew up in Salvador, Bahia, where the presence of Afro-Brazilian religion, especially Candomblé and its associated deities, is very strong (see Chapter 6). The influence of African and Afro-Brazilian music is prominent in *RAW*; though Chagas has invented most of the rhythmic material himself, he employs a $\frac{12}{8}$ bell pattern used by the Ewe people of southern Ghana. His long residence in Germany inspired him to depict war and religion as universal features of human society. The performing forces are truly impressive in number and variety and include electronic keyboards, computers, synthesizers, and a large battery of percussion instruments, as well as five singers and a dancer. The staging includes a bank of televisions tuned to real-time programming.

The 75-minute opera itself does not tell a story or have a plot. Rather, it consists of 60 separate scenes, each with its own distinctive textual, musical, and dramatic character, but all dealing with the topic of war.

Film Music

Writing music for film requires a great deal of versatility, because the composer needs to draw on the widest variety of media and musical styles to convey, complement, or even contradict the drama onscreen. This can involve all of the techniques just encountered, as well as the ability to write in a variety of styles, both historical and contemporary, and to cross from folk to popular to classical styles with ease.

Gustavo Santaolalla

Among the most successful composers of film music today is Gustavo Santaolalla (b. 1951) of Argentina, one of only four composers ever to win

FIGURE 9.6 Gustavo Santaolalla

back-to-back Oscars for his music. In 2005, he won the Academy Award for best original score for *Brokeback Mountain*. He won again the following year for *Babel*. In addition, he has won other prestigious awards for his film scores and other recordings, including Grammy, Latin Grammy, and a Golden Globe in 2006 for best original song, "A Love That Will Never Grow Old" from *Brokeback Mountain*.

In the context of this chapter, Santaolalla's career is somewhat unusual. Like Heitor Villa-Lobos (see Chapter 6), he launched his career by playing popular music and learning from his immediate musical environment. Unlike the other composers discussed in this chapter, he did not attend a music conservatory or university to study composition. Nonetheless, he is actively and successfully involved in both popular and classical music. In fact, it is his remarkably diverse musical background and versatility that have enabled him to succeed as a film composer.

As a young man, he founded the group Arco Iris (Rainbow), which pioneered a fusion of rock with Latin American folk music as part of the *rock nacional* movement in Argentina (see Chapter 7). He moved to Los Angeles in 1978, and he remains based there today. In addition to performing with rock groups, he has cut several solo albums. His innovative blending of rock with the sounds of Latin American folklore, especially that of the Andes, distinguishes his compositions for television and film.

He is active as a producer, having coproduced the Kronos Quartet's *Nuevo*, an album that celebrates the musical heritage of Mexico. In addition, Santaolalla has collaborated with Argentine composer Osvaldo Golijov and soprano Dawn Upshaw, who commissioned the opera *Ainadamar*, based on the murder of Spanish poet Federico García Lorca, and *Ayre*, a collection of folk songs, in which Santaolalla performs with a group called The Andalucian Dogs.

In 2004 Santaolalla won the BAFTA (British Academy of Film and Television Arts) Award for best film music for his score for *Diarios de motocicleta*, which tells the story of a young Che Guevara on his motorcycle tour of South America. The poverty and injustice he encounters transform his worldview and his life. Santaolalla's score often draws on folk music for inspiration. Such references in the music not only establish the setting of the action but also represent the culture of the people Che encounters and to whose cause he will commit himself. In the overture to the movie, the composer plays guitar and is accompanied by members of the Argentine rock group Bersuit.

⊚ Santaolalla: Overture to *Diarios de motocicleta* (The Motorcycle Diaries)

Composer: Gustavo Santaolalla

Date of composition: 2004

Date of recording: 2004

Performers/instruments: Gustavo Santaollala, guitar; Aníbal Kerpel, guitar; Braulio Barrera, percussion; Don Markese, flute; and Javier Casalla, violin

Genre: film score

Form: binary, **AA′**, in which the **A** section is restated in a varied manner

Tempo/meter: slow triple meter with syncopated rhythms suggesting indigenous music

What to Listen for:
- Use of plucked string instruments and percussion (charango and bombo) to suggest traditional Andean music
- Repeated syncopated rhythmic pattern in imitation of traditional Andean music
- Gradual layering of instruments and musical ideas to create escalation in intensity

Time	Description
0:00	**Section A** Suggestion of folk music through syncopated rhythmic opening played on a charango
0:15	Entrance of guitar playing repeated chord progression over rhythmic accompaniment
0:30	Addition of flute line to harmonic progression
0:45	Strident, bold chords in the guitar increase intensity
0:54	Percussion enters (bombo)
1:28	**Section A′** Sudden decrease in intensity as all parts drop out, except opening syncopated rhythm on the charango
1:42	Return of all parts at maximum intensity; violin and bombo prominent
2:23	New melodic idea in flute and violin
2:32	Final cadence as music fades away, to the syncopated rhythm in the charango and long notes in violin and flute

Conclusion

It is clear throughout this book that the boundaries separating traditional, popular, and classical styles are very permeable, and that for centuries performers and musicians have routinely crossed these borders in search of new sounds and means of expression. The composers highlighted here are no exception to this rule, and even in the context of very new music that challenges our ability to listen and respond, they have consistently drawn upon instruments, sounds, and traditions that we recognize. Their art remains grounded in what is familiar, even as it presents us with types of musical expression that may seem strangely, even wildly, unfamiliar. In short, Latin American composers possess an inexhaustible storehouse of musical inspiration to draw upon. Their music will continue to surprise, challenge, and move us for a long time to come.

KEY TERMS

arpegina	microtonality
etude	trill
extended techniques	zampoña

FURTHER READING

Gidal, Marc M. "Contemporary 'Latin American' Composers of Art Music in the U.S.: Cosmopolitans Navigating Multiculturalism and Universalism." *Latin American Music Review* 31, no. 1 (Spring–Summer 2010): 40–78.

Lusk, J. "The Last Tango (interview with Gustavo Santaolalla)." *fRoots* 30, no. 5 (November 2008): 43–5.

Rivera, José. "Roberto Sierra's *Missa Latina (Pro Pace)*." *Choral Journal* 50, no. 8 (March 2010): 6–23.

Slayton, Michael. *Women of Influence in Contemporary Music: Nine American Composers*. Lanham, MD: Scarecrow Press, 2011.

Starobin, David. "A Conversation with Mario Davidovsky." *Guitar Review*, 92 (Winter 1993): 5–8.

FURTHER LISTENING

Paul Desenne, *Tocatas Galeónicas*. Dorian Discovery, 1995.

Gabriela Frank, *Leyendas: An Andean Walkabout*. Chiara String Quartet. New Voice Singles, 2007.

Tania León, *Indígena*. Composers Recordings, 1994.

Gabriela Ortiz, *Altar de Muertos*. Urtext Records, 2006.

FURTHER VIEWING

Motorcycle Diaries (*Diarios de motocicleta*). Focus Features, 2004.

10

Twenty-First Century Latin American and Latino Popular Music

DANIEL PARTY

<table>
<tr><td>Introduction</td><td>This chapter discusses recent trends in both Latin American popular music and Latino popular music (Latinos are people of Latin American</td></tr>
</table>

heritage who live in the United States). In the new millennium, Latin American and Latino popular music are so deeply intertwined that it has become increasingly difficult to draw a clear line between them, as the songs considered here illustrate. Strikingly, the United States is today the second-largest consumer market for Latin American music after Brazil. The market for **regional Mexican music** (an umbrella term that includes styles like norteña, banda, and ranchera) is larger in the United States than in Mexico itself! Accordingly, the production center for regional Mexican music is now in Southern California, not Northern Mexico. And the largest market for Dominican bachata is not on the island of Hispaniola but on the East Coast, largely due to the increase in Dominican immigration and the popularity of Aventura, a *Dominicanyork* band from the South Bronx.

Not only is the United States an important consumer of "Latin/o American" music (this term will be used when it is appropriate to encompass both Latin Americans and U.S. Latinos), but it is also the most prolific production center for Spanish-language popular music, the vast majority of which is produced by the four major international recording labels (Warner, EMI, Sony, and Universal). Each of these labels has a subsidiary that oversees music for the Latin American and Latino market. Notably, these Latin music subsidiaries are not located in Latin America but in the United States (three in Miami and one in Los Angeles). Some artists based in Latin America travel to the United States to collaborate with producers and take advantage of cutting-edge studio technology. Some relocate permanently to the United States in

LISTENING guides

Shakira, "La tortura"
Juanes, "Me enamora"
Los Tigres del Norte, "De paisano a paisano"
Venegas, "El presente"
Calle 13, "La Perla"
Kumbia Kings featuring Ozomatli, "Mi gente"
La India, "Selúceme"
Aventura, "Su veneno"

397

order to internationalize their careers (Miami remains the preferred hub for artists with hemispheric appeal). And some Spanish-language pop stars are U.S.-born Latinos who are bicultural, equally comfortable in U.S. and Latin American cultures.

One of the most salient features of twenty-first-century Latin/o American popular music is its **hybridity**. Hybridity, the mixing of various elements, is certainly not unique to Latin American music. All popular music from around the world is the result of combinations of features from multiple sources from the distant and recent past. What is noteworthy about recent Latin/o American popular music is that it embraces hybridity as an aesthetic. More often than in Anglo pop music, Latin/o American artists are likely to combine the local with the global in their hit songs. Colombian Juanes may play a Jimi Hendrix–inspired guitar solo over a Colombian cumbia rhythm, Puerto Rican MC Residente may rap over Balkan brass band music, and Los Angeles band Ozomatli may mix a shout-out in Jamaican dancehall style with tejano accordion and Indian *tabla*. The songs discussed in this chapter illustrate that Latin/o Americans are in dialogue not only with other nations from the Americas but also with the rest of the world.

An important inspiration for the foregrounding of musical hybridity is the recent increase in interaction among different Latino communities in the United States (the adjective **inter-Latino** is used to describe this type of interaction). Latin American immigrants to the United States not only encounter dominant Anglo culture, but also other Latin American cultures, often for the first time. The marked diversification of the Latino population since the 1990s has resulted in a noticeable growth in the number of inter-Latino marriages and other cross-cultural affiliations. An increasing number of young Latinos today thus experience an added layer of hybridity, since they may embody two or more national groups (e.g., MexiRican, CuBolivian). Inter-Latino diversity is challenging the long-standing approach to thinking about Latinos in terms of a single external national affiliation (such as "Cuban-American"). Inter-Latino interaction in the United States has become an important trend in popular music, as exemplified by the international hits of Shakira and Wyclef Jean's "Hips Don't Lie" (Colombian and Haitian), and Café Tacuba and producer Gustavo Santaolalla's "Eres" (Mexican and Argentinean, discussed in Chapter 3).

There is much to laud in such music. A hybrid aesthetic rejects notions of racial and cultural purity and instead celebrates the multiple associations and influences in our lives, regardless of our ethnicity. For Latinos in particular, hybridity is a feature of **Latinidad**, the shared culture and experience of Latin American immigrants and their descendents in the United States. Thus, hybrid music ("neither here nor there" or "both here and there") can speak powerfully to the life experiences of Latinos and other immigrant communities.

Although the notion of hybridity may suggest egalitarian cultural exchanges, one needs to be aware of the power dynamics that often surround them. In hybrid expressions, one culture almost always dominates. For example, in **Nor-tec** music (the hybrid style of techno and Mexican banda discussed in the book's introduction), DJs sample banda music to create electronic music pieces, not the other way around. (Although the idea of a brass band emulating the blips and beats of techno is intriguing, most likely the resulting music would not be considered banda by banda fans, and might not be appealing to them.) Moreover, hybridity can easily contribute to ethnic ambiguity, functioning to create a common-denominator product to maximize potential consumer audiences. From a marketing perspective, the more styles included in an album, or even within a single song, the larger number of communities that may purchase it. But in creating ethnic ambiguity, hybridity can function as a homogenizing force that conceals or downplays socio-cultural differences.

This chapter provides a sample of important trends in popular Latin/o American music of the twenty-first century's first decade. It emphasizes artists who have one foot in Latin America and one in the United States, who have a sizeable following across the Americas, who win Grammy and Latin Grammy awards, and whose music is widely available for purchase. Although contemporary popular musics created by Latin Americans and U.S. Latinos have many things in common (and often sound very similar), it is important to recognize that U.S. Latinos are a distinct group from Latin Americans. U.S. Latinos constitute an ethnic minority with a long history of struggle for civil rights and social recognition. As such, the music of U.S. Latinos holds a different set of meanings as the expression of a historically disenfranchised minority. For that reason, this chapter is divided into two sections. The first section covers contemporary Latin American popular music (with examples by Colombian, Mexican, and Puerto Rican artists), and the second examines recent trends in popular music by U.S.-born Latinos.

Contemporary Latin American Popular Music

Colombian Hit-Makers

Shakira and Juanes, the most commercially successful Latin American artists of the new millennium, have a lot in common. Both are Colombian singer-songwriters who grew up in **cosmopolitan** environments that exposed them to a wide range of music, with British and U.S. rock at the core. Both relocated to the United States in the late 1990s to reinvent and internationalize their careers. Both use a hybrid approach to commercial pop rock; that is, they borrow from a wide range of local and international styles to "spice up" their radio-friendly hits. Both are popular beyond the Spanish-speaking Americas, and have become de facto cultural ambassadors for Colombia and Latin America.

In the United States, where they still reside, Shakira and Juanes are the most visible faces of "**new Latinos**." The marked increase in migrant populations from South and Central America since the 1990s has challenged the perception of U.S. Latinos as primarily Mexican, Puerto Rican, or Cuban—the three historically dominant Latino communities—and has shifted attention away from stateside Latino culture to Latin American culture. The two songs discussed in this section are among the most popular Latin/o American hits of the twenty-first century. Shakira's 2005 "La tortura" (Torture) holds the record for longest run (25 weeks) at the number one spot on the U.S. Billboard *Latin Pop* chart. Juanes's 2007 "Me enamora" (She Seduces Me) follows right behind it, having stayed at number one for 20 weeks. Shakira's piece won Latin Grammy awards for best song and record of the year, and so did Juanes's two years later.

Shakira: Resisting Categorization

Shakira (Shakira Isabel Mebarak Ripoll, b. 1977) is the most successful Latin American singer worldwide of recent years. She is a global phenomenon and has recorded songs in Spanish, English, and Portuguese. Shakira has been described as "pop's twenty-first-century Latina bombshell," a moniker that echoes the way Brazilian Carmen Miranda was characterized in the late 1930s (see Chapter 6). Yet she is also known for her intelligence; in an interview she once explained the choice of covers for her albums with references to Freud's psychoanalysis and Jungian archetypes.

Shakira is a fascinating example of a global Latin American who resists easy categorization. Born in Barranquilla, an important port town on Colombia's northern Caribbean coast, she is of Lebanese and Spanish ancestry, and describes herself as a mix of "raw kibbeh and fried plantain." She grew up in a cosmopolitan environment, and her early musical preferences were divided between Anglo bands like Nirvana, Led Zeppelin, and The Cure and songs derived from her Arabic heritage.

Shakira's international popularity began with her third album, *Pies descalzos* (Bare Feet, 1996), which she cowrote and coproduced with Luis Fernando Ochoa. Already in this early album one can hear Shakira's eclectic approach to popular music. The song "Un poco de amor" (A Little Bit of Love) featured a Jamaican **dancehall** beat and guest vocals by reggae singer Howard Glasford. Two years later she released what many critics and fans consider her best album, *Dónde están los ladrones?* (Where Are the Thieves?),

The Latin Music Explosion and Crossover

At the dawn of the twenty-first century, Latin American and U.S. Latino popular music seemed unstoppable. Ricky Martin's electrifying performance in the 1999 Grammy Awards ceremony landed him a *Time* magazine cover and countless media appearances. Martin's achievement paved the way for a cadre of Latin/o American artists who found commercial success in the United States and beyond with English-language pop albums.

The artists of the so-called "Latin explosion," who besides Martin included Marc Anthony, Jennifer Lopez, Enrique Iglesias, and Shakira, followed the model of 1980s crossover stars Gloria Estefan and the Miami Sound Machine. This is not coincidental; Miami Sound Machine founder and Gloria's husband Emilio Estefan Jr. produced several of the "Latin explosion" albums. The tenants of Estefan's crossover model include the use of standard American verse–chorus song format; the incorporation of subdued Latin American music influences, such as the syncopated keyboard style of salsa (derived from the salsa montuno; see Chapter 5), nylon-string guitar runs, and—most importantly—lyrics in English, peppered with a few easy-to-pronounce Spanish words.

The financial appeal for Latin/o Americans of reaching the U.S. Anglo music market is undeniable. The United States is the largest market for recorded music in the world, accounting for 27 percent of global revenues in 2008. By comparison, the largest Latin American market for music is Brazil (which represents 1.2 percent of global revenues), followed by Mexico (0.8 percent), and Argentina (0.3 percent). The urge to record in English is especially strong because the English-speaking United States has a long history of resistance to popular music in other languages. In 2007, for example, the market

FIGURE 10.1 Ricky Martin on stage in Miami in 1999

for Spanish-language albums represented only a modest 5 percent of total sales.

At first, Latin/o Americans were thrilled to see crossover stars achieve what seemed to be a realization of the American dream. But as the media craze subsided, fans grew disenchanted with what began to sound like a predictable musical formula that actually included relatively few influences from Latin America. Since then, several of the "explosion" artists have returned to recording in Spanish in order to reconnect with their original audiences. From today's vantage point, the "Latin Explosion" illustrates the limitations of a one-size-fits-all formula in Latin/o American music, and the dangers of catering too slavishly to the English-speaking mainstream.

a considerably more ambitious CD featuring mariachi trumpets ("Ciega, sordomuda," Blind, Deaf and Dumb), bolero-style percussion on the bongos ("Moscas en la casa," Flies in the Home), and the Middle-Eastern *oud*, a fretless pear-shaped precursor of the guitar ("Ojos así," Eyes Like That).

Interested in expanding her popularity to include the U.S. market, Shakira did what many Latin American artists have done since the early 1980s: move to Miami. Riding the wave of the late 1990s "Latin Explosion" (In Depth 10.1), she released her first English-language album, *Laundry Service*, in 2001. The album topped charts around the world, yet many Latin American critics felt that Shakira had sold out and overly "Americanized" her sound. They pointed out the changes in lyrical themes on the release (mostly about love, whereas she had sung about political or socially engaged issues previously) and in her image. Shakira had dyed her signature dark hair blonde, and she appeared to be skinnier and wearing considerably skimpier clothes. All of this elicited rather unfavorable comparisons to Britney Spears.

On her follow-up album, Shakira took a different strategy. Instead of producing a one-size-fits-all crossover release, she divided her audience and provided two distinct products, one in Spanish (*Fijación oral, Vol. 1*, 2005) and months later one in English (*Oral Fixation, Vol. 2*, 2005). Although the album titles suggest that one release is a translation of the other, there are only two songs that appear on both albums. Shakira has explained that the musical elements used in a song lead her naturally to the language she should use to record it. You can hear this: the album intended for an Anglo audience is more homogenous, incorporating mostly rock influences. The Spanish-language one, by contrast, is strikingly eclectic. A *New York Times* review labeled it "blissfully pan-American"; an even better descriptor might be "worldly," given that many of its influences come from beyond the Americas. Tracks include nods to Brazilian bossa nova, 1960s French pop, 1980s British synth pop, reggaeton, and Argentine *rock nacional*. In *Fijación oral, Vol. 1*, she comes across as an informed listener with a profound knowledge of popular music from many countries, and the album proved an important point to her Latin American critics: that she had not replaced her Colombian/Latin American identity with a U.S. one. Instead, she absorbed what the United States and Europe had to offer and used it creatively, in conjunction with her Latin American heritage.

The first single of *Fijación oral, Vol. 1*, "La tortura" (Torture, Listening Guide 10.1), is a duet with Spanish balladeer Alejandro Sanz, a major pop star in Spain and in Latin America. Structured as a conversation, the song tells us that Sanz cheated on Shakira and is now apologizing, but only halfheartedly. The true feelings of each singer are ambiguous until the second half of the song, in which Sanz acknowledges he wants forgiveness but plans to continue misbehaving (on Saturdays!). The story's twist comes at the

⊚ Shakira: "La tortura" (Torture)

Composers: Shakira, Luis F. Ochoa

Lyricists: Shakira, Alejandro Sanz

Date of recording: 2005

Performers/instruments: Shakira with Alejandro Sanz; accordion, electric and acoustic guitars, electric bass, Cuban tres, keyboards, drums, and percussion

Form: strophic verse–chorus with bridge

Tempo/meter: moderate duple

What to Listen for:

- Prominent reggaeton beat, often accompanied by a tresillo-style bass line
- Eclectic studio production: many electronic sound effects, instruments such as Colombian vallenato accordion and Cuban tres featured, as well as Sanz's Spanish flamenco-inspired singing
- Backbeats strummed on electric guitar, a style taken from Jamaican ska and reggae

Time	Text	Translation	Description
0:00	Ay payita mía . . .	Hey girl . . .	Entrance of reggaeton beat, together with an electronically echoed acoustic guitar and an electric guitar playing chords on beat 2 (the backbeat) during the introduction. Later, bass and accordion play over the same beat, imitating cumbia vallenato (see Chapter 4)
0:19	No pido que todos los días sean de sol . . .	I don't ask for sunshine every day . . .	Stripped-down verse section features female voice prominently as well as accordion chords and sparse percussion hits; other instruments silent
0:39	Ay amor me duele tanto . . .	Oh, love, it hurts so bad . . .	**Pre-chorus**, with vocal harmonies; entrance of bass with tresillo pattern over reggaeton beat; guitar plays sparse, occasional chords
0:54	Yo sé que no he sido un santo . . .	I know I haven't been a saint . . .	**Chorus;** full ensemble sound featured with ska-inspired backbeats on the electric guitar, along with reggaeton rhythm and heavier bass pulse on strong beats
1:22	No puedo pedir que el invierno . . .	I can't expect winter. . . .	**Verse;** music becomes sparser again, with reggaeton pulse and bass prominent, but less drum set and guitar
1:42	Ay amor me duele tanto . . .	Oh, love, it hurts so bad . . .	**Pre-chorus;** Cuban tres plays prominent fills
1:56	Yo sé que no he sido un santo . . .	I know I haven't been a saint . . .	**Chorus;** full ensemble sound featured again; accordion solo at 2:16
2:25	No te bajes, no te bajes . . .	Don't let go, don't let go . . .	**Bridge;** most instruments fall silent for a time, except male voice and bass; slow buildup of pulse and percussion again

(continued)

Time	Text	Translation	Description
2:45	Yo sé que no he sido un santo . . .	I know I haven't been a saint . . .	**Chorus**
3:00	Todo lo que he hecho por ti . . .	Everything I've done for you . . .	**Outro;** section features electronically generated melodies and electric guitar on backbeats; texture slowly thins; acoustic guitar strums in the final seconds

FIGURE 10.2 Cover of Shakira's *Fijación oral, Vol. 1,* 2005

end when Shakira recognizes that he will not change and then breaks off their relationship. Musically, the song is a catchy mix of reggaeton, Colombian vallenato accordion playing, and Jamaican dancehall, together with the flamenco-stylized vocals of Sanz.

The music video for "La tortura," directed by the renowned Michael Haussman, broke MTV's unspoken language barrier when it aired on the station without translation or subtitles. The video is largely about the male singer's voyeuristic gaze, as he peeks at Shakira from an adjacent apartment window. Through the use of fragmented narrative, Haussman undermines the possibility of understanding the song in a monolithic way. There are times in the video when we are likely to empathize with Sanz, a few second later to despise him. Most interestingly, as Sanz watches Shakira lasciviously, we—the viewers—become voyeurs as well, complicit in his transgression.

Shakira's savvy use of images brings to mind an artist like Madonna, an early star of the music-video era. Like Madonna in the 1980s, Shakira plays with various female stereotypes, for instance, the naïve virgin when she sings in a childish voice ("Día de enero," January Day), the sexually charged bombshell ("Las de la intuición," Women with Intuition), or the nurturing mother (on the CD's cover art; Figure 10.2). Also like Madonna, Shakira uses her body and dancing to garner attention, and once we are looking at her, she manages to make us aware of the very act of looking.

Juanes: A Triple Threat

Singer-songwriter and guitarist Juanes (Juan Esteban Aristizábal Vásquez, b. 1972) started his career in his home country of Colombia as lead singer for a heavy metal band. In 1998 he moved to Los Angeles to start a solo career, and the half-dozen albums he has released since have topped the charts throughout Latin America, the United States, and Europe. To date, he has more Grammy awards than any other Latin American or U.S. Latino artist. Perhaps the most striking feature of Juanes's international success is the fact that he has achieved it singing in Spanish. When prodded as to why he does not sing in English he responds: "I prefer to play guitar in English and sing in Spanish."

In his music and appearance, Juanes combines three important types of Latin American musician. He is part urban, scroungy rocker who can solo on the electric guitar; part romantic crooner with a smooth voice; and part socially conscious singer-songwriter. Although he borrows from all these styles, his sound is considerably more homogenous than Shakira's. His songs are arranged for a traditional rock combo of electric guitar, electric bass, keyboards, and drum set—and he regularly performs his songs live with a small band. Gustavo Santaolalla, an Argentine composer and producer who lives in Los Angeles, has been behind Juanes's entire solo career. Not only has Santaolalla produced or coproduced all of Juanes's records, but he is responsible for encouraging Juanes to incorporate elements of Colombian traditional music into his pop-rock mix, adding yet another layer to his hybrid style.

Juanes manages to be a pop star and still sing about social issues. A recurring theme in several of his songs is the problem of landmines in Colombia, an ever-present threat. Since 1990, landmines have led to more than eight thousand amputees there, and some estimates suggest that they claim three victims a day. Juanes has also taken an active role in organizing concerts with a sociopolitical agenda. He organized a Peace Without Borders concert in response to the diplomatic crisis that affected Ecuador, Colombia, and Venezuela in 2008. A year later he organized a controversial second Peace Without Borders concert in Havana, Cuba (Figure 1.3). Given Juanes's massive following, these activities have resulted in public acknowledgments by the presidents of Venezuela, Colombia, Cuba, and the United States.

FIGURE 10.3 Juanes in concert in the Dominican Republic, 2010

Juanes's international hit "Me enamora" (2007, Listening Guide 10.2) is one of his best-known songs. An upbeat love song with a lilting guitar intro, a strong downbeat, and a memorable chorus, "Me enamora" topped the charts in over a dozen countries and won two Latin Grammy awards. The electric guitar solo borrows from classic Anglo blues rock, illustrating well what Juanes means by an "English-speaking" guitar.

Although there are many important similarities between the music of Shakira and Juanes, some key differences should be

⊚ Juanes: "Me enamora" (She Seduces Me)

Composer/lyricist: Juan Esteban Aristizábal Vázquez (Juanes)

Date of recording: 2007

Performers/instruments: Juanes; electric guitar, keyboards, electric bass, drums, and percussion

Form: strophic verse–chorus

Tempo: moderate duple

What to Listen for:
- Strong rhythm-and-blues/rock influences, less overtly associated with Latin America
- Elements of Jamaican ska and reggae, and of international pop
- Sudden shifts of texture from full to sparse, corresponding to lyrical sections

Time	Text	Translation	Description
0:00			**Instrumental introduction** in electrified blues style; electric guitar and full ensemble sound with electric bass and drum set prominent in this section
0:19	Cada blanco de mi mente . . .	Each blank in my mind . . .	**Verse;** texture becomes thinner initially, with bass on strong beats and high hat on backbeats behind vocals
0:39	Hay tantas cosas . . .	There are so many things . . .	**Pre-chorus;** texture builds slowly, adding electric guitar strumming on the backbeat, more percussion, and electric organ
0:49	Me enamora . . .	I love how . . .	**Chorus;** section features vocal harmonies and a strong backbeat feel, reminiscent of Jamaican ska and reggae, as in "La tortura" (Listening Guide 10.1)
1:15			Return of introductory melody, followed by a solo on the electric guitar; loud section with full ensemble sound
1:44	Yo no sé si te merezco . . .	I'm not sure I deserve you . . .	**Verse;** texture becomes sparser again, as in the first verse
2:04	Hay tantas cosas . . .	There are so many things . . .	**Pre-chorus**
2:14	Me enamora . . .	I love how . . .	**Chorus**

noted. Perhaps the most controversial is their choice of language. As part of her crossover effort, Shakira learned English and began to write and record in English alongside Spanish. Juanes, on the other hand, has continued to sing in Spanish. Language is just one of many aspects in which Shakira is open to experimentation. Her singing is notably versatile. She can sound soothing and comforting at one point, intense and angry on the following track, only to be close to sobbing on the next. And in her music she has embraced a plethora of international styles. Comparatively, Juanes's style has changed considerably less during the past decade. His lyrics have evolved with each album, but musically he has remained close to the sound he and Gustavo Santaolalla developed for his first solo album in 2000, a compelling mix of classic rock with Colombian traditional music elements.

Shakira and Juanes demonstrate that Latin American artists can achieve worldwide success in the commercial music market, and in different ways. Their urbane and cosmopolitan music represents their status as global citizens. It is of utmost importance to recognize that for cosmopolitan musicians like Juanes and Shakira, hybridity is a choice, the result of individual aesthetic decisions as well as of education and privileged social position. For many others, like the poor Mexican migrant workers discussed in the next section, hybridity is an imposed reality, the result of fragmented lives and the need to fit in a host society.

At the Boundary: Two Case Studies from the Mexico–U.S. Border

The Mexico–U.S. border is a musically rich region that spans almost two thousand miles and represents home for more than ten million people. The border region can be described as a contact zone, a place where cultures meet and identities are challenged by the encounter. Unlike the experience in the heartland, border inhabitants are constantly reminded of their national identity through contrasts with others. Yet for many who live by the border, *patria* or homeland is truly the border itself, not Mexico or the United States. Chicana author Gloria Anzaldúa has famously described the U.S.–Mexico border as "two worlds merging to form a third country."

Northern Mexico has a distinct identity, historically estranged from that of the capital, Mexico City, and comparable to the relationship between those in Texas or the southwest United States and Washington, D.C. Mexican northerners have a self-sufficient mindset, developed from decades building communities in harsh terrains without aid from the central government. Understandably, given the region's proximity to the United States, the far North is Mexico's most "Americanized" region—a sore point for the Mexican government. From Mexico City, the northern frontier appears as a porous zone where Mexicanness is diluted and U.S. culture is all too prevalent. Government officials do not always recognize the rich culture that exists at the border, reflected in the various music traditions that have blossomed there. Border culture is particularly diverse in terms

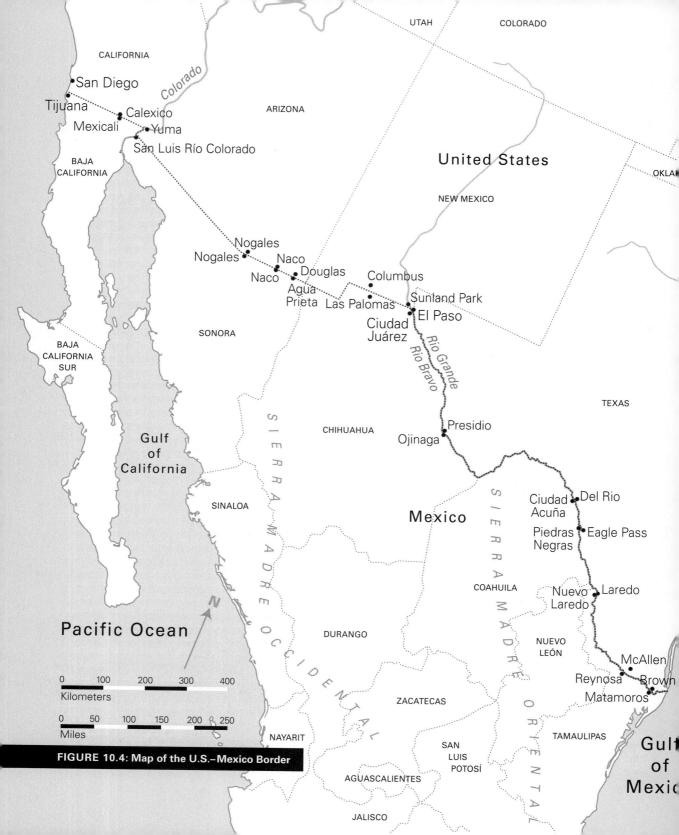

FIGURE 10.4: Map of the U.S.–Mexico Border

of well-established popular music traditions, everything from working-class, largely unrecorded rural styles like huapango (see Chapter 3, p. 96) to the mass-mediated **tejano** style of the late Selena Quintanilla.

Throughout the twentieth century, a common theme in border music was the border experience itself. Songs celebrated self-reliance and discussed legal and illegal border crossing, the difficulties of working far from home and of staying true to oneself in the midst of the constant push and pull from north and south. As a result of changes in migration patterns, in recent decades the themes of border music have undergone important transformations. This section's examples represent two cases of twenty-first-century border music: music of working-class northern Mexicans and undocumented migrants, and alternative pop by cosmopolitan performers.

Música norteña: Neither Here nor There

Mexican laborers have been crossing over to work in U.S. territory since the end of the Mexican-American War in 1848. In the mid-twentieth century, the Immigration and Naturalization Service's Bracero Program streamlined the process by which Mexicans could enter the United States to work temporarily in agriculture and railroad building. Bracero is a Mexican Spanish term for temporary laborer (from the Spanish word for arm). By the time the controversial Bracero Program was terminated in 1964, the use of Mexican labor had been institutionalized. Farms and factories still relied on cheap Mexican labor, and the vast numbers of Mexican nationals in need of work resulted in an exponential growth in illegal immigration. In 2010, there were about twelve million Mexican immigrants (foreign born) in the United States, of which about half were undocumented.

Changes in immigration laws and border control during the last twenty years have resulted in new migration patterns that have transformed the lives of undocumented migrant workers. Border control has tightened, thus migrants are crossing less often, opting instead for longer stays in the United States. While historically the vast majority of migrants had been working-age men, in the last two decades an increasing number of women and children have joined them. In the past, Mexican migrants had remained close to the border, primarily in California and the Southwest. Today, they find work all across the United States; thus, some of the fastest-growing Mexican communities are now in the Pacific Northwest and in the Northeast, as well as in the Carolinas and the Southeast.

Another important shift is that recent migrant workers are considerably less invested in **assimilation** into the United States, as demonstrated, for example, through a lack of interest in learning English or in becoming a U.S. citizen. This can be partly explained by the hostility they encounter: in the new millennium the United States has become a considerably less welcoming place for immigrants than it used to be. Also, recent developments in technology and travel have allowed immigrants to maintain long-distance communication with their families and places of origin. In a sense, these newly arrived peoples remain closer to their hometowns than ever before.

The most concrete way in which migrants remain connected to their hometowns is by sending back part of their earnings to family. These monies, called **remittances**, have grown so much in recent years that they have become a key component of several Latin American countries' economies. For example, in 2007, remittances sent from the United States to Mexico reached almost $24 billion dollars. The Mexican government, aware that migrants who remain connected with their hometowns are more likely to contribute to their local economies, has developed policies that aim to maintain such links. For example, since 2005, Mexicans abroad have been able to vote in local elections in their former places of residence.

Migrant workers have been quick to adopt new technologies for music consumption. Their inherent mobility and the need to maintain regular communication with people back home have made the cell phone an essential part of migrant workers' lives. Not only is the cell phone their primary means of communication, but also their main means of acquiring music. In 2008, Latinos were twice as likely to buy ringtones as were non-Latinos. And when it comes to digital purchasing of regional Mexican songs, 85 percent of the time fans download them to their cell. Regional Mexican, an umbrella category that includes **música norteña**, ranchera, and banda, is by far the dominant style of Spanish-language music in the United States (in 2008, it accounted for 62 percent of all U.S. Latin music sales). Given the strong ties between regional Mexican and cell-phone use, phone carriers have built more partnerships with regional Mexican artists than with any other genre, Latin or not.

The most popular music among Mexican migrant workers, particularly undocumented ones, is música norteña (p. 107). The standard instrumentation of a norteña ensemble features a three-row button accordion, bajo sexto, electric bass, and drums. Set to dance-oriented styles like polka and waltz, música norteña repertoire incorporates many pieces with socially conscious lyrics that might be described as contemporary corridos, traditional Mexican narrative ballads (for more on corridos, see Chapter 3). In norteña, the emphasis is on lyrics rather than instrumental virtuosity; in fact, only minimal accordion soloing is used. (If you enjoy virtuosic accordion playing, check out **Texas–Mexican conjunto,** the north-of-the-border version of *norteña* that focuses on instrumental dancehall numbers and features striking accordion solos.) Norteña's lyrics deal with the experience of migration and celebrate Mexican traditions as well as resistance to assimilation.

FIGURE 10.5 Los Tigres del Norte performing at the Latin Grammy awards in Houston, 2006

Norteña songs contribute to the development of a sense of community at a time and place when identities are most frail and in flux. As Cathy Ragland puts it, norteña creates "a nation between nations."

The main audience for música norteña is in Northern Mexico (Tamaulipas and Nuevo León) and among Mexican immigrant laborers in the United States. But in recent years, norteña's popularity has extended as far south as Mexico City. With one out of ten Mexicans living in the United States, norteña's stories of displacement are striking a chord even with the ones who stay behind. The most famous norteña acts are Ramón Ayala y Los Bravos del Norte, Los Tucanes del Norte, and Los Tigres del Norte.

Los Tigres del Norte have made a four-decade career of singing about border crossing and immigrant life. In 1968, while still teenagers, the four brothers Hernández from Sinaloa entered the United States hoping to make money playing music. They eventually settled in San José, California, began recording with Fama records, and went on to sell more than thirty million albums. Los Tigres specialize in the performance of corridos that deal with contemporary social issues. They are largely responsible for modernizing the corrido by replacing the genre's traditional poetic speech with a plain, working-class language.

In the early 1970s Los Tigres del Norte found fame recording **narcocorridos**, a subgenre of corrido that chronicles the lifestyle and tragic adventures of border-crossing drug smugglers (p. 93). Though still known for their popular narcocorridos, in the new millennium Los Tigres del Norte have moved beyond the style to sing more broadly about the life of the *mojado* or wetback, the poor immigrant that crosses the border illegally. They have also added songs that address sociopolitical issues in Mexico itself (listen to "La granja," The Farm, from 2009, an allegory of political corruption which was censored by concert promoters in Mexico). The recent immigration

EXAMPLE 10.1: Basic música norteña pattern

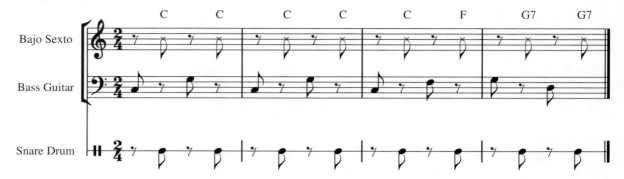

trends outlined above are reflected in Los Tigres's recent de-emphasizing of border crossing itself and newfound interest in the struggles of migrants within the United States, particularly assimilation.

One representative example of Los Tigres's recent work is "De paisano a paisano" (From Countryman to Countryman, 2000, Listening Guide 10.3). Like most Tigres songs, "De paisano a paisano" is in duple meter, and the arrangement and production are straightforward. At its core lies a regular pattern of a bass guitar note on the downbeat followed by a chord on the bajo sexto played together with the snare drum (Example 10.1). This is the typical manner of interpreting polka music in norteña repertoire. The accordion plays the introductory melody and the fills between verses; accordion lines are simple and memorable, rather than showy and virtuosic. Vocal harmonies are used only during the chorus.

Although Los Tigres's concerts attract both men and women, their songs bear traces of a tradition of performance that occurred in male-only spaces, such as local cantinas. Thus, song lyrics often describe conversations among men. Even in songs about love or heartbreak, the lyrics do not address a woman directly, but rather a buddy or a relative. As the title suggests, "De paisano a paisano" (From Countryman to Countryman) recounts a story told man to man. It celebrates the untamable character of the *mojado*, who could be from anywhere in Latin America, bravely crossing borders to provide for his children, and his anti-assimilationist attitude. The song presents the *mojado* as a heroic outlaw.

"De paisano" illustrates Los Tigres del Norte's uncanny ability to embrace commercialism while maintaining a populist, even oppositional stance vis-à-vis the mainstream. On the one hand, the song appeared in TV ads in which the band promoted a money-transferring company. On the other, Los Tigres used the same song to record a different ad promoting a campaign of Mexico's Secretaría de Gobierno; the campaign aimed to inform Mexican workers abroad of their rights and privileges and was appropriately

⊚ Los Tigres del Norte: "De paisano a paisano" (From Countryman to Countryman)

Composer/lyricist: Enrique Valencia

Date of recording: 2000

Performers/instruments: Los Tigres del Norte; accordion, bajo sexto, electric bass, drums

Form: strophic verse–chorus

Tempo: moderate duple

What to Listen for:
- Accordion fills
- Polka rhythm, created through alternation between a bass note and the bass drum playing on the downbeat and a bajo sexto chord and a snare drum on offbeats
- The simple, clean arrangement and production

Time	Text	Translation	Description
0:00			**Introduction;** accordion begins alone, accompanied only by occasional percussion taps on strong beats; polka rhythmic pattern begins at 0:07
0:20	Como el águila en vuelo . . .	Like a flying eagle . . .	**Verse;** instruments mostly maintain constant patterns, deferring to the vocals, but bass fills follow the first half of the text at 0:29; accordion fills between verses, at 0:42
0:47	Si la muerte me alcanza . . .	Should death take me . . .	**Verse;** similar instrumental fills at the end of vocal phrases
1:13	De paisano a paisano . . .	From countryman to countryman . . .	**Chorus;** second voice enters a third higher than the original and harmonizes with the lead singer; accordion fills at 1:21 and 1:32, and 1:42
1:54	De paisano a paisano . . .	From countryman to countryman . . .	Section spoken while accordion plays the introductory melody
2:33	De paisano a paisano . . .	From countryman to countryman . . .	**Chorus**

named the "*Paisano* program." Los Tigres's popularity has extended the appeal of corrido beyond its original border audience to include people in Mexico City and in places as far off as Chile and Spain. The group has even shared the stage with mainstream Latin pop artists like Ricky Martin and the Mexican ska/pop/rock group Maná. For millions of undocumented workers (throughout Latin America), Los Tigres del Norte tell an inspiring story of a *mojado*'s triumph against all odds.

Cosmopolitan Tijuana: Both Here and There

Nothing represents border culture better than the Mexican city of Tijuana. Tijuana is the busiest port of entry in the U.S.–Mexico border, stamping over forty million crossings a year. For most of the twentieth century, Tijuana had a bad reputation in both countries. In the United States it was conceived as a city of sin and debauchery; and in Mexico, Alejandro L. Madrid writes, as "the barbaric land where U.S. cultural imperialism threatens Mexican, Latin American, and Hispanic culture in every bar where you order your beer in Spanglish and pay with a mix of dollars and pesos." Tijuana appears from both these perspectives as a place where a large transient population prevents the emergence of a lasting social or cultural identity, a town neither here nor there.

In the new millennium, however, Tijuana-based artists have been challenging stereotypes of the border region. Authors, visual artists, musicians, and dancers argue that their culture has been misunderstood and that foreign critics miss the point by expecting a static Mexican identity from Tijuana. Instead, they posit, Tijuana needs to be understood as a multicultural place, and scholars agree. Researchers argue that *tijuanenses* have a strong national identity, fueled in no small measure by the experience of constant contact/ friction with the United States. What is unique about *tijuanenses*, Jennifer Insley suggests, is that they "incorporate signs and symbols from elsewhere without perceiving a contradiction between these and a fluid but strong sense of national, ethnic, and linguistic selfhood."

The Tijuana multimedia art form known as Nor-tec, discussed briefly in the Introduction, is a perfect aural representation of contemporary Tijuana culture. Nor-tec stands for a hybrid of norteña and techno, the local and the global. Musically, this means that Nor-tec DJs take samples from classic norteña and banda sinaloense (see Chapter 3) tracks and fuse them with the beats and loops of electronic popular music. Rather than an amorphous "neither here nor there" style, Nor-tec is better thought of as both here *and* there.

Singer-songwriter Julieta Venegas (b. 1970) represents yet another kind of border pop musician, similar in some respects to Shakira and Juanes (Figure 10.6). Born in Long Beach, California, to Mexican parents, she spent her formative years in Tijuana. Like many young *tijuanenses*, Venegas had more contact with

FIGURE 10.6 Julieta Venegas performing her MTV Unplugged concert in Mexico City, 2008

San Diego, California, than with the far-away Mexican capital. Venegas and her music can be best described as cosmopolitan. On the one hand, she is strongly rooted in Mexican culture: despite being fluent in English she has shown no interest in writing songs in that language, nor in moving to the United States. On the other hand, she grew up listening to Anglo rock and borrows freely from it. The international quality of her music makes it equally appealing and meaningful to Argentineans as to Spaniards and North American critics, who have celebrated her music since the release of her first album, *Aquí* (Here) in 1997.

While Venegas's first instrument is the piano, she is most widely recognized for playing the keyboard accordion. Interestingly, Venegas picked up the accordion after being inspired not by música norteña repertoire but by alternative rock musicians Tom Waits's and Joe Jackson's use of the instrument. Her 2008 *Unplugged* album for MTV illustrates Venegas's keen musicality. The most common pitfall of acoustic pop-rock albums is their aural monotony; stripped of guitar pedals and other sound effects, there is often little except the melody to distinguish one song from the next. Aware of this, Venegas worked with Brazilian Jaques Morelenbaum, long-time collaborator of bossa nova founder Antônio Carlos Jobim, to re-create her songs for live concert settings. Relying on several multi-instrumentalists, the elegant yet lively arrangements present an eclectic kaleidoscope of sounds, from a classical string quartet to tuba, from cavaquinho (see Chapter 6) to a saw blade played with a bow.

"El presente" (The Present, Listening Guide 10.4), the first single off the album, showcases Venegas's cosmopolitan aesthetics. The song opens with

---

⊚ Venegas: "El presente" (The Present)

Composer/lyricist: Julieta Venegas

Performer/instruments: Julieta Venegas; accordion, acoustic guitar, string quartet, keyboards, bass, drums and percussion

Date of recording: 2008

Form: strophic verse–chorus

Tempo/meter: brisk duple

What to Listen for:

- Polka rhythmic pattern heard in the introduction (and at later moments) drawing from norteña but speeding up the pulse and mixing the traditional sound with backbeat guitar strumming

- Elements from pop and European classical music (synthesizer, cello, etc.) contrasting markedly with references to traditional border repertoire

Time	Text	Translation	Description
0:00			**Introduction;** accordion takes the lead melody, accompanied by bass, drum set, and backbeat guitar strumming; one of the more "traditional" segments of the music

(continued)

Time	Text	Translation	Description
0:13	Ya sé lo que te diga . . .	I know that nothing . . .	**Verse;** thinning of texture as the accordion largely drops out to feature Venegas's vocal; another female voice enters in harmony during second half
0:26	Quién nos dice que la herida . . .	Who says that the wound . . .	**Pre-chorus;** louder and with more of a pop feel with syncopated acoustic guitar strumming and keyboard, held chords in accordion
0:40	El presente es lo único que tengo . . .	The present's the only thing I've got . . .	**Chorus;** section seemingly out of time; percussion thins; lyrical cello countermelody plays prominently under the lead vocal and backs vocal harmonies; guitar (plays more softly) and tambourine heard
1:03			Repetition of instrumental introduction, with addition of trumpets
1:20	Con el mundo como va . . .	The way the world turns . . .	**Verse**
1:32	Quién nos dice que la herida . . .	Who says that the wound . . .	**Pre-chorus**

Venegas playing a lilting line on the accordion over a lively polka rhythm and bass pattern. In the chorus, the percussion drops off and is replaced by sustained string notes and Beatlesque vocal harmonies, producing an out-of-time feel.

Hip-hop en Español

As we saw in the previous section, remittances by Latin Americans working in the United States are so large that Latin American economies have begun to depend on them. Latino-studies scholar Juan Flores suggests that migrants' influence in their home countries extends far beyond monetary contributions. Flores proposes that migrants also transmit what he calls "cultural remittances," by which he means ideas and expressive forms, like music, that arrive in Latin America when migrants return home to visit or to relocate. In addition to physical visits, recent technological developments in communications have made the transmission of expressive forms from the diaspora to the homeland considerably easier than in previous decades.

One of the musical styles that arrived in Latin America as a cultural remittance is hip-hop. Spanish-language rap first found international popularity in the 1990s. It did not take root in a single location; instead, all across the Americas, MCs and DJs tried their hand at this exciting style that originated in New York City. Some of the most important 1990s Latin American rappers include Panamanian El General, Puerto Rican Vico C., and bands Illya Kuryaki and the Valderramas from Argentina, and Control Machete and Molotov from Mexico. The most important international break for rap *en Español* came in the new millennium with the worldwide success of reggaeton (see Chapter 5).

In the United States, Latinos have been involved in hip-hop culture—DJing, graffiti, breakdancing—since its early days in the South Bronx in the late 1970s. By the late 1980s, a few Latino artists had crossover success rapping in English, sometimes peppering the lyrics with Spanish phrases and slang. Examples include Cuban-American Mellow Man Ace ("Mentirosa," 1989), Chicano Kid Frost ("La Raza," 1990), and Ecuadorian-American Gerardo ("Rico Suave," 1991). More recently, Nuyorican Fat Joe and Cuban-American Pitbull have released chart-topping albums in the United States.

Throughout Latin America there also is an important, albeit less commercially successful, form of hip-hop that raps about sociopolitical issues. Political rap, known as "hip-hop *social*" in Colombia and as "rap *consciente*" in Cuba, has been particularly important among Afro-Latin American youth. Inspired by African American rappers who use hip-hop to celebrate a shared African diasporic experience, Latin Americans rappers adopt the style to decry social and racial inequality and challenge the status quo. This grassroots rap can be considered the torchbearer of 1970s political song (see Chapters 4, 5, and 7).

Since 2000, one hip-hop group that has managed to create catchy party tracks *and* politically engaged rhymes *en español* is the Puerto Rican duo Calle 13 (Figure 10.7). Calle 13 consists of rapper and frontman René Pérez

FIGURE 10.7 Eduardo Cabra (left) and René Pérez (right) of Calle 13 performing in Los Angeles, 2008

(aka Residente) and multi-instrumentalist and producer Eduardo Cabra (aka Visitante). They first achieved international popularity in 2006 as reggaeton artists with the song "Atrévete-te-te."

Calle 13's third album, *Los de atrás vienen conmigo* (Those in the Back Are Coming with Me, 2008), is to date their most ambitious both musically and lyrically. Its eclectic musical mix (the *New York Times* described it as "omnivorous") includes influences from polka, Balkan brass bands, 1980s synth pop, and Nigerian Afro-beat. Lyrically, *Los de atrás* is an aggressive, albeit humorous, album: rapper Residente takes on, among other things, reggaeton's frequent glorification of consumption and excess, and its misogyny; dancehall singer Sean Paul's accented English; and Latin American social climbers who pretend to be American and reject their heritage wholesale ("gringa wannabe"). But there is an important exception to such biting commentary: the third single, "La Perla" (Listening Guide 10.5) is a heartfelt, nostalgic ode to the San Juan working-class neighborhood of the same name.

Like many Calle 13 songs, "La Perla" disparages the *bling* lifestyle, celebrating instead the simple pleasures of family life in the *barrio*: brightly-painted houses, boys jumping across rooftops, an adolescent's first kiss, grilled food, cold beer, and shooting hoops with friends. In evocative and highly visual vignettes, Residente raps that he's not interested in modernization, but in staying true to his heritage, represented by the image of his mom's food and his grandmother in a rocking chair. The chorus boasts of barrio pride: "I have everything/I don't lack anything/I have the night, which is my blanket/I have the best skyscapes/I have a cooler stacked with iced beer." The musical arrangement, by Visitante, is sparse, to keep the listener's attention on the lyrical flow. It features an Afro-Uruguayan style called candombe (see Chapter 7), played by Argentine percussion group La Chilinga (notice how candombe shares the 3-2 clave pattern of Afro-Caribbean music).

The second half of "La Perla" includes a rap and a *soneo* (an improvised vocal in call-and-response form) by renowned Panamanian salsa singer-songwriter Rubén Blades, known for his socially conscious songs. Blades continues Residente's celebration of barrio life and its matrilineal culture, but suggests that La Perla is a "barrio universal" in that it represents working-class life across the Americas. His collaboration with the hipsters in Calle 13 introduced Blades to a younger generation, while his socially conscious rap lent credibility to Calle 13's political leanings. The music video, a beautiful realization of the song's narrative, won a Latin Grammy for best video.

⑥ Calle 13: "La Perla" (The Pearl)

Composers/lyricists: Eduardo Cabra, René Pérez, and
Rubén Blades

Performers/instruments: Calle 13 featuring Rubén
Blades and La Chilinga; horns, electric bass,
keyboards, and percussion

Date of recording: 2008

Form: strophic verse–chorus

Tempo/meter: moderate duple

What to Listen for:
- Uruguayan candombe percussion
- Rubén Blades's rap and *soneo* sections

Time	Text	Translation	Description
0:00	Oye, esto va dedicado . . .	Hey, this is dedicated to . . .	**Introduction/Dedication;** begins with 3-2 clave pattern
0:21	Yo tengo actitud desde los cinco años . . .	I've had attitude since I was five . . .	**Verse;** entrance of keyboard, then bass
0:53	Allá abajo en el hueco, en el boquete . . . [2x]	Down there in the hole, in the gap . . .	**Chorus;** Blades sings lead (half sung/half spoken), full ensemble: backing vocals, piano, organ, trombone notes held
1:16	Un arcoíris con sabor a piragua . . .	A rainbow that tastes like a canoe . . .	**Verse;** return to sparse percussion in 3-2 clave; keyboard and synth riff starts at 1:26, then horns added
1:58	¡Oye! Esto se lo dedico . . .	Hey! I dedicate this . . .	**Verse;** bass drops, horns join riff, then bass returns with a thicker percussion arrangement
2:31	Allá abajo en el hueco, en el boquete . . . [2x]	Down there in the hole, in the gap . . .	**Chorus;** Blades sings lead (half sung/half spoken), full ensemble: backing vocals, piano, organ, trombone notes held
3:15	¡Oye!, Esto fue por la inocencia de Jonatán Román . . .	Hey! This goes for Jonatán Román's innocence . . .	Spoken dedication uttered by Residente
3:24	Esa risa en La Perla la escuché en el chorrillo . . .	That laughter in la Perla, I've heard in the stream . . .	Blades raps over candombe percussion and repeated three-note bass line
3:47	¡La noche me sirve de sábana! . . .	The night serves me as a blanket! . . .	**Chorus;** call-and-response *soneo* between Blades and group; only percussion and isolated bass hits; at 4:08 entrance of large ensemble with a salsa groove: bass, keyboard, new voices
4:30	Allá abajo . . .	Down there . . .	**Chorus**

Recent Trends in U.S. Latino Popular Music

Latinos or Hispanics, the two terms used in the United States to refer to people of Latin American ancestry living in the country, totaled an estimated 50.5 million people as of 2010. At 16 percent of the total U.S. population, they are the country's largest ethnic minority. If the U.S. Latino communities lived in a separate country, it would be the third-most-populous nation in Latin America. People of Mexican and Puerto Rican ancestry still predominate among Latinos, in 2010 accounting for 63 percent and 9 percent of the total demographic, respectively. But shifts in immigration beginning in the 1990s led to a marked increase in new migrants from Colombia, the Dominican Republic, Ecuador, Guatemala, and El Salvador—a group collectively referred to as "new Latinos."

A common misconception about U.S. Latinos, partly fueled by the growth of "new Latino" immigration, is that most Latinos are foreigners. In fact, people of Latin American heritage have been living and making music in what is now U.S. territory since the sixteenth century, and more than 60 percent of Latinos in the United States today were born there. Some artists make music primarily for Latino audiences, while others aim at crossing over to the mainstream Anglo market. Some emphasize their Latin American heritage, while others downplay it. Latinos have been instrumental in the development not only of Latino popular-music styles, such as New York City salsa, Texas conjunto, and Los Angeles Chicano rock, but also of styles traditionally considered Anglo, like rock and roll, country, and hip-hop.

This section focuses on twenty-first-century popular music created by U.S.-born Latinos for Latino audiences. The Listening Guides represent three of the largest Latino groups: Mexican Americans, stateside Puerto Ricans, and Dominican Americans. Each of the next three guides—illustrating **cumbia tejana**, **salsa romántica**, and **urban bachata**, respectively—presents a modernized version of a Latin American style studied in previous chapters. The artists behind these innovations are bilingual and bicultural second- and third-generation Latinos. They have hybridized Latin American genres, fusing them with contemporary rhythm-and-blues and hip-hop elements to make them more appealing for urban U.S. Latino audiences.

Twenty-First-Century Cumbia Tejana

U.S.-born Mexican Americans—that is, the descendents of Mexican immigrants—have a considerably different experience from that of the undocumented migrants just discussed. Second-generation Mexican Americans have historically assimilated well into U.S. Anglo culture. Research has shown that second-generation Mexican Americans speak English better than they do Spanish and regularly move out of immigrant neighborhoods into multiethnic ones. This process plays an important role when it comes to musical preferences. For many second-generation Mexican Americans, their first music interests are styles in English, such as rock and hip-hop, not Mexican music in Spanish.

Many U.S.-born Mexican American musicians first performed Anglo styles like rock and roll and country, and only later embraced their Latin American heritage. Examples include Ritchie Valens, Freddy Fender, Los Lobos, Selena Quintanilla, and Los Lonely Boys. Their stories speak loudly of their complex bicultural worlds. For example, the great tejano singer Selena Quintanilla, born in Lake Jackson, Texas in 1971, started singing in English and only reluctantly switched to Spanish at the request of her father, who thought that she had a better chance of success by targeting Spanish-speaking Americans than by aiming for crossover to Anglo audiences. In her early Spanish-language recordings, Selena didn't understand what she was singing, so her father had to coach her. Only after she had secured a massive fan base among Mexican Americans did Selena begin to fulfill her long-time dream of recording an album in English. Sadly, she never saw the project to fruition because a fan shot and killed her in March 1995, while she was still working on the album.

After Selena's passing, the torch of hip tejano music passed to her older brother, A.B. Quintanilla III (b. 1963), who played in Selena's back-up band and also composed several of her hits. Quintanilla has enjoyed widespread popularity in the new millennium with his band Kumbia Kings. The Kumbia Kings updated the tejano sound by replacing the traditional sparse production, used for example in Selena's early 1990s albums, with elaborate techniques and studio effects typical of contemporary rhythm-and-blues, hip-hop, and boy band music. Kumbia Kings vocals also borrow extensively from smooth rhythm-and-blues crooners, like Usher or Ne-Yo.

True to their name, Kumbia Kings often feature the cumbia rhythm in their dance-oriented songs. Cumbia is a style originally from Colombia's northern coast that in the mid-twentieth century became popular throughout Latin America. In previous chapters you have encountered various local variants, such as Argentinean *cumbia villera* (Chapter 7), Peruvian *cumbia andina* and technocumbia (Chapter 8), and Mexican cumbia (Chapter 3). The Mexican variant is markedly simpler than Colombian cumbia. The original polyrhythms are replaced by a straightforward rhythmic pattern and small combos (*grupos*) consisting of electric guitar, electric bass, organ/synthesizer, *güiro* and drum set that take the place of traditional big bands. Example 10.2 shows

EXAMPLE 10.2: Mexican cumbia rhythmic pattern

Mexican cumbia's core rhythmic pattern. Note that in the conga line, the two different pitches in black heads represent open tones on two different conga drums, one tuned higher than the other. The golden age of Mexican cumbia spans the 1970s and 1980s, with groups such as Los Bukis and Bronco. Kumbia Kings can be considered a modernized version of such groups.

In 2003, Kumbia Kings released the album *4* in which they mix cumbia, reggae, vallenato, rhythm and blues, and hip-hop. The album's first half features songs in Spanish while the second half is in English. The third single released off the album is an exciting collaboration, cowritten and coperformed by Kumbia Kings and critically acclaimed alternative rockers Ozomatli, a Los Angeles, California, band that formed in the mid-1990s, and is known for its musical hybridity. In Nahuatl, an indigenous Mexican language, Ozomatli refers to a figure in the Aztec sun calendar and to the god of dance. While borrowing most consistently from Latin American dance rhythms, the multiracial band incorporates elements from a wide range of world music sources. In the following quote, Ozomatli's Mexican American trumpet player Asdrubal Sierra jokingly describes what an ad for the band would look like:

FIGURE 10.8 Kumbia Kings at the Premios Juventud Awards in Miami, 2004

Looking for a classical Indian music/tabla player of Japanese decent; a Jewish American bassist influenced by Sly and Robbie; a Mexican guitarist that can play Cuban tres, a strat, a Veracruzan jarana; a half Spanish/Mexican tenor sax player that doubles on requinto jarocho and piano; and a Mexican American singer who can sound Middle Eastern, *gitano* [Gypsy], salsa, or rock in English or Spanish—play trumpet is a must.

Before collaborating with Kumbia Kings on "Mi gente" (My People), Ozomatli's 2001 album *Embrace the Chaos* won the Grammy for Best Latin Rock/Alternative Performance. "Mi gente" (Listening Guide 10.6) thus represents a collaboration between the hit-making, chart-topping Kumbia Kings and the less commercially successful but critically acclaimed Ozomatli (Figure 10.9). The song also bridges the gap between the Latino cultures of Texas and Southern California.

"Mi gente" takes inspiration from first-generation immigrants. It tells the story of a migrant worker who comes to the United States following a promise of opportunity. He wonders "if I'm honest and I work from dawn until dusk, why am I treated like I don't belong here?" The infectious chorus expresses a string of contradictory emotions: "I suffer, feel, laugh, cry, don't speak up, scream, with my people . . . because they don't understand me." The song opens with a striking mix of hip-hop scratching, Brazilian cuica friction percussion, Caribbean timbales, and Mexican accordion. The bridge section borrows from Jamaican dancehall, and is followed by a bluesy electric guitar

Kumbia Kings featuring Ozomatli: "Mi gente" (My People)

Composers/lyricists: Luigi Giraldo, Raúl Pacheco, Justin "Niño" Porée, Abraham Quintanilla III, Nir Seroussi, Asdrubal Sierra, and Jiro Yamaguchi

Performers/instruments: Kumbia Kings featuring Ozomatli; accordion, electric guitar, electric bass, horns, keyboards, drums, and percussion

Date of recording: 2003

Form: Strophic verse–chorus with bridges and montuno

Tempo/meter: Moderate duple

What to Listen for:

- Eclectic introduction opening with hip-hop scratching, Brazilian cuica, timbales, and accordion
- Anthem-like, politicized quality conveyed by using several singers, and a chanting chorus
- Cumbia rhythmic pattern

Time	Text	Translation	Description
0:00	Ozomatli, Kumbia Kings, Exclusivo, Cumbia!		**Introduction;** whispered voice, hip-hop scratches, keyboard and horn hits in crescendo, cumbia beat starts at 0:11, bird calls at 0:14, horn riffs, timbales fills
0:22	Sufro, siento, río, . . .	I suffer, feel, laugh, . . .	**Chorus;** group vocal
0:33	Si yo trabajo de sol a sol . . .	If I work from dawn 'til dusk . . .	**Verse;** pair of voices
0.44	Si yo vine de lejos a esta tierra . . .	If I came to this land from far away . . .	**Verse;** single voice
0:53	Sufro, siento, . . . [2x]	I suffer, feel, . . .	**Chorus;** timbales fills, bird calls
1:15	Yo quiero que entiendan . . .	I want you to understand . . .	**Bridge;** musical shift to a quieter sound, almost out of time, less percussive; vibraslap; freer bass and sax lines, then at 1:24 locks in again, leading up to chorus
1:35	Sufro, siento, . . . [2x]	I suffer, feel, . . .	**Chorus;** horn melodies and percussion hits accompany the voices during the chorus, and in introduction
1:57	Sufro por ti para que no sigas así . . .	I suffer for you to not continue like this . . .	**Bridge 2;** dancehall style; voice quasi-spoken or chanted, sparse percussion rhythm (hits on the first two beats of a tresillo)
2:07			**Solos;** electric guitars (2:07), then trumpet (2:28), timbales fills
2:49	Sufro, siento, . . . [2x]	I suffer, feel, . . .	**Chorus**
3:10	Por mi gente es que grito yo . . .	For my people I shout today . . .	**Montuno;** lead voice alternates with chorus; horns drop out, Brazilian cuica, accordion, and timbales play fills

solo and a jazzy trumpet line. The music video combines scenes of Kumbia Kings and Ozomatli performing (separately) with footage from the Chicano rights movement of the 1960s. The video brings home the song's message of unity, ending with the image of a wall graffiti that reads "Brown is together."

Salsa for the Hip-Hop Generation

A lot has happened since the golden age of the raw and edgy sound of 1970s New York City salsa discussed in Chapter 5. After a rough patch in the 1980s when Dominican merengue dominated the East Coast Latino club scene, salsa came back in full force with an updated, smoother sound and an aesthetic that made it more commercially successful than ever before. In the twenty-first century, salsa artists like Marc Anthony and La India have begun to close the gap between the hard-driving barrio salsa of the 1970s and the romantic spirit of the 1990s.

The 1980s was a trying decade for salsa. It started with the closing of Fania Records, the epicenter of salsa production in the 1970s and, to many, the label that created the best salsa records ever produced. As Latino youth turned to Dominican merengue and the new Bronx style later known as hip-hop, salsa became "old-folks' music." The most successful effort to modernize salsa came from the collaboration of arranger Louie Ramírez and producer Isidro Infante. They came up with the idea of recording cover versions of already-popular **baladas** (romantic pop ballads, a style wildly popular across Latin America that is associated with soap opera sound tracks) using salsa arrangements.

This new style, first known in Puerto Rico as *salsa sensual* and in New York City as salsa romántica, differed from the Fania model in a number of important ways. First, it avoided the Spanish Harlem–centered and politically charged lyrics of 1970s salsa. Even as the style moved beyond cover songs and new ones were composed, lyrics dealt mostly with romantic themes. Second, a smooth-sounding crooning style of singing replaced the nasal quality of 1970s salsa vocals. Third, the brash, rough-around-the-edges sound of the salsa bands, particularly of the brass and percussion, was replaced with a polished and refined sound, molded in the studio. Finally, salsa romántica shifted the attention from the bandleader to the singer, and from improvised lead vocals in the montuno to entirely precomposed songs. Instead of experienced *soneros*, most salsa romántica featured youthful and attractive singers that appealed to younger audiences.

In 1987, concert promoter Ralph Mercado founded the label RMM Records with the purpose of recording and marketing this new style of salsa. RMM's music directors Isidro Infante and Sergio George are largely responsible for shaping the salsa sound of the 1990s and are behind the success of a cadre of singers including Tito Nieves, La India, Marc Anthony, and Johnny Rivera. Infante and George aimed at crossover, but not in the traditional sense of pushing a Latin/o American style into the mainstream United States. Their goal was primarily crossover within Spanish-speaking Latin/o American communities. As previous chapters in this book demonstrate, musical preferences vary widely across Latin America, making hemispheric crossover a challenging enterprise few artists have achieved. While purists continue to mourn the death of the classic Fania salsa of Willie Colón and Héctor Lavoe, RMM's formula produced the best-selling salsa artists of all time, and, notably, brought to fruition Fania's dream of a pan–Latin American embrace of salsa.

FIGURE 10.10 La India performing in Hollywood, Florida, 2008

One of the most compelling singers in the RMM roster was *Nuyorican* La India (b. Linda Viera Caballero in 1969) (Figure 10.10). Like many young second-generation Nuyoricans in the 1980s, La India initially rejected salsa because she considered it old-fashioned and corny. She started her music career singing in English in the house-music scene, and only turned to salsa after encouragement from salsa singer Héctor Lavoe. Her breakthrough album, *Dicen que soy* (1994), is a perfect example of producer Sergio George's new approach to salsa. George combined La India's soulful rhythm-and-blues vocals (including melismas and blue notes), covers of famous baladas arranged as salsa, and elements of hip-hop and house music. The winning result was somewhere between 1970s "hard salsa" and 1980s salsa romántica; the lyrics were too romantic and melodramatic to be "hard salsa," the singing too fiery and intense to be salsa romántica. (*Dicen que soy* closes with an exciting duet with then up-and-coming Marc Anthony, called "Vivir lo nuestro," roughly "Live Our Lives").

A comparison of La India's 2002 song "Sedúceme" (Seduce Me) with the salsa song included in Chapter 5, Celia Cruz and Ray Barretto's "Ritmo en el Corazón," will help us elucidate the new features of twenty-first century salsa. While "Ritmo en el Corazón" is not a classic salsa from the 1970s golden age, it serves our purpose here because in 1988, when it was recorded, the song looked back nostalgically to earlier decades, as represented by two older and well-established artists. "Ritmo" celebrates tradition both lyrically and musically. Celia Cruz sings about her undying passion for music while outlining the history of salsa, from Africa to Cuban son and rumba. Musically, the song acknowledges the two main sources for salsa, Cuban son and Puerto Rican bomba.

Like many salsa romántica songs, "Sedúceme" contrasts stylistically with older repertoire, represented by songs such as "Ritmo en el corazón." It opens with an airy keyboard and synthesizer introduction reminiscent of late 1990s boy-band production; only twenty seconds into the song, with the entry of the percussion, do we realize that this is actually going to be a salsa number. Also characteristic is the fact that the song is about heartbreak and seduction rather than tradition or politics. In "Sedúceme," the singer pleads for a final night of passion with her lover before parting ways. There are no references to salsa's history except for a clever allusion to the title of La India's own duet with Marc Anthony, "Vivir lo nuestro." The target audience for "Sedúceme" is a younger crowd that is open to salsa, yet may not be interested in thinking about it as a style with a long history, or a political one.

The crisp, clear pop sound of songs like "Sedúceme" is the result of **overdubbing**, a recording technique in which each part is recorded individually and the final song is produced by layering the tracks. The downside of overdubbing is that it limits opportunities for improvisation and interaction among musicians that can occur in live performance. Ray Barretto's own opinion was that most of the young salsa singers who emerged in the early 1990s were unable to *sonear*, to improvise in rhyme like classic salsa singers could. While India has developed into a great vocalist in terms of her overall abilities, improvisation plays a less central role in her music than it did with earlier performers. When I saw La India performing live in Philadelphia in 2003, "Sedúceme" was the climax of the show. She belted the song out with aplomb and passion, making everybody in the audience move. Yet her *soneos* in the montuno section were identical to the recording, and so were the brass section's *moñas*. Old-timers may resent the declining role of improvisation in salsa, yet nobody in the audience at that show, including me, seemed to mind.

The "pop" quality of this new salsa is only part of the reason why it resonates with younger-generation Latinos. Most importantly, for many second-generation Latinos, this new salsa resonates with their bilingual and

⊚ La India: "Sedúceme" (Seduce Me)

Composers/lyricists: India, S. Marte, R. Contreras, and J. Greco

Performers/instruments: India; trumpets, trombones, keyboards, electric bass, and percussion

Date of recording: 2002

Form: strophic verse–chorus with bridge and montuno

Tempo/meter: moderate duple

What to Listen for:

- Rhythm-and-blues inflected vocals and overall sound influenced by U.S. pop
- Other salsa romántica qualities: synthesizers, strings, overdubbed vocals, strings, smooth, sweet-sounding horn arrangement, extremely polished studio production
- Horn lines change in each verse, each time growing more complex
- Shorter vocal call-and-response section (the montuno) in contrast with the multiple montunos in Celia Cruz's "Ritmo en el corazón"

Time	Text	Translation	Description
0:00			Synthesized keyboard, warm bass notes, and a lack of Latin percussion make the introduction sound like a pop ballad
0:29	Bésame, pronto va a amanecer . . .	Kiss me, it's almost dawn . . .	**Verse;** entrance of congas and bongo accompanying the voice along with sparse synthesizer lines and bass notes
0:50	Mírame, quiero ver en tu mirada la pasión . . .	Look at me, I wanna see passion in your eyes . . .	Section features slap bass, fills by the trombones, and later trumpets that enter for the first time
1:10	Sé que mañana no estarás . . .	I know tomorrow you'll be gone . . .	**Chorus;** percussion switches to bells, lead vocal moves to a higher register; synthesized strings accompany syncopated keyboard patterns; trumpets and trombones alternate hits
1:42	Porque tú eres parte de mi vida . . .	Because you're part of my life . . .	**Verse;** texture becomes thinner again, percussion switching off bells; more horn arrangement accompanies the verse vocal
2:04	Sé que mañana . . .	I know tomorrow . . .	**Chorus;** same as above; African American–style melisma in India's voice toward the end of this section
2:37	Solamente tenemos unas horas . . .	We only have a few hours . . .	**Bridge;** percussion becomes softer at first; timbales continue to play bell. For most of the bridge, the bongo plays on the head, while the piano and bass stop the driving montuno style, which resumes at 2:57 as excitement builds
3:24	Sé que mañana . . .	I know tomorrow . . .	**Chorus**
3:58	Bésame, abrázame, sedúceme . . .	Kiss me, hold me, seduce me . . .	**Montuno;** emotional climax of the song, involving call-and-response singing between India and a male chorus; short montuno section broken into two halves, with an instrumental break in between; romantic and soft finale, like the introduction

bicultural experience. It allows them to reconnect with their heritage without giving up the hard-earned right to assimilate into U.S. society.

Urban bachata: To the White House and Back

Dominican Americans are the fifth-largest Latino population in the United States. Unlike the Latino groups just studied, most Dominican Americans are first-generation immigrants. In fact, over half of the Dominican American population arrived in the United States after 1990. The economic, political, and cultural importance of the Dominican Republic's U.S. diaspora is undeniable. As George Lipsitz notes, Dominican political candidates campaign in New York City, Dominican political parties have offices in the United States, and the remittances of Dominicans abroad shape the country's economy.

A music style that beautifully illustrates the transnational nature of contemporary Dominican identity is bachata. As outlined in a Chapter 5, bachata is traditionally a Dominican acoustic love ballad characterized by its lyrics about heartbreak and quick, high-pitched, lilting countermelodies on the lead guitar. It originated in the 1960s as a local variant of the Cuban and Mexican bolero and Puerto Rican *jíbaro* music. As Dominican immigration to the United States skyrocketed in the 1990s, the musical preferences of migrants, with their higher incomes, began to shape the Dominican music industry from abroad. In the new millennium, as Deborah Pacini Hernandez explains, it is *Dominicanyork* bachata that dominates the scene in both countries, rather than the other way around.

By far the most influential and commercially successful *Dominicanyork* bachata group is Aventura, a quartet formed in the mid-1990s in the South Bronx. Aventura's breakthrough came in 2002 with the hit "Obsesión," which topped the charts in places like Italy and Germany and helped define their bicultural style. The "Kings of Bachata," as they call themselves, modernized bachata by adding melismatic rhythm-and-blues singing, rapping in English and Spanglish, collaborating with reggaeton artists, and adopting a hip urban fashion sense and a big-city attitude. In the words of frontman Anthony "Romeo" Santos, Aventura "put the cool in bachata."

Musically, the most recognizable features of Aventura are Romeo's suave and expressive **falsetto** and Lenny Santos's rapid-fire guitar countermelodies. Aventura follows a trend that started in the 1990s of composing bachata with clean, family-friendly lyrics and marketing it to young women. Lead singer Romeo unmistakably addresses his song lyrics and frequent ad-libs to women. The band presents a striking combination of old and new, rural and urban sensibilities. All their major hits are essentially acoustic bachatas accompanied with guitar and light percussion on bongos, congas, and güira (a metal version of the gourd güiro preferred

FIGURE 10.11 Aventura
performing in Hollywood,
Florida, 2010

by Cuban and Puerto Rican performers). Their gallantry is definitively old-fashioned, tame in comparison to hypersexualized rap and reggaeton. Yet their looks are unquestionably urbane: designer jeans and tight shirts, shiny bling and light-colored suede.

So far, Aventura has not crossed over to the mainstream U.S. market. Arguably, however, the massive audience that follows the group challenges the very concept of mainstream. In early 2010, Aventura played four sold-out concerts at New York City's Madison Square Garden, a feat unheard of since Madonna's peak in the 1990s. By comparison, that same month Lady Gaga sold out for four nights too, but in Radio City Music Hall, a much smaller venue. If bachata is a niche market, then the niche may soon grow larger than the mainstream.

The flow between homeland and diaspora is circular. The same advances in technology that allow immigrants to stay connected to their homeland permit the reverse flow of music back to the sending country. First-generation Dominicans brought bachata with them. Second-generation *Dominicanyorks*, like the members of Aventura, are sending it back, transformed, as a cultural remittance. In 2010 Aventura presented the same show they developed for the U.S. market to a sold-out Santo Domingo arena; fans fainted and critics raved.

In 2009 Aventura dominated the Billboard Latin charts with their album *The Last*. Its massive popularity landed them an invitation to perform at the White House for a televised concert hosted by President Barack Obama and First Lady Michelle Obama in celebration of Hispanic Heritage Month.

⊚ Aventura: "Su veneno" (Her Venom)

Composer/lyricist: Anthony "Romeo" Santos

Performers/instruments: Aventura; acoustic and electric guitars, electric bass, percussion

Date of recording: 2009

Form: strophic verse–chorus

Tempo/meter: moderate duple

What to Listen for:

- Intricate nylon-string guitar countermelodies, hearkening back to the acoustic origins of bachata and contrasting at times with flanged electric guitar
- Smooth crooning tenor voice
- Sung in Spanish, but partly spoken in English

Time	Text	Translation	Description
0:00			Solo acoustic guitar in the introduction, along with synth effects
0:12	En el proceso de dejarla . . .	In the process of leaving her . . .	**Verse;** bongos, guitar countermelody, electric bass; guitar fill style derived from the bolero tradition
0.29	(Tal vez) mi futuro está en sus manos . . .	(Perhaps) my future is in her hands . . .	Flanged electric guitar in the background, referencing more-recent bachata sounds
0:52	Su maldito veneno . . .	Her damned venom . . .	**Chorus;** all instruments continue as before, but the güira more prominent in this section, switching from straight hits to more-syncopated variations
1:25	[Spoken] *Romeo's not gonna die like that . . .*		Introduction with acoustic guitar and effects as before, then electric guitar solo
2:10	(Tal vez) mi futuro está en sus manos . . .	(Perhaps) my future is in her hands . . .	**Verse;** strummed guitar

Aventura's members were the only performers who were not from the three historically dominant U.S. Latino communities: Mexican Americans, Puerto Ricans, and Cuban Americans. At the White House they performed their bachata "Su veneno" (Her Venom), the third single off *The Last*.

Conclusion

This chapter has explored contemporary Latin/o American popular music, emphasizing the concept of hybridity and the interconnections that exist across the Americas. All the artists in this chapter can be described as having one foot in Latin America and one in the United States. For contemporary

Latin American artists, the U.S. serves as an attractive center of music production and, given the size and economic power of the Latino community in the United States, a highly profitable market as well. For U.S.-born Latinos, on the other hand, Latin America remains an important source of musical inspiration and a powerful referent for the construction of Latino identities.

This chapter has also addressed the impact of migratory trends on popular music. In the future, migration is expected to continue to be a transforming force in both Latin America and the United States (some estimate that by 2050, U.S. Latinos will account for 30 percent of the country's population). Through economic and cultural remittances, the influence that diasporic communities have in their originating countries is likely to persist, if not grow. In the United States, it is conceivable that the growth of the Latino population will lead to an increase in inter-Latino interaction. Stronger bonds across U.S. Latino communities may contribute to a weakening of national identification with countries of origin. In its place we may find a bolstered sense of Latinidad. The music that will speak to these new identities remains to be heard.

KEY TERMS

assimilation	inter-Latino	regional Mexican music
balada	Latinidad	remittances
cosmopolitan	música norteña	salsa romántica
cumbia tejana	narcocorrido	tejano
dancehall	new Latinos	Texas-Mexican conjunto
falsetto	Nor-tec	urban bachata
hybridity	overdubbing	

FURTHER READING

Cepeda, María E. *Musical ImagiNation: U.S.-Colombian Identity and the Latin Music Boom*. New York: New York University Press, 2010.

Flores, Juan. *The Diaspora Strikes Back: Caribeño Tales of Learning and Turning*. New York: Routledge, 2008.

Madrid, Alejandro L. *Nor-tec Rifa!: Electronic Dance Music from Tijuana to the World*. New York: Oxford University Press, 2008.

Madrid, Alejandro L., ed. *Transnational Encounters: Music and Performance at the U.S.–Mexico Border*. New York: Oxford University Press, 2011.

Pacini Hernandez, Deborah. *¡Oye como va!: Hybridity and Identity in Latino Popular Music*. Philadelphia, PA: Temple University Press, 2010.

Ragland, Catherine. *Música norteña: Mexican Americans Creating a Nation Between Nations*. Philadelphia, PA: Temple University Press, 2009.

Rivera, Raquel Z. *New York Ricans from the Hip Hop Zone*. New York, NY: Palgrave Macmillan, 2003.

Washburne, Christopher. *Sounding Salsa: Performing Latin Music in New York City*. Philadelphia, PA: Temple University Press, 2008.

FURTHER VIEWING

Chulas Fronteras. Les Blank, director. Arhoolie Records, 2003 [1976].

Latin Music USA. Jimmy Smits, Adriana Bosch, et al., directors. PBS Distribution, 2009.

The Elements of Music

WALTER AARON CLARK

Introduction

The purpose of this appendix is to explore the world of sound as music, treating the various means of manipulating sound to create music and the terms and concepts associated with doing so. In this way, you can acquire a vocabulary for describing and understanding what you hear in music. Reading this appendix in advance will help you to assimilate the material in the previous chapters much more easily, and it will facilitate discussion of the musical examples to which you will be listening.

Each Listening Guide provides you with a summary of information about the piece, its composers and performers, the performing media involved, its form, rhythm, and other salient aspects. Then a table lays out the major events in the piece, providing both descriptions and timings so that you can follow along. The following text includes references to Listening Guides, figures, and musical examples throughout the book that help to illustrate the terms and concepts in question.

Sound as Music

It may seem an obvious thing to state that all music consists of sound. But sound is a phenomenon that requires thoughtful treatment, for it is more complex than you may imagine. To begin, what constitutes musical sound? Is any kind of sound potentially music, regardless of its origin or purpose? The authors of this textbook prefer the definition that John Blacking provided in his 1973 book *How Musical Is Man?*: "music is humanly organized sound." It is crucial to bear in mind, however, that this is only one perspective and not relevant to all cultures. In many languages, such as Quechua and Náhuatl in Latin America, there is no single word for music itself, but many terms and phrases referring to various kinds of musical performance. In fact, there are many ways that people can relate to the sounds of their immediate environment, and those they make themselves, as music. These are inevitably based in local culture.

Unpitched versus Pitched Sounds

There are two basic kinds of sound in music: unpitched and pitched. Unpitched sounds are sometimes called **noise**, a word people often use in a pejorative sense to describe music they do not like, to assert that it is not really music at all. But the reality is that unpitched sound plays a crucial role in most kinds of music (for instance, the sound of a cymbal crash, or the beat of a bass drum). The difference between unpitched and pitched sounds is easy to summarize: an unpitched sound has an unfocused waveform or vibration, while the waveform of a pitch is uniform and regular in shape.

Like pitches, unpitched sounds may be lower or higher, but they lack peaks of intensity occurring over regular periods of time (cycles per second, or cps). Instead, their frequencies are spread more evenly across a broad spectrum. **Pitches** have measurable frequencies. For instance, in the United States, "concert A," the pitch to which orchestras tune, is currently 440 cps. Every pitch has its own rate of vibration. The distance between any two pitches is called an **interval**. The most basic interval is an **octave,** the point at which the frequency of a pitch is doubled or halved. An octave above A-440 is A-880; an octave below, A-220 (other intervals will be treated further on).

In short, when you snap your fingers, the resulting sound is unpitched; when you hum a tune, you use pitches. Both are musical sounds. In a rock band, the drum set consists largely of unpitched instruments. Electric guitars produce mostly pitches. Both unpitched and pitched sounds combine to create music (Figure A.1).

Sound Generators

In fact, there is a universe of sound generators, some of which produce unpitched sounds, some pitched, and many both. The most obvious examples are the human voice and body. The human voice is capable of great subtlety and variety in the sounds it can produce, and **vocal production** is the term one uses to describe the quality of a singer's voice, whether it is rich, full, nasally, pinched, throaty, and so on. The basic types of vocal categories correspond to how high or low they sing: female voices from high to low are soprano, mezzo-soprano, and alto; male voices, tenor, baritone, and bass. In addition to the voice, the fingers, hands, and feet can all be used as percussion instruments through snapping, clapping, and stomping.

FIGURE A.1 Rock groups such as Maná utilize instruments that produce both pitched and unpitched sounds

Beyond the body, there are four traditional categories of sound generators, as well as a more recent addition. The first is **membranophones**: instruments that are meant to be struck (called percussion) and that produce sound by means of a membrane, made of animal hide or synthetic material, that vibrates when hit with the hands or with sticks (mallets). An Aztec huehuetl is an example of a membranophone (Figure 2.4).

The second is **idiophones**: percussion instruments that do not employ a membrane and whose sound derives directly from resonance of the object itself. Woodblocks, cymbals, or chimes are all idiophones, because sound results from striking wood or metal directly. Again, the striking element may be hands, sticks, or some other object. The Aztec teponaztli is a good example of an idiophone (Figure 2.3).

The third category consists of **chordophones**: instruments that produce sound by means of a vibrating string, as on a guitar (Figure 5.4 and Miguel Matamoros, "Beso discreto," Listening Guide 5.4, 0:00–0:09, 0:32–0:43). Strings may be set in motion with a bow (violin), the fingers or a plectrum (guitar), or with hammers (piano). The root word—chord—does not refer to harmony (see p. 445) but rather to a string of some kind, whether of animal sinew, silk, metal, or nylon.

The final traditional category is **aerophones**: instruments that produce sound by means of a vibrating column of air, as on the Andean panpipes (Figure 8.4 and "Sikuri taquileño, " Listening Guide 8.2, 0:00–0:35). The flute, trumpet, and saxophone are all aerophones. The column of air may be set in motion by blowing over a notch or hole (flute), or by blowing on a reed or double reed pressed between the lips (clarinet, oboe, bassoon). All brass instruments use a cup mouthpiece, into which one buzzes one's lips to create the vibrating column of air. Holes, keys, or valves on an aerophone allow for adjusting the length of the instrument to accommodate different pitch frequencies.

One additional, more recent, category consists of electronic instruments, or **electrophones**, such as synthesizers and computers. These produce electronically generated signals that can be modified in an almost limitless number of ways (Gabriela Ortiz, Five Micro Études for Solo Tape, No. 5, Listening Guide 9.5).

Obviously, some instruments represent a sort of hybrid, like the electric guitar or electric piano. The organ, an instrument very prominent in Latin American churches and cathedrals, is basically an aerophone, as its sound is produced when air is forced through pipes. Before the age of electricity, wind entered a pipe opened by means of mechanical keys. In modern times, this mechanism is often electronic. A synthesizer can simulate the sound of almost any instrument.

A composer thus has a very wide variety of sound generators to choose from when writing a piece of music. The term **instrumentation** refers to the instruments that a composer or musicians have chosen to use in a particular piece. **Orchestration** refers to the art of deciding how to combine various instrumental parts in a composition (Figure A.2).

Tone Color

What distinguishes the sound quality of Colombian gaita flutes (Figure 4.8) from that of a guitar, even if they are playing exactly the same pitch? The physical characteristics of a sound generator (i.e., the parts of it that

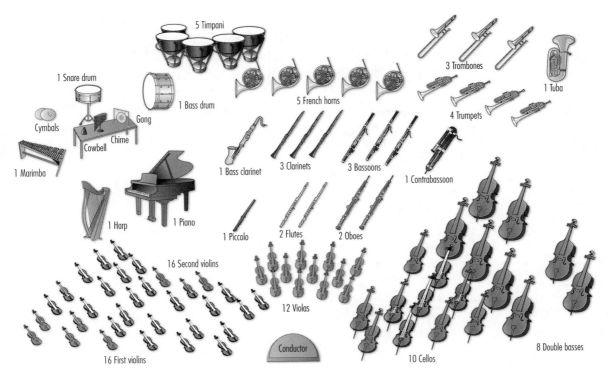

5 Timpani

1 Snare drum

1 Bass drum

Cymbals

Gong

Cowbell

Chime

1 Marimba

3 Trombones

1 Tuba

5 French horns

4 Trumpets

1 Bass clarinet

3 Clarinets

3 Bassoons

1 Contrabassoon

1 Harp

1 Piano

1 Piccolo

2 Flutes

2 Oboes

16 Second violins

12 Violas

Conductor

16 First violins

10 Cellos

8 Double basses

FIGURE A.2 The modern symphony orchestra consists of a wide variety of chordophones, aerophones, membranophones, and idiophones

resonate) determine its sound quality, known as **tone color** or timbre. In fact, it is possible to elicit a variety of timbres from the same instrument. For instance, if I pluck the string of an acoustic guitar with a hard plectrum, or pick, the resulting sound will be rather strident and tinny. If I pluck it with a pick made of felt, the sound with be much mellower. The same effect can be produced by plucking it first back by the bridge (where the strings attach to the body of instrument), and then over the sound hole or neck. To understand how this is possible, and how different timbres are created in the first place, it is necessary to understand the concept of **overtones**.

Just as white light is a composite of various colors (frequencies), so any pitch produced on an instrument or by the human voice is comprised of many notes called overtones, which form the **overtone series**. This is a sequence of higher notes that combine together in the background when a fundamental note is played and help generate its characteristic timbre. For instance, if you play a C in the lower register of the piano, above that fundamental note will sound (even if you cannot hear them easily) another C, then G, C, E, G, B♭, C, and many other pitches beyond those. These are the overtones (also called **partials** or harmonics). They provide richness and variety to musical sound.

Because of its unique construction, when a gaita flute plays a C, certain overtones are stressed more than others. This pattern gives it a timbre that is different from that of a guitar, because the guitar will stress other overtones. To return to our example on the guitar, if I play with a hard pick (or fingernails) or back by the bridge, where the string tension is very high, I will bring out the higher overtones, producing a strident timbre. Conversely, playing with a soft pick or the flesh of my finger, or over the sound hole where the tension is lower, will bring out the lower overtones, lending a softer quality to the sound.

Intensity

One last crucial element of sound pertains to its intensity or **dynamics**, how loud or soft a sound is. If pitch is determined by the frequency of a sound wave's vibration, and if tone color is the product of its overtone series, then intensity arises from the amplitude of the sound. That is to say, the actual height of the sound wave, not the frequency of its movement past a fixed point, determines how loud or soft a sound is. The guitar again provides a useful means of illustrating this simple point. If I pull a string back as far as it will go, it will vibrate back and forth across a wider area than if I use minimum force to displace it from its point of rest. In other words, the farther back I pull the string, the louder the sound it makes. For the same reason, the harder I hit a drumhead, the louder the resulting sound will be, because I have displaced the head farther than by hitting it gently. The sound waves thus generated will be larger (though not faster), that is, they will have greater amplitude.

An electric amplifier takes the signal from an instrument, via a pickup, and increases (amplifies) the size of the sound wave. Until you plug it into an amp, a solid-body electric guitar makes a very soft sound, because the thick wood does not resonate easily. An acoustic guitar has its own built-in amplifier: the soundboard and hollow body of the instrument amplify the sound made by plucking or striking the strings, and it projects out of the hole on the front. High volume or intensity is often referred to by the Italian word for strong, *forte*, while passages of lower intensity are described as *piano* (soft). A gradual increase from soft to loud is called a *crescendo*, and from loud to soft, a *decrescendo*.

EXERCISE A.1: Intensity

Listen to Revueltas: *Sensemayá* (Listening Guide 3.10) and compare the intensity level of the opening (0:00–2:00) to that of the conclusion (6:01–7:04). Does the work get softer or louder?

Rhythm

The term rhythm describes the way time is organized in music. In its most basic sense, rhythm refers to the relative durations of musical sounds. I say "relative" because one perceives the length of any musical event in relation to events around it. A note of some absolute duration may seem longer or shorter depending on what goes on before and after it. For instance, a note one second in duration will seem very long if preceded and followed by notes lasting only a fraction of a second. Conversely, it will seem quite short if surrounded by notes of several seconds' length. There is an almost infinite number of possible sound durations and combinations of rhythms, which musicians exploit to great effect.

Beat and Meter

Another dimension of rhythm has to do with **beat**, a regularly occurring form of rhythmic organization in a piece of music. Though most music has a beat, it is not necessary in a musical composition, and there are kinds of music without a pronounced beat or pulse; they are referred to as **ametrical** or unmetered. A sense of beat occurs, as mentioned, when one can hear regular emphasis or stress in the rhythm. Such stress often encourages sympathetic physical movement, and "toe-tapping" rhythms are popular around the world.

When these pulses are organized into recurring patterns of weak and strong beats (i.e., some beats are stressed more than others), the phenomenon of **meter** arises. This term has been borrowed from poetry, where a similar phenomenon occurs. Take, for example, the popular rhyme "**Jack** and **Jill** went **up** the **hill** to **fetch** a **pail** of **wa**-ter." The syllables in bold note recurrent stresses in a regular pattern, that is, on every other syllable. These regular stresses give a sense of meter to the poem. In notated Western music, one such unit of meter is called a **bar**, or measure.

There are many kinds of metrical rhythm, but the most common ones are based on two and three. For instance, marches are always composed in groupings of two, also known as **duple meter**: ONE-two, ONE-two, or ONE-two-THREE-four. This is because the march's primary purpose has been to accompany and regulate the movements of soldiers in the field or on parade. Human beings with two legs move in binary ways, which suggest duple meter (Carlos Gardel/Alfredo Le Pera, "Por una cabeza," Listening Guide 7.4, 0:00–1:19). Fortunately, our range of motion is not quite so limited. The waltz is a very elegant dance that exhibits **triple meter**, and one that humans imitate through motion: ONE-Two-three, ONE-Two-three, and so forth. The waltz, which features three beats per measure, emphasizes the first beat strongly, the second less so, and the third weakly (Graciela Olmos, "El Siete Leguas," Listening Guide 3.3, 0:00–1:14). Another type of meter is called **compound** because its metrical stresses take place on multiple levels. In compound duple, for instance, there are two (or four) primary pulses, but each pulse is subdivided into three subordinate beats ("El Sapo," Listening Guide 4.1, 0:00–1:24). Compound triple exhibits three pulses at both levels. Some pieces in compound meter may also be written in aggregate segments, for instance three beats followed by two, or more complicated groupings (3 + 3 +2, etc.), such as the rhythm discussed next.

EXERCISE A.2: Meter

Listen to Miguel Matamoros, "Beso discreto" (Listening Guide 5.4) from the beginning and see if you can identify the meter—in other words, is it duple, triple, or compound duple?

Any musical composition can use none or all of these, or it may alternate various meters. Hispanic music very often alternates compound duple meter with triple meter, a type of rhythm called **hemiola** (in Spanish, sesquiáltera): ONE-two-three, ONE-two-three/ONE-two, ONE-two, ONE-two/ONE-two-three, ONE-two-three/ONE-two, ONE-two, ONE-two ("El son de la negra," Listening Guide 3.4, 0:00–0:56). A classic example of this device is the number "America" from the musical *West Side Story* by Leonard Bernstein (text by Stephen Sondheim). Bernstein employs the rhythm as a kind of musical marker to identify the Puerto Ricans who sing and dance it. Hemiola also occurs when compound duple meter is juxtaposed against triple meter (Example 7.1).

The juxtaposition of two or more different meters in a piece of music is called **polymeter**, and the foregoing example (Example 7.1) is a perfect illustration of it. **Polyrhythms** result from the juxtaposition of two or more different rhythmic patterns, even though all the parts may be in the same meter (Example 6.2). Polymeters and polyrhythms are very characteristic of Afro-Latin music in general, especially in Cuba and Brazil, being derived as they are from West African music, in which this kind of rhythm predominates (see the discussion of West African music in Chapter 5).

A rhythmic (and/or melodic) pattern that is repeated over and over is called an **ostinato**, the Italian word for "obstinate" (Example 6.4 and "Elegguá, Oggún, Ochosi II," Listening Guide 5.2, 0:00–0:27). This technique appears frequently in Latin American music with an indigenous or African character, which often incorporates looped rhythms or melodies of various sorts as a basis for improvisation and dance.

Syncopation and Tempo

When music emphasizes musical pulses between beats (upbeats) that are normally weak, one creates **syncopation**. This device is especially characteristic of African-derived music (Tote Gira and Daniela Mercury, "O canto da cidade," Listening Guide 6.6, 1:16–1:33). In fact, syncopation is absolutely central to jazz, because it lends "swing" to the rhythm. In similar fashion, rock relies heavily on syncopation to give it its characteristic motion. Rock is almost always in duple meter, four beats per bar. Normally in such a situation, the first and third beats of the measure would be emphasized: ONE-two-THREE-four. But in rock, the pattern works like this: one-TWO-three-FOUR. This pattern, also called a backbeat, is articulated in the drum set, while the melody usually hews to the meter in a more conventional way. The resulting rhythmic contrasts and interactions give rock its infectious beat (Juan Esteban Aristizábal Vázquez (Juanes), "Me enamora," Listening Guide 10.2, 0:00–1:14).

Regardless of how many beats there are or how they are accentuated, **tempo** (Italian for "time") refers to how rapidly the beats are moving. Performing a particular piece at a slow tempo will yield a much different effect from a performance of the same work at a faster tempo. No other parameter of the music changes, yet it may sound altogether like a different work. For instance, think of any song you enjoy and imagine it at different tempos. A march, in particular, will sound ridiculous if played either too slowly or too fast. There is a rather narrow range of march tempos that will produce a satisfying effect, for instance, somewhere around 120 beats per minute, or 2 per second. Often a composer will specify either the precise tempo in terms of beats per minute, which can be determined with a device called a **metronome**, suggesting a particular tempo.

EXERCISE A.3: Tempo

Listen to Carlos Chávez, *Sinfonía india*, Listening Guide 3.9 (0:00–2:05 and 2:06–5:49) and try to discern any difference in tempo between the two passages. Are they slow, fast, or somewhere in between?

Subdivision

Finally, any rhythm can be **subdivided**, that is, broken down into smaller parts by dividing it into twos or threes. For instance, two normal beats, ONE-two, can be divided by two to become ONE-&-two-&, that is, each beat consists of a **downbeat** followed by an **upbeat**; another subdivision by two can be expressed as ONE-e-&-ah two-e-&-ah. Dotted rhythms represent not a division but rather an addition to a note of one half its value. The Cuban habanera features a prominent dotted rhythm that can be expressed by saying aloud only the first and last syllables of the following pattern: ONE-e-&-ah. This pattern becomes a kind of ostinato in the habanera and is one of this song's distinguishing traits (Example 2.4 and Ignacio Cervantes, "Los delirios de Rosita," Listening Guide 2.10, 0:00–0:39). It is very similar to the syncopated beat of a much more recent and familiar style of music called reggaeton. You can see this rhythm in Example 5.7 and Shakira, Luis F. Ochoa, "La tortura," Listening Guide 10.1. Try tapping it out against a basic pulse, as in the transcription, to get a feeling for how syncopation works.

Melody

It is quite possible to have a musical composition without a melody, but never without rhythm. As soon as you make a single sound intended as music, rhythm occurs. Nonetheless, most styles of music depend heavily on melody to convey emotion and meaning. All songs, for instance, rely on melody as well as text for this purpose. Whereas one could easily organize a work utilizing only unpitched sound, melody requires pitches.

Phrase and Motive

The best way to understand the concept of melody is to make analogies to speech. A melody is essentially a succession of single pitches forming a musical sentence, a complete musical idea that has an identifiable beginning and ending. A melody may be preceded and followed by other kinds of music, and other music may be going on at the same time, but it can stand alone as a recognizable and coherent statement. And, like any sentence, a melody can be broken down into constituent parts. A **phrase** is like the musical version of a clause in a sentence. Western melodies are typically made up of two or more phrases, even as this sentence is made up of two clauses. The smallest subdivision of a melody, however, is not the phrase but the **motive**. Motives are short musical ideas, consisting of only a few notes, which give a melody its distinctive character. A motive is very much like a phrase in language. Many well-known songs are made up of two- or four-bar phrases, to make for a very logical structure. Think, for example, of the U.S. national anthem, "The Star-Spangled Banner." Its melodic structure is very symmetrically laid out in four-bar phrases. The opening three-note motive gives it a distinctive and immediately recognizable character.

Of course, the concept of melody is common to almost all music cultures. Yet, the way melody is structured may or may not resemble what was just described. Just as different languages have their own syntax and sentence structure, so different musics can exhibit unique ways of organizing melody. For example, the melodies sung by the Kayapó-Xikrin people of the Amazon, treated in Chapter 6 ("Nhuiti ngrere," Listening Guide 6.1, 0:00–1:01), do not resemble the melodies people commonly sing in the United States, especially since the distinction between speaking and singing is not always clear in indigenous Brazilian songs.

EXERCISE A.4: Melodic Styles

Listen to "Huistan, Fiesta of San Miguel, 1974. Three Drums and Small Flute" (Listening Guide 3.1); Lucho Bermúdez, "Gaita de las flores" (Listening Guide 4.5); and Silvio Rodríguez, "En estos días" (Listening Guide 5.7). Compare the melodies in terms of their structure.

Scales

A composer or performer uses a series of notes called a **scale** on which to base a piece of music. The composer or improviser is not limited to the notes in a particular scale but will rely on them more than any others to give the piece a sense of unity and coherence. The notes of a scale are sometimes called **degrees**, as in the "third degree" of a scale, meaning the third note up from the first. The greater the distance between degrees of the scale, the larger the interval.

Principal Scale Types

Most but not all scales span an octave. In the European tradition (and, by extension, much Latin American music), scales of many types have appeared, but the two most common scales are called **major** and **minor**. As their names imply, many in Europe and the United States associate the major scale with a bright, happy quality, while describing the minor scale as sad and brooding. However, these are culture-specific associations. In Latin America, minor scales appear much more frequently in traditional and popular repertoire than in the United States, and the key does not necessary seem sad to listeners.

A minor scale can be created by playing a major scale beginning on the sixth degree and continuing upward for an octave. Because certain keys are related in this way, one speaks of relative major and relative minor scales—for example C major is the relative major of A minor, and vice versa, because to get an A minor scale, you play on the white keys of the piano starting on A, not C.

EXERCISE A.5: Major and Minor

Listen to Víctor Jara, "Plegaria a un labrador," Listening Guide 8.6 (0:00–1:47) for changes between major and minor keys.

Major and minor scales consist of a series of tones either a **whole step** or a **half step** apart. A whole step is equivalent to moving from one white key

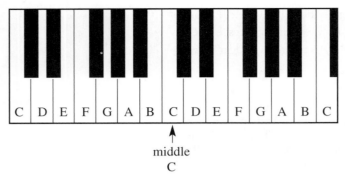

middle
C

FIGURE A.3 A keyboard indicating the names of the white keys of the piano an octave above and below middle C

to another on a piano, provided there is a black key between them (Figure A.3). The distance from a white key to an adjacent black key is a half step. On the piano, half steps occur between white keys in only two places, E–F and B–C. It is a particular sequence of whole and half steps that gives any scale its characteristic quality, although scales are not limited to whole and half steps and may have larger or smaller gaps between notes. For instance, in other music cultures the steps themselves may be larger or smaller; intervals smaller than a half step are called **microtones**, and they figure prominently in music of Amerindians in the Amazon region ("Nhuiti ngrere," Listening Guide 6.1, 0:00–1:01).

It should be obvious by now that there are many other scale possibilities than these. In fact, there are hundreds of other possibilities. The Western system is not a universal standard: scales can have a variable number of notes in them, with different kinds of steps arranged in a myriad of sequential patterns.

Fortunately, there are only a few other scale types that appear in most of the examples throughout the textbook. One is the **chromatic** scale, consisting entirely of half steps, that is, all the keys on the piano (a scale consisting entirely of whole steps is called a **whole-tone scale**). *Chromos* is the Greek word for color, and as the name suggests, this kind of scale can have a colorful quality (Leo Brouwer, *La espiral eterna*, Listening Guide 5.9, 0:00–2:04). One other scale type that is of crucial importance in Andean music in particular is the so-called **pentatonic** scale. One common version of this five-note scale can be rendered by simply playing the black keys of a piano. There are no half steps in many pentatonic scales, such as those found in traditional Andean music; instead, they consist entirely of whole steps or even larger intervals ("Sikuri taquileño," Listening Guide 8.2, 0:08–1:35).

Notation

You have noticed the use capital letters to refer to particular notes. This is a Western convention dating back hundreds of years. Rather than run through the entire alphabet, however, early on people decided it would be easier to use the first seven letters of the alphabet and then repeat them after reaching the octave: C, D, E, F, G. A, B, C. Half steps between these notes are indicated by using sharp (♯) and flat (♭) signs, called **accidentals**. For instance, an F♯ or a G♭ both refer to the same note halfway between F and G. A natural sign (♮) negates a sharp or flat.

In the Western system of musical notation, notes are represented as ovals (white and black) on a series of five parallel lines called a **staff** (plural staves).

The music for an ensemble of any size contains several staves and is called a **score**. A clef sign indicates which line corresponds to which note. A G (or treble) clef is in the shape of the letter G and circles the second line from the bottom of the staff, indicating that it is G (Example 8.2). It is used to notate higher pitches, typically above middle C on the piano. The F (or bass) clef and C clefs are similarly stylized versions of letters and indicate those respective pitches on the staff. They are used to notate lower pitches.

Notating pitch is much easier than notating rhythm, simply because there are so many more possible rhythms than pitches in the Western system. A system of stems, flags, dots, and beams gradually developed to indicate the relative durations of the oval notes on the page. Basic durations are indicated as fractional subdivisions of the whole note (a large goose-egg shape): half, quarter, sixteenth, thirty-second, and sixty-fourth (subdivisions beyond this one are possible but rare). **Time signatures** appear as a fractional number at the beginning of a piece to indicate what meter the piece is in, such as $\frac{2}{4}$ or $\frac{4}{4}$ (duple meter), $\frac{3}{4}$ (triple meter), $\frac{6}{8}$ or $\frac{12}{8}$ (compound duple), $\frac{9}{8}$ (compound triple), and so on. The numerator refers to the number of beats in a measure, and the demoninator designates what type of note (e.g., quarter or eighth) gets one beat.

Key

The **key,** or **tonality**, of a piece is determined by two things: the scale type that predominates in the composition, and the note on which that scale begins. A piece in C major is based principally on a major scale beginning on C, without any flats or sharps. A piece in D major has sharps on F and C; however, instead of writing these out on every note, it has been found more convenient to indicate them once, at the beginning of each line of music, in a **key signature**. The number of flats or sharps in the key signature will indicate what key the piece is in, depending on what the starting note of the scale is (Example 8.2). It is possible to have two or more keys occurring at the same time, something called **polytonality** (Alberto Ginastera, First Piano Sonata, first movement, Listening Guide 7.9, 0:00–1:01). Scales and keys are the basis for the vertical dimension of musical sound, called harmony.

Harmony

Up to this point, the discussion has focused on notes in a horizontal sequence, happening one at a time. However, most of the music in this text features two or more notes occurring simultaneously. This vertical dimension of music is called **harmony**. Harmony refers to any collection of two or more different pitches sounding at the same time. Harmony is found in many music cultures around the world, and it has been especially characteristic of Western music for the past thousand years. The most common type of vertical assemblage of pitches is called a **chord**. There is almost no limit to the number of possible chords, but the most common kinds are triads, meaning that they consist of three different notes (regardless of how high or low they are or how many performers play them). The triad has been the harmonic foundation of Western music for the past five hundred years, coinciding with the period of continuous European presence in the western hemisphere.

Types of Triads

As you might already have guessed, there are different types of triads. Two basic types are crucial to our understanding of harmony. The first kind is called a major triad. In this chord, there is a root note and two notes above it. The first upper note is separated from the root by two whole steps, an interval called a major third. From C to E, for example, is a major third (C to D and D to E constituting the two whole steps). In a major triad, the interval between the two upper notes is a minor third (one and a half steps). From E to G is a minor third. So, a C major triad consists of the notes C, E, and G, sounded anywhere on the keyboard or on any instrument or in a group of voices. A minor triad is the reverse of the major in that there is a minor third below and a major third above it.

Generally speaking, however, major and minor chords sound pleasing and restful to our ears, or **consonant**. Not all chords are consonant, however, and many sound harsh and unsettled, or **dissonant**. There are many other kinds of dissonant chords, but notions of dissonance and consonance are highly subjective and change from one period or culture to the next. (See Lôbo de Mesquita, Salve Regina, Listening Guide 2.4, 0:00–1:01, for some music that is highly consonant, and Mario Davidovsky, *Synchronisms No. 10* for Guitar and Electronic Sounds, Listening Guide 9.6, 4:50–5:53, for some that is highly dissonant.)

Triads can be built on every degree of the major or minor scale. For reasons that have to do with acoustics as well aural conditioning, the first and fifth degrees of a scale, and consequently the triads built on them, are the most important in both major and minor keys. They are called **tonic** and **dominant**, respectively. The tonic chord will predominate, and it is the harmony with which a piece will usually begin and end. But the dominant triad will always be the next-most-frequently used chord in a composition, as it usually "leads" or "resolves" to the tonic chord. Third in importance is the so-called **subdominant**, on the fourth degree of the scale. Roman numerals are often used to indicate these chords: I, IV, V. In most popular music, especially rock, these three chords form the substance of the piece's harmony and are used far more than any other chords. Chords played in a predictable sequence form something called a **chord progression**. Much traditional and popular music is based on the chord progression I–IV–V–I (Atahualpa Yupanqui, "Malambo," Listening Guide 7.1, 0:18–2:00).

Atonality

Not all music is tonal (has a key or traditional harmony). When music has no tonal center and uses mostly dissonant chords, it is called **atonal** (Leo Brouwer, *La espiral eterna*, Listening Guide 5.9, and Mario Davidovsky, *Synchronisms No. 10* for Guitar and Electronic Sounds, Listening Guide 9.6, which are both atonal throughout). This type of music can be highly expressive, but in a disturbing and unsettling way that conveys particularly intense emotion. Indeed, there are some extreme states of feeling and experience that cannot really be expressed as effectively in any other style of music. For a piece to be atonal, it is necessary that every note in the chromatic scale receive equal emphasis in the music and that no one note be perceived as more important than any other, that is, as a tonal center. Very often this music will also seem to lack a sense of regular pulse or meter (Listening Guides 5.9 and 9.6). This type of music is very characteristic of the post–World War II avant-garde.

Texture

It may seem odd to refer to the **texture** of a piece of music, as if it had a tactile quality like a rug or paint on a canvas. In fact, some of the terminology used in music (line, color, texture) is borrowed directly from art history. Just as one can draw analogies between language and music, so one can use visual metaphors to describe what one is hearing. In many ways, one "looks" at music with his or her ears instead of eyes.

Monophony, Heterophony

When talking about the texture of music, one is referring to the ways in which voices and instruments combine and interact melodically and harmonically. The simplest kind of texture is called **monophony**, in which there is a single melody without any chords or other melodies. Monophony does not refer to how many people are performing the melody. There may be one, or there may be a hundred; they may be singing or playing instruments. Sometimes a soloist alternates with a group in singing monophonically, a technique known as **call-and-response** ("Elegguá, Oggún, Ochosi II," Listening Guide 5.2). This is characteristic of West African and Afro-Latin singing.

In any case, all the word monophony indicates is that there is a single melody, nothing else. This texture is typical of Gregorian chant (Lôbo de Mesquita, Salve Regina, Listening Guide 2.4, 0:00–0:07). Much Native American music exhibits a closely related texture called **heterophony**, in which slightly different versions of the same melody are taking place simultaneously ("Nhuiti ngrere," Listening Guide 6.1, 0:00–1:01, and "Harawi," Listening Guide 8.1).

Homophony

Homophony indicates the presence of chords, either by themselves or accompanying a melody (Gaspar Fernandes, "Xicochi conetzintle," Listening Guide 2.3, 0:27–0:32). All the notes in the chords move in the same rhythm, hence the prefix "homo-," suggesting uniformity. A singer accompanied by a guitar is a classic example of a homophonic texture. In fact, homophony is the characteristic texture of most popular music.

Polyphony

Polyphony is the most complex of textures because there are two or more independent melodies taking place at the same time. Polyphony appears in a wide variety of music contexts, both traditional and classical. For instance, parallel polyphony, in which different lines move together, is characteristic of much Andean music ("Sikuri taquileño," Listening Guide 8.2). The sacred music of the colonial period in Latin America was usually polyphonic in texture (except for chant). A special kind of polyphony involves the presentation of a melody, or theme, and its subsequent imitation in other voices or instruments (or "voices" on the same instrument). This is known as imitative polyphony. The most common type of imitative polyphony is the **fugue** (José Mauricio Nunes Garcia, "Cum Sancto Spiritu," from *Missa de Nossa Senhora de Conceição*, Listening Guide 2.5, Fugue: 0:00–1:36). In a fugue, a melody (subject) is subsequently repeated (answered) by other lines, sung and or played, entering one at a time against a countermelody.

EXERCISE A.6: Texture.

Listen to Tania León, *Horizons*, Listening Guide 9.2 (0:00–1:04) and try to determine its texture—whether it is monophonic, homophonic, or polyphonic.

Form

The German author Johann Wolfgang von Goethe once described architecture as "frozen music." In some ways, music is a kind of architecture. All musical compositions, whether written down or not, have a structure, a way that they are put together so that they make sense. Even the apparent absence of structure is in itself a method of organizing musical sound over time. Form is one of the first things we try to perceive when listening analytically to a piece of music for the first time.

The form of a piece of music is normally classified according to the number and sequence of the various themes (melodies) presented. Each section of a piece is dominated by a particular theme, and that section is identified with a capital letter (which does not designate notes or keys). A very common form is **AB**, in which the initial section is followed by a contrasting theme (and key). This is called **binary form** (Carlos Gardel/Alfredo Le Pera, "Por una cabeza," Listening Guide 7.4, **A**: 0:15; **B**: 0:49). If there is a return to the opening section, perhaps in a slightly varied way, this results in the form **ABA**, or **ternary** (Domenico Zipoli, "In te spero," from *In hoc Mundo*, Listening Guide 2.6, **A**: 0:24; **B**: 1:20; **A**: 2:20). This is typical of many opera arias, and of popular song. Another form, called **rondo**, presents a recurring section separated by contrasting themes: **ABACABA** (Agustín Pío Barrios, *La catedral*, Listening Guide 7.10, 4:02–6:28 has a very similar form, **AABCAB'AB**). It is possible to have a sequence of contrasting sections without any return of previously stated ideas: **ABC** (or **AABBCC**) ("Sikuri taquileño," Listening Guide 8.2, **A**: 0:08; **B**: 0:22; **C**: 0:36).

As mentioned previously, the formal structures of much traditional indigenous and Afro-descendant music do not fall easily into such categories. Often its formal structure derives from cyclic, open-ended rhythmic or melodic patterns that are repeated many times in variation as a complement to dance, religious worship, or other activity. This sort of expression must be analyzed not in terms of discrete sectional shifts, but rather in terms of subtle changes to the texture, the addition or elimination of melodies, rhythms, or other elements, the incorporation of improvisatory passages, changes in tempo or intensity in relation to other sections. In short, there are many different types of form.

Song form represents a special case because of the close relationship of the music to the text. Most song texts are poetic and consist of two or more stanzas. If each stanza is set to different music, the song's form is **through-composed**. If each succeeding stanza (or strophe) is set to the same music as the first, the form of the song is **strophic**. Most traditional songs, anthems, carols, and other popular songs are strophic in form. Many vocal works consist of a verse and refrain. The verse presents new text while the refrain repeats the same text and music. In Spanish, their names are **copla** and **estribillo**, respectively (Café Tacuba, "Eres," Listening Guide 3.7, copla: 0:27–1:17; estribillo: 1:18–1:42).

Aesthetics and Culture

The various kinds of music treated in this text reflect the diverse cultural heritage of Latin America, including indigenous, mestizo, Afro-Latin, and European elements. These often determine the salient features that a particular piece of music exhibits. Listen to the following four excerpts, each representing one of these facets of Latin American heritage. Apply the

Indigenous: "Harawi" (Listening Guide 8.1)

In this example, take specific note of how the sound is organized.

1. What accompaniment, if any, do you hear?
2. What sorts of pitches or scales are used?
3. What sorts of phrasing and motives appear in the melodies?
4. How would you characterize the form?
5. How would you describe the texture?
6. Assuming you were hearing it for the first time and did not know, what clues would you pick up that this is traditional indigenous music?

terms and concepts introduced in this appendix when listening to them. Notice the vocal production and instrumentation (if any), rhythm, melodic structure, harmony, form, and texture of each piece. Then make your own Listening Guide for each based on what you perceive as you listen.

While this example from the Andes features only singing, various percussion and wind instruments are often used in indigenous music. These include trumpets and flutes made of various materials (bamboo, wood, metal, terra cotta), as well as membranophones and idiophones of assorted kinds and sizes. String instruments introduced by Europeans have been adapted to suit local tastes, as in the case of the Andean charango (Figure 8.7) and the harp. A prominent scale in Andean music is the pentatonic scale. Several forms appear, but they usually involve varied repetition of melodies, whose different phrases and motives follow the text closely. Textures feature monophony, heterophony, homophony, and polyphony. Finally, the music is part of an oral tradition and not written down. The musicians require not only a keen sense of pitch and rhythm but also excellent memories.

Mestizo refers to a blending of native and Spanish ancestry, and the resulting hybrid forms of culture. We noted indigenous elements in the previous

Mestizo: "La bruja" (Listening Guide 3.2)

In this example, see if you can identify the elements that make this mestizo. Here are some questions to ask:

1. What language are they singing in?
2. What is the relationship of the poetic structure to the piece's form?
3. What sorts of instruments are used? Are any of these different from instruments used in Spanish music?
4. How would you characterize the rhythm?
5. Does it have a meter, and if so, what kind?
6. Are there several melodies at the same time, or does it feature mainly one melody with chordal accompaniment?

example. The European and Spanish-derived elements are conspicuous in this one. Among the most obvious is the use of a European language, Spanish, as well as related poetic forms. The structure of the music conforms to that of the poetry, in this case a copla form with paired four-line stanzas. In any event, the purpose of the music is to complement and intensify the song lyrics, not compete with or obscure them. A popular instrument is the guitar, which originally came from Spain. It is light, portable, relatively inexpensive, and musically versatile. It can play chords and melodies, either accompanying or playing solo. Yet, this piece utilizes varieties called the jarana and requinto, which are Mexican and not Spanish. Another popular string instrument is the harp. In terms of rhythm, though there is frequent syncopation, there is also a strong sense of pulse, in which certain meters prevail, especially duple and triple. Songs and instrumental music utilize major and minor scales, and the texture is often homophonic, with a melody and chordal accompaniment.

Afro-Latin music like the *batucada* usually demonstrates a high level of rhythmic density or polyrhythm, with many different beats sounding simultaneously. Pieces may be in duple or triple meter, or they may involve simultaneous rhythms that emphasize both groupings of two and three. The relationship *between* rhythms is very important because many performers of traditional percussion music do not read Western notation and therefore orient themselves solely on the basis of how their part fits in with the others. Moreover, many of the individual rhythms fit together to form aggregate melodies. That is to say that each performer will play certain notes of

---

Afro-Latin: Tote Gira and Daniela Mercury, "O canto da cidade" (Listening Guide 6.6)

Afro-Latin music possesses distinctive traits that distinguish it from other styles. Address the following points in your listening:

1. What kinds of instruments do you hear in this selection? Are there membranophones? Idiophones? What sorts of materials do think these instruments are made of?
2. How would you describe the rhythm in this piece? Does one rhythm predominate, or is there approximate equality between the rhythms?
3. Do the rhythms constantly evolve and change, or do some of them repeat over and over?
4. What is the sense of beat here? Do you sense one basic sort of meter, duple or triple, or can you perceive different meters at the same time?
5. What is the melodic structure like? Is the melody restricted to one instrument or voice, or is it broken up among various performers?
6. How would you characterize the overall formal organization of this music? Does it exhibit a sequence of different melodies, or do rhythmic patterns determine its structure?
7. Would you describe this music as polyphonic? Why or why not?

the melody, which can only be heard in its entirety when the various parts of it interlock. Thus, multiple parts seem to form a single pattern.

In terms of form, much West African and Afro-Brazilian music is based on repeating cycles and patterns, resulting in an open-ended form that lasts as long as the performance event requires. There is often a hierarchy of instruments in African-influenced repertoire, with some instruments like the bell playing a basically static, unchanging line that serves to keep the pulse. Others vary their parts a bit more, while still others feature prominently as solo instruments, fighting the relatively constant rhythms laid down by the rest. Call-and-response singing is an African-derived characteristic in much of this repertoire, featuring a soloist alternating with the group. Finally, much Afro-Latin music incorporates a vast array of sounds from metal, wood, animal skin, and plant material, giving the music a colorful abundance of timbres.

In addition to a wide variety of string instruments, the Europeans introduced keyboard instruments, along with many new wind and percussion instruments. In the twentieth century, electronic instruments became prominent. The textures of European music include monophony, homophony, and polyphony, especially imitative polyphony. The harmonic language is basically tonal, utilizing major and minor scales, but over time, the music has become increasingly chromatic, with the actual breakdown of tonality in the twentieth century. This tendency towards innovation and stylistic change over time (which is not the same as progress) is characteristic. The rhythm of European music is basically downbeat oriented and relies on duple, triple, and compound meters. Here, too, the quest for rhythmic novelty eventually produced increasingly complex rhythms and metrical

European: Mario Davidovsky, *Synchronisms No. 10* for Guitar and Electronic Sounds (Listening Guide 9.6)

This work is quite unlike the three previous examples, especially in its use of electronic technology with a performer. It is also different in other important respects.

1. What is your emotional response to this work? Does it seem to express traditional emotions like sorrow and joy, or does it strike you as emotionally neutral?
2. What is the relationship between the electronic and acoustic sounds? Are they equally prominent, or does one tend to dominate?
3. Do you think this music allows for improvisation on the part of the performer, or does the composer intend that the piece sound the same way with each performance?
4. How would you describe the harmony of this work? Is it dissonant or consonant? Tonal or atonal?
5. Is there any sense of beat or meter in this music? If not, how would you describe the rhythm?
6. What sort of form does this work exhibit? Can you describe it using letters for different melodic sections, or would you have to devise some other way to describe it?

patterns, and even the abandonment of any feeling of beat whatsoever (ametricality). Electronic technology, atonality, and ametricality are defining traits of Davidovsky's work.

Though these four categories do no exhaust all the possibilities, they still represent the great diversity of Latin American music in its various cultural contexts. It is important to remember, however, that these are not impermeable categories. Rather, it is quite possible to form hybrids and cross boundaries. In fact, each of them is the result of earlier such mixtures, and that process of hybridization will persist and intensify.

KEY TERMS

accidental	hemiola	polyphony
aerophone	heterophony	polyrhythm
ametrical	homophony	polytonal
atonal	idiophone	rondo
bar	instrumentation	scale
beat	interval	score
binary form	key	staff
call-and-response	key signature	strophic
chord	major scale	subdivision
chord progression	membranophone	subdominant
chordophone	meter	syncopation
chromatic	metronome	tempo
compound meter	microtone	ternary form
consonant	minor scale	texture
copla	monophony	through-composed
degree	motive	time signature
dissonant	noise	tonality
dominant	octave	tone color
downbeat	orchestration	tonic
duple meter	ostinato	triple meter
dynamics	overtone	upbeat
electrophone	overtone series	vocal production
estribillo	pentatonic	whole step
fugue	phrase	whole-tone scale
half step	pitch	
harmony	polymeter	

Glossary

Academic music See **Classical music**.

Accidental A symbol used in music notation to indicate that a note is to be raised a half step (sharp), lowered a half step (flat), or played without a flat or sharp (natural).

Acculturation The cultural modification of an individual, group, or people by adapting to or borrowing traits from another culture; often the result of prolonged contact.

Aerophone A wind instrument, that is, one that produces sound by means of a vibrating column of air within a resonator or tube. Aerophones include the trumpet, saxophone, panpipes, chirimía, and flute.

Agogô An African-derived double bell used in the samba bateria.

Ametricality The absence of meter or sense of a regular beat.

Andalusian cadence A descending sequence of four chords based on a minor descending tetrachord, that is, a series of four bass notes, with a distinctive half step between the last two. This progression conveys tonal ambiguity because it begins on a minor chord (such as D minor), proceeds through two other chords (such as C major and B-flat major), and ends on a major chord (such as A major), thus arriving on the dominant, rather than the tonic. See also **Dominant** and **Tonic**.

Antiphony (adj. **antiphonal**) A term referring to a practice whereby two halves of a choir sing back and forth to one another.

Aria An extended composition for solo voice that is found in opera as well as in large-scale vocal and instrumental genres such as cantatas and motets.

Arpa llanera A harp with 32 gut or nylon strings, found in the Colombian and Venezuelan Llanos. The arpa llanera gives *música llanera* its distinctive sound and provides the harmony, melodic solos, and a great deal of the rhythmic foundation.

Arpeggiation The presentation of chords in arpeggios—that is, playing the pitches of a chord in a linear series rather than all at once.

Arpegina A bowed stringed instrument identical to the viola but with five strings instead of the traditional four.

Arrabal (pl. **arrabales**) Term for an impoverished district on the outskirts of Buenos Aires and Montevideo where the tango arose.

Art music See **Classical music**.

Assimilation The process by which immigrants are integrated into host societies or cultures.

Atonal A type of music that has no tonal center or key. In an atonal work, no one note is more prominent or important than any other.

Aymara An indigenous language spoken in southern Peru and Bolivia. The word may also be used to describe those who speak the language, as in the "Aymara people."

Bachata A style of commercial dance music from the Dominican Republic, derived from local reinterpretations of the Latin American bolero. It first developed in the 1970s and gained an international audience in the 1990s.

Baião A social dance for couples with a fast-paced melodic line played on the accordion and a marchlike accompanying rhythm.

Baile funk A type of dance party held in the impoverished suburbs of Rio de Janeiro. The local youth dance to the beat of electronic drum machines and sampled sounds from African American music of the 1970s and 1980s, mixed with Brazilian percussion. See also **Tamborzão**.

Bajo sexton A guitar-like instrument with twelve metal strings used in Mexican norteña music from the northeastern border region.

Balada The Latin American variant of the international pop romantic ballad. It features lyrics about love and romance, crooner-style singing, and sophisticated studio production.

Bambuco A Colombian song form, primarily of European background, first called *canción colombiana* (Colombian song). It started as a trio of different guitar-type instruments from the interior provinces and was reinterpreted by big bands for urban audiences in the 1930s and 1940s.

Banda sinaloense A style of wind-band dance music from the northernwestern state of Sinaloa, Mexico.

Bandolim A stringed instrument similar to the mandolin, with four double courses of strings, used in the Brazilian choro.

Bandoneón An accordion-like instrument of German origin associated with the tango that is also used in contemporary traditional-music ensembles. It has 38 buttons in the upper and middle registers and 33 buttons in the lower register.

Bar One unit of meter (also called a measure). See also **Meter**.

Baroque The historical period from about 1600 to 1750. Baroque musical characteristics include elaborate ornamentation, contrasting textures and dynamics, and extended melodies.

Batá A double-headed, hourglass-shaped drum traditionally played in groups of three in Santería ceremonies in Cuba and elsewhere. The consecrated drums are believed to contain a sacred force.

Bateria A huge percussion ensemble, including European and African-derived instruments, that performs in samba-school parades during Brazilian carnival.

Beat A regularly occurring stress, or emphasis, in the rhythm of a piece.

Berimbau A musical instrument used in capoeira, the berimbau is a musical bow made out of wood in the shape of an arc and strung with a steel wire. The player strikes the wire with a small stick. A dried gourd, attached at the bottom of the bow, functions as a resonator. Berimbau performers hold a small rattle with the right hand and coordinate it with a rock or coin held between the thumb and index finger.

Binary form See **Form**.

Bolero The Latin American bolero is a romantic song genre that first developed in Cuba at the turn of the twentieth century but has since become popular throughout Latin America. It is characterized by complex chords, slow tempos, and refined, poetic lyrics. Unlike the Spanish bolero, it is in duple meter rather than triple.

Bomba (1) An Afro–Puerto Rican drumming tradition of which many variants exist. It is performed on large, round drums made from wooden barrels. Bomba has influenced salsa and other commercial Latin dance music. (2) An Afro-Ecuadorian dance music genre performed with guitars, vocals, and a small hand drum, which is also known as a bomba.

Bombo A large, double-headed cylindrical drum played with sticks and known throughout the Andes and parts of Argentina. Goat or llama hair is typically left on the leather drumheads, giving the instrument a muffled sound.

Bordón A term used in the Andean region for a syncopated bass line.

Bossa nova A popular song style that emerged in the 1960s in Rio de Janeiro. Bossa nova musicians sing in an intimate singing style accompanied by syncopated, samba-derived rhythms and jazz-derived harmonies played on the guitar.

Bumba-meu-boi A dramatic dance popular in Brazil that tells the story of the death and resurrection of an ox.

Caboclo (var. **caboco**) A Portuguese term referring to a person of mixed native Brazilian and European ancestry. The word is also used to refer to a person of mixed race, usually settled in a rural area.

Cadenza Literally, "cadence" in Italian, a passage near the end of a movement that features the soloist alone, in virtuosic display, without orchestral accompaniment.

Cajón A rectangular, wooden box drum struck with the hands. In Afro-Peruvian music, the performer sits on top of the instrument and plays on the side facing forward. In Cuba, the instrument is smaller and generally is held between the knees, allowing the performer to play the top side.

Call-and-response A musical style in which a solo voice and a group alternate, with the group responding to the soloist's call. Call-and-response is typical in African and African-influenced vocal performance, as well as some European genres.

Canción mexicana A form of Mexican art song or parlor music, usually written for voice with piano accompaniment, and sometimes based loosely on Mexican traditional melodies.

Candombe A term with multiple meanings (that should not be confused with Brazilian Candomblé). Most commonly, it is defined as an Afro-Uruguayan song and dance genre performed at carnival that uses a specific drum call played by a percussion ensemble. See also **Tamboril**.

Candomblé An Afro-Brazilian religion that blends mostly West African (Yoruba) elements and beliefs with others derived from Roman Catholicism. Drumming and singing are central to Candomblé worship. See also **Oricha**.

Canto necesario The specifically Venezuelan name for a genre of music with lyrics of social consciousness; most often called nueva canción (new song) in the rest of Latin America.

Cantoria A Brazilian tradition of sung improvised poetry lyrics over the strumming a viola (guitar); sung by itinerant peasants in rural areas of northeastern Brazil. It is similar to the Cuban *controversia* and the rioplatense payada.

Capoeira An Afro-Brazilian secular fight/dance/game, with movements similar to those in martial arts yet coordinated with music.

Cavaquinho A ukulele-like, four-string instrument used in various styles of Brazilian popular musics, including choro and samba.

Chacarera A lively Argentine couples' dance that alternates between $\frac{3}{4}$ and $\frac{6}{8}$ meter and is traditionally performed by an acoustic violin, guitar, and bombo. Today, the chacarera beat also appears in contemporary popular music.

Chamamé A song and couples' dance genre that originated in northeastern Argentina as a synthesis of the European polka with local musical features. It has a romantic character and sentimental lyrics.

Charamela A colonial Brazilian ensemble made up of double-reed instruments.

Charango A small lute played in the Andean region. It usually has five sets (courses) of double strings, tuned G–C–E–A–E, which can either be plucked or (more typically) strummed.

Chéquere An idiophone of Yoruba origin used in the Caribbean, for example, in some Cuban rumba ensembles. It consists of a dried gourd around which a net of beads or seeds has been tied. The net is manipulated to make percussive sounds.

Chicha A type of popular music originating in Lima, Peru, during the second half of the twentieth century that combines traditional music of the Andean highlands with cumbia and other elements of Latin pop. It is named after a local alcoholic beverage.

Chirimía A term used to refer to various early predecessors of the oboe. These double-reed instruments were played throughout Latin America during the colonial period.

Cholo A derogatory term used in the Andes to refer to an urbanized indigenous person, particularly a rural migrant to a large city who has not fully adapted to the new environment.

Chorale A hymn melody, or a four-part setting of a hymn.

Chord A vertical assemblage of two or more pitches. The most common type of chord is a triad, a chord with three pitches. Major and minor chords, for instance, are distinguished by the kind of intervals separating the three pitches. A major triad features a minor third (two pitches separated by one and a half steps) on top of a major third (two pitches separated by two whole steps). A minor triad inverts this order.

Chord progression A series of chords that follows a standard or predictable pattern, such as I–IV–V–I, where roman numerals represent distinct triads.

Chordophone An instrument that produces sound by means of a vibrating string. Strings may be set in motion by a bow, by the fingers or a plectrum, or by hammers. Chordophones include the violin, charango, vihuela, harp, and piano.

Choro An urban popular instrumental style that originated in early twentieth-century Rio de Janeiro. Choro performances blend European dances, such as the polka and waltz, with group improvisation and virtuoso display.

Chromatic Refers to music based on all twelve pitches within an octave, equivalent to the white and black keys on a piano.

Chuscada A variant of the Andean wayno from the Ancash region of northern Peru.

Cinquillo A five-note syncopated rhythmic pattern characterized by a "long-short-long-short-long" rhythm and found throughout the Caribbean. In Cuban dance music it often alternates with a measure of two or three quarter notes, creating the Cuban "three-two" clave pattern.

Classical music In the Latin American context, music originally associated with the Catholic Church and with the Spanish aristocracy that was imported to the Americas during the colonial period. It continues to be performed, composed, and listened to among elite and middle-class urban audiences.

Clave (rhythm) Rhythmic patterns informing African-influenced Latin American music and typically consisting of a two-measure repeating figure, one measure with a relatively straight rhythm, and the other with a more syncopated rhythm.

Claves An idiophone of Cuban origin and consisting of two rounded wooden sticks. Claves are played in rumba and son music, as well as in other genres.

Cofradía A religious confraternity, or brotherhood.

Coloratura In vocal music, elaborate ornamentation, such as fast, virtuosic runs on one syllable.

Compadrito A stereotype of a rioplatense male from the lower classes, associated with the marginal social environment of the early tango. Tango lyrics and rioplatense literature portray the compadrito as a courageous fighter, an arrogant bully, and a sensuous dancer.

Compás The Spanish term for "meter," or for a measure (or bar) of that meter. It has a more specific meaning in mariachi repertoire. See also **Meter**.

Commercial music See **Popular music**.

Compound meter See **Meter**.

Concertato style Refers to a composition consisting of relatively short, contrasting segments, typical of Baroque musical style.

Conjunto de gaitas An Afro-Colombian music and dance genre that spread from the Caribbean coast in modified form to national and then continental popularity under the name cumbia. The term gaita refers to an indigenous flute, a pair of which are accompanied by drums and usually by singing.

Consonance Musical sounds that seem pleasant and stable.

Continuo A shortened form of basso continuo, this Baroque-era term refers to a bass line that outlines a composition's harmonic structure.

Contradanza A dance genre popular in Cuba in the nineteenth century. Based on English, French, and Haitian antecedents, the genre features a simple two-part (binary) structure while introducing African-derived syncopations or repeated rhythmic ostinatos, especially in the bass line. The most notable ostinato is the habanera rhythm.

Copla A rhyming poetic couplet, often consisting of four eight-syllable lines.

Corrido A ballad, that is, a song that tells a story, in the Spanish language. Corrido music is associated primarily with rural Mexico.

Cosmopolitan In music, an urbane style free from provincial or regional features.

Counterpoint (adj. **contrapuntal**) Specifically, the juxtaposition of two or more melodies; in more general terms, the juxtaposition of musical ideas. See also **Texture**.

Course On a string instrument, two or three strings tuned in unison or octaves, laid next to one another on the neck, and usually played together as if they were a single string. A course can also be a single string on an instrument whose other courses are multistringed. Instruments with at least one multistringed course are referred to as coursed. Instruments with only single strings are referred to as uncoursed.

Criollo A term used to describe music descended from Spanish roots and that developed in the Americas. It also has specific local meanings. In Argentina, it is used to describe music that is sung in Spanish and has predominantly European characteristics. In Peru, it refers to the people, culture, and music of the coast, as distinct from the indigenous and mestizo Andean highlands.

Crumhorn An early bass aerophone, first developed during the Middle Ages. It consists of a cylindrical tube that curves upward at the end. The player blows through a capped double reed to produce a bracing, bright tone. Its loud volume made it especially suitable for outdoor performances.

Cuatro (1) A small guitar-like instrument with four nylon strings found throughout Venezuela. (2) A traditional string instrument from Puerto Rico. It consists of five courses of metal strings, most of them doubled to produce a bright, twangy sound.

Cuíca A friction drum used in carnival samba that improvises high- and low-pitched notes on top of the surdo beats.

Culo'e puya (or **Redondo**) Thin cylindrical drums hung from musicians' necks and played in sets of three; from Barlovento, an African-influenced region on the northeast coast of Venezuela.

Cumbia An African-Colombian music and dance genre that has spread from the Caribbean coast throughout almost all of Hispanic America. Cumbia originally was used as a term for the conjunto de gaitas, then was applied to several related Colombian music and dance forms.

Cumbia tejana A variant of Colombian cumbia most popular among Texas-born Mexican Americans.

Cumbia villera A genre of music, associated with Argentine rock of the late 1990s, that took hold among impoverished youth. It featured images derived from gangsta rap combined with cumbia rhythms.

Da capo aria An aria whose opening section is followed by a contrasting section (usually in a different key), after which the opening material returns, creating the formal structure **ABA**. Convention allows the singer to embellish the return of the **A** section material, providing an opportunity to display his or her virtuosity.

Dancehall A style of electronic dance music from Jamaica that emerged in the 1980s and '90s.

Danza A two-part, 32-measure solo piano work based on the Caribbean habanera rhythm.

Décima A ten-line poetic form derived from medieval Spain. Many forms of sung décima continue to be performed throughout Latin America.

Declamation In music, the manner in which a text is sung, either syllabic (one pitch per syllable) or melismatic (many pitches per syllable).

Degree The place a note occupies in a scale, as in the "second degree" or the "fifth degree" of a scale. The most important scale degrees are the tonic, the first degree of a scale; the subdominant, the fourth; and the dominant, the fifth. These terms also refer to the chords built on those degrees.

Descending tetrachord A four-note descending scale. The repetition of this pattern in the bass line is a structural feature in Baroque dance and vocal music.

Descriptive music See **Program music**.

Development The second section of a sonata form. The development manipulates and varies the main musical themes of the piece.

Diatonic Refers to music based on a selection of eight pitches within an octave and equivalent to the white keys on a piano.

Dissonance A harsh or unpleasant musical sound that creates a sense of tension, as if it needs to resolve. Unresolved dissonances frequently occur in contemporary music.

Divine Office The canonical prayers recited daily by Roman Catholic religious orders (priests, monks, nuns). The Catholic day is broken up by eight periods of prayer (Matins, Lauds, Prime, Terce, Sext, None, Vespers, and Compline), each with its own rituals and texts.

Dominant (1) The fifth note of a major or minor scale. (2) The chord that is built on this pitch.

Downbeat The initial half of a beat, usually emphasized.

Duple Meter See **Meter**.

Dynamics The loudness or softness of musical sound, determined by the amplitude of the sound waves.

Electroacoustical Refers to a type of music that employs both electronic instruments, such as the synthesizer, and traditional acoustic instruments, such as the piano or violin. Electroacoustical music gained favor with classical composers during the second half of the twentieth century, when advances in electronic technology made synthesizers and computers suitable for a wide variety of musical purposes. Electroacoustical media greatly expand the universe of sound that composers have at their disposal.

Electrophone An electronic instrument, such as a synthesizer or a computer, that produces electronically generated signals that can be modified in an almost limitless number of ways.

El perreo Literally, "doggie style." A dance move associated with reggaeton music of an explicitly sexual nature, with the man grinding his pelvis into the woman's backside.

El Sistema A system of community-based, European classical orchestras in Venezuela, consisting primarily of economically disadvantaged youth, with an emphasis on communities of color. The most advanced musicians graduating from El Sistema play in the internationally recognized Simón Bolívar Youth Orchestra.

Estribillo A refrain.

Ethnography The systematic study of human societies through extended, close observation and interaction. The techniques of ethnography derive from sociocultural anthropology.

Ethnomusicology A discipline in the humanities heavily influenced by anthropology and concerned with studies of present-day traditional and popular musics. Ethnomusicologists often conduct extended fieldwork, living with particular communities.

Etude A piece of music with the pedagogical purpose of developing one or more aspects of technique. Some etudes are only for use in practice, while others are intended for concert performance.

Exposition The first section in sonata form, presenting the main musical themes of the piece in two different keys.

Extended techniques Nontraditional ways of playing traditional acoustic instruments, such as striking, blowing, plucking, or otherwise generating sound on them in ways not utilized by earlier composers.

Falsetto A method of voice production used by men to sing in a high vocal range. It has a thinner and lighter quality than ordinary singing.

Fandango An eighteenth-century popular dance genre that was performed by a couple and was characterized by its use of zapateo and erotic choreography.

Folk music See **Traditional music**.

Folklorization A process in which music and other cultural traditions are removed from their original context and displayed in new contexts. In Latin America, it describes the common practice, since the twentieth century, of presenting highly stylized or professionalized versions of rural traditions as staged heritage for tourists.

Form The structure of a piece of music, normally classified according to the number and sequence of the various themes (melodies) presented. Common forms include binary (**AB**), ternary (**ABA**), and rondo (**ABACABA**).

Forró An umbrella term used in northeastern Brazil to describe a party with dancing. The baião is one of the most popular rhythmic patterns and dance choreographies performed in a forró.

Fugue Literally, "flight." The fugue is a structured classical genre that consists of two or more independent lines, called voices. It begins with a main theme that the voices present in turn as they "flee" from each other.

Furro A friction drum from northwest Venezuela used in traditional *gaita de fulia* and gaita music. The player strokes a stick protruding from the drum skin with a damp cloth to produce a resonant "grunting" sound.

Gaita (1) A long cane duct flute, played in pairs in Colombian gaita. (2) Traditional, rural-based music from Colombia's Caribbean coast, more accurately known as the conjunto de gaitas. (3) A Colombian urban popular dance form that combines conjunto de gaitas and Caribbean popular-music influences. (4) A Venezuelan musical genre from the northwest state of Zulia, currently popular nationwide during the Christmas season.

Galant A mid-eighteenth-century musical style that moved away from the complexities of Baroque music and stressed symmetry, balance, grace, and simplicity. Music in the galant style features less ornamentation, greater use of homophony, and fewer contrasts in texture.

Gaucho A South American horseman from the plains regions of Argentina and Uruguay or from Rio Grande do Sul in Brazil (where he is known as gaúcho). Gaucho music features solo singing and dancing accompanied by the guitar.

Grupo Renovación A group of Argentine composers, founded in 1929, that aimed to modernize classical music by implementing the latest international trends.

Guaraní A South American tribe from Paraguay and northeastern Argentina. The language of this group is also known as Guaraní.

Güira A metal version of the güiro used in the Dominican Republic, often in genres such as merengue and bachata.

Güiro A small, hand-held idiophone, often made out of a dried gourd, into which notches have been cut. A wooden or metal striker is used to scrape the notches, producing a scratchy, percussive sound.

Guitarilla A small Nicaraguan guitar with four metal strings that accompanies the marimba de arco. The guitarilla is strummed, adding rhythmic support to the music.

Guitarrón A large, guitar-like instrument tuned a fifth lower than the standard guitar and commonly used in mariachi ensembles.

Habanera A Cuban song genre incorporating the habanera rhythm that gained international popularity during the second half of the nineteenth century.

Habanera rhythm A syncopated rhythm found throughout the Caribbean, also known in Cuba as "ritmo de tango." It became one of the building blocks for the Cuban contradanza and danza, the habanera song genre, and later the Argentine tango.

Half step See **Step.**

Hapsburg A Germanic royal family that controlled the Holy Roman Empire from 1440 to 1806. Through political marriages and land acquisition, descendants of the family came to rule over much of Europe, including Spain from 1516 to 1700.

Harawi An indigenous Andean song genre dating to the Inca era. It is performed today by small groups of unaccompanied female singers at agricultural and life-cycle ritual events in rural areas of Peru.

Harmonic See **Overtone series.**

Harmony The vertical dimension of music, referring to any collection of two or more different pitches sounding at the same time. See also **Chord.**

Hemiola A type of meter in which two groups of three beats ($\frac{6}{8}$) alternate with three groups of two beats ($\frac{3}{4}$). It is typical of Spanish and Spanish-influenced musical traditions.

Heterophony (adj. **heterophonic**) The simultaneous performance of two or more variations of the same melody.

Hocketing The practice of dividing the pitches of a melody between two different musicians or groups of musicians; it is used in the sikuri panpipe music of Peru and Bolivia.

Homophony (adj. **homophonic**) Music that consists of a dominant melody and a subordinate accompaniment. In homophonic music, all voices in the accompaniment move simultaneously.

Huapango An alternate name for son huasteco. Huapango is the Nahuatl word for the raised wooden platform on which dancers frequently perform.

Huayno See **Wayno.**

Huehuetl A sacred, single-headed membranophone drum used by the Mexica.

Hybridity A term popularized by postcolonial theory to explain cultural fusion. In the Latin American context it is often used as a synonym for mestizaje.

Idiophone A musical instrument made of a resonant solid material, such as wood, bone, or metal, that vibrates to produce sound, rather than producing sound by means of a vibrating membrane (see **Membranophone**). Idiophones include claves, the güiro, cymbals, the marimba, and the teponaztli.

Impressionism An artistic movement that emerged in Paris in the second part of the nineteenth century when painters started to emphasize changing light and movement in their work. Composers such as Claude Debussy used sounds to suggest feelings and ambiance, moving away from strict classical structures and traditional harmony.

Indigenismo (adj. **indigenista**) An intellectual, cultural, and political movement that championed indigenous cultures and heritage in Latin America. Especially strong in Mexico and Peru in the early to mid-twentieth century, the indigenista movement was primarily led by the mestizo elite, including composers, who emphasized indigenous themes in their classical works.

Indigenista See **Indigenismo.**

Instrumentation Refers to the instruments that a composer or musicians have chosen to use in a particular piece.

Intensity See **Dynamics.**

Inter-Latino An adjective referring to the interaction among different Latino communities in the United States.

Interval The distance between any two pitches. Prominent intervals include the third, fourth, fifth, and octave. For example, E is a third above C; F, a fourth; G, a fifth; and C, an octave. Two identical pitches form the interval of a unison.

Irmandade A Brazilian confraternity or brotherhood. Organized along lines of class or race, irmandades had tremendous influence in colonial times, building churches and hospitals, maintaining clergy, overseeing funerals and feast days, and providing music.

Jácara (xácara) One of the most popular dances of the Baroque period, the jácara features a repetitive hemiola rhythmic base and alternating major and minor harmonies.

Jarabe A potpourri genre consisting of a series of different but connected short dance pieces played in succession as a single unit, often with contrasting tempos, rhythms, keys, and choreography.

Jarana In Mexico, a small, guitar-like instrument used in the son jarocho. In coastal Peru, a festive gathering of friends and family featuring criollo music, dancing, and food.

Joropo llanero A music and dance form of the Colombian and Venezuelan Llanos. It features the Venezuelan cuatro (a small guitar-like instrument), maracas, and usually a diatonic harp.

Kena (var. **quena**) An end-notch flute with six anterior holes and one posterior (thumb) hole, variations of which are played throughout the central Andes. Contemporary kenas may be constructed from cane, bamboo, wood, bone, or even plastic.

Key The scale used as the basis for a piece of music, such as C major, D minor, and so forth. See also **Tonality**.

Key signature The accidentals placed at the beginning of each line of the staff indicating the key of the piece. The absence of accidentals indicates C major, or any scale derived from it, such as A minor.

Ladino In Guatemala, the equivalent of mestizo, denoting mixed Amerindian and European race and culture.

Latinidad The shared identity of people of Latin American heritage living in the United States.

Liberation theology A reform movement within the Catholic Church that rose in prominence in the early 1960s in reaction to the rapid rise of Protestantism, especially in Latin America. Named from the influential 1971 book *A Theology of Liberation* by Peruvian Gustavo Gutiérrez, the movement's primary leaders were young priests who called for a closer relationship between church and followers that included working for social justice.

Littoral In Argentina, the northeastern region that lies between the Paraná and Uruguay rivers whose music features couples' dances of European and local origin and uses the accordion as a signature musical instrument.

Llanos Meaning "flat," the large region of plains in southern Colombia and Venezuela.

Lunfardo A rioplatense dialect that blends Italian linguistic characteristics with local patterns of speech. Lunfardo words appear frequently in the lyrics of tango songs.

Major scale See **Scale**.

Malambo An improvised Argentine dance performed by two competing gauchos. It is characterized by variations on a repeated chord progression played by the guitar, along with vigorous zapateo dancing.

Maraca A small, handheld idiophone that may have indigenous or African origins, or both. Maracas consist of roundish spheres of wood or dried leather that have seeds or pellets inside. The instrument is shaken to produce percussive sounds.

Mariachi The form of Mexican music best known abroad. It first developed in the state of Jalisco (west-central Mexico) in the mid-nineteenth century. Performers of mariachi repertoire are also known as mariachis.

Marimba de arco A 22-key diatonic (one row) marimba with an arc, found only in western Nicaragua. Like the Guatemalan marimba de tecomates, it is diatonic with a single row of keys and has a wooden arc that the player sits on. However, the marimba de arco's resonators are now made of hollow cedar tubes.

Marimba de tecomates A 25-key diatonic (one row) marimba constructed in the form of an arch and now found only in rural Mayan areas. Named for the resonators suspended under keys that are made from different-sized gourds, or tecomates.

Marimba doble, or **grande** A large, chromatic marimba developed at the end of the nineteenth century. With the addition of a row of keys like the black keys on a piano, the marimba doble (double) can be used to play urban and cosmopolitan music. It is especially popular in Chiapas, Mexico, and cities in Guatemala, often accompanied by drum set, bass, and sometimes horn sections. The marimba doble was the prototype for metal resonator vibraphones and buzzless marimbas now used worldwide.

Marimba sencilla A diatonic marimba found in rural and urban Mayan areas and some ladino populations in Guatemala as well as other regions. It is named for its single (sencilla, simple) row of keys.

Marinera A $\frac{6}{8}$ meter music and dance genre from Peru, historically related to the Chilean and Bolivian cueca. Regarded as the national dance of Peru, it is a social couples' dance with significant regional variations in choreography and musical accompaniment and is primarily associated with coastal criollo culture today.

Mazurka A Polish dance in triple meter with a distinctive accent on the third beat. It became popular throughout Europe and the Americas during the nineteenth century.

Measure See **Bar**.

Melismatic See **Declamation**.

Membranophone Any percussion instrument that produces sound by means of a vibrating membrane, usually made of animal hide or a similar synthetic material. Membranophones include the conga drum, snare drum, huehuetl, bongo drum, and surdo.

Merengue An up-tempo dance genre from the Dominican Republic.

Mestizaje (Portuguese **mestiçagem**) A Spanish term meaning "mixture," referring to the blending of indigenous, African, and European peoples in the Americas over time, and by extension to their hybrid cultural forms.

Mestizo An adjective referring to racial or cultural hybridity, usually a European and indigenous mixture, or a noun referring to a person of mixed-race ancestry. (The feminine form is mestiza.) In Latin America it can refer to any racial or cultural blending. See also **Mestizaje**.

Meter The organization of beats into recurring patterns of strong and weak, usually in groups of two (duple) or three (triple). Compound meter results when each beat of either duple or triple meter is further subdivided into three parts. See also **Time signature**.

Metronome A device that makes a clicking sound to maintain a steady beat at any tempo.

Mexica The historical term for Nahuatl-speaking peoples, often referred to as the Aztecs, who formed the Meso-american empire at the time of the Spanish conquest.

Microtone (adj. **microtonal**) A pitch that lies between the half steps of the traditional Western chromatic scale. For example, quarter tones lie halfway between the outer two pitches of a half step.

Milonga A traditional song genre of Argentina and Uruguay in syncopated duple meter with guitar accompaniment. Alternatively, this term may refer to an urban popular dance, or to any place where tangos are performed.

Mina A large drum from Barlovento, an African-Venezuelan region on the northeast coast of Venezuela. Constructed from a tree trunk, the mina is more than six feet long; it is propped up on one end and played both on the sides and on the skin-covered head.

Minor scale See **Scale**.

Mode (adj. **modal**) A term used to describe certain eight-note scales in the Western tradition that are neither major nor minor. These include Dorian, Phrygian, Lydian, and Mixolydian. Modes were commonly used in Gregorian chant and polyphonic music before 1600. Music based on one or more modes is called modal.

Moñas Literally, "ribbons," a term that salsa musicians use to describe interlocking melodies played by trumpet and trombone players in the hotter instrumental interludes of the montuno section. Moñas are frequently improvised.

Monophony See **Texture**.

Montuno The final call-and-response section of rumba, son, and salsa.

Motet A vocal or choral composition based on a sacred text, for use as part of a church service.

Motive A brief musical idea whose melody or rhythm gives a phrase, and hence a melody, its character.

Movimiento Urbano Acústico The Venezuelan Urban Acoustic Movement, an ongoing attempt to unite the many musicians who interpret traditional repertoire in a semi-Euroclassical style.

MPB An acronym for Música Popular Brasileira; an umbrella term that refers to Brazilian popular songs of the 1960s, 1970s, and 1980s that include lyrics with sociopolitical content and that stylize traditional Brazilian musical genres for urban audiences.

Mulato Originally derived from the word mule and rife with negative connotations, this term has been used in Latin America since colonial times to describe people of mixed African and European heritage. It is still used today, though generally not in a pejorative sense.

Música caipira The Brazilian equivalent to "hillbilly," or country, music. See also **Música sertaneja**.

Música guajira Rural music in Cuba associated with immigrants from Spain and the Canary Islands. It is played primarily on stringed instruments and is often in triple meter.

Música norteña A popular music style originally from northern Mexico that features the accordion, bajo sexto, bass, and drum set.

Música ranchera Literally, "music of the countryside." The dominant genre associated with mariachis, it emphasizes full-throated, emotional singing on a wide range of themes strongly felt by ordinary people.

Música sertaneja "Country music," a popular-music genre derived from the cantoria tradition of the Brazilian Northeast. As in música caipira, pairs of sertaneja performers typically sing romantic ballads, accompanied by viola, guitar, and accordion. See also **Música caipira**.

Música tropical Literally, "tropical music." A generic term in South and Central America for dance music based loosely on the cumbia, or for salsa music.

Musical nationalism Originally a nineteenth-century movement to create music derived from the cultural resources of one's nation as a source of identity.

Musicology A discipline in the humanities generally devoted to the historically oriented, scholarly study of classical repertoire.

Narcocorrido A subgenre of the Mexican corrido that chronicles the lifestyle and adventures of border-crossing drug smugglers.

Neoclassicism A classical musical style that emerged after World War I. Its hallmark is the return to forms and practices of the past from a contemporary perspective.

Neophyte A new religious convert.

New Latino A twenty-first-century term used to refer to a Latin American immigrant from a country such as Colombia, the Dominican Republic, Ecuador, Guatemala, and El Salvador.

Noise An unpitched sound with an unfocused waveform, or vibration, and lacking peaks of intensity occurring over regular periods of time (cycles per second, or cps).

Ñongo One of approximately thirty common rhythm patterns played on the batás to accompany the songs and dances of Santería ceremony.

Nor-tec A hybrid musical style combining Mexican banda with techno music.

Nueva canción Literally, "new song." A term used in Spanish-speaking Latin America to refer to socially engaged music, often of a political nature. The term has numerous local variants, for instance nueva trova in Cuba and canto necesario in Venezuela.

Nueva trova See **nueva canción**.

Octave The point at which the frequency of a pitch is doubled or halved. An octave above A-440 is A-880; an octave below, A-220.

Orchestration The art of writing for orchestral instruments and combining various instrumental parts in a composition.

Ordinary of the Mass Texts of the Roman Catholic Mass that are used every time the Mass is celebrated, regardless of the occasion.

Oricha (var. **orisha, orixa, orixá**) A common term for the many divinities associated with the Santería (Cuba) and Candomblé (Brazil) religions. Orichas are believed to be ancestors of Yoruba peoples who continue to guide and advise those in the present. They are also believed to represent forces of nature and fundamental aspects of human personalities.

Ornament The embellishment of a melody through the use of rapid nonessential notes such as trills.

Ostinato From the Italian for "obstinate," a repeating melodic or rhythmic figure that is the structural foundation for a piece of music.

Overdubbing A recording technique in which a sound is recorded and layered over a previously recorded sound.

Overtone series The series of pitches that sound above a fundamental note when it is played or sung. These pitches are also called partials or harmonics. For example, if C is played, C, G, C, E, G, B-flat, and C sound above it as the first seven overtones. Although overtones are inaudible unless isolated, they are responsible for the tone color (or timbre) of any pitch, depending on which overtones an instrument or voice emphasizes.

Pampas The plains region of Argentina, Uruguay, and southern Brazil that was home to the gaucho and that also encompasses the modern capital cities of Montevideo (Uruguay) and Buenos Aires (Argentina).

Pandeiro A handheld frame drum with a wooden frame, metal jingles, and a skin head that can be tuned to provide high or low pitches. It is used throughout Brazil in traditional and popular musics.

Partial See **Overtone series**.

Participatory performance Performance events in which few divisions exist between performer and audience and everyone's active involvement in music and/or dance is encouraged.

Pasacalle An Andean musical genre marked by a steady pulse and heavy downbeats, performed for processions and public dancing. It may be played on a wide variety of instruments.

Pasito duranguense A style of wind-band music from the northwestern state of Durango.

Patronato system A system under Pope Alexander VI that allowed Portuguese and Spanish rulers, not the Vatican, to make and control all clerical appointments in the colonies.

Payada A rioplatense vocal competition that derives from the tradition of improvised sung poetry of the Iberian Peninsula. The payada is based on the improvisation of sung stanzas of poetry by two singers, accompanied by guitars. It can be compared with the Cuban *controversia* genre and Brazilian cantoria.

Pedal A sustained bass note in any kind of composition. Named after the pedals on an organ, which are used to play bass notes.

Pentatonic Refers to a scale or piece of music based on five pitches, such as C–D–F–G–A. Pentatonic melodies are common in the Andean region and in much indigenous music throughout the Americas.

Phrase The musical equivalent of a clause in a sentence. Two or more phrases make up a melody.

Pitch A sound whose waveform is uniform and regular in shape, with measurable frequencies.

Pizzicato A technique employed on string instruments like the violin, viola, cello, and bass whereby the performer plucks the strings rather than bowing them (a technique called *arco*).

Plainchant Monophonic liturgical chant of the Roman Catholic Church.

Polka A lively dance in duple meter that originated in Poland and became popular throughout Europe and the Americas during the nineteenth century.

Polo A song form from Sucre state on Venezuela's eastern coast featuring a chordal pattern systematically alternating between major and minor tonalities.

Polychoral style A term referring to compositions that juxtapose and contrast two (or more) choirs, which may be accompanied by instruments.

Polymeter The juxtaposition of two or more different meters in a piece of music.

Polyphony (adj. **polyphonic**) Music that combines multiple independent lines of equal importance.

Polyrhythm (adj. **polyrhythmic**) The juxtaposition of two or more different rhythmic patterns.

Polytonality (adj. **polytonal**) The presentation of two or more tonalities (keys) at the same time.

Popular music Urban music associated with the mass media. It tends to be performed and sold for profit and to incorporate influences of instrumentation and style from the international music industry.

Prelude A short piece intended as an introduction to a more extended piece.

Presentational performance An event in which a group of musicians or dancers provides music for a relatively passive group of spectators.

Program music (adj. **programmatic**) Music that has non-musical associations, that is, music that tells a story or depicts a scene.

Proper of the Mass Texts of the Roman Catholic Mass that change according to the liturgical calendar.

Punteado A style of playing the guitar or lute in which the strings are plucked to produced individual pitches.

Quechua An indigenous language of the Andean region. Once the language of the Inca Empire, today it is the most widely spoken indigenous language in the Americas, with many regional dialects. The word may also be used to describe those who speak the language, as in the "Quechua people." In Ecuador, the dominant dialect is known as Quichua.

Ranchera See **Música ranchera**.

Rasgueado A style of playing the guitar or a similar instrument in which the hand strums across the strings, producing multiple pitches.

Recapitulation The third section of a sonata-form piece, which restates the main musical themes of the piece in their original form, all in the home key.

Recitative Declamatory singing in which the pitches and rhythms mimic spoken text in prose narration and dialogue in opera and oratorio.

Redoble A fast series of three strums used as a flourish in strummed son jalisciense music.

Redondo See **Culo'e puya**.

Reggaeton A modern dance music that has gained widespread popularity among Spanish-speaking youth since about 2003. It is defined by rapped or sung vocals performed to a backbeat of a particular rhythm consisting of a tresillo against a steady bass drum beat.

Regional Mexican music An umbrella term that includes several musical styles popular in Mexico and the United States, including norteña, ranchera, and banda.

Relative minor/major scale See **Scale**.

Remittance Money sent home by an immigrant working abroad.

Repinique A two-headed drum used in samba baterias. Its high-pitched sound provides the rhythmic calls that cue the other instruments of the bateria.

Requinto A small guitar tuned a fourth higher than the regular instrument. It is commonly used by Mexican *trios románticos* and most famously associated with Trio Los Panchos who invented it.

Revista A musical review, a form of stage entertainment involving a string of song and dance pieces connected loosely by a plotline. Revistas are similar to vaudeville entertainment in the United States, or performances by the Ziegfeld Follies.

Rioplatense An adjective describing music (as well as people, places, and things) from the region encompassed by the Río de la Plata estuary and including Argentina, Uruguay, and Paraguay, and parts of southern Bolivia.

Ritornello (pl. **ritornelli**) In Baroque music, an instrumental refrain alternating with sections of an aria or a choral or orchestral work.

Rock en español A term that can cover any type of rock or rock-related music in Spanish-speaking Latin America (and even Spain). In the 1990s the term was used especially to describe the new fusion of traditional vallenato and other forms with rock in Colombia.

Romance A form of extended secular poetry, often accompanied by music, that developed in Spain during the Middle Ages. The musical form is similar in many respects to the ballad.

Romanticism A style period in Western classical music from roughly 1820 to 1900. Romantic music emphasizes emotion, subjective experience, and fantasy. It also seeks "unity" with the other arts, drawing inspiration from literature and painting in compositions that tell a story or paint a picture (see **Symphonic poem**).

Rondo A form in classical music that is based on a recurring theme (**A**) alternating with contrasting episodes (**B**, **C**, etc.). A simple rondo form can be diagrammed as **ABACA**.

Rubato Literally "stolen," as in tempo rubato ("stolen time"). In this performance style, the tempo is elastic rather that rigid; the performer takes slight liberties with the rhythm by slowing down and speeding up.

Rumba A form of secular Afro-Cuban traditional music and dance that has influenced the development of salsa. Rumba music is often performed on three conga drums, claves, and a pair of wooden sticks, and is accompanied by singers.

Sackbut An early predecessor of the trombone, first developed in the Middle Ages.

Salsa A dance music style developed in New York City in the 1960s and 1970s. It derives from the Cuban son but combines musical elements from Cuba, Puerto Rico, the United States, and elsewhere.

Salsa romántica A subgenre of salsa developed in the 1980s and influenced by balada. It features lyrics about romantic love, a polished and refined sound, and sophisticated studio production.

Samba An African-derived, duple-meter song or dance accompanied by percussion. There are several versions of traditional samba, but the most popular can be heard during carnival season in Rio de Janeiro.

Samba-canção Literally, "samba-song," an urban samba style in which the lively and syncopated rhythms of traditional samba are softened by slower tempos, longer melodies, and romantic lyrics.

Samba-enredo Sambas composed each year to be performed by samba schools during carnival season.

Samba-reggae A hybrid form of percussive carnival music performed in Salvador, Bahia, in the northeast of Brazil. The music combines influences from traditional Afro-Brazilian drumming with others derived from Jamaican reggae.

Santería An Afro-Cuban religion, primarily of Yoruba origin. Santería worship involves extended musical performances and dance.

Scale A series of tones on which a composition or performance event is based. There are many different types of scales, but the most common are major and minor.

Score The music for an ensemble of any size that contains all of the staves of the various parts.

Sequence The repetition of a melodic idea at different pitch levels, either higher or lower.

Serialism (adj. **serial**) A twentieth-century technique of musical composition in which pitches and sometimes other parameters—such as dynamics, rhythms, and tone colors—are arranged in repeatable series, providing internal organization and coherence to a work that has no tonal center and possibly no sense of beat or meter.

Sertaneja See **Música sertaneja**.

Sesquiáltera The Spanish term for hemiola. See also **Hemiola**.

Shaman See **Shamanism**.

Shamanism A collective term for various indigenous healing practices and spiritual beliefs found through Latin America. Ritual specialists, often known as shamans, act as intermediaries with the spirit world. Shamanic practices may include trance, song, dance, the use of musical instruments such as rattles and drums, and in certain parts of the Amazon region, the use of native hallucinogens.

Shawm A double-reed woodwind instrument of the European Middle Ages and Renaissance; the ancestor of the modern oboe.

Siku A double-rank panpipe made of bamboo or cane, played in the Peruvian and Bolivian Andes.

Sikuri A term used to describe both a specific genre of double-rank panpipe (siku) music from Peru and Bolivia and the ensemble that performs the genre.

Solfège A system that uses a set of syllables to refer to fixed musical elements, such as pitch or rhythm. In Western music, the term refers to the syllables *do–re–mi–fa–sol–la–ti*, which are applied to pitches of the musical scale, often for pedagogical purposes.

Son (pl. **sones**) In Cuba, Mexico, and elsewhere, a term for one of the most important kinds of traditional dance music. A cognate of the English word "song," the term can be used in a general sense by Spanish-speakers to mean song or tune, but can also refer to specific regional or national styles of music. Mexican son styles are especially diverse.

Son huasteco A musical form in a syncopated triple meter, traditionally intended for dancing. The term huasteco refers to the Huastec region in northeastern Mexico. The name derives from the Huastec people, a Nahuatl-speaking indigenous group in the area. See also **Huapango**.

Son jalisciense A prominent genre of mariachi music from the state of Jalisco, along the Pacific coast. The basic meter of son jalisciense consists of a measure of strumming that emphasizes beats 1, 3, and 5 of the $\frac{6}{8}$ measure followed by another that emphasizes beats 2 and 5.

Son jarocho A regional son variant from the state of Veracruz, along the coast of the Gulf of Mexico. Instruments in jarocho ensembles typically include the *arpa jarocha* (harp), various types of jarana (a small guitar), the requinto (another guitar-like instrument), and voices.

Sonata A genre of instrumental music consisting of one or more movements with contrasting characters. Sonatas are often written for solo instruments, especially piano, but can involve two to four instruments.

Sonata form A standard form of classical music that consists of three main sections: exposition, development, and recapitulation. This form is typical of the outer movements of sonatas from the late 1700s to the present, as well as symphonies and other genres of instrumental music. See also **Exposition**, **Development**, and **Recapitulation**.

Staff (pl. **staves**) A set of five parallel lines on which musical pitches are notated.

Step The distance between two adjacent pitches. The distance between two adjacent keys on the piano is a half step. The distance between any two keys with one key in between is a whole step. From E to F is a half step, and from C to D is a whole step. (The black key C-sharp/D-flat is between the two white keys C and D.)

Strophic A term describing the organization of a song in which each verse of the text is set to the same music; the opposite of through-composed, in which each verse or stanza is set differently. Hymns, anthems, and folk songs are often set strophically; art songs are sometimes set in a through-composed style.

Subdivision The breaking down of any rhythmic pattern into smaller rhythmic components. For example, a quarter note can be subdivided into two eighth notes or four sixteenth notes.

Subdominant (1) The fourth note of a major or minor scale. (2) The chord that is built on this pitch.

Surdo A bass drum that provides the basic marching rhythm in samba.

Syllabic See **Declamation**.

Symphonic poem Sometimes called a tone poem, a one-movement composition for symphony orchestra inspired by a poem, novel, painting, or even a landscape. Franz Liszt (1811–1886) invented this term for his many works in this genre, inspired by Beethoven and Berlioz's earlier narrative orchestral works.

Syncopation The placing of rhythmic emphasis on weak beats or upbeats.

Tambor Afro-Venezuelan dance and music from the coastal Choroní region that has gained national popularity.

Tambora A traditional double-headed drum from the Dominican Republic. It is used in various forms of rural music as well as in the merengue.

Tamborazo A style of wind band–based dance music from the northern state of Zacatecas, Mexico; named after a large bass drum used in the ensemble.

Tamboril A common name for a single or double-headed drum found in various regions of Spain and Latin America. In Uruguay, the tamboril is an important national instrument associated with candombe. The tamboril played in candombe is a single-headed drum of African origin that is carried over the player's shoulder and is played with two hands, one of which holds a stick.

Tamborim A small-frame hand drum played with a drumstick; part of the samba bateria.

Tamborzão Music based on the electronic sampling and remixing of samba bateria percussion sounds; it is used as dance music in Rio de Janeiro's bailes funk.

Tango An Argentine and Uruguayan popular genre that arose at the turn of the twentieth century in the surroundings of Buenos Aires and Montevideo. The tango uses a duple or quadruple rhythm and features an accordion-like instrument known as the bandoneón.

Tarka A wooden six-holed duct flute played in the Peruvian and Bolivian Andes. Carved from a rectangular or octagonal block of wood, tarkas have a distinctively hoarse timbre.

Technocumbia A Peruvian variant of the Colombian cumbia that gained popularity in the late 1990s and early 2000s.

Tejano A popular music style originally from Texas that is traditionally performed by Texas-Mexican conjuntos. It is based loosely on Mexican-style cumbia and polka, but adds elements such as synthesizer from U.S. popular culture.

Tempo The speed of beats—in other words, how quickly or slowly a piece moves. Common tempo designations include the Italian words *allegro* (fast), *andante* (walking speed), and *largo* (slow).

Teponaztli A pre-Columbian idiophone, a split-log drum used by the Mexica.

Ternary form See **Form**.

Texas-Mexican conjunto A musical ensemble and a dance form popular in south Texas and the southwestern United States. Its music style is similar to música norteña but features more virtuosic accordion playing.

Texture The ways in which voices and instruments combine and interact melodically and harmonically, in particular, how many melodies are going on at the same time. Monophony features a single melody line with no accompaniment. Homophony is characterized by melody with chordal accompaniment, or just chords. Polyphony features two or more independent melodies at the same time. Imitative polyphony is a texture in which a single melodic idea is juxtaposed against itself.

Through-composed See **Form**.

Timbales A percussion instrument of Cuban origin played with sticks and used in modern salsa bands. It consists of two drums (membranophones) with plastic heads and metal rims that are mounted on a stand. A wood block and bells of various sizes are often attached to the stand as well, and a ride cymbal often sits to one side.

Timbre See **Tone color**.

Time signature A fractional number used to indicate the meter of the music. Common duple meters include $\frac{2}{4}$ and $\frac{4}{4}$; triple meters, $\frac{3}{4}$; and compound meters, $\frac{6}{8}$, $\frac{9}{8}$, and $\frac{12}{8}$. See also **Meter**.

Toada A Brazilian term for a short, strophic song with a refrain. A toda typically deals with themes of romance or nature.

Toccata A type of Baroque piece in free form, usually for keyboard, intended to display technical virtuosity.

Tonality (adj. **tonal**) The characteristic of a piece of music whereby it has a key or tonal center, a note that is more prominent than any other note.

Tone cluster A small collection of notes close to one another in pitch and played at the same time.

Tone color The distinguishing quality of a vocal or instrumental sound, determined by which harmonics in the overtone series are emphasized.

Tone poem An orchestral work that tells a story or depicts a literary idea or image. See also **Symphonic poem**.

Tonic (1) The first note of a major or minor scale. (2) The chord that is built on this pitch.

Traditional music Music typically associated with rural contexts and/or with specific communities or ethnic groups. It is often learned by ear and performed as part of everyday community activities rather than as staged entertainment.

Transubstantiation The Roman Catholic doctrine that the sacred host, consecrated by the priest and distributed during the Mass, becomes the literal body of Christ.

Tres A small, guitar-like instrument from Cuba. It is played in música guajira repertoire and especially in Cuban son.

Tresillo A three-beat rhythm of Kongo origin that is found in many forms of Caribbean folkloric music, and elsewhere in Latin America. It is also prominent in modern-day reggaeton.

Triad See **Chord**.

Trill A rapid alternation between two notes, usually employed as a kind of melodic embellishment.

Triple meter See **Meter**.

Tritonic A term describing a scale or piece of music based on three notes or pitches, usually the pitches of a major triad.

Tropicália A musical and artistic movement that emerged in Brazil during the 1960s. Tropicália musicians mixed electronic instrumentation from rock and roll with traditional Brazilian musical styles and instruments.

TUBS Time Unit Box System, a form of rhythmic notation and analysis developed in the United States in the 1960s and 1970s. It employs series of boxes to represent units of time in a given piece of music, with percussive notes or beats shown by filled boxes and rests shown by empty boxes.

Tun A Mayan slit drum made from a hollowed tree trunk. An "H" cut into one side creates two tongues of wood, each of which produces a tone when struck with a rubber-tipped mallet. Essentially the same instrument is called teponaztli in Nahuatl in central Mexico and in Central America south of Mayan Guatemala.

Tundete An onomatopoeic term for the guitar accompaniment pattern to a Peruvian vals.

Upbeat The second half of a beat, usually weak.

Urban bachata A subgenre of bachata developed by New York Dominicans in the 1990s. It combines the romantic lyrics and virtuosic guitar lines of Dominican bachata with North American rhythm and blues and hip-hop.

Vallenato Created by combining *nato* ("born in") and *valle* ("valley"), the term refers to the name of a song and dance genre and ensemble from the rural northeast of Colombia; the music is also popular in western Venezuela. Vallenato ensembles include lead and backup singers, a button accordion, a *caja* (small drum), and a *guacharaca*, a gourd scraper.

Vals A Peruvian adaptation of the waltz, closely associated with criollo music from the city of Lima during the early to mid-twentieth century. See also **Waltz**.

Viceroyalty (adj. **viceregal**) A country, province, or colony ruled by a viceroy.

Villancico A poetic and musical genre popular throughout Latin America, Spain, and Portugal from the fifteenth to the eighteenth centuries. Usually, a refrain (estribillo) in the villancico alternates with rhymed verses (coplas). Although the villancico developed in Europe as largely a secular genre, in Latin America it was used for devotional events and was particularly associated with the Christmas season, although it retained its rustic character and the use of the spoken vernacular.

Villancico de negros A style of villancico that attempted to depict black speech, music, and culture through stereotypical speech dialects and syncopated rhythms.

Viol A bowed instrument that developed during the Renaissance and that came in a number of sizes. Viols are distinguished from instruments in the violin family by a deeper body and a flat back, sloping shoulders, and a fretted fingerboard. Viols were used frequently in chamber music and to emphasize the bass line of a composition.

Viola A stringed instrument smaller than the guitar with five double metal courses and played in Brazilian cantoria and música sertaneja.

Vocable A nonlexical syllable used in a song; one example of vocables is the phrase "fa-la-la."

Vocal production The quality of a singer's voice, whether it is rich, full, nasally, pinched, throaty, and so on.

Walking bass A melodic pattern in the bass line of a piece characterized by a steady and even rhythmic motion, suggestive of walking.

Waltz A triple-meter couple dance originating in Austria that became popular throughout Europe and the Americas during the nineteenth century. The waltz was initially controversial because it involved close physical contact between the dancers. See also **Vals**.

Wayno (var. **huayno, huayñu**) The most widespread and popular genre of music and dance found in the Andean highlands of Peru and Bolivia.

Whole step See **Step**.

Whole-tone scale A scale made up entirely of whole steps.

Xácara See **Jácara**.

Yaraví A slow and halting romantic song genre from the southern Andes, particularly associated with the Peruvian city of Arequipa.

Zabumba A double-headed bass drum common in the north and northeast of Brazil. The performer holds the instrument in place with a strap on the left shoulder and plays the top head with a mallet in the right hand.

Zampoña Spanish term for "panpipe." Unlike the siku, zampoñas are usually played by a single musician, who holds the two interlocking halves together. See also **Siku** and **Sikuri**.

Zapateado See **Zapateo**.

Zapateo (var. **zapateado**) A specific dance style derived from Spanish sources, characterized by motion primarily from the waist down and the tapping of the dancers' shoes against the floor to create percussive sounds or rhythms. Such dancing characterizes many genres of Latin American music. The term may also refer to specific dance genres that use this gesture.

Zarzuela A Spanish-language light opera alternating musical numbers with spoken dialogue.

Additional Resources

 Extended bibliographies are available at wwnorton.com/studyspace

CHAPTER 1

Reading

Aharonián, Coriún. *Conversaciones sobre música, cultura e identidad*. Montevideo, Uruguay: OMBU, 1992.

Béhague, Gerard. "Reflections on the Ideological History of Latin American Ethnomusicology." In *Comparative Musicology and Anthropology of Music. Essays on the History of Ethnomusicology*, edited by Bruno Nettl and Philip Bohlman, 56–68. Chicago: University of Chicago Press, 1991.

Bethell, Leslie. *A Cultural History of Latin America. Literature, Music and the Visual Arts in the Nineteenth and Twentieth Centuries*. New York: Cambridge University Press, 1998.

García Canclini, Néstor. *Hybrid Cultures: Strategies for Entering and Leaving Modernity*. Translated by Christopher L. Chiappari and Silvia L. López. Minneapolis: University of Minnesota Press, 1995.

Green, Duncan. *Faces of Latin America*. London: Latin American Bureau, 1997.

Koetting, James. "Analysis and Notation of West African Drum Ensemble Music." *Selected Reports in Ethnomusicology* 13 (1970): 115–46.

Nettl, Bruno. *The Study of Ethnomusicology: Thirty-one Issues and Concepts*. Urbana: University of Illinois Press, 2005.

Rowe, William, and Vivian Schelling. *Memory and Modernity. Popular Culture in Latin America*. London: Verso, 1991.

Treitler, Leo. L. *Music and the Historical Imagination*. Cambridge, MA: Harvard University Press, 1989.

Turino, Thomas. *Music as Social Life. The Politics of Participation*. Chicago, IL: The University of Chicago Press, 2008.

CHAPTER 2

Reading

Baker, Geoff. *Imposing Harmony: Music and Society in Colonial Cuzco*. Durham, NC: Duke University Press, 2008.

——. "Latin American Baroque: Performance as a Post-Colonial Act?" *Early Music* 36, no. 3 (2008): 441–48.

Dean, Carolyn. *Inka Bodies and the Body of Christ: Corpus Christi in Colonial Cuzco, Peru*. Durham, NC: Duke University Press, 1999.

Knighten, Tess, and Alvaro Torrente, eds. *Devotional Music in the Iberian World (1450–1800): The Villancico and Related Genres*. Aldershot, UK: Ashgate, 2007.

Manuel, Peter. *Creolizing Contradance in the Caribbean*. Philadelphia: Temple University Press, 2009.

Olsen, Dale. *Music of El Dorado: The Ethnomusicology of Ancient South American Cultures*. Gainesville: University Press of Florida, 2002.

Reily, Suzel Ana. "Remembering the Baroque Era: Historical Consciousness, Local Identity, and the Holy Week Celebrations in a Former Mining Town in Brazil." *Ethnomusicology Forum* 15, no. 1 (June, 2006): 39–62.

Russell, Craig. *From Serra to Sancho: Music and Pageantry in the California Missions*. New York: Oxford University Press, 2009.

——. *Santiago de Murcia's Códice Saldívar No. 4: A Treasury of Guitar Music from Baroque Mexico*, vol. 1. Urbana–Champaign: University of Illinois Press, 1995.

Stein, Louise K. "'La música de dos orbes': A Context for the First Opera of the Americas." *The Opera Quarterly* 22, nos. 3–4 (Summer–Autumn 2006): 433–58.

Stevenson, Robert. *Music in Aztec and Inca Territories*. Berkeley and Los Angeles: University of California Press, 1977.

Listening

El Milagro de Guadalupe. San Antonio Vocal Arts Ensemble (SAVAE). Iago Records, 1999.

Esteban Salas: Un barroco cubano. Coro Exaudi de La Habana. Jade, 2005.

Juan Gutiérrez de Padilla: Música de la Catedral de Puebla de los Ángeles. Ars Longa de la Habana. Almaviva, 2006.

Matins for the Virgin of Guadalupe. Chanticleer. Teldec, 1998.

Norton Anthology of Western Music, vol. 1, Ancient to Baroque (6th ed.). W. W. Norton, 2010.

CHAPTER 3

Reading

Bitrán, Yael, and Ricardo Miranda, eds. *Diálogo de resplandores: Carlos Chávez y Silvestre Revueltas*. Mexico City: CONACULTA, 2002.

Burr, Ramiro. *The Billboard Guide to Tejano and Regional Mexican Music*. New York: Billboard Books, 1999.

Parker, Robert. *Carlos Chávez: Mexico's Modern-Day Orpheus*. Boston, MA: Twayne Publishers, 1983.

Pedelty, Mark. *Musical Ritual in Mexico City: From the Aztec to NAFTA*. Austin: University of Texas Press, 2004.

Ragland, Cathy. *Música Norteña: Mexican Migrants Creating a Nation between Nations*. Philadelphia, PA: Temple University Press, 2009.

Russell, Craig. *From Serra to Sancho: Music and Pageantry in the California Missions*. New York: Oxford University Press, 2009.

Simonett, Helena. *Banda: Mexican Musical Life Across Borders*. Middletown, CT: Wesleyan University Press, 2001.

Stevenson, Robert. *Music in Mexico*. New York: Crowell, 1952.

Zolov, Eric. *Refried Elvis: The Rise of the Mexican Counterculture*. Berkeley: University of California Press, 1999.

Listening

La Bamba: Sones Jarochos from Veracruz. José Gutiérrez and Los Hermanos Ochoa. Smithsonian Folkways, 2003.

The Mexican Revolution: Corridos about the Heroes and Events 1910–1920 and Beyond! Arhoolie, 1997.

Revueltas: The Centenial Anthology. RCA Red Seal, 1999.

¡Viva ed Mariachi!: Nati Cano's Mariachi Los Camperos. Nati Cano and Los Camperos. Smithsonian Folkways, 2002.

Viewing

Chulas Fronteras. Les Blank, director. Brazos Films, 2003.

CHAPTER 4

Reading

Brandt, Max. "African Drumming from Rural Communities around Caracas and its Impact on Venezuelan Music and Ethnic Identity." In *Music and Black Ethnicity: The Caribbean and South America*, edited by G. Béhague, 267–84. Miami: University of Miami North-South Center, 1994.

The Garland Encyclopedia of World Musics: South America, Mexico, Central America, and the Caribbean. Edited by D. Olsen and D. Sheehy. New York/London: Routledge, 1998. See the entries on each nation.

List, George. *Music and Poetry in a Colombian Village*. Bloomington: University of Indiana Press, 1983.

Navarrete Pellicer, Sergio. *Maya Achi Marimba Music in Guatemala*. Philadelphia: Temple University Press, 2005.

Scruggs, T.M. "Central America: Marimba and Other Musics of Central America." In *Music in Latin American Culture: Regional Traditions*, 80–125. New York: Schirmer Books, 1999.

Scruggs, T.M. "The Rise of Afro-Venezuelan Music to the Present Day Hugo Chávez Era." 2007. http://afropop.org/hipdeep/HipDeep.html#programId=690&view=1

Sider, Ronald R. "Contemporary Composers in Costa Rica." *Latin American Music Review* 5, no. 2 (1984): 263–76.

Wade, Peter. *Music, Race and Nation: Música Tropical in Colombia*. Chicago: University of Chicago Press, 2000.

Viewing

El Sistema: Music to Change Life. Simón Bolívar Youth Orchestra. Paul Smaczny and Maria Stodtmeier, directors. Euroarts, 2009.

Shotguns and Accordions—Music of the Marijuana Regions of Colombia. Nafer Durán, director. Shanachie, 2001.

CHAPTER 5

Reading

Allen, Ray and Lois Wilcken, eds. *Island Sounds in the Global City: Caribbean Popular Music and Identity in New York*. New York: New York Folklore Society, 1998.

Manuel, Peter. *Caribbean Currents*. 2nd ed. Philadelphia: Temple University Press, 2006.

Moore, Robin. *Music of the Hispanic Caribbean*. New York: Oxford University Press, 2010.

Rivera, Raquel, Deborah Pacini Hernández, and Wayne Marshall, eds. *Reggaeton*. Durham, NC: Duke University Press, 2009.

Waxer, Lise, ed. *Situating Salsa. Global Markets and Local Meanings in Latin Popular Music*. London: Routledge, 2002.

Listening

Africa in America. Music from Nineteen Countries. Cambridge, MA: Rounder Records, 1993.

Latin Jazz: La Combinación Perfecta. Smithsonian Folkways, 2002.

Viewing

In the Tradition. Miami: Warner Brothers, 1996.

Salsa: Latin Music of New York and Puerto Rico. BBC "Beats of the Heart" series. Newton, NJ: Shanachie Records, 1979.

Routes of Rhythm with Harry Belafonte, 3 vols. Cultural Research and Communication, Inc., 1989.

CHAPTER 6

Reading

The Brazilian Sound: Samba, Bossa Nova and the Popular Music of Brazil. Philadelphia, PA: Temple University Press, 1998.

Crook, Larry. *Northeastern Traditions and the Heartbeat of a Modern Nation.* Santa Barbara, CA: ABD-CLIO, 2005.

Listening

Forró in the Dark, *Bonfires of São João.* Nublu Records, 2006.

Babel Gilberto, *Tanto Tempo.* Six Degrees, 2000.

Paralamas do Sucesso, *Arquivo.* EMI, 1990.

Rio Baile Funk: Favela Booty Beats and *Rio Baile Funk: More Favela Booty Beats.* Essay Recordings, 2005.

Chico Science and Nação Zumbi, *Da lama ao caos.* Sony Music, 1996.

Sepultura, *Roots.* Roadrunner Records. 1996.

Tropicália Essentials. Hip-O Records, 1999.

Viewing

Beyond Ipanema: Brazilian Waves in Global Music. Guto Barra and Béco Dranoff, directors. Beyond Ipanema Films, 2009.

Favela on Blast. Leandro HBL and Wesley Pentz, directors. Mad Decent, 2008.

CHAPTER 7

Reading

Collier, Simon. *¡Tango! The Dance, the Song, the Story.* New York: Thames and Hudson, 1995.

Florine, Jane L. *Cuarteto Music and Dancing from Argentina: In Search of the Tunga-Tunga in Córdoba.* Gainesville: University Press of Florida, 2001.

Gorín, Natalio. *Astor Piazzolla: A Memoir.* Translated, annotated, and expanded by Fernando González. Portland, OR: Amadeus, 2001.

Ruiz, Irma. "Musical Culture of Indigenous Societies in Argentina." In *Music in Latin America and the Caribbean: An Encyclopedic History,* edited by Malena Kuss, vol. 1, 163–80. Austin: University of Texas Press, 2004.

Schwartz-Kates, Deborah. "The Popularized Gaucho Image as a Source of Argentine Classical Music, 1880–1920." In *From Tejano to Tango: Latin American Popular Music,* edited by Walter Aaron Clark, 3–24. New York: Routledge, 2002.

Trigo, Abril. "The Politics and Anti-Politics of Uruguayan Rock." In *Rockin' las Américas: The Global Politics of Rock in Latin/o America,* edited by Deborah Pacini-Hernández, Héctor Férnández L'Hoeste, and Eric Zolov, 115–141. Pittsburgh: University of Pittsburgh Press, 2004.

Vila, Pablo. "Argentina's *rock nacional*: The Struggle for Meaning." *Latin American Music Review* 10, no. 1 (Spring–Summer 1989): 1–28.

_____. "*Rock nacional* and Dictatorship in Argentina." *Popular Music* 6, no. 2 (May 1987): 129–48.

Viewing

Afro-Uruguayan Rhythms: Candombe. Surmenages, 2006.

Argentina: Chamamé crudo. Films Media Group, 2007.

CHAPTER 8

Reading

Bigenho, Michelle. *Sounding Indigenous: Authenticity in Bolivian Music Performance.* New York: Palgrave, 2002.

Bolaños, César, et al., eds. *La música en el Perú.* 2nd ed. Lima: Fondo Editorial Filarmonía, 2007.

Feldman, Heidi. *Black Rhythms of Peru: Reviving African Musical Heritage in the Black Pacific.* Middletown, CT: Wesleyan University Press, 2006.

Mendoza, Zoila. *Shaping Society through Dance: Mestizo Ritual Performance in the Peruvian Andes.* Chicago: University of Chicago Press, 2000.

Romero, Raúl. *Debating the Past: Music, Memory, and Identity in the Andes.* New York and Oxford: Oxford University Press, 2001.

Stobart, Henry. *Music and the Poetics of Production in the Bolivian Andes.* Aldershot, UK: Ashgate, 2006.

Turino, Thomas. *Music in the Andes: Experiencing Music, Expressing Culture.* New York: Oxford University Press, 2007.

Wibbelsman, Michelle. *Ritual Encounters: Otavalan Modern and Mythic Community.* Urbana and Chicago: University of Illinois Press, 2009.

Listening

Traditional Music of Peru, vols. 1–8. Smithsonian Folkways Recordings, 1995–2002.

Viewing

Ciudad chicha ("Chicha City"). Omar Ráez and Raúl Romero, directors. Instituto de Etnomusicología, Pontificia Universidad Católica del Perú, 2005.

El derecho de vivir en paz ("The Right to Live in Peace"). Carmen Luz Parot, director. Warner Music Chile, 2003.

CHAPTER 9

Reading

Gidal, Marc M. "Contemporary 'Latin American' Composers of Art Music in the U.S.: Cosmopolitans Navigating Multiculturalism and Universalism." *Latin American Music Review* 31, no. 1 (Spring–Summer 2010): 40–78.

Lusk, J. "The Last Tango (interview with Gustavo Santaolalla)." *fRoots* 30, no. 5 (November 2008): 43–5.

Rivera, José. "Roberto Sierra's *Missa Latina (Pro Pace)*." *Choral Journal* 50, no. 8 (March 2010): 6–23.

Slayton, Michael. *Women of Influence in Contemporary Music: Nine American Composers*. Lanham, MD: Scarecrow Press, 2011.

Starobin, David. "A Conversation with Mario Davidovsky." *Guitar Review*, 92 (Winter 1993): 5–8.

Listening

Paul Desenne, *Tocatas Galeónicas*. Dorian Discovery, 1995.

Gabriela Frank, *Leyendas: An Andean Walkabout*. Chiara String Quartet. New Voice Singles, 2007.

Tania León, *Indígena*. Composers Recordings, 1994.

Gabriela Ortiz, *Altar de Muertos*. Urtext Records, 2006.

Viewing

Motorcycle Diaries (*Diarios de motocicleta*). Focus Features, 2004.

CHAPTER 10

Reading

Cepeda, María E. *Musical ImagiNation: U.S.-Colombian Identity and the Latin Music Boom*. New York: New York University Press, 2010.

Flores, Juan. *The Diaspora Strikes Back: Caribeño Tales of Learning and Turning*. New York: Routledge, 2008.

Madrid, Alejandro L. *Nor-tec Rifa!: Electronic Dance Music from Tijuana to the World*. New York: Oxford University Press, 2008.

Madrid, Alejandro L., ed. *Transnational Encounters: Music and Performance at the U.S.–Mexico Border*. New York: Oxford University Press, 2011.

Pacini Hernandez, Deborah. *¡Oye como va!: Hybridity and Identity in Latino Popular Music*. Philadelphia, PA: Temple University Press, 2010.

Ragland, Catherine. *Música norteña: Mexican Americans Creating a Nation Between Nations*. Philadelphia, PA: Temple University Press, 2009.

Rivera, Raquel Z. *New York Ricans from the Hip Hop Zone*. New York, NY: Palgrave Macmillan, 2003.

Washburne, Christopher. *Sounding Salsa: Performing Latin Music in New York City*. Philadelphia, PA: Temple University Press, 2008.

Viewing

Chulas Fronteras. Les Blank, director. Arhoolie Records, 2003 [1976].

Latin Music USA. Jimmy Smits, Adriana Bosch, et al., directors. PBS Distribution, 2009.

Endnotes

Chapter 1

5. "Put aside ideological differences": *Soundspike*, August 24, 2009, http://www.soundspike.com/news/2/19933-juanes_news/.

Chapter 2

27. "Western parts of the Ocean Sea, toward the Indies": Edmundo O'Gorman, *The Invention of America: An Inquiry into the Historical Nature of the New World and the Meaning of its History* (Indiana University Press, 1961), 82.

36. "Upon realizing that all their songs were composed to honor their gods": Robert M. Stevenson, *Music in Aztec and Inca Territory* (University of California Press, 1968), 93.

56. "Triumph over heresy": Carolyn Dean, *Inka Bodies and the Body of Christ* (Duke University Press, 1999), 1.

56. "The entire course of the procession is a continuous altar": Geoffrey Baker, *Imposing Harmony: Music and Society in Colonial Cuzco* (Duke University Press, 2008), 36.

57. "Inventions and games": Alejandro de la Fuente et al., *Havana and the Atlantic in the Sixteenth Century* (University of North Carolina Press, 2008), 220.

61. "They have many songs to sing in their dances": Craig Russell, *From Serra to Sancho: Music and Pageantry in the California Missions* (Oxford University Press, 2009), 287n.

66. "Visibly representing the action of satisfied love": Giacomo Casanova, *The Story of My Life*, trans. Stephen Sartarelli and Sophie Hawkes, selections by Gilberto Pizzamiglio (Penguin Classics, 2000), 462.

Chapter 3

119. "Rooted in its intrinsic variety": Carlos Chávez, *Sinfonia India* (Schirmer, 1950).

Chapter 7

301. "La cumparsita" was "the worst": Ricardo García Blaya, "*La Cumparsita*," *Todo Tango*, http://www.todotango.com/english/biblioteca/cronicas/la_cumparsita.asp.

304. "Our music is what we do so that they cannot invade us": Michael Seamus O'Brien, "Contemporary Tango in Buenos Aires, Argentina: A Globalized Local Music in a Historicized Present" (Master's thesis, University of Texas at Austin, 2005), 92–3.

313. "General characteristics of the Italian Renaissance": Mario García Acevedo, "Teatros: Argentina," *Diccionario de la música española e hispanoamericana*, ed. Emilio Casares Rodicio (Sociedad General de Autores y Editores, 2002), vol. 10, 214.

314. "Now joyful, now melancholy": Gilbert Chase, "Alberto Ginastera: Argentine Composer," *Musical Quarterly* 53, no. 4 (October 1957): 445.

316. "Populated by symbols": Pola Suárez Urtubey, *Alberto Ginastera* (Ediciones Culturales Argentinas, 1967), 72.

Chapter 8

359. "Was a call to the peasants": Joan Jara, *Victor: An Unfinished Song* (Bloomsbury, 1998), 126.

Chapter 9

384. "My concept of the mass": José Rivera, "Roberto Sierra's Missa *Latina (Pro Pace)*," *Choral Journal* 50, no. 8 (March 2010): 9.

384. "The orchestration reflects my interest": ibid.

392. "I was put in the 'fridge'": e-mail message to author, April 1, 2010.

Chapter 10

400. "Pop's twenty-first-century Latina bombshell": Jon Pareles, "The Shakira Dialectic," *New York Times*, November 13, 2005.

400. "Raw kibbeh and fried plantain": María Elena Cepeda, *Musical Imagination: U.S.-Colombian Identity and the Latin Music Boom* (NYU Press, 2010), 136.

402. "Blissfully pan-American": Jon Pareles, "Critic's Choice: New CD's," *New York Times*, June 13, 2005.

405. "I prefer to play guitar in English and sing in Spanish": Maya Jaggi, "The Juanes Success Story," *The Sunday Times*, January 27, 2008.

407. "Two worlds merging to form a third country": Gloria Anzaldúa, *Borderlands/La Frontera: The New Mestiza*, 2nd ed. (Aunt Lute Books, 1999), 25–26.

411. "A nation between nations": Cathy Ragland, *Música Norteña: Mexican Migrants Creating a Nation Between Nations* (Temple University Press, 2009).

414. "The barbaric land where U.S. cultural imperialism threatens Mexican, Latin American, and Hispanic culture": Alejandro Luis Madrid, *Nor-Tec Rifa!: Electronic Dance Music From Tijuana to the World* (Oxford University Press, 2008), 14.

414. "Incorporate signs and symbols from elsewhere": Jennifer Insley, "Redefining Sodom: A Latter-Day Vision of Tijuana," *Mexican Studies/Estudios Mexicanos* 20, no. 1 (Winter 2004): 107.

416. "Cultural remittances": Juan Flores, *The Diaspora Strikes Back: Caribeño Tales of Learning and Turning* (Routledge, 2009), 9.

418. "Omnivorous": Jon Pareles, "Critic's Choice: Calle 13," *New York Times*, October 20, 2008.

429. "Put the cool in bachata": Jody Rosen, "Crossover Dreams of a Bronx Bachatero," *New York Times*, June 3, 2009.

Appendix

434. "Music is humanly organized sound": John Blacking, *How Musical Is Man?* (University of Washington Press, 1973), 10.

448. "Frozen music": letter to Johann Peter Eckermann, March 23, 1829.

Music and Lyrics Credits

Ruben Isaac Albarran Ortega, Enrique Rangel Arroyo, Jose Alfredo Rangel Arroyo, and Emanuel Del Real Diaz, "Eres." Words and music by Ruben Isaac Albarran Ortega, Enrique Rangel Arroyo, Jose Alfredo Rangel Arroyo, and Emanuel Del Real Diaz. Copyright © 2003 Editora Azul, Editora Bachiller, Editora Musica de Tubos and Editora Oso. All rights controlled and administered by Songs of Universal, Inc. All rights reserved. Used by permission. Reprinted with permission of Hal Leonard Corporation. Adolfo Alfonso and Justo Vega, "Controversia." Translated by Robin Moore. Cortesía de la familia Adolfo Alfonso/Reprinted by permission of the family of Adolfo Alfonso. José Alfredo Jiménez, "El hijo del pueblo." Copyright 1952 by Editorial Mexicana de Musica, S.A. Administered by Peer International Corporation. All rights reserved. Used by permission. Reynaldo Armas, "El indio," from *Historia Musical del Llano, Vol. 1.* Reprinted and translated into English by permission of the composer. Ary Barroso, "Aquarela brasileira (Aquarela do Brasil)" (Brasil). Words and music by Ary Barroso. Copyright © 1939 by Irmaos Vitale. Copyright renewed. All rights for the world excluding Brazil administered by Peer International Corporation. International copyright secured. All rights reserved. Reprinted with permission of Hal Leonard Corporation. Tego Calderón, "Loíza." Translated by Robin Moore. From *El Abayarde*, Malito Music, Inc. dba Hecho en PR Entertainment, Inc. (ASCAP). Reprinted and translated into English by permission of Kenya Calderón-Rosario. Félix Calderón Chacin, "Los dos titanes," as performed by Daisy Gutiérrez. Reprinted and translated into English by permission of the performer. Jose Augusto Pinto Cardoso and Antonio Carlos Moreira Batata, "Pássaro sonhador." Words and music by Jose Augusto Pinto Cardoso and Antonio Carlos Moreira Batata. Copyright © 1999 Mercury Prod. E Edicoes Musicales Ltda. All rights controlled and administered by Universal Musica Unica Publishing. All rights reserved. Used by permission. Reprinted with permission of Hal Leonard Corporation. Rómulo Castro, "La rosa de los vientos." Reprinted and translated into English by permission of Fuerte Suerte Music. Chabuca Granda, "Flor de la canela." Copyright 1958 by Southern Music Publishing Co., Inc. Southern Music Publishing controls in the USA and its possessions. Copyright renewed. All rights reserved. Used by permission. Elvis Crespo, "Píntame." © 1999 Sony/ATV Music Publishing LLC and CD Elvis Music Publishing. All rights administered by Sony/ATV Music Publishing LLC, 8 Music Square West, Nashville, TN 37203. All rights reserved. Used by permission. Manuel Esperón and

Ernesto M. Cortázar, "¡Ay! Jalisco no te rajes." Copyright 1941 by Promotora Hispano de Americana de Musica, S.A. Administered by Peer International Corporation. All rights reserved. Used by permission. Sindo Garay, "En opuestas regions." Transcription by Robin Moore, by permission of Ned Sublette. Charly García, "Los sobrevivientes." Translated by Tony Beckwith. From *Grasa de las Capitales*. Reprinted by permission of SADAIC Latin Copyrights, Inc. Luiz Gonzaga and Humberto Teixeira, "Asa Branca." Words and music by Luiz Gonzaga and Humberto Teixeira. Copyright © 1947 Fermata International Melodies, Inc. Copyright renewed. All rights administered by Wixen Music Publishing, Inc. All rights reserved. Used by permission. Reprinted with permission of Hal Leonard Corporation. Juan R. Ortiz González, "Ritmo en el corazón." Words and music by Juan R. Ortiz Gonzalez. Copyright © 1988 Fania Music. All rights controlled and administered by Universal Musica Unica Publishing. All rights reserved. Used by permission. Reprinted with permission of Hal Leonard Corporation. "Hanacpachap cussicuinin." Translated by Rosaleen Howard. *Fire Burning in Snow* (Ex Cathedra Baroque Ensemble, Jeffrey Skidmore, conductor), 2008. Reprinted by permission of Rosaleen Howard, Newcastle University, Chair of Hispanic Studies. "Harawi." Translated by Jonathan Ritter from the recording *Traditional Music of Peru, v. 6: The Ayacucho Region* (Smithsonian Folkways, 2001). Reprinted by permission of Institute of Ethnomusicology, Av. Universitaria 1801, Lima 32, Peru. Víctor Jara, "Plegaria a un labrador." Words and music by Víctor Jara. © 1963 (renewed) Editorial Lagos (SADAIC). All rights administered by WB Music Corp. Used by permission of Alfred Music Publishing Co., Inc. All rights reserved. Agustín Lara, "Solamente una vez." Translated by John Koegel. Used by permission of Peer International Corporation. Miguel Matamoros, "Beso discreto." Translated by Robin Moore. Used by Permission of Peer International Corporation. Carlos Mejía Godoy, "Credo" from *La misa campesina nicaragüense.* Reprinted and translated into English by permission of the composer. Daniela Mercuri De Almeida and Antonio Jorge Souza Dos Santos, "O canto da cidade." Words and Music by Daniela Mercuri De Almeida and Antonio Jorge Souza Dos Santos. Copyright © 1993 by Paginas Do Mar Edicoes Musicais Ltda. All rights administered by Universal Music-MGB Songs. International copyright secured. All rights reserved. Reprinted with permission of Hal Leonard Corporation. "Neblina blanca." From the CD *Huayno Music of Peru, Vol. 1* (Arhoolie Records, 1989). Courtesy Arhoolie Records. Transcribed by Oswaldo Voysesí. Sixto Palavecino,

Photo Credits

Index

in Guatemala, 4
hip-hop and, 417–19
in Latin America, 16, 405
in Mexico, 80, 108
Mexico-U.S. border region,
411–13
Peru, 351–52
in Venezuela, 160, 164
Soda Stereo, 309
Sojo, Vicente Emilio, 170
"Solamente una vez" (Lara), 103–5
"Soldado do Morro" (MV Bill), 4
solfège, 33, 35, 36
Solo Pueblo, Un (group), 166, 170
"Somba de ums nota só" (Jobim),
259
Somoza, Anastasio, 127, 134, 136
Sonata andina (Frank), 378–80
son, Cuban, 194–96
clave, 191
influence in Colombia, 147
contradanza as precursor, 70
son, Mexican, 82, 87–90
son huasteco, 87, 96, 98, 409
son jalisciense, 87, 95–96
son jarocho, 87–90
sonata form, 316–17, 367
sonatas, 116
son chapin, 173
Son de Madera (group), 88
soneo, 418–19, 426, 427
son huasteco, 87, 96, 98, 409
Sonido Trece method of composition,
115
son jalisciense, 87, 95–96
son jarocho, 87–90
son nica, 134–35
Sony, 397
Sosa, Mercedes, 285–86, *286*, 358
Soto, Carlos, 200
sound as music, 434–38
sound generators, 435–36
sound-reproduction technology,
13–14
Spain
casta (caste system) employed
by, 78
colonies in Latin America, 7–8,
25, 27–29, 35–50, 78, 79, 126,
153, 178–80, 276–77, 362
exploration of Latin America, 27
Latin American dance music in,
372–73

Spanish-American War, 181
Spasiuk, Chango, 292
staff, 444–45
Stampiglia, Silvio, 64
Starobin, David, 390
Stein, Louise K., 62
Sting, 234
Strauss, Johann, Jr., 139
string instruments. *See* chordophones;
specific instruments
Stroessner, Alfredo, 311
strophic form, 449
Studio for Electronic Music of the
WDR, 391
Suárez Paz, Fernando, 302
Suazo Lang, Sergio, 140
subdivision of rhythms, 441–42
subdominant, 282, 446
Sucre, Bolivia, 31
Sucre, José Antonio, 161
"Sueños de Guillermo" (Grupo
Mina), 166–69
Sumac, Yma, 364
Sumaya, Manuel
La Partenope, 64
surdo, 248, *248*, 250, 251–53
"Su veneno" (Aventura), 431
symphonic poems, 115
Synchronisms (Davidovsky), 388,
390–91, 446, 447, 452–53
syncopation, 38, 48, 49, 50, 71, 254,
395, 441, 451
synthesizer, 355, 436

Tacón, Miguel, 215
Taínos, 178
Tamayo, Rufino, 82–83
tambor, 166, 173, 378–79
tambora, 106, 144, 145, *203*, 203–6
tambor alegre, 144, *144*, 145
tamborazo, 106
tamboril, 293–94
tamborim, 248, *248*, 250
tamborito, 173
tambor llamador, 144, *144*, 145
tamborzão, 264, 266
tambourines, 65
tango
in Argentina, 12, 275, 277, 279,
295–305
bandoneón in, 282
in Brazil, 254
in Colombia, 147

contemporary, 303–5, 382–83
contradanza as precursor, 70
habanera's influence on, 215
La Guardia nueva, 299–300
La Guardia vieja, 297
Nuevo tango, 300–303
origins, 296
rioplatense, 295–303, 320
in Uruguay, 295–303, 310
tango canción, 297–99, 303–4
Tango Sabatier (Desenne), 382–83
Tañón, Olga, 5
Taquile, Peru, 334–36
tarantella, 310
tarima, 88
tarka, 332
tarol, *248*
tarola, 106
Tavárez, Manuel Gregorio, 215
tayil ritual, 280
Teatro Colón (Buenos Aires), 313,
313, 314
Teatro Solis (Montevideo), 319
Teatro Tacón (Havana), 215
techno, 3, 414–15
technobanda, 107
technocumbia, 356–57, 421
Teixeira, Humberto, 240–41
tejano music, 409. *See also* música
tejana
Telemundo, 5
tempo, 441
Tenochtitlán, 7, 32–33, 79
Templo Mayor massacre, 34
"Teponazcuicatl," 35
teponaztli, *32*, 32–33, *33*, 117, 128,
129, 436
ternary form, 449
Terzián, Alicia, 318
Texas, conjunto in, 107, 410, 420
Texas Republic, 79
texture, 447–48
Theatro São Pedro de Alcantara, *267*
"They Don't Care About Us"
(Jackson/Olodum music
video), 251
34 Puñaladas (group), 303–4
Three Souls in My Mind (group), 108
through-composed form, 66, 449
thumb piano, 203
Tierra Caliente, 346, *346*
Tijuana, Mexico, 3, 414–19
timbales, 21, 196, 199–202, 423–24

Yoruba people
    in Brazil, 228, 242–46, 252, 393
    in Caribbean region, 179, 185–89, 191, 440
Y tu mamá también (film), 109
Yungas valley, Bolivia, 344
Yupanqui, Atahualpa, 319
    "Malambo," 284–85, 440, 447

zabumba, 235, 236–41
Zacatecas, Mexico
    wind bands, 106
zamba, 216, 281, 320
zambo, 328

zampoñas, 378–80
Zapata, Emiliano, 78
zapateado, 85, 94
zapateo, 66, 282, 284
Zapatistas. *See* EZLN (Ejército Zapatista de Liberación Nacional)
Zapotec language, 83
zarabanda, 27, 372
zarzuela, 61
    in Argentina, 312
    in Mexico, 98, 112–13
    in Peru, 362, 363–64
    in Spain, 373

Zarzuela, Héctor, 200
Ziegfeld Follies, 113
Ziegler, Pablo, 302
Zipoli, Domenico
    In hoc Mundo, 58–60, 449
Zitarrosa, Alfredo
    "Milonga para una niña," 282, 286–88
Zoque people, 84
Zulia, Venezuela, 163
Zumaqué, Francisco "Pacho," 153
Zumbi, Rei, 244